I KILL KILLERS
Omnibus Edition

S. T. ASHMAN

DEDICATION

To my beloved mother and father-in-law.
You have been my unwavering cheerleaders,
holding faith in my potential even when others questioned it.
Thank you for being my steadfast believers.

CONTENTS

WE KILL KILLERS

FINAL KILL

I KILL KILLERS

PROLOGUE

When I was eight years old, I stabbed a boy.

He came from a troubled home, the kind where violence was the solution to any problem. His piercing eyes were a window to his sadistic soul, revealing a weariness far beyond his years. At thirteen years old, he tortured and killed cats and dogs. There were also rumors that he had molested a kindergartner in the school's bathroom.

I did my best to avoid him until one day, after school, I saw him lingering in front of the grocery store. At the time, he'd been suspended from school. He looked unkempt. His brown hair was sticky and long, and his face was smudged with dirt. Our eyes met for a split second before I stepped past him and into the store.

I was on my way home when I felt the unmistakable sensation of being followed. Glancing around, I saw his shadowy figure darting between cars, keeping pace with my strides. I felt no fear, only a nagging annoyance that he might make me late for my piano lesson.

I kept walking and entered a quiet street, where he managed to pull me behind a small patch of rosebushes. Concealed from the road, he threw me onto the leaf-littered ground and pulled out a knife, its blade glinting in the September sunlight. He told me he'd cut me open if I screamed. I nodded and asked him what he wanted.

"Kiss it," he said, grabbing his crotch.

I agreed but asked him to sit on the ground. "You're too tall," I said, which seemed to make sense to him.

He sat down in front of me. I knelt between his outstretched legs and waited for him to put the knife on the ground to unzip his pants. As soon as he did, I snatched up the blade and slashed his neck with a single smooth movement.

I'll never forget the look of horror on his face as he frantically pressed his hands against the deep crimson that gushed relentlessly from the wound in his neck. I'll also never forget the odd sense of emptiness I felt as I stood there watching him. No sadness or joy. Just a numb void that left me feeling detached from myself and the world.

When the first group of people gathered around the scene, gasping and screaming, I calmly walked straight to the police station and told them everything, bloody knife still in hand.

The boy survived, but my parents left me to rot in the Kim Arundel Psychiatric Hospital for the Severely Mentally Ill for the rest of the school year. I'd told the police that it was self-defense, and they'd believed me. But the composed and emotionless way I'd handled myself created a ripple effect in my small town, and CPS branded me a high-risk child in need of immediate intervention.

The therapeutic period that followed was mostly unremarkable. There were the standard programs designed to help normalize me: the grippy socks, the endless talk sessions. But what really left its indelible mark on my mind was the time I spent in the treatment center's library, a space shared by the children and adult units.

It was there, between the picture books and cleavage-filled romance novels, that I discovered a book about German National Socialism during World War II. Judge me how you want, but strangely, this book, as thick and heavy as three books combined, gave me hope.

My fascination with the book wasn't related to the horrific atrocities committed by the Nazis, nor was I fool enough to admire one of the greatest mass murderers in history. My obsession with Hitler stemmed from the peculiar fact that the same monster who was responsible for sending millions of people to concentration camps was also a vegetarian who had a deep affection for his dog, Blondi. At a time when a human's life meant close to nothing, Hitler passed some of the strictest animal protection laws ever written. He introduced penalties for animal cruelty and banned free hunting rights.

As I sat there on the library's torn and dusty couch, the worn book spread open on my lap, something stirred inside me. This, by itself, was shocking because I rarely felt any kind of emotion—hatred, joy, contentment, nothing. I understood the difference between right and wrong and derived no pleasure from witnessing animals or people suffer. Yet, on most days, I simply felt nothing—as if my inner world was a merciless desert devoid of even the slightest hint of life. Feeling that warm flicker inside me meant everything. Eventually I realized what it was: It was hope.

If a man as evil as Hitler could unearth the slightest bit of love within the depths of his icy, rotten heart—even if it was for animals—then perhaps, one day, I might be able to do the same.

ONE

I'm here ☺, Tim texted.

My phone's bright light illuminated the glass of water sitting beside it. It was 5:36 p.m. Tim was thirty-six minutes late. Men like him often were.

I was in a cheap Chinese restaurant, listening to the sounds of forks clinking against plates, the occasional peal of laughter, and the sizzling of grease against hot pans in the kitchen.

I picked up my phone.

About time ☺, I texted. *Waiting inside. Blonde girl with short hair, holding a red rose.*

The familiar bouncing three dots indicated Tim was answering.

I'm late, and you got me a rose? That was my job. Want me to grab one real quick? Feel like a douche now. LOL

I took a sip of my ice water. *Just kidding. No rose. But I'm the only one in a red dress.* ☺ *Get your sexy butt in here.*

Exhaling deeply, more out of annoyance than anything else, I turned toward the window overlooking the parking lot. The sky was a canvas of fading orange and purple hues fighting against the encroaching gray of the night. Several streetlights illuminated the handful of scattered cars in the dim parking lot of the small shopping mall, which consisted of nine-to-five businesses such as an outdated fitness studio and a shabby tattoo parlor.

As I scanned the cars, my phone remained silent. A whole two minutes ticked by without a response.

He's debating leaving.

Many debated internally over whether to do 'it' just one more time, each motivated by their own reasons, in a constant back-and-forth.

I glanced at my phone, noticing the three dots bouncing again.

Shit, Tim texted. *I'm so sorry, but work just called me in.* ☹

Oh no, I replied, hoping I could persuade him to change his mind. If he backed out now, it would complicate things significantly. My upcoming weeks were packed with concerts.

This late? I texted.

My boss says some older woman has a major leak in her ceiling, and our on-call guy won't pick up the phone. I'm so sorry. I feel terrible.

That's a shame. But don't feel bad. Work pays the bills. I get it. It's nice you're helping that elderly lady. You sound like a keeper.

There was another silence. Disappointed, I continued to stare out the window. I needed something to push him—*quickly*—or he might not bite. Something that preyed on his most primal instincts as a man.

Possessiveness. Jealousy.

My friend Mike is having a beer close by anyway, I texted. *He begged me to meet up tonight. I'll just join him. No biggie.*

Suddenly a pair of headlights turned on from the far end of the parking lot.

Bingo.

He'd been watching all along. I knew it.

He texted again: *Hey, this might seem super weird...but do you want to tag along?*

My green eyes narrowed at the headlights. *Attaboy.*

I just really want to get to know you, he continued. *Could be a fun story at our wedding reception. LOL*

Wedding reception? That was a little forward. He was attempting to exploit the loneliness of the type of woman I was pretending to be. A sweet and kind soul. One that longed for love and stability like a flower craves the sunlight.

Won't you get in trouble for that? I asked. *Bringing me along to work?*

Nah. It won't take me long to fix the leak. We could bring donuts and coffee and just talk in the car. Or grab dinner after. I know a fancy place and could make a reservation for nine thirty.

I waved at the young Asian waitress and reached inside my purse to grab twenty dollars. She hurried over. "Are you ready to order?"

"Sorry, but I have to go." I placed the twenty on the table. The soft fabric of my knee-length red dress slid over my thighs as I rose. I was wearing matching red ballerina shoes.

"Thank you," the waitress said, fingering the bill.

The door's bell tinkled as I stepped out into the parking lot and inhaled the cool autumn breeze. It smelled like a mixture of Chinese food and the fake floral scent of detergent from a nearby Laundromat. I waited a moment, then texted:

I'm outside. Just promise me you're not a serial killer. LOL

More dancing dots.

I promise. ☺

The vehicle with the bright headlights at the far end of the parking lot started rolling toward me. Slowly. Under the dim light of a nearby streetlight, it revealed itself as a gray van that read EAST COAST PLUMBING. WE DO IT RIGHT! on its side. The van came to a stop in front of me. For a moment I stood there, waiting for Tim to get out. When he didn't, I walked around the front to the passenger's side. The door stuck a bit when I opened it.

As I got a closer look at Tim, I noticed the overwhelming difference between his dating-app pictures and reality. The photos were fake, of course. His once handsome cheekbones were now hidden beneath quite a few extra pounds. The striking blue eyes that could ignite a woman's wildest fantasies had lost their luster, appearing weary and dull. He was clean-shaven with an obscenely wide nose; only his brown hair and tall, imposing stature matched his photos. He wore a white protective coverall. Brand-new. Industrial, disposable.

He's a two out of ten, I thought and climbed up onto the seat.

"Wow," Tim said as I closed the door and strapped on my seat belt. It tightened against my chest, outlining my small breasts. Tim stared at them. Shameless. "You look even prettier than in the pictures," he continued.

I forced a playful giggle. "Stop it."

"No, really." Tim grinned, shifting the van into gear. "I'm a lucky man." His eyes lingered on me. "I don't think I've ever been with a woman as pretty as you." His gaze dropped to my legs before traveling back up to my breasts. "You could be a model."

He conveniently didn't address his own looks—or more the lack of them when compared to his pictures. Many of his kind were like this. Manipulative, dishonest, and yet with an air of entitlement, always prepared with an excuse to justify their self-serving actions.

Tim maneuvered his van out of the parking lot, smoothly merging with the flow of traffic as he joined the bustling street.

"Is the woman's house far?" I asked as the van snaked its way through the southern Boston suburb of Dorchester without stopping. I peeked over my shoulder into the back of the van—rusty toolboxes, pieces of white PVC piping, sponges, and buckets. Then my eyes settled on a very familiar five-gallon white-and-blue bucket of Fixx. The cleaning detergent used oxygen instead of chlorine. It was a fairly new cleaning product that erased all traces of hemoglobin, the oxygen-transporting protein in blood that was crucial in forensic tests.

Tim focused on the road. "No, not far at all. She lives close to the Blue Hills Reservation State Park."

The forest.

I stayed quiet. He laughed. "Don't worry. I promised not to be a serial killer, remember?"

Adjusting my dress, I forced out a chuckle. "Yeah, you did."

The houses gradually spread apart until the dark silhouettes of trees rose in the distance, marking the entrance to the large state park. I shifted in my seat. He glanced at me out of the side of his eye but didn't say anything.

Tim's headlights beamed into the darkness as he steered the van onto a dark road leading into the park. It was a smaller road, not the one that passed through the park's entrance and parking lot.

"She's pretty secluded out here," I commented, looking out my window at the endless black trunks of the trees now surrounding us. I sensed Tim smiling beside me, but he remained silent, driving deeper into the darkness of the woods until the road transitioned from concrete to gravel.

The stuffy air in the van grew even thicker, almost unbreathable. My heart started pounding against my chest as an icy adrenaline rush raced through my veins. This was the only time I felt excitement, and I often wondered why. Why did I feel this way *before* the storm hit? Why not later when his sweaty body violently pressed against mine?

I snapped out of my thoughts before Tim became suspicious of my silence.

"I...I think I want to turn back," I said in a weak, trembling voice. My fingers fumbled with the leather strap of my purse.

Tim remained silent, his dark profile starkly outlined against the window.

"Are we almost there?" I asked. "I think it's better if I go home. It's getting late."

Nothing but that stupid grin.

The van shook on the uneven gravel road as we ventured deeper and deeper into the woods. No one would ever come this way tonight. No one would be here to *save me*.

"I...I have to go home. Can we please turn around?" I pleaded, my voice rising in desperation.

His grin persisted, but he still offered no response.

Suddenly Tim stopped the van at a small bend in the road. End of the line. The headlights illuminated the never-ending rows of dense bushes and trees. To the left of the van, I could barely make out a narrow, overgrown path obstructed by branches, leaves, and rocks.

Turning toward his window, Tim gazed out into the night. Abruptly his hand jerked up to his hair, and he ran his fingers through it repeatedly, mumbling something to himself that sounded like "You're all the same."

"Tim?" My voice was a frightened whisper.

"Be quiet."

My throat started burning, suddenly dry, and I rubbed my hand against it.

There was nothing normal about any of this, and he not only knew it, but he loved it. He lived for these moments, craved my fear like a drug.

"Please," I said in a shaky voice. "I want to go—"

"I said shut up!" he snapped. His wide eyes locked with mine, and I noticed something flickering in his pitch-black pupils. Hate. Rage. Lust for pain.

Ah, the crude savage. Among the myriad of killers, I detested his kind the most, with their raw ferocity and absence of finesse.

Helpless whimpers escaped my lips.

"Stop that," Tim demanded, balling a fist.

I bit my lower lip and covered my mouth with my hand. The first tear rolled down my cheek, landing wetly on my dress. Whimpers emerged once more.

"I said shut up!" he yelled, slamming his fist onto the steering wheel. The loud honk of the horn echoed through the still night, making me jump in my seat.

"Please," I begged. "I won't tell anybody."

"Tell anybody what?" Tim yelled, pounding his fist on the horn again and again. "Tell anybody what, what, *what*, you cunt!"

I reached for the door handle, but just as my fingers wrapped around the metal, Tim grasped my arm and yanked me toward him.

"No!" I screamed. "Help! Help!"

In a matter of seconds, Tim was on top of me, his heavy body like a boulder crushing me into the soft seat. My stomach churned at his stale body odor and onion breath.

"No!" I screamed again as his large hand found my throat and wrapped around it. He used his free hand to lift up my dress and tear at my panties. The fabric cut into my skin until it finally snapped.

Scratching, biting, kicking, I fought every second, but it was no use.

"Please," I begged, my eyes beginning to water. "Please!"

But the hand around my throat tightened, cutting off all air. My eyes felt like they were bursting from my skull.

"You loose little whore," he huffed above me. "Want to abandon me to fuck that Mike, huh?" His dark eyes met mine, and I saw the evil flicker of a monster in them.

Trembling with excitement, he pushed my legs open with his knee and maneuvered his hips between them.

"A cunt is a cunt," he mumbled over and over again as if summoning a demon.

I thought about screaming once more. For help, to make him stop, but I knew it was futile. So I didn't scream. And he didn't stop.

I waited until he was fumbling with the coverall's zipper on his chest. Then I went still, dropping my arms abruptly like a puppet without strings.

That was when I started to laugh.

At first a weak chuckle escaped my lips, tentative and shy, but as soon as he loosened his grip around my neck, my giggles rose in volume and turned into a burst of uncontrollable, full-bellied laughter.

Tim's eyebrows furrowed in confusion as he removed his hand from my neck and pushed himself into a sitting position. Disbelief was written all over his face as he struggled to process the situation unfolding in front of him.

"What...what's so funny?"

I just kept laughing, gasping for air, my chest heaving up and down.

"What's so funny?" he yelled. The anger in his voice had returned, but this time it was the rage of a pissed-off man, not a manic psychopath.

With practiced ease, my hand reached into the pocket of my dress, finding the syringe. I slid it out and removed the needle cap with one hand, almost poking myself.

"You want to know...," I said, steadying my voice, "what's so funny?"

For a moment, the van lay in complete silence, as if time itself had stopped. Neither of our sweat-slicked bodies moved.

I narrowed my eyes at Tim. Emotionless. Cold.

"It's amusing that most of your kind share the same traits. Not one of you keeps going when I laugh. You need the screaming to feel powerful, don't you? But the truth is, there's nothing powerful about you."

I rammed the syringe into the side of Tim's neck and pushed the contents into him. Tim jerked as if he'd been shot. Then he grabbed for my hand, yanked the needle out, and stared at it.

Quickly, from underneath him, I tugged at the door handle and kicked it open. Before he realized what was happening, I angled my legs and kicked him backward out of the van so he wouldn't collapse on top of me. With a heavy thud, Tim's large body crashed onto the ground, snapping a branch underneath it.

I scooted to the edge of the seat and carefully smoothed out the creases in my dress with my hands. "The propofol acts fast," I said. "We'll talk some more when you wake up again."

I stepped out of the van and onto Tim's chest. He coughed under my weight.

"Then you'll tell me where the bodies of Kimberly Horne and Janet Potts are."

Gasping for air, Tim somehow managed to squirm onto his side before he stopped moving. His vacant eyes stared into nothingness while his mouth was torn open, as if frozen in a scream.

I reached into my purse for my gloves and carefully slipped my hands into them. Bending down, I took off Tim's leather boots and slid them onto my feet. They were too large for me, and I was slightly unsteady in them, but I made my way to the back of his van just fine.

"Let's see what we're working with here," I said, adjusting the short blond wig on my head. It had shifted to the side a little during the fight. Short-haired wigs were my first choice when hunting. They perfectly covered my long hair, disguising one of my most identifiable features. The police rarely considered a good wig when searching for their persons of interest.

"You still with me, Tim?" I asked as I opened the doors of his van and climbed in.

No answer.

"Good."

The van's headlights cast bright beams of light, illuminating Tim, whose head and torso were securely duct-taped to a large tree. He groaned and slowly opened his eyes, drool trickling down his chin and pooling on his chest. At first his eyes rolled back, displaying only the whites. But then, with a jolt of sudden awareness, his eyes snapped wide.

"You bitch!" he coughed, gagging on the spit that had built up in his mouth and throat. He shifted his shoulders impotently, trying to free his arms. "Cut me loose!" he demanded, hacking up more saliva.

Dressed in a protective coverall—borrowed from his collection—I stepped out of the van with a cordless drill in my gloved hand. The bucket of Fixx was already positioned next to the van.

"Silly, silly Tim," I said, pressing the drill's trigger switch. I stared at the spinning tip of its tile bit and then watched as it halted the moment I released the switch. "You went through the trouble of wearing a coverall to a date but then would have left DNA behind by raping me? Which really wasn't nice, by the way. With such amateur moves, the FBI could have found you before I did."

Tim blinked rapidly, as if he'd just realized his mistake.

"Well, let's not dwell on the past." I leaned over and opened my purse, which was next to the Fixx bucket on the muddy ground. From it, I pulled out several syringes. One was full, the others were nearly empty. With an expression as blank as if I were watching paint dry, I reached into the purse again and pulled two severed fingers from a zipper-lock bag. They were tinged blue and reeked of rotten meat. One by one, I pressed the tips of the fingers onto the syringes.

Tim observed my movements closely. He was stunned into silence, and his lips quivered—but no words came out.

"Heroin," I said. "The full one has a lethal dose. And these fingers will leave fingerprints of a deceased criminal."

"Wh-what?"

I walked up to Tim and knelt beside his outstretched, motionless legs. Calmly I selected one of the syringes with only a trace of heroin in it.

"What the fuck are you doing?"

"I need to collect DNA from you so that the heroin needles will be linked to you. I'll scatter them throughout your van to portray you as a heroin addict. That's almost half the cover-up work. It's a tragedy, but once drugs are involved, law enforcement agencies perceive the victim as less significant and are less diligent in their pursuit of justice."

"What? Get that shit away from me!"

Tim jerked and squirmed, attempting to get free, but he barely moved an inch. I knew my way around duct tape.

I sighed and nodded at his legs. "If you're worried about the needle poke, you won't feel a thing."

Tim stared at his legs, his brow raised high and pushing against the duct tape wrapped around his forehead. Then he began gasping for air as if he were drowning. "My legs! I can't feel my legs!" His neck veins popped like a tangle of snakes as he tried to free his head. "You stupid cunt! What did you do to my legs?"

I pursed my lips. "You didn't bring enough tape. So, I had to cut through your lumbar spine intervertebral space, leaving you paralyzed from the waist down."

"You what?" His rage gave way to a whimper of sheer desperation.

"I can see you're upset. But if you think about it, you should be grateful. You won't feel any pain from your waist down. It's a courtesy you didn't extend to Samantha Hayden. Her medical report stated that she was beaten so badly her femur had snapped in two places. The sheer force necessary to accomplish that..." I shook my head in disgust.

"I don't know what you're talking about! You're crazy!" he babbled, like they always did. They were predictable that way. I didn't need to hear any more.

With a steady hand, holding the syringe at a ninety-degree angle, I pushed the first needle into his upper thigh.

"Wh-what are you doing? Stop!"

"Her bone snapped right about here," I said, grabbing another needle and inserting it a few inches below the first one. "And here."

My hand returned to the needles on the ground and hovered briefly above the one containing the lethal dose of heroin.

"I know death," I said in a raw tone. "That haunting stillness that takes over when the last flicker of light leaves the eyes. It's beautiful and terrifying at the same time."

I reached for the drill.

"Samantha's head was battered so brutally the forensic team had to freeze it at the crime scene to be able to transport it without it falling apart." I tapped the trigger switch of the drill. Its high-pitched whirring echoed through the night as Tim's eyes fixed on it in horror. "I wonder if it would bring her family joy if something similar happened to the man who killed their little girl."

Tim's teeth ground together, his gums whitening from the pressure. He strained against the duct tape, his face turning dark red with the effort, but ultimately, he slumped backward with a whimper. "Help!" he screamed. "Heeeeelp!"

I rose slowly, towering over the pathetic remains of the monster who had stolen the lives of countless young women in the most horrific ways imaginable. "Help?" I asked calmly. "Is that what Kimberly Horne and Janet Potts screamed when you brutally murdered them?"

"I...I don't know what you're talking about." Tim sniffled like a child. "Please don't hurt me." Tears began streaming down his face. But they weren't tears of regret. No, he was weeping for himself.

"Ah...there they are." I gave a sharp nod toward his face. "People think psychopaths like you can't feel emotions, but I know your tears are genuine. Soon you'll be bawling and begging like the true coward you are." I couldn't help the sarcastic scoff that slipped out. "It's ironic, but in some fucked-up way, you can feel more than I can." It was empathy for humans and sometimes animals that antisocial personalities like him lacked. I could feel plenty of that for normal people and animals. But when it came to feeling intense emotions, I was utterly incapable.

"Please let me go. I have children," Tim sobbed.

"Wonderful." A hint of excitement replaced my apathetic facial expression. "They'll be much better off without you. Especially once the world finds out what a monster you truly are."

"I'm not the guy you think I am. I didn't hurt those women. I don't know any of them! You have to believe me!"

"Don't worry. You'll remember soon enough. Men like you always do as soon as the slightest bit of pain is involved. Kind of ironic. For someone who loves violence, it's striking to see how poorly you handle it when the tables are turned."

I pressed my finger on the drill's trigger and maneuvered it toward Tim's teeth. The sound of its whirling and high-pitched screeches echoed through the woods.

"Noooooo!" Tim shrieked. He clenched his eyes shut as I inched closer. In a sudden movement, he clamped his mouth shut. That didn't stop me or the drill. With steady force, I drilled through the soft flesh of his lips and reached his teeth effortlessly. There was a rasping sound of metal against enamel as pieces of bloody flesh and white tooth chips shot off left and right. Tim's mouth flew open reflexively, and he let out a long, shrill shriek.

I stopped and stared at his mutilated front teeth, which were drilled halfway off in uneven chips. Blood mixed with spit streamed down his chin, dripping onto his chest.

"Stop!" Tim cried. His mouth gaped open as he spoke, trying to avoid touching the open nerve ends of his broken teeth. "Please stop! Please! It hurts so much. Please."

"I know," I said. "Shall we keep going?"

"No." He wept, his body trembling uncontrollably. "Please...no!"

I scrunched my eyebrows, aiming the drill once more. "Tell me where those missing bodies are, and then I'll stop."

Tim blinked at me. "I don't know what you're taaaaaaa—"

I pushed the drill into his upper row of teeth, this time more violently. I ran the drill over the whole set of upper and lower front teeth. Blood, flesh, and large tooth chips launched in all directions, some striking me in the face. Tim's screams rose over the sound of the drill's screeching.

I stopped once more, noticing that this time his lower gums were an unrecognizable mess. Tim kept screaming as his voice grew weaker and weaker until it was just a hoarse sob.

"I usually start out smaller and then go big," I said as if making casual conversation. "Like a crescendo of a colorful sonata. But I don't have much time tonight." I allowed a hint of irritation to show through my tone. "You were late. Now let me ask you again, where are the bodies?"

When Tim didn't answer, I pointed the drill at one of his eyes.

"Waiy!" he cried, unable to enunciate the word as he spat up blood. "Waiy, waiy, please waiy...please..."

"Finally, you understand the situation," I said, nodding at him.

"Dey..." He sobbed. "Dey are uuried in a semetay in Newuuyoot."

I cocked a brow at him. "A cemetery in Newport?" I clarified.

Tim just kept sobbing, but I took that as a yes.

"New graves without headstones would be obvious and raise suspicion," I wondered aloud, then paused. "Unless you placed the bodies into the graves of recently deceased people. Right after the funerals, before grass or flowers had a chance to grow over them." I tilted my head. "Timmy boy, I have to admit, that's quite clever. I assume you don't remember which graves you used?"

Tim continued sobbing. If I hadn't seen his work in the FBI's files, I would have felt pity for him. But a monster like this didn't deserve sympathy.

Determined, I grabbed the syringe with the deadly dose of heroin.

"Whah...whah are you 'oing!" His widened eyes revealed a ring of white around his pupils. "I...I 'old you 'ere dey are! You sai' you sop if I 'ell you 'ere dey aaa!"

"I did. And I will stop with the drill." I rammed the syringe into his leg and emptied it. "As I said earlier, I don't have much time, and I still have to drill your face apart. It'll go faster without you sobbing and soiling yourself, and honestly, unlike you, I don't enjoy this."

A soft smile ran over Tim's brutalized face the moment the warm, golden rush of the heroin hit him. On some more profound level, it bothered me that he'd be spared the suffering his victims endured. But I had a concert to perform in less than two hours, and his whining was irritating me.

Tim's gasps for air grew more labored as his eyes rolled back into his head. Soon his skin would turn purple and his breathing would slow. Until it stopped altogether.

I had cleaned the front of the van with Fixx earlier, but I still had to do some more cleaning and staging before making my way back to Boston. The sound of a ticking clock echoed in my head, urging me to move more quickly.

I picked the drill back up and was on the verge of completing my work with Tim when I realized I'd made a mistake. I hated mistakes. They meant sleepless nights tossing and turning, replaying the error in my mind again and again and again.

Staring at Tim, I shook my head in disappointment. After years of practicing basic human emotions, I'd made an obvious error!

"Joy is not the right emotion," I mumbled to myself. Earlier, I had told Tim that the families of his victims would experience joy over his miserable end. But thinking about it now that his mouth was drilled into an unrecognizable mousse, I realized joy wasn't the right emotion at all.

Joy. I shook my head. *Why would any of this bring anyone joy? Joy is for family birthdays, holding a puppy, or kissing a loved one...not this!*

In my defense, I grappled with both the intricacies of Savant syndrome and the challenging world of alexithymia. While each presented its own set of challenges, it was the shadow of my severe alexithymia, not the Savant syndrome, that cast a deeper veil over my ability to experience emotions and connect with others. Despite dedicating my whole life to understanding feelings, I found it a constant struggle. When to smile, when to laugh, when to look upset or yell in anger.

Sucking in a deep breath, I looked at Tim's mangled face.

Of course it won't bring them joy.

I turned on the power drill again and aimed it at Tim's left eye.

But it might give them closure.

The muffled sound of people rushing by my room, exchanging urgent whispers, told me I was late. Fifty-seven disrespectful minutes late. I hated it when others were late. I hated it even more when I was late.

Hastily I placed the plastic bag with my red dress and blond wig under my gold-plated makeup table. I stowed the ballerina shoes away too. I'd dispose of them after the concert.

A gentle knock came at my door. I quickly tied my long brown hair into a bun and wiped my face with flushable wet wipes to remove any leftover blood. The coverall I'd worn had shielded me from most of Tim's mess, but my face and neck still needed a few more rounds of wiping down.

"Leah?" Erik Hieber's voice sounded from behind the closed door. As always, the staff had fetched the CEO to handle the situation. I ignored him and slid into my black pumps, pulling my long satin evening gown over my head. Its cool, silky fabric brushed against my skin, sliding over my bare breasts down to my ankles.

"Leah, is everything all right?" Erik asked.

I took a look at myself in the bathroom mirror one last time. My mascara had made it through the event in decent shape, and with a few quick dabs of concealer rubbed over my forehead and cheeks, I looked presentable enough.

"We can cancel the concert if you're not well, Leah. Just say the word, and I—"

I flung the door open and strode confidently past the tall, silver-haired man who emanated arrogance and authority with every step he took. Undeterred, I continued down the hallway toward the stage. Relieved faces greeted me every step of the way, from stagehands to Crystal, the red-haired operations manager. Erik scurried after me, barely keeping up.

We reached the back of the stage where the stairs would lead me in front of the thousands of people who had traveled from all over the world for tonight's concert.

"Well, just let me know if you need anything. Your wish is my command," Erik said, a fake smile playing on his lips. A signature red satin scarf was elegantly draped over his shoulders, eerily mirroring the crimson hue of Crystal's glasses and hair.

"Thank you. I will." I nodded at him and ascended the stairs into the bright, warm light of the stage. The moment I walked in front of the crowd, a thunderous ovation erupted. People rose to their feet, cheering and chanting my name.

I approached my maple-colored Bösendorfer grand piano, the only piano I would play, and finally faced the crowd. It was difficult to discern faces against the blinding floodlights, but there was no mistaking the elegant man applauding from the private balcony on the first floor.

Luca Domizio. One of my biggest admirers. Dressed in a hand-tailored tuxedo, he was one of those men who had aged extremely well, projecting an aura of authority that warned others not to mess with him. His silver-streaked black hair was slicked back. He looked sophisticated as always. In his hand, he held a red rose that he would toss onto the stage after the concert, just as he always did. I gazed at him to acknowledge his nod, bowed to the crowd, and took my seat at the piano bench.

The crowd fell into a quick and complete silence. There wasn't a single cough, sneeze, or shuffle to be heard.

Taking a deep breath, I studied the black and white piano keys before me. I spread my fingers wide and struck the keys, initiating the heavy, slow chords of Rachmaninoff's *Prelude Op. 3, No. 2 in C-sharp minor*. Each note seemed to captivate the crowd, their collective focus creating a tense excitement in the room. The audience was under my spell, completely immersed in the witchcraft of my music. I played in Boston—nowhere else—and my concerts were sold out two full years in advance.

As always, in the aftermath of a kill, I would end my concert with the intricate melodies of Liszt's *La Campanella*. The piece wasn't technically as difficult as Cziffra's arrangement of *Flight of the Bumblebee* or Balakirev's *Islamey,* but the precision and control required for *La Campanella's* blistering speed and daunting technicality were still extraordinary. Playing it at its intended speed was a feat achieved by only a select few pianists, with most others crumbling under the weight of its rapid, chromatic scales cascading across the keyboard.

But I, perhaps the only person on this planet, had mastered the challenge of the piece in under three minutes and forty-five seconds.

And my performance didn't just hit every note correctly; it transcended the usual cacophony, weaving a clear, compelling melody.

Years ago, MIT researchers had conducted a study using *La Campanella* with new software to assess the technical accuracy of musicians in comparison to computers. They included my renditions in the study, and the results were mind-blowing. I stood alone as the only pianist who came close to matching a computer's precision. No one else had achieved my speed and accuracy.

Nobody.

That study had catapulted me to the top of the classical music world. Overnight, I was transformed from a musician into a legend—a machine in human form, my music a haunting echo of my dark soul.

I was celebrated as the greatest pianist of the century.

The very ground I walked on was cherished.

I'd been called the reincarnation of Bach and Beethoven themselves.

I could bring my audience from tears to laughter in seconds.

And yet...I was a fraud.

A crook.

A swindler.

As I felt absolutely nothing when I played.

Not the slightest bit of joy or anguish. Nothing. Nada. Zero. Null. Void.

If I were a color, I wouldn't be yellow, green, blue, or even black or white. I would be gray.

Playing the piano only stirred up an endless sea of gray inside me. I could spend an hour on a treadmill and feel the same way: sweaty and tired with a few calories burned.

Yet playing the piano had saved me. I learned more about emotions through music than I ever did interacting with people or during the countless, dull years I'd spent in therapy. Each set of tones had a corresponding emotion that people felt. Minor notes were associated with sadness, while major tones were linked to lively and colorful moods. Those were emotions I should have felt and couldn't, but at least now they had a sound. I was like a hacker deciphering a code.

To this form of art, I owed my life. My existence. It had liberated me from mental institutions and endless therapy sessions. And every single time I touched those piano keys, even if my only emotion was gratitude, I vowed never to forget.

TWO

The "Mama Is Calling" ringtone blared from Liam's phone as he slid into the booth styled like a classic car. Elly, the attractive yoga teacher in front of him, had chosen this rock-and-roll-themed diner for a breakfast date. Liam had no idea that breakfast dates were a thing now, but since it suited his schedule better than evening dinners, he didn't mind.

The diner was filled with the aroma of freshly brewed coffee and bacon. An older waitress was moving from table to table, refilling mugs and cheerfully chatting with guests.

"I'm sorry." He offered an embarrassed smile and silenced the call using the side button on his phone.

Elly tugged a curl of her long blond hair behind her ear as her blue eyes looked up at him from behind the menu. "Is that actually your mom calling?"

"As embarrassing as it is, yes. The boys over in cyber thought it'd be funny to hack my phone and install this ringtone when I turned thirty-five."

"That's quite the violation of privacy," Elly remarked, frowning.

"They were just joking." Liam thought it was pretty funny, but for some reason, it had struck a chord with Elly. "We joke around a lot at the office. It keeps us sane. But I don't know how to change it back. Now it's a running joke." His grin widened as he held up his phone. "I suck at tech. I only use my phone for calls, texts, and to take pictures of those rare moments when my daughter isn't throwing a tantrum over absolutely anything."

Elly's eyes widened. "You...have a daughter?"

"Yes, I thought my online profile mentioned th—"

"Mama Is Calling" rang out again, interrupting Liam.

He sighed. "I've been dodging her calls since last night. I better take this real quick, or she'll call the Bureau to look for me."

And she would. Liam's helicopter mom had done it before. It was one of the reasons his coworkers had changed his ringtone in the first place. Liam had never been the type of man who lived in his mother's basement or was overly dependent on her. His mother just happened to be batshit crazy when it came to boundaries; the situation had worsened when his younger sister left for college and his father passed away. But he loved his mom, so he put up with it as much as he could, especially since he knew how lonely she was.

Liam rushed out of the restaurant, heads turning as "Mama Is Calling" blasted once more. He stepped into the fresh morning air, only to be greeted by the overpowering smell of burnt traffic. He quickly picked up the phone as the cool breeze brushed against his face.

"Mom? Everything all right?"

"Nothing is all right, Liam," her shrill voice sounded through the phone. "I still have that rash on my arm from when you first told me about you and Sara splitting up."

Liam threw his hand up in frustration. "Are you kidding me? You're calling about your rash again? This early in the morning?"

"I called last night as well."

"At eleven p.m. I'm getting old. I was asleep."

"Oh, I'm sorry," his mother replied sarcastically. "I guess the possibility of never seeing my granddaughter again isn't a good enough reason for me to call."

Liam sighed. "Who said you'll never see Josie again?"

"The judge will when you lose the custody battle."

"Mom, even heroin addicts who neglect their kids are granted visitation rights these days. Don't you think a devoted dad and FBI agent who pays his taxes would be given the same rights?"

There was a brief silence.

"But you have a record. Remember when you stole that doll from Aunt Jane's collection to undress it in your closet? She called the police on you, remember?"

God have mercy, not the doll story again. "Yeah, but as soon as they saw her talk to the dolls and realized I was six, they left."

"Most likely thinking you might be a future criminal."

This conversation was going nowhere.

"Can I call you back? This is not a good—"

"This divorce is killing me, Liam."

"Killing you? It's my divorce."

"I still don't understand why you just couldn't work it out with Sara."

"Work it out?"

Liam shook his head in disbelief. He had done it again. Swallowed his mother's bait for drama like a starving fish swallowing a worm on a hook. Throughout his career, he'd had guns pointed at him and looked into the eyes of cold-blooded killers without losing his shit. But something about his mother—most likely her constant judgment and talent for twisting the truth to her liking—made him come unhinged.

"You make it sound like I'm the one at fault here," he said, feeling the heat of anger rising in his chest.

"I'm not saying that, but it takes two to tango."

"Two to tango?" Liam couldn't hide the outrage in his voice. "And how am I supposed to tango when my wife is sleeping with her twenty-year-old fitness trainer?"

His mother hesitated. "I...just wish you would care more."

"Oh, I do care, Mom. I'm the one losing my house, my daughter, and even my goddamned Peloton bike, so believe me, I care. But right now I'm in front of a restaurant, trying to put my life back together. And all I want to think about is whether my date likes bacon with her eggs or fake fucking tofu sausages!"

"A date? It's only been a year, and you're already on a—"

"Love you, gotta go."

And with that, he hung up. Immediately his mom called back—the screen lit up, the music played—but he dismissed the call. Shoving his phone in his pocket, he faced the large glass restaurant windows and noticed the customers inside staring at him. A mother with two kids held her toddler son's ears shut as she scowled at Liam.

"Damn it," Liam mumbled, walking past the judging eyes and returning to his date.

"I'm sorry for—" Liam nodded toward the windows "—for that."

Elly's blue eyes followed him as he sat across from her. The slick tie around his neck suddenly felt too tight. He loosened it with a quick tug and smoothed out a few wrinkles on his suit pants.

"No worries," Elly said.

"At least the date can't get much worse from here, right?" Liam said.

But just as Elly's tense expression relaxed into a smile, Liam's phone rang again. This time it wasn't his overbearing mother.

SAC Larsen, the screen read.

"I...I'm so sorry." Liam ran his hand through his short brown hair. "But I think I have to go."

THREE

Liam parked his new car behind one of the many mud puddles dotting the gravel road. Rain had drenched the area all week, but today the sun had finally emerged, shimmering golden through the tree canopies as birds chirped among the branches. It would have been a beautiful morning scene if not for the dead body.

Liam stepped out of his car, plunging his foot right into a puddle. Cold water drenched his leather shoe and sock. "Damn it," he said.

Shaking off the mud, he made his way down the gravel road toward the forensic and police officers bustling around the crime scene. A patrol officer standing among the many police cars lining the wooded road exhaled after taking a hit from his vape pen. The crisp morning air highlighted the white cloud rising above him. His gaze was fixed on the ground, an empty look in his eyes.

Farther down the road, Liam made eye contact with Tony, his partner of five years. He stood next to a forensic officer wearing a white coverall and face mask. A Boston Italian in his late forties, Tony was a portly man whose love for barbecues and beers was evident by the pouch hanging over his waistband. But what he lacked in physical fitness he offset with loyalty, and he was blessed with a sharp mind. This was evident in his large, curious eyes, which noticed every detail, no matter how small.

Tony nodded at Liam and strode over, carefully dodging another mud puddle. "Hope you didn't eat much breakfast," he said as he stopped in front of Liam, adjusting his belt to accommodate his belly.

"I didn't eat breakfast at all," Liam grumbled.

"I thought you went on a breakfast date, or whatever the hell it's called, with that yoga teacher."

"I did go on a breakfast date."

Tony raised an eyebrow.

"But I didn't get to eat breakfast," Liam clarified. "The date had gone to hell even before Larsen called me in, if you really need to know."

Tony threw him a curt nod. "Sorry to hear. But it might be for the best. You don't want a full stomach at this crime scene."

"That bad?" Liam asked.

Tony opened his mouth to say something, but the roaring sound of a sports car interrupted him. Neither one had to look to know whose it was.

"For Christ's sake," Liam cursed. "What the hell is Cowboy doing here?"

"Getting on our fucking nerves," Tony muttered. "That's what he'll be doing here. Apparently, there were drugs involved, so they sent someone from narcotics. Forensics just told me there are used needles and heroin all over the van. Not exactly a serial killer's signature."

"Then why are we here?" Liam wondered. Tony and Liam belonged to the Behavioral Analysis Unit of the FBI, a department dedicated to profiling and investigating serial criminals like killers, arsonists, and rapists.

The bright yellow Porsche screeched to a stop a few feet away from them, splashing muddy water onto Liam's legs and shoes. Tony chuckled, having been just out of the water's reach.

"This fucking guy," Liam cussed.

Both watched silently as a flamboyant blond man in his late twenties, wearing an expensive suit, stepped out of the car. He was clean-shaven. His smug grin, Armani sunglasses, and shaggy hairstyle made him look like a member of a failed boy band.

With confident strides, Cowboy approached them like he was on a catwalk.

"What, no coffee, ladies?" he asked, grinning.

Tony arched his eyebrows. "What do you think this is? A fucking breakfast date?"

Liam shot him a disapproving glance. Tony shrugged.

All three men made their way toward the small army of forensic officers who swarmed around a tree at the end of the gravel road.

"So why did Larsen send us out here together?" Liam asked as they walked.

"The crime scene reminded the Mass police chief of some other crime scene he'd seen or something," Cowboy explained. "So he wanted to make sure they're not connected."

"Or something?" Tony repeated. "Really got the facts sorted out, huh?"

"Wait." Liam stopped, blocking Cowboy's way. "Did you just say that the chief of the Massachusetts State Police was out here and called the Bureau himself?"

Nodding, Cowboy walked around Liam. "Not *was* out here...*is*. Some lieutenant colonel...something. I forgot his name."

Liam cursed under his breath as they both followed Cowboy toward the crime scene. "What the hell do you mean, 'some lieutenant colonel something'?" Tony pulled his golden badge out to hang it onto his belt. Liam did the same. Cowboy didn't.

"That means I forgot his name," Cowboy retorted, his tone slightly defensive.

"Unbelievable," Liam scoffed. "Get your fucking badge out, and don't you dare pull some Wild West shit."

Cowboy rolled his eyes like a child but pulled his badge out of his jacket pocket.

"If the chief of the state police called this in, we're going to make it a picture-perfect visit, you hear me?" Liam warned.

Cowboy fastened his badge to his belt as his gaze drifted to a young police officer who was nervously rubbing his pale face. An older officer was talking to him, his comforting hand resting on the younger man's shoulder.

"Calm your titties," Cowboy said. "This is probably just a classic gang murder, but the police chief called it in 'cause his boys can't handle anything beyond raccoons vandalizing Granny's trash ca—"

His voice cut off as they reached the tree at the end of the gravel road. The air seemed to grow heavy and unbreathable the moment their eyes settled on the dead man tied to the tree. The body was dressed in a blood-soaked white coverall that extended down to the victim's socked feet. Chunks of flesh lay strewn about the corpse. Most horrifying of all, the victim's face, taped to the tree by the forehead, had been carved like a gruesome Halloween pumpkin. The eyes, nose, and mouth were nothing but a gory mess of fleshy pulp and blood.

"What the fuck!" Cowboy gagged.

Tony, the most seasoned officer on the force, staggered back a few steps while Liam looked skyward and inhaled deeply, only to be hit with the overwhelming stench of rotten meat. Moments later, Cowboy spun around, dashed a short distance, and retched violently into the bushes.

A short, older man approached Liam and Tony and cast a disdainful look over at Cowboy. He had a weathered appearance, and his face bore the deep-set wrinkles of years in the line of duty. A neatly trimmed silver mustache adorned his upper lip while his high forehead revealed his receding hairline.

"I apologize for ruining your morning like this," the man said, shaking Liam's and Tony's hands. "Chief Murray."

"Special Agent Liam Richter from Behavioral Analysis." Liam introduced himself.

"Tony Russo. Also Behavioral Analysis."

Chief Murray looked in Cowboy's direction.

"Cowb—Theo McCourt," Tony said as Cowboy rose slowly, his face pale. "Violent Gang Task Force."

"McCourt?" Chief Murray asked. "Like the associate deputy director of the FBI?"

"Yup. His nephew," Liam confirmed, focusing back on the crime scene. With a slow, deliberate motion, he shook his head as if that would ease the shock of the surreal image in front of him. In the years he'd worked hunting serial killers, he'd seen some of the most horrific crime scenes one could imagine, but this...

"Jesus Christ," Cowboy murmured, rejoining the group. He wiped the corner of his mouth with his suit jacket's sleeve.

"You won't find Jesus here," Liam said.

"This is the work of the devil," Chief Murray added, dropping his gaze to the ground. "Have you guys ever seen anything like this before?"

The forest fell silent except for the clicking sounds of forensic cameras capturing the scene around them.

"Never," Tony finally said, glancing at the plumbing van parked a few feet from the victim. Its doors were wide open, and blood-soaked tools and cleaning supplies were scattered everywhere.

Liam walked up to the van and stopped before a bucket of Fixx. "Me neither," Liam said.

"You mean this brutal?" Chief Murray asked.

Liam's eyes remained on the bucket of Fixx. He retrieved a glove from his suit pocket and pulled it over his right hand. Lost in thought, he picked up a bloodied rag beside the bucket. The watchful eyes of Tony, Cowboy, and Chief Murray followed Liam as he stood and walked over to a small firepit filled with charcoaled wood. The strong odor of gasoline radiated from its dying embers. Liam's gaze settled on the charred remnants of what appeared to be fabric or plastic.

"It's not the brutality of the crime that's throwing me off here," Liam finally said, his eyes still fixed on the firepit.

"What do you mean?" Chief Murray asked.

"I mean—" he scanned the area, his eyes darting from one item to the next "—I've never seen a crime scene with this much evidence, yet nothing adds up."

Cowboy crouched in front of a small pouch containing a white substance that looked like heroin. "What are you talking about? There are plenty of goodies around. Seems like a drug gang crime to me. I bet the needles they found come back with the victim's DNA and heroin residue."

Tony joined Liam by the pit, peering into it as well. "Why did the killer only burn some of the evidence? Seems like a half-hearted job."

"I have no idea," Liam admitted.

Tony gestured toward the van and the words printed on it: EAST COAST PLUMBING, WE DO IT RIGHT.

"Why on earth would a plumber in a coverall be driving around in the woods with a bucket of Fixx? Maybe the victim isn't the owner of this van, and it was stolen," Cowboy said.

"Could be. But the Fixx could belong to the plumber to clean up leaks," Chief Murray suggested.

Liam glanced over his shoulder at the chief. "Have you had leaks before?"

The chief furrowed his brow. "I've owned four houses in my life. What do you think?"

Tony left Liam's side and moved closer to the corpse, examining it intently, shuddering briefly. "Then how many plumbers do you know who clean up after themselves in a coverall using a cleaning product? They arrive late, spend fifteen minutes on the job, leave you with damaged drywall, overcharge you, and then take off. No mopping up floors. Especially not with a bucket of product capable of destroying DNA evidence."

Cowboy shrugged. "I think the victim's drug dealer brought the Fixx here and left it after killing the drug-addicted plumber. Most likely because the plumber didn't pay back his debt or snitched on him. The cartels kill people for less than that."

"Possible," Liam said. "But whoever killed this guy went through a lot of effort to leave no trace behind. Just look at the footprints in the mud." Liam crouched down to examine a footprint. "Those seem to come from the same pair of shoes. Most likely the plumber's, considering he's missing his shoes. Why would someone go through all the trouble to leave no footprints behind but then get careless and leave behind a bucket that could easily be picked up and placed in the back of a car?"

Murray and Tony traced the footsteps etched in the mud, observing a trail that led away from the crime scene.

"I agree with Liam that the killer must have worn the victim's shoes," Tony said, nodding toward the victim's socked feet.

"It would explain why the victim's shoes are missing," Murray agreed.

"The butchers working for drug gangs aren't exactly known for their cunning tactics to outsmart law enforcement," Tony said, looking around for the missing boots. "It's a stretch to suggest that one of them went through the trouble of putting on this poor guy's shoes and then erased DNA evidence with a bucket of Fixx."

Liam hovered over the corpse once more, his blue eyes fixed on the bloodied remains that had once been a breathing human being. He ran his hand through his hair, feeling lost.

Tony was right. None of this screamed cartel to him.

"Maybe we aren't standing in the mess left behind by a bunch of cartel brutes," he said, narrowing his eyes at the corpse. "But a carefully orchestrated crime by a brilliant killer who knew exactly what he was doing."

All four men stared at the crime scene again, frowning like they were trying to fill a strainer with water.

"What murder?" Cowboy suddenly asked, breaking the silence.

"Huh?" Tony asked.

Cowboy looked at Chief Murray. "You said you called this in because this reminded you of another murder. Which one?"

The chief opened his mouth to answer but then stepped aside to make way for a couple of officers carrying an empty body bag and what looked like an oversized cooler with vents. The younger of the two officers, a skinny man with a long nose that seemed out of place, caught Liam's interest in the cooler. "A freezer. To prevent the head from falling apart during transport," he explained.

A look of disgust washed over Chief Murray's face as he watched the portable freezer a moment longer, then turned to face the group.

"Samantha Hayden," Liam interjected just as the chief was about to speak. "The crime scene here reminds Chief Murray of the murder of Samantha Hayden up in Maine."

Chief Murray took a moment, as if gathering strength, then nodded. "Samantha went to school with my daughter before her family moved to Maine," he explained, throwing Liam a long, intense gaze. Then he pulled out a card from his pants pocket and handed it to Liam. "Not a day goes by that I don't think of Samantha, and no matter how hard I try to remember her smile, all I can see is the way she was left behind in the woods." His thin lips curled into a pained grimace. "You keep me in the loop on anything you find on the son of a bitch responsible for this. I won't allow some wannabe Ted Bundy to kill college girls and plumbers in my state or any other, you hear me?"

"If this is the work of a serial killer, then this is federal now," Cowboy said in an arrogant tone. "The state police have no—"

"I will," Liam promised, cutting Cowboy off.

Chief Murray maintained eye contact with Liam. "If you need anything, let me know. And by anything—" his gaze briefly drifted off, as if he was thinking about Samantha, but then his focus snapped back to Liam "—I mean fucking *anything*."

Liam and Tony nodded as Chief Murray clapped his hands.

"Boys!" the chief said to the police officers. "Leave everything where you found it. This is the FBI's playground now."

As he squeezed past them, Chief Murray shot a final irritated glance at Cowboy before sliding into his car.

Tony shook his head at Cowboy.

"What?" Cowboy shrugged.

"Disrespecting the head of the Mass State Department," Tony said. "This is a BAU now—you can leave too. Violent Gang Unit has no business here."

Whipping out his cell, Cowboy smirked and walked off. "We'll see about that."

"Calling your uncle to cry, huh?" Liam hollered after him. "Ask him for some balls while you're at it."

Without turning, Cowboy flipped him off over his shoulder and kept walking.

"Just be glad he's gone for a bit." Tony sighed, pulling out his phone. "That'll give us some time to analyze the crime scene without his stupid jokes and cotton-candy breath on our necks." Tony lifted his phone over his head. "Bad reception. I'll call this in from one of the cruisers."

"Try to get a K-9 unit as well. We need to find those damn boots."

Liam turned back to the crime scene, hands on his hips.

Fucking nothing made sense here. Nothing. The bucket of Fixx, the firepit, the needles, the sad remains of the plumber wearing a coverall—what the hell was going on?

As always, when he first examined a crime scene, a drowning feeling of self-doubt washed over Liam. This sensation, deeply rooted in his self-esteem, stemmed from a mother who never acknowledged his achievements, no matter their size or importance. But unlike previous times when he'd questioned his ability to solve a case, Liam felt that this time—maybe for the first time ever—his doubts were entirely justified.

FOUR

The steady beat of my feet hitting the treadmill filled my workout room, spilling out into the hallway of my luxurious Beacon Hill town house. I pushed into a sprint for the final thirty seconds of my thirty-minute morning run.

As I stepped off the treadmill, the familiar beep of the alarm system announced Ida, my house aide, entering the home.

I wiped my forehead with a towel and stepped out into the hallway. My home struck a perfect balance between vintage charm and modern technology, featuring smart lights, an advanced heat-pump system, a top-of-the-line gourmet kitchen, spa-like bathrooms, and an expansive private roof deck with panoramic views of Boston. Double doors, high ceilings, and exquisitely carved fireplaces exemplified its fine Victorian craftsmanship. In the backyard, the former servants' quarters had been converted into a cozy two-bedroom guest house. Ida and her adult children lived there rent-free. A comparable residence in Beacon Hill could fetch thousands per month, but Ida was worth every dime to me, so I covered all utilities.

"Good morning, Ida."

Ida wore black pants and a white shirt, the same style of uniform she had worn for the 15 years she had worked for me. As usual, her black hair, threaded with silvery strands, was neatly pinned into a tight bun.

"Good morning," she said. "Breakfast will be ready soon," she added, giving the shopping bag in her hand a brief shake before turning in to the kitchen right off the dining room.

"Thank you," I replied and ascended the stairs to my master bedroom, which occupied the entire second floor. I took off my sweaty shirt and jogging pants, tossed them into a laundry bin, and stepped into my bathroom, which boasted a rainfall steam shower and freestanding bathtub. Its white marble surface shimmered in the morning sunlight.

"Turn the shower on to one hundred degrees," I instructed my smart system. The shower activated as I examined my slender body in the large mirror hanging on the wall. I noticed a football-sized bruise, purple and yellow in color, on my chest. Tim had managed to leave me with this memento when we'd fought in the front of his van. I stared at it briefly, expressionless, before stepping into the shower.

There, my gaze was immediately drawn to the shampoo, conditioner, and bodywash in my shower niche. Its usual impeccable spacing was off. Presumably, one of Ida's daughters had helped her mother clean the bathroom yesterday to receive some cash in return. This subtle disruption in the arrangement bothered me deeply, messed with my keen sense of detail and order. I reached out with wet hands, carefully adjusting the three items until they were in perfect alignment.

Ida worked diligently to maintain my five-thousand-square-foot home. It was a full-time job that wasn't too demanding considering I lived alone and kept the house completely clutter-free. I could stab a murderer without flinching, but the thought of clutter made me physically ill. Throughout the years, I'd learned to limit my obsession with orderliness to my personal spaces rather than allowing the chaos of other people's lives to affect me. It made life easier—especially considering that Ida had littered every free inch of her living quarters with useless stuff and pictures of her five children and twelve grandchildren.

I dressed in black designer pants, no panties, and slipped into a cream-colored silk shirt. Then I pulled my black hair into a casual ponytail and stepped into my fifteen-hundred-dollar vibrant red high heels. My wardrobe consisted strictly of black, cream or white, and red, with most pieces made from cashmere or silk.

After approving my look in the bathroom mirror, I decided to go without makeup that day.

My entire appearance was merely a facade, portraying a woman I was not. I cared for none of this. Not the nine-million-dollar town house in Beacon Hill nor the five-hundred-dollar face cream made with stem-cell technology from a rare Swiss apple.

To me, it was all part of the charade I had to maintain in order to meet the world's expectations of who I was.

I entered the kitchen, where Ida was preparing several small dishes at my usual seat at the white kitchen island. The meal included watermelon, almonds, raw tuna with shoyu, plain oatmeal, and a vegetable smoothie with moringa powder—all organic and fresh.

A small package at the end of the island caught my attention.

"Did it arrive last night?" I asked Ida, who was washing dishes across from me.

"Yes." She dried her hands on a kitchen towel and handed me the package.

"Thank you."

I narrowed my eyes at it. It was addressed to Olivia Nachtnebel. Only two people used my middle name, "Olivia," when sending me letters. It was given to me by my father when I once told him, as a little girl, that I disliked the name Leah, which I always thought lacked melody. But my father hadn't sent me mail in years, so I had no doubt who this package was from.

My expression remained emotionless as I opened the package, revealing a flip phone—simple and outdated.

Of course he would want to talk to me. The way I had left Tim was, well, not how I usually settled matters. For a brief moment, his angry face flashed before me. As much as I understood the rationale behind his anger, I was already annoyed.

"Is anything the matter?" Ida asked.

"No. Could you please tell my driver to pick me up in ten minutes? I'll practice at the Symphony Hall today."

"Yes, Miss Leah."

Ida took out her phone and briefly fumbled with it, then resumed washing the dishes.

This was the extent of our conversation most of the time. We both preferred it that way, and I paid her extremely well for her quiet nature—a trait uncommon among us humans, who generally love to talk, mostly about ourselves.

My eyes flicked over to the flip phone. I would need to adjust my evening schedule to accommodate him and meet at our usual location. He would be in an awful mood, yet I had nobody but myself to thank for that.

I stared at the raw tuna and thought about Tim's gums. This was probably the moment I was supposed to feel shocked, repulsed, or remorseful. Well, I didn't.

"Play Edith Piaf, please," I said to my smart kitchen. "*No Regrets*. The French version."

As the built-in Bose speakers in my kitchen ceiling played the song's instrumental introduction, I started my breakfast with a faint smile on my lips.

Now that Tim was taken care of, I could shift my focus back to enemy number one: the Train Track Killer.

FIVE

Liam parked his SUV in front of Josie's school and watched as a bunch of kids headed to the main entrance, their colorful backpacks slung loosely over their shoulders. Though the rain had stopped, a few drops still trickled down the window on the passenger side, where Josie was sitting. She was the one thing Liam loved more than life itself. She wore a colorful beanie over her blond pigtails. Even though it was early fall and too warm for a wool beanie, all her friends wore one, and at almost ten, Josie could argue quite convincingly if Liam dared to question the logic behind sweating for a trend.

"Your mom will pick you up today," Liam reminded her, feeling their weekend together had passed faster than a heartbeat again.

Josie frowned and twirled one of her pigtails around her finger. "Can't you ask Mom if I can stay another day with you?"

It hurt like hell just looking at her right now, but Liam knew Sara would never allow it. His ex might even accuse him of kidnapping his child. Out of spite, or whatever other reason, she had made it her quest to destroy the man *she* had cheated on.

A boy standing on the school stairs caught their attention. He waved enthusiastically at Josie with a cheerful smile. Her blue eyes lit up in response.

"Cute little fellow," Liam mumbled. "And look, he's wearing a rainbow beanie. But nope."

In a swift motion, Liam leaned over and pressed his badge against the passenger-side window, then made an overly dramatic *I'm watching you* gesture with two fingers.

"Dad!" Josie scolded.

"What?" He leaned back in his seat, faking remorse.

"He's nine!"

"Exactly my point. You kids these days go to college at eleven and marry at seventeen."

Josie giggled. It was heartwarming to hear that innocent laugh—a sound that had become all too rare lately because of the divorce Sara was dragging out in court. Liam had agreed to shared custody and offered more than the required alimony. After all, it was for his daughter, and what man would leave his child with nothing? But then out of the blue, Sara had a change of heart and wanted more money and fewer visitation rights for Liam. Well, that wasn't going to fly.

"Am I still spending Thanksgiving with you this year?" Josie asked, her voice soft, her eyes on her yellow Converse. It broke his heart to see her insecure like this. But he also couldn't agree to be his ex-wife's joke until she "figured things out." Sara had brazenly requested that he ignore her affair while acting like nothing was wrong. And when Liam mustered the remnants of his dignity and packed his bags, Sara's fury erupted, transforming him into her number-one enemy. In the aftermath, she'd claimed their house, savings, and stocks, and even the damn cat that Liam had come to love but lost in the end as well.

Liam knew marriage wasn't easy, and once the honeymoon phase was over, he had tried to put in the required work to keep it alive. But like many clueless husbands, he didn't realize how unhappy his wife was until another man stepped in and slapped a Band-Aid on a wound that needed stitches.

"Sweetheart," Liam said and grabbed Josie's hand. "I don't think your mom—" His voice broke off. What was he supposed to say? That Sara wouldn't allow him to have one Thanksgiving even though she'd spent most of the summer and last year's Thanksgiving with Josie? Because she wanted to hurt him?

Josie's eyes widened at Liam in anticipation.

"I...I don't think your mom should be alone on Thanksgiving. It would make her sad, sweetheart."

Goddamn, it sucked being the only grown-up in this relationship.

"But she won't be alone. Rick will be there. He's moving in," Josie said.

Liam pinched his lips. So Sara's bare-chested TikTok boy was now getting comfortable in Liam's hard-earned home for good?

"Well, he won't be enough for your mom on Thanksgiving. Do you know why?"

"Why?"

"Because Rick is just a normal dude, and you, my girl, you are an angel. And who wouldn't want an angel at their table over some normal dude?"

Josie's chuckle warmed his heart.

"And you know what else?" Liam said.

"What?"

"Christmas, you'll be mine this year!"

"Really?"

"I swear on your Aunt Jane's insane doll collection. I already called Santa to make sure he won't skip my apartment this year."

"Daddy," Josie said, rolling her eyes. "Santa ain't real."

"What? Says who?"

"Rick."

Fucking Rick.

"Ah, yeah? That's what Rick says, huh?"

"Mm-hmm." Josie smirked.

"Well, you tell Rick that making his bare-chested TikToks shouldn't be real."

Josie laughed loudly, bending forward onto her legs.

"Now you better go, or you'll be late for school."

We don't want to give your mother ammo for the judge.

Josie leaned over and hugged Liam tightly before unbuckling her seat belt.

"Wait, sweetheart!"

Josie turned with a curious frown on her face.

"Do Daddy a favor and don't tell Rick I said that about his videos, okay?"

Josie nodded.

"Or at least make sure your mom isn't there when you do."

Josie laughed again, then grabbed her backpack and opened the passenger door, eager to join a group of beanie-wearing girls who hysterically greeted Josie as if they hadn't seen each other for years.

Before the divorce, Liam had left the school as soon as he knew his daughter was safely with her friends and teachers. But that was before he'd lost the right to make his girl her toast and cereal every morning. Now he stayed in his car and watched her until she disappeared from sight. He treasured every moment no matter how long it lasted.

His phone interrupted him. The screen read *Tony*.

"I'm dropping off Josie," Liam said, hiding his frustration that the call was ruining his last few moments with his daughter.

"I'm sorry. We found out who the plumber was. Some guy called Greg Harris. Do you want me to call you back in a few?" Tony's voice crackled through the phone.

Liam's attention was still on Josie as he leaned forward onto the steering wheel. "No, tell me now. Who is it?"

"You gotta see it to believe it."

Despite the exciting news, Liam remained fixated on Josie, watching her intently as she waved goodbye before disappearing inside her school.

"I'm on my way."

SIX

Liam navigated the maze of busy phones and coworkers typing on keyboards at the new Chelsea FBI headquarters across the river from Boston. It was a stylish eight-story glass complex, yet the offices had the same outdated gray carpets and light blue wall paint one would find in older branches.

The entire Behavioral Analysis Unit was crammed in a single spacious room without cubicles, as if everyone were at a big family picnic. Only the Boston FBI headquarters' supervisor, Special Agent in Charge Larsen, enjoyed the luxury of a private office.

Liam stopped at Larsen's open door, but the chair behind the desk was empty. He continued toward the meeting room designated for the investigation of the serial killer believed to be responsible for the deaths of both the plumber and Samantha Hayden.

Liam had reached the desk of Heather Connor—who was on the serial-rapist task force—when the unmistakable aroma of McDonald's wafted through the air. He locked eyes with Heather, who heaved a sigh and rose from her seat.

"Can't he get a freaking salad for once?" Heather grumbled, rolling her eyes. Her radiant ebony skin was a stunning contrast to her white suit shirt. High cheekbones and deep, expressive brown eyes complemented her short-cropped hair. "I've put on five pounds since Cowboy slimed his way into BAU. Do you have any idea how many miles I have to jog on my treadmill to get that shit off again? I'm in my thirties and have three kids."

She grabbed a folder from her desk and followed Liam to the meeting room.

BAU was composed of agents who investigated mass murders, serial murders, serial rape cases, and kidnappings. But at the end of the day, everybody stuck together and helped one another. And when it came to finding a person of interest, Heather was the queen bee. She used to do the whole field-agent-with-gun thing, but when her third kid was born, she'd asked for a transfer to research.

"Don't complain until you hit your late thirties like me, Heather," Liam said, joking. "People think we thirties folks are all the same, but there's a huge difference between thirty-one and thirty-eight. I have to work twice as hard to shed those extra pounds. Besides, Rob doesn't care about them anyway. So you have the loving-spouse thing going for you too."

Upon entering the modest, two-hundred-square-foot meeting room, they were greeted by a central desk and a sizable whiteboard displaying a summary of their evidence, complete with photographs.

Tony and Cowboy were already sitting at the table—Cowboy in front of leftover fries, a grin on his face like always.

"That love is being tested," Heather said as she took her usual seat across from Cowboy. "Rob bought a new truck without telling me. I. Was. Furious."

Tony looked up from a pile of pictures in a manilla folder. The table was littered with papers and pictures related to the investigation. "Are you seriously expecting a man to condemn another man for buying a truck?"

"It was almost fifty K," Heather countered.

"A man always has money for a truck," Tony said. "No matter what."

Heather shot Cowboy's fries a disapproving glance.

"So what do we have?" Liam asked, taking a seat next to Heather. This was the usual seating arrangement: Tony and Cowboy across from Heather and Liam, Larsen at the end seat like a lord.

Tony pushed a low-res picture across the table. It depicted a white sedan at a gas station with a woman in a red dress sitting in the back. She was wearing a baseball cap over her short blond hair and was watching a young man in a white T-shirt pumping gas. A pink sign in the windshield identified the car as a rideshare vehicle.

"The guy in the white shirt? Who is he?"

Heather handed Liam a picture from the folder in her hand. "Not him," she said. "Her."

Cocking a brow, Liam examined the close-up of the woman. Her face was angled downward, as if she were aware of the gas station camera, but her short blond hair and red dress could be helpful in recognizing her in other footage.

"I'll be pretty impressed with our plumber if the lady in red is really the woman who was last seen with him." Cowboy joked like a juvenile. "She's a nine."

"You can't see her face. How do you know she's a nine?" Heather asked.

"Oh, I'm not looking at her face." Cowboy smirked. "I'm talking about—"

"This is the FBI, Cowboy, not Hooters," Larsen interjected sharply as he entered the room. The short man with round silver glasses and a slim face with a large forehead always reminded Liam of a scientist studying rock samples. His attire, featuring a bow tie instead of a standard necktie, and the slightly higher pitch of his voice, placed him more in the realm of geek than the stereotypical "manly man." But none of this meant that Larsen was someone to mess with. He had a solid military record with five tours in Afghanistan. His rate of clearing cases was the highest in the entire building, including the cybercrime unit, for which hackers did the work.

Larsen sat at the table, maintaining his intense stare at Cowboy. "Please refrain from degrading women with sexual remarks, or make sure you have a damn good reason to explain this childish insecurity to your uncle once I file a complaint. Here at BAU, we respect every man, every woman, and everything in between, you hear me?"

Liam, Heather, and Tony all bit down a laugh, shifting their focus to random items in the room to avoid Larsen's penetrating gaze. Liam almost made the mistake of grinning, but he knew that if he did, Larsen would target him next, likely questioning what he found amusing about witnessing a coworker, who might take a bullet for him in the field, being reprimanded like a child.

Like a spider waiting for a fly to get caught in its web, Larsen waited a moment, studying each of the agents in the room through his old-fashioned glasses. When no one dared to challenge him, he proceeded to distribute photos and documents from the folder in front of him.

"Caucasian female," he said in an unemotional tone. "Age between thirty and fifty, approximately five-seven and a hundred and fifteen pounds, wearing a red dress and shoes of an unknown color...and that's about all we have on her."

Liam glanced over the paper in his hands, which appeared to be a witness statement. "What do you mean that's all we have?" he asked. "It looks like we interviewed the Lyft driver. The guy in the white shirt at the pump."

Larsen nodded. "We did. I talked to him myself. Owen Wilkers. College kid. He doesn't remember much about the woman other than her red dress and long legs. He said it was dark."

Shuffling through the papers, Liam discovered another witness report, that of an Asian waitress. "And this?" he asked, holding the report up. "Another witness statement."

Larsen nodded again. "A statement from a waitress working at a restaurant called the Dragon's Palace, a run-down Chinese restaurant in the Rancher's Shopping Center."

"Is that the shopping center we tracked Greg Harris's van to using traffic cams?" Cowboy asked.

"The exact one," Larsen confirmed. "Tony interviewed the staff of the businesses in the shopping center and got lucky with the waitress from the Dragon's Palace. She claims she noticed the van on the night of the murder."

Tony cleared his throat, his voice steady and deliberate. "Ms. Liu said she served water to a woman matching the description of the red-dress lady. The woman graciously tipped her a twenty just for sitting there for about forty minutes. After that, Ms. Liu saw her climb into a van identical to Harris's. Her testimony led us to the woman in the red dress in the first place, and Heather managed to link her to the woman in the Lyft car at the gas station."

"Dang, good work, H!" Cowboy said, nodding his approval.

Heather's forehead wrinkled. "H?"

Liam ignored him. "This all sounds...promising, doesn't it? We've identified a person who was with Harris right before the murder—maybe even witnessed it."

"Or who did it," Heather said.

"Come on," Cowboy scoffed. "Have you seen the pictures of the crime scene?" He pointed at the gruesome photos of Harris's body pinned to the whiteboard, their presence casting a dark shadow over the room.

Heather shuddered, and Liam couldn't blame her. The pictures weren't something any normal human being could easily stomach, seasoned FBI agent or not.

"The autopsy report states that Harris had enough heroin rollercoasting through his blood to kill him," Cowboy argued, his voice ringing with pride. "And considering used needles with his DNA were found in his van and next to him by the tree, I'd like to seize this moment while I have everyone's undivided attention to offer my assistance to you. In my modest, yet seasoned, opinion, Greg here—" he paused for effect, nodding at the whiteboard again "—was an addict who pissed off the wrong folks, so they took care of him, sending a message to other blue-collar junkies. The cartels do this all...the...time. Period."

"Then why would they leave the woman alive? Cartels don't care about killing women and children," Heather said.

"Who says she even witnessed the crime?" Cowboy argued. "Maybe she and Harris fought before all this happened. Maybe she took a Lyft back to town after she got out of the van and was stranded on the side of the road."

At this point, Liam thought, anything was possible. "Do we have the time of the ride?" he asked.

Heather shuffled through her papers. "Pickup time near the gravel road was 9:21 p.m."

Tony scrutinized the documents in his hands, his eyes narrowing. "So it's entirely possible that the Lyft ride was just before the murder. Our estimated time of death falls between nine and ten p.m. What name was the ride booked under? Do we have a cell number associated with it?"

"We do," Heather said. "The booking was made under Greg Harris, using his credit card and phone."

A feeling of defeat settled in Liam's gut like a boulder. "The victim's..." he mumbled. Nothing on the lady in red so far. Nada.

Heather nodded with pinched lips. "That's how I was able to trace the Lyft ride and the lady in red in the first place. I combed through the call logs of nearby cell towers for the victim's phone number and discovered that a call was placed from Harris's phone to the Lyft ride."

"And the phone itself?" Cowboy asked.

Heather shook her head.

Another major evidence item missing. The damn phone.

Cowboy cast Liam an all-knowing look. "Harris's cunning girl in red probably stole his shit right before he was murdered. Who knows? She might even be a prostitute for the dealer who offed him."

"What about the fingerprints we found on the needles and on the door handle of Harris's van?" Liam looked at Heather. "Were we able to match them with anybody?"

"Nope. Only those of Harris. The other set of fingerprints remains unidentified."

Liam's shoulders sagged, the weight of defeat pressing down on him as his gaze wandered to the evidence board. A harrowing crime scene, reminiscent of a *Saw* film, had yielded no DNA evidence except for a set of unidentified fingerprints and some heroin. No tire tracks or footprints but the plumber's—whose boots were still missing after a weeklong search through the woods with K-9 units. And, to top it off, the entire crime scene painted a vivid picture of a drug crime. The only problem? "No cartel or drug gang I've ever come across works like this," Liam said, crossing his arms. "Drug dealers don't care about buckets of Fixx or erasing footprints. Hell, a hit job costs less than fifty bucks from where they recruit in Mexico. The cartels send butchers, not Mr. Brooks."

"Speaking from your years of experience working drug crimes?" Cowboy asked.

"So," Tony said, exhaling loudly, "all we've got is the possible smashing-heads signature of a serial killer who might not even exist. What a waste of fucking time."

Tony's words left a bitter taste on Liam's tongue—because they were true. But an unshakable feeling nagged at him. The same feeling that had helped him crack every other case. The same feeling he'd gotten the last night Sara had said "I love you" before he'd uncovered her cheating. It was a suspicious, gut instinct that now whispered to him that there was more to this case than drugs. He couldn't ignore it.

"If we follow logic, we might not even have a consistent signature here," Larsen said. "The head injury could be a mere coincidence and unrelated to Samantha Hayden's killing. Our boys in Maine told me they're linking her death to a serial killer called the College Snatcher. As his name states, he snatches and kills college girls, not drug-addicted plumbers. The evidence we have so far strongly indicates that Greg Harris is just an unfortunate drug addict who crossed the wrong people."

"The College Snatcher is still out there, as far as I know," Liam objected. "Sure, Harris didn't match his victim profile at first glance, but who knows why these psychos do what they do. Maybe he killed Harris for some kind of revenge. I would love to pay our boys in Maine a visit and go over the evidence."

Larsen's brow furrowed. "Sorry, Richter. But unless we find something more substantial to connect Harris to the College Snatcher, I won't be able to push that through with McCourt. No suspects. No prints. No DNA. No cell. You can give the team in Maine a call, but a trip is out of the question under the current circumstances. We're understaffed as it is, and Heather is too behind on the Newcastle well-water-poisoning case to help with this one. And if that poisoning son of a bitch walks, not even Jesus can save us from McCourt."

"So where do we stand now?" Tony asked. "The case. Is it Drugs—" he gave Cowboy a pointed look "—or BAU?"

"Uh, drugs at the crime scene and in the victim's blood. Drug crime," Cowboy chimed in, his tone dripping with smug certainty.

"Wherever McCourt wants it to be after we talk to Harris's mother," Larsen said, ignoring Cowboy. "We've identified and located the poor woman."

A silence hung in the air like a dense fog.

"Dear God," Heather mumbled. "I hereby withdraw from that visit."

"I'm not part of this unit. Officially," Cowboy declared.

"Great. I won't go alone, that's for sure," Tony said. "Freaking face drilled in...That's too much for one agent to deliver."

Liam nodded. "I'll go with you."

"Good." Larsen straightened his papers and rose. He must have been barely five feet five inches tall. "Well, if nothing else comes up, I'd say we talk to the mother, and then McCourt will hand the case over to..."

His voice trailed off midsentence as Cowboy tapped his two index fingers against the table's edge in a drumroll as if this were an AC/DC concert. Larsen shot him a glare that could kill.

"Sorry," Cowboy muttered like a terrified schoolboy. "I got caught up in the moment."

"We'll debrief this again tomorrow," Larsen said coldly before heading toward the door.

Tony and Heather rose as well, but Liam leaned back in his chair, his eyes glued to the picture of the woman in the back of the Lyft.

"The woman," he said, halting everyone in their tracks as they gathered their papers to leave. "Let me guess. She asked to be dropped off at a park or street corner? Somewhere without an address?"

That's what the smarter substance abusers usually did so they couldn't be traced.

Cowboy, Tony, and Heather shuffled through their papers. Since Larsen had interviewed the driver, Liam looked directly at him, bypassing the search for the witness report in his folder.

"Not...exactly," Larsen admitted. All eyes turned to him.

"Where, then?" Tony asked.

"Downtown Boston," Larsen said.

"Downtown? Where?" Heather pressed.

"Not that it matters much," Larsen said, pausing briefly, "but she was dropped off at the Boston Symphony Hall."

Heather, Liam, and Tony exchanged curious glances while Cowboy's lips curled into a smug smirk. "For a fucking cello concert?" he said, joking.

"Did she go inside?" Heather asked, a confused look on her face.

Larsen frowned. "She did. But we don't know what she did there or how long she stayed. She might have just used the bathroom to shoot up for all we know. It's not like that hasn't happened in a major city before."

Liam cocked a brow. Out of all the possible drop-off locations Larsen could have named, the symphony seemed...off.

Tony shrugged, conceding that it was odd but likely wouldn't change much. "Maybe she likes to be high to the sound of Mozart. Remember that homeless guy on Eighth who shot up at that burger place every night because he liked the smell of fried meat? The owner of the place had to install blue bathroom lights to get rid of the dude."

"Why blue?" Heather wondered.

"They can't find their veins in blue light," Cowboy said, tapping his elbow pit.

"But what if she works at the Symphony Hall," Liam said, "or was meeting someone there?"

"Sorry, Richter," Larsen said. "I already checked. No woman matching the description of our lady in red works there. Nobody even remembers seeing her. All we have is the driver claiming he saw her walk inside in his rearview mirror after he dropped her off."

"Shit," Liam muttered. Another dead end.

"Same time tomorrow." Larsen threw the team a curt nod and was almost out the door when Liam stopped him once more.

"I'd like to check it out, just in case."

Larsen's brow furrowed, maybe rightfully so. It was most likely a waste of time, but the freaking Boston Symphony Hall? That familiar gut feeling nudged Liam once more. Something was off here. Really, really off.

Placing his hands on his hips, Larsen lingered, clearly thinking. He looked up at the whiteboard as the room lay in silence, eagerly awaiting his response.

"Be my guest," he finally said, annoyed. "But unless you come back with something substantial, we take care of the poor mother and let McCourt hand the case over to the Wild West, you hear me?"

Liam offered a military salute. "Yes, sir!"

"And don't upset anyone over there. That damn Symphony Hall sees more politicians come and go than the Senate."

With one final icy glance from his piercing eyes, Larsen strode out of the room.

"Damn," Cowboy muttered. "Larsen is literally the only person on this planet who could make a grown man wet his pants."

"Is it just me, or does Larsen seem grumpier than usual?" Tony scratched the thinning patch on the back of his head.

"It's the Newcastle well-water case," Heather explained, squeezing past Liam. "Better get that visit to the Symphony Hall done and then call it good. Larsen wants all hands on the Newcastle case to prepare for court. Apparently, we got a confession from the guy who poisoned the well water, but then his wealthy aunt hired a top-notch lawyer right before he signed it. One of those TV OJ lawyer types. And we all know how Larsen gets when one of the bad guys might walk."

"Like a starving grizzly finding a campsite filled with Girl Scout cookies," Tony said.

"Mm-hmm," Heather agreed, heading back to her cluttered desk in the large operations room.

"You want me to come with you? We could go over the imminent transfer of the case to my boys in the car," Cowboy offered.

Liam scratched his head. "Erm...thanks, but this is a one-man job. Why don't you and Tony visit the victim's mother together? It'd be a great transition, considering you might have to talk to her again while working the case in the future."

"What?" Tony protested. "Liam, come on!"

"I better go before some concert starts and it gets busy over there," Liam said with an apologetic look. He felt bad for saddling Tony with Cowboy, but there wasn't enough time to stop at the Boston Symphony Hall and visit the victim's mother. The case might be with Drugs before the week was over. Larsen seemed convinced that this case belonged with Drugs. And maybe it did...yet something didn't add up here. What substance abuser would take a Lyft to the Symphony Hall, using her boyfriend's stolen card and phone right before he was slaughtered?

Nah, something was off about this whole damn case. And Liam would find out what it was.

SEVEN

Rain or shine, the Boston Symphony Hall maintained its glamour. The combination of towering brick walls and elegant white marble pillars created a striking, castle-like presence. Gazing at it long enough made Liam feel as if he'd been transported back to a time when men still wore top hats and women corsets.

Circling a large puddle, Liam made his way up the white flight of stairs and into the entrance hall. Given the time of day, the hall was pretty empty. Concerts likely wouldn't start until late afternoon or evening, and even the ticket booths were closed.

Liam scanned the hall, locking eyes with a young man carrying a cello case over his shoulder.

"Excuse me, do you happen to know who manages the operations at the Symphony Hall?" He pulled out his badge and flashed it.

The young cellist's eyes widened in scared curiosity.

"No need to be alarmed. Nobody's in trouble. I just have a few questions."

The young man seemed to relax a bit. He nodded toward the ticket booths. "Just follow the hallway behind those booths, and you'll find Erik Hieber's office. He's the one in charge. Just a heads-up though, he can be a real dick."

Liam grinned. "Thanks."

The helpful cellist had neglected to mention that Mr. Hieber's office was tucked away in the staff-only area, a labyrinth of seemingly never-ending windowless hallways adorned with red carpet. These hallways were a symphony in and of themselves, with musicians practicing in various rehearsal rooms. The air was alive with harmonies and practice runs.

After what seemed like an eternity, Liam finally stumbled across Mr. Hieber's office. The door was larger than the other doors and made of wood with a golden nameplate on it. While it stood out, it wasn't overly extravagant. Liam knocked, carefully, like someone who didn't want to intrude.

"Yes?"

He stepped inside to find a tall, skinny man sitting behind a large mahogany desk in an otherwise simple office. The man appeared to be in his late sixties with silver hair neatly combed back and a well-groomed mustache. He wore a cream-colored suit with a crisp white shirt and red necktie. There was an air of arrogance and authority about him. A blood-red satin scarf hung loosely over his shoulders. Across from him sat a younger woman with red hair, glasses, and lipstick that eerily matched the color of Mr. Hieber's scarf.

Mr. Hieber looked up from a disorganized pile of papers he seemed to be reviewing with the woman and narrowed his eyes at Liam. "What is it? Can't you see I'm busy?"

Liam grinned. The cellist was right—Hieber was a bit of a dick.

"I'm sorry to interrupt you, Mr. Hieber." Liam pulled his badge out and held it up. "Agent Richter with the FBI. I'd like to ask you some questions if that's all right?"

Mr. Hieber's thin lips twisted into a frown while the young woman's eyes widened in shock.

"FBI?" she said.

"Let me take a closer look at that badge," Mr. Hieber demanded, gesturing Liam to come closer. It was rare for someone to ask to look at his badge, but not unheard of, so Liam walked over to his desk and handed it to him.

Leaning forward in his chair, Mr. Hieber scrutinized the badge for a few moments before handing it back. "Make it brief."

The woman quickly rose to her feet and nervously grabbed her papers.

"Stay, Crystal. This won't take long."

Crystal glanced between Liam and Mr. Hieber.

"It won't take long," Liam confirmed.

Crystal hesitantly sat down again.

"Nobody's in trouble—"

"Of course not," Mr. Hieber interjected. "This is one of the most prestigious symphony halls in the world. Not Woodstock."

Liam nodded with a forced smile. "I'm here about a possible witness. On the night of the twelfth of last month, she was seen entering the Symphony Hall."

"So? Thousands of people do that every weekend. We're an international attraction."

"Right. Of course. I'm not suggesting anything here. I was just wondering if there's anybody who might remember a woman dressed in a short red dress with short blond hair? It's possible she was distressed that night and acted unusual. Did anybody mention anything?"

Mr. Hieber furrowed his brows. Liam knew it was a long shot but still worth a try. One never knew when it came to who had seen what.

"Do you have cameras?" Liam already knew the answer to that question. He had seen them in the ticket hall, and there was even one in this office. Crystal opened her mouth, but Mr. Hieber was faster.

"Why are you asking me questions to answers you already know?" He nodded at a corner in his office.

Liam smiled innocently. "Could I have a look at the footage from that night?"

Mr. Hieber scratched his chin, thinking.

"It most likely won't yield anything," Liam said, "but it'll help us close the matter of the symphony's role in the case before it gets any unnecessary attention from the public. It's in relation to a rather gruesome crime. Not exactly the publicity a prestigious place like this deserves."

With narrowed eyes, Mr. Hieber leaned back in his chair. "We have a security team. It's small, but the Symphony Hall is monitored twenty-four seven. Connor is the man in charge of security. Crystal will take you to him."

Poor Crystal took a little too long to process his command.

"She will take you *now*," Mr. Hieber added dismissively.

Crystal swiftly rose to her feet. "Connor is right down the hallway, Mr.—"

"His name is Agent Richter," Hieber answered before Liam could.

Crystal smiled nervously and led the way to the door.

Before Liam followed her into the hallway, he turned to Mr. Hieber. "Thank you," he said, only to receive a dismissive wave as Mr. Hieber returned his attention to the papers scattered across his desk.

"Mr. Hieber doesn't mean anything by it. The holiday concerts are coming up," Crystal explained as she knocked on the door marked SECURITY. "Things can get pretty stressful around here, especially for Mr. Hieber."

Liam nodded. "I get it."

An awkward silence filled the air as they both stared at the door. Moments later, a tall man opened it from the inside. He looked like a retired version of G.I. Joe, and despite appearing to be twice Liam's age, he seemed capable of taking on Liam any time of day.

"Connor, so sorry to bother you," Crystal said, pushing her glasses back on her nose. "This is Agent Richter from the FBI. He would like to look over some security footage."

Connor furrowed his brow.

"Nobody's in trouble," Liam said. "We're just looking for a potential witness."

"Mr. Hieber okayed it," Crystal chimed in.

"Well, come on into the dungeon then," Connor said, turning toward a dim-lit, windowless room filled with security monitors showing various areas of the Symphony Hall.

"Thanks, Connor. This won't take long," Crystal said, pulling a chair from the table placed in front of the state-of-the-art monitors mounted on the wall. The room boasted 4K touchscreen displays, cutting-edge computers, and even a security alarm on the wall.

"Nice setup," Liam said, genuinely impressed. The computers at the Bureau were twice as old.

"There's a lot of money in Mozart," Connor said, sitting down in a high-end massage chair.

"No kidding," Liam mumbled.

"So what footage are you looking for?" Connor's voice was laced with curiosity. "I suppose you can't spill all the beans?"

"Unfortunately not," Liam replied. "We're searching for a woman with short blond hair in a red dress. She entered the Symphony Hall on the twelfth of September around nine-thirty p.m. Do you keep footage that long?"

"When I was still a young stud, this would've been a problem," Connor said, gesturing toward the sky. "But thanks to that, we can go sniffing back months."

Crystal and Liam exchanged puzzled glances. Connor noticed their confusion.

"The cloud. You don't get it? Cloud...as in the fluffy thing in the sky."

Crystal forced a smile. Liam followed suit and leaned over Connor's shoulder as the big man scanned his badge with a device attached to the computer, then pulled up the file from the night of the twelfth.

"This should be around 9:28 p.m.," Connor said, playing a video of the hall's grand entrance doors. A smattering of people, dressed to the nines, gracefully navigated the white stairs, entering or exiting the building. It didn't take long before the woman in the red dress appeared on the stairs, walking toward the entrance doors.

"There!" Liam said, his finger jabbing at the computer screen. The baseball cap, the vibrant red dress, and her statuesque figure—it was undoubtedly the woman from the pictures. Swiftly she ascended the stairs and vanished through the imposing double doors of the entrance, seamlessly blending into the elegant evening crowd.

"Can we follow her with the other cameras?" Liam asked.

"We sure can." Connor's fingers danced across the keyboard; moments later, another video played on the screen. This one showed the entrance hall where the woman in red strode confidently past the ticket booths. Her head was lowered, as if she was aware of the need to shield herself from the prying lenses of the cameras. Then she disappeared around a corner.

"On it," Connor said, swiftly pulling up the next video. It showed her navigating one of the lengthy hallways, only to vanish behind another corner.

Connor sighed, leaning back in his chair.

"Well?" Liam inquired, his impatience growing. For the first time today, he actually felt like progress was being made.

"That's it," Connor said, steepling his fingers.

"What do you mean?"

"That's the last camera that captured her journey. Around that corner is the staff entrance and the hall's best-kept secret. An unknown restroom. Only the most frequent concertgoers know about it, and they'd rather die than share that toilet with newcomers."

"There are no more cameras?" Liam's voice carried more outrage than he'd intended. To come so close to even the smallest breakthrough, only to be met with this setback, was a crushing blow.

"We ain't recording no women's bathroom doors. That's a legal line no venue as profitable as ours wants to cross. And the staff area is too large to monitor. We ain't got the sort of musicians here that would require that investment. We're Mozart, remember? Not Mötley Crüe. Besides a few junkies shooting up in the bathrooms in the winter and the occasional homeless person looking for a warm spot to sleep at night, we ain't got much trouble here."

Liam pursed his lips, his disheartened gaze fixed on the monitor still playing the video. A few people carrying instruments in cases came and went, and a woman with a cleaning cart appeared—but no woman in red.

All three of them watched for another minute or two, but still no woman in red came back out of the bathrooms.

Connor leaned forward in his chair again. "Would you mind if I fast-forward? We have a shift change soon."

"No. Go ahead," Liam said.

The video played through several more minutes—still no sign of the lady in red.

"Where the hell is she?" Liam wondered.

"I have no idea," Connor admitted, squinting at the screen.

"Maybe she passed out in the bathroom stall for a while?" Crystal suggested.

"Nah," Connor said. "Melinda cleaned that bathroom around 9:55. See? Here she is." He paused the video as a short, stout woman with a cleaning cart entered the frame from the direction of the bathroom.

"Then where is she?" Crystal asked, her voice laced with confusion.

"Well, she either snuck into the staff-only area, or the video glitched," Connor explained. "I'd have to watch the whole video in real-time to catch the glitch. It's very rare, but it happens sometimes."

"A glitch. That's gotta be it," Crystal said, trying to sound convinced. "She would've been noticed in the staff-only area."

Liam looked at her. "Are you sure? Things look like they can get hectic around here."

Crystal chuckled. "Absolutely. You've met Mr. Hieber. We have very expensive instruments in the back rooms."

"A Stradivari worth a million bucks among them," Connor added.

"None of us would open the door to unknown faces. If you forget your badge, you have to get a temporary replacement from Mr. Hieber for that day. So you just don't forget it in the first place if you know what I mean."

Liam nodded. "Who performed that night?"

"Leah Nachtnebel," Crystal and Connor said simultaneously, then grinned at each other like children who were about to shout "jinx."

"Who is that?"

Connor's and Crystal's smiles vanished, replaced with looks of utter disbelief.

"Leah...Nachtnebel?" Crystal raised a brow at Liam.

"I'm sorry, but I have no idea who that is."

"Jesus, Miss Nachtnebel is someone even I know," Connor said, "and I'm just security."

"Why? Is she like the Bruce Springsteen of classical music?" Liam asked.

"Hah!" Connor barked. "More like the Bruce, the Backstreet Boys, Elvis, and Johnny Cash combined in one pretty face. Add Michael Jackson too and you're getting closer to what this woman is in the classical music world."

"Jesus, that big, huh?"

"Even bigger," Crystal added. "Her concerts are sold out two years in advance. People fly from all around the world to see her. She just played for the president."

"Damn," Liam mumbled.

"Damn is the right word for sure." Connor nodded.

Another dead end, Liam thought as he stared at the frozen footage of the cleaning lady. "Could I have a copy of the recording?"

"I'll have to ask Mr. Hieber. Everything has to be okayed by that man first. Even the air I'm breathing in here."

"I figured," Liam said. "How often has the footage glitched before?"

Connor scratched his chin. "Maybe a couple of times. It's not too unusual for a few seconds, but it would have to freeze for at least thirty seconds to miss the woman in red walking back down the long hallway. But if she somehow entered the staff-only area, she could have left through one of the many back exits."

"Very unlikely," Crystal said. "The staff-only area is a maze of locked doors you need a keycard for. Again, I doubt people just let her through the whole backstage area without asking who she was."

Liam thought about this for a bit. "Connor. Do you remember anything from that night that seemed out of the ordinary? Anything at all?"

"I can ask Nilson. He was on duty that night. But if there was, he would have told me."

Liam looked at Crystal.

She shook her head. "It was a crazier night than usual. Backstage, I mean. But other than that, not really."

"Why was it so crazy?"

Looking over her shoulder as if to make sure Mr. Hieber wasn't there, Crystal sighed. "Well, Mr. Hieber and Leah have their differences. The atmosphere is not ideal on any given day, but that night, the concert started late, which pushed Mr. Hieber to the brink of a nervous breakdown."

"Thank God I wasn't there for that," Connor said.

"What differences do they have?" Liam asked.

Connor grinned mischievously. "He pissed her off big time. She canceled a concert last year, and he was cocky with her after, like he is with everybody else. But Leah Nachtnebel isn't everybody else. This woman propelled the Boston Symphony Hall to become the biggest classical moneymaker in the nation. So when Hieber had a big lip with her, she threatened to cancel her concerts for the whole year. We're talking close to sixty mil of loss here."

"Mil as in millions?" Liam repeated, stunned.

"Mm-hmm, and that's only her annual ticket sales, not even counting the city's financial boom from tourists flying in for her. The mayor of Boston himself made Hieber beg on all fours for forgiveness. Wanted Hieber fired right after that, but Leah, for reasons we'll never know, prevented it."

"Thanks, Connor," Crystal said, smiling thinly, her teeth barely visible. "If Agent Richter wanted drama, he would buy a ticket to one of our operas."

Connor cleared his throat. "Sorry."

Interesting drama indeed. But nothing useful had surfaced so far. Dead ends all around once again—unless someone had witnessed something in the staff area. But most likely, even that wouldn't be enough to keep the case. As it stood, Cowboy would soon be in charge of all this.

Maybe rightfully so, an inner voice nagged at Liam. Maybe Greg Harris's murder was the drug-fueled freak show Cowboy claimed it to be, and there was no serial killer's signature at all. Just a bizarre coincidence of brutal savagery tearing heads apart. Completely unrelated.

"Do you know why the concert was late?" Liam asked.

"Not really," Crystal said. "It happens all the time. It's only unusual because it was Leah's concert. She's never late."

"What time did the concert start?"

"Shortly after she arrived. Around 9:50."

"Close to the time my lady in red vanished," Liam mumbled. With this little to work with, every stone had to be turned, even the most unremarkable one. "Is Miss Nachtnebel in right now? Maybe she noticed someone in the hallways?"

"Impossible!" Crystal scoffed. "Mr. Hieber would never stand for it. If anything upsets Leah ever again, she'll pack her bags and leave."

Liam furrowed his brow at Crystal. "Well, fortunately, Mr. Hieber doesn't seem to be in charge of Miss Nachtnebel. This is an FBI investigation, not a meet and greet."

He was just getting warmed up when Larsen's words forced their way back into his memory. *Don't upset the Symphony Hall*, he'd warned.

Liam shifted in his stance and offered Crystal a warm, charming smile. "If someone could ask Miss Nachtnebel for just a few minutes of her time, it would help me out a lot."

Not that he was an expert in flirting—ten years of marriage had left him a bit rusty—but he was aware that his tall, toned body had a certain appeal to some women, and the whole FBI agent thing didn't hurt either. It was worth a shot. And today it seemed that luck was on his side, as Crystal appeared to soften at his smile.

"Miss Nachtnebel might have crossed paths with this woman in a hallway," Liam pressed. "Perhaps she saw or heard something. A large scar on the suspect's face or even just a distinct accent during a brief hello. Any little detail would be incredibly helpful. All she can do is say no to seeing me, right? No harm done."

Crystal and Liam locked eyes for a moment.

"Please."

Finally Crystal sucked in a deep breath and smiled. "I happen to be in charge of her schedule this month. Tomorrow I have a short debrief with her. If you have a card, I can let you know if she agrees."

Liam's lips curled into a smile. "It's my lucky day. Thank you so much! Here's my card."

Crystal accepted it and read both sides. "Special Agent Liam Richter. FBI." She shook her head, but she was still smiling. "Just like in the movies."

"I can assure you it's nothing like in the movies," Liam replied. "They never mention the endless hours of paperwork and how underpaid we are."

Crystal slid the card into her pants pocket.

"I'll call you tomorrow, and I can also let you know about the copy of the video," she said.

"That would be fantastic. Thank you."

The crisp fall breeze was a welcome relief from the stuffy atmosphere of Mr. Hieber's world. Liam strode down the grand steps of the Boston Symphony Hall with his phone pressed to his ear, listening to its monotonous dialing sound, when a tall, slim woman in an expensive, cream-colored coat passed him. Her long, dark hair was neatly pulled back into a ponytail. Something about her drew him to fully turn and look at her.

Tony picked up the phone. "You done at the hall?"

Liam opened his mouth to answer, but right at that moment, the woman stopped in front of the large entrance doors of the Symphony Hall and turned, her gaze locking onto Liam's as if she felt he was watching her. Her green eyes were as sharp as a blade of grass.

Liam was stunned, transfixed by her stare. For a moment, he could feel each beat of his heart, each circuit of the blood as it pulsed through his body.

"Liam?" Tony asked.

Expressionless, the woman stood still, staring at Liam like a lion staring at its prey. It was the strangest thing. Did she know him?

"Liam! You kidding me? You there?"

Then, out of nowhere, she turned as if nothing had happened and disappeared inside.

"Y-yes, I...I'm here."

"What the hell are you doing?"

"Nothing. Just got done at the Symphony Hall."

"And? Anything?"

As if under a spell, Liam continued to stare at the doors where the woman had just disappeared.

"I don't know yet."

"Jesus Christ. Well, if you're done playing Mr. Mysterious, why don't you meet me at the victim's mother's house? Fucking Cowboy was called in to some Drug emergency, and I'm sitting in the car waiting in front of the house. I can't do this by myself. I really can't."

Having spent considerable time with Tony at the Bureau, Liam knew him well. Tony could put a bullet into a serial killer's chest and never lose a night of sleep over it. But delivering such devastating news to an elderly woman would gnaw at him for weeks to come.

"Text me the address. I'm on my way."

"Thank God. Please hurry. I've been sitting here for a while."

"Hang tight. I'm already at my car."

EIGHT

It felt like they'd stepped into the opening scene of a low-budget horror film. Liam and Tony found themselves perched on a worn-out, grime-covered couch that reeked of cat urine. A macabre collection of taxidermy cats surrounded them, their dull glass eyes seeming to watch the agents' every move.

Mrs. Harris sat across from them, dressed in stained pink leggings and a purple pullover with an image of a cat sipping wine on it. An overwhelming assortment of random items like cat toys and dirty laundry cluttered the space between Mrs. Harris and the agents. Maybe it wasn't a horror scene; maybe it was a scene from the reality TV show *Hoarders: Buried Alive*.

Cats darted past Liam's and Tony's feet here and there, adding to the eerie ambience.

Suddenly a tabby cat leaped onto Liam's lap. Tony, who hated cats and was allergic to them, sneezed violently and edged away from Liam, trying to put as much distance as possible between himself and the feline hit man.

"That's Donald," Mrs. Harris said with a smile, leaning over her walker in front of her. Her yellow teeth shimmered in the dim light of the stuffy living room. "He likes to get scratched under his chin."

Liam smiled and scratched the tubby fellow, eliciting a loud, contented purr in response.

The whole visit was nothing short of surreal. The cluttered house, the abundance of cats, and most strikingly, Mrs. Harris, who appeared completely unfazed by the most heart-wrenching news a mother could ever receive.

"Again," Tony said in a saddened voice. "We are so sorry for your lo—"

"Are you sure you don't want coffee and cookies?" Mrs. Harris interrupted him as if she was weary of his condolences. "You two look like hardworking fellows who deserve a treat." Her expression twisted to disapproval. "Unlike that no-good I had to raise. Unable to hold a job, always drinking at bars, fraternizing with tramps."

Liam tried hard not to, but he couldn't help but glance over at Tony, who looked completely lost.

"No...erm, no, thank you, Mrs. Harris," Tony stumbled. "I...erm, I know this must be very hard for you, but it would help us out tremendously if we might ask you a few questions."

She shrugged. "Be my guest."

Liam leaned forward, Donald digging his claws into his legs. "Did Greg have any disagreements with anybody lately? Maybe with a girlfriend?"

"Girlfriend?" Mrs. Harris scoffed. "I thought he was into men until I overheard those horrendous, dirty videos he watched at night on his computer. Those were women screaming, not men. I told him if he ever watched something unholy in my house again,

I would have the Lord's blessing to cut it off." Mrs. Harris mimed snipping with her fingers as if they were a pair of scissors.

"Right..." Tony muttered.

Liam looked away and focused on petting Donald, his mind racing. This entire case was growing increasingly bizarre. "Did he have many friends growing up?" Liam asked.

Mrs. Harris opened her mouth as if to say something, then closed it again. "I don't remember his childhood much. I have dementia, you see." She tugged at her ear and looked away, a possible sign of lying.

Eager to dig deeper, Tony leaned forward, but Liam cleared his throat as a signal to hold back. Pushing her too much about something she didn't want to talk about might get them kicked out. "I'm sorry to hear about your health struggles," Liam said. "Do you know who your son worked for? We were unable to locate the plumbing business advertised on the side of his van."

"That's because he made it up. The liar pretended to be a plumber. What failure of a man pretends to be a plumber? Not that he had what it took to be one. I pray for the poor people who he did work for. If any of them are asking for their money back, tell them he drank it all away."

"Greg struggled with alcohol?" Liam asked.

"Struggled? He drank like a Russian!"

Tony cleared his throat. "What about harder drugs?"

"Not that I know of, but it wouldn't surprise me. But if that's what you think killed him, you're wrong. I know who did it."

Liam and Tony both scooted to the edge of their seats as Mrs. Harris reached for a cigarette and lit it, taking a long drag before coughing violently on the first puff. She paused for effect.

Finally, she spoke. "You wanna know who killed my son?" Mrs. Harris exhaled a cloud of smoke and looked them dead in the eye. "The devil did."

Tony cussed inaudibly under his breath while Liam kept his cool, nodding emphatically.

"The devil wanted Greg from the day he was born," she continued. "Put a part of his evil in that boy. Now he finally has him. So don't waste our tax dollars on him anymore." Suddenly her eyes widened as if she had an epiphany. "You know what you should do? You should look into that case I saw on TV, where that young girl went missing in Texas forty years ago. Annabel. Annabel Kneebling. Beautiful angel. Golden curls and so much love for Jesus in her heart. God knows how often I prayed for her. But the Lord decided to test me instead."

"Right," Tony said, rising as Donald the cat stepped off Liam's lap and made his way over to him, leaving a trail of cat hair on Liam's dark business pants. Tony turned toward the entrance door, but Liam shifted his gaze to the dark, cluttered hallway.

"You said Greg lived with you?" Liam asked.

Tony shot Liam a weary look.

"Would you mind if we take a look at his room?"

"Be my guest. It's down the hallway. But if you find anything valuable, it's mine, right?"

Fading posters of naked women adorned the grimy walls of Greg's room. The eyes of some of the women had been scratched out, giving them a demonic appearance. The room was old and simple, but everything was impeccably organized down to the tiniest detail. Books were neatly arranged by size on the windowsill, shoes were stored in a clean closet, and the bed was made. A small table with an outdated desktop computer sat against the wall under the window. Various action figures were lined up on the windowsill like a small army. The room was such a strong contrast to the rest of the house, Liam needed a moment to take it in.

Tony's lips moved silently in what Liam read as *What the fuck?*

Both agents slid on rubber gloves they'd taken from their pockets and began to search the room.

"Looks like Greg had some interesting fantasies," Tony said, picking up pink pantyhose from a small pile hidden under Greg's pillow.

"Fantasies that need further investigation," Liam said, nodding at the action figures on Greg's desk. On the female ones, the breasts had been cut off and the private areas burned, as evidenced by the warped plastic.

Liam approached the desk and tapped on the computer keyboard. The screen lit up, requesting a password under the username *GregTheRipper*.

An eerie feeling spread in Liam's stomach. The hunch he'd had all along about this case finally started to form into something more substantial.

"Good God," Tony gasped, pulling a Polaroid from under the mattress. He stared at it with wide eyes, shaking his head before handing it to Liam. "What the hell is going on here?"

An ice-cold lightning bolt struck Liam as he looked at the close-up of a woman's privates—covered in blood.

"I...I honestly have no idea," Liam mumbled, still gazing at the disturbing photo in shock. "But even if I have to challenge Larsen to a duel, this case ain't going anywhere."

Tony nodded and walked over to the computer. "I have a bad feeling about what we might find on here."

"Me too," Liam said, slipping the photo into his pocket before heading back into the hallway. "Let me work on Mrs. Harris to release the computer to us voluntarily. You might wanna take your allergy pills. I have a feeling the price for the computer will be a few hours of cat stories and cookies."

"Damn it," Tony grumbled. "Those cats will be all over me."

"My friend, those cats are the only thing that feels normal about this house." Liam frowned, looking into the hallway at a taxidermy cat that had tipped over. "The ones that are still breathing at least."

NINE

I parked my Audi in the small parking lot behind the boarded-up factory near the abandoned pier at Lynn Shore Reservation. As usual, there were a few abandoned cars with flat tires. It was late afternoon, and dusk would soon blanket the sky.

The smell of the ocean and fish greeted me as I made my way past the PRIVATE PROPERTY sign and onto the small wooden dock behind the factory.

The ocean's unpredictable waves lapped against the wooden dock's posts. While I found the water fascinating, I didn't feel the calming or longing sensations others often described when gazing at the endless blue expanse.

A gentle autumn breeze carried the salty scent of seaweed as seagulls noisily squabbled over an old sandwich nearby.

A man's figure appeared in the corner of my eye as I reached the end of the dock and observed the seagulls. The man stopped right next to me, staring at the ocean briefly before balling a fist and placing it on the weathered wood of the pier's railing.

"What the hell, Leah?" Larsen cursed.

My focus remained on the seagulls. Intently, I watched the largest one nipping at the smaller ones. Nature usually favored the larger creatures—a tale as old as time. Until a species called humans decided to use their oversized brains and change the course of the world forever.

"The crime scene looks like Jack the Ripper and Dahmer had a psychopathic child who went on a murder spree!" Larsen barked, pulling me from my thoughts.

"I guess I got carried away."

"Carried away?" His outrage echoed through the air. "Carried away? The man was carved out like a damn jack-o'-lantern!"

"So was Samantha Hayden." I looked directly at Larsen as I spoke. "I thought I might return the favor."

His gray eyes narrowed slightly as his facial muscles softened a bit. "You know I don't care about what you did to him. God knows that piece of shit deserved it. It's *how* you did it, Leah. You left the body in a state that drew attention. And then you took a freaking Lyft back to the Symphony Hall? Why not flag down a patrol car while you were at it?"

"I was late for my concert."

Larsen placed his hands on his hips. "Late for your concert, huh? What's the number one rule, Leah? The number one rule we live by?"

My eyes turned back to the restless waves. The water was murky, tainted by mud and dirt.

"Never, ever shit where you play," Larsen said when I remained silent. "You never, ever shit where you play, remember? My guys at the FBI and the Mass police chief are asking questions they shouldn't be asking. And damn Agent Richter, that man will do anything to fight for justice and stand up for the underdog. Soon he'll be up my ass so deep I'll be able to taste his determination. He already went to Harris's house and took his computer, and I highly doubt he'll find a family video of that sicko getting his first puppy for Christmas." Larsen paused for breath. "And to make matters worse, I did a little digging, and it turns out Greg Harris went to the Kim Arundel Psychiatric Hospital for the Severely Mentally Ill, Leah. Freaking Kim Arundel! Did you know that?"

I remained silent. The same mental institution I had been sent to as a child. An interesting turn of events, indeed.

"I never met him," I said. "The children's unit was closed shortly after I left due to abuse charges brought by a few parents. He must have been there as an adult. But in any case, my files have been destroyed. No connection will be made."

"I'll double check that," Larsen huffed, then leaned over the railing to stare at the undulating water. His eyes conveyed an intense look as if he were in there among the waves, fighting to remain afloat.

To be fair, I understood why he was upset. It was only logical. Larsen and I had worked together effectively for years, taking out quite a few monsters while adhering to strict rules and guidelines. Greg Harris's death deviated from our usual methods, so Larsen's anxiety over the possibility of being discovered and the consequences that might follow seemed reasonable.

"I am aware that the circumstances of this case are not ideal," I said. "But Greg was slipping away from me. And rule number one isn't *don't shit where you play*, it's *never engage in person with a target more than once*. I had to strike that night or risk creating traceable evidence that could link me to Greg. I had to pursue him that night or let him go. And as you know, I don't let them go."

My eyes met his. "The FBI won't be able to link anything to me," I continued. "They'll chase dead ends and eventually deem Greg a drug-related crime. Did the autopsy indicate that Greg was a long-term substance abuser?"

"It couldn't, but the physician performing it ruled it a strong possibility."

I nodded. "Were the fingerprints on the drill and needles traced back to a drug-related criminal?"

Larsen shook his head. "No, they didn't match anyone."

"Interesting." That required my attention. "I'll find the name of who those fingerprints belonged to."

"That would help. But we still have the problem of Greg's true identity. My guys are going to find out what a sick fuck he really was."

"Good."

He furrowed his brow. "Good?"

"Yes. It'll expedite the end of the investigation. Your agents are overworked and underpaid. They'll move on to another case more quickly if their motivation for seeking justice is taken out of the equation. Not many people are interested in bringing a killer's killer to justice."

"Maybe. I'll arrange for the case to be transferred to the Organized Crime Division, so it gets buried among other cartel cases. If the footage of the woman in red entering the Symphony Hall doesn't yield anything, we might get away with just a slap on the wrist."

"It won't. I changed my clothes in the bathroom and burned the evidence later. All people saw backstage was me entering my dressing room late."

"All right." Larsen's voice was steadier now. I wasn't concerned about his emotions, nor was I intimidated by him. In fact, his emotional outbursts only irritated me. Emotional people were prone to mistakes, and the success of our entire operation relied on careful planning and rational thinking. Ensuring that he remained calm and focused was part of my responsibility.

I handed him a printed map of Newport, marked with a black *X* over the cemetery. The names "Kim and Jan" were written just above the *X*.

"What's this?" he asked.

"It's the location of Kimberly Horne's and Janet Potts's bodies."

Larsen studied the map and took a deep breath. "If that's true, their families will finally find some peace."

"They'll find even greater solace when the news breaks that the man responsible for their daughters' deaths has faced justice."

He nodded.

My gaze fell upon a rolled-up envelope sticking out of his jacket pocket. I held back, allowing him to present it to me on his own accord.

For a brief moment, we stood there, observing the seagulls as they glided gracefully against the backdrop of the vivid orange-and-blue sky.

"Damn it." He sighed loudly, finally pulling out the envelope. "But hold off for now. We need to lie low until Greg's case is written off as just another unsolved cartel murder. It won't take long with the drug epidemic tearing through this country." He handed me the envelope, which I slid into my coat pocket.

"Are you sure you included all of them?" I asked.

He nodded. "Every single report of train-related suicides from Maryland to Maine."

"Good. Have you taken a look at them?"

Larsen shook his head, his expression darkening. "No. Your 'Greg masterpiece' pales in comparison to what a train does to a body. I'll leave the fun of combing through the evidence to you."

I checked my wristwatch, realizing it was getting late. "I have to go."

I turned to leave, but Larsen grabbed my arm—a bold move. He knew better than to touch me, ever. My eyes fell to his hand gripping my arm, and he immediately let go.

"Sorry...I just wanted to say I really hope you find something in those reports." He gestured to the folder. "I've started waking up at night thinking about this son of a bitch."

The Train Track Killer—a son of a bitch indeed. Throughout the years Larsen and I had worked together, he had remained the one serial killer who kept eluding us. He was as brilliant as they came, his methods ingenious. A savage brute like Greg Harris could only dream of possessing such skills. Larsen and I had struggled for years to identify his victims and had failed to find a signature beyond the gruesome act of positioning his victims on train tracks, making their deaths look like suicides.

No one ever questioned the circumstances when a body was discovered by the railroad police—a specialized unit untrained for handling murder cases yet responsible for every body found on the tracks. They ruled the gruesome aftermath left by the trains as suicide, and no one ever said otherwise except for the grieving families, who insisted their loved ones wouldn't take their own lives. But even that was tricky—loved ones were often in denial.

My hope rested on meticulously examining each case involving a body found on the tracks and searching for a pattern. Anything. The Train Track Killer was a genius, but he was human after all. Unlike brutal savages like Greg, who merely indulged in their violent fantasies, most ingenious serial killers sought to convey something deeper through their murders.

"I'll let you know as soon as I find something," I said, holding Larsen's gaze for a moment. Long enough to see his hopeful nod. Then I headed back to my car.

Lie low, he'd advised. But we both knew that if I managed to uncover anything about the Train Track Killer, the hunt was on. No matter the cost, no matter the pain. I'd repay him using the very gruesome method he used on his victims: tying him up on the tracks as a massive 286,000-pound train barreled toward him.

TEN

As I walked through the front door, the inviting aroma of turkey and ginger enveloped me. Ida must have prepared turkey breast in a ginger-basil sauce. I wasn't particularly fond of meat, but Colin loved it, so I had her prepare his favorite dishes whenever he came over.

"Is there anything else I can do for you, Miss?" Ida asked, lighting the candle on the dinner table. The white tablecloth shimmered softly under the dimmed lights, elevating the room's ambience. Wineglasses glistened, their polished surfaces reflecting the flickering candlelight, while the expensive Chinese porcelain dinnerware added an air of sophistication. The romantic gesture of a single white rose and a bottle of expensive wine completed the perfect dinner scene.

"No, that'll be all. It looks beautiful, thank you."

Ida smiled warmly before leaving through the back patio door to her cottage. I wouldn't see her again until tomorrow morning. She was reclusive—another thing I liked about her.

I walked into my office and placed the thick brown envelope on my desk. I was tempted to open it, but the doorbell rang—Colin was early for once. Maybe there was still hope for him after all. But it also meant I would have to change into my evening dress.

My hand turned the doorknob. Much to my surprise, the man before me wasn't Colin but a strikingly handsome, tall man with distinct Italian or Spanish features. The sun's golden evening rays cast a warm glow on his chiseled face, highlighting his high cheekbones and strong jawline. Thick, perfectly arched eyebrows framed his dark, lively eyes, and his tousled chestnut hair danced playfully in the gentle breeze. He was wearing a blue raincoat and jeans, giving off the vibe of a nature-loving college student.

A moment of confusion passed between us.

"Are you...Leah?" he asked. He had a pleasant tone tinged with a hint of shyness.

"The more pressing question would be who you are," I remarked.

"I'm Emanuel. I'm here for Colin."

My eyebrows arched in surprise. "And why isn't Colin here?"

"He...um..." Emanuel glanced around, seemingly to ensure the coast was clear.

"Let's discuss this inside," I suggested, stepping aside.

As soon as the door closed, Emanuel offered an innocent smile. "Nobody told you?" Emanuel peeked into the living room, his expression filled with awe.

"No."

"Colin moved to San Francisco for college. I guess he met a girl from there."

This revelation caught me off guard. I had been employing Colin's services for over a year. For him to vanish like this, sending someone else to relay the news, was highly unprofessional.

With a sigh, I took off my coat and hung it in the closet near the entrance.

"It's quite a place you have here," Emanuel said.

"Do you know what Colin's line of work entailed?" I asked, disregarding his comment.

Emanuel picked up an antique Roman vase from a sideboard table and examined it. "You...paid him to be with you."

"That's only partially true."

Emanuel carefully placed the vase back on the side table, avoiding my gaze.

"Are you here to take his place?" I asked bluntly.

"If you think I'll do. The escort agency said you need to approve."

"I see."

I stepped closer and gently took both his hands in mine. He stood only inches away, towering nearly a head taller than me. The scent of his inexpensive cologne wafted through the air. Surprisingly, I found it appealing.

I examined his hands, paying particular attention to his fingers. They were long and slender. Good. Beautiful hands were incredibly important to me; I couldn't stand the sight of dirty fingernails or misshapen fingers when a man's hand caressed my thighs.

"Open your jacket and lift your sweater," I instructed.

"W-what?" Emanuel stammered, grinning shyly as his cheeks reddened.

"Have you never done this before?"

He bit his lower lip. "Of course I have."

"Then lift up your sweater, or you can leave."

After a brief pause, he unzipped his blue raincoat and lifted his gray wool sweater. His abdomen had a lean, muscular build. Just how I liked it.

"Would you like to eat dinner?" I asked abruptly, holding up my hand for his jacket. Nodding, he handed it to me.

"Then sit and tell me about yourself," I said as I walked into the dining room. I grabbed our plates and headed into the kitchen. I filled one with turkey breast and asparagus for him and the other with asparagus and a mushroom risotto for me.

"What do you want to know?" Emanuel asked as he sat down, staring at the candle as if it were all a dream.

I set our plates on the table and took a seat across from him. "What do you do besides this?"

Emanuel watched my movements as I poured red wine for both of us. He picked up his glass, twirling it between his thumb and index finger without taking a sip. "I'm a veterinary student."

I savored a sip of my wine and began eating. Ida had truly outdone herself with the risotto. "That's an interesting profession. May I ask why?"

"Why?" He took a sip of the wine. "Oh God. That's really good." He cleared his throat and grinned. "I guess I like animals better than humans."

"Because of their raw honesty or the loyalty of species like dogs?"

He seemed surprised by this question. "Both, I guess."

I nodded. "Did you know Colin well?"

Emanuel bit his lip again, then nodded.

I placed the cutlery on the plate and delicately dabbed my mouth with my white napkin. I met Emanuel's gaze, holding it for a moment before speaking. "If you ever lie to me again, I'll ask you to leave and never come back."

"What?" Emanuel sat up straight in his chair.

"You bite your lip when you lie. You did it earlier in the hallway when I asked if this was your first time meeting with a client. And you lied to me just now about knowing Colin. I don't waste my time on liars. In fact, I do not like them."

"I..." Emanuel stared at his plate. "I'm sorry. I usually don't lie."

My eyes followed his fork as it pushed the asparagus away from the meat. "You don't like meat?"

He pinched his lips. "Yes, I mean, no. I'm a vegetarian."

"Then don't eat it. I still have more of the mushroom risotto. Would you prefer that?"

"Thank you. But I ate right before I came here. I had no idea that Colin, that lucky bastard, got a Michelin-star dinner in a multimillion-dollar home with someone like you."

A heavy silence filled the air. I leaned back in my chair and looked at Emanuel, who was avoiding my gaze.

"This is your first time, isn't it?" I asked.

"It is."

"Are you sure this is the type of work you want to do? I pay incredibly well, but I ask a lot of my escorts, and you seem to lack experience."

"I'm a quick learner," he countered. "I'm sure I can deliver. No ex of mine has ever complained in that regard if that's what you're worried about."

There it was. Finally some confidence.

"Very well. Let me explain to you what this position requires first. Then you can make your final decision." I rose and walked into my office to grab the script along with one of the golden wedding bands I kept in my desk.

Emotionless, I placed both items next to Emanuel's wineglass, then sat across from him again. His deep brown eyes settled on the document and ring.

"What is this?" he asked.

I nodded at the script and ring. "When you are here, I need you to wear that ring."

Emanuel slipped the ring onto his finger and furrowed his brow in puzzlement. He turned his hand this way and that to examine it from every angle. "Like we're engaged?"

"Married. Just inside these four walls, of course. You will find instructions in the script in front of you. Assume the role of the husband as portrayed in the script and perform accordingly."

"Like an actor?"

"Yes. We'll act out detailed scenes of a happily married couple's life together."

Emanuel raised an eyebrow and skimmed through parts of the manuscript. "You...want me to hug you from behind when you're in the kitchen and kiss your neck?"

"When I cook. You will address me with a tender nickname and tell me that it smells delicious."

He looked at me a bit longer than he probably meant to before diving back into the manuscript. "Hug you on the couch while watching movies," he mumbled, still reading.

I hated the TV, but I agreed. "Yes. Among other things."

His eyes snapped up from the manuscript to meet mine. "No condoms?"

I shook my head. "I expect you to undergo a full STD screening before our first intercourse. I will do the same. If you're worried about children, I had a tubal ligation procedure, so pregnancy won't be a problem."

Emanuel's lips parted as he focused back on the document, his cheeks turning a rosy shade. "So you want me to say 'I love you' when I—" He stopped midsentence, glancing at me again.

"I want you to tell me that you love me when you fill me with your cum," I clarified. "Or when I swallow it."

The fiery glint of desire danced in his eyes. I didn't need to glance at his pants to know he was hard. He wanted me, badly, and the feeling was mutual. Psychopaths like myself often found comfort in lust and sexual pleasure, experiencing it intensely. However, unlike those monsters with their violent fantasies, I was fascinated by the intimacy of a loving, monogamous relationship. This fixation had puzzled me my entire life and would likely remain a mystery forever. The methods I used to satisfy my sexual cravings were shocking, but I didn't know how to love. And who could ever love me, anyway?

I stared into his eyes, slowly licking my lips. His gaze followed my tongue as his breathing quickened.

"I'll pay you twenty thousand per month," I said. "You'll be exclusive to me. No other clients. Do you have a girlfriend?"

Emanuel shook his head.

"Good. Do you have any questions?"

He shook his head again.

"Well then, do you need time to think about—"

"No," Emanuel interrupted confidently as he straightened in his chair. "I'll take the job."

"Are you sure?"

"Yes."

I nodded, rising from my seat. His gaze followed me intently as I approached. "We won't have sex until you present me with a negative HIV test, but you can come in my mouth," I said, leaning over to gently brush my lips against his.

He moaned. Excited. Thrilled. Horny...shocked.

I ran my hand down his chest to his erection and unbuttoned his jeans.

"Would you like that?" I asked, kissing him passionately. "Come in my mouth?"

"Y-yes." His chest heaved as his beautiful eyes gazed into mine.

Gently, I wrapped my fingers around his manhood. He groaned, throwing his head back in pleasure. A fiery heat built between my legs—a sensation I craved as much as the air I breathed. I knew it was lust, not love, but it made me feel alive.

I knelt between his legs and took in his entire length.

"God." He gasped for air.

"Does that feel good?"

He nodded, speechless.

"Then say it."

"Yes."

"Yes, baby," I corrected him.

His gaze smoldered, reflecting the fire within him. Then, to my surprise, he smiled at me and softly ran the back of his hand down my cheek. "You are so beautiful," he said, looking directly into my eyes.

I moved my lips in rhythm with his rapid breaths. Loud moans escaped him as flaming-hot arousal coursed through both our bodies.

"I...I...love you," he gasped, rehearsing the script.

"Not bad," I responded. "But you'll get better at this over time."

ELEVEN

The meeting room echoed with a woman's agonizing screams from the video playing on Greg's computer. Its flickering light threw eerie shadows across the faces of Liam, Tony, Larsen, and Heather. Liam was standing closest to the computer, and his hand was clenched in a fist against his mouth. Behind him, the others had risen to their feet, frozen in place.

"No!" the woman screamed over and over again as Greg bashed a hammer into her battered face. How she was still alive at that point was a mystery. Cowboy had left for the bathroom once the first video, titled "Olivia," had twisted everyone's stomachs to the point of throwing up. But this one, titled "Samantha," seemed like something that would have been cut from a horror film due to its brutality.

"Turn it off," Larsen murmured weakly, his gaze dropping to the floor. The woman's screams finally subsided, but Greg kept pounding his hammer into the now unrecognizable face. Liam gagged, the taste of bile rising in his throat.

"I said turn it off!" Larsen snapped, gripping the backrest of his chair as if he were afraid to fall.

In a flash, Tony reached for the mouse connected to the laptop and paused the video. The air in the room was stifling, and the silence that followed was suffocating. Yet no one dared to speak until the surreal moment passed, leaving behind a brutal reality.

"Tony," Larsen finally said, his voice tense and shaky, "get a search warrant and send a unit to Greg Harris's house. We also need to contact our people in Maine and let them know we might have found their College Snatcher. If we're lucky, we'll find something at this monster's home to locate the bodies of the missing victims and bring those girls home to their families at last."

No one said it, but the thought was on everyone's mind: Bring them home? In what condition?

"Does all this mean the drug-addicted plumber is a serial killer?" Cowboy asked, stepping back into the room. "Can someone explain all this to me? 'Cause I'm kinda losing it here." His face was snow-white.

"Thank God it's almost five. I need to go home, hug my kids, and wash the past ten minutes off me with a long shower," Heather said, her face twisted in disgust.

"If you could please reach out to Maine headquarters first," Larsen said in an understanding tone. "Those guys need to know about this ASAP."

Heather nodded and left.

Tony let out a heavy sigh. "I'll get that warrant taken care of. What a fucking shit show."

Liam lingered, staring at the floor, feeling strangely detached. The horror of what they'd just seen weighed heavily on him. He heard every word they said, but it all felt surreal.

"Who do you want to execute the warrant?" Tony asked Larsen. "Does the case now stay with us, or does it move to Cowboy's department?"

Larsen pursed his lips.

"Of course it stays with us now," Liam interjected, speaking for the first time since they'd started watching the videos. He sounded both exhausted and agitated. "Greg Harris is a serial killer, and serial killers fall under BAU jurisdiction, not Drugs. This is our case now."

"Is it?" Larsen countered. "All BAU has is a dead serial killer. As insane as this all is, the evidence so far points to a drug-related crime in regard to this monster's killing. Some drug gang unknowingly did the world a favor by taking out a serial killer. Maybe there's a god after all."

"We don't know for sure if Harris's dealer killed him. We don't even have a match for the fingerprints yet," Liam argued. "And the only possible witness has also not been located."

Cowboy let out a mocking laugh. "Who cares, Columbo? The needles and heroin littering the crime scene are pretty conclusive to everyone but you. Why don't you help Maine clean up the mess left by this College Snatcher, and my boys and I will find the gang who solved the Snatcher case for you. If you're lucky, the cartels will keep doing your job for you. Seems like you could use the help."

Liam narrowed his eyes. This case was getting under his skin, and so was Cowboy. "Think you've got some big balls to talk to me like that, huh?" Liam stepped closer. "Why is your rookie ass so obsessed with this case in the first place? Got something to prove to your uncle after he finally caved to your mom's nagging to get you on the force?"

"The only thing I have to prove to my uncle is that some folks here at BAU shouldn't be trusted to ring up worn panties at Goodwill, let alone work for the FBI," Cowboy retorted.

"Funny," Tony sneered at Cowboy, paying no attention to Larsen. "Swinging some big-boy punches now, huh? There's only one person here who just bolted to the bathroom with—"

"I said stop it!" Larsen bellowed, slamming his hand on the table. "We have the biggest mess on our hands since the Boston Strangler. The press is about to crash down on us like a tsunami, and all you can think about is brawling like drunks at a bar? I'll take this up to McCourt, and whatever he decides will be the end of it."

The room fell silent.

"Liam, go help Heather with the team in Maine while Tony works on getting us that search warrant," Larsen instructed.

"What about me?" Cowboy asked.

"You'll join me in executing the warrant."

"What? Why him?" Liam objected. It was uncommon for Larsen to execute warrants, but choosing to honor this special occasion by bringing Cowboy's ass along was too much for Liam to handle.

"Is there a problem?" Larsen raised an eyebrow at Liam. "Because last time I checked, Special Agent in Charge was written on my door, not yours."

Liam's mouth flew open, ready to fire back, but Tony turned on him, shaking his head. Meanwhile, Cowboy stood there grinning like the annoying little prick he was.

"Let me ask you again, Agent Richter. Is there a problem?" Larsen asked, locking eyes with Liam. He was a head shorter than Liam, but his gaze could intimidate Goliath. And given Larsen's power to suspend agents, Liam had no choice but to tuck his tail between his legs or get kicked off the case altogether.

"No, sir, no problem at all."

"Good. Then fucking get to it, and prepare for a media firestorm unlike any we've faced before."

"I'll help with the press!" Cowboy interjected.

"Well, isn't that just perfect?" Liam exhaled. Cowboy's favorite thing in the world—attention.

"Enough," Larsen snapped. "All of you." He shook his head as if trying to ease the pain. "If anyone asks about the case, you know what to say. Nothing. That's what you'll say, you hear me?"

Nobody answered—which meant *yes*.

"Goddamn this case," Larsen muttered, grabbing the folder on the table. He glanced once more at the paused video, his face contorted with disgust as he murmured something inaudible. Then, with a heavy stomp, he left the room. Cowboy trailed behind him, flashing one last grin at Tony and Liam.

"I can't stand that fucking guy," Tony grumbled.

"Larsen or Cowboy?"

"Right now? Both."

Liam rested his hand on Tony's shoulder before moving past him. "Go ahead and get that warrant, will ya?"

Tony's head jerked back. "Why do you sound like you're leaving?"

"Because I am."

"What? Didn't you hear Larsen?"

"I did."

"Then where the hell are you going?"

"I'm going to find that lady in red before Cowboy can jerk off to my case."

"Please don't! Larsen will kill you."

Liam nodded. "I know." Despite the risk of infuriating Larsen to the brink of catastrophe, he had to locate that woman. Time was of the utmost importance. If McCourt decided to assign this case to Drugs, spurred on by Cowboy's whining, Liam would be out, and the case would go cold among countless other unsolved cartel murders. As much as he wanted to believe in the drug gang theory, he couldn't. The pieces didn't fit. A gruesomely mutilated plumber who, it turned out, was a monster himself—killed in the same manner as one of his victims? And all the while, his supposed drug-addicted girlfriend vanishes at the Boston Symphony Hall?

The pieces didn't add up. And it was up to Liam to find the evidence to support his suspicions and unearth the hidden secrets deeply rooted in this goddamn case.

TWELVE

The entrance hall of the Boston Symphony Hall bustled with eager concertgoers. Dangling chandeliers cast a warm glow, highlighting the elegant architecture. Guests, dressed in their finest, chatted and laughed, creating a lively atmosphere. The scent of perfume mingled with the aroma of wine. Friendly staff welcomed arriving guests and handed out programs as the ticket booth buzzed with activity.

Liam decided not to waste time with Mr. Hieber's bullshit today and cut straight to the chase. The first person on his list was already in sight, innocently pushing her cleaning cart toward the staff-only section. He quickly approached the short, middle-aged woman with brown hair pulled back in a tight ponytail.

"Excuse me," Liam said, flashing his badge. "My name is Agent Richter with the FBI. May I ask you some questions?"

The cleaning lady from the surveillance tape—Melinda, if he recalled correctly— didn't even glance at his badge. "Sorry, but I'm busy."

"Of course. I remember the horrific mess people leave behind as if it were yesterday." He nodded in the direction of the restrooms. "I worked my way through college as a janitor, among other jobs. To this day, I'm looking for answers to the question of how a rubber duck once clogged one of the toilets."

Melinda hung on his every word. "If you ever find out, please let me know," she chipped in enthusiastically. "I found an iguana in one of the stalls in the men's room once."

"The animal?"

Melinda nodded.

"Jesus..."

"Yup. I took him home. His name is Frank. Love him to pieces."

Liam nodded with a soft smile. "Would you mind if I asked you a few questions? It will only take a minute. You're Melinda, right?"

She nodded, tilting her head to reveal her growing curiosity.

"I have some questions about the night of October twelfth. It was a Saturday. Were you working that night?"

"I always work late on Saturdays."

"Did anything out of the ordinary happen that Saturday?"

Melinda shook her head.

"It was the night Ms. Nachtnebel's concert ran late," Liam added, hopeful.

"Oh yes, I remember now."

"I'm looking for a woman in a red dress with short blond hair. She might have been in the restroom near the staff entrance just before you cleaned it that night. Did you happen to see her?"

"No, I didn't. Sorry."

Disappointment weighed heavily on Liam's shoulders. Melinda had been one of his very few promising leads.

"The restroom was empty after Ms. Nachtnebel finished in there," Melinda added.

"The famous pianist?"

Melinda nodded.

A spark of excitement ignited in Liam's chest. It was like metal detecting in the rain for days and finally getting a hit. Perhaps Ms. Nachtnebel saw something. One door closed, another opened.

"Are you sure it was her?"

"Yes. It was the first time I'd ever seen her use that restroom, and she greeted me as usual. Most people don't greet me."

"That's because a lot of people are idiots," Liam said warmly.

Finally, Melinda smiled.

"You said it was the first time you saw her in that restroom. Do you know why she never used it before?"

Melinda answered with a shrug.

Damn it.

"Thank you for your help," Liam said. He was about to leave when his gaze fell upon the hallway leading to the restroom and, more importantly, the staff-only area. "Could you let me into the back?" he asked.

Melinda hesitated. "I don't know, Mr. Hieber—"

"Will never find out. And if he does, I'll tell him I forced you under the threat of obstruction of justice." Liam ensured his smile was warm so as not to frighten her. "I know how he can be." He sucked in his cheeks and widened his eyes, mimicking Mr. Hieber's haughty expression as accurately as possible.

Melinda chuckled. "All right, but please don't tell him it was me."

THIRTEEN

Liam did his best to avoid eye contact, but Crystal was right: People in the hallways closely observed those who navigated the staff-only area. Three times some wannabe sheriffs stopped him, and each time he'd had to show his badge and explain himself.

Ms. Nachtnebel's private room was deep within the maze of backstage tunnels, storage rooms, and practice spaces. From the last person who stopped him, Liam learned it was highly unusual for an artist to have a permanent private room at the Symphony Hall—Leah was the only artist granted this privilege. He was told to follow the piano music to find her. So he did.

The rapid notes of a classical piece Liam couldn't identify echoed through the door as he raised his hand to knock. But for some reason, he hesitated, his hand frozen in the air, paralyzed by the music's beauty. As the notes of the classical piece filled the air, Liam found himself slowly drifting away. The captivating melody transported him to joyful memories of his youth, as vivid images gracefully danced in harmony with the mesmerizing tune.

"This is a staff-only area!" a woman's voice exclaimed, abruptly pulling him from his profound memories. Locking in on the woman's gaze from afar, Liam knocked—this time with a sense of urgency—before she could catch up with him.

The music stopped abruptly.

"Who is it?" a woman's confident voice asked from inside the room.

"Erm, Agent Richter, FBI. I have a few—"

"Come in."

He slowly opened the door and found himself in a lavish dressing room radiating sophistication and elegance. Rich, deep-toned wood paneling adorned the walls, complemented by a majestic, full-length mirror that stood beside an opulent makeup table. The seating area boasted a luxurious, tufted chaise, an exquisitely carved coffee table, and two adjoining rooms. It was an inviting and refined space to prepare for concerts.

"Hello?" Liam called out when he didn't see anybody.

"The room to your right," the woman instructed.

He followed the voice and froze in surprise when he saw, seated behind a grand piano, the woman he had met on the stairs before. Her stunning green eyes locked on him as she turned her head. Slim and graceful, she wore a black evening gown with a daringly deep cut that extended almost to her buttocks. No bra. Her long, dark hair was pinned into a tight bun. Though her nose was slightly crooked, there was no denying her beauty.

"How may I assist you?" Ms. Nachtnebel asked in one of the most serene tones he had ever encountered.

"I'm sorry for intruding..."

Usually this was the moment people reassured him that he wasn't, but Leah said nothing.

"You are Ms. Nachtnebel, I assume?"

"It's a stage name, but yes, I am."

"I didn't know it was a stage name. What's your real name?"

"Miller," she replied, her expression unchanging. "Like the beer. But the people who attend my concerts generally aren't the sort of crowd who would appreciate associating Bach with a beer."

"Makes sense," he said.

"Agent Richter, wasn't it?" She pronounced his name in a perfect German accent.

Liam raised a curious brow. In all the times he'd heard his name said aloud, he'd heard only one other person pronounce the hard *ch* as *kh*, just like a native German speaker.

"You know how to say my name better than I do," Liam said, joking. "Do you also know that it means—"

"Disciplinary or judge."

"That's...right." He furrowed his brow in astonishment.

"Quite fitting," Ms. Nachtnebel said. "Do you come from a long line of judges or police officers? Or are you the rebel who broke free?"

"Maybe I came from a long line of FBI agents, not judges or cops," Liam responded, glancing around the small practice room. Nothing out of the ordinary. The walls were lined with sheet music neatly stacked in rows. A rack with expensive-looking dresses stood next to a shelf filled with matching shoes.

"That lineage wouldn't be very long since the FBI was established in 1908 in the United States, and the name Richter originated in medieval Germany, named after its profession."

Damn. This woman would make a hell of a detective.

"I guess you caught me. Both my father and grandfather were police officers. Some great-great-great-whatever might have been a judge. I stepped right into their footsteps." He smiled.

Leah nodded curtly and arranged the sheet notes on her grand piano. "So how can I help you?"

Liam stepped into the small practice room. "I have a few questions if you don't mind?"

"I wouldn't have asked you in if I did. Go ahead."

Straight to the point. Fair enough.

Liam cleared his throat. "The night of October twelfth, you arrived late to your concert?"

"I did."

"May I ask if you noticed anything unusual when you arrived?"

"I did not," Leah responded without a moment's hesitation.

Liam gave a brief, affirmative hum. "I'm looking for a woman in a red dress with short blond hair. She was wearing a baseball hat that covered most of her face. Some people placed you near her around the time she disappeared by the bathrooms at the staff entrance."

"I have a photographic memory. I would remember running into her. I'm sorry."

"Damn it." Liam dragged his fingers through his hair, only to notice Leah's watchful gaze moments later. He quickly lowered his hand to his side. Although his training had taught him to control and manipulate body language while interacting with witnesses and suspects, his current reaction sprang from his unguarded self as though he were with Tony at that moment. Something about this woman threw him off, which was highly unusual.

It wasn't the way she talked—an emotionless calm that felt both mysterious and confident. Given that she was one of the world's most renowned artists, particularly in the classical world, Liam had anticipated a certain degree of eccentricity. However, there was something else about her, something he couldn't quite put his finger on.

"May I ask why you were late to your concert that night? I heard it's unusual for you."

"It is."

There was a moment of silence.

"But I'd rather not say. It's a personal reason."

Liam offered a subtle nod. "I apologize for pressing you on this, but any information about this unusual night could be helpful."

"Unusual night?" Leah inquired, a hint of curiosity in her voice.

Liam nearly blurted out, "The lady in red is a witness to a murder where the victim turned out to be a serial killer," but he caught himself, his lips still parted. Who was interrogating whom now?

"I'm sorry, but I can't discuss the case," he finally managed to say.

"Well, Agent Richter, I apologize, but unless I'm being charged with a crime, I'll keep my personal reasons for delaying my concert...personal."

Liam's mouth curved into a smile. "Of course you're not being charged. I'm sorry if I came across as pushy. I really appreciate you taking the time to answer some questions."

Ms. Nachtnebel offered him a nod—no smile. "I'm sorry I couldn't be more helpful."

It was a dismissal. Liam heard it clearly in her voice. *Fair enough*, he thought. He had nothing else here. Nothing at all.

"Thank you." Liam was about to leave, then added, "You play beautifully, by the way. I don't know anything about classical music, but even I couldn't help but listen before I knocked. It's like a drug. Amazing, really."

As she studied Liam, Leah narrowed her eyes slightly. It was as if she were analyzing his thoughts. Or maybe like a tiger observing its prey. Then her facial features softened.

"Thank you. If you're interested, I could get you a ticket for my concert. It's not possible today, I'm afraid, but I could get you a seat for the next one at the end of the month. This is not a bribe, of course."

Liam frowned as Leah walked into the adjoining room and approached her makeup table. She leaned over to write something on a piece of paper. With swift, graceful steps, she strode up to Liam and handed him a signed ticket.

"The bribery reference was a poor attempt at humor," Leah said.

Brows still furrowed, Liam examined the ticket's signature. The N, the T, and the L of Nachtnebel were written as if from the eighteenth century—curvy and precise. He had never seen a signature like this in real life. None of the people he knew ever signed so artistically. But then again, none of the people he knew were famous.

"Show this to security at the balcony doors and ask them to seat you. They'll know it's from me. My signature is difficult to forge."

"No kidding. Did you have to practice this?" Liam asked.

"Yes, I did. Handwriting is a lost art. Keyboards and phones have deprived us of the ability to write or spell properly. And with the advent of AI, soon we won't even need to form our own sentences in our minds. Humans, by nature, will always seek shortcuts. I doubt there are more than a handful of people in this entire building right now who could handwrite a full-length page without misspellings or poor penmanship."

"But technology makes life easier in these hectic times we live in. Most of us barely have time for anything beyond what's necessary for basic survival," Liam countered.

"Perhaps, but research has linked handwriting to cognitive development and information retention. I would argue it's important for people to maintain the ability to communicate and think independently without assistance. Otherwise, who's to say that we are the ones controlling AI and not the other way around?"

"Looking at it that way, I suppose you might have a point," Liam said.

One corner of Leah's mouth curved upward, forming a faint smile. It made her appear even more attractive, but something about the smile seemed disingenuous.

The standard ringtone of Liam's phone interrupted their conversation. The display read *Tony*.

"Excuse me," Liam said, turning away slightly. "Is it important?" he said into the phone.

"Where the hell are you?" Tony asked, his voice strained with stress.

"At the Symphony Hall."

"Well, get over here ASAP. We got the search warrant for the Harris residence. Larsen just called from the scene. They've broken into the basement, and he said it looks like fucking Dahmer's apartment down there—his exact words. And guess what they found? A map with the victims' names on it."

Liam turned his back farther away from Leah and lowered his voice. "A map?" He glanced over his shoulder. She was staring right at him, a certain satisfaction in her eyes.

"A fucking map, Liam. With marked locations!" Tony confirmed.

"I'm on my way." Liam hung up and slid the phone back into his suit jacket. "Well, I'm sorry for taking up your time. Thank you for answering my questions. I can't wait to hear you play soon."

So he was going to her concert? How was that even benefiting the case?

"I hope you enjoy it. Best of luck with the case." With that, she turned and resumed practicing.

Liam stood rooted to the floor for a moment, captivated by the way her hands danced up and down the piano keys, producing otherworldly sounds. Then he snapped out of his reverie and rushed into the hallway.

A map. They had found a fucking map and yet...something else was on his mind.

Leah Nachtnebel.

World-famous pianist.

Beautiful.

Mysterious.

Maybe the most interesting person he had ever met.

And he couldn't shake the gut feeling that their paths would cross again—beyond next week's concert.

FOURTEEN

Liam turned onto the street where the Harris home was located, just twenty minutes north of Boston. Suddenly he had to slam on his brakes so hard that the seat belt yanked him back into his seat. The once-quiet residential street was now buzzing with chaos, swamped by media crews, all trying to get a prime spot. Bright lights flooded the area, illuminating the Harris residence like a movie set.

"Fuck," Liam mumbled, staring at the buzzing media circus. Larsen had been right. The press had caught on quickly.

Finding a parking spot near the Harris residence was out of the question, so Liam pulled over to the side of the road. Just as he was about to shift his car into park, a black SUV approached at a rapid pace. It had to be Larsen.

"Crap."

Larsen's vehicle screeched to a halt beside Liam's. Both men rolled down their windows, Larsen frowning in disapproval.

"Are we wrapping up?" Liam asked, feigning ignorance.

"You'd know if you'd been at HQ helping the other agents like I told you to."

Liam didn't want to mention the meeting with Nachtnebel because it hadn't provided any leads, so why provoke his SAC until he had goodies? "I had to run a case-related errand," Liam explained.

"Oh, all right. Then don't worry about vanishing during a critical stage of the Harris case cleanup."

"Really?"

"No! If you keep going rogue, I'll give Heather time off and hand you her admin duties for the next month."

Liam grinned. "I'm sure she'd appreciate some quality time with her fam."

Larsen's eyebrows snapped together so quickly Liam swore they made a cracking noise.

"Come on, Larsen. It's me, Liam. The same guy who covered Christmas for you when Eileen was sick, remember? Which, by the way, I now have to justify in family court during my custody battle because my ex wants to make it look like I was neglecting Josie."

Larsen's face softened—for the first time since the case began, now that Liam thought about it. Why was this case pissing him off so much? Granted, it was one of the most disturbing cases Liam had encountered since he'd joined the Bureau, but Larsen had already been on the force, chasing serial killers when Liam was still battling teenage acne. What was it about Greg Harris that threw him off?

Larsen seemed to notice Liam's intent gaze and sighed. "All right. Our team will be busy here all night. The place is like Dahmer's apartment. Greg didn't even try to hide evidence in that basement. We even found a hand in the freezer, buried beneath expired peas and a meatloaf." With a vacant stare at his steering wheel, Larsen slowly shook his head. "Sick bastard."

"Do you want me to snoop around a bit with them?" Liam offered.

"No. Tony and Cowboy will meet up with our colleagues from Maine in Newport. They're working on obtaining a warrant to use ground-penetrating radar on the cemetery to determine which graves have multiple remains in them. Burying his victims on top of other bodies was clever. I have to give Harris that."

"What about the families of the people buried in those graves? Will they let us exhume them?"

Larsen pressed his lips together, frowning. "It's going to be a shit show, no doubt. But the families of those murdered women deserve to bring their girls home. If that means we have to step on some toes, then so be it. Besides, I doubt the families of the bodies in those graves would want a brutally murdered woman resting alongside their loved ones—can't imagine that makes for a peaceful afterlife."

Exhaling deeply, Liam leaned back in his seat. "What a mess. Nothing about this case makes sense."

Larsen raised an eyebrow at him. "How so?"

Surprised, Liam locked eyes with Larsen. "I mean, a serial killer found mutilated in a forest in the same style as the victim he mutilated? And his alleged girlfriend stealing his wallet to take a Lyft to the Symphony Hall?"

Straightening in his seat, Larsen gripped the steering wheel. "It doesn't have to make sense. Serial killers don't make sense. They never have, and they never will. They do what they do because they're sick fucks. I hate to break it to you, but this is just another twisted case like so many others we've dealt with. As we speak, the state's attorney is preparing for court to hold that psycho accountable for poisoning the public well system in Newcastle. That guy killed twenty people, including five children. How does that make sense to you? It doesn't. Greg Harris is a monster who ran with the wrong crowd, and they did us a favor by offing him. Many serial killers have had drug or alcohol issues. Dahmer drank heavily. Harris shot up. It's as simple as that."

Liam let those words unfold in front of him as Larsen glanced at him from the corner of his eye.

"You have a lot on your plate right now with the divorce, Liam," Larsen continued. "Sometimes we throw the orange out the window because the guy at the store was a jerk."

With an empty stare, Liam ran his hands along the steering wheel. Maybe Larsen was right. Maybe that feeling in his gut was being triggered by his divorce and this whole case was just a drug deal gone wrong involving a serial killer.

"You might be right."

"I tend to be," Larsen said. "Which court is handling the custody battle?"

"Hillson County."

"Hillson...I know a few people there. How has the judge been treating you so far?"

"Like I'm at fault for getting cheated on."

Larsen nodded. "I'll make some calls. You're a good dad, and from what I've heard, you were a damn good husband too. We'll make sure you don't lose your daughter because the judge is some randy old man who falls for Sara's puppy eyes."

Liam's brow furrowed. "Really?"

"I can't promise anything, but at least we'll try to get you someone fair."

For the first time in months, Liam felt as if he could breathe. The custody case had been swinging more in Sara's favor simply because she had the better lawyer—and the puppy eyes.

"I...I don't know what to say," Liam said.

"Yeah, yeah. Don't go all soft on me now, will you? I need you in top shape. We have a hell of a time ahead of us. Those families of the victims deserve answers. And we're the ones who'll have to find them."

Liam was about to express his gratitude to Larsen once more when the fast-moving figure of a young woman in a pink suit caught his eye. "There's the guy in charge!" she shouted, pointing the microphone in her hand at Larsen.

Within moments, her cameraman and a crowd of journalists were surging toward them like an avalanche.

"Is it true that Greg Harris is the College Snatcher?" the woman demanded.

"Why hasn't his autopsy been released yet? Is it true that he was found decapitated in the woods?" another journalist asked.

"I'll text you the address for Newport's cemetery," Larsen called to Liam, rolling up his window and driving off.

Liam nodded and swiftly turned his car around to avoid being trapped by the swarm of reporters. He had barely shifted his car into drive when the first flood of blinding camera flashes assaulted him from all directions. If this were a movie, he would have floored the gas pedal and sped off. But in the real world, he had to inch forward at a snail's pace until even the last reporter blocking his path was several feet away from his car. The last thing Liam needed was to hit one of these sensationalist reporters.

As Liam slowly navigated his way up the street, bombarded by a cacophony of questions and blinding flashes, he couldn't help but ponder Larsen's words. The more he thought about it, the more he agreed with him. Maybe it *was* just a drug deal gone wrong.

The heavy weight that had been tied around Liam's neck ever since he'd set foot on the Harris crime scene was finally loosening its grip.

Cowboy's division would investigate Greg's killer while Liam would collaborate with the FBI in Maine to tie up loose ends in the College Snatcher case. This included finding the bodies of the women who remained missing. There would be a unique sense of satisfaction in returning the bodies to their loved ones, especially because the monster responsible for taking their lives was not basking in the prison's library or enjoying daily walks in a sunny courtyard. Liam took grim satisfaction in the fact that this killer now lay in a body bag himself. But none of this would stop the cameras from clicking. The world would relish this macabre tale: a monster slain by another monster, truly an eye for an eye.

FIFTEEN

Bover, NH, 1980

My little arms stretched wide as I stood in the rain, feeling the cool drops explode off my skin. It poured relentlessly, soaking through my underwear and white undershirt. To avoid damaging my leather shoes again—a mistake that had gotten me into trouble before—I chose to go barefoot, welcoming the rain's cool embrace. The rhythmic sound of the raindrops formed a comforting melody, revealing a pattern in the way the beads of water fell and spread around. Once I'd watched long enough, the raindrops began to shimmer in a spectrum of colors, like a kaleidoscope. It was a fascinating and beautiful distraction from the void I felt inside.

"Nick!"

My mother's voice, sharp with alarm, cut through the rain from the living room window. I turned to find her pressing her hands against the glass, her eyes wide with urgency. The curling iron caught in her hair was a clear sign she'd been interrupted mid-preparation for today's church event.

"Niiiiiick!" she called out again, this time with a hint of hysteria. "She's doing it again!"

She disappeared from the window just as the front door of our modest home burst open. My mother, moving carefully over the wet porch steps, quickly made her way to me. Her fingers, cold and filled with tension, tightly dug into my arm.

"What are you doing out here!" she yelled, her voice laced with panicked aggression. "Are you simple in the head?"

Her gaze suddenly shifted to the street, landing on Mrs. Schmiegel and her poodle, both sheltered under an expansive, black umbrella. Mrs. Schmiegel's grey eyes peered with a sharp, judgmental gaze from under her outdated, pointy cat-eye glasses, scrutinizing every second of the scene in front of her.

My mother cleared her throat. "Good day, Mrs. Schmiegel," she said, her tone unnaturally friendly, reminiscent of the fraud it was. "I'll see you at the church brunch later. I'm bringing my ginger-mint cookies."

Mrs. Schmiegel managed a tight smile, then turned, leading her dog away in a hurry. After we'd watched for a few seconds, my mother dragged me back inside, past my father, who stood in the hallway with a dazed expression.

"I can't do this anymore, Nick," she barked, pausing by the TV chair. My father, a simple man of working-class roots, had no particular stance on me standing in the rain but adhered to my mother's household rules—a successful arrangement between them.

"Do it harder this time," she instructed. "People will talk again, Nick. Just last week Angela Houser had that tone when she asked about Leah."

My father calmly took his seat in the chair. Barely waiting for him to settle, my mother positioned me over his knees, stomach down.

"There was that tone in her voice. As if she was mocking me. And now Mrs. Schmiegel stood right there in the rain with us. Everyone will know, Nick. Everyone!"

I lay obediently across my father's lap, my arms and knees dangling, eyes fixed on the yellow carpet below. My mother paced to the coffee table, lighting a cigarette with trembling hands and taking a long drag, her red-painted thumbnail caught between her teeth.

She glanced at us, frowning at my father, prompting him to start.

The rhythmic smacks of his hand against my bottom rocked me like a boat in a stormy sea. Back and forth. Back and forth with every hit.

"This is from your side of the family," she nagged. "We don't have lunatics in mine. We are respected people."

"You're right, Nance. I'm sorry," my father murmured, the sound of his smacks leaving no doubt about their force. It took several more before my mother's attention snapped to me. She watched in utter shock as I remained unflinching, emotionless, as if I were a soulless doll, feeling absolutely nothing. Of course I felt the physical pain, but what use was there in screaming or crying? The pain would fade, as it always did.

Her eyes widened as she stared at me, her teeth sinking into her nail even harder now. In the brief silence of her shock, I seized the moment to offer what I thought would calm her anger. "I took off my shoes and dress this time so they wouldn't get ruined."

Wasn't this why she was so angry? Wasn't she worried about the clothes?

Her eyes widened even more. My father let out an apologetic sigh. Then she dropped her head into her hands and stormed off. "I should have listened to my mother and married Ben Schuster," she sobbed.

My father gently placed me on the soft rug—an odd contrast to the recent violence—and followed her. "Nance," he called. "Nance, wait!"

How long I stood there, drenched, my bottom sore and swollen, I couldn't tell. Time was often distorted in my mind, leaving me to question the reality of my life.

I struggled to understand my mother's reactions—a common theme with most people I encountered. Since birth, I had been different, a challenge for my family. Even my entrance into this world was peculiar: without a single sound, nor did I ever cry after that. From a young age, I could understand that my parents genuinely perceived me as a mistake, a faulty model that should never have left the factory. And with my limited capacity to fit in, no matter how hard I tried, I couldn't help but wonder the same thing.

Boston, now

My gaze was fixed on the flat-screen TV ingeniously concealed behind a large golden mirror adorning the wall across from my work desk. When turned on, the TV magically appeared through the glass; when turned off, it vanished completely.

The news played silently while Bach's *Fugue in G minor, BWV 578* filled the room from the built-in ceiling speakers. I cradled a glass of Japanese whiskey against my chest as the vibrant hues from the TV screen and the warm, orange-red glow of the flickering fireplace flames danced across my face and desk. The room was otherwise steeped in a somber darkness.

I watched intently, reading the captions of the news footage covering the crime scene at the Newport cemetery. Major news outlets had been following the story all week. The FBI and police had doubled their efforts since finding Kimberly Horne's body in an older man's grave. Now they had discovered another woman, clad in a blue-flowered dress—the same one Janet Potts had worn the night she'd vanished from campus.

The camera zoomed in on a hysterical woman, tears streaming down her face as she pushed herself against a police officer, desperately trying to reach the grave where the body of Janet Potts had been found. MRS. POTTS, a caption read as the woman's frenzied movements grew out of control, her face torn into a grimace of unbearable pain and grief. Another police officer entered the scene, attempting to grab Mrs. Potts by the arm and drag her away from the scene. But suddenly she collapsed to the ground, pounding her fists against her chest, her mouth wide open in a silent scream. After several attempts, the officer managed to grasp her upper arm and tried to yank her back onto her feet. But just then, a familiar face brushed him aside, knelt beside Mrs. Potts in the dirt, and wrapped an arm around her for support.

Agent Liam Richter.

My eyes narrowed at the TV as Agent Richter turned toward the camera in anger as though he were staring directly at me through the screen. His lips furiously formed words that the captions failed to capture. Moments later, the camera was switched off. A female anchor, her face overly made-up, appeared in the NewsChannel studio and apologized for the graphic content before turning her attention to the awaiting discussion panel.

"Turn the TV off please," I requested of my smart system, shifting my focus to the dancing flames in the fireplace. The intimate and raw moments of the woman mourning her daughter had stirred something deep within me: an empty flicker accompanied by a subtle ache in my throat. I'd never experienced emotions like this before. It felt strange. Alongside this rare emotion stirring within me, another thought persisted:

Agent Richter.

Agent Richter's empathy and composure at the scene with the victim's mother perfectly aligned with the impression I had formed of him after our initial encounter. Undoubtedly, he was a man of integrity and honor. Larsen had been right about him. Where others might concede in defeat, Richter was the kind to redouble his efforts. Fueled by the three *D*s of success—determination, dedication, and discipline—this man lived for his beliefs and would readily sacrifice himself for them.

I couldn't help but think that if he made it his task to destroy me, he might succeed.

I took a sip of my whiskey and leaned over my desk. Gruesome images of dismembered bodies strewn across train tracks occupied nearly every inch of the surface except for the small area where I set down my wineglass. Night after night, I sat here, allowing these horrifying scenes to haunt me. The task of identifying the remains of over a hundred victims hit by a train was beyond daunting. It was torture. The impact of a train was similar to that of a grenade—only much worse. A grenade's grisly effects were contained to a small radius. In contrast, a train could drag severed limbs for miles before they finally detached. And a monstrous individual was deliberately inflicting this unimaginable torment upon unsuspecting people and their families.

But why and how?

As much as I despised every breath the Train Track Killer took, I couldn't help but admire the twisted ingenuity behind his heinous acts. For years, I'd found nothing on him. Studying gruesome images night after night, searching for patterns or clues, was a last-ditch effort to salvage the case. But distinguishing between a genuine suicide on the tracks and the Train Track Killer's murders based on the photos and rudimentary reports from the untrained railroad police was nearly impossible. Moreover, the statements from the victims' loved ones in the reports offered little assistance.

"He would never do that."

"She was happy. She loved her friends and college."

"He couldn't wait to see the grandkids for Christmas."

None of that provided any concrete evidence; it only highlighted the tragic nature of these deaths. Suicide was a complex matter. One could spend a lifetime with someone and never truly know the depths of their depression. The situation was further complicated by the Train Track Killer's erratic choice of victims. Men, women, old, young—he seemed to have no particular preference. The only demographic he appeared to avoid was children, at least for now. His motive remained yet another mystery. If it hadn't been for the murder of Mike Bauer on the commercial railway tracks south of Boston, Larsen and I might never have learned about the existence of the Train Track Killer in the first place.

Mike Bauer was a male accountant in his late forties. His family had filed a complaint with the FBI, accusing the railroad police of losing evidence and wrongfully ruling his death a suicide. After Larsen looked into it, he discovered that Bauer's car was found at the Green Street subway station—along with one of his shoes, which was right next to his vehicle. He had disappeared after a work party on a Friday evening. The railroad police had insisted Bauer had walked four miles without shoes, in less than an hour, to a secluded part of the woods where he had then thrown himself in front of a commercial train. But both his white socks were clean when the police took pictures of his body at the accident site. If he'd walked even ten feet without shoes on, his socks would have been muddy or dirty, especially given that it had rained heavily that day.

Considering this evidence, the most reasonable conclusion was that somebody had placed Mr. Bauer on those tracks.

After investigating additional complaints, Larsen uncovered two more suspicious cases involving the railroad police: Thomas Griffon, an older male from the Boston area, and Kelly Dorns, a young female nursing student from New York. The night before Kelly's body was struck by a commercial train north of New York, she had managed to send a text to her sister that read, *Help he kill me.* Such a message was hardly the kind of farewell one would expect from a suicide victim. On the other hand, clues from Thomas Griffon's case were revealed during his autopsy. Despite the absence of any rope at the crime scene, the autopsy report described bruises consistent with marks left by a tight rope around his ankles and wrists. But the railroad police insisted that Thomas had committed suicide and that the autopsy report was inaccurate.

"You're up late again." Emanuel's voice pulled me out of my thoughts. He was standing in the doorway, his lean, muscular body naked except for boxers.

"What time is it?" I asked. For the past few days, I'd fallen asleep at the desk, my arms and head resting on pictures of horror.

"Two in the morning."

"I'll be right with you," I said, then straightened in my chair when Emanuel stepped into the office. "I'd wait in the hallway if I were you," I warned him, but he walked up to the desk anyway like a child drawn to a hot stovetop. The shadows from the fireplace flickered across his face as he picked up one of the victim's photos and scrutinized it, his eyes narrowing. Almost immediately he gagged, reaching for the desk to steady himself.

"Oh my God." He gasped, pressing a clenched fist against his lips. The picture in his hand slipped from his grasp, fluttering to the floor along with several others from the desk. "What...is this?"

"Unsolved murders," I replied and walked around the desk to retrieve the scattered photos. Emanuel watched me intently, his eyes wide.

"Are you one of those amateur detectives on forums and podcasts who try to solve murder cases or something?" Emanuel asked.

"Not exactly, but something along those lines," I replied.

Emanuel tugged on his ear. "That's an unusual hobby. Most people read books, go hiking, or binge Netflix in their free time."

"They do indeed," I agreed, shuffling the pictures into a neat stack. It was then that I caught a slight inconsistency in color on the rusty tracks next to the body of Emma Mauser, a young woman who had vanished after a college party in Philadelphia.

"But then you're not like most people," Emanuel said, attempting to lighten the mood.

I seized the picture and strode to the desk. Could this be more than just dirt or a dent in the tracks? I retrieved the magnifying glass from the top drawer and switched on the small desk lamp.

"Actually, you're not like anyone I've ever met before," Emanuel continued.

I disregarded his comment, focusing instead on the photograph. Holding it beneath the lamp, I positioned the magnifying glass over the peculiar color inconsistency on the rusty metal tracks. It took a few seconds for me to realize what I was looking at, and the inconsistency wasn't dirt or a dent. It was a tiny symbol, almost resembling a needle's eye atop a cross.

I drew in a sharp breath as a tingle of excitement coursed through me—a sensation I rarely experienced. It felt amazing, incredible.

"What is it?" Emanuel asked, leaning over the picture.

"A mark. Right here," I said, pointing at it.

He scrutinized the mark, and after a few moments, his expression shifted to one of fascination. "Holy shit, I think you might be right. What does it mean?"

I stared at it with wide eyes. A mark! A goddamn mark on the tracks next to the body. It could be nothing, or it could be the breakthrough I desperately needed.

"I...I don't know yet," I said, deep in thought, "but I'll find out."

I left a puzzled Emanuel behind and walked into the hallway, opening the closet door.

"What are you doing?" he asked.

Grabbing my coat, I glanced at him. "Stay here. I'll be back as soon as I can."

"Are you kidding? It's two in the morning! Where are you going?" Emanuel stood beside me, a look of shocked disapproval on his face.

"As I said, I'll be—"

"I'm coming with you," he insisted.

Sitting on the small bench in the hallway, I put on my hiking boots. "I'm afraid that's not possible."

Emanuel marched straight up to me. "The hell it is. I won't let you go alone this late. I know you think there's nothing the world-famous Leah Nachtnebel can't do, but this is Boston, and unless you're hiding a judo gold medal or an Iron Man suit, I'm coming with you. I'll only be a minute."

As Emanuel hurried up the stairs, I weighed my options. Although I'd prefer to go alone, leaving him behind might raise more questions than simply bringing him along. There wasn't much he could ruin by coming, and if I encountered a threat, two people would be better than one.

I reached underneath the shoe rack and pulled out a small gun. Quickly I slipped it into the back of my pants.

"Ready," he announced, sitting beside me to put on his white sneakers.

I nodded at them. "Those will get dirty."

He shrugged. "They're shoes. They tend to do that."

A faint smile crossed my lips as I watched him tie his shoe. It had been a few weeks since he had started working here. According to our arrangement, I would reach out when I wanted his company. Yet Emanuel often texted me, asking if he could come over—and more often than not, I said yes. He acted out the script I'd provided him more convincingly than Colin ever had, and his overall personality was more pleasant and engaging too.

I had never had a preference in escorts before.

"Where are we going?" he asked, tying his other shoe.

I pulled open the side table drawer next to me and handed Emanuel a flashlight. "Somewhere very, very dark."

SIXTEEN

We found ourselves enveloped in darkness, our flashlights cutting through the trees and bushes. The black mass seemed endless, ready to swallow us whole.

I had parked in the lot of an abandoned liquor store near the tracks where Mike Bauer's body was discovered after he had vanished from the Green Street subway station. A refreshing autumn breeze carried the crisp scent of moss and damp earth to my nostrils as I led the way along the narrow, leaf-littered path.

"So what are we looking for?" Emanuel asked.

"The exact location where Mike Bauer's body was hit by a train."

"Is that the guy from the picture with the weird sign on the tracks?"

"No, that was a woman named Emma Mauser. She was also hit by a train under questionable circumstances."

"Questionable circumstances, as in..."

"As in I don't think they killed themselves."

"Wow," he said. "Whatever this is, you're really deep into it, aren't you?"

"I don't engage in matters unless I intend to give them my best efforts."

I stepped over a fallen tree branch and slid a few inches on the wet mud, managing to avoid a fall.

"There you go," Emanuel said. "What if the next obstacle is a crazy pervert? You should let me walk ahead."

"To perpetuate the conventional belief that navigating through uncertain times is a responsibility designated primarily to men?"

"No. Because I can punch harder than you. Not to be stereotypical."

"And that's why you'll be more useful from behind. Men usually are."

"Oh my God." I didn't have to turn around to see his beaming grin. "Did Leah Nachtnebel crack a dirty joke?"

I let out a playful sigh and continued walking. To my surprise, as much as his, Emanuel's unwavering loyalty and infectious optimism occasionally coaxed out a lighter, more playful side of me.

"So you think Mike Bauer's and Emma Mauser's deaths could be connected somehow?" Emanuel asked, his tone turning serious.

That was a very observant question. "What makes you think that?" I asked.

"I'm obviously new to all this, but if you didn't think whatever you found in Emma's picture was related to this place, we wouldn't be here."

I smiled—another thing I seemed to do more frequently than usual around Emanuel. "Your observation is correct."

We hiked for about five minutes when the dense tree line gave way to a small clearing. The dark, gray clouds overhead obscured the sky, and the opening was hardly noticeable. It wasn't until we had stepped into the clearing and onto the train tracks that we could truly see it.

"Keep an eye out for bloodstains." I pointed my flashlight onto the rusty brown tracks and the coarse gray gravel surrounding them. "We should be right at the spot where Mr. Bauer met his end."

Emanuel let out a loud sigh. "You do realize this is kind of creepy, right?" He aimed his flashlight toward the rustling bushes at the tree line. "It's like the perfect opening scene for a low-budget horror movie."

I swept my flashlight along the tracks, walking over the sharp gravel.

"Jesus Christ, I think I found something!" Emanuel exclaimed.

I hurried to his side. His flashlight's beam revealed a dark red stain on the gravel beneath the train tracks. The contrast between the stain's vibrant hue and the gray stones created an eerie sight, with the surrounding darkness amplifying the scene's spine-chilling ambience.

"I assume this is blood?" Emanuel asked, his eyes widening with unease.

"Yes," I confirmed.

"Good God." Emanuel sucked in a deep breath. "So you think this man was murdered right here where we stand?"

I walked over the tracks, examining various angles with my flashlight. "I can't say for sure if he was killed here or elsewhere, but his body was placed here—dead or, more likely, alive."

Emanuel's face contorted in disgust. "Why would anyone do that? I mean, putting bodies on tracks for a train to..." His voice trailed off.

A crisp breeze rustled the leaves of the dark woods surrounding us.

"Because humans are as complex as they are troubled. For some, violence stimulates the brain's reward centers or eases the pain of a hidden darkness."

I paced along the inner side of the tracks for a short distance, preparing to retrace my steps on the outer side when my flashlight revealed a subtle inconsistency in the tracks' color. My feet became rooted to the ground as a shiver raced up my spine. That elusive thrill of excitement tingled in my chest and fingertips once more.

I gazed at the sight in awe. After years of fruitless searches and chasing dead ends, not to mention countless nights spent studying photographs of gruesomely disfigured bodies, there it was.

The very same symbol found in the picture of Emma Mauser.

A cross, approximately two inches in size, with a looped top. Etched into the metal of the rusty tracks like a heart carved into a tree.

"Holy shit, it's the same bizarre symbol," Emanuel said, standing beside me. His voice quivered as he asked, "Why do both murders have the same fucking symbol carved into the tracks?"

"The most plausible explanation would be that the murders were committed by the same person who etched these symbols into the tracks as a signature," I replied.

"So those suicides were actual murders..." Emanuel whispered, his voice laced with shock. "Do you know what the symbol means?"

The darkness around us seemed to close in as we contemplated the sinister reality of the situation becoming increasingly apparent.

In the photograph of the Hauser murder, the symbol was more challenging to identify due to the poor image quality. However, now, examining it from just inches away, I recognized the symbol without a doubt. "It's an ankh, an ancient Egyptian symbol representing life or immortality."

"Life? Is this some kind of a sick joke?"

"I don't know why the killer associates the ankh with his victims. The symbolism of an ankh at a death site could have numerous interpretations. But one thing is clear—" I stood up, my gaze still fixed on the ankh "—whoever is doing this isn't acting out of a blind thirst for blood. He wants to tell a story. A story that's likely tied to his past."

"His?"

I nodded. "Not that women aren't capable of such crimes even if they are statistically less likely to be violent, but transporting a body this far would require immense strength. I've dragged a body a few feet before, and it was incredibly exhausting."

"Very funny. Like a serial killer, huh?" Emanuel said, joking.

A tree branch snapped in the canopy, and Emanuel spun around. "Shit." His light shot up in the direction of the noise. "You don't think that guy is still out here?"

As I took pictures of the ankh symbol, I glanced at the source of the noise before refocusing on the tracks. "Unlikely but possible. Don't worry. I won't let him hurt you."

"Isn't protecting us my job?" He aimed the bright beam of his flashlight into my face. I didn't flinch at its blinding light but frowned in annoyance. He redirected the light back at the woods.

"We should go," I said.

"Ready when you are."

SEVENTEEN

The headlights flickered as I unlocked my car. They cast a brief flash across the parking lot. By the time I reached the driver's side, Emanuel had settled into the passenger seat, the door clicking shut behind him. Just as I was about to slide into my seat, I noticed a shadow flickering through the eerie darkness of the woods. My pulse quickened as I stared into the forest, my hand moving with deliberate slowness beneath my jacket to rest on the cold handle of the gun.

"What is it?" Emanuel asked, his voice tinged with concern. I ignored him, straining my senses to detect even the slightest sign of movement. The wind itself seemed to hold its breath, the night unnervingly still.

After waiting a moment longer, I reluctantly withdrew my hand from the gun and climbed into the car. "It's nothing," I reassured him, pulling the door closed behind me with a soft thud.

"Can we get out of this spooky place then?" Emanuel asked.

I reversed out of the parking lot and onto the road, my hands gripping the wheel. Casting one last glance into the rearview mirror at the path where I had thought I'd seen something, all I found was emptiness.

Strange.

"So what now? Are we going to the police?"

The suffocating fog of exhaustion began to cloud my mind. For days, I had been awake at night, poring over the Train Track Killer's gruesome handiwork. And with this recent breakthrough, my workload had just increased.

"No," I replied.

"No? Why not?" Emanuel's eyebrows knitted together.

Because I'll take care of this twisted son of a bitch myself. "This symbol won't give the railroad police anything. They're underfunded, and for them to admit their inadequate investigative work, we'd need something more concrete."

"But we could report this to the FBI. They're the big guns."

"We could, but the railroad police would still have their incompetent fingers all over the investigation and most likely leak the ankh symbol to the press. That would inform the killer that someone's onto him."

"So what will your crime group do about any of this then?"

Driving with one hand, I propped my elbow against the car door and leaned my weary head against my palm. "I'll gather more evidence by visiting all the crime scenes to see which ones have the symbol and were actual murders by the Train Track Killer. A pattern might emerge from that."

Emanuel nodded, his expression both satisfied and weary. "There were so many photos on your desk. Won't this...hobby mess with your concerts? The holidays are coming up."

My body stiffened in my seat as my head snapped up. I stared at Emanuel, my gaze locked on his as the car rolled to a stop at a red traffic light. "You know who I am?" I asked, taken aback.

His forehead creased as if I had just asked him to find a cure for cancer. Colin had never really known who I was or where the money he spent out of my pocket had come from. "Something with music," he'd always say with a smile on his handsome face. But he was good in bed, and his performance as my fake husband was generally satisfactory, so I never cared about his lack of interest in me.

"What kind of a question is that?" Emanuel jerked his head back. "Of course I know who you are. How the hell could I not?" Emanuel's lips curled into a melancholic smile. "I've known you for longer than you know. My father took my mother to one of your concerts a few years back when she was diagnosed with stage four lung cancer. She used to play the piano. To her, you walked on water."

He turned his face to gaze out the passenger window.

"In her final days, she just wanted to go back home to Italy, to be with her sisters in that small town just outside of Rome," he continued. "Dad and I, we were there with her. She was loaded up on pain meds, and all she kept talking about was your concert. She would tell me about it over and over again. I played along, pretending I hadn't heard that same story a million times before. She would stare at the ceiling like she was still there, listening to you play. My dad wants to get buried next to her. And I kinda do too."

Damn.

This was one of those moments when more than a simple "I'm sorry for your loss" was expected. But what did he want to hear from me? What emotion would be appropriate? A touch of sadness in my voice but not too much? Or empathy? But how could I truly empathize if I had never witnessed someone I cared for waste away from cancer? Both my parents were still alive, and even if they were to die, I feared I might not be able to shed a tear for them.

"I..." I hesitated, searching for the right words as Emanuel turned to look at me. Why did I even care about saying the right thing? "I hope my music brought her some comfort during those dark times."

My response seemed to resonate with Emanuel, as he gave me a soft nod. "Thank you. It really did." Clearing his throat, he said, "Wow, I seriously just managed to worsen the creepy serial killer mood. I'm real fun to be around, huh?" He offered a sad smile.

"I think you're more pleasant than most," I replied, simply being honest. But my words made him laugh.

"I guess that's a compliment in Leah Nachtnebel's world," he said, grinning.

"You do have a sense of humor," I acknowledged.

"Yup. Train track murders always make me jolly," he replied.

This time I actually chuckled a little and glanced at him. There was something about this man, something that brought out the little good in me.

"Wait a minute." Emanuel glared at me, feigning outrage. "Was that a giggle? First that dirty joke in the woods, and now you laugh? I think I deserve some credit here."

"Maybe you do." I smiled, pulling into the empty parking lot of a church. I parked the car away from the glow of the street lamps and turned off the engine.

"What is it?" he asked, growing serious and looking out the window as if expecting the Train Track Killer to come knocking.

"You can't come with me to the murder scenes."

"Of course I can," he protested.

I unbuckled my seat belt and climbed over the center console, settling on his lap. His dark eyes flashed with excitement and something else I couldn't quite make out.

"Not this time. I'll drop you off at my house when I grab a few things. You can stay there if you like."

I traced a path of tender kisses up and down his neck. "I'll be gone for only a few days." Our breaths quickened as I unzipped my pants and slid them down over my ankles. Emanuel followed suit, clumsily lowering his pants over his muscular thighs to reveal his already hard shaft. I parted my legs and positioned myself above him, guiding him inside me.

"Fuck," he murmured as I started to glide up and down. His eyes darted nervously out the window before returning to me.

"Slow down," he moaned, gripping my hips. "Otherwise, I'll cum."

Instead, I intensified the rhythmic motion of my body against his massive size.

"Then fill me up," I said, kissing him passionately. A sultry moan escaped my lips, my hunger for him growing. Each penetration drove me wild. My cheeks glowed like embers, and it felt as if a wildfire was engulfing my whole body.

He tensed, and I could feel the pressure building within me, propelling us both closer to the brink.

We shared feverish kisses as I rocked against him a few more times until we both reached the height of pleasure. He groaned loudly, his load filling me up, trickling from the tip of his mass down my thigh.

"I love you," he moaned against my lips, his body shuddering. "I really fucking do."

As the sincerity of his words washed over me, an electrifying warmth cascaded through my body. The sensation swirled from the pit of my stomach, radiating outward to the tips of my fingers and toes.

I felt incredible. Amazing. Alive.

"Say it again," I groaned against his lips.

He pulled back from our kiss and looked deep into my eyes. "I love you."

The heat inside me persisted for a few more glorious seconds before dissipating, leaving me hollow and shivering in the icy void that had plagued my existence for far too long.

I clambered over the center console and returned to the driver's seat. "You are getting really good at this. I might add a few more scenes to your script if you don't mind."

Emanuel watched me, his eyebrows arched high as I cleaned myself with a tissue and slipped back into my pants.

"We should go. I need to be back before my concert on Saturday," I said, restarting the engine.

Emanuel remained silent, his gaze fixed on the dark scenery beyond the passenger window. Something was off. Even a blind chicken stumbled upon a seed now and then, and right now I had no doubt that I'd unsettled him somehow. But how was I to proceed? Should I ask him about his concerns or pretend everything was perfectly fine?

Damn it.

I could scrutinize a thousand individuals and accurately decipher the emotions and intentions of 991 of them, all through their body language and verbal cues. I could pinpoint their aspirations, motivations, fears, hatreds, and passions. But when it came to understanding my own emotions, I was absolutely useless, like a fish floundering in the desert.

I shifted the car into drive and eased out of the dark, deserted parking lot. The headlights cut a path through the inky darkness as I redirected my attention to the elusive Train Track Killer.

At last I had picked up a clue, and I would pursue it relentlessly until that monster was finally put to rest...by one who was more bloodthirsty and brutal than him.

EIGHTEEN

The phone had been ringing nonstop. Journalists and senators from New Hampshire and Maine were relentless with calls to Liam's extension. There he sat, buried under piles of paperwork and evidence, when—surprise, surprise—the phone rang again.

"I'll bet you a buck it's the senator from Massachusetts. He's late to the party," Tony quipped, tapping away at his computer. His desk was adjacent to Liam's, across from Heather's, with Martin sandwiched in between. Martin had been newly assigned to the Greg Harris case, helping tie up loose ends and clean up the mess left in its wake.

The whole world had its eyes on the FBI, demanding answers. And Larsen had made it abundantly clear that his unit would provide them. "As soon as humanly possible" were his words.

Taking a deep breath, Liam picked up the phone. Before he could utter his name, the voice on the other end blurted out, "Is the hammer that Harris used for his victims going to be auctioned?"

Liam promptly hung up.

"Jesus, not another one of those," Martin grumbled, typing away on his computer without glancing up at Liam. Martin Neeble, a gentle giant in his late fifties, reminded Liam of a peach-skinned goliath.

"I had a guy call me and ask if I could email him a picture of Greg's privates," Martin continued. "Now Larsen wants me to look into that sicko too. These past few days have been the worst of my career."

Many agents on the floor shared that sentiment. The phone rang incessantly with callers ranging from unhinged fanatics to vengeful vigilantes. One person had threatened Tony for not finding Greg Harris sooner, while another invited him on a trip to Disneyland with his family.

"Just wait until Netflix turns this into the next *Tiger King* documentary," Tony griped. "They'll put us in those ridiculous interview chairs with fake backgrounds and make us look like total idiots."

"God, I hope I'm long gone before that happens," Liam chimed in.

Martin leaned back in his chair and pushed his glasses up his nose. "Name one profession that was once highly respected but is now a joke," he huffed.

"FBI agent," Heather replied from behind the towering stacks of document boxes on her desk.

"President," Liam said just as the phone rang again. He shook his head and stood up. "Nope. I'm done for today."

"Where're you going?" Tony asked.

Liam strode over to Heather's desk. Tony grabbed his jacket from his chair and followed him.

"Didn't you say you might have a possible identity for our Jane Doe?" Liam asked Heather.

The ground-penetrating radar had uncovered the bodies of not only Kimberly Horne and Janet Potts but also two more unidentified females, both too severely decomposed to match with missing person reports. One was dubbed Jane Doe and the other Janet Doe.

Heather pulled a manila folder from under her keyboard and handed it to Liam. "Not just possibly. Her name is Ami Lee. College student. Her DNA sample came back about half an hour ago with a match from an unsolved missing case report. I was waiting for Larsen to assign an agent to drive out and inform the family."

With Tony peeking over his shoulder, Liam opened the folder and felt a sharp stab in his chest. The high school graduation picture of a beautiful young woman smiling from ear to ear stared back at him. She had a fresh, optimistic look on her face as if she had the whole world ahead of her.

He closed the folder again and put his hands on his hips. "Fuck," he mumbled.

Heather shook her head, disbelief etched on her face. "I know. I just hope I'm not the one who has to break the news to the family that their little angel is no longer with us. I have kids of my own. I don't think I can bear to look another mother in the eyes and tell her that the most precious thing in her life is gone." She glanced around, as if ensuring that Larsen wasn't within earshot. "If you ask me, whoever chopped this bastard up should get a free pass from us."

"An eye for an eye," Martin agreed, folding his arms across his chest.

"An eye for an eye? Did I miss the memo for the Bible study group?" Cowboy chimed in as he approached Heather's desk from the hallway, noisily slurping a McDonald's milkshake. The overpowering scent of cheap cologne assaulted Liam's nostrils like an invisible avalanche.

Time to go.

"Tell Larsen I'll talk to the family," Liam said. He was about to walk out when Cowboy blocked his way.

"That wouldn't happen to be Jane Doe, aka Ami Lee?" Cowboy nodded at the folder in Liam's hand. "As fate has it, Larsen asked me personally to pay the family a visit."

"What?" Liam frowned.

"Yup! Let's go together." Cowboy slapped Liam on the back with such force that he stumbled forward and coughed. "I'll wait for you downstairs." Then Cowboy pulled a vape pen from his jacket and held it up as if it were evidence in a court trial. "If I get caught in the bathroom one more time, my uncle will have me by my gigantic balls!"

At that, he left, half skipping like a child.

"Why the hell does Larsen involve him in grown-up work?" Tony asked.

Martin shrugged. "Maybe McCourt is pressuring Larsen. A tale as old as time. Big shark eats small fish."

"I'm kinda over this case," Heather said, picking up her cell from her desk, fumbling with it. "If we're lucky, Cowboy will take this damn case and disappear with it into the Wild West of Drugs before the week is over."

As much as Liam had initially hated the idea, he'd come to terms with it. The mess surrounding Greg Harris seemed endless, and because their only evidence pointed to a drug deal gone wrong, he was no longer opposed to Cowboy taking over. Everything about the case still felt strange, but Liam was tired of following a gut feeling like he was battling an inner conspiracy theory.

"Anyone else want McDonald's?" Heather asked, scrolling through her phone.

"Get me a meal," Tony said, sitting back down.

Liam ran his hand through his hair, scoffing at Tony. "Seriously? You're just going to sit here and eat burgers?"

Tony turned his back to him. "I'm not going anywhere with Cowboy ever again. On the drive up to the cemetery, he talked about his endoscopy for over an hour."

Heather and Martin also turned back to their work.

"Great. That's real team spirit right there." Liam turned to leave, muttering just loud enough for them to hear, "One for all and all for one."

Heather was right. The sooner Cowboy took the murder case and rode off into the sunset with it, the better. Then Liam's team could focus on cleaning up the nightmare that Greg Harris had left behind and put the case to rest. Let some grass grow over it.

NINETEEN

The Lees' home in Newport, Massachusetts, was a quintessential middle-class residence about an hour north of Boston. A white picket fence surrounded slightly overgrown bushes and neatly trimmed grass in the front yard. A new SUV was parked in the driveway, just a few feet from the wooden porch.

Liam approached the door first, stepping onto the large rug that read DOG LOVERS. Taking a deep breath, he knocked. Cowboy stood next to him, looking around the porch with a curious, helpless expression.

"Please tell me you've done this before," Liam said. But Cowboy's silence confirmed his worst fears. "Just don't say anything stupid. Or better yet, don't say anything at all," Liam added, just before the door opened to reveal a man in his late forties.

"Mr. Lee?" Liam asked kindly.

Mr. Lee didn't respond or give Liam time to identify himself with his badge. Instead, his eyes widened behind his gold-rimmed glasses, and he stumbled backward until he collapsed onto the hallway stairs that connected the first and second floors. Tears streamed down his face as he removed his glasses to wipe them with the sleeve of his sweater.

"In a way, I'm glad we finally know," his trembling voice mumbled before his head fell into his hands and he started sobbing uncontrollably.

Liam had seen this too many times before, and it never got easier. The heartbreak and loss families experienced in moments like this would be etched into his memory for life. As a father himself, he found it heartbreaking.

Eventually they moved to the living room, where Liam and Cowboy sat across from the broken man. Family portraits decorated walls and side tables—Ami Lee's whole life on display all around them, from a lavish little girl's birthday party all the way to a family picture in front of Newport University. From the pictures, it appeared she had a younger brother. By God, Liam hoped he was still alive.

Mr. Lee's eyes followed Liam's gaze at the pictures. "She was always such a happy girl, our Ami. God couldn't have blessed us with a sweeter child."

Liam's mouth curled into a sad smile. "She looks like a kind and gentle soul."

"She was."

To think this beautiful family had been destroyed for no other reason than a monster's thirst for gore was enough to drive Liam mad.

"Would your wife like to join us?" Liam asked.

Mr. Lee shook his head, his gaze fixed on the carpeted floor. "She took our son to the trampoline park. This is the first time they've been out together like a normal family in a long time. Let him be happy even if it's just for an afternoon. None of this is his fault."

Liam nodded. "Of course."

A heavy silence settled in the room. Liam always gave the families of victims time to ask questions and digest his presence.

"When..." Mr. Lee began in a solemn, slow voice, "can we expect Ami's body to be returned to us? We would like to have a funeral so she can rest in peace."

Cowboy adjusted his tie. "The autopsy took longer than usual, as the body was in pretty bad shape."

Mr. Lee's face contorted with fresh sobs.

"Do you have any questions about her murder?" Cowboy added quickly, seeming lost.

"No," Mr. Lee cried. "It won't change anything. She was taken from us. What, how, or where doesn't matter. The only thing that matters now is that we can help our little girl return to our Lord and Savior with a proper funeral."

"Of cour—" Liam barely managed to say when Cowboy interrupted him.

"If it's of any comfort, the man who did this to your daughter has been tortured and killed himself."

Mr. Lee's red, swollen eyes widened. "How...how would that be a comfort? We are a family of faith. We get no pleasure from hate." He slowly shook his head. "I...I think it would be best if I spent some time alone now. Let me show you out."

Cowboy, that idiot, opened his mouth again, but Liam leaned forward in his seat and pressed his elbow into Cowboy's side. Cowboy got the message and leaned back into the couch—silently, thank God.

"Of course. We are very sorry for your loss," Liam said. "If there's anything we can do for you or your family, please let us know." He placed his card on the table under Mr. Lee's watchful gaze.

Mr. Lee nodded slightly, then rose to his feet. Liam and Cowboy followed suit.

"Thank you, but the body of our beloved Ami is all I'm asking for."

"I'll have that arranged the moment I get back to the office," Liam promised.

"Thank you."

As if in a trance, Mr. Lee walked into the hallway and opened the front door. Liam and Cowboy followed him.

Cowboy was out the door when someone grabbed Liam's arm. He turned to find an older Asian woman, small in stature, staring at him with narrowed eyes. "You said the monster who did this suffered?"

"Mother, please," Mr. Lee pleaded, then added something in Korean.

But Mrs. Lee ignored him and only tightened her grip. Liam knew exactly what she wanted from him. So he nodded.

Her bony shoulders slumped, and Mrs. Lee released his arm, contorting her wrinkled face. "Good. I hope it was slow and painful. May God bless whoever granted me this little bit of closure. It might be all I can cling to during the endless nights of torturous pain."

"Mother, enough," Mr. Lee scolded her as Liam stepped outside to join Cowboy.

Without another word, Mr. Lee closed the door. Shortly after, Liam heard him through the door, angrily speaking in Korean.

Liam took a deep breath, sighed at the thought of all those family portraits, and walked to the car. Cowboy followed closely.

"How does a father not want to know what happened to his own daughter?" Cowboy asked. "I'm not a father, but—"

"Exactly!" Liam cut him off. "You're not a father. Please enlighten me with your endless wisdom on how a grieving parent should act so I can update the FBI's training manual with that literary treasure of yours."

They both got in the car.

"Come on, Richter," Cowboy said. "I'll give you that I'm not a parent, but don't you find that whole 'Jesus love boat' the dad is cruising on a little weird?"

Liam turned on the car and stared out the window at the Lees' home. There was some truth to what Cowboy was saying. Many families of victims became obsessed with the murders of their loved ones. Sometimes that grief pushed a family to the point of delusional conspiracy theories. But then Liam was not a man of deep faith nor had he ever lost a child.

"Listen," Liam said, "the Lees acted well within the normal limits of a grieving family—both of them, the father and the grandmother. We already know who did it, so we came here only to bring the tragic news to the Lee family and offer our assistance in every possible way. They asked us to give them space, so that's what we'll do. Roger?"

Cowboy folded his hands behind his head. Then, in a jerky movement that startled Liam, he pulled something out of his jacket.

"Jesus!" Liam said.

Cowboy held up a piece of folded paper. "So you don't think I should leave this in Mr. Lee's mailbox then?"

"What the fuck is that?" Liam grabbed it and opened the folded paper. It was a copy of the map of the Newport cemetery that the evidence crew had found at Greg Harris's home. "You—" Liam paused to take a deep breath "—wanted to leave a copy of evidence in a victim family's mailbox? Are you for real?"

Cowboy raised his hands in defense. "No. I wanted to give him the map in person, if you really need to know. But then he was all Jesus and shit."

"This is evidence, Cowboy! If this leaked to the press....For Christ's sake, did you get any training at all, or did Uncle Bob wrap your badge as a birthday gift?"

"Why are you so pissed? We already have the killer." Cowboy suppressed a grin. "Well, parts of him."

Liam cussed and massaged his temples.

"Come on. I meant well," Cowboy said. "I thought the Lee family might want to lay flowers at the site where we found their daughter."

In his own twisted way, maybe Cowboy was trying to be kind, but it was too stupid to let go. "Listen," Liam said, "we have three lawsuits from the families of the graves we had to open. Do the Lees look like the kind of folks who want to fight with another family over who gets to lay roses at a grave?"

Cowboy opened his mouth, but Liam glared at him. For a second, Liam thought Cowboy might actually have learned when to shut up, but then again, cowboys liked to shoot.

"The grandma does," he said in a weak voice.

Liam dropped his head into his hands and shook it. How did he get stuck with this guy? How could Larsen let Cowboy do anything that required him to actually talk?

"Unbelievable," Liam muttered through his fingers. Then he put on his seat belt and refolded the map. He was about to put the map into his coat pocket when he froze as if struck by lightning.

Frantically he unfolded the paper again and held it closer to his face. His wide eyes narrowed.

"Impossible..." he mumbled and quickly pulled out his wallet. In between dollar bills and receipts was the ticket for Leah's concert. He tore it out, dropping a ten onto his lap, and held it next to the writing on the map.

Cowboy jerked his head back. "Dude. You okay?"

Liam ignored him, staring at the writing of the names "Jan," "Kim," and "Newport Cemetery."

Cowboy sighed. "Look, man. I'm sorry, okay? But I think you're overreacting a bit now."

Liam held up a hand to tell him to be quiet. His eyes scanned the handwriting again and again and again. The curves, the way the letters were shaped.

It was unmistakable. His heart raced as the implications began to sink in. There was no doubt. Not even the slightest.

The handwriting on this map belonged to Leah Nachtnebel.

"What. The. Fuck?" he mumbled in utter shock.

How did this make sense? How? Did she know the woman in the red dress? How could they possibly be connected? A world-renowned pianist with a lowlife drug dealer? If Ms. Nachtnebel bought drugs, like many artists did, it would definitely not be from someone like Greg Harris or his missing girlfriend.

"Earth to Liam. I really don't think the map thing is that big of a deal, but if it triggered some underlying anxiety or something, I have some Valium in my car at headqua—"

"Oh, be quiet, will you?" Liam said. "Let's get back to headquarters. I need to speak to Larsen."

"About the map?"

Liam shot Cowboy a look that went beyond annoyance; he hoped it conveyed a sense of finality, as if he were done talking to Cowboy for good. Then he put the car into gear.

He needed to talk to Larsen about this and have the map's and ticket's handwriting analyzed to confirm his suspicions in writing before the case was handed off to the Drug Unit. That nagging feeling in his gut he'd been told to ignore had returned, and this time it was back with a vengeance.

TWENTY

Larsen was seated at his desk, lost in a sea of paperwork. The door to his office was wide open, yet the serious and tense look on his face made Liam hesitate. Given the severity of the Harris case, it was understandable that Larsen wasn't exactly Mr. Sunshine. Yet his mood was something else—like a bull you wouldn't want to poke.

As their gazes met, Larsen gestured for Liam to enter.

"Tell me something good, no matter what it is," Larsen requested, closing a folder on his desk and leaning back into his black massage chair.

Liam furrowed his brow. "The tiger population has increased by forty percent in the wild."

Larsen thought about this for a moment before nodding in approval. "Good. A majestic creature like that doesn't deserve to go extinct because of us human assholes."

Liam closed the door behind him and placed the results from the forensic handwriting examination on Larsen's desk.

"What is this?" Larsen asked, picking it up.

"You tell me. It makes absolutely no sense, but the handwriting on the map we found at the Harris residence matches that of Leah Nachtnebel's signature on my concert ticket. Ms. Nachtnebel is a world-famous pia—"

"I goddamn know who Leah Nachtnebel is," Larsen snapped.

"Of course. You might also recall that she performed the night the woman in red disappeared at the Boston Symphony Hall. Her concert was delayed, beginning around the same time the woman in red was last seen near the restroom right before the concert."

Larsen scrutinized the papers in his hands. Liam thought he detected a brief twitch in the muscles around Larsen's eyes before he placed the documents on the desk and looked up. "The College Snatcher was likely stalking her and imitated her handwriting for some twisted sexual reasons or something," Larsen said.

Liam shook his head. "I thought about that. So I had handwritten notes from his residence analyzed as well. Page four of the results indicates that it's highly improbable, with less than a one percent chance, that he could replicate such artistic writing to this level of precision. He could barely sign his own name."

Larsen narrowed his eyes at Liam. "The only question crossing my mind right now is how you suddenly got all this useless information, including a ticket to her upcoming concert, when I specifically told you to stay away from these cold leads?" Larsen's eyes sparked at Liam from underneath his glasses.

Liam adjusted the tie around his neck as if the heat in the room had just exploded. "Well, I asked around a bit and—"

"Asked around a bit?" Larsen's voice was getting louder. "So while McCourt is breathing down my neck like a hungry python, and the whole unit is desperately trying to dig itself out of a pile of shit the size of the Giza pyramid, you're chasing handwriting and concert tickets from Leah Nachtnebel? To suggest what? That a world-famous artist...no, let me rephrase that. That the artist the world hails as the second coming of goddamn Mozart himself—" Larsen sucked in an angry breath "—the same woman who has played for the President of the United States on more than one occasion—" he was yelling now "—has anything to do with Greg fucking Harris and his drug-addicted girlfriend?" He slammed his fist on his desk so hard it shook. "Because of how she writes her fucking name?"

The room lay in utter silence.

Hearing him say it out loud like that, it did sound a little crazy. And yet...

Liam dragged a chair over to face Larsen and took a seat. "I understand your skepticism, but just listen. Something isn't right here. The custodian at the Boston Symphony Hall confirmed that Ms. Nachtnebel was in the same vicinity as the woman in red when she was last seen. Ms. Nachtnebel possesses a photographic memory, and both the witness account and surveillance footage reveal no one else was in the restroom besides the two of them. However, Ms. Nachtnebel claims she has never encountered this woman—"

"Claims?" Larsen's face turned red. "You interrogated Leah Nachtnebel behind my back?"

Shit.

"No, no." Liam raised his hands in defense. "I wouldn't call it that. I just asked her a few questions, which she gladly answered. And I think if we can keep the case a little longer, I can get her to tell me what she knows about the woman in red and how her handwriting ended up on that map. She might be scared of whoever murdered Greg Harris."

Larsen dropped his head into his hands and exhaled heavily. "Dear God, if you're out there and can hear me, please, I beg you, help my agents listen to me." With a mix of desperation, exhaustion, and lingering frustration, Larsen raised his gaze to meet Liam's once more. "Why are you so hung up on this case? What's really going on here? This bad attempt to keep it, manically chasing empty leads, these crazy theories...Liam, this is not *you*. You used to be my best. What happened? Did Harris get to you? The divorce? Some midlife crisis? Did you get into a dick size contest with Cowboy? Does Cowboy remind you of Sara's new b—"

"No," Liam said firmly. "It's nothing like that."

"Then what—" Larsen's mouth moved, grasping for words "—then what's going on?"

Liam pursed his lips. Was he totally out there in la-la land? Had the divorce really gotten to him? Maybe Cowboy did subconsciously remind him of the TikTok boy toy Sara had cheated on him with.

"Nobody likes Cowboy," Liam said. "That's not it."

"Then what is it?" For once, Larsen sounded empathetic.

Battling frustration directed mostly at himself, Liam raked a hand through his thick hair. "There's something about this case, Larsen. Something I just can't make sense of. The moment I stepped onto the crime scene, nothing about it has screamed drug murder. The way the person cleaned up after himself. Almost as if he left evidence behind to confuse us."

Larsen pinched his lips.

"And the woman in red. She's still missing," Liam continued. "Along with the boots and Harris's phone. I mean, aren't you curious about where she is? Don't you want to know if she's still alive? Whom do the fingerprints on the needles and drill belong to?"

For a moment, Larsen appeared to genuinely consider Liam's words instead of dismissing him outright. But then his expression shifted to a frown. "I already know what happened to the woman in red. And deep down you do as well."

That was true. Liam had worried about it every time he thought of her. Whoever killed Harris most likely killed her too.

"Let Drugs handle this. We have enough bodies to take care of. Cowboy's guys know how to follow the white powder. They know the dealers, the small fish, and the sharks. We'd just waste time on all that, and if the public starts questioning why the BAU is devoting more resources to finding a serial killer's murderer than locating missing victims and reuniting them with their families, some of us might end up as scapegoats and have to answer with our badges."

Damn it. Larsen always had a way of taking the wind out of his sails.

"You know Drugs will bury this as just another unsolved cartel murder."

"Then fucking let them."

"If it was only about justice for Harris, I'd agree. But what if the woman in red is still alive and hiding? What if she wasn't his girlfriend but one of his victims who somehow made it out of there, hoping someone would find her and help? No one left behind, that's our slogan. Remember?"

Larsen just stared at him. Burned out. Over it.

Liam saw this as a moment of opportunity and jumped on it. "Let me talk to her one more time, Larsen."

"No."

"Come on. I have a ticket to her concert. Nobody can forbid me to go there in my free time anyway."

"Oh yeah?"

Shit. That had pissed him off again.

"Okay, you could forbid it. But why not let me talk to her just one more time? If you're right, nothing will come of it, but at least I can assure myself that I've exhausted all possibilities and can finally move on. I promise I'll be the first to deliver those evidence boxes to Cowboy and his boys."

Larsen exhaled a weary sigh, retrieving a vape pen from his desk. "See what you fuckers did to me? I quit cigarettes ten years ago."

Liam smiled faintly. "Is that a yes?"

Larsen turned on the small vape pen and took a puff, coughing as if this was his first time.

"I'll take Tony with me. And then that's it. I promise."

"Goddamn it. All right. But if she doesn't want to talk—"

"Then I'll leave her be."

"You'll treat her like she was your mother."

"Even better. No good-cop, bad-cop shit. I promise."

Larsen leaned over his desk and nodded. "And you'll take Cowboy with you, not Tony."

"Come on!"

Larsen frowned.

"All right, all right. We'll be like Starsky and Hutch."

Larsen's face tightened, and his nostrils expanded. "Will you please get the hell out of my office?"

"Yes, sir!" Liam playfully saluted and left. But the minor triumph of persuading the SAC to allow another interview with Ms. Nachtnebel was only a drop of water in a deadly hot desert. Larsen was right about one thing: Unless Liam could uncover substantial evidence, the case would be transferred out of BAU. Whether justified or not, that was the reality.

TWENTY-ONE

Rain hammered my car as if the clouds had chosen buckets over mere drops to drench the world. My windshield wipers worked furiously against the relentless downpour. A burst of headlights briefly flashed in my rearview mirror. The vehicle weaved through the vacant lot, throwing up sheets of rainwater, before coming to a stop beside mine. I pressed the button to unlock my vehicle. Within moments, a figure dressed in a black coat yanked the door open and swiftly climbed in.

"The Lord must feel my anger," Larsen grumbled, wiping his face with a handkerchief. He was soaked from the short walk between his car and mine.

I ignored his usual sarcasm and pulled out the folder from the side of my car. I held it up toward him, but he just looked at it over his rain-speckled glasses.

"You never told me that Richter paid you a visit and you two had a little story time."

"Because no stories were exchanged, and I've got better things to do than set up a meeting and drive all this way just to soothe your nerves over nothing," I shot back.

Larsen raised both eyebrows at me. "Richter is all over this. He was clever enough to match your handwriting from the map you gave me to the ticket you handed him. Which, now that we're opening up here, you also failed to mention. Is it true then? You invited him to your concert?"

I nodded.

"Damn it, Leah. Are you trying to get caught?" Larsen stared out at the rain.

I lowered the folder in my hand. This conversation would take longer than I had anticipated.

"Calm yourself. I need to be razor sharp for the Train Track Killer. I found something in those files you gave me."

I held the folder back up, but Larsen merely glanced at it before turning his attention back to the downpour outside the windshield. "I don't know what games you're playing with Richter, but I don't think I can stop him if he were to find something else on you," Larsen said. "He's one of those guys—"

"Who won't stop until it's done. Determination. Dedication. Discipline. Quite admirable if you ask me."

Anger flashed in Larsen's eyes. "Not if it will destroy us and all we've worked for."

"You'll be relieved to know, then, that I invited Agent Richter to the concert so he could have a chance encounter with Luca Domizio."

Larsen's eyes widened. "The former head of the Domizio mob?"

I nodded. "Everybody knows about his involvement in drug smuggling."

"It was the trial of a lifetime. The whole world was shocked when he was found not guilty. The boss of one of the biggest drug syndicates in history. If they ever find out about me, I'll hire his lawyer no matter the cost."

"You should spend your money on his assassin, not his lawyer. There were no witnesses left at the trial."

Larsen furrowed his brow. "Regardless of how he got off the hook, the feds monitored him for years. Domizio has since left the drug trade behind, so this chance encounter won't help us. He's now involved in the contracting business. We can't prove it, but Domizio likely used extortion to secure the government's highest-paying construction bids, making them pay twice the price. Nearly every bridge and government building in this state was built by him. This won't help us at all."

"The world still remembers his old days," I countered. "Richter will as well. We're not trying to frame Domizio for a crime he didn't commit. We only need to create the impression that drugs play a role in the Harris case, and who better to do so than a former drug kingpin?"

I gave Larsen some time to think about everything, then held the folder in front of his chest.

His eyes narrowed at it. "How are you involved with Luca Domizio anyway?" he asked as if he wanted to clear that up before touching the folder.

"In no way that will endanger our operation. That's all you need to know."

Larsen sighed, then finally took the folder and opened it. I watched as his eyes scanned the papers inside. "Holy shit. You found this exact same symbol at sixteen different sites?"

I nodded. "The puzzle piece to unlock the patterns we've been hunting for. Look at the markings on the Boston subway map."

In nervous awe, Larsen shuffled the papers in the folder until he found the map I was referring to.

"The bodies are always placed at the commercial line tracks closest to a subway end station."

Larsen's lips parted as he forced out a shocked breath. "Oh my God, you're right!" It was like watching the sun rise on his face. "Why is he doing this?"

That was the terribly frustrating part of all of this. "I'm afraid I don't know for certain. I assume the location is based on convenience. End stations are less busy at night so preying on commuters is easier. Placing them on a commercial train line avoids problems because those run mostly through woods and away from possible witnesses. So far, all his victims have been placed on the SEATRAK line. He uses different locations for his bodies to avoid drawing attention from a specific railroad police force."

"And since the railroad police is untrained in murder and different stations don't communicate about incidents..."

"No pattern was established, and his murders have gone undetected as suicides."

Larsen stared at the printed map of Boston in his hands, a shocked expression on his face. "Fucking genius," he concluded.

"Quite so," I agreed, running my hands over my heated leather steering wheel.

"No wonder this bastard has given us the runaround for so long."

We sat there in a moment of silence as if we both needed time to admit who had been running the show so far: neither of us.

"The sign the killer leaves behind," Larsen said, looking at me. "Do you know what it means?"

"Ankh. An ancient Egyptian symbol for life or immortality. Unfortunately, I don't know why he carves it into the tracks. The meaning of the symbol has changed throughout the thousands of years it was prevalent in ancient Egypt. Pharaohs used it as much as common people. Even the gods wore it as a talisman. The sun god, Ra, wore it as a symbol of creation while the god of the dead, Anubis, wore it as a symbol of his power over life and death. Our killer might as well have carved a question mark into the tracks. But I'm planning on connecting with an Egyptologist at the Boston Museum of Fine Arts."

Larsen shuffled through the papers. "So it's a dead end until then?"

I looked straight at him. He lifted his gaze to meet mine. "No. If you look at the train lines map again, you'll see that there is only one stop that he hasn't used. There's another train stop in New York that also fits the criteria. Both are end stations. Within a few miles of the SEATRAK line."

Larsen stared at the map. "Hill Park Station in Boston," he mumbled and shuffled his papers. "And Summons Heights in New York. You think he'll drop his next body at either one of these two stations?"

"Nothing is certain, but he seems to follow the pattern of killing on the fourteenth of every month. There is no regularity in the month itself, but most of the murders happen every two to three months. As if he's trying to stop but can't. His killings are driven by what he believes to be great symbolism. Unlike Greg Harris, the Train Track Killer is a highly intelligent individual who plans his murders in genius detail. His profile is most likely that of a privileged male with a college degree and maybe even a family."

Larsen's tense shoulders stiffened even more. His eyes ran over the papers I'd handed him. Then he closed the folder and looked at me.

"Leah—"

"I'll do it anyway," I countered. I knew precisely what he'd been about to say. I knew it long before he had entered my car.

"You can't be involved with the Train Track Killer right now!" His voice was raised over the sound of the rain. "Richter is all over the Harris case."

"Then you'd better have it handed to Drugs as soon as you can. I'll have the ID to the fingerprints I left at the crime scene for you soon."

Larsen threw his hands up. "Please, Leah. Let me handle this and just wait it out for a little while. The fourteenth is coming up this weekend. I'll wait in the parking lot for this guy at the train station. No need for you to endanger your cover."

He was asking the impossible. For years I had chased the Train Track Killer. A chance to finally kill him was now in reach.

"There are only two more end stations left for him to place his bodies on the fourteenth. And you and I know he won't stop killing after that. He'll simply move to another pattern. Something else just as genius, maybe even better. Who knows how many years and lives will pass until we get a chance like this again." I shook my head.

"You can't wait for him at the train station. He's too intelligent for that. And we don't even know if he kidnaps all his victims from the stations or from somewhere else."

Larsen slapped his thigh with his hand. "Fine. I won't wait at the train station. I'll wait for him at the location you predicted on the commercial lines and shoot that son of a bitch."

"There are two," I countered.

"Then I'll wait for him at one of them and again if I miss him the first time."

He made it sound like running into a friend at the mall. "It's too risky. This might be our only chance, and he's smarter than you are."

This was no insult said in anger; it was just a simple fact.

Larsen took no offense. "I don't need to be smart, just a good shot. Which I am."

I clenched my fingers around my steering wheel. Larsen was starting to waste my time. I had made up my mind; he should know better than to try to change it.

"I'll take Hill Park Station. You'll wait for him at Summons Heights in New York," I said.

Larsen opened his mouth to say something, but I was faster.

"Now please get out," I said in a firm but calm voice. "I've told you all you need to know. Be ready on the fourteenth."

For a moment, we both sat there, listening to the rain patter against the roof of my car. Then Larsen tucked the folder under his coat, pressing it to his chest, and mumbled something under his breath. By now, he knew what I was capable of. In some ways, he feared me as much as he needed me—the only combination that could keep a man like him in check.

"Damn it, Leah. At least promise me you won't turn this guy into another Harris," he said as he opened the door and stepped into the rain. As the downpour drenched Larsen, he bent over to look at me through the open door. "Why Harris? Why did you pick him to do what you did?"

I was surprised he hadn't asked this question sooner. I remained silent, so he wiped water out of his eyes and sighed.

"Do I at least have your word that the Harris situation won't repeat itself?" he demanded.

I narrowed my eyes at him, reflecting the darkness I had carried within me since I had stabbed a boy when I was a little girl. "It won't be another Harris," I assured him. "You have my word."

TWENTY-TWO

Liam and Cowboy were sitting in a private balcony close to the stage. The room was filled to the last seat. Both men were wearing tuxedos. Much to Liam's relief, he had listened to his mother for once and not worn a shirt and suit pants, as most of the men attending the concert wore tuxedos as well. The conversation with his mother had taken place right before she had started a fight with him about the fact that he was going to the concert without her. She hadn't been assuaged even though Liam had explained, many times, that he was on the job and had to go with a coworker.

"If I fall asleep, leave me be," Cowboy said as the lights dimmed and the chattering died down. "This was supposed to be my weekend off, and I partied too hard last night." He leaned back in his seat and crossed his arms.

Liam ignored him and scanned the private balconies across from and next to theirs. The crowd included a few senators and their wives, as well as some of the richest people this money-driven country had produced. He almost couldn't believe that his balcony was closer to the stage than theirs. It had earned him jealous as well as curious gazes. Only one other private balcony, to his left, was closer to the stage. It was still empty, and with only five minutes to go, Liam wondered if it might be the only seat with a no-show. But just then, Cowboy hit Liam on his arm with the back of his hand, interrupting his thoughts.

"Holy shit." Cowboy perked up in his seat and nodded at the empty balcony.

A man dressed in a white tuxedo and holding a red rose stepped in. Two bear-sized men dressed entirely in black were behind him.

"It's Luca fucking Domizio!" Cowboy mumbled. "As in former drug kingpin. Another strike for Drugs."

"Holy shit," Liam cussed under his breath as well.

He was right there. Only feet away from them.

"So it's true." Cowboy lowered his voice to a whisper. "The former head of all East Coast drug operations is a huge fan of your lady friend. I'd heard he was obsessed with her."

Liam stared at one of the most famous mobsters in history.

"Now here's another goodie for you," Cowboy continued. "Domizio was here the same night as our lady in red—a witness to a drug-related slaughter."

Frowning, Liam looked away to avoid getting caught staring. "How do you know he was here?"

"Drugs still has someone follow him at all times. And most likely will until his last breath. We haven't been able to place him with the woman in red yet. But it's worth looking into."

"Someone is still following him? The trial was years ago. How is that even authorized?"

Cowboy leaned in. "It's not. It's off the books. But what went down there was the biggest embarrassment in law enforcement history since Al Capone. And Domizio had his fucking taxes in order."

The whole room rose to its feet and frantically started clapping. Leah Nachtnebel entered the illuminated stage in a black dress that exposed her whole back—no bra. She looked stunning.

Liam rose to his feet as well, but Cowboy remained seated. The clapping continued for almost a minute while Leah bowed a few times next to her wooden grand piano and then sat down.

"Jesus," Cowboy cussed. "My hands hurt."

Finally the crowd sat and waited in great anticipation. The room was dead silent except for the occasional cough, including one from Cowboy.

Nervous excitement filled the air, all eyes on the bright stage. Liam briefly looked at Luca Domizio, whose face was torn in restless anxiety.

Suddenly Leah raised both hands, held them still for a moment, and then dropped them onto the elegant grand piano's keys. Liam had no idea what she was playing, but as the sad notes filled the room and swallowed him in a cloud of mystery, he closed his eyes and let his emotions wash over him like a wave on the beach. He had listened to millions of songs before, but never had music reached into his soul like this, tugging at his deepest fears and desires. It was as if she knew them and was laying them bare. It was unreal.

"What the fuck," he heard Cowboy mutter in awe and saw him lean over the balcony railing, staring at the stage as if under a spell.

Liam sat perfectly still, his whole body absorbed in the music. The world around him seemed to evaporate like a warm breath in the bitter cold. All that mattered were the glimpses of memories that started flashing in front of him. Exciting ones. Sad ones. The beauty of reliving them almost overwhelmed him.

He opened his eyes to look at the woman who was making all this possible.

Leah Nachtnebel.

Whoever she was, he would never forget the way her music moved him.

When the last note of the concert was played, the room rested in utter silence once more as Leah rose to her feet and faced the crowd. She looked unemotional. Almost detached.

Then all hell broke loose.

Chants, tears, clapping, and shouts for more. Liam and Cowboy rose to join them, and so did the man who, according to Cowboy, might be the answer to the riddle that brought them here.

Luca Domizio.

After a few more bows, out of nowhere, Leah looked straight up at Liam. Without blinking, she stared at him, her beautiful face emotionless, her red lips slightly parted.

Her gaze wandered over Cowboy to Luca Domizio. And her lips curled into a faint smile that almost seemed fake. He nodded at her. She nodded back.

Then she turned and walked off the stage.

TWENTY-THREE

"Hey, you can't be back here!" a woman yelled the moment her sunken eyes scouted Liam and Cowboy in front of Leah's backstage room. She rushed over, pulling her headset back.

"I'd have to disagree," Cowboy said, arrogantly flashing his badge.

The woman looked at it, her eyes widening in shock. "Is something wrong?" she gasped.

"Can't say. Official FBI business," Cowboy said as if he were the star of a Hollywood B movie.

The woman covered her mouth in worried disbelief.

"Nobody's in trouble," Liam cut in. "We just have a few questions for Ms. Nachtnebel. She's waiting for us."

The woman slowly nodded, calmer, then pulled her headset back on and left. Liam threw Cowboy an annoyed glance, but Cowboy ignored him and knocked.

"Come in." Leah's voice was muffled through the door. Cowboy opened it eagerly, but before he could step in, Liam blocked the way and leaned over.

"Why don't you find Luca Domizio and feel him out a bit? Might not get a chance to talk to him again."

For a moment, the two men stared at one another. It was Cowboy who looked away first.

"You still think this is your case, don't you?" Cowboy said. "Keep a box of tissues close, because it won't be for much longer." Then he left.

Liam stepped in and closed the door behind him. He turned to find Ms. Nachtnebel on her silken couch, her green eyes narrowing at him. The side slit on her elegant evening dress revealed the evenly tanned skin of her long, crossed legs.

"Agent Richter, I hope you enjoyed the concert."

Stepping closer, Liam ran his hand through his hair, looking for words. "It was...I'm kinda lost for words, to be honest. Truly amazing. I think I even recognized one or two of the pieces you played."

"That's because I chose a program of the world's most-known masterpieces for today."

Liam grinned. "Thanks for keeping it light for people like me."

"Quite the opposite," she countered, her face serious. "The easier the technical part of the piece is, the harder it becomes to play."

"Really? Why is that?"

"Mistakes are easier to notice. It's extremely hard for a drop of red blood to hide on a plain white canvas." She paused. "Few of us will ever master that skill, but for the ones who do, the rewards are truly worth the effort."

Liam let those words run through his head. Was she referring to Luca Domizio? Did she know something about him and the woman in red? Were they hiding right in front of him like a drop of red blood on a canvas?

Liam voiced his suspicion. "You mean kinda like Luca Domizio?" he asked, watching every inch of her response.

Her foot turned. She smoothed a wrinkle in her dress, then looked back at him. "I'm afraid I don't follow."

Liam walked around the room, his eyes wandering over musical sheets and the empty makeup table. Not one freaking note with her handwriting on it.

"Luca Domizio. Do you know him well?"

"Not really. He comes to all my concerts and sometimes takes me out for dinner afterward. He has a deep love for classical music. That's mostly all we talk about."

Liam nodded. "He was here the night the woman in the red dress vanished."

"As I said, he attends most of my concerts."

Liam nodded again but this time turned to look at her. "A few people at work commented on your beautiful handwriting. On the..." He paused and watched her eyes briefly widen. "The ticket," he finally said.

Leah's lips curled into a faint smile. "Thank you. You can actually take a class that teaches you how to write like that. It's quite popular."

"Really. Is it an online class or in person?"

Her mouth dropped open slightly, and she hesitated before answering. "I...don't know. A friend mentioned the class to me. He is the one who taught me." She gave her ear a quick tug. A sign she was lying?

"Do you think I could talk to this friend? I'd love to get more information about this class."

A brief silence swallowed the room. Then Leah rose and walked over to the closet next to the door to grab her coat. "I am otherwise engaged, but if you like, you can walk me out."

Liam jumped on that offer and opened the door for her. She stepped through and led the way down the hall toward the stage.

"When you were a child, who taught you right from wrong, Agent Richter?" she asked as they walked past curious staff in the hallway.

Liam frowned. Personal questions. He shouldn't answer. No way.

He answered anyway. "My...father."

"You mentioned he was a police officer?"

"He was."

She nodded. "So you were raised with the moral compass of those who enforce the law, not write it?"

He didn't have to answer this question, but she would most likely shut down if he didn't. This was his last chance. He needed something. Anything.

"He raised me to follow the law and respect it, if that's what you're asking."

They passed the backstage area and followed a hallway Liam had never been in before.

"So you distinguish right from wrong based on laws and social norms?"

"I guess."

Leah stopped and turned to look at him. "But the law is not always right. People are not always right."

Liam frowned as she continued walking. "I guess you have to trust the people around you then," he said. "My father was a good man. He threw the ball with me and never touched a drop." Liam pictured his father in the dim light of a lamp, sitting on his bed when Liam was a teen dealing with his first heartache. "His hand was always on my shoulder when I needed it to be," he continued, the memory fading. "Poor devil's only mistake was to marry my mother, who dragged him through hell and back."

"I'm certain that wasn't his only mistake," she said with confidence as if she'd known his father all her life.

"It kind of was. He was just one of those good guys who are hard to find these days."

The hallway ended at an emergency exit. Leah placed her hand on the door and was about to push it but paused. "And why would making mistakes change that?" she asked, then pushed through the door.

Considering what she'd just said, Liam followed Leah into a dark alley. A cat launched out of a nearby trash can and darted off.

Leah walked toward the end of the alley and turned to face Liam. At the same time, the headlights of a Maybach luxury limousine turned on as the vehicle rolled up to her. One of Luca Domizio's bodyguards rushed out of the front passenger side and opened the door to the back of the car. Luca Domizio himself leaned forward and looked straight at them with an intense curiosity.

"The canvas, Agent Richter," Leah said and looked deep into his eyes, serious, mysterious. "The canvas."

Without another word, she walked up to the limousine and slid in. The bodyguard closed the door behind her, then looked Liam up and down, disapproval written on his face as he got back into the passenger side seat.

In awe, Liam watched the limousine merge with the chaotic Boston downtown traffic. Everything was wrong here.

Everything.

It was obvious she'd lied about the friend teaching her the handwriting. The strange remarks about hiding in plain sight also haunted him. So did her psychological analysis of his moral standards.

"Did she tell you anything?" Cowboy asked, joining him as they watched the limousine in the distance. It was now stuck behind a red light several intersections down.

The canvas, Liam thought.

"Nothing but vague hints."

Cowboy frowned. "About Domizio?"

The noise of the surrounding traffic grew louder as Liam remained silent.

"I guess that's it then, huh? But don't worry, sweetie—" Cowboy gave him a demeaning pat on the back "—I got it from here."

TWENTY-FOUR

The limousine's soft orange light cast a warm glow on Luca's face. His black hair, flecked with silver, was neatly combed. With a slim, long nose and face, he looked elegant. His sophisticated style was complemented by a hand-tailored white tuxedo and a cashmere coat draped over his shoulders.

I was sitting across from him, smiling faintly when he handed me the red rose—and shortly after, a small piece of paper.

My smile deepened as I held the rose to my nose and smelled its sweet scent.

"Bravissimo," Luca said in his typically calm tone. "You haven't played Mozart for me in months. Or did you play it for somebody else?"

I carefully placed the rose on the fine leather seat beside me but kept the paper in my hand. "I play for everybody."

Luca grinned, revealing a golden tooth in the far left of his mouth. "Including the FBI."

"Including the FBI," I said impassively. "Does it worry you?"

"Why would it?" he asked, shrugging innocently. "I build bridges. Bridges normal people drive on. Bridges the FBI and even the president drive on. I also build their offices. Many of them. Almost all of them. And I always keep a spare key."

My eyes dropped to the note in my hand. This was the first time I'd had to ask my source to identify the body to which the fingers I used for planting fingerprints belonged. Up until now, every single fingerprint had been successfully identified by law enforcement and traced back to a missing or diseased criminal. Case closed. This time they'd been unable to trace the prints.

I opened the note.

Eduardo Garcia was all it read.

Luca looked out the window through the tinted glass. A drunk couple was yelling on the sidewalk next to the traffic light where the limousine had stopped.

"An illegal immigrant who worked for the cartel in Mexico before he came here to sell drugs for them," Luca said, focusing on the fight outside. The sobbing woman was yelling at the man, who was trying to calm her with soft words and forced hugs. "That's why there were no police files on him. He stole from the cartel. A few hundred dollars, but they killed him and his whole family for it. Even the children."

His eyes narrowed as the limousine started moving again.

"When the Italians and Irish were still running things, there was a code of honor," he continued. "Women and children were not to be touched. The filth from Mexico and Russia that are ruling the trade now are a disgrace to humankind."

I grabbed my flip phone from my coat pocket and texted the name and cartel information to Larsen.

"We humans have gravitated toward darkness since the beginning of our existence," I remarked, closing the phone with a strong snap. "We are too afraid to admit what we truly are. People pretend it's the lack of humanity that is responsible for the atrocities we're capable of when, in fact, humanity is the root of it."

Luca's head tilted as he stared at me with softening features. "May I steal you for dinner? I saw you renamed Beethoven's *Moonlight Sonata* in your program. I am dying to hear more about it."

The limousine turned, and I saw the familiar brick town homes of my neighborhood in Beacon Heights. "I apologize. But I am otherwise engaged tonight."

Luca remained silent as he stared at me. This relationship was built on give and take. I just took, so now I had to give.

"But how about after my next concert? If Luigi tunes his piano, I will play for you and the guests."

I disliked that piano. It was old and had two broken keys—a typical item placed in Italian restaurants as decor.

Luca's lips curled into a smile. "I would like that very much."

The limousine came to a stop in front of my town home. I grabbed the rose and opened the door, then paused and turned to Luca. "I changed it in the program because Beethoven never named his Sonata No. 14 after the moonlight. He called it *Quasi Una Fantasy.*"

"Like a fantasy."

I nodded. "After Beethoven's death, a poet compared the sonata to a boat floating in the moonlight on the Vierwaldstättersee in Switzerland."

Luca scratched his chin. He loved stories like this. "The world decided it knew Beethoven's music better than the maestro himself."

"Pretty much."

There was a brief silence in the car.

"Who would I turn to if I needed to obtain someone's phone number and address?" I asked.

"The internet. It runs about forty bucks on the dark web."

"And if...it was an FBI agent?"

The leather seat creaked under Luca's movement. "Then me," he said with a grin.

I nodded. "Tell Luigi to tune that old thing." I stepped out.

Luca smiled. "I will."

TWENTY-FIVE

The red taillights of the vehicles ahead of him twinkled like little stars, leading Larsen down the dark highway. He was making his way down US 20 from Boston to New York.

The radio was playing a song Larsen had never heard. Its beats mixed with the humming sound of the tires on pavement. He was navigating through the steady stream of traffic toward an exit when his flip phone vibrated in his coat pocket.

Leah.

He pulled it out and opened the message. The ID of the fingerprints.

"Fucking finally," he cussed, tossing the phone onto the passenger seat. He almost missed the exit as he fumbled with his work phone to call the associate director of the FBI. His eyes glanced at the radio's clock: eight p.m.

Late but not too late for a call like this. Ever since the news of Greg Harris broke, McCourt had been breathing down his neck like a vulture waiting for a feast. A case that shook the nation always landed on the desks of big fish.

"Larsen," came McCourt's low voice from the phone. "Please tell me you have something that will stop the damn press from blowing up my office lines."

"I'm afraid not even the second coming of Jesus would stop them. But there might be a way to take some heat off the case."

"Give me a minute, we have the grandkids tonight," McCourt said as the noise of screaming children in the background rose. It died down with the sound of a closing door. "Damn little devils. So what you got for me?"

"We were able to match the fingerprints at the crime scene. It's very safe to say that the College Snatcher was killed by a drug dealer working for the Mexican cartel. He was here without papers, so it took us a bit to identify him."

"Thank fucking God," McCourt said. "Just in time. My daughter showed me some fucking YouTube videos of a guy insisting Harris was killed by a serial killer who killed serial killers. A few smaller news stations picked up on it without the slightest evidence. These conspiracy assholes need to find real jobs."

"How would you like me to proceed? Hand the murder investigation of Greg Harris to Organized Crime?" Larsen asked.

"No need. I want this fucking case buried to the center of the earth."

Silence filled the stuffy air of the car.

"Sir, could you elaborate?"

"Do you speak English? Close the damn case, Larsen. Make this dealer responsible for Harris's death and return the bodies of the Snatcher's victims to the families. End of story."

Larsen almost sighed in relief. He hadn't noticed the sweat on his forehead until a droplet entered his eye. "What about other victims? There might still be some women we haven't found yet. If we close the case—"

"There're always others. I said close the fucking case. That's the end of it."

"Yes, sir. Do you want me to—?"

With a click on the line, McCourt hung up.

"Prick," Larsen mumbled as he slipped his work phone back into his pocket and grabbed the flip phone off the passenger seat.

Thirty minutes to destination, he texted Leah.

He was surprisingly eager to confront the Train Track Killer in the dark woods so that he could shoot him at first sight, bypassing the court system and saving taxpayers from funding a killer's life in prison. Plain old justice on the spot.

Larsen had served several tours in Iraq. Sometimes after a killing, he felt guilt, but most of the time, he didn't. The rush of adrenaline was like a drug. He hoped the Train Track Killer would show up in New York, not at Hill Park Station in Boston. Not that he didn't trust Leah to deal with him. There was no monster like that woman. The things she was capable of doing were straight out of a nightmare. She was a genius, literally—in music as much as in everything else she touched. But after the Harris case, Larsen was starting to question her ability to prioritize clean operations over personal objectives. Because of her mistakes, Agent Richter had come close. Not close enough for Larsen to have to think about plan B but still too goddamn close for comfort.

If Lady Luck smiled at him tonight, he could simply put a bullet in the Train Track Killer and then leave the body out there for someone else to find. He would be back in Boston before anyone knew he was gone.

Open-and-shut case. Another monster returned to the pits.

TWENTY-SIX

I had been waiting for several hours. In utter darkness, completely still, my loaded Glock handgun relaxed in my gloved hand. There was something peaceful and serene about the darkness enveloping the world around me, casting deep shadows among the trees and underbrush. The moon shined its silver light onto the train tracks ahead. The cool air smelled of moss, and the rustling of leaves in the wind was the only noise that sliced through the silence of the night.

Despite my deep desire for the Train Track Killer to feel the same pain and terror he'd caused others, I couldn't let my years of pursuit go to waste by allowing him to escape. My plan was straightforward: shoot him, and with any luck he'd survive so I could lay him on the train tracks—alive. He would hear the distant rumble of an approaching train and be overtaken by the terror of an imminent, grisly end. He deserved nothing less and so much more.

A branch cracked to my left. Turning quickly, I saw a rabbit dash by. It leaped over the train tracks and vanished into the woods beyond.

I found myself wondering if Larsen would be the one to secure our grim win tonight. I had instructed him to maintain radio silence until the Train Track Killer was dead or dawn broke. Even a slight glow or buzz from a phone could give us away.

Another branch snapped, echoing from the woods across the train tracks where the rabbit had disappeared. Then came another snap, and the rustle of leaves grew steadier, hinting at something approaching. Suddenly a large, dark shape emerged at the forest's edge. Excitement surged through me, leaving me momentarily breathless as I watched the figure. It moved with a hunch, pausing only to straighten up and listen for danger. I froze, barely daring to breathe.

For a moment, the forest was quiet and still. Then, at last, a towering figure stepped into the moonlight, carrying the lifeless form of a woman over his shoulder as if she weighed nothing. Her wrists and ankles were tied up tight. This massive man, easily over six feet tall, had the muscular build of an athlete. A hood was drawn low over his face, hiding his identity.

He glanced left and right, then strode up to the tracks and unceremoniously dumped the woman's body onto them as if she were no more than a sack of rocks. The impact jolted her awake. She began to move her limbs groggily before thrashing violently, struggling to free her tied wrists and ankles. A cloth muffled her screams and groans as she failed to escape the tracks. Unmoved by her sobs, the man rolled her onto her stomach, pressing her face into the gravel. Then he knelt beside her and began etching something into the tracks.

This was my moment. Now or never!

In what felt like slow motion, I raised my weapon, aiming at the figure hovering beside his prey. My finger found the trigger, poised to fire.

Suddenly the man rose and stared my way, with his gun aimed directly at me.

How was this possible? I hadn't made a sound. Could he feel my presence? Two killers alone on the devil's playground?

The world stood still as we stared at each other. Eye to eye, monster to monster. It was too dark to make out any facial features, but his eyes had a glow to them, like those of an animal. Why wasn't he shooting? Why wasn't I?

Calmly he lowered his gun about an inch, as if to ask for a truce. No, as if to let me know he wouldn't kill me. But this was what he didn't know about me. This was where he and I differed.

I wasn't afraid to die.

Take away the warm glow one feels when watching their children play. Remove the comforting love that surges through one's body when embraced by a loved one. Erase the unbridled laughter shared with friends at a lively bar table after one too many drinks. Take it all away, and you're left with me. I was lucky to experience the occasional sense of passion or gratification when I killed a killer.

So his gun failed to intimidate me. I rejected his offer of peace.

The distant blare of a train horn signaled its imminent arrival. With no time to waste, I pulled the trigger.

In seconds, the Train Track Killer stumbled and fell to his knees, clutching his chest. I burst from the woods and fired again, missing as he leaped to his feet and disappeared into the shadow of the trees. I fired two more rounds into the darkness before sprinting to the woman on the tracks.

She thrashed and screamed, face down, as the train's whistle grew louder, closer. I yanked her off the tracks just moments before the train roared past us. Blood was smeared across her forehead from a head wound, but she would live. I quickly took out a knife and cut her loose, careful to keep my face hidden, then turned and charged after the Train Track Killer.

My heart pounded as I raced through the darkness, the moon casting a faint light through the branches above. I stumbled over a fallen branch, nearly losing my balance, but quickly regained my footing and pressed on. Periodically I paused to listen as the sounds of snapping branches and rustling leaves grew more distant. My target was increasing the distance between us.

I pursued the faint sounds until I spotted the glow of a road ahead, near the edge of the woods. With a final burst of energy, I broke through the tree line just as a van sped down the road, its engine roaring and tires screeching against the pavement.

The license plate read *1432 GG.*

Gasping for breath, I watched as the van dwindled into the distance.

1432 GG.

TWENTY-SEVEN

The office was bustling with agents moving around as if they were in a disturbed ant pile. Liam passed the break room and could smell fresh coffee. The sound of typing on keyboards mixed with the nonstop trilling of ringing phones.

Liam found Tony and Heather huddled around Martin's computer, chatting and pointing at something.

"What the hell is going on here?" Liam asked. "Did Greg Harris rise from the dead?"

Heather looked up at Liam, her glasses magnifying her eyes. It was always a bad sign when Heather didn't have enough time to put in her contact lenses in the morning. "Where the hell have you been?" she asked.

"I got a call from Josie's school. She had a fever, so they made me pick her up and test her for Covid at an urgent care."

Tony, Heather, and Martin looked at him with eyebrows raised.

"Calm down, it was negative."

All three returned their focus to the screen.

"It's the storm before the calm," Heather explained. "I'm so glad it's almost over. I can't wait for this floor to smell like cheap air freshener and coffee again."

Now that she mentioned it, the air didn't smell of its usual fast-food spices.

"I kinda liked the burger smell," Tony said.

Heather rolled her eyes at him.

"What do you mean? What are you guys talking about?" Liam asked.

Tony and Heather exchanged glances while Martin kept his focus on the screen.

"You haven't heard yet?" Tony asked.

"No. As I said, I was stuck in urgent care for five damn hours. Healthcare has gone to shit in this country."

"Well," Heather said, "Larsen closed the case."

If she'd punched Liam in the face, it would have been less of a blow.

"What do you mean he closed the case? You mean transferred it to Cowboy?" Liam's voice was strained and filled with tension.

"No. He closed it," Martin said. "They matched the fingerprints on the murder weapon with some Mexican cartel dealer."

"What?" Liam's head jerked back in surprise.

"Pretty crazy, huh? This case solved itself for us," Heather said.

This all sounded too...simple. All of it. Nothing made sense here, and then at every dead end, some simple explanation presented itself?

"Who has him in custody?" Liam pressed.

If this guy would at least talk, Liam might get some answers.

"Hell does," Tony said. "The guy washed up on Carson Beach. Some kid was poking his blue, soaked face with a stick before his screaming mom finally discovered the corpse."

Heather shook her head. "Kids these days are desensitized little monsters."

"My fifteen-year-old nephew made me watch *Saw* with him. I felt nauseated the whole time, but I couldn't look away," Martin said, staring over his computer screen as if he was reliving the trauma.

Liam turned on the spot and strode off.

"Don't do it!" Tony yelled after him, but Liam didn't care. Something was amiss here. Every case he had ever worked on had been a disaster, but they were never simply closed and swept under the rug.

The door to Larsen's office was ajar. A heavy sigh escaped Larsen's lips as Liam entered and closed the door behind him. Like everyone else since the Harris case, Larsen appeared weary and burned out. But today he looked as though he had partied all night, having arrived at the office in the same clothes he'd worn the night before.

"Please don—"

Liam cut him off. "You closed the case? Just like that? What about the possible victims we're still missing? When did we start doing half-ass work here, Larsen? Because I think I didn't get the memo."

Larsen took off his glasses and rubbed his reddened eyes, then faced Liam with a frown. "Let me put this in toddler language for you so this fight will be as short as my temper today. McCourt called me and said Organized Crime found a match of the fingerprints. The murderer of the College Snatcher. Close the case, he said. End of story."

He put his glasses back on and focused on a folder in front of him. Liam waited for a moment to see if he would add anything else, but he didn't.

"End of story?" Liam repeated, agitated.

"End of story," Larsen countered, weary.

"And the college girls who vanished from the College Snatcher's hunting grounds around the same time he was active there...end of story for them as well?"

Larsen frowned. "Yup. End of story," he repeated.

"I went to see Leah Nachtnebel again, remember? The woman who was in the same bathroom at the same time our woman in red disappeared. A drug-crime victim. On the same night Luca Domizio was there as well."

"And?" For the first time, a spark of interest flashed in Larsen's eyes.

"She's lying to me. I know it. There's something going on between the two of them, maybe the three of them if the woman in red is still alive. Don't you want to get to the bottom of all this? If McCourt doesn't care, maybe the state's attorney will. I know he's been going crazy on this case. He wants justice for those families and counts on us to deliver it."

Larsen sighed loudly. "Fine. Then give me what you got."

Liam hesitated. The way Larsen said it sounded almost like a bluff.

"You insist there's more to this case, so give me something. Anything."

Liam bit his lower lip as his gaze dropped to the floor. He had nothing...yet.

Larsen nodded. "So you want me to ask the state's attorney to overrule the associate director of the FBI to challenge a woman who plays piano for the president and a man with half of DC in his pocket, all based on a hunch in your gut?"

It was quiet. Larsen had done it again—twisted and turned the truth to make Liam sound like a lunatic.

Larsen started tapping his fingers on his desk. "Let me tell you what the state's attorney will tell me. He will tell me, with all due respect, to take a fucking laxative to help with the gut feeling and move the fuck on!"

Larsen had actually yelled those last words.

"So," Liam said cautiously, adopting a softer tone. "Do we just ignore the truth and leave Harris's other victims to decay in the ground? Let their families spend the rest of their lives wondering what happened to their girls? I have a mother of a missing girl from the same college that Samantha Hayden was taken from calling me daily in tears, begging me to find her daughter. And there's a father standing outside this building right now. What do you want me to tell them, Larsen? 'Sorry, folks, case closed'?"

"I hate this as much as you do." Larsen yanked open his desk drawer and slammed a thick folder onto the desk. "But here's the reality of our world, Richter. This is just Boston."

Liam didn't need to ask about the folder's contents. Every agent knew the ominous black folders filled with photos of missing people, their eyes full of accusations of abandonment. Delving into those cases was a plunge into a world of despair. Thousands of people were missing from the city alone with no leads or hope.

"We don't have enough hands to save them all," Larsen said. "So please, listen to me just this fucking once. Don't piss up McCourt's tree. You might not like what the wind blows back to you. Take a few days off to cool down. I can't afford to lose one of my best."

The stuffy air in the room filled with awkward silence.

Defeat. The sour taste of it burned on his tongue like acid.

Larsen was right. There was nothing to be done. The food chain had slapped them right across the face. Darwin's law had come knocking. The big dicks had all the swag.

Liam turned and opened the door.

"Richter, wait!" Larsen called after him. But for today Liam had had enough. He'd been pulling long hours and even weekends since the Harris case like none of the others. Then, today, he'd spent all day driving his sick daughter around to get her tested for Covid when the whole damn town was out of tests.

He'd had enough. He would listen to Larsen and take a few days off, then come back to work as a new man with twice the drive and triple the effort.

Liam was already halfway through the office when he stopped and looked over at Martin's desk for Heather. She wasn't with him any longer, but Liam knew exactly where she was.

A voice deep inside him urged him to simply return home as Larsen suggested. But he had an idea. One last thing before he let it all go.

He followed the smell of coffee and burgers and found Heather sitting in the break room, burger in one hand, fries in the other.

A grin flashed over Liam's lips as he leaned against the doorframe and folded his arms. Heather looked up and rolled her eyes.

"Not a word," she said before stuffing a fry in her already-full mouth.

"All right," Liam said, grinning even wider.

Heather narrowed her eyes at him. "You're not here for a lunch date, are you?"

Liam shook his head. It took Heather a few more moments before she put the burger down and wiped her mouth with a napkin.

"No. I won't do it," she said.

"Come on, Heather!" Liam begged as he approached her, dragging a chair across from her.

"No need to sit," she said. "My answer is no. Larsen said close the case. And that's what I'll do."

Pinching his lips, Liam took a fry from her and ate it. "I swear it won't get you in trouble."

"Hell yeah, it will."

"No, because I'll say it was all me."

"Then whatever it is, you do it."

"I can't. You're the file whisperer, not me. You know people in every law enforcement organization there is. If anybody can find something, it's you."

"If..." Heather remained firm.

"Come on, Heather. Remember when I gave you almost a week of my PTO when you and Rob were struggling and went on that couples therapy retreat?"

"Oh really? You pulling that card now?"

"I got a lot of shit for that from Sara. But hey, sure. Let's just all come to Liam when we need something, but if he needs us in return—"

"All right, all right." Heather sighed. "But if I help you, I never want to hear about the PTO thing again."

"I swear on my Aunt Jane's life."

Heather dismissed him with an eye roll, already familiar with Liam's Aunt Jane and her crazy doll collection. "And I won't give you back that PTO."

Liam hesitated.

"Fine, then forget about—"

"Keep the PTO," Liam cut in.

Heather nodded. "So what do you want?"

"I need you to look into Leah Nachtnebel."

"The pianist?" Both her eyebrows shot up.

"The very one."

"Fuck. If Larsen finds out I'm wasting time and resources—"

"He won't," Liam promised.

Heather sighed again, then took a bite of her burger. "All right."

Liam rose with a smile. "You're the best! Call me when you got something. I'll be out for a few."

"What do you mean you'll be out for a few?" Heather yelled after him as he walked toward the door. "Where the hell are you going?"

Liam turned. "Taking a few days off. Larsen's orders. Don't wanna piss him off. You know how he can be." Then he walked out.

"You got off? That's bullshit!"

Heather's voice was muffled by the bustling office sounds as he made his way to the elevator. A mix of disappointment and hope stirred within him as he pressed the call button.

If anyone could uncover something useful, it would be Heather. All he had to do now was wait.

TWENTY-EIGHT

The screams from a rollercoaster combined with the smell of popcorn as Liam grasped an old baseball. He aimed at the two tin cans left between him and the stuffed animal prize. With a deep exhale, he hurled the ball, but it soared past both cans, falling into the basket below.

"Damn it!" Liam grumbled, reaching for his wallet once again.

"Dad—" Josie sighed "—you can stop now. I really don't need it that bad."

"How about we go on the water ride again?" Liam's mother suggested. She was a petite woman with an unwavering confidence. Known for her strong bite and critical nature, she had a stern demeanor with deep frown lines and a tightly pressed mouth. Her hair was dyed brown, and her signature oversized glasses amplified her piercing gaze.

With a grumpy sigh, Liam slapped a ten-dollar bill onto the carpeted table of the tin can stand. The grumpy woman working there placed five balls in front of him in a robotic motion.

"My pumpkin wants a stuffed animal, so she will get one, and I'm already ninety in. I can't stop now," Liam said.

"You sound like a gambler," Liam's mother scolded him.

"Here. Spit on it for good luck," Liam said and held the balls in front of Josie's face. Josie grinned.

"No spitting on balls," the tin can lady grumbled in a monotone voice.

Liam and Josie shared a chuckle before he launched another assault on the cans. Finally, with the last of the balls and a surge of justified aggression, he sent the ball crashing into the cans with a satisfying metallic clang.

"Touchdown!" Liam bellowed, celebrating as if he had just won the lottery. Josie jumped up and down beside him.

"Which one do you want?" the tin can lady asked gruffly, nodding at the sun-bleached collection of stuffed animals dangling from the ceiling of the stand.

"The rainbow poop," Josie blurted.

"What?" Liam objected. "I practically threw my retirement savings away for poop?"

Josie laughed. "I want the poop, Dad. Everybody has one now."

The lady handed her the stuffed rainbow poop with an expressionless face. Josie's smile stretched from ear to ear as she hugged it against her chest.

"There's something disturbing about watching you embrace poop, pumpkin." Liam teased her, his eyes bright with affection.

She teased him back. "I'll always think of you when I hold it. Promise."

"You know there were cheaper ways to get you rainbow poop."

"Ew, Dad!" Josie smacked his arm, but she was laughing.

"Really, Liam. Ew," his mother added.

"Look, Dad!" Josie pointed excitedly at a food truck. "Can I have a chocolate funnel cake?"

"I don't know, pumpkin. That's a lot of sugar," Liam said.

His mother, sensing the opportunity, opened her purse and handed Josie a ten-dollar bill. "Here you go, sweetie."

Josie's face lit up, but she still glanced at her dad for approval. With a reluctant frown, he finally nodded.

"Parents these days are terrified of sugar, but they let their kids post videos of themselves in bikinis on TikTok," his mom remarked as they watched Josie cheerfully bound to the truck and join the line, her rainbow poop tucked securely under her arm.

A gentle smile spread across Liam's face, accompanied by a warm feeling that radiated through his body. He loved this girl more than life itself. The thought of losing a child and never knowing what happened to her was unbearable.

"The canvas, Agent Richter." Leah Nachtnebel's words suddenly intruded upon his thoughts. The strange questions she had asked about his father and upbringing had lingered in his mind. The roles in his family had always been so clear. His father was the beauty and his mother the beast. Who was Leah Nachtnebel to question that?

Liam's gaze fell upon his mother's glittering purse. It was adorned with key chains and an assortment of other trinkets, covering every available inch, reminding him of something out of a Japanese anime. Ever since his sister had moved out to go to college, his mother's constant belittling of Liam had escalated to new heights, and she had developed an obsession with collecting items from garage sales and thrift stores. If he didn't keep an eye on her, she was sailing straight to the TV show *Dr. Phil*.

"Mom? Can I ask you something?"

His mother turned to look at him, her wrinkled eyes widening with curiosity. "Sure," she replied, her eyes narrowing. "If this is about Sara trying to take Christmas from us, then I—"

"It's not." Liam interrupted her before that volcano erupted. "It's about...Dad."

His mom looked at him in shock, her eyebrows arching in surprise. "Your father?"

Her confusion was understandable. Anytime he brought up his father, it was usually to share a fond memory with a smile on his lips. But now he didn't sound like a doting son; he sounded like Agent Richter, and his mom was cunning enough to notice the change.

"What about him?"

His mind flickered with an image of Leah's captivating green eyes as they had walked backstage to the exit. He shook the thought away.

"Is there anything...I mean...did he ever do anything..." Liam struggled to find the words to form an accusation when it came to his dad. The man was nothing short of a saint. Or was he? "Is there anything about him you're not telling me?"

His mom froze, her hand flying to her lips. "What did Aunt Jane tell you?"

"What...what do you mean? What could she have possibly told me about Dad that's freaking you out like this?"

His mom shook her head, her expression a mix of confusion, anger, and fear. "Why now, Liam?"

"Why now what?"

Their tense exchange was interrupted by the loud ringing of his work phone. He ignored it for a few rings, staring at his mother as if waiting for her to reveal the truth. When nothing followed, he reluctantly turned and answered the call.

"Hello?" He walked over to a quieter corner behind a Mexican food stand.

"Where the hell are you?" Heather wondered.

"Seacoast Amusement Park with Josie and my mom."

"Stay away from the tin can games. They make the cans heavier to steal money from naive dads like you."

Liam bit his lip. "Did the search come back with anything?"

"Not much. Not even a parking ticket. Her boyfriend, Emanuel Mancini, is a young veterinary student who works for an escort service. However, it's difficult to determine whether their encounters are financially compensated or if they're actually dating. Such agencies are quite adept at conducting their operations discreetly. Other than that, it looks like there might have been an expunged incident in her childhood that has no records."

Liam wasn't discouraged yet. He knew Heather wouldn't quit so easily. "But you didn't stop there after running her name through the database, did you?"

"God." Heather laughed. "We spend too much time together. But no. I didn't. I called the police station of the small town she grew up in. Bover in New Hampshire. About an hour north of Portsmouth. They also didn't find anything in the computer."

"Aaaaaand...of course you didn't stop there either."

"No. I had them go through all the paper records. Those dusty things nobody ever touches anymore. That's why it took a few days."

Heather paused.

"Jesus, Heather. Do you want a drumroll or something?"

"Would be nice, considering Larsen will kill me if he finds out I'm helping you, but fine. Looks like your lady friend was a party in an incident in which the police were involved."

"What happened?"

"It's hard to say. It happened a long time ago, in the eighties, and most of the file has been destroyed or is missing. However, there's a psych evaluation that recommended treatment at a place you won't believe."

Liam felt a surge of adrenaline spreading from his stomach to his fingertips. "Tell me!"

"The Kim Arundel Psychiatric Hospital for the Severely Mentally Ill," Heather said, her tone triumphant and laced with excitement.

"The place they shut down in the eighties due to child abuse and trafficking?"

"The very one," Heather confirmed. "A private group bought the place from the state a few years ago and turned it into a star-powered wellness residence for the ultrarich and famous to do hot yoga and essential oil massages."

"Did you stumble upon any old files?"

"Unfortunately, the place burned down in the nineties and most of the files with it. I only have the final recommendation page from her old police file."

"What about the Bover Police Department? Any old-timers there that might still remember something?"

"It's a small town. I'm sure there are. But it won't help."

"Why not?"

"Because they won't talk. I've tried, but we're living in the age of Netflix. Every documentary they release exposes the questionable practices of law enforcement back in the day and all the messed-up things that occurred. We're talking about a time when a cigarette pack at the crime scene was considered sufficient evidence to send people to death row. Unless you make this an official investigation, nobody will be willing to help you with a side mission down there."

Shit.

"If you get Larsen's approval, you could pay the hospital a visit. Who knows what might be hiding in an old attic or basement."

"Larsen won't ever hop on this train. According to him, it's like that train in the apocalyptic show with all that ice...*Snowpiercer*."

Liam waved at Josie, who was sharing a funnel cake the size of a basketball with his mother.

"I loved that show," Heather said. "But listen, you know you're my favorite guy at work and all that, so please don't take this personally—" Liam detected a *but* coming "—but from here on, you're on your own. Larsen is super edgy these days, and I have three kids to feed. Steve was laid off during Covid."

"I get it. Really. Thanks for helping me out on this one. You did more than enough to earn those vacation days back from me."

"So you really going to stay on the case?" Heather asked.

Liam made his way back to Josie and his mom, almost running into a group of high school kids. "I have to, Heather. The case was closed too soon. Something isn't adding up here. I can't just leave those missing women in a pile of unknown dirt for people to trample on. Those families deserve to bring their loved ones home. Those girls deserve to go home."

There was a heavy silence. "I agree with you. This case has never made sense to me."

Liam froze. This was the first time somebody else had expressed concern with the whole damn case.

"I wish I could do more. I really do," Heather said.

"You've done enough."

There was another heavy silence.

"Liam?" Heather finally said.

"Yeah?"

"Be careful."

Gazing at his beautiful daughter, her face now smeared with chocolate, Liam nodded as if Heather could see him. He was confident that Larsen wouldn't fire him over this decision. And even if he did, it wouldn't matter. Pursuing this case was the right thing to do, and he would have a hard time wearing the badge if he didn't.

"I will. I promise," he said.

TWENTY-NINE

Liam pulled his car up the gravel driveway past a lush green garden with colorful flowers. He parked in front of the imposing brick building of the historic Kim Arundel Psychiatric Hospital for the Severely Mentally Ill. The tall windows and large stone stairs gave it a castle-like feel. He got out of his car and smiled back at a nurse walking by with a middle-aged patient wearing a hospital wristband.

The place was in top shape. Even the entrance hall had a modern waiting area with a flat-screen TV and one of those expensive Nespresso coffee makers next to a tray of donuts. Liam grabbed a vegan donut and was about to take a bite when an older woman wearing a white dress suit approached with a smile.

"Agent Richter?"

Liam wondered for a moment what to do with his donut, almost putting it back on the plate, but then he slipped it into his suit pocket and wiped the powdered sugar on his pants before accepting her handshake.

"I'm the director, Leanne Stadtman," Mrs. Stadtman said, revealing her coffee-stained teeth. Her gray hair was tied into a firm bun, and her skin was layered with heavy makeup.

"Thank you for squeezing me in," Liam said.

"Not a problem. Shall we take a stroll in the garden?"

Liam noticed the curious stares of a few patients as they walked down the large hallway with redone wooden floors and fancy silk couches.

"Whatever works best for you," he said with a smile.

They walked through the large double doors and took a small path around the main building.

"I hope I'm not too much trouble," Liam said.

"Oh no. It's just, after the whole Greg Harris news broke, we wanted to keep it as quiet as possible. So far, we've been fortunate enough to avoid camera crews altogether. We have some high-profile clients who come here to get away from cameras. You can see how this could financially hurt us."

Liam stopped in his tracks. "Wait a minute. Greg Harris was a patient here?" He stood there, frozen, trying to process the information.

Mrs. Stadtman turned to face him. "Isn't that why you're here?"

"No. I had no idea Greg Harris was a patient here. What do you know about him?"

Greg Harris was a patient at the same institution where Leah Nachtnebel was. What if they had known each other?

"Not much, I'm afraid. When we bought the place, it was in a terrible state. Most of the files were burned during a fire, but a few group therapy session notes from the nineties survived. Greg Harris is named as an attendee. But that's as much as I can say without a warrant. HIPAA, you see."

The dates didn't match to connect Greg to Ms. Nachtnebel, but he could have been a repeat patient here. Without Mrs. Harris's cooperation, who knew what else was hiding in the shadows about this man?

Liam nodded and stopped to look at the rose garden to his left. The bees were buzzing around the flowers' strong, sweet scent.

"Not quite what I expected," he said, feeling almost at peace out here.

Mrs. Stadtman smiled. "You mean patients screaming profanities as we strap them down and electrify them?"

"You don't even have the dim-lit corridors or forced ice baths?" Liam joked back.

"As I mentioned earlier, our focus is on serving the one percent. When the investor group purchased the institute from the state, following the fire in ninety-eight, it underwent extensive renovations for several years. The objective was to cater exclusively to the one percent, providing them with top-tier treatment for substance abuse and mental health challenges. Although we do have ice baths in our Turkish sauna area. They're quite popular now that they're voluntary."

Liam frowned. "I guess even mental illness is better when you're rich."

"This is America, Agent Richter. Everything is better when you're rich. So how can I help you if you're not here for Greg Harris?"

"I know you bought the place from the state years ago, but I was wondering if there are any traces of its past still left. Old boxes in a dusty basement, an old computer disk, or even just a former staff member you decided to keep on?"

"There were some boxes left indeed. One included the group therapy session attendance sheet with Harris's name on it. During the renovation, they were found in the attic. They'd somehow survived the fire."

A tingle of hope formed in Liam's chest. He could have sworn Larsen had said that *nothing* had survived the fire. "Would you mind if I take a look at those boxes?"

Mrs. Stadtman turned them onto a loop around the back of the building. Away from people.

"I hate to be the bad guy here, but again, I'm afraid without a warrant, that won't be possible. When we bought the institute, we signed a contract that any private information about patients found during renovations is property of the state and protected by HIPAA. When you operate at levels of financial profits like we do, every law and rule needs to be followed."

"Of course," he said, trying to hide his disappointment.

Mrs. Stadtman gazed at him with soft, understanding eyes. "I'm really sorry. Please believe me that I would love to hand you these boxes and be rid of them once and for all. They've been sitting in our storage for years. Any attempts to have the state send someone to pick them up were a waste of time."

"Why don't I place a hundred-dollar bill on one of the benches here and you accidentally forget to lock the room they're in?" he said, joking.

Mrs. Stadtman laughed. "A hundred dollars won't even pay for my own therapist. This place isn't as much fun if you have to run it."

Liam looked around the quiet grounds and perfectly cut grass. "So I assume you can't give me much information about a Leah Miller. She was here in the eighties."

A look of curious puzzlement came over her face. "I don't know her, but some of the leftover boxes in the attic are from the old children's program. But again, as I said, you would need a warrant to look through those."

Liam scratched his chin. "Made out to the state or you?"

"I would have to ask our lawyer, but, considering this is a tricky legal situation, most likely both. Also, the warrant would have to be made out to a specific person. HIPAA laws are rather strict with those matters. A mental health state employee or I would have to comb through the boxes for you to look for files related to this Leah Miller."

Another dead end. No judge would grant a warrant for Leah Nachtnebel's childhood files without charges against her. And mental health files were among the most fiercely protected by the institutions that held them.

"Well, thank you for your time," Liam said, curling his lips into a smile.

"I'm sorry you came all this way for nothing."

Liam nodded, his face filled with disappointment. He was prepared to leave when Mrs. Stadtman suddenly shrugged.

"But you might want to check with your office. Someone from the FBI was here a few weeks back with a warrant for some of the files in the attic. Maybe you can reuse the warrant if it's the same person of interest."

Liam's eyes grew wide in disbelief. "Are you sure it was an FBI agent? What did this person look like?"

Mrs. Stadtman nodded. "I wasn't here that day, but I'm pretty sure that's what our HR director said. She was the one who complied with the warrant."

"When did you say that was?"

As the closest field office to this hospital, Boston headquarters would have been notified of any FBI warrants from out of state. Hell, most likely they'd have been asked to execute it.

"Would I be able to speak with the HR director?"

"I don't see why not. But she's currently on maternity leave. If you have a card, I can let her know to call you as soon as she's back in."

Liam handed her a card from his pocket.

"Again, I'm sorry I couldn't be of more help," she said as they arrived outside of Liam's car.

"You were of more help than you think. Thank you."

Liam climbed into his car and watched as Mrs. Stadtman vanished into the building. It seemed someone, likely posing as a federal agent, had come to retrieve old files from the time Leah Nachtnebel had been a patient here. The situation had grown increasingly bizarre, gradually revealing the faintest outlines of an intricate web.

And the thing about webs was, even if their patterns seemed indecipherable at first, once completed, they all connected perfectly, ready to catch a fly.

He had been right all along. Something bigger was going on here. But what? A sex-trafficking operation selling women to monsters like Greg Harris maybe? The dark web was full of disgusting shit like that. But why kill him so brutally? Had he gotten smug and blackmailed the people who sold the women to him? And what the hell was a world-famous pianist's role in all this?

"Nothing makes fucking sense," Liam mumbled as he turned on the car and pressed the voice-command button on his steering wheel. "Siri, which restaurant in Boston has the most Michelin stars?"

The speakers beeped. "The restaurant with the most Michelin stars in Boston is Oui. Its dishes are inspired by French cuisine with a four-point-nine Google rating by customers. Would you like me to call Oui for you?"

Fuck. That sounded expensive.

"Yyyyyy-yes," he spat out as if the words were acid.

The dialing sound of his phone reverberated through the speakers as Liam pondered whom to invite. His mom? He hadn't seen Elly since their breakfast weeks ago, and he'd barely managed to exchange a few texts with her since. Moreover, it felt wrong to involve her in work matters.

"Damn it."

He loathed this situation. He truly did. But he needed a cover, and his mom would inadvertently blow it from a mile away. And since he was hoping Elly would give him another chance after the terrible breakfast date, why not kill two birds with one stone and ask Elly out again—this time a bit fancier?

A man with a French accent answered Liam's call over the speakers. "Hello?"

Liam hesitated.

"Hello?"

"Damn it," he grumbled, furrowing his brow. To get the waiter not only to squeeze him in but to also reveal when Leah would dine there again—if at all—he'd have to concoct some story. If this failed, he'd have to repeat the whole charade with the second most expensive restaurant in Boston. And this endeavor would undoubtedly cost him a fortune.

"Hello?" The waiter's voice grew more assertive.

"Yes," Liam finally replied. "I am—" he took a deep breath "—I'm calling to inquire about a table for two. I know I'm asking a lot, but could you possibly glance at your reservations book? My wife has just been discharged from the hospital and happens to be Leah Nachtnebel's biggest fan. I know she's got a reservation with you tonight, right?"

THIRTY

"Then he had the balls to burst into the operating room and lunge at Dr. Flores. The guy was trying to stop lifesaving surgery on his pregnant cat."

I savored an exquisite bite of my Jerusalem artichoke served atop black truffle paste and garnished with roasted quail eggs. I glanced at Emanuel before meticulously slicing the tiny quail eggs into even smaller pieces. Emanuel raised his wineglass, allowing the tuxedo-clad waiter to refill it. After murmuring a gracious "thank you," he continued his story.

"Dr. Flores is a hundred and forty pounds, if that, and most of that is organic tofu. So I jumped on the guy. He swung at me a few times, but he was drunk and slow, so I was able to get behind him and keep him in a chokehold until the cops arrived. And thaaaaat's how I got the bruises on my arms."

I placed the knife and fork onto my plate and dabbed my mouth with the bright white napkin from my lap. Emanuel's voice was the loudest in the restaurant, but I paid no mind to the occasional glances from other guests whenever his enthusiasm elevated his volume. I wasn't much of a talker myself and generally didn't enjoy listening to others either, but Emanuel had a unique ability to captivate my attention longer than anyone else in my life. He exuded a magnetic aura that drew people to him like moths to a flame, and his storytelling was always filled with intriguing twists and turns.

"What happened to the cat?" I asked. Surprisingly, I found myself genuinely intrigued. As I said, moths and flames.

Emanuel bit his lip and paused. "The mother cat and most of the kittens died. One of the vet assistants took it really hard. She's been mumbling about messages from the afterlife ever since."

"Messages from the afterlife?"

"Yeah. She keeps telling us about a pact she made with her mother, using some rare word or something. If one of them dies and the other hears the rare word somewhere, that means it was a message from the afterlife."

"What utter nonsense."

"But what if it's not? We should come up with our own word. So we can send messages from the afterlife to one another." Emanuel grinned.

"Ridiculous."

"Come on. Just having some fun here."

"All right then. Our word would be lēros," I countered, giving him a small smile.

"Lēros?" He looked equally amounts amused and puzzled. "What does that mean?"

"It's old Greek and means nonsense."

He laughed, then grew serious again. "As fate had it, one kitten managed to survive. She lives in my closet for now."

I frowned. "In your closet?"

"Well, the shelters are full, and I'm trying to find a home for her. My roommate, who's on the lease of the apartment, is allergic to cats and won't allow them. So my other roommate Ginny and I are closet-sharing the kitten to hide it until we find a home." Emanuel looked into my eyes. "Someone with a lot of room. A house, hopefully. And no kids or dogs."

I ignored his blunt attempt at pushing the cat on me and focused my attention on the food again.

"Someone who needs a companion when her boy toy is at university," he added in a colorful voice. I didn't even have to look up to know that he was grinning from ear to ear.

"I don't care for pets, Emanuel. They are too needy for your love."

"Well, that's the point of them. Love."

I glanced up at him, encountering precisely what I had anticipated. His deep brown eyes were fixed intently on me, accompanied by that mischievous grin of his. I reclined in my chair, allowing the rich flavor of the truffle to pair with the exquisite 2006 Barolo Riserva Monfortino—fourteen hundred dollars per bottle.

"I really have no time for a ca—"

My voice faltered when a couple was escorted to their table not far behind Emanuel. The woman, a slender blonde in her thirties, appeared rather unremarkable. But the man I could have picked out from a crowd of thousands.

Agent Richter.

"What are you staring at?" Emanuel's voice registered faintly as background noise while Richter and I locked gazes. He didn't smile; he just stared at me long enough for it to convey a message.

This encounter was no coincidence.

He was here for me.

"Leah?" Emanuel repeated, now glancing at Richter as well. He then shifted his gaze back to me. "Do you know that guy?"

I was about to respond when my phone's ringtone interrupted me. As I reached for my purse, I realized it wasn't my usual smartphone ring—it was the flip phone.

I retrieved it and flipped it open.

"We have a problem," Larsen's voice urgently declared on the other end.

I observed Agent Richter as he pulled out a chair for his date before casting another curious glance in my direction.

"I can see that," I said, locking eyes with him once more before rising and leaving the table.

The clatter of cutlery against plates and subdued conversations trailed me as I made my way out the door, down the long hallway past the restrooms and elevators. Approaching the floor-to-ceiling glass window, I gazed down upon the bustling scene of the city's nightlife.

"We said no calls," I said.

Encrypted texts only.

"I know, but this can't wait. Tomorrow…"

I put one and one together. "Tomorrow you won't make it to our meeting point to provide me with the information I requested," I concluded. Which was the address of the license plate of the Train Track Killer.

"Things are getting too hot. I closed the Harris case, but Agent Richter just won't stop. He's like a bloodhound on the scent."

"I still need that information about the plate," I insisted.

A couple emerged from the elevator, offering me a friendly smile as they strolled down the hallway and entered the restaurant.

"Are you listening to a word I'm saying?" Larsen said. "Richter has been to Kim Arundel, Leah."

"There is nothing to be found there."

"Maybe not, but he won't stop until he finds something. I know him."

I agreed with Larsen on that one. Richter was precisely that kind of man: a tireless knight, brandishing his sword not for king or country but for justice. He hailed from a lineage spanning hundreds of years with generations of men in his family dedicated to the same pursuit. It was bred into him.

"Regardless, I need that information," I said. "This time it will be quiet and quick, I promise."

"No, Leah. I can't. You need to lie low. I'm putting one of my agents on the case. Going by the book this time."

A fiery tingle erupted in my stomach—the rare sensation of anger. For years, I had pursued the Train Track Killer, and now I'd been so close. He was mine to kill, not the world's to parade through a broken justice system that he could manipulate with a cunning lawyer and his well-groomed white-male privilege.

"Are you sure the woman you saved didn't see your face?" Larsen asked for the third time since the incident.

"Certain," I confirmed.

"Still, I'm taking you off the case."

I was on the verge of responding when the restaurant door at the end of the hallway swung open and Agent Richter emerged. With measured strides, he fixed his gaze on me, looking pleased with himself as he approached.

"You know better than to cross me," I said into the phone.

"Leah. Wait. Listen to me. It's just until—" Larsen's voice begged, but I snapped the phone shut. I waited for Agent Richter to join me by the window moments later.

"That sounded intense," he said, nodding at the phone, which I slipped back into my purse. "Is that a burner phone you got there?" he added, looking for a reaction.

"Is that what they call them?"

"Pretty much. Mostly used by innocent elderly who aren't so tech-savvy or, well, criminals. Which one are you, Ms. Nachtnebel? You don't look that old to me, if I may say so."

I smiled. "I am the exception, Agent Richter. Always the exception."

He nodded. "What a lucky coincidence I ran into you here tonight. A few more questions have popped up since we met last."

"Coincidence," I echoed. "This restaurant is filled with the nation's wealthiest patrons, as well as couples who spend their last dime here, naively believing that it will salvage their marriage. So which one are you?"

Agent Richter smiled at me. "The exception, of course."

I nodded. There was something truly fascinating about this man. He was a diamond in the rough. By now he must have assembled some of the puzzle pieces before him even if it meant risking his job in the process. If the world had more men like him, maybe monsters like myself wouldn't be necessary.

"I'm afraid my partner is already wondering where I am. I'd better return to the table," I said. But Richter blocked my way. A bold move. I was now only inches from his face. The scent of his aftershave wafted through the air, a captivating blend of soap and a hint of spice that added a subtle warmth. Towering a head taller than me, he was far too close for anything but two people romantically involved. Undaunted, I tilted my head back and met his gaze directly, neither flinching nor blinking. I added a subtle smile to convey my fearlessness and self-assurance. I wasn't afraid of this man or any other. Caught off guard by my boldness, his lips parted in surprise as he fumbled for words. Eventually he stumbled a few steps back, clearly unsettled by the intensity of our unexpected encounter.

"That, erm, that handwriting class," he said, steadying his voice. "I'm afraid I need to talk to that friend to find out more about it."

I shrugged. "Of course. I will get that information for you in a timely manner."

I started walking back to the restaurant. This time he made way.

"And maybe a copy of anything you might still have of your time at the Kim Arundel Psychiatric Hospital for the Severely Mentally Ill," he said just as I passed him.

I froze.

"Funny thing is," he continued, "Harris, the guy who was killed the night the lady in red disappeared right where you were last seen, well, Harris went to the same institution you did. The coincidence is striking, don't you think?"

I turned to look at him. "Those are very private matters you are inquiring about. That was a dark time in my life. One that I'd like to forget. I'm afraid there are no files left on my end. I moved on, and as you can see, I did quite well."

His sharp blue eyes analyzed my face as if searching for the lie. "I understand, and I'm really sorry. Do you remember anything about it? Such as running into one of the most brutal serial killers in Boston history?"

I tipped my index finger against my lower lip, pretending to think. "I'm afraid it's all rather blurry. As I said, it was a long time ago and I was only a child. And as you know, back then, mental health wasn't quite what it is now. People from all over the East Coast were shipped to large institutions like the Kim Arundel Psychiatric Hospital for the Severely Mentally Ill. Luckily, these days, there's less stigma attached to mental health struggles. Maybe I should join the movement on social media and come forward with my past struggles so it's out in the open. Some might find strength and inspiration in my personal journey."

Agent Richter frowned. "Yeah, maybe," he conceded. I assumed the matter was settled, but Richter stepped closer again, his demeanor shifting. "Or you can just answer my questions truthfully and stop playing games. Did you know Greg Harris? Back then or—" he narrowed his eyes at me, the atmosphere growing tense as if he were aiming a gun at my chest "—or did you first meet him in the woods?"

We stood there for a moment, locked in a silent battle, our eyes boring into each other.

"Not personally," I finally responded, choosing a lie that skirted the truth to avoid detection.

Agent Richter scrutinized my answer. He had opened his mouth to speak when Emanuel approached from down the hallway.

"Leah! Is everything okay?" Emanuel's gaze swept over Richter, nostrils flared like a bull ready to charge.

"Yes," I replied quickly, moving toward Emanuel. "Just ran into an acquaintance." I grabbed Emanuel's arm and guided him back to the restaurant.

We had nearly reached the restaurant's entrance when Richter called after me, "I got a ticket to your next concert! I'm looking forward to running into each other again!"

As we continued walking, I couldn't help but feel the weight of his words, the thinly veiled threat, a shadow cast over the evening.

THIRTY-ONE

"Look who's gracing us with his presence," Tony said as he stopped typing on his keyboard and leaned back in his chair. "You should have let us know you were coming back today. I could have rolled the red carpet out for you."

Liam looked around the office. The phones were still ringing here and there, but it was definitely quieter. Closing the Harris case was already having an effect, the best one being Cowboy getting transferred back to Organized Crime.

"I was gone for a week, Tony. So unless I unknowingly time traveled, I don't want to hear it."

"Gone during a week of hell," Tony countered. "You're welcome for carrying your load as well. But I won't bust your balls anymore. Not when *it* has already asked for you twice this morning. You in trouble or something?"

Liam instantly looked at Heather, who shrugged. "Not a word from me," was all she said.

"Shit," Liam mumbled and threw his blazer over his chair. "I swear this guy has a third eye or something."

With a worried frown, Liam made his way to Larsen's office, his footsteps slow and measured. He was about to knock on the wide-open door when Larsen caught sight of him and eagerly waved him in.

"It's Monday," Liam said. "I drop Josie off on Mondays. That's why I'm late."

"I know," Larsen said in a calm tone. "Close the door, will you?"

With a puzzled frown, Liam complied. Larsen's voice was calm, but he only ever asked his agents to close the door when trouble was brewing.

Liam took a seat and sighed. "All right. If this is about the Harris case, hear me out."

"The Harris case?" Larsen looked perplexed, and Liam's confusion mirrored his. "Why on earth would this be about the Harris case? The damn case is closed."

"Yeeeees. Of course it is." Liam pinched his lips. "So what is this about then?"

Larsen played with a pen in his hand and looked at Liam from over his glasses, a gesture he often made before presenting a significant case. But this time he also seemed torn. As if whatever he wanted to ask was controversial.

Liam straightened in his seat. "So? What do you have?"

"I...need some eyes on a guy who might be a real jewel," Larsen finally said.

"Who is it?" Liam's curiosity was evident in his voice.

Larsen leaned over his desk, closer. "This needs to be off the books for now. I don't have enough on him to make it official, but the leads are solid. I checked them myself."

"What leads?"

"Some family members of suicide victims have filed complaints with the FBI that their loved ones might have been victims of murders, not suicide."

"Sounds like a bad podcast to me. Any pattern like that would be picked up by forensics even at the lowest level of law enforcement."

Larsen nodded. "You're right. It would. If the lowest level wasn't the railroad police."

Liam scratched his head. "The folks who chase off the homeless from trains and return runaways?"

"Yup. The same poor devils who also have to scrape off the remains of people run over by trains."

Shit. Liam had forgotten about that aspect. He'd once had a friend who'd dated a woman who was part of the railroad police. Horror stories she had shared at a birthday party came rushing back to him. He shuddered, trying to shake off the unpleasant memories. "Yeah, that's some awful stuff. But what does that have to do with us?"

Larsen's face grew dark. "I'm afraid, if any of the complaints are true, there might be a killer out there who is placing his victims on train tracks...alive."

Liam heard the words, but their meaning was surreal even for someone like him. He shook his head, confused, leaning forward as he steepled his fingers under his chin. "Are you seriously saying that some sick fuck out there is kidnapping people, putting them on train tracks, and letting a train smash them to bits?" A wave of disgust rose in Liam's throat. For a moment, he felt hollow. Could humans truly sink this low?

Larsen pressed his lips together. "I'm afraid there's a genuine possibility that a monster like that might be out there."

"Are you sure it's not just one of those attention-seeking prank callers? I mean, how could something this massive go unnoticed?"

"I'll tell you how." Larsen shook his head. "If this is true, we're not dealing with a monster like Harris but a psychopathic mastermind."

Liam's head jerked back. "Mastermind?"

"Consider this. The railroad police aren't trained for complex murder investigations. They barely communicate with one another and deal with enough suicides that a skillfully staged homicide could easily go undetected in a small, underfunded department like a local railroad police station."

"You're freaking me out," Liam said.

"I know. The thought of a case like this makes me sick to my stomach, but I looked over the complaints from these families more than once, and some of it looks suspicious."

"Why didn't you say something sooner?"

Larsen let out a heavy sigh. "Because that's all I had: suspicion. I need a hell of a lot more than distraught family members and a gut feeling before I accuse not just one but dozens of railroad police departments of utter incompetence. If this becomes public, the Harris case will seem like a walk in the park compared to the Train Track Killer."

An eerie atmosphere enveloped the room. "Train Track Killer," Liam murmured, as if uttering the words alone could summon the beast. He shook his head. "It doesn't matter how it looks. If this is true, we need to focus all our resources on this immediately."

"I agree, but we need more juice before we open a lemonade stand. I've had my contacts at the police stations look out for anything that could be relevant."

"And?"

Larsen slid over a manila folder. Liam promptly opened it, only to be confronted by a photo of a young woman with a bruised and bloodied face, her expression etched with terror. Her black hair looked sticky and covered in mud, while her blue eyes seemed dull, as if they'd lost their spark.

"Those photos are from the hospital. There's a report included as well. The woman is Anna Smith. She claims that a man kidnapped her from Hill Park Station after the last train and drugged her. She woke up when he threw her onto the train tracks of the SEATRAK commercial line."

Liam struggled to find words. This was insane. First Harris, now this.

"There's a police report, but I thought you might want to visit Anna yourself."

Liam nodded. "Yes, of course."

"She might be able to provide a description that matches our suspect."

The folder nearly slipped from his grasp. "We have a suspect?"

Larsen hesitated but then nodded. "Someone anonymous called in about a man dragging a woman into a van at the Hill Park Station around the time Anna claims to have been kidnapped."

"Please tell me that the witness was smart enough and—"

"Wrote down the license plate," Larsen finished the sentence.

Hope. Adrenaline. Rage. Joy. Disgust.

A whirlwind of emotions welled up inside Liam. The past few weeks had been taking their toll—the Harris case, the grieving families, Leah freaking Nachtnebel. And now this. If all this was true, and he had a chance to take down a killer like that, he might find redemption after all.

"Richter," Larsen said.

He looked up. "What?"

"I said this is still unofficial. All I need you to do is talk to the girl and follow the suspect for a while. His name is Robert Patel. Some city employee in his forties. If we bring him in for questioning with the little we have, he'll walk. As smart as this bastard is, he won't even need a lawyer to get us hard and then throw us out into the cold."

Liam rose. He had to talk to Anna Smith. Now.

"Got it. I'll brief with the others and ensure we have eyes on this guy twenty-four seven."

Larsen nodded. Then he rose too, looking Liam straight in the eyes. "If you get the slightest chance, put a bullet in his head, you hear me?"

A deafening silence settled on Liam's shoulder like an iron curtain. Larsen had never asked something like that. Had he even heard it right?

"Sir?"

"I meant it the way you think I did," Larsen confirmed, not even blinking. There was something raw in Larsen's voice. Something Liam couldn't place.

"I'll promise you I'll do my job," was all Liam said.

Larsen studied him a moment longer, then nodded. "Good. Now get this son of a bitch. I need this taken care of ASAP."

THIRTY-TWO

The scent of coffee and disinfectant hung in the air as Liam accompanied Dr. Sensling, the ICU's attending physician that day, to room 301. Medical equipment beeped incessantly, creating a background soundtrack that filled the entire floor from every direction.

"If she doesn't want to talk, I'll have to ask you to leave," the tall doctor said. Like most doctors Liam encountered during official hospital visits, he was skinny and had dark rings under his eyes.

"Of course, thank you," Liam said.

Dr. Sensling nodded at him, then knocked on the door and entered. Liam stepped in behind him and almost took a step back at the sight of the poor young woman in front of him.

She was lying in bed, staring at the colorful get-better balloons, eyes wide open and dull. The ghostly pale skin on her face was spotted with dark purple bruises. She had a large bandage on her head, and her left arm was in a cast. Tubes hooked up to various machines monitored her closely and provided her with fluids.

Liam's stomach churned as his chest tightened to the point where it felt hard to breathe.

"Anna," Dr. Sensling said softly. "This is Agent Richter from the FBI. He was wondering if he might talk to you for a moment."

"You can call me Liam," Liam added with a smile.

Anna turned her head to gaze directly at Liam—expressionless. Then her face contorted with pain, and tears streamed down her cheeks.

"I think you should come another time," Dr. Sensling suggested, but Liam strode to Anna's side, gently grasping her hand.

"I'm so sorry this happened to you. I'll find the monster who did this to you or die trying."

It was dramatic. Intense. But he meant every word. Maybe it was her large eyes or pointy chin, but Anna Smith, barely twenty years old, reminded him of Josie. And some twisted individual had done this to her—tried to kill her by placing her on train tracks. Ever since Larsen had assigned Liam to this case, he had struggled to comprehend the cruelty. In all his years working with serial killers, he had seen some horrific things, including the Harris case, but placing people on train tracks...

"It's okay," Anna whispered weakly, her reddened eyes turning to Liam's.

Dr. Sensling lingered a moment longer, giving her a chance to change her mind, and then left the room. "Call me if you need anything," he said before closing the door behind him.

Still holding her hand, Liam pulled a chair next to her bed and sat down. For a moment, they just sat there, Anna crying, Liam comforting her, assuring her that everything was okay now.

"You're the first one who actually cares," she sobbed, catching her breath. "The others just acted like I'm crazy. It seems like it's not as important to the police if you survive."

"It's important to me," Liam promised.

Anna shook her head. "You won't believe me. Just like the others. I was asked ten times by different officers if I was high, but only one asked for a detailed description of the guy who hurt me."

Liam let her settle a little, then looked deeply into her eyes. "I believe you. And I meant what I said earlier. I will find that son of a bitch or die trying."

She nodded, this time in relief and with an expression of gratitude.

"Do you think you could tell me what happened?" Liam asked. "I know it'll be hard, but I need to know what happened so I can catch this guy."

She nodded again as her tears slowed. "I don't remember much. Things happened so fast, and I was unconscious for most of it. I don't know if he hit me on the head or what."

Liam nodded. "And that's okay. You went through a lot, and the mind can play tricks on us when we're under great distress."

Her thin hands grabbed the blanket, and she took a deep breath. "I was on my way back from a bar. I was meeting this guy from a dating app downtown, and we kind of hit it off. But he didn't do this," she added hastily. "I kept telling the cops that, but they kept circling back to him. The guy who did this was twice his size. Like a bear. Muscles as hard as steel." Anna shifted in her bed.

"I believe you," Liam said calmly, and she relaxed.

"I almost missed the last train home."

"Do you live with your parents or a roommate?"

"With my grandma. She raised me. My parents...they have drug issues."

Liam already knew that from her file. He had all the basics about Anna. She had graduated high school last year and took waitressing jobs here and there, most likely trying to find herself like most young kids growing up in troubled homes.

"I ran so hard to catch the last train and felt this huge relief when its doors closed behind me. A cab ride would have been an easy fifty bucks. Now I wish I would have missed the train."

Gently patting her hand, Liam comforted her as tears welled up in her eyes once more. "What happened next? Was the man on the train with you?"

Anna shook her head. "I don't know. I got off at Hill Park. There were only a few people getting off with me. I'd missed the bus and wanted to call my grandma to pick me up, but then this van pulled up. Some guy asked me if I needed a ride, but I told him no and walked away."

"Did you see his face?"

Anna shook her head. "It was too dark."

"Was his voice young or old?"

"Like yours."

Liam nodded. "What happened next?"

"I...I don't know. Someone grabbed me from behind and pulled me into a van. I passed out or something, and when I woke up again, I was thrown on the tracks of a train." She sucked back a ragged breath. "I tried to run, but my arms and legs were tied up. There was blood everywhere and my head hurt so bad. Then the train came. I could hear its horn and felt the tracks vibrate underneath me." One of the machines monitoring Anna beeped faster, and she broke into sobs. "I thought the train would kill me. I thought I would die."

Liam squeezed her hand as her fingernails dug into his palm.

"Suddenly there were loud bangs. Like...like gunshots."

"Gunshots?"

"Yes. Then out of nowhere, somebody pulled me off the tracks and cut my arms loose. Only seconds before the train would have hit me."

"Somebody cut you loose?"

Anna nodded.

"Did you see who?"

She tightly shut her eyes, as if that would make it all go away.

Liam leaned in close. "Breathe, Anna. You're safe now." Her eyes met his. "Breathe," he repeated in a slow, soothing tone. Her initial attempts were quick and shallow, but after Liam started to breathe with her, slow and steady, she managed to follow his lead and calm down.

At that moment, the door opened, and Dr. Sensling hurried to the machine that had been beeping rapidly just moments before. "I think we've had enough for today," he said.

Liam gently squeezed Anna's hand and left his card on the nightstand next to her bed. "You can call me anytime, day or night, rain or shine. For anything. Even if you just want to talk."

Anna nodded.

"Now rest. I'll check in on you again in a few days if that's all right."

She nodded again.

Liam was halfway across the room when Anna called out to him. He glanced over to find her propped up in bed.

"Do you think...you can catch this guy?"

Her eyes, wide with a mix of fear and hope, reminded Liam of Larsen's request to shoot this train killer bastard on sight, whether he was armed or not. For a fleeting moment, Liam contemplated the idea. But his training and principles resurfaced, reminding him of the oath he'd sworn to uphold the law. He wasn't the embodiment of the law, merely its enforcer.

"I promise, I'll give it all I've got," he assured her.

THIRTY-THREE

Liam watched raindrops gently tapping the windshield from the FBI undercover van parked a few houses down from Robert Patel's address in a southern Boston neighborhood. Robert was a divorced man in his forties who worked at the tax collector's office of the City of Boston. The past three weeks of surveillance had provided absolutely nothing. Robert went to work in his 1999 Toyota Camry, then came straight back home. Aside from a few trips to the grocery store and one to Men's Clips for a haircut, he went absolutely nowhere—ever.

Tony and Liam were watching, bored, as Robert Patel avoided the rain by holding his black work suitcase over his head as he ran from his car to his house. He was a beast of a man, well over six feet, and had horrible taste in clothes. Khaki pants, purple business shirt, a cartoon tie, and golden glasses that looked straight out of the sixties. He even combed over the few black strands of hair he had left, which did nothing to cover his shiny bald head.

His house, though generally well-maintained, displayed some wear and tear—the yellow paint was peeling in places, and dry rot marred the edges of the windows on his Victorian middle-class home.

Tony slurped on a milkshake. "So far, Patel's fashion choice is the only crime that has been committed. This must be the most boring surveillance job I've ever been on."

Liam stared at Patel as he closed the front door behind himself. "There's plenty more awkward shit about Patel besides that."

Tony cocked a brow. "Oh yeah?"

"The ink on his divorce papers dried five years ago, but in the past three weeks, he hasn't managed to make time for a single visit to his children, who live, like, five minutes away."

"Maybe they're on vacation with the mother."

"They're not. I stopped by their school and saw them on the school's playground. Something weird is going on."

"Maybe he doesn't like kids. Family court said it was a pretty clean divorce. No restraining orders, no accusations of abuse. Maybe Larsen is wrong about Patel. This guy sure as hell is strange, and his clothes make him look like a pedophile, but he doesn't seem like no Train Track Killer to me."

Liam shook his head. "Nah. Something is off with this guy. I mean, no social media, no phone calls in or out, no visitors, not even a fucking trip to the mall or grimy dive bar. What the hell is he doing all weekend long in this house? Which raises another red flag. Why the hell did his ex-wife move into a one-bedroom apartment with two kids and just leave Patel this large house? I have a feeling she might be afraid of him."

Tony shrugged. "Could be, but that doesn't make him a serial killer. Who knows? He might just be watching TV all weekend. If I could watch TV all weekend long without Lilly nagging or the kids calling for money, I'd be doing that for the rest of my life. But instead, I'm stuck in here sniffing some other dude's sweaty armpits."

Liam opened the glove compartment and retrieved a stick of deodorant. "That's your smell, my friend. As a single man, I never travel without this." He held the deodorant spray in front of Tony's face. "I literally forgot my wallet twice last week but not *this* wingman."

With a furrowed brow, Tony sniffed his armpit before begrudgingly accepting the deodorant, muttering something to himself.

"You're welcome for not shaming you and for taking your stench like a real man," Liam said.

"I sweat a lot in my sleep."

"Wait, you're sleeping on your night shift?"

Tony straightened in his seat. "No."

Liam cocked a brow at him.

"Not on purpose," Tony finally confessed. "But what do you expect? I'm almost fifty. This surveillance thing is some G.I. Joe shit, it's not me anymore. Why didn't you ask for somebody else to do this?"

"'Cause I trust you."

Tony accepted that with a silent nod as Liam reached for the door. "I have something to do this morning, but how about I take the afternoon and the night shift after that, and you get some sleep tonight?"

"Really?"

"Yup. Just don't tell Larsen that I gave you the morning shift and left for a few hours."

"Why? What the hell are you up to now?"

"Paying someone a visit. Regarding the Harris case."

"Oh hell no! Don't tell me this shit! What I don't know I don't know."

"You asked," Liam countered, opening the front passenger door of the van and stepping out into the rain.

THIRTY-FOUR

The veterinary university near Boston looked more like a state-owned brick orphanage than a modern academic institution. Surrounded by fields and stables, it lacked the vibrancy of a bustling city campus. Sporadically, the sun broke free from the heavy clouds, casting a warm glow on the lush grass surrounding the university as the occasional student strolled by.

Liam drove to the rear lot where the students parked their cars. He had managed to obtain the schedule of mandatory classes for third-year students like Emanuel Mancini.

Growing impatient, he glanced again at the time displayed on his car radio. It was 12:33 p.m.; class had ended three minutes ago.

Soon enough, the first students began streaming out of the building, making their way to their vehicles. A few moments later, Leah's dashing gigolo emerged from the glass doors and headed toward the parking lot as well.

Shifting his car into drive, Liam pulled up beside Emanuel. A look of surprise washed over Emanuel's face as Liam rolled down the window and flashed his badge.

"Need a lift to your car?" Liam offered.

Emanuel frowned. "I don't."

"All right, then we can do this right here, outside, in front of everyone. I'll be sure to flash my badge a few more times so the whole world can see it. If I angle it right, the sun reflects off it like a disco ball. How's that for the campus rumor mill?"

Emanuel mulled this over for a moment before swearing under his breath and climbing into the passenger seat.

"Good decision," Liam said as he began driving. It took only a few turns for him to pull up beside a beat-up 2000 black Jeep. He stopped and observed as Emanuel registered, with shock, the fact that Liam knew which car was his.

"Nice move. So what do you want?" Emanuel asked. "I know who you are."

"How come? Has she told you not to talk to me?"

"No, but you harassed her at the restaurant, and now you're playing *True Detective* out here with me. Plus I can read. Your badge says FBI."

"Well, first of all, let me assure you that I'm not here to cause you any trouble in case you were wondering."

"I wasn't," Emanuel retorted.

"Oh, that's good. Some straight-A students like you might worry about their side gig as a prostitute in a state where it's illegal. One trip to jail and all this—" Liam gestured at the campus "—is gone, my friend."

"Oh yeah?" Emanuel pulled out his phone and held it up. "Some FBI agents might worry about using blackmail in the age of smartphones." His phone's display showed an active recording button. Then he slipped the phone back into his pocket.

Liam grinned. Clever little shithead.

"All right, let me ask you on the record then: What do you know about your client Leah Nachtnebel? Has anything suspicious caught your attention? Connections with serial killers or former drug-cartel bosses like Luca Domizio?"

Bingo. That brief widening of Emanuel's eyes, followed by the drop in his gaze. He knew something.

"Let me remind you, also on the record, that lying to a federal agent is a felony."

Liam allowed those words to hang in the air for a bit before continuing.

"I'm not the bad guy here, Emanuel. And I'm not asking about whatever it is she pays you for. Honestly, I couldn't care less. Your body, your choice. But look at me, Emanuel."

He did.

"I'm talking about terrible things here. Brutal murders, if you really want to know."

Emanuel pressed his lips together. He knew something. He fucking did!

"Are you seriously suggesting that Leah hurt somebody?" he finally asked. "That's crazy. Like, what are we even talking about here?"

Liam was about to clarify that he didn't believe a world-famous pianist like Leah was actually getting her own hands dirty with anything—he suspected she might be involved in a drug- or human-trafficking operation at the higher levels—when a realization struck him like a lightning bolt.

The shock hit him like a jolt of electricity, causing his body to tense and freeze in disbelief.

Idiot! Fool! Amateur! The woman in red!

He reached for a folder in the glove compartment, pushing Emanuel's legs to the side.

"Hey!" Emanuel protested.

Frantically Liam rifled through the evidence folder from the Harris crime scene. Some pictures fell out.

"Jesus." Emanuel cursed in disgust as one of the images—Harris's mutilated head from the autopsy report—landed on his lap. He pushed it off and onto the floor like it was burning-hot charcoal.

"This woman!" Liam exclaimed, holding up a photo of the woman in red taken from the surveillance footage at the Boston Symphony Hall. She had short blond hair and wore a baseball cap, but the stature, the height, and even the shape of her chin and cheeks...

Jesus.

Fucking.

Christ!

"Who does this woman remind you of? The height, the figure." He shoved the picture into Emanuel's face.

Emanuel jerked back and looked at it. Liam watched in what felt like slow motion as Emanuel's eyes and mouth widened right before he reached for the car door handle. Liam was losing him.

"Wait!"

Emanuel paused.

"I...understand how a woman like her can leave quite an impression on anyone. But is that really worth lying for? Innocent girls were hurt, Emanuel! You seem like a good guy who wants to do the right thing."

Emanuel stared out the window.

"You seem like someone who wants to protect those girls. Women just like the ones in your own class—young and full of life with the world at their feet. Don't you want to help protect them? To stop whatever is going on here that Leah might be a part of?"

The car was dead silent, as if time had stopped. Emanuel was on the fence; Liam could see it in his intense gaze.

But then, suddenly, a young man approached the SUV and knocked on the window, right on the passenger side where Emanuel was sitting.

"Hey, Emanuel," the guy said through the window. "I'm so sorry, man. But can you give me a ride to town? Ben left without me again."

Emanuel turned to face Liam, his eyes narrowing as they met his gaze. If there had ever been a moment when he had considered changing sides, it had passed.

"I have absolutely no idea what the hell you're talking about," he said firmly. He opened the door. "But stay the hell away from Leah."

With a loud slam, Emanuel shut the door behind him and headed toward his car. His friend glanced at Liam before joining Emanuel in the black Jeep.

Liam watched as Emanuel pulled out and drove away, not even sparing him a glance. He knew something. He definitely did. The way he'd looked at the woman in red...

"No," Liam mumbled.

Not the woman in red.

Leah Nachtnebel. She was there with Harris the night of his murder, the last person to see him, talk to him. Then there was the connection to Kim Arundel Psychiatric Hospital—both Harris and Nachtnebel had spent time there.

Liam gripped the steering wheel tightly as he recalled the day he had driven out to Harris's crime scene. Chief Murray had told him to call if he ever needed anything.

Frantically he rummaged through his wallet, looking for the card Chief Murray had given him. Of course it wasn't there; he'd left it on his desk at the office. He quickly pulled out his phone and searched for the contact information of the Massachusetts police chief's office. A woman answered the phone.

"Hello? *Massachusetts state police chief's office.*"

"Yes, erm, this is Agent Richter from the Boston Federal Bureau of Investigation. Could you please transfer me to Chief Murray if he's in?" He checked his watch: 12:56 p.m.

There was a brief silence, as if the woman was deciding what to do.

"I know he might be on his lunch break," Liam said, "but he'll want to be interrupted for this, believe me."

"What was your name again?" the woman asked.

"Richter. FBI. Tell him I was on the scene of the Harris case."

"One moment please."

There was no hold music—nothing. As he waited, Liam wondered if the woman had hung up on him.

"Hello?" Murray's voice answered.

Liam straightened in his seat. "Chief Murray. Thank you for accepting my call."

"Of course. How can I help you? Good job on the Harris case, by the way. This is between you and me, but I'm glad the bastard is dead."

Liam looked up at the gray fabric ceiling of his SUV. Another fan of Harris's butcher. The club was growing.

"Thank you. I'm really sorry for disturbing you during your lunch break."

"No worries. Now I have a good excuse to skip my wife's meatloaf. I married her for many reasons, but cooking wasn't one of them."

Liam nearly chuckled, especially because his ex, Sara, had also been a terrible cook. He had been the one to do all the cooking in their relationship. The absence of her Christmas goose every year was one of the best things that had come out of their divorce.

"So what can I do for you?"

"I...uh...I'm calling regarding the Harris case, actually."

"What about it? As far I know, it's closed. You guys were the ones who closed it."

"Yes. But there seem to be a few loose ends," Liam said as confidently as he could. "And I need help tying them up. For the families."

There was a brief silence. "Yes, of course. What ends?"

"There is a woman—"

"The woman in red?"

Of course he'd stayed up to date on the case. Liam was one of the people who kept him informed as a courtesy.

"Yes. I need to find her."

"Why?"

What was Liam supposed to say? That he suspected the reincarnation of Mozart to be involved in the brutal mutilation and death of a serial killer? That he was conducting this investigation behind the back of Larsen, who likely believed he was crazy?

"I...suspect the woman knows a lot more about Harris than we believe. They knew each other from the Kim Arundel Psychiatric Hospital. And so far, she might be the only woman who has ever survived this monster. There are still a lot of families looking for their girls." Liam rested his head on the headrest. "I want to be able to look them in the eyes and promise them I've exhausted every road before I close the door."

"I see. Does Larsen know about this?"

"No."

There was an awkward silence. Then Murray cleared his throat. "When your guys in Maine found whatever was left of Sam up in that swamp Harris had left her to rot in, her mother called me to thank me. I'd never heard a more devastated woman in my life. And yet after we had both prayed together and cried, her mother said to me, 'Robert...at least...at least I finally know. Now I can stop dreaming about finding her.'"

Liam's heart ached for Sam's mother. What a fucked-up world this was.

"What do you need from me?" Chief Murray asked.

"There's a police station in Bover, New Hampshire. In the eighties, there was an incident involving a girl named Leah Miller. I need to find the officer who handled her case. He might hold the key to solving this puzzle."

"I'll let you know when I find him."

Fucking amen!

"Do you think you can get him to talk to me?"

"He'll talk like my Grandma Sue, God bless her chatty soul. You'll hear from me soon."

THIRTY-FIVE

The rain was hammering onto the surveillance van like a flood sent from the gods to wash Liam away. With the engine turned off, the temperature inside the van had dropped significantly, becoming so cold that he could see his breath.

Liam took a sip from his cold coffee and buttoned his wool coat all the way up to his neck. Tony was right. This surveillance job sucked. Day after day and night after night, the two of them took turns watching and waiting, and literally nothing of interest ever happened.

With plenty of time on his hands, Liam tackled the puzzle that had taken root in his mind like fungus on moldy bread. Theories and dead ends pushed him to the brink of sleep deprivation, aiding him during night shifts but straining his sanity.

As much as he tried to focus on the Train Track Killer case, he could think only about *her*.

Leah goddamn Nachtnebel.

She was a genius, there was no doubt. A classical superstar who lived a life of Michelin-star dinners and handsome escort boyfriends. Most men and women would kill to trade with her. So why did she bother with a lowlife like Luca Domizio? What role could she possibly play in all this? Liam had thought about it from all angles. Really. All of them. Drugs, human trafficking, the dark web, mental illness, you name it. He had assigned Leah Nachtnebel the role of matchmaker to the rich and powerful for child prostitutes and then tried her as the drug queen of a Mexican cartel. But no matter the thought, it always resulted in the same conclusion.

Nonsense.

The rain intensified, making it almost impossible to see anything. Especially not without the windshield wipers on.

"This summer fucking sucks," he cussed just as his phone vibrated. He looked at the illuminated screen and almost dropped the damn thing.

It was Sara, calling him at two in the morning.

Fuck.

A storm of emotions washed over him as he watched the round green symbol on his display bounce up and down. The lawyer said no contact. Not until the trial was over. And why the hell would he pick up anyway? Sara had cheated on him, literally making him a laughingstock in front of the whole world with a TikTok video labeled WHEN YOUR SEX LIFE GOES FROM OLD LAME VANILLA TO BURNING HOT. Even Josie had seen the video in which Sara's new stud flexed his abs. So why in the world would Liam throw out the little bit of dignity he had left and pick up?

Because she gave him Josie, and for that alone, a part of him would love her until the day she died.

"Hello?" Liam answered, his hand slightly trembling.

"Liam?" Sara's voice was almost a whisper.

A painful sigh escaped his lips as he raised a hand to his forehead. He didn't say anything, just sat there in silence.

"I...I'm so sorry. I—" Sara's voice broke off.

Was that fucking club music in the background?

"I...I just wanted to hear your voizzzz. I mizz you," she slurred.

He shook his head.

Goddamn her. She's wasted.

"You...you don't mizz me at all?"

It was pathetic, but yeah, he did. He missed the family they had. But she'd ruined it all.

"Liam, say something," she demanded. "Anything. Tell me you love me or to pizz off. Just fucking break that perfect little shell of yours for once and stoop down here to my level!"

Drunken nonsense.

"Sara...I—"

The bright red taillights of a vehicle blazed as it backed out of Robert Patel's garage. Liam watched in shock as the vehicle rolled out of the driveway and onto the rain-soaked road. Despite the heavy downpour, Liam could discern the shape of a van.

The van!

"Drink lots of water. I gotta go," Liam said before hanging up. He held his phone in his hand, waiting a few moments before starting his own van. The windshield wipers sprang to life, but even with their hard work, visibility remained terrible on these treacherous roads, with only the taillights of the van in the distance to guide him.

Cautiously he followed the van as it left the quiet neighborhood. Liam gradually closed the distance while maintaining enough space to avoid raising suspicion.

The roads were dangerously slick with water encroaching from every direction.

Hunched over the steering wheel, he maneuvered with one hand and dialed Larsen.

"Hello?" he answered in a husky, two-in-the-morning voice.

"It's me. Patel is on the move. In a freaking white van!"

"Holy crap," Larsen mumbled in disbelief. "Stay on him. I'll wake the others."

"All right."

Liam focused intently on the road ahead, sliding the phone back into his pocket. The van led him down I-95 for a while before taking the exit to Lexington, located about twenty minutes west of Boston.

Lexington? Liam's heart began pounding against his chest. That was close to Hill Park Station! Where Anna Smith had been attacked and lived with her grandmother! Patel must have had someone follow her home from the hospital.

Patel finally slowed in a run-down neighborhood with toppled fences and unkempt front yards. The heavy rain flooded gutters and turned the road into murky streams.

Liam switched off his headlights and cautiously trailed Patel's van, which eventually parked next to a blue house with overgrown grass and a rusty old swing set in the front yard. Liam positioned his SUV behind a large truck a few cars behind Patel's van on the opposite side of the road. The heavy rain and dimly lit streetlights made visibility almost nonexistent.

Swiftly he turned off the car and pinpointed his location on his phone's map.

"East Lincoln Drive," he mumbled, grabbing Anna's file from the passenger seat. Anxiously he leafed through the papers, glancing up every few seconds to ensure the van was still there. It remained parked and running, its red rear lights glaring like eyes.

At last he found the statement summary of Anna Smith's attack. And her address: *1445 East Lincoln Dr*, he read in shock, his gaze snapping back to the van as the folder nearly slipped his grip. The van's headlights had been turned off!

"Fuck."

Liam's blood surged with icy adrenaline as he dialed Larsen. Instinctively he reached for the gun in his hip holster and flung the car door open.

The loud, pounding noise of the rain striking cars and roofs, along with the whooshing sound of the downpour, made it difficult to hear Larsen answer.

"He's at Anna's house! Fourteen forty-five East Lincoln Drive!" Liam yelled into the phone before hanging up and raising his gun to aim at the van. Cold rain streamed down his body, drenching him with each step he took toward the vehicle. Cautiously he circled it to the front driver's side and pointed his gun directly at the window.

"Patel!" he shouted as loud as he could, trying to be heard over the relentless rain.

Nothing.

Slowly he stepped closer, within reach of the door handle, then wrenched the door wide open with one hand while keeping the gun aimed.

The van was empty. He peered into the back, but Patel was nowhere to be found.

He spun around to look at the blue house right behind him. The mailbox read 1445—Anna's home.

In a frenzy, Liam charged up the porch stairs, nearly slipping, and tried the front door. It was locked.

"FBI!" he yelled, pounding his fist against the door. "Open up!"

Nothing happened.

Shit.

Liam weighed his options. He could either waste time circling to the back, searching for Patel or a potential entry point, or...he could kick down the old wooden front door.

With a resounding bang, the old door flew open under the force of Liam's kick. Wood chips scattered across the floor as the handle slammed into the wall.

The house was eerily silent and pitch black.

Liam flicked the light switch next to him, but it didn't work; the darkness remained unbroken. His eyes strained to adjust.

"FBI!" he bellowed into the void, anxiously navigating room to room around shadowy, indistinct pieces of furniture.

"Anna!" he called up the stairs after clearing the kitchen and living room, finding himself in the hallway.

Suddenly a loud bang echoed from upstairs. It was followed by the rapid thumping of footsteps.

Cold sweat formed on his brow as Liam quickly ascended the stairs and swept the upstairs hallway with his gun, aiming first to the left and then to the right.

Nothing.

His eyes narrowed at an open door at the end of the hallway. First, he noticed a flicker of a shadow, then what appeared to be movement.

Liam's grip tensed around the cool metal of his gun, his knuckles turning white. He moved cautiously toward the cracked bedroom door. Muted streetlight from a window cast eerie shadows on the floor.

"FBI! Hands where I can see them!"

Silence.

As he reached the doorframe, his eyes were drawn to the gruesome sight that dominated the room: a bloody bed, its white sheets drenched in vivid crimson. On it was an older woman, her pink nightgown soaked with blood.

"Shit!" Liam cursed, rushing over to the lifeless body. He checked for a pulse at her neck, all the while casting wary glances around the room, ready for a surprise attack.

His stomach churned, knots twisting and tightening.

No pulse.

The woman was dead.

From the corner of his eye, Liam caught a subtle movement by the closet door. He whirled around, gun aimed at the door, his reflection staring back at him from a mirror hanging off it.

"FBI! Come out with your hands up!" he yelled.

When nothing happened, he slowly crept up to the door and reached for its handle, his gun pointing at the door as if it were frozen in place.

He opened the door to find Anna sitting on the floor, half concealed by dresses hanging from the closet rod. Her gaze was vacant, eyes wide with terror, the whites starkly visible around her pupils.

"Oh God, Anna." Liam leaned over, placing his hand on her shoulder.

She remained statue-like, unresponsive.

"Anna, is he still here?" Liam pressed. As he turned to make sure nobody was creeping up on him, he saw a large, dark figure towering behind him. Realizing it was too late to turn, aim, and shoot, Liam acted on instinct, throwing himself at the man and sending them both crashing to the ground. The dim light filtering in from the window revealed Patel's face beneath a rain-slicked coat. In a matter of seconds, Liam was on top of him, but Patel managed to knock the gun out of Liam's hand. With a powerful twist of his mighty torso, Patel used his legs to leverage himself out from under Liam's weight, tossing Liam aside and sending him sprawling onto the floor.

"Anna, run!" Liam bellowed as he and Patel twisted and turned on the ground. Against all odds, Liam managed to obtain the upper hand and pinned the six-foot-three beast of a man to the ground once more. However, just when he thought he had the situation under control, he felt something cold slam into the side of his chest.

First once, then twice, then a third time.

A burrowing, burning pain flared to life in his chest as a loud groan escaped Liam's lips. He collapsed to the side, clutching the throbbing, agonizing wounds where Patel had stabbed him. Pain radiated through his chest as warm blood seeped between his fingers. Gasping for air, he watched as Patel rose to his feet, towering over Liam like Goliath. A flash of lightning briefly illuminated the room, casting an eerie glow on Patel's blood-smeared glasses and the lifeless body of Anna's grandmother. Despite the excruciating pain, Liam tried to rise and fight, but Patel struck again, this time driving the blade deep into his stomach. With a guttural cry, Liam crumpled back to the floor.

Patel loomed above him, his expression cold and detached as if he were looking at a perplexing work of modern art rather than a dying human being.

A mixture of cold and hot sweat dripped from Liam's forehead as he mustered the strength to push himself into a slumped sitting position against the bedframe. Waves of pain washed over him. He cast a fleeting glance at Patel and the gleaming, bloodstained knife in his hand, then let his head drop to the side to ensure Anna had escaped and was no longer in the closet.

But his heart shattered into a million pieces when he realized the poor girl was still sitting there, staring at him with the same empty gaze she'd had when he'd first found her.

"Anna..." Liam coughed up blood. "Run, Anna...r-run," he groaned, feeling his energy ebbing away.

"Ann..." he attempted once more, but his strength failed him, and he flopped sideways to the floor. His vision blurred as he watched Patel step over him, the glinting blade of the knife edging closer to his throat.

"Piece...of...shit, let her...go," Liam choked out as a flood of regret and despair consumed his final moments. The emotional pain far exceeded the physical pain of the gaping wounds in his chest. He had failed Anna, her grandmother, and, worst of all, Josie. His beautiful girl would grow up bearing the pain of losing her father. If he had managed to save Anna at least, he could have found peace in that. But this? This was the most agonizing end imaginable.

He'd vowed to protect the innocent and those he loved. He'd failed at both.

"Run...Anna...please," he whispered. Liam squeezed his eyes shut, unwilling to let the last thing he saw be Patel's nasty face. Any moment now, and he'd be gone.

He tried to think of Josie, her smile, her laugh, but all he saw before him were Anna's eyes, wide with fear and unspeakable horror.

"Josie," he mumbled, bracing himself for the cold metal cutting his throat.

Suddenly a loud gunshot rang out. It was followed by the thud of a heavy body collapsing onto his legs.

Liam forced his eyes open, but his blurry vision could discern only the dark silhouette of a small figure standing a few feet away. The weight of Patel's lifeless body cut off the blood supply to Liam's legs.

"Anna?" Liam mumbled as the shadow moved closer and knelt beside him. Wordlessly, the figure guided both of Liam's hands from the wound on his side to the one on his stomach, pressing firmly against it. A pained moan escaped his lips, but he continued to apply pressure even after the person's hands withdrew.

Suddenly the world began to spin and darken, the distant sirens fading into silence. Was he dead?

"The canvas, Agent Richter," a woman's voice said, somehow both distant and near.

"A drop of red blood on a snow-white canvas," the voice whispered once more before an all-consuming darkness swallowed Liam whole.

THIRTY-SIX

The beeping of the hospital machines drilled their way into Liam's consciousness first. Then the voices.

"He moved!" Josie said.

"Oh my God, you're right!" his mom gasped in a shaky voice.

"Dad!" Josie cried. "Dad, wake up!"

Slowly Liam opened his eyes to blurry faces hovering above him.

"Josie." Liam coughed as his vision returned and he made out the faces of his daughter and mother.

"Dad!" Josie cried and clutched Liam's arm.

His mother wiped away tears and grabbed his hand with such force, he flinched. "You scared us," she scolded him as her long fingernails dug into his palm.

"Ouch." Liam winced. "Your nails are sharper than the knife that stabbed me."

Josie faintly smiled as Liam's mom let go of his hand with an eye roll.

He placed his hand on Josie's golden head and smiled. "Good to see you, pumpkin."

Tears were rolling down her red cheeks as she smiled back. "I'm so happy you're alive. Even Mom cried."

"That...is kind of her," Liam said.

"Very kind," his mom said with a hint of sarcasm.

Liam shook his head at his mom as she sat on his bed.

"You might be happy to hear that the bastard who did this to you is dead."

"Mom." Liam frowned and nodded toward Josie, who was listening to every word with wide eyes.

"What? It's the truth, and at least she won't have nightmares wondering if the man might come for you again." She turned to Josie. "Don't worry, pumpkin, the bad guy is in a morgue freezer somewhere. Just like he deserves."

"Good God, Mom!"

Josie wiped away tears with her sleeve. "It's okay, Dad. It does make me feel better."

"See what you're doing to this poor girl?" he said.

Liam's mom shrugged. "I'm making a strong woman out of her. The world needs those, believe me."

A gentle knock interrupted their conversation. Larsen appeared, grasping the string of a pink *Get Well Soon* balloon while Tony carried a bouquet of flowers.

"Going above and beyond to avoid repaying the fifty bucks you still owe me, huh?" Tony said, placing the flowers on the stack of gifts and get-well cards.

"Last time I checked, it was thirty, but yeah, it almost worked."

"You guys shouldn't joke about this," Larsen said, awkwardly handing Liam the string to the balloon.

Liam inspected the glittery pink balloon and cocked a brow at Larsen.

"I know. My wife chose it."

Josie snatched the glittery balloon from Liam's hand, her eyes sparkling with delight.

"Hey, Mom, why don't you take Josie to grab some muffins from the cafeteria?" Liam suggested.

She nodded and gently took Josie's hand. "Let's go, sweetheart."

The trio watched them depart before Larsen and Tony approached the bed.

"The doctors said that by focusing pressure on your stomach wound instead of the side wound, you saved your own life," Larsen said.

A hazy memory of the silhouette shifting his hands to his stomach flickered in Liam's mind.

"Patel did quite a number on you," Larsen said, shaking his head. "But you did well sending him to hell." He continued speaking, but Liam's thoughts drowned out his words as he revisited the moments before he lost consciousness.

Anna hiding in the closet. The searing pain in his chest. Patel looming over him. Liam mustering his final breath to plead with Anna to flee.

Anna...Liam could barely summon the strength to ask about her. If she hadn't made it, the guilt would haunt him for the rest of his days.

"...they'll be asking questions about the gunshots you fired and—"

"Anna." Liam cut Larsen off, his voice cracking.

Tony placed a reassuring hand on his shoulder. "She's alive, buddy, thanks to you."

The crushing weight on his chest lifted, allowing him to breathe easier. Liam tried to sit up but winced at the pain.

"She's alive?"

"Yes," Larsen confirmed. "She's been treated for minor injuries, but she'll be fine."

"What about her grandmother?"

Larsen shook his head, his expression somber.

Poor Anna.

"She'll sleep better knowing Patel is dead," Larsen said. "In fact, many women will. We found Anna's DNA in the van. It was the same one that was used to kidnap her the night she was placed on the train tracks."

"Holy shit," Liam mumbled.

"You can say that again," Tony huffed. "That freaky geek was the Train Track Killer. A monster we didn't even know existed. Makes you wonder what else is out there."

Liam attempted to adjust his bed to a sitting position, but a sharp pain halted him midway. He grimaced.

"Well, we'd better let you rest," Tony said.

Larsen nodded. "We'll come visit you again. Heather mentioned she'd stop by later too. If possible, try to recall how you shot Patel. Forensics is hounding me about a missing bullet. They've matched one of the bullets in his chest to your gun, but the other bullet is unaccounted for even though it didn't pass through his chest."

As Tony and Larsen began to turn toward the door, Liam bit his lip. "Wait."

They did.

"I...I didn't shoot him."

"What do you mean?" Tony asked.

"I mean, I didn't shoot Patel. Someone else was in the room with me."

Larsen and Tony exchanged worried glances.

"Anna?" Larsen mused. "Are you saying Anna shot Patel?"

Memories of the incident overwhelmed Liam: the pain, the darkness, the deafening thunder and rain, Anna's eyes wide with horror, and then the mysterious silhouette.

"I...I don't know," Liam said, massaging his temples. "Everything happened so fast."

"Could've been you, and you just don't remember?" Tony wondered. "The bullet in Patel's chest matches your gun, and your gun was fired out of your hand."

"What?" Liam jerked up, ignoring the pain.

Larsen placed a hand on Tony's shoulder. Tony looked worried out of his mind, as if Liam was talking crazy.

"Your gun's gunpowder was on your hand," Larsen explained. "It means—"

"I know what that means," Liam muttered, lost and confused. What the hell was going on here? "And I know this sounds crazy, but I didn't shoot him."

"All right," Tony said, lifting his hands as if to calm a cornered animal. "Why don't you just rest a little more. All of this is so fresh, and the mind can play tricks on us after highly traumatic events."

"He's right," Larsen agreed. "Rest up. We'll talk more in a few days."

Liam nodded, but there was nothing wrong with his memory. He didn't shoot Patel. Period. Maybe Anna did it. But why would she place the gun in his hand first?

"Did one of the gunshots hit Patel in the back?" Liam asked.

Larsen shook his head cautiously. "No. Both were frontal shots."

Liam wrinkled his forehead at Larsen in utter disbelief. "But that would mean whoever shot Patel walked around him first, without him noticing, and then shot him from right next to me. How is that possible?"

Larsen and Tony shared another worried glance. Tony appeared on the verge of breaking down at any moment.

"It'll be fine. Give him some time," Larsen mumbled to Tony, who nodded and rubbed his eyes like they were burning. "Get some rest, Liam. We'll see you in a few days," Larsen added.

"Later, bud. Let me know if you need anything," Tony said before they left.

Liam sank back into his pillows, staring at the door in disbelief. What on earth was happening? He could clearly recall the events until Patel stabbed him. The gun he'd allegedly used to shoot Patel had been knocked out of his hands. And Anna...she was in shock and wouldn't even run for her life. The idea that she suddenly transformed into John Wick and killed Patel seemed highly unlikely.

A tall, slender man in blue hospital scrubs entered the room, followed by a young red-haired nurse who appeared to be maybe half Liam's age. The man's name tag read DR. WILLERS beneath a prominent Mass General Hospital logo. Hers read NURSE KELLY.

"How are you feeling?" Dr. Willers asked.

"Good. How long was I asleep?"

"For about twelve hours after surgery. Your vitals were stable, so we knew you'd wake up sooner rather than later. You've been recovering better than we expected when they brought you in."

Liam watched as Dr. Willers lifted his hospital gown to inspect the bandages covering the side wound. Then he repeated the process for the stomach wound.

"Looks good, no excessive inflammation. We'll keep you on antibiotics just in case and monitor you for a few more days. But surgery went really well, and we were able to close the damaged artery in your stomach. You chose the right wound to put pressure on, that's for sure."

"So I've heard," Liam mumbled, his gaze drifting to a tree outside the window. His mind felt trapped in a dreamlike state, as if lingering in another world.

He needed to talk to Anna as soon as possible.

"How soon can I leave without risking my life?" he asked.

The doctor gave him a don't-even-think-about-it look, but when Liam maintained his serious expression, he relented. "Technically, you could leave right now if you sign a waiver, but I strongly advise against it."

"Why? Would it kill me?"

"No, but as I said, I don't recommend it. We'd like to keep you a bit longer to ensure the wound doesn't reopen."

Liam frowned. "I don't mean to sound ungrateful, but I need to leave."

The room fell silent for a moment before the doctor nodded. "All right. I've warned you. It's your call. I'll send the discharge admin to you with the paperwork. I'll also prescribe antibiotics and pain medication."

"I don't need the pain meds. That stuff is addictive."

Dr. Willers frowned. "I'll prescribe them just in case. I bet you ten bucks you'll take them."

Liam was about to accept the bet when his eyes landed on a single red rose in a clear vase on a small table next to the door. It stood out in stark contrast to the white wall, like a drop of red blood on a white canvas. "Who put that there?" He pointed at it.

Nurse Kelly and Dr. Willers both turned. "The rose?" Kelly asked.

For a moment, Liam was relieved they both saw it, as this reassured him that he wasn't losing his mind.

However, they both looked at Liam as if he were, in fact, going crazy.

"I don't know," Dr. Willers said, like the question was a waste of his precious time.

"Is anyone allowed on this floor?" Liam persisted, staring intently at the rose. "I mean, someone must have seen who left it."

Nurse Kelly scratched her head and looked at Willers. "I think Jenny mentioned a flower delivery guy dropping something off this morning."

"But who sent it?" Liam asked, immediately realizing how foolish that sounded. How could they possibly know who sent him flowers?

"Well, do you have any other questions? If not, I'll check in on you over the phone tomorrow." Every word the doctor said seemed distant. Liam couldn't tear his gaze away from the rose.

"The canvas," Liam mumbled.

"All right," Dr. Willers said. "Kelly will check your vitals." He stood up and left while Kelly checked the machines Liam was hooked up to. Then she glanced over her shoulder at the rose. "It's pretty," she said, checking Liam's pulse. "The red against the white. Like a—"

"Like a red drop of blood against a white canvas," he mumbled. The memory of the silhouette whispering those same words into his ear came flooding back.

The same words he had heard before from one person and one person alone.

"Nachtnebel." He said the name like a vow.

As if on autopilot, Liam's legs swung out of bed. He felt the cool sensation of the floor through his grippy hospital socks.

"Mr. Richter, you have to stay in bed until the meds wear off!" Nurse Kelly insisted, holding out a hand as if to physically stop him.

"Get me those discharge papers," Liam demanded, aware of how intense he sounded. So he added, "Please."

"That will take a little bit."

"I don't have time."

He needed to talk to Larsen, then arrange for Leah Nachtnebel to be brought in for a formal interview at the FBI headquarters.

But on what grounds? He had absolutely no proof of anything. Perhaps he could find her DNA at the crime scene if he retraced her steps. Time was of the utmost importance.

"Please get back in bed!" Kelly urged, but Liam had already removed the needles from his veins. "Mr. Richter, stop!"

"Dad!" Josie shouted from the door, nearly dropping the plate of muffins in her hands.

"Are you crazy?" his mother scolded him.

"I...I need to—"

"You need to rest and stop scaring your daughter, who spent all night crying and praying!" His mother gestured to Josie, who looked horrified.

"Pumpkin, Daddy just...needs to go to the bathroom," Liam lied with a weak smile.

Josie's face instantly relaxed. Good. She bought it. However, Nurse Kelly and his mom both narrowed their eyes at him.

"The discharge papers?" Nurse Kelly whispered to him so Josie couldn't hear.

"We'll talk about them tomorrow," Liam said.

Kelly sighed and nodded. "All right. I'll need to assist you if you need to go to the bathroom. If you fall, it's my fault."

Liam shook his head. "Absolutely not."

Nurse Kelly crossed her arms. "Fine. But I'll wait in the bathroom with you until you're done."

"Well, go, Liam," his mother said and grabbed a laptop bag from the couch. "And after that, we'll watch a movie on the laptop together and eat muffins. Isn't that right, pumpkin?"

Josie grinned wide and stretched out on Liam's bed, already eating a muffin. "We have three movies you can choose from."

Liam stared at her, but his mind was still occupied with Leah Nachtnebel. Her soft voice echoed through his mind: "Like a drop of red blood on a white canvas."

"Dad!" Josie shouted at him. "Are you listening?"

"Of course. You choose the movie. Just don't let Grandma talk you into *Doctor Zhivago* again." He limped past an annoyed Nurse Kelly toward the bathroom door.

"And why not?" he heard his mom bark after him as Nurse Kelly closed the door behind them.

"Because the damn song gets stuck in my head for weeks!" he hollered back. He gestured at Kelly to turn around. "Would you mind?"

Nurse Kelly rolled her eyes and turned away.

He needed to get out of there as quickly as possible, preferably tomorrow or, at the latest, the day after. If Murray stood by his word, by now he should have found the police officer who handled Leah Nachtnebel's case, the one that had sent her to the Kim Arundel Psychiatric Hospital...just like Harris. They were around the same age. Despite what others had said, nobody had any concrete evidence that they didn't meet there during group talk therapy and choir practice. If he was lucky, that would be the smoking gun he needed to confront her. Even if it cost him his job, he would solve her mystery and, if possible, expose her crimes.

THIRTY-SEVEN

Chief Murray lowered the window of his red Tesla and gave Liam a brief nod as Nurse Kelly wheeled him out of the bustling hospital entrance, holding a trash bag containing his few belongings. To add to his embarrassment, Liam wore an old Britney Spears T-shirt and salmon-colored pants—clothes his mother had brought from his old room at her house, not his apartment.

A group of young med students in scrubs parted for Liam like the sea for Moses. He could hardly bear the chief's gaze. It was humiliating for any man to be wearing a Britney shirt while being pushed around by a woman nearly half his age, but it was part of the deal to get released. After several unsuccessful arguments, Liam relented to the persistent nurse with the steely gaze.

The moment they were through the entrance, Liam rose from the wheelchair, earning yet another disapproving glance from Nurse Kelly.

"Thank you, Kelly. I got it from here."

"You take care of yourself, Mr. Richter."

"I will," Liam said as a sliver of pain radiated from the stab wounds.

Kelly shook her head as she walked back inside.

Murray got out of the car and hurried around to open the passenger side for Liam.

"Please, not you too," Liam said, getting in and wincing as he fastened the seat belt.

"Not me too what, Richter?" Murray furrowed his brow as he got behind the wheel and started driving. "Treat you like you just got stabbed and nearly died?"

Liam pursed his lips.

"I really think you should be in the hospital right now." Murray's small eyes briefly glanced at the worn-out T-shirt.

"I appreciate the concern, but I'm fine."

With a frown, Murray's gaze wandered to the pink pants. Then he nodded.

"So who is this Leah Miller? You really think she's the lady in red?"

When speaking with Chief Murray, Liam had cautiously avoided linking Leah Nachtnebel to her former identity as Miller. He feared Murray would side with Larsen if he learned Liam was targeting the world's most celebrated pianist as a suspect without solid proof.

"I'm pretty sure," Liam said. "But since this is an off-the-books mission for now, it's better if I keep details to myself until I have proof. I made a choice knowing it might ruin my own career, but I don't want to drag others down with me."

"It would take someone extremely powerful to bring me to my knees."

Leah had performed for queens and presidents in their homes and was somehow connected to the mob as well. Narrowing his eyes at the GPS to clear his blurry vision, Liam frowned. "I'm afraid she might have the connections to do that."

Murray took the ramp onto I-95 up north to Maine and followed the flow of traffic.

"So anything I need to know about this guy?" Liam asked.

Murray focused on the road. "Not much to tell you. His name is Chris Davis. Worked as a cop his whole life. Then his mother died, and he inherited her farm up near Portland. He seems to be pretty old school and by the books. Went a little nuts after he moved out into the country by himself."

"Nuts? How?"

"Mostly conspiracy theories. Alien abductions and fake moon landing kinda shit. Don't tell him you're FBI. He watched a few too many *X-Files* episodes and thinks the FBI is in on it."

"In on what?"

Murray's thin lips curled into a grin. "Everything."

Liam rolled his eyes and gazed at the farmland next to the highway. "Great."

The drive up went by pretty quickly, thanks to the pain meds that were still in Liam's system. About thirty minutes into the drive, Liam could no longer resist the weight of his heavy eyelids, and they closed involuntarily.

"Wake up," Murray said, touching Liam on his shoulder. Liam jerked awake, his hand instinctively reaching for the spot on his hip where his gun usually was.

"It's me, Richter," Murray reassured him. "We're here."

"I..." Liam rubbed his face with his hands. "I'm sorry."

With a knowing expression, Murray nodded. "I'm an Iraq vet. I get it. I really do." Then he got out of the car and pulled his pants up by his leather belt.

The afternoon sun broke free from the clouds and reflected warmly off Davis's run-down farmhouse. Rusty junk cars were scattered around the property, and wild bushes and trees grew all over the place. There were no animals except for a few chickens and an old golden lab that limped toward them, wagging its tail.

Liam stroked the animal's soft fur.

"You Chief Murray?" the voice of an old man hollered as he stepped out of the red farmhouse with a shotgun in his hand. His dirty baseball cap was hanging sideways, and his jean coverall pressed tightly against his potbelly. With one eye significantly larger than the other, his distinct face was hard to forget.

"The one and only," Murray said, pulling out his badge. He threw Liam a curt nod. "This is my nephew."

Mr. Davis pulled his baseball cap up to scratch his bald scalp. "What's wrong with him?" Davis asked, nodding in Liam's direction, his eyes narrowing at his outfit.

Murray walked up to Davis, unfazed by the shotgun or the harsh tone. "He's from a new generation. They just ain't cut like you and me."

Davis grinned and leaned the shotgun against the porch post. "Now ain't that the truth."

With a weary sigh, Davis sat on one of the outdoor chairs under his porch's overhang. Murray took a seat across from him and waited for Liam to do the same. The damn chair was wet, but Liam refused to be the only one to get up and wipe his pants.

"So how can I help you?" Davis asked. "I'll tell you whatever you need to know. Once a cop, always a cop."

Now that was great news for once. Liam cleared his throat. "You worked at the Bover Police Department in the eighties?" he asked.

A look of pride crossed Mr. Davis's face as he straightened in his seat. "I did."

"There was a case," Murray said, "of a little girl."

"Her name," Liam chimed in, "was Leah—"

"Miller," Mr. Davis said. "Her father owned the gas station in town."

Murray and Liam exchanged glances.

"I remember it as if it were yesterday. Something like that don't ever leave you. In all my years as an officer, I've never encountered anything like it again."

"What happened?" Liam asked, leaning forward.

"I don't know the full story. The girl never spoke. Not to me or anyone else. So if there's any issue with the file or any lawsuit involving the hospital she was transferred to—"

"It's nothing like that," Murray interjected. "Just tell us everything you know. We won't cause trouble."

Davis wiped his sweaty brow and set his baseball cap on the chair's armrest. "I was making coffee in the kitchen when I heard gasps coming from the entrance hall of the station. Eileen, our secretary, called out for me. She sounded panicked. I had my gun drawn as I rushed into the entrance hall, spilling coffee powder and water all over myself. When I arrived, it felt like I'd been struck by lightning. The room was eerily silent. You know that cold feeling in your stomach when something is just wrong, don't you?"

Liam and Murray nodded.

"So what happened?" Liam asked, trying to cut through some of the drama.

"Well, there in the middle of the entrance hall, leaving a trail of blood behind her, was little Leah Miller. She held a knife in her hands, covered in blood."

Ignoring his penchant for dramatic embellishment, Liam tried to focus on the facts. "A blood-covered knife?"

"As I sit here before you, a blood-covered knife," Mr. Davis confirmed. "But that wasn't the most chilling part of it all. When her green eyes met mine, she walked straight up to me and handed me the knife. Then she said, 'I stabbed a boy.' Just like that. Like it was the most natural thing in the world."

Liam nearly gasped out loud, envisioning Leah as a blood-soaked little girl. "Did you say she stabbed a boy?" he asked.

Davis nodded as if reliving the scene in his mind. "She sure as hell did. The tone of her voice...it was as if she were possessed. That's the part that still haunts me."

A million questions raced through Liam's mind, but he struggled to articulate even one of them.

"What happened?" Murray asked.

"As far as we know, the town's bully tried to molest her. It's believable, considering he had already killed Mrs. Garcia's cats and we had several other complaints against him. He was a little psychopath, that one, that's for sure. So nobody wanted to make a big deal out of it. We recommended she stay at the Kim Arundel Psych Ward, and as far as I know, her parents followed up with that recommendation."

"Do you know who the boy was?"

Please say Harris. Please say Harris. Say. Fucking. Harris!

Davis rubbed his nose. "Ethan Green. As worthless as they come."

"What happened to him? Does he still live in Bover?" Murray asked.

Mr. Davis shook his head. "His mother wasn't right in the head. She married a former priest who was brought up on molestation charges after Ethan was arrested. They moved out of state and had Ethan's case transferred, so I'm sorry, but I can't help you on that one."

Fuck.

"And Leah Miller? What happened to her?"

The old lab limped onto the porch, settling down in front of Mr. Davis. The dog placed its paw on the man's knee, as if requesting affection. Davis obliged, tenderly stroking the dog's head.

"Bover is a small town," Mr. Davis continued. "You don't just forget a scandal like that. Her father sold the gas station, and the Millers moved away."

It would have been too good to be true if Mr. Davis had connected Harris to Leah. But this visit was still worth it.

"Well, if you don't have any more questions, I'll go inside and finish my episode of *Wedding at First Sight*." Davis rose and shook his head in laughter. "These idiots, marrying someone they don't even know," he mumbled.

The two made their way back to the car. The old yellow lab limped after them, tail wagging enthusiastically.

"Do you think the woman in red could be Leah Miller and that the boy she stabbed might be Harris?" Murray asked, pausing to pet the dog, which had finally caught up and blocked his path.

"It's possible. There's a significant gap in Harris's childhood that his mother refuses to discuss with us," Liam said.

They both climbed into the car. But instead of debriefing, they sat in a heavy silence.

Then a wildly crazy idea struck Liam. It was so nuts that he was too scared to share the thought with anybody at this point. What if the woman in red, Leah Nachtnebel, not only knew Harris but, given her violent past, was the one who...

Liam exhaled sharply and shook his head. It was almost too crazy to even think. But then again, why the hell not? Nothing else had made sense so far. And the words the silhouette had whispered to him right before he lost consciousness...the likelihood of anyone other than Leah uttering those words was nearly nonexistent. But if she was the woman in red *and* the silhouette at Anna's house, why would she save him?

"Richter?"

"Hmm?"

Liam's eyes met Murray's. He noticed the other man hadn't started the car yet.

"Ultimately, it's your decision, but I think it's time to tell Larsen about all this. He comes across like a jerk sometimes, but he's a good guy. I served with him in Iraq."

"You served with Larsen?"

Murray's gaze wandered out the windshield and settled on the yellow lab sitting in the middle of the gravel road. "Not in the same platoon, but I did co-op on a few missions with him in the Middle East. There are many things to be proud of when you serve. And equally as many that haunt you at night. But at the end of the day, Larsen was one of the good guys who had our backs. You can trust him to do the right thing."

It made sense. Liam couldn't keep his investigation secret any longer. In fact, he needed not only Larsen but the full force of the FBI if he wanted to bring down justice on the most famous classical wunderkind of the century.

"You might be right."

Murray nodded and started the car. "Where to? Home?" he asked, his finger hovering over the car's GPS, then typing in Boston.

Liam almost nodded but then straightened in his seat. "Actually, would you mind dropping me off somewhere else? It's on the way. It's time sensitive. Otherwise I wouldn't ask."

"Of course."

When Murray still didn't start driving, Liam turned to look at him.

Murray's hands were gripping the steering wheel. "This Harris case will haunt me until the day I die. I've seen a lot of messed-up things, but this serial killer shit...I don't know how you do it."

"I wonder that myself," Liam said, noticing the rawness in Murray's eyes.

"I've met a lot of people in my life, Richter, but you are quite something. If you ever need my help again, you have it."

Liam held his gaze, then nodded. "Thank you. That means a lot."

"Now are you allowed to have a beer with whatever they gave you for the pain? I'll buy." Murray smiled and started driving.

Liam smiled back. "You bet. I was told it would make the meds more fun."

Murray laughed. "That might not be a good thing. Another time then."

"If you're still buying...because I might be out of work then."

THIRTY-EIGHT

Contrary to Liam's expectations of encountering another horror scene like he had the night of his fight, East Lincoln Drive looked vastly different. Despite the rundown homes, the neighborhood that had nearly cost him his life just days before was now bathed in the idyllic glow of the evening sun. As Murray parked in front of Anna's house, a group of children on bicycles rode by, laughing and howling like wolves.

"I'll wait," Murray said and leaned back in his seat, but Liam shook his head.

"No need. I'll catch an Uber home."

"You sure?"

"Yeah, this might take a bit, and I've already taken enough of your time. Plus it's better if she sees I'm alone."

"All right. Let me know if you need anything."

Liam stretched his hand out for a handshake. "Thank you, Chief."

Murray nodded. "You're a good guy, Richter. If the feds don't want you anymore, call me. I could use a man like you."

"I might take you up on that sooner rather than later," Liam said and got out of the car. Murray honked once and drove off.

Liam didn't notice the wide-open front door until he crossed the street. An icy shock wave jolted him with the horrors of that night. The plastic bag containing his belongings slipped from his fingers, and he hobbled quickly toward the porch, his face twisted in pain.

As he ascended the front steps two at a time, Anna emerged from the house, carrying a large moving box. Their near collision startled them both, and they exchanged curious glances. The yellow CRIME SCENE DO NOT CROSS tape that had once barricaded the door now lay on the ground. It took Liam a few moments to connect the dots between Anna, the stuffed car in the driveway, and the open door.

"Probably a good idea," Liam said, eyeing the box in her hands. He heard the sound of a car door opening and turned to see a woman around Anna's age stepping out of the vehicle parked in the driveway. Liam turned back to Anna, who was shaking her head, signaling the other woman to stay put.

"It's okay," Anna called.

The woman responded with a curt nod before returning her focus to the phone in her hand.

"They said it's okay to grab a few things," Anna mumbled, placing the cardboard box on the ground. She tucked a strand of brown hair behind her ear, her gaze fixed on the box, avoiding Liam's eyes.

"Of course."

"I...I already told the police and FBI everything I remember," Anna said, her voice tinged with frustration.

"I know," Liam replied calmly.

"I can't remember anything else. I swear to God. All I remember is waking up in the closet with the police shining their flashlights at my face."

"That's okay."

And yet the way she avoided his gaze, as if feeling crushed under immense guilt, Liam knew she wasn't telling the truth.

The last time he'd seen Anna, she'd been in a state of total shock. She hadn't even flinched when he'd screamed her name, begging her to run. It was a miracle she was walking and talking again instead of lying in an inpatient psychiatric unit, staring blankly at the ceiling. There was no way in hell she killed Patel. Something had happened that night after he'd passed out, and whatever—or to be more precise, *whoever*—it was had known exactly what to say to Anna to keep her from talking.

"I'm so sorry you got hurt because of me," Anna said. Her tone left no doubt that she was sincere.

"I'm not," Liam said with a smile. "I just wish I could have stopped him sooner."

Tears started running down her cheeks. "Me too. But thank you for saving me. If it wasn't for you—" Her voice broke off.

If it wasn't for me what, Anna? Then the person who really killed Patel would have been too late to save us both?

Liam stared at her with a gentle yet inquisitory smile. "Of course."

The same group of boys rode their bikes down the street again, barking now instead of howling.

"Anyway. I gotta go," Anna said. "Your guys have my phone number in case you need me. But as I said, I don't remember anything."

"All right, let me know if you need anythi—" A stab of pain flared in Liam's side, and he took a deep, painful breath, wincing. "Sorry," he groaned and pulled out the small orange medicine bottle from his pants pocket. Under Anna's careful eyes, he popped two pills and swallowed hard. One of the pills got stuck in his throat. He really didn't want to take this shit—he'd skipped most of the doses—but this was important.

"Do you need water?" she asked.

"Yes, please."

She disappeared inside and quickly came back with a glass of water. Liam accepted it gladly and flushed down the pill stuck in his throat.

"Thank you." He handed her the empty glass. The look of guilt on her face made it clear she felt responsible for his injuries.

"Don't worry, I'll be fine, but—" Liam pulled out his phone and pulled up a picture of Leah from her concert website, holding it up in front of her "—could you just take a look at this woman and let me know if—"

His voice broke off the moment he saw Anna's eyes widen in shock. She stood still, staring at the picture of Leah.

"Anna?" Liam asked. "You don't have to say a single word to me right now. But I beg you, I risked my life for you and would do it again in a heartbeat. All I ask in return is a simple nod, nothing more. It can be tiny. Or even just a blink of your eyes."

Anna kept staring at the picture. Then her eyes found his.

"Please," Liam begged. "Please. Is that the person who killed Patel?"

She glanced back and forth between Liam and his phone. Then, just when he thought he was losing her, Anna finally nodded at the same time she tore the door behind herself shut and grabbed the box from the ground. Within seconds, she was inside her friend's car, and they were pulling out her driveway.

Liam slowly lowered his phone, watching as Anna and her friend drove away from him like he was part of the life they were fleeing—which, in all honesty, he was.

But it didn't matter at this point. The missing pieces of the puzzle had finally started to fall in place, creating a picture so mind-blowing and horrific that he struggled to comprehend it.

The world slowly faded as his thoughts took him hostage. Over and over again, he ran through all the evidence and events.

Harris.

The lady in red.

Patel.

Anna.

Even Domizio.

They were mere moths flying toward a wildfire, attracted by the light. And in this case, the wildfire was Leah Nachtnebel.

Beautiful.

Mysterious.

Genius.

Secretive.

A red drop of blood on a white canvas, hiding in plain sight for the whole world to see.

A serial killer of serial killers.

THIRTY-NINE

Liam sat alone by the window in the dimly lit burger joint across from the Boston Symphony Hall. The bar lights cast a gentle glow over his expressionless face. The city was cloaked in darkness, yet the Symphony Hall's bright facade stood out like a spotlight on a stage. Liam's lips curled into an empty smile as he downed the last of his whiskey, his mind clouded and weary.

"The canvas," he mumbled and placed the empty glass on the table, along with a fifty. Then he slowly rose, briefly running his hand over the cold metal of the gun tucked in the back of his pants. He'd grabbed it from his apartment before coming here.

The cool night breeze sobered him up just enough to realize it wasn't all a dream. He wasn't drunk, but the pills mixed with the two glasses of whiskey did make him feel out of it. The rest of his foggy state was the result of the mind-fuck he'd been trapped in by the most genius being he had ever come across.

"Who am I in your masterpiece, Leah Nachtnebel?" he muttered, crossing the street. The first cars with concert guests lined up in front of the entrance.

Liam stepped inside the Symphony Hall, past curious stares and mumbles, and flashed his badge at the security guards rushing toward him. He couldn't blame them, given the way he looked.

He proceeded straight to the staff-only area, flashing his badge at a musician to gain entry. It wasn't long before he heard the soft melody of a captivating piano piece. As if in a trance, he followed the sound, moving past Leah's room and arriving at the stage.

"If I'm just a pawn, why did you let me live this long?" Liam murmured as the music swelled around him.

Liam couldn't stand the thought of a world where individuals like Leah Nachtnebel operated behind the scenes without repercussions. His entire life had been dedicated to upholding justice and the law. Without order, chaos reigned. Leah's mere existence challenged everything he believed in.

With his hand on his gun, Liam climbed the stairs toward the stage, stepping out of the shadows and into the light of the illuminated platform.

FORTY

Mozart's Requiem in D minor, K 626.

The cool piano keys obeyed my fingers' every command, creating a sound that was tear-provoking to most yet meaningless to myself. Or at least, that was how it used to be. Much to my surprise, as I played, the music began to stir something profound within me. The tiniest bit of warmth tingled in my chest when I played. It was almost unnoticeable, yet for me, when this feeling first emerged a few days ago, it was one of the greatest moments of my life. I felt reborn with the hope that one day I might feel deeply and passionately about something.

The concert hall was dark, the stage I practiced on illuminated with bright floodlights.

I saw Agent Richter's long shadow even before the hardwood flooring creaked under his deliberate yet careful steps.

I didn't flinch or turn. My fingers continued to move effortlessly over the keys. "You can put the gun away, Agent Richter. I can promise you I have no weapon taped to the underside of my grand piano."

He stood in silence, right behind me, his tall shadow swallowing me whole, darkening the keys beneath my fingers. The gentle notes were the only sound in the room, slowing down time and creating a dreamlike state.

"Thank you for the rose. That was very considerate," he finally said, circling around me. His hand moved with practiced ease as he slipped the handgun back into his belt. He stopped at the end of my grand piano. "So tell me," he said, "was Greg Harris the boy who tried to rape you as a child? The one whose neck you slashed with his own knife?"

Something was off about him. His words were slightly slurred.

I kept playing. Unfazed. "You really shouldn't mix alcohol with your medication."

A sarcastic chuckle escaped his lips. "Is that a threat?"

"Quite the opposite."

Another silence settled between us, like a short truce.

"Are you here to arrest me, or is Larsen unaware of this visit?"

"I see you've done your research on my superiors."

"Something along those lines."

"Well, then you might be relieved to hear that this is a private visit."

I leaned in for a crescendo as the requiem reached its peak. "With what purpose?"

Slowly, as if approaching a timid horse, he stepped beside me and placed his hand on the grand piano. "To ask you to look me in the eyes and tell me that you're not the lady in red. That you didn't kill Harris or Patel. That I'm crazy and that none of this is true. Just look me in the eyes and tell me that you didn't do any of it, and I'll turn around and never come back."

Abruptly my hands rose from the keys, cutting off the melody prematurely. I turned and gazed straight into Agent Richter's deep brown eyes. He stared back in defiance and determination. His sharp cheekbones and strong jawline were covered in a three-day beard, and the dark rings under his eyes left no doubt about the extent of his exhaustion. Yet I knew what a tired, desperate man was capable of doing.

My eyes widened slightly as I inhaled the air, now laden with my unspoken words.

Captivating. That was all that came to my mind when I stared at Agent Liam Richter. I knew I'd chosen wisely. As seconds passed without a response, his eyes narrowed. Then he began to clap, the slow, resonant sound reverberating throughout the empty hall.

"Bravo, Ms. Nachtnebel."

His applause ceased, and his arms fell to his sides.

"But you see, the thing is, when you play in shit for too long, even someone like you gets dirty enough for someone like me to notice." He shook his head. "I suppose there's no point in asking why if you won't even admit to any of it." His lips twisted into a sardonic smile. "You know what plagues me the most about all this? I know you were the one who killed Patel that night. What I can't comprehend, no matter how hard I try, is what you said to Anna to make her side with a murderer."

I gave a slight nod as if to concede that I would grant him at least this one answer. "People tend to be more cooperative if they're threatened. Or truly grateful. According to your stated events, the girl would have a stronger sense of gratitude toward me than you, as I, according to you, was the one who killed her killer. Anna seems to be one of the many people who believe the world is a better place without a monster like him." I tilted my head to the side. "Many people...but not *you.*"

"Oh no, you're wrong. I'm one of the many people who agree. How could I not? Kill the killer. Make the world a better place. I just also happen to think it's an awful lot of power for one person to be the judge and executioner."

I nodded. "Many people wield this kind of power to enrich themselves without ever breaking a single law. It would be an insurmountable task to pursue them all."

He gazed at me with a raw emotion I couldn't place. "I'm not coming after all of them. I'm coming after you."

The intense silence was cut like a knife by one of the stage assistants who hollered over from the stairs at the other end of the stage. She was merely a silhouette against the darkness of the room. "Leah, do I have your permission to open the doors in ten?"

I maintained eye contact with Agent Richter, as if asking permission. He offered a subtle nod before turning away. "Go ahead," I replied to the woman, who hurried off immediately.

Agent Richter had reached the edge of the stage, mere steps from being enveloped by the room's darkness, when he turned and looked at me one last time.

Determined.

Dedicated.

Passionate.

"You are the drop of red blood on a white canvas for the whole world to see, aren't you, Ms. Nachtnebel?"

I stared at him in silence.

He nodded. "Brilliant. Truly. Fucking. Brilliant."

He stepped forward, and his figure slowly began to fade into the darkness until his silhouette was nothing more than a memory.

FORTY-ONE

A loud knock jolted Liam awake. Startled and disoriented, he shot up to find himself on his couch. Judging by the sunrays filtering through the blinds of his two-bedroom apartment, Liam concluded it was late morning. The blurry memory of getting back to his apartment was mixing with sleepless hours of pain and mind-bending thoughts. Both his wounds had gotten worse with every hour that passed last night, but Liam needed his head clear and refused to take any more pain pills.

"It's me." Tony's voice accompanied another knock.

Liam stumbled through his living room and opened the door. The bright sunlight briefly blinded him, and he squinted as Tony stepped inside, his gaze filled with worry.

"Jesus. You look like shit." He stared at the Britney Spears T-shirt. "Maybe we should take you back to the hospital?"

Liam squinted and walked back to the couch. "What time is it?"

"Three."

"In the afternoon?"

Tony nodded and looked around. The apartment itself was clean, but when Liam caught his own reflection in the hallway mirror, he couldn't deny that he looked like shit indeed.

"Why don't you clean up a bit? Your mom is picking up Josie and wants to stop by. She called me to check in on you to make sure you're less crazy than you were last night when you called her. She said you sounded like E.T. on meth, and you kinda look like it too."

"For Christ's sake." Liam rubbed his temples. "I'm glad you and my mother are getting along so well all of a sudden. Guess you're not just 'the man who smells like sausages' to her anymore."

Tony shrugged. "Everybody deserves a second chance. And I did eat a lot of brats back then." Tony sat in the chair next to the couch. "Rough night?"

Liam lowered himself to the couch, the soft cushions folding beneath his back. "Yes. Really rough night. But I don't want to drag you into it."

"Well—" Tony slapped his leg "—it's a little too late for that now. I already saw you in the Britney Spears T-shirt and the tight pink pants. So why don't you talk to me? I'll help out as much as I can."

Liam stared at the floor with a distant gaze. "I need more evidence. If I tell you right now, you'll just think I'm crazy."

Despite reviewing the evidence and recounting his conversations with Leah countless times, Liam realized that nothing she had said would hold up in a court of law. He lacked any definitive proof to build a solid case against her. Anna's nod wouldn't even be enough to warrant Leah's detainment for formal questioning at the police station. Furthermore, although Leah's escort boyfriend recognized her as the woman in red from the photo, he had no intention of admitting to this in a courtroom setting.

"No, my friend, I got absolutely nothing to nail her with. Nada. Zero. Null. It's better if you stay out of it."

Liam waited for Tony to brush it all off with a joke and drag him into the shower, but Tony nodded attentively and gave him a serious look. "By *her*, I take it you mean that pianist?"

Liam straightened in his seat. "I do."

"Well, then tell me everything you got."

"You might think I'm nuts."

"I already think that. Have for some time, actually."

Cautiously Liam weighed the consequences of sharing his case with Tony. But there wasn't really anything to lose here. Tony was a friend, and the worst he could do was tell Larsen about all of it. And that might not be such a bad idea at this point. Any help, even one that might begin with a brief suspension, would be a bottle of water in the desert. Besides, he sure as hell already looked crazy, so that ship had sailed.

Liam hesitated a moment longer, then leaned forward. "I don't even know where to start."

"You're really selling the case to me here."

"Fine." Liam slapped both his hands on his thighs. "Leah Nachtnebel killed Greg Harris."

It was as if the words echoed several times more, like in a cave, before fading into an uncomfortable silence.

Tony steepled his hands, looking away, opening his mouth, and then looking away again. "Liam," he finally said in the soft tone they were taught at the academy to use on victims.

"No. Don't do that." Liam cut him off and scooted to the edge of the couch. "Don't talk to me like I belong in a psych ward."

"But what you're saying—"

"Is the truth, Tony." Liam rose and pointed at himself. "Look at me."

Tony sighed.

"I said look at me, Tony."

His friend finally met his gaze.

"If there was ever a time when we were more than just two colleagues navigating a fucked-up job with stupid jokes that nobody outside our bubble would find funny, then I need you to look at me right now and listen. It's still me, Tony. Liam. The same man who would take a bullet for you and the same man who just took three stab wounds for a woman who was about to get murdered. We've worked together for ten years, Tony, ten goddamn years. And now you want to treat me like a lunatic? Look at me, Tony. Look at me and tell me that's what you really think."

The room fell silent again but this time only briefly as Tony shook his head. "No. I don't think that."

Liam dropped backward onto the couch as if he had just unloaded a truckload of concrete blocks. "Good," he huffed. "Fucking finally somebody treating me normal again."

Scratching his scalp, Tony frowned. "So you really think Leah Nachtnebel killed Harris, mutilated him like some Dahmer psycho, then took an Uber to play a piano concert?"

"As insane as it all sounds, I do. She has a history of violence. When she was eight, she slashed a boy's neck with a knife and was sent to a mental institution right after that."

"Are you serious?"

Liam nodded, encouraged by Tony's change in tone. "This isn't even the craziest part. Guess who the boy was?"

Tony shrugged.

"I have reason to believe the boy she almost killed when he was eight was Greg goddamn Harris."

Tony let that settle for a moment, then shook his head in disbelief. "How do you know all this?"

"Because I met the cop who processed her as a child. Somebody had gone through a lot of trouble erasing all her files, but Heather found the original psych ward recommendation in an old paper file."

Shock was evident all over Tony's face. "And the cop said the boy was Harris?"

"No. But it's the most logical conclusion. Just think about it. We have nothing from Harris's childhood. The man is a ghost up until he turned fifteen, and his mother refuses to share any information about his childhood. Then there's the fact that not only was Leah Nachtnebel present at the crime scene, but Harris was also a patient at the Kim Arundel Psychiatric Hospital—the very same institution where Leah Nachtnebel received treatment during her childhood."

"How do you know that?"

"When I visited the facility to get records of Leah's stay, the director mistakenly assumed I was there for Harris's files."

"Why the hell didn't they reach out to us with this information?"

"Why would they? Harris was dead, and it's not exactly good for business to have housed a serial killer. Wouldn't go well with the thirty thousand monthly price tag the one percent pays to find their inner peace."

"Holy shit," Tony mumbled.

Liam was on the verge of diving into another crazy story, how Leah Nachtnebel was likely responsible for Patel's death, making her a serial killer who targeted other serial killers, but he had even less evidence to support the Patel claim, so he chose to set it aside for now. If he could rally support and arrange for Leah to be brought in for an official interview, he could revisit the topic of Patel.

"What the fuck is going on with this world?" Tony said, his face twisting as if he were tasting something sour.

"I know. My nightmares have been less fucked up than the shit happening in the real world."

"We have to tell Larsen about all this," Tony said. "There's just no way we can do anything without him."

As much as he hated to hear it, it was the truth. The time for the final tango with Larsen had come.

"I know." In slow motion, Liam reached for his phone on the coffee table.

"You gonna call him now?" Tony asked.

"Might as well before Ms. Nachtnebel flees the country."

"Why the hell would she do that? It's not like she knows you're onto her."

Liam held his phone next to his ear, avoiding that question.

Tony sighed. "Nooo. Tell me you didn't confront her."

Liam turned his back to Tony.

"What the fuck, Liam! Why would you do that?"

"I had to be sure."

"Oh yeah, and how did that go?"

Shitty. "We have a complicated relationship, all right!"

"What the fuck are you two talking about, Richter?" Larsen's voice snapped through the phone. "Are you two sniffing your pain pills?"

Even from his seat, Tony could hear Larsen's angry voice. He lowered his gaze like a child caught with his hand in the cookie jar.

"All hell has broken loose here," Larsen said. "The guy who poisoned the well and killed all those people might get off the hook thanks to the next OJ lawyer. So unless this is important, tell Tony to get his ass back here, and we'll talk another time, all right?"

For whatever reason, this time Liam didn't take well to Larsen's aggression. Maybe it was the fact that he'd almost gotten killed only a few days ago on the job and deserved more respect than this. Or maybe it was the fact that the past few months had been, hands down, the craziest of his life. Either way, he didn't give a fuck anymore.

"It's important, so you can allocate me a minute of your time, Larsen, or I'll call Murray and handle the situation with him. Might make the FBI look really bad, though, once shit hits the fan. But I'm sure McCourt will understand."

Larsen was silent on the other end. Liam glanced at Tony, who looked more shocked than he had when Liam had told him that the most genius pianist of all time had drilled a man's face in.

"I," Liam continued, "have strong reason to believe that Leah Nachtnebel is the lady in red and that she killed Greg Harris."

Still silence, which was better than Larsen yelling and hanging up on him.

"She most likely knew him from an incident from her childhood. She slashed a boy's throat when she was eight, and I have reason to believe that boy might have been Harris."

For a few seconds Liam heard nothing but heavy breathing on the other end of the line.

"Do..." Larsen's voice was shaky, and he cleared his throat. "Do you have any evidence?"

"I can prove that Harris was treated at Kim Arundel, the same place Leah Nachtnebel was sent as a child. I was also able to locate the police officer who handled the case in the eighties. I'm sure he would testify if Murray told him to do it."

"Murray? You involved Murray?" Larsen sounded beside himself. "What...what did you tell him?"

"Not much. He just drove me. He doesn't know that I suspect the lady in red to be Leah Nachtnebel."

A loud breath sounded through the phone. "Good. What about Tony?"

Liam looked up at him. "He knows. And he believes me."

Liam extended his phone toward Tony, who shook his head vigorously in protest. However, after Liam shot him an angry glare, he reluctantly cleared his throat and leaned into the phone. "Hello, erm, sir. I apologize for all of this. But...I...I have reason to believe Richter might be onto something here."

Liam rolled his eyes and held the phone back against his ear. He could almost taste the tension in the air when he took a deep breath and prepared for his final pitch. "Larsen, in all the years I've worked under you, I've never really caused you trouble. I've taken over shifts when nobody else would and had your back no matter what. Now I need you to believe me because if you won't, I'll get in a cab right now, put my badge on your desk, and take Murray up on his offer to close this case as one of his."

Clutching his phone tightly, Liam waited for Larsen to say something. Anything. To yell or laugh or just hang up. But Larsen remained on the line in silence, breathing heavily. It felt like a fog had filled the air between them and was about to swallow the apartment with Liam and Tony in it.

Finally Larsen cussed under his breath. "Okay."

Liam's head twitched back. "Okay?"

"Okay?" Tony echoed with an open mouth.

"I said okay. I wanted to wait until I had more, but I stumbled across something regarding Harris myself yesterday. Are you able to meet?"

"Yes!" Liam said eagerly, straightening his slumped back.

"Then meet me at the Harris crime scene. There's something I need to show you."

A sudden rush of adrenaline erupted inside Liam, forcing his heartbeat into a quick rhythm. "What did you find?"

"You gotta see it for yourself. When can you get there?"

"I'll leave right away." Liam reached for the car keys and clumsily put them into his pockets.

"Good. Don't talk to anybody about this anymore until you meet with me. And—" he exhaled deeply "—and bring Tony."

FORTY-TWO

The SUV rattled along the gravel as Tony navigated the final stretch of forest road to the Harris crime scene. Sunlight filtered through the dense canopy, painting intricate patterns of shadows on the ground and the car. Dust rose from the gravel, accompanied by the crunching sound under the tires as the SUV rumbled along the road.

Soon enough, they caught sight of Larsen's car parked near the tree, its surroundings still marked with the yellow CRIME SCENE DO NOT CROSS tape.

Exiting the SUV, Liam and Tony breathed in the scent of moss and pine as they approached the tape. Liam had reached out to tear it down when his phone suddenly rang—a call from an unknown Boston number.

He picked up.

"Hello?" A woman's voice was cutting in and out, giving him not much more than "...HR director...Kim Arundel."

"I can't hear you well. You said you're calling from Kim Arundel?"

"My name...Susan...call...tell you what...FBI agent looked like...got the files."

"Ah, yes. Thank you for calling me. I was told you might be able to identify the person who picked up the boxes that remained intact during the fire," Liam said as he greeted Larsen with a nod when he emerged from behind a tree. Tony stepped under the yellow crime scene tape and joined Larsen on the scene.

"Short..." the woman's voice said, cutting out again. "...glasses...bow..."

Liam cussed under his breath. "Damn reception. What was his name again?"

"...en," the woman said.

"What?"

"...en."

This was going nowhere. "I'll call you back later, thank you," Liam said before hanging up and turning to face Larsen.

"It's almost as if none of it was ever real," Larsen said as he gazed at the idyllic forest scenery.

Liam listened to the birds for a moment and nodded in agreement. Leaves and fallen branches concealed any evidence of human presence. If not for the yellow tape, the area would have been an ideal backdrop for a family photo session.

"But it is real," Tony said. "In my memories and my nightmares, and I pray to God it won't be the last thing I think about when I draw my final breath."

Larsen pursed his lips, glanced at the sky, then shook his head.

"I'm so sorry, Tony—" his voice sounded pained "—but it actually will be." With practiced ease, he lifted a gloved hand, drew his gun, and shot Tony in the head.

For a split second, Tony's eyes and mouth opened in terror before his lifeless body collapsed to the ground, causing leaves to swirl momentarily before settling atop the blood and fragments of his brain.

Liam stood frozen, his eyes locked on Tony's horrified expression. The shock left Liam breathless. He grappled with the thoughts and words necessary to comprehend the horrifying turn of events. He felt alternating chills and fiery heat, and then suddenly bile surged upward, causing him to vomit violently onto his own feet.

Unbridled fury washed over Liam like a tsunami. Instinctively his hand reached for his gun, only to clasp at empty air. Of course he hadn't brought his weapon. After all, he was meeting with two FBI agents—his colleagues and friends.

"What did you do?" he screamed at Larsen, wiping the corner of his mouth. His face contorted into disgust as his voice rose in a fevered pitch. "You shot Tony! You son of a bitch. You shot Tony!"

His fists were clenched so tightly his nails cut into the flesh of his palms. He was on the verge of lunging at Larsen, but then he found himself staring directly into the barrel of the gun aimed unwaveringly at him.

"You did this!" Larsen yelled at Liam, using his gun as an extension of his arm to point at him. "You just couldn't let it go! I told you to stop, but you just...fucking...didn't! Now look at what you've done!" Spit flew from Larsen's mouth as he yelled. "Was this worth it?" He shook his gun at Tony's dead body before turning the weapon back to Liam. "Was it fucking worth it?"

"I didn't do this!" Liam snapped. "You're the psycho who shot him! You!"

As if triggered by Liam's words, Larsen straightened, adopting a tall, composed posture. Exuding confidence, he crouched beside Tony's lifeless body, extracted Tony's gun from its holster, and momentarily fumbled to place it into Tony's lifeless hand while still holding his own weapon. After a brief struggle, he managed to position Tony's limp hand, now wielding the gun, to aim it at Liam.

Liam immediately understood Larsen's plot. Larsen would use Tony's gun to kill Liam, and then place the gun he'd used to kill Tony in Liam's hand. This would make it appear as though the two agents had engaged in a shootout most likely initiated by the mentally unstable Agent Richter. Liam's current scattered state, fueled by the traces of opiates and alcohol in his system, would only serve to support Larsen's fabrication.

"But why?" Liam sucked in a weak breath, completely lost. He knew he was going to die, but why?

A sad smile curled onto Larsen's lips as he looked Liam straight in his eyes. "For what it's worth, I'm really sorry. But I've been brought into this world to shoulder a tremendous burden. My purpose here holds more value than the combined lives of all three of us. I know that if you and Tony really understood what I'm doing here, both of you would willingly sacrifice yourself for this cause. If it's of any reassurance," he said, aiming Tony's gun at Liam, "Josie is in no danger. I do what I do to save lives, not take them. I'm not a monster like Harris or Patel."

Larsen adjusted the aim of the gun in Tony's lifeless hand, sending a chilling shiver down Liam's spine.

"I'm sorry, Richter. It's nothing personal."

"It's very personal, you asshole." He shook his head in disbelief. "Why, Larsen? Fucking why?"

Larsen took a deep breath. "Let's not do the whole confession thing they do in movies. It's a waste of time and solves nothing. Sorry, Richter."

"Go to fucking hell, you piece of shit."

Liam closed his eyes, embracing the sun's warmth on his face as he pictured Josie's smile. He braced himself for the explosive sound of the gunshot and the endless darkness that would follow.

But then, just when Liam thought this was truly it, Leah Nachtnebel's voice pierced through the crisp forest air like an arrow seeking its target.

"Put the gun down, Larsen," she said calmly.

Liam's eyes snapped open, half expecting his mind to be playing tricks on him, only to find Leah standing there, bathed in the golden glow of the setting sun. The waning sunlight glistened off her white suit, enhancing her surreal presence. Her makeup and hair were as flawless as ever, matched by the gleaming metal of the gun in her hands—aimed unwaveringly at Larsen's temple.

FORTY-THREE

Agent Richter glanced back and forth between Larsen and me like wounded prey with a newfound will to live.

Slowly Larsen let go of the gun in Tony's dead hand but not the one in his other hand.

"Drop the gun and step back," I instructed.

He hesitated.

"Unless you want your wife to find something similar to Harris when they call her to identify your body," I added.

Finally Larsen dropped the second gun and stepped back. Sweat was dripping from his brow when he turned to face me.

"You—" Agent Richter's eyes were still darting between us "—know each other?"

"We do. Rather well," I said. "Isn't that so, Agent Larsen?"

Liam barked out a sad laugh and looked at Larsen. "It was you who destroyed the files from the Kim Arundel Psychiatric Hospital, wasn't it?"

At first Larsen said nothing, but then he frowned. "Our work had to be protected."

"Your work?" Liam's piercing gaze was now directed at me like a pair of sharpened knives. "You mean killing people?"

"Monsters," Larsen corrected him. "They were monsters, not people."

"Whatever you want to call them, I was right all along," Agent Richter concluded, shaking his head. "You killed Harris and Patel," he said to me.

"I did," I confirmed unemotionally.

This didn't seem to satisfy Agent Richter. "But why?" he pressed. "Because Harris tried to rape you when you were a little girl?"

"Not quite." The last rays of the sun flashed across my face as I put a few feet between Larsen and myself. No need to get blood on my clothes. "Do you want to tell him, or should I?" I asked Larsen, who bit his lip in a tense silence.

"Tell me what?" Agent Richter demanded.

I granted Larsen a moment to speak, but he didn't.

"Everything you said is true," I said. "When I was eight years old, I stabbed a boy. He was a tormented soul, the very prototype of the monsters I hunt down today. I was walking home from the store when he began to follow me. He forced me onto the ground and took out a knife. I was just an innocent little girl. But I refused to be his victim." I narrowed my eyes at Larsen. "However, you're mistaken about one thing, Agent Richter. The boy I stabbed when I was a little girl, he wasn't Harris."

A fleeting silence intensified the already-charged air.

"It was me," Larsen suddenly said, pulling down his suit shirt and tie to expose a large scar on his neck.

Agent Richter's eyes widened in astonishment as they fixed on Larsen. "You?"

Larsen sucked in a sharp breath and exhaled it. "I was a deeply troubled boy who'd already caused a lot of pain. I was angry all the time. That anger had to go somewhere. So I followed a little girl home from the grocery store to do something unthinkable." His lips curled into a sarcastic smile. "But that little girl was unlike any other I'd ever encountered or would ever meet again. She was a rarity, a creature one in a billion, if even that. She taught me what fear was that day...and pain. It was as if fate had brought us together—the same fate that led my mother to marry the man who sent me to a military school for troubled juveniles, where the army snatched me after graduation and molded me into a man overseas. It was fate when the FBI accepted my application from among thousands. And on the day of the funeral, fate was by my side again."

"What funeral?" Agent Richter asked.

The memory of the funeral flashed in front of my eyes like a faded photograph. Relentless rain had hammered down on us that day as mourners wept under their black umbrellas. The pastor's words were barely audible under the downpour. I must have been the only one who noticed *him* standing under a tree in the distance, watching, moving his lips as if in prayer.

"The suicide of a common acquaintance," Larsen said.

"A boy Larsen molested as a child," I clarified. "The pain Larsen had inflicted on him in his childhood turned out to be more than he could carry, so he killed himself."

Larsen nodded and wet his lips. "That night when she paid me a visit, I knew it was to finish what she had started a long time ago."

"I couldn't accept the fact that he lived while a boy who had done nothing wrong but cross paths with a monster was gone," I explained.

"So what happened? You seem to be pretty good at killing. How did Larsen transform from a target to a partner in crime?" Agent Richter asked.

"I was determined to end his life and expose him for who he truly was, but then Agent Larsen pleaded for just a minute of my time, to show me his work. And what he revealed was intriguing."

"Killing serial killers?"

I nodded. "At that time, he hadn't managed to kill anyone yet, but his preparations were detailed enough that, with outside help, it seemed like it could be a successful operation."

Shaking his head, Agent Richter glanced briefly at Tony's lifeless body, his jaw quivering. Then he looked back at me. "Now what? Shoot Larsen and me to cover your tracks and continue until the next Richter stumbles upon your mistakes and starts asking the wrong questions?"

A brief silence hung in the air. Then, completely unexpectedly, Larsen burst into laughter, like a man pushed to his breaking point.

"Mistakes." He laughed at Agent Richter. "You really still believe she made mistakes? There were no mistakes, were there, Leah? I asked you why Harris, but now I understand." His laughter transformed into a deep scowl. His eyes narrowed, and his lips pressed tightly together. "Think, Liam, think, goddamn it! Harris and his connection to Kim Arundel. She deliberately chose Harris as our next target because of the link between her and him through the Kim Arundel Psychiatric Hospital. His bashed-in face was a calculated move to remind the investigators of Samantha Hayden's case. Another critical piece in her puzzle. And the Uber—" he gestured in the direction of the main road in the far distance "—she took the Uber not because she had no other choice but because it was planned. To leave a trail for you to follow. Why else would she ask the driver to drop her off at the Boston Symphony and not somewhere nearby?"

Agent Richter hung on every word. "The ticket," he interjected, stepping forward. "You signed it on purpose, knowing you could later point out your unique handwriting. Then you placed the same handwriting on the map, hoping I would connect it to the ticket after you instructed Larsen to plant it." Liam let out a humorless laugh. "You even told me it was you. From the start. The canvas...like a drop of red blood on a white canvas—it's incredibly difficult to hide in plain sight. You told me that over and over again. And Patel. You most likely had me followed by then. But—" He tilted his head, both eyebrows lowered in confusion "—why? Why go through all this? Why save me only to kill me now?"

Larsen's laughter violated my ears like the sound of a cat being strangled. He clapped his hands together violently as his chest heaved up and down. "Bravo!" he yelled. "Bravo, Leah. Bravo." He turned to Liam. "You idiot. Don't you see? She's not here to kill you, she's here to kill me and replace me. Aren't you, Leah?"

I was indeed. My eyes narrowed at Larsen in disgust. "All those years ago, when I visited you after the funeral, you asked me how I knew who you were."

Larsen's body abruptly stiffened, his muscles coiling like a spring. "I did. Nobody else recognized me after I got out of the military. It was as if I had become a ghost to the world. Not even my own mother recognized the son she despised. But you, you knew it was me the moment our eyes met on that cold and rainy day of the funeral. You promised that one day you would tell me how you knew who I was."

I nodded. "It's your eyes. When I first looked into them as a little girl, I saw the darkness of a monster lurking within. All you monsters have it—a mark placed upon you at birth. When I gazed into your eyes at the funeral, the mark was still there."

"A monster," Larsen mumbled, raising his trembling fingers to his glasses, briefly closing his eyes as he slid them off his nose. He looked incredibly fragile now, his shoulders sagging like those of an old man.

"You were testing him, weren't you?" Agent Richter asked me, stunned. "To see if he'd really changed."

Wearily, Larsen glanced at Tony's body, waiting for my response. Instead of saying anything, I steadied my aim at his head.

He grinned and then gazed into my eyes. "What makes you think you're any better than me? We're the same, you and me. We're both monsters who kill for a greater good."

I shook my head. "You and I are not the same. You kill people. I...I kill killers."

I pulled the trigger.

"No!" Agent Richter screamed, just as the deafening sound of my gun reverberated through the woods, sending a sudden flurry of wings into the air as a group of birds took off from the branches above us. "Fuck!" He twirled around.

I lowered my gun, walked over to Larsen's lifeless body, and examined his head wound. His empty eyes stared straight at me as if he were judging me.

A perfect shot to the head. Another monster gone. *Good.*

With a deep breath, I straightened my posture and strode over to Liam. I extended my arm and held my gun in front of him with an air of certainty. "Here. The gun is registered to your name."

Agent Richter accepted it, briefly glancing at my gloved hands, then stared at the gun like it was some exotic object. In a trance, he slowly pointed it at me. I ignored the motion and kept staring into his glossy, shocked eyes.

"Fire one shot so that gunshot residue particles will be found on your clothes and hands. When the police arrive, report that Larsen shot Tony and you had to shoot Larsen in self-defense. We'll use Larsen's hidden identity as his motive. Tell the FBI that you discovered his true identity, a teenage psychopath named Ethan Green."

I pulled out the unregistered phone I had purchased recently.

"I recorded a video of Larsen shooting Tony and will send it to the police anonymously tomorrow," I continued. "It will look like it was sent by a frightened witness who doesn't want to get involved. Tell them you thought you saw a jogger but were in too much shock to be certain."

"You...you recorded Tony's death? Why the hell didn't you save him?"

"There wasn't enough time, and I assumed you were suspicious of this meeting and armed as well. My logical conclusion was that you would shoot Larsen after he drew his gun on Tony. Larsen suspected Tony of being armed, making it more logical to neutralize him first. At least, that's what I would have done. But don't blame yourself. The medications in your system are still clouding your judgment, and you didn't kill anyone. Larsen did." I tried to look empathetic. "I'm sorry about your friend."

Agent Richter frowned, the gun in his hand still pointing at me.

"In time, I will reach out to you. I expect you will have made your decision by then."

"What decision?"

I looked into Agent Richter's eyes. "Whether I'm a monster or just the villain who kills them. One you can work with. The other you need to kill."

We stood there, frozen in silence, staring at each other as the world around us seemed to fade. His amber eyes looked lost, determined, confused, yet confident. If there was such a thing as the fate Larsen had gone on about, then fate had brought this man to me. A righteous man who knew right from wrong. A man who gave more than he took and pledged to live his life with unwavering determination, dedication, and discipline until his very last breath. I could trust him to make the right decision even if, in this moment, I couldn't predict what that decision might be.

With a faint smile on my lips, I turned. The gravel crunched beneath my feet as I started walking down the road. At first there was only tense silence as the sky above turned from the vibrant colors of the setting sun into the blue and orange tones of twilight.

"Stop!" Liam shouted after me.

I kept walking.

"Stop, Leah, or I'll shoot!" His voice was trembling.

I had no idea if he would, but it really didn't matter. Whatever he decided to do, it would be the right decision one way or the other.

"Leah! Goddamn it! Stop!"

I didn't.

Suddenly a strange ache burned through my throat, then moved into my chest. I stopped and looked down, wondering if he'd actually shot me, but there was no sign of a bullet wound. In awe, I froze. The cool evening air brushed against my neck and face as I realized that I was experiencing an unfamiliar emotion, one that I had never felt before. It was as if I had swallowed pieces of glass that were cutting me from the inside.

Pain.

I felt *pain*.

I embraced the beautiful feeling, appreciating its intensity. I loved the way it burned, the fact that I could feel it at all.

But what had triggered it? Why was it surfacing now, after all these years of lying dormant?

"Absolutely magnificent," I marveled, resuming my stride toward my car parked at the side of the main road where Emanuel was waiting for me. He promptly swung open the passenger-side door, his eyes brimming with relief.

The first stars were appearing through the canopy, as they had since the beginning of time. I stepped further and further into my new life, ready to embrace whatever fate had in store for me—or, in my case, Agent Liam Richter.

FORTY-FOUR

Three Months Later

Liam's hand tightened around the leather handle of his bag as he walked down the eerily quiet hallway. Since Tony's death, silence had become his least favorite companion, inviting tormenting thoughts.

An agent from another division rushed past him, clutching a large folder under his arm.

Liam took a deep breath, pausing briefly in front of the door to the Behavioral Analysis Unit.

"Please, God, please no surprise party."

He tilted his head back, huffed out a long breath, and then opened the door.

A sudden burst of applause greeted him the moment he stepped in. Colorful balloons and yellow crime scene tape decorated the whole place. His coworkers surrounded him with laughter and excited handshakes under a large banner that read WELCOME BACK SAC RICHTER!

The room was packed. It must have been the whole damn headquarters squeezed in.

Towering a head over everybody else, Martin gently smacked Liam on the back in a brotherly manner. Heather, on the other hand, came in for a long hug and handed him a book-sized gift wrapped in yellow crime tape. Jumping out of the crowd, grinning widely, Cowboy did wild shooting motions with both hands as if he were in a shootout. He had been given Tony's position, and the whole office knew it was because he'd begged his uncle to make it happen. Something about serial killers seemed more appealing to him—most likely the publicity and press the fucked-up cases got.

Overwhelmed but thankful, Liam forced a smile. "Thank you, everybody. It's good to be back. I missed you all."

Cowboy let out a cheerful yodeling cry.

"Good God." Liam sighed. "Even you, Cowboy."

The room erupted into laughter as Cowboy shot Liam a thumbs-up.

Liam lifted his hands to command attention. Quiet anticipation replaced the noise of the crowd. "I also want to thank my superiors, wherever they are—"

Suddenly an older, tall man dressed in a navy-colored suit lifted his hand. It was the associate deputy director of the FBI, McCourt, in flesh and blood.

His piercing blue eyes were those of a man who noticed everything around him, and his perfectly coiffed silver hair matched his confident posture. He was standing next to a young Black woman also dressed in an immaculate suit. Her natural curls were pulled back into a sleek and tidy bun that made her look disciplined and focused.

Liam simply nodded at them with a smile.

"Anyway," he continued. "I wanted to thank you all for the honor of awarding me the position of Special Agent in Charge. I'll try everything in my power to earn the trust you've placed in me. I hope I won't let you down."

The crowd clapped again. Liam stared at them, hoping the heavy feeling of disappointment weighing him down over this position wasn't obvious. The added responsibility and strength it would take to lead Boston's units had given him sleepless nights. It felt more like a setback than a well-earned victory. The fallout from the Larsen affair had severely tarnished the FBI's reputation, reaching depths not seen since the days of the Boston Strangler. Time and again, Liam was tempted to turn his back on everything, but at his core, he was not one to abandon a sinking ship and leave those he cared for to drown.

None of the circumstances Liam was in were reasons for celebrations, especially not when *she* was still out there. He complied with her demands because, at the moment, he had no other options. Exposing Larsen as Leah's accomplice in a string of murders would have unleashed a maelstrom of unprecedented magnitude, posing a grave threat to the FBI's reputation for generations to come. That could lead to a loss of funding, the erosion of the Bureau's recruitment efforts, and a wave of resignations. To make matters worse, the loss of Tony had taken an immense toll on him as well.

Liam pursed his lips, wondering if he should mention Tony now, but there had already been five memorial services in his honor. Two here at headquarters, one at the funeral, and two more by his family in the park for the public and press. If it were up to Liam, he'd talk about Tony all day, but the people in front of him needed to start healing—and to get back to work.

"You're here with us, Tony," Liam mumbled, then cleared his throat loudly. "Well, thanks again, everybody, for this amazing welcome-back party. But if you think I'm gonna tell you to take the morning off to eat cake and shoot the shit in my honor, you're wrong."

A loud wave of collective sighs and murmurs washed over Liam, who quickly lifted his hands in the air.

"Just kidding. Go eat cake, and whoever brought those bottles of champagne, wait for McCourt to leave before opening them."

The mood in the room flipped. The crowd clapped and yelled their approval.

Liam made his way through the chattering crowd toward Larsen's office, which was now his. McCourt and the woman he came with joined him. Liam's attention was on McCourt, but his focus occasionally drifted to faces in the crowd, who were wishing him well.

Liam, McCourt, and the woman entered the sanctuary of his office, and Liam closed the door behind them. The animated conversations of the party became subdued mumbles.

McCourt reached for Liam's hand and squeezed it. "Congrats again. You deserve this position."

Liam nodded respectfully, then turned his attention to the woman, who also reached for his hand.

"Agent Valery Rose," she said with a smile, revealing perfect white teeth that complemented her confident, amber-colored eyes. "People call me Rose."

"Nice to meet you, Agent Rose, and welcome to BAU. We need all the help we can get right now."

McCourt grinned, showing his own coffee-stained teeth. "I see you put one and one together."

Liam did. The only question was why he hadn't been involved in hiring Rose. He'd been kept informed about Cowboy and any other departmental changes.

"Smart and drama-free," McCourt concluded at Liam's silence. "And I like drama-free. That's exactly what the Bureau needs right now, thanks to the mess that piece of shit Larsen left behind. Between the two of us, I'm glad you took him out."

Agent Rose pursed her lips, clearly disapproving.

The brief, awkward silence was disturbed by a synchronized buzzing of McCourt's and Liam's cell phones.

"What shit hit the fan now?" McCourt grumbled, fishing his phone from his pocket. Liam approached his desk, setting his bag down and pulling out his own phone.

"Good God!" McCourt exclaimed, his eyes widening as they remained glued to his phone's screen. A blend of shock and anger colored his expression as he tapped the screen, initiating the playback of a video.

"A city in shock," a female news reporter's voice rang out from his phone, her tone filled with urgency. "Ladies and gentlemen at home, we have live footage here from the Newcastle courthouse. It appears that Harvey Grand, the man responsible for poisoning Newcastle's well water, has been released from jail."

"What?" Agent Rose gasped, squeezing beside McCourt. Liam hurried over as well. They all watched the live footage of the reporter wrestling for a spot close to the large double entrance doors.

"We don't know much yet, only that there seems to have been a request of dismissal based on a technicality error that Grand's defense submitted late last night to the judge, demanding immediate release."

"Damn it!" McCourt charged out of the office and into the room filled with cheerful chatter. "The party's over!" he declared, his voice booming.

The atmosphere shifted dramatically, and a wave of confusion followed McCourt as he made his way to the wall-mounted TV. Liam and Agent Rose observed from the doorway of his office as the TV flickered on, revealing the tumultuous scene on the courthouse steps where protestors clashed with police officers.

Grand released without bail! the bold caption announced above the distressing footage. The room buzzed with murmurs as disbelief and anger filled the air.

"How is this possible?" Rose shook her head. "He killed fifty-five people!"

Leaning against the doorframe, his eyes narrowed and gaze distant, Liam retreated into his mind, which was haunted by Leah Nachtnebel.

Day and night, he replayed every encounter he'd ever had with her. It consumed him, regardless of where he was or what he was doing. The way she'd made him feel when he'd first heard her play. Her green eyes gazing at him as she'd asked about his childhood. Her firm hands applying pressure to his stab wound, saving his life. And the cold, detached manner in which she'd killed Larsen without so much as a blink.

A killer of killers.

The drop of red blood on a white canvas for the whole world to see.

Her voice echoed through his mind. Was she the monster or just the villain who killed them?

Even from wherever she was, Leah was still controlling him like a puppet master its toy. Was she the evil hero whom a fractured and unjust world needed?

Anna was alive because of her, and so was he, and most likely countless other people.

"We are a family of faith," Mr. Lee, the father of Ami Lee—one of Harris's victims—had said. "We get no pleasure from hate."

"I hope it was slow and painful," Mrs. Lee had said. "May God bless whoever granted me this little bit of closure."

Two completely opposite views. Neither wrong...

"If we don't see to his justice, God will." Agent Rose's voice pulled Liam back from his thoughts.

"Well, let's hope God kills him for us," Heather said bluntly, appearing from the muttering crowd glued to the spectacle on the TV.

Agent Rose kept her eyes on the screen, then pushed off the wall. "Excuse me," she said, joining McCourt.

"Uh-oh," Heather said, her gaze fixed on Agent Rose. "Please don't tell me they hired the fun police."

"Be nice." Liam grinned at her.

"Mm-hmm." She crossed her arms. "So what you gonna do about this?" Heather nodded toward the TV.

As he combed through the layers of horrific memories and intense emotions of the past few months, a sudden clarity took hold of Liam. It was as if he finally knew the answer to the question that had plagued him.

The room fell eerily silent as footage showed Mr. Grand descending the courthouse stairs with a frenzied mob clamoring around him. He was shielded by a group of police officers acting as his personal bodyguards.

Abruptly Mr. Grand halted in front of the small army of journalists, leaned over the microphones, and flashed a wide grin that exposed his yellowed teeth. "I want to say to the families of the victims...justice was served. And if any publishers or TV producers are interested in my story, they can contact my lawyer to place their bids."

As the room erupted in angry mumbles, Liam felt a strange sensation of peace. As if things would be all right from here on. Not because of the justice system but because of *her*.

"Not a monster but the dark hero who kills them," he mumbled to himself as he grabbed his coat from his office chair.

"What was that?" Heather asked as he passed her.

"Nothing."

"Where are you going?" she shouted after him, but Liam ignored her and pushed through the crowd and into the hallway.

He had to see her.
His villain.
His nightmare.
His salvation.
His doom.
His promise of a new beginning or worthy end.

EPILOGUE

Emanuel and I sat down for breakfast, the morning sun casting a warm, golden glow across the room as Ida bustled around in the kitchen. Savoring a cup of freshly brewed sencha tea, imported from Japan, I lost myself in a classical music magazine. Suddenly Emanuel looked up at me, his gaze intense.

"What is it?" I asked.

He looked down at his coffee like a child about to confess to some mischief. "A few months back, some FBI agent visited me on campus," he began, his voice steady but soft. "He accused you of some terrible things."

I nodded. "I see." I briefly hesitated. "Would you...like to know if any of it is true?"

Determined, he shook his head. "I honestly don't care about your secrets. I know you would never hurt me. And that's all I care about."

His words caught me off guard. For once in my life, I was speechless.

I offered him a reassuring smile. "I was wondering," I said, taking a sip of my tea, "if you'd like to travel through Europe with me this summer."

The question hung in the air as the sunlight continued to pour in, casting a warm glow on the tranquil scene before us.

Emanuel's face brightened. "Is that a trick question? Of course!"

"It's decided then," I said. "Do you want me to drop you off at the library downtown?" The new Beamer I had purchased for him had broken down last night at the side of the road.

"Nah. Traffic is awful. I'll take the subway."

I nodded and returned my attention to the magazine in my hands.

Emanuel stood at the bustling subway station, waiting for the train to arrive. The station was a lively mix of people of all ages and from various walks of life, swiftly making their way to their destinations. The hum of conversations and the rhythmic tapping of footsteps on the platform filled the air. Somewhere in the distance, a baby cried.

Emanuel was scrolling through the news on his phone when a very tall and muscular man with a hood pulled low over his forehead approached him. The stranger wore sunglasses and a disposable face mask, blending in with the many other passengers on the platform.

The mysterious figure stopped in front of him and held up a piece of paper. Emanuel cocked a curious brow at the stranger.

"Sorry, dude, I think you've mistaken me for someone else."

But the man grabbed Emanuel's hand and placed the paper into it.

"What the hell is this?" Emanuel asked, his brow furrowed in confusion.

The man stared at Emanuel for a moment, then leaned in to whisper into his ear: "It's your message from beyond." His low voice churned like gravel. "Lēros."

Before Emanuel could react, the man pushed him in front of the oncoming train.

The train's screeching brakes and blaring horn drowned out the hysterical screams around him. In the chaos, an unbearably sharp pain shot through Emanuel—a sign of the worst to come. The world around him seemed to blur and waver in his agony, and in that dream-like state, Leah's voice suddenly reached him.

"Lēros," it seemed to whisper, a trick of his mind as he neared death. "Lēros, my love."

As darkness enveloped him, the echo of her voice became his final grasp at life.

WE KILL KILLERS

PROLOGUE

The winter wind lashed mercilessly against the young boy's face, cutting through his skin like a blade. As his teeth clattered uncontrollably, a deep, desperate wish took root within his broken heart: that both his parents were dead.

Clad only in a dirty T-shirt and underwear, he stood on the slippery stairs of the backyard porch. His bare feet had turned an alarming shade of blue, while his ears throbbed from the cold.

"Put the knife down, you bitch!" his father's raging voice echoed from the house in Slovenian.

"I'll kill you!" his mother screamed, a threat made so often that its familiarity was chilling.

Even at his tender age, the boy couldn't understand why such broken people would choose to have children. Their pitiful lives were a series of devastating choices, each worse than the last, including that of having kids.

The jarring slam of the porch's storm door was quickly followed by the violent shatter of glass somewhere inside the house. In an instinctive reaction, Mojca pressed his eyes shut. Footsteps approached from behind, igniting a paralyzing fear within him. Escape seemed impossible, as if he was caught between his violent father and intimidating mother.

"Mojca, it's me," whispered the familiar voice of his older brother Anton, who nudged Mojca's eyes open. Standing before him, Anton gently guided Mojca's slender arms through the sleeves of a worn coat.

In a kinder world, Anton, hovering between youth and adulthood, would be somewhere else. Maybe on a date at the mall or secretly puffing his first cigarette behind a corner store with friends.

But this wasn't a kinder world. Not for them, anyway. So, Anton was here, by Mojca's side, as he had always been.

His brother's comforting smile warmed Mojca even more than the snug fit of the dirty boots and pants that Anton quickly dressed him in.

"Let's go ride on the train, okay?"

Anton's voice was so calm, one would never suspect that their parents had been dangerously close to murdering each other just moments before. But Mojca played along, faking a soft, sad smile.

Hand in hand, they navigated the grim streets of 1980s South Bronx, making their way to the 167th Street train station—the epicenter of American ruin.

They passed the homeless, cocooned in makeshift beds. Rusted bodegas, buzzing liquor stores, and shady pawn shops lined the gloomy streets. Not even the biting winter winds could cover the nauseating stench of urine and shit. A group of men loomed at the side of a street—probably gangs selling crack to zombie-like creatures, their vigilant eyes darting, ever-watchful for the cops.

The train station was just around the corner, and the inside warmth felt like a friendly hug.

As they climbed over the ticket barrier, Mojca realized that Anton had forgotten his coat. Given how things had unfolded earlier at home, this wasn't exactly surprising.

Mojca cast a hesitant glance back in the direction of their house, worry and uncertainty evident on his face.

"I'll be fine. It's warm on the train," Anton assured him.

"But . . ." Mojca began, "your pills. What if—"

His words were cut off by the shouts of two drug addicts getting into a fight. Just a typical Saturday morning in the Bronx. Around here, every moment felt like a living hell.

"Come on, let's go." Anton tugged Mojca by the hand onto the cold train platform.

They had done this countless times before, but today felt different to Mojca. He couldn't quite explain it, but it felt like the darkness that had always lingered at the edges of his life was suddenly encroaching, ready to finally swallow him.

Determined, Mojca paused.

"What is it?" Anton asked.

Mojca couldn't quite find the words. Everything was the same as always, but today, the shadow of mortality felt more palpable, its cold breath on his neck like a warning from the afterlife.

"I . . . want to go home." Mojca's voice was firm.

Anton's forehead creased. "We can't."

Discouraged, Mojca dropped his gaze to the stained concrete floor of the station, its discarded gum and scuffs. Deep down, he knew his brother was right. They couldn't go back until one of their parents was arrested or left the house for a few days to go on a drinking spree. This pattern was all too familiar.

But in that moment, as crazy as it was, their home seemed like the better option to Mojca. Better than that horrific feeling in his gut, at least.

Anton gently tugged Mojca along the platform. "I'm cold, Mojca."

Glancing at the approaching train, Mojca wanted to protest again, but Anton's quivering, blue-tinged lips silenced him. For the first time, Mojca noticed Anton's swollen eye. It was almost half-shut. Clearly, his father had gotten a hold of him while he was fetching Mojca's clothes.

"Are you a brave warrior or a scared princess?" Anton asked, smiling as he fished out Mojca's necklace from beneath his shirt. He gently pulled it free, exposing a small stone ankh symbol on a worn leather chain—a gift from the Metropolitan Museum of Art during one of their free admission days for families in need. Fascinated, Mojca and Anton had spent hours at the Egyptian exhibition, lost in discussions about life and death, the gods living in the stars, and the powers that the Egyptians believed they wielded.

Anton nodded at the necklace. "What do I always tell you?"

"That there are many stars up there with special powers, and someday, one of them will shine down on us," Mojca recited.

"Yes, that's right." Anton tousled Mojca's hair just as the train roared into the station.

As they boarded side by side, Mojca tightened his grip around his brother's hand, realizing one stark truth: that without his brother, he was utterly alone.

Bover 1981

Leah

The early rays of the sun were still soft and weak, barely illuminating the thin layer of snow on the ground. I sat on the orange couch by the living room window, watching my parents in the driveway as they loaded more suitcases into the back of their station wagon. Their breath was visible in the chilly air, rising in soft puffs. My mother ignored me, not sparing a single glance in my direction. She usually did that when she sensed she'd done something wrong. Not that she felt guilty—I was sure her contempt for me would turn into relief the moment they pulled out of the driveway and I was out of sight. But deep down, they both knew that leaving their child alone for weeks wasn't something their friends would do. My father's expression made that clear.

My mother was in the passenger seat, filling letters into a magazine puzzle, when my father paused before sliding into the driver's seat. He caught my gaze. Shame was etched across his face. But all my mother had to do was clear her throat—loud and annoyed—and my father got in the car and drove off.

I never knew how long they'd be gone. If they went to our small ski cabin at Stowe, they'd be gone for about seven days. If it was a road trip south or west to warmer weather, it could be weeks. A good indicator was the amount of non-perishable food they left behind. A scan of the pantry this morning suggested this trip would be a very long one.

I stared at the empty driveway a moment longer, then turned and walked to the piano in the small dining room. It had belonged to my grandmother and was completely out of tune, but it was the only thing in the world that provided me with distraction.

I sat and sank my little fingers into the keys, striking them aggressively. Then I started Chopin's Étude Op. 10, No. 12 in C minor, also known as the Revolutionary Étude. I ran my hands forcefully up and down the length of the keys as if the loud, angry roars of the music were my only voice.

As always, time blurred when I played, and eventually, I found myself sitting in the rays of the afternoon sun. My hands throbbed with pain, and blood from my wounded fingers speckled the keys.

Calmly, I rose and walked into the kitchen to get some Band-Aids and a glass of water. I rarely felt hungry. The thought of perishing was almost a relief to me, but in the end, I always forced myself to eat.

I was halfway through my cheese sandwich when I heard the giggle of children outside. At first, the sound was joyful to my ears, the warmth of their laughter cutting through my endless emptiness like no music ever could. But as I approached the living room window, I knew the group of kids gathered on the street wasn't here for comfort—they were here for torment.

"There she is, the witch girl," one of the girls yelled before hurling a snowball against the window. It burst upon impact, scattering snow dust across the glass.

"Get her!" yelled one of the boys, launching another snowball.

The group of kids started a relentless attack, throwing more and more, laughing and screaming until the first rock hit the window. It struck with a sharp crack, leaving a hole in the glass and hitting my forehead.

The group instantly ran off, laughing and screaming.

My first concern wasn't the blood trickling down my face. Instead, it was the broken window. Would my mother feel anger? Would she feel rage? Or would she wish I were dead again? Was there even a difference among these three? Which emotion would make her hate me less? Distinguishing these feelings was incredibly difficult. I vividly recalled the day the psychiatrists diagnosed me with severe alexithymia. The condition blurred my ability to understand my emotions and those of others. That same day, my mother coldly confessed she wished I had never been born. The specialists credited my exceptional musical abilities to Savant syndrome, but my mother, indifferent to the arts, saw me as nothing more than a mistake—a burden placed in this world to torture her.

As I stood there, watching the kids bolt down the street as if they were being chased by the devil himself, I couldn't help but wonder if anyone else in the world felt this hollow emptiness deep inside.

ONE

Boston, Now

Under the silvery glow of the moon, the quiet graveyard was pierced by the distinct sound of metal meeting earth. Across the scene, the moonlight draped eerie shadows that danced and shifted with every movement. The men's methodical shoveling joined the restless sway of tree branches in the night wind. White beams of flashlights added an artificial touch. They illuminated the fresh mound of dirt and the tombstone inscribed with the words:

Emanuel Marin. Born 1998, Died 2023. Loved & Loving Son. He is now with his beloved mother.

The warm breaths of the three men formed misty clouds as they unearthed the coffin. Their shovels dug relentlessly into the soft earth, each scoop revealing the darker, damp soil below.

When the first shovel hit wood with a muted thud, all movement ceased. The three men locked eyes. The skinniest among them, looking to be in his late forties, quickly made the sign of the cross, murmuring something in Italian.

The bulky man of the trio shook his head, his voice dripping with a mix of mockery and a Boston-Italian accent. "Seriously? You kill without blinking, but this has you wetting your panties?"

"It's holy ground, alright?" the skinny man snapped back.

"Would you two shut up?" the tallest interjected as he knelt on top of the walnut coffin, clearing from it a thin layer of dirt. He pried open the top, revealing a face hardly recognizable anymore, its skin a patchwork of green and brown, dried out and sunken in places. The foul stench that emerged made all three turn their heads and gag.

"Father, forgive us. We're just doing our job," the skinny one muttered, his face twisted in disgust. He got a saw from a black duffle bag and passed it to the tall man, who was kneeling over the corpse again. Eyeing the situation, he nodded in approval as his eyes narrowed from the odor.

"I think I can cut out the heart without opening the rest of the coffin."

"Then do it," the shorter one urged. "If we can get that shit cremated soon, we can be done with this before dawn and never talk about it again."

WE KILL KILLERS | 191

TWO

Rome, Italy
Leah

The blue and red lights from the police escort cut through the dark streets of Rome like a cavalry launching its attack. My limousine was part of a caravan transporting Europe's most powerful politicians. Every street was barricaded, with countless pedestrians raising their phones to record this event of a lifetime. Traffic had been redirected, allowing us to sail through red lights as though we were a plane in the endless, free sky.

I glanced at one of the Italian military snipers atop a tall apartment building and wondered if my silhouette was in his sight as we thundered by.

Before long, we rounded the final corner and arrived at our destination: the mighty Colosseum.

Illuminated under a starry sky, it stood as a testament to the long-forgotten glory of the ancient world. On an ordinary day, the Colosseum stood as a breathtaking reminder of ancient glories. But today, it was poised to etch its greatness into history once again, having been transformed into an energetic concert arena.

As the caravan approached, a massive crowd cheered. Metal barriers held them back from the main entrance. Awaiting us was a lavish red carpet flanked by a battalion of cameras, their flashes as blinding as lightning. Circling above the arena, news helicopters were like vultures on the hunt.

For a moment, I was awestruck, marveling at the fact that the Italian prime minister had actually pulled this off. When Emanuel passed away, I canceled my Europe tour without explanation. The sudden cancellation of my only overseas concerts in a continent that loves classical music as much as Americans love the Super Bowl struck its people with profound disbelief. Especially at a time when Europe itself struggled to hold on to its dream of unity.

The French prime minister personally called me, offering me the chance to play at Versailles. The Greeks followed with the Epidaurus Amphitheatre, Spain with the *Sagrada Familia,* and the UK, much to the outcry of post-Brexit Europe, with Wembley.

I rejected them all and directed my assistant to send a message to the Italian prime minister: I might consider playing at the Colosseum—not just using its exterior as a backdrop like at other performances but utilizing its heart, resurrecting it from its grave of ancient glory.

Even I couldn't hide my surprise when, the next day, I received a photograph via email depicting an army of engineers walking the Colosseum. The subject line read: We have a deal.

It was a task of gigantic proportions.

But the outcome was a masterpiece: fifty thousand seats, a central stage that seemed to echo the battles of ancient gladiators, and front-row seating reserved for Europe's elite.

Staring at this wonder of time in front of me, I adjusted the silk scarf draped over my naked shoulder. My dress, tailored exclusively for this occasion, was crafted from the finest black chiffon. The back revealed my slender frame, devoid of undergarments. The sides featured a slit extending to my upper thighs, showcasing a delicate thigh chain made of gold and diamonds. At the back, a prominent bow with a long train added a touch of nobility. This garment was an intersection of ancient Roman style and modern sex appeal, conceived solely for this event and costing me a whopping $200,000, not counting the jewelry. It was an unspoken truth that today's spectacle demanded unparalleled grandeur. The Colosseum wouldn't settle for anything less. Europe wouldn't settle for anything less.

"Could you drop me off at the back entrance?" I asked my driver in rusty Italian.

The middle-aged man glanced apprehensively in the rearview mirror, his eyes darting out the window to the procession of Europe's caravan of politicians. Ultimately, he made the right choice and veered the car aside. "Of course . . . La Imperatrice."

I stood beneath the enormous stage, feeling the presence of ancient gladiators who had once prepared in these depths to face their fate above. The Hypogeum, the Colosseum's intricate subterranean maze of tunnels and chambers, had housed both gladiators and wild animals before their turn in the arena.

From above, thin beams of light seeped through the cracks of the temporary stage, piercing the darkness to cast an ethereal glow around me. It was as if I had stepped into an eternal underworld.

The orchestra had just concluded Beethoven's 9th, and the applause reverberated through the structure, causing the ground beneath my feet to vibrate.

I bent down, took a handful of dirt in my hand, and squeezed it. For a fleeting moment, I felt as if I could hear the distant screams of the souls once sacrificed here.

"You have outdone yourself, La Imperatrice." Luca Domizio's voice resonated from behind me. "What you've achieved here . . . it's a marvel that will etch itself into history, never to be forgotten or replicated."

When I turned, I saw him clad in a pristine, hand-tailored white tuxedo. His fingers brushed the cold walls where gladiators and slaves had once stood. He belonged to the class of men who aged with grace, radiating a powerful presence that silently cautioned others against challenging him. His hair was a mix of black and silver and neatly combed back, complementing his long nose and thin lips.

His wide eyes reflected awe. "To witness this . . . here . . . bravissimo, La Imperatrice. Truly, bravissimo."

My gaze shifted upward. Through the stage's gaps, I caught fleeting glimpses of the orchestra members departing. I always performed solo; the risk of another musician ruining the performance was too great.

"I'm not fond of that title," I remarked, my voice devoid of emotion.

"You've revived the era of Rome's great emperors," he countered in a respectful tone. "It's their way of celebrating you. No woman since Maria Callas, The Divine, has been given such an honor. Calling you 'The Empress' is a fitting tribute considering where we stand, don't you think?"

As I reflected on this, I realized that emperors were often ruthless murderers. "Perhaps," I conceded hesitantly.

He nodded.

"Do you have it?" I asked, letting the dirt slip from my grasp.

"Yes." From his pocket, Luca produced a golden locket. It looked grotesquely opulent, swathed in diamonds and gold, each detail screaming of lavish extravagance.

"You shouldn't have." I fixed my gaze on the locket as its diamonds shimmered in the ambient light filtering in from the stage above.

I reached out to grab it but hesitated inches away. How could I ever dare to touch him again after he had died because of my mistakes?

Still, I allowed my fingers to graze the gold surface. Emanuel's gentle smile flashed before my eyes.

Pulling back, I handed Luca a note with the details of the resting place of Emanuel's mother at a cemetery outside Rome. As a first-generation immigrant, she had expressed her wish to return to Italy during her final weeks so that she could pass away surrounded by her four sisters. Emanuel had always told me that someday he'd reunite with her. It was his heart-felt wish.

Now he would.

"Could you have the locket buried at this grave?" I asked.

Holding the locket in one hand and the note in the other, Luca studied me, a hint of curiosity in his eyes. When I offered no further explanation, he tucked both items into his pocket. "A sad love story? Is that what this is all about?" With a sweep of his arms, he encompassed the grandeur of the Colosseum. "I didn't know you had a romantic side." He smirked playfully.

"I'm afraid my answer would leave you disappointed then," I replied.

Guilt and regret over Emanuel's death haunted me. The events leading up to it, my own blunders, tormented my sleepless nights. Reliving every mistake that led to this, over and over, threatened my sanity.

But no . . .

Emanuel's death hadn't transformed me into the stereotypical grief-stricken victim. I hadn't suddenly found faith in the afterlife or God. But Emanuel believed in it. So, honoring his beliefs by reuniting him with his mother felt like the least I could do. After all, who was I to insist that my perception of the world was the only truth?

"Miss Nachtnebel." A young stage worker called for me.

I stepped into the dark corridor of the tunnel system.

She spotted me instantly, with a large crew of stagehands in tow. "It's time. We're ready when you are."

I acknowledged her with a nod and followed, leaving Luca behind.

We navigated through the ancient tunnels like famous gladiators, heading toward the massive stage entrance that had withstood the test of over two thousand years. With each step, spontaneous applause erupted from the concertgoers waiting for me in the hallways. Our group grew rapidly, coming to resemble the tail of a massive, applauding comet.

"Thirty seconds away," reported the stage worker into her headphones. Anxiety laced her voice.

As we neared the gate to the stage, the crowd around me grew rapidly into a large mass of people, their voices rising to manic shouts, their hands reaching out in a desperate attempt to grab at me.

"Bravissimo!"

"Bella!"

An older Italian woman, tears streaming down her face, managed to briefly grasp my arm. "La Imperatrice," she sobbed, as if our connection would bestow a blessing upon her like the touch of a saint.

Bodyguards swiftly aligned themselves into two protective lines flanking me, shielding me from the tidal surge of the frantic crowd.

"Twenty seconds," the woman ahead of me relayed into her headset as we approached the final tunnel to the stage. The tunnel's end radiated with a luminous light like a gateway to the beyond. "Three, two, one," she counted.

As we climbed the last set of stairs to the stage, all movement halted—except mine.

"Europe, your La Imperatrice has arrived!" a commentator announced ecstatically through the speakers of the mighty Colosseum.

In a breath, I transitioned from the shadowy passageways to the brilliantly illuminated stage of one of the seven wonders of the world. The gigantic arena erupted in an overwhelming cacophony, with tens of thousands leaping to their feet in an impassioned display of excitement.

The male commentator's voice resonated through the speakers: "The Colosseum lives again!"

For a moment, I stood there, taking it all in. Flowers started raining down on the stage, thousands of them, before I'd even touched a key.

Under the watchful eyes of its leaders, Europe had made a spectacle of this event, and the results were overwhelming. In the crowd were people dressed like ancient Romans, screaming and hollering as if this were a World Cup final. I wasn't a fan of such drama, yet I played my part.

With elegance and determination, I approached the applauding European delegates placed to the left of the stage, not far from my grand piano. I recognized them, all from the news and some from my concerts in Boston. Leaders from France, Germany, Italy, Spain, Portugal, Greece, the Netherlands, Norway, Belgium, Austria, Croatia, and Poland, a few kings and queens, the Pope, and the rest of Europe. They were all here for this classical version of the American Super Bowl.

Catching fleeting images of myself on the colossal screen strategically placed high above the temporary stages, I stopped before them and fluidly swirled the train of my dress. I dipped my head toward them—a gesture of respect but devoid of submission.

Then I turned to all four directions of the ecstatic crowd and expressed my gratitude with four similar nods.

The arena resounded with chants of "La Imperatrice," as though I had emerged victorious from months-long games of life and death in ancient Rome.

I paused for a moment, a fake smile on my lips, then gracefully made my way to my piano and took my seat behind it.

It was my first and only concert abroad. Europe's elite had spent ridiculous sums for their rare stage seats. But a glance at the politicians reminded me of the true message that this spectacle was conveying to the world. It wasn't solely in my honor. It was also intended to demonstrate that Europe, after years of struggles, stood united through one of the most magnificent events in its modern history.

And I was OK with that, as I, too, had come here with a hidden agenda. I had come to celebrate not Europe's light but its underworld.

For something priceless in return.

Liam

Rain blasted against my apartment window as if it were trying to break through. I sat on the couch, staring at the TV, my arm wrapped around Josie, who was absorbed in funny kitten videos on her tablet.

"What a concert!" the commentator announced euphorically.

On the screen, Leah was standing in the middle of the mighty Colosseum. Flowers were being thrown onto the stage as if it were raining there too.

"Angela, you've been quiet for some time now," the male announcer said.

"Yes, Bob . . . I'm just speechless, to be honest," answered Angela, the female commentator. "This was undoubtedly the most spectacular event I've ever had the honor of witnessing. To be here tonight and watch the Colosseum come to life like this . . . I'm fighting back tears."

"A feeling many probably share with you. They say that tickets sold out within a second of going live," Bob said.

I stared at the screen, my eyes fixed on Leah. She looked stunning in that black dress. Josie and I had caught only part of her performance after we'd returned from the mall, but it was the best I'd ever seen. Villain or not, this woman was truly one in a billion. Larsen was an asshole. He'd gotten what he deserved, but he sure as hell was right about that.

"Dad," Josie said, putting her tablet aside. "Can we watch the movie now?"

I was still glued to the TV, watching Leah accept roses from the Italian prime minister as the crowd cheered. Would Leah be able to make it to our meeting this weekend?

I pulled out the flip phone from my pocket.

"Earth to Dad!" Josie said.

"What, sweetheart?"

"You said we'd watch that new anime after the concert." She nodded at the TV.

I let out an exaggerated sigh and quickly texted Leah *MNY*, then put the phone on the table. "If you think," I said, turning to Josie and raising both hands, imitating claws with my spread fingers, "that I'd rather watch some big-eyed, neurotic cartoon characters with my daughter than one of the most important classical concerts of our time . . ." Josie started giggling the moment I tickled her side. ". . . then you are absolutely right!"

We both laughed as Josie wriggled under my attack like a worm on a hook.

Leah

My fingers flew over the aged piano keys in front of me as I played Liszt's "Grand Galop Chromatique," Cziffra's Version. It was known as one of the hardest pieces ever written if played at its intended speed.

The notes of Liszt's masterpiece echoed over the heads of Europe's political powerhouse and their fifty thousand guests as I delivered an immaculate performance of this extraordinary test of a pianist's capabilities. If every note was played correctly—which, due to the technical inability of the player, was the case less than 0.01 percent of the time—the piece would mimic the sound and rhythm of thundering hooves.

I entered the piece's intense finale at two minutes and forty seconds. My fingers turned into a hurricane, every single one of them tirelessly playing across the entire span of the keyboard, pushing the limits of my reach and control with precise strokes unmatched anywhere in the world. The treacherously wide stretches at a relentless pace required everything I had. I was renowned for being the only pianist in history—next to Liszt himself and Georges Cziffra—to play this piece in under three minutes and five seconds.

I played it in two minutes and fifty seconds.

Many years ago, MIT students employed a new software to detect the accuracy of musicians. They used it on the biggest names in music.

Nobody matched my speed and accuracy.

Nobody.

Their study catapulted me to the top of the classical music world overnight. A star was born. A machine in human form.

I was sweating as I finished this madness of a piano piece. I played it seldom and only at the end of my concerts. I hated the feeling of sweat dripping from my forehead onto the keys, creating a slippery mess and endangering my accuracy.

With a last stroke, my hands hammered the end of the piece. A second of silence passed. Another.

Then the crowd of fifty thousand erupted into chaos. The air vibrated with chants and thunderous applause. Their voices melded into a harmonious roar, chanting "La Imperatrice," hailing me as their divine empress.

Yet...

Amid this frenzy, I stood completely still, an island in a stormy sea. I listened and observed, feeling an overwhelming sense of emptiness, a profound solitude that contrasted starkly with the chaos around me. Despite being the epicenter of one of the biggest events in the history of the European Union, I felt utterly alone.

Leah

The Colosseum faded behind me, its ancient stones still echoing the applause and melodies of the evening. The balmy Roman air enveloped me, mingling the scent of traffic and an earthy aroma.

Ahead, a gleaming black limousine stood in stark contrast to the illuminated Roman ruins in the background.

"Miss Nachtnebel!" a young assistant to the Italian prime minister called out, rushing after me.

I continued walking, but she managed to catch up.

"Miss Nachtnebel," the pantsuit-clad woman huffed, catching her breath.

I stopped to face her.

"The prime ministers and their guests have another gathering now. I apologize for the confusion."

I was about to answer her when my flip phone buzzed in my pocket. *MYN?* read the message from Agent Richter.

It made sense; I was still in Rome, and we were scheduled to meet this weekend at our usual spot. The *Meet Yes No?* inquiry was justified.

Y, I quickly texted back, then slid the phone into my purse. Finally, I turned to the waiting assistant, my face emotionless. "Please convey my deepest apologies to the prime ministers and their special guests, but I have other commitments. Thank you."

"W-what?" the young woman stuttered, her face reflecting utter disbelief.

Earlier in the evening, I had dined with the prime ministers and entertained their guests, consisting primarily of Europe's most influential manufacturers. After the concert, there had been a champagne reception. The prospect of yet another event with the stifling entitlement of the ultra-rich was as daunting as my next commitment.

"I said cancel it," I asserted with calm authority and resumed walking.

A tall man in a black suit got out of the passenger seat of the limousine and opened the door for me.

Inside, in the back, Luca Domizio glanced at the stunned assistant. A hint of amusement played on his lips.

"Drive," I instructed as I got in. I didn't share Luca's joy. A scandal like this could ignite global backlash—maybe not enough to destroy me but certainly enough to be extremely bothersome.

The limousine journeyed for about thirty minutes before the urban sights of Rome transitioned to the tranquil Italian countryside at night, with its rolling hills and iconic cypress tree silhouettes.

We ascended a gravel path leading to a majestic Italian castle whose façade glowed under gentle golden lights. A rustic dinner setting awaited outside, tables graced with grapevines, candles, and sumptuous Italian spreads. The bright sound of laughter filled the air as children darted among the tables, occasionally earning reprimands from the adults. Meanwhile, discreetly stationed security personnel in sleek black suits surveyed the scene.

As the limousine stopped, a diverse group of Italian men and women ceased their conversations and looked straight at us. The men, radiating both anticipation and respect, began to approach the vehicle, keen to welcome us.

I cast a wary glance at a grand piano positioned beneath an olive tree and, more importantly, at the gathering of Europe's top mafia dons. Their presence in these modern times was a testament to the enduring corruption that existed within global political systems.

"What am I doing here, Luca?" Frustration tinged my voice.

"Bellissima, you know exactly why you're here," he replied, a cunning smile gracing his elegant features as a security guard opened our door.

We remained seated.

"You're indebting me to you," Luca continued, his grin broadening. "A debt far beyond providing you with a dead junkie's fingers for false fingerprints or stalking FBI agents for you. A debt so profound, only I could repay it. And whatever it will be, you'll collect on it someday, whether that's in weeks or years. Or am I wrong?"

A lock of silver hair cascaded onto his forehead, emphasizing his intense gaze. I stayed silent, shifting my attention to the approaching group of mafiosi.

Luca chuckled. "Oh, my La Imperatrice." He stepped out and extended his hand to assist me. "May the gods who created you be eternally blessed."

Accepting his gesture, I emerged from the car. "Or the underworld they reside in," I countered. I faked a smile as an elderly mafioso, his skin weathered with age but his eyes sharp, gently took my hand. With a respectful nod, he pressed his lips to the back of my hand, the gesture exuding an old-world charm.

"Makes no difference to me," Luca interjected, taking his place beside me. "I was never afraid of the dark."

THREE

Liam

I was standing at the end of a weathered wooden dock, the gray sky casting a depressing shadow over what should've been a sunny fall day.

The growl of a bike caught my attention. I turned to find a light-colored dirt bike, its rider encased in a red and black leather suit. The bike skidded to a halt at the end of the dock. For a moment, the person just sat there, staring at me from behind a dark helmet visor.

My hand instinctively moved to the gun in my chest holster. Then the rider pulled off the helmet to reveal herself: Leah, strands of hair tumbling out of her lazy bun. She clutched her helmet and rode the dirt bike at full throttle down the long dock, coming to an abrupt halt just a few feet from me. Damn, she knew how to handle those things.

She dismounted with a smooth grace and stepped beside me. I caught a glimpse of her deep green eyes. Then my gaze shifted back to the waves crashing against the dock's old foundation.

"I didn't think you'd make it," I said.

"Didn't you get my text?" she replied.

"I did."

A brief, awkward silence followed. These meetings were still so weird to me, especially out here, next to this rundown old factory sprawled across a shitload of acres north of Boston.

"That was quite a concert. Maybe one of the most spectacular things I've seen on TV."

"The Colosseum did most of the work," Leah countered.

"Won't you need to lay low after pulling off such a spectacle?" I asked.

She shook her head and stepped even closer, entering my personal space and catching me off guard with her proximity. Her perfume filled my senses: an elegant floral scent with notes of yasmin, white peach, bergamot, and cedarwood. "For a short while, maybe. But the sort of people who attend my concerts aren't the type to stalk me for TikTok videos or want to read about me in trashy magazines."

I nodded. Thinking about it, I realized that I could walk past any classical superstar on the street without recognizing them.

"Do you have the files?" she asked, her voice as calm as ever.

"Yes." I handed her the folder with the reports and pictures from Emanuel's crime scene at the train station. "The photos are quite—" I started, wanting to warn her of their graphic nature.

However, she was already looking at them with an emotionless expression as if she were checking the weather.

I cleared my throat, attempting to be sensitive. It was hard to know what she was thinking. "I'm sorry about what happened to him," I continued. "I . . . eh . . . left his case with the police. I thought it best not to draw attention or have people wonder why the FBI was involved. The police wrote it off as just another case of a homeless person pushing someone in front of a train."

"Good," she said as she turned and made her way to a weathered wooden bench close by. As she sat there, her piercing green eyes scanned the reports and pictures. I watched her in silence before cautiously taking a seat beside her. Everything about this felt odd, especially considering I was sitting next to a serial killer of serial killers. A whirlwind of questions raced through my mind as her expensive perfume enveloped my senses again.

Who was she really? And how did she end up this way?

Was a storm of emotions raging behind her composed exterior as she sifted through the gruesome pictures? Or did she really feel nothing at all?

My eyes fell on the picture in her hands: Emanuel, his head and left arm severed cleanly by the train.

Jesus.

"I'm . . . so sorry," I mumbled again.

She remained silent, then shifted slightly in her seat. "You mentioned a note?"

I nodded. "One of the reports mentioned it. It was clenched in his fist, but those idiots lost it."

Her lack of surprise told me she knew the messy procedures of law enforcement all too well. "Does the report mention what was written on it?"

"There's a picture of his hand with the note. That's how I found out about it. I think it said something like—"

"Leros," she cut in, pulling out the close-up of Emanuel's hand with the blood-soaked note. Her eyes narrowed, and for a fleeting moment, something dark flickered in them.

"Do you know what it means?" I asked.

"Yes. It means nonsense."

"Nonsense?"

"Yes."

I frowned as Leah's expression darkened even more.

"Were you able to get a picture of Patel's autopsy?" Her voice had shifted and was now slightly lower.

"Yes." I leaned forward to retrieve it from the back pocket of my pants and handed it to her. "Sorry. I just got it this morning from the closed files. Work has been crazy, and this new agent, Rose, it's like she's spying on me for McCourt. Every time I turn around, she's right there."

Leah barely glanced at the picture before suddenly rising and handing it back to me. "It's not him," she declared, then walked to the dock's railing, where she gazed at the enigmatic expanse of the ocean.

"It's not who, Leah?" I asked.

"Patel," she said. "Patel isn't the Train Track Killer."

I sprang to my feet and joined her, the picture still in my grasp. "What? What do you mean Patel isn't the Train Track Killer?"

It looked as though she was collecting her thoughts. "Patel's shoulder. It should have a bullet wound."

I frantically examined the photo of Patel's bluish body on the steel autopsy table. "But there *is* a bullet wound, right here on his chest, at his heart," I protested.

"I know. I put it there," Leah admitted, openly disclosing how she had killed Patel. "But I also shot the Train Track Killer in the shoulder the night he dropped Anna on the tracks."

The gravity of her words hit me like a punch, and I stumbled back a step. "But . . . there's no bullet wound on Patel's shoulder," I said, stating the obvious.

"Precisely," she confirmed.

I took in a deep, shaky breath. "Are you trying to tell me that the Train Track Killer—" I couldn't even finish the sentence.

"Is still alive," she finished for me, turning to look straight into my eyes.

It took a moment for me to steady the sudden whirl of dizziness that clouded my thoughts. But then it set in. All of it. "Fucking Christ, Leah!" I scoffed. "Do you even realize what that means?"

"I do. And it makes sense when you think about it. Patel's profile never matched that of a genius serial killer. He was a brainless, sadistic follower."

"Maybe Patel didn't match the profile of a Hannibal, but what about all the other evidence?" I countered. "Anna's DNA was found in his van, and her grandmother's blood was also found all over him, confirming him as her killer. Anna testified it was him who killed her grandmother. Are you saying he was innocent?"

"Far from it."

Thank God. The relief came before nausea could hit.

"Patel did kill her grandmother and was most likely there when Anna was kidnapped the first time. His vehicle was probably also used for that. But he wasn't the man I met in the woods that night. The missing bullet wound confirms it."

A moment of silence passed. "He was working for him," I finally said in a weak voice. "It does make more sense that way. Patel was a struggling psycho, yes, but a genius?"

"Not so much," Leah confirmed.

"Goddammit."

She bit her rosy lower lip, an unusual gesture for her. "I've suspected for weeks that I made a mistake," she said. "But now it's confirmed. The Train Track Killer has outsmarted us."

Frustrated, I ran my hand through my hair as my eyes stared into nothingness.

"My daughter!" I suddenly exclaimed. "If this son of a bitch is still alive, I have to get her into protective custody ASAP."

I frantically patted down my pockets, searching for my phone, only to remember it was back at the apartment—ensuring I couldn't be traced. As I turned to sprint off, Leah's grip on my arm halted me. I froze, my gaze dropping to her small hand, clad in a leather glove. Touch like this was a new thing for her. Us.

"That won't be necessary. He won't hurt her," she assured me in a low, soothing voice.

"We don't know that. He killed Emanuel."

"Emanuel was an adult. The Train Track Killer has never harmed children. Not once. He must see them as innocent, almost sacred, maybe a reflection of his own painful view of childhood."

I stared into her eyes, wrestling with her words. Gradually, the tension in my muscles eased, and the dread of losing my daughter diminished. I trusted Leah. Trusted her instincts. But I had to be sure.

"Anna was barely a woman, and he tried to kill her."

"Anna is nineteen," Leah countered.

"Exactly. Still a kid."

A faint smile flickered across her lips. "Many men would consider Anna in the prime of their lust-driven pursuits."

I frowned. "Well, those old bastards have some soul-searching to do."

Her smile briefly widened, then disappeared. Under my watchful gaze, she slowly removed her hand from my arm, staring at it as if questioning why she had let it linger there for so long.

"Regardless, your daughter is safe. Which is more than I can say for us. But then, if he wanted us dead, it would have happened already."

"So, you think he knows who we are and that we're on to him?"

"Most likely, yes."

"That makes no sense. Why leave us alive but kill Emanuel?"

Leah's gaze returned to the waves. "I . . . don't know."

It felt like an admission of failure.

We stood in silence, lost in thought, listening to the relentless crash of the waves.

"What do we know about him besides the fact that he's one of the smartest sons of bitches I've ever come across?" I asked. "And that he doesn't hurt children?"

"He's more than just smart." Her eyes darkened with intensity. "He's a genius. One in a billion. Probably highly successful and powerful, maybe even with a family of his own. He counted on me juggling too many chess pieces at once and starting to slip up. And he was right about that."

I caught the harsh self-criticism in her tone. "Leah, this isn't your fault."

"Of course it is," she shot back.

A pause lingered between us once more.

"Do we have any leads? Any clues we can pursue?" I asked, desperation seeping into my voice. "What about the symbol he leaves at the crime scenes?"

"The ankh."

"Isn't it the Egyptian symbol of life and death?"

She nodded. "I had a meeting scheduled with an Egyptologist in DC. I didn't follow through because I thought we had identified the killer with Patel's capture."

"We should follow up on that now. Do you want to meet with this expert, or should I?"

"I will. On my way back from Ocean City."

My expression darkened.

Ocean City. Fucking Harvey Grand.

"So, we're really doing this?" I asked hesitantly.

"Of course." The certainty in Leah's voice was astonishing. "Is he still in Ocean City at the Caribbean Dreams Inn?"

I took a deep breath and exhaled slowly, preparing myself for what lay ahead. "Yes," I finally said. "The inn is booked until the end of the week. He just got another advance from his publisher."

"The timing is perfect. People don't expect me back from Europe yet."

"Is there no other way?" I asked.

"Of course there is," she said, "but it all depends on what you're hoping for. We could accept the outcome of our broken justice system—a system where a man who killed dozens of people and was found with more evidence than Dahmer gets to whore around, gamble, and then write a book about it. But will we accept what happens next?"

"Which is?" I probed.

"I assume you know the difference between a sociopath and a psychopath?" she asked.

"There are many, but overall, a sociopath is an out-of-control savage while a psychopath is a calculated genius."

She nodded. "We both know what Harvey Grand is. A thirteen-year-old could have dumped his Googled poison mix into a public well. Harvey even used a credit card to purchase the supplies and didn't even bother to disguise himself. This man is a sociopath with the IQ of an average pig. To him, it's always been about attention, rage, and financial gain. Once one of those diminishes, he'll strike again, probably in the same manner, seeking the same result. We all know he'd end up in prison when that happened, but by then, more people would have paid the price for the unimaginable luck life has bestowed upon him."

I leaned over the old wooden railing, staring into the ocean.

"There were women and children among the victims," Leah added.

"There were," I confirmed, balling a fist. Leah was right. Families were mourning at their loved ones' graves while this monster was gambling and snorting coke in casinos across the country. "Let's get him," I said, my voice laced with determination. "But no Harris crime scene, you hear me? The image of Harris's face tied to that tree in the woods still haunts me at night."

Leah pushed off the railing beside me. "Don't waste your dreams on a piece of shit like Harris. They don't deserve to live on through us."

I met her gaze. "I mean it, Leah. We'll use drugs. It worked with Harris, really threw our investigation off. Grand has a long history of substance abuse. Nobody will question an overdose."

Her eyes narrowed briefly—was it disappointment at missing out on the thrill of torture? Or did my commanding tone unsettle her?

Eventually, she nodded. "Drugs," she conceded, then turned and walked over to her bike. "Do you know how to ride a dirt bike?" she asked, gracefully swinging a leg over one side.

I raised an eyebrow. "I grew up white and poor. What do you think?" Confidently, I approached her bike, examining it closely. "Looks like this bike was meant for someone much heavier. The suspension's too stiff for you. Must be hard to control." I pointed out the insufficient sag.

A wide grin spread across Leah's face, showing a mix of admiration and amusement. "Impressive, Agent Richter." She pulled a piece of paper from the bike's storage bag and handed it to me. "These are coordinates for alternative meeting locations. Memorize them and burn the paper. If you ever think you're being followed, don't return here. Text me a different meeting location using this map, and ride a bike through the woods to reach it. No calls."

I accepted the map as a mix of astonishment and worry crept in. She'd thought of everything. If Leah ever turned against me, how in the world would I outplay her?

"What about Anna?" I asked. "Is she safe from him as well?"

"He hasn't killed her yet, though that doesn't mean we're in the clear. As I said, she's not a child, and she was already on his list."

"I need to talk to her ASAP," I said.

"That won't change much. I've already spoken to her."

"To Anna?"

Leah nodded. "I wasn't sure he was still alive, but I warned her, nonetheless. I offered her a substantial sum and a fake passport from her country of choice, but she declined."

My head snapped back in surprise. "Why the hell would she do that?"

Leah shrugged. "Probably for the same reason most make foolish choices."

I raised an eyebrow. "Which is?"

"Matters of the heart, of course."

"You mean she met a guy?"

"Or a woman. This is the twenty-first century, Agent Richter," she teased with a smirk.

"Yeah, yeah. Man or woman, the foolish girl still needs protection."

"She made her choice. And explaining to law enforcement why you're protecting her could severely complicate things, especially if the FBI catches wind that the Train Track Killer is still out there."

"I'll figure something out. Blame it on a copycat or something."

Leah raised an eyebrow, doubt shadowing her features. "If he really wants her dead, the only way to ensure her safety is to eliminate him or send her away. Far enough for him not to bother with it. A simple patrol car outside Anna's place won't cut it."

I cursed under my breath, hating everything about this situation yet knowing Leah was right. "Then why not go public with it? Announce he's still alive. Put everything the FBI has behind this."

"I'd advise against that. Parts of the investigation would leak to the media, and we'd be openly at war with him. Not wise when you don't know who your enemy is or what motivates him."

I mulled over her words.

Leah watched me carefully, then put on her helmet. "At least wait until I've handled this other matter. Then do as you wish," she said, her voice wavering slightly. "And keep that gun with you at all times," she added, kicking down the kickstarter lever to revive the engine. "We're up against someone who might be cunning enough to take us both down. Just because it hasn't happened yet doesn't mean we're safe. I'll reach out after Grand is neutralized and I've met with the Egyptologist. Let me know if you find anything else."

I nodded, watching her ride off into the distance past the decaying factory complex and disappear down a narrow trail in the woods. I sighed as the weight of our reality sank in. The whole situation was utterly surreal.

The Train Track Killer was still out there, slipping through the FBI's grasp, outsmarting the most brilliant mind I'd ever known. My new reality rang with the clarity of a bell in a graveyard. I needed Leah more than ever. It wasn't just about Anna or the countless others in the crosshairs of the Train Track Killer; it was about me too. She had become my sole ally in a game in which I'd crossed the point of no return. But could I truly place my trust in someone who regarded the dismembered remains of her former lover with less engagement than someone scrolling through reels on Instagram?

But what other option did I have? Leah Nachtnebel wasn't a hero, but in an era when darkness brought order to justice, a villain of her caliber was exactly what the world needed. She was the most ingenious person I'd ever met. As things stood, she was our only hope in capturing one of the worst killers to walk the earth.

FOUR

Leah

The darkness provided my only solace as I stood in the moldy closet of a room at Caribbean Dreams Inn, a decrepit seaside motel in Ocean City. It was around 3:00 a.m., two torturous hours after Harvey Grand had stumbled back from the casino, completely wasted. My senses were assaulted as I witnessed this five-foot-five abomination fucking two drug-addicted prostitutes he'd brought along. Their inability to hide their contempt was evident, their moans of fake pleasure a pathetic attempt to continue. One of them was so high she fell asleep with his dick still in her mouth and inadvertently bit down on him. Enraged, the yellow-toothed piece of shit struck her and broke her nose. Blood streamed down as it hung grotesquely to the side. But she was so high that she barely seemed to notice the pain and passed out on the couch with a wide grin.

The other prostitute, a bony figure with bruises all over her limbs, remained silent, clutching her next hit as Harvey decided to take her doggy style. With a pitiful grunt, he dismounted. Then she, too, succumbed to the heroin, collapsing on the filthy couch with a vacant smile.

"Stupid whores almost used all the smack," he cursed, scavenging through the debris on the table—empty beer cans, used needles, crumpled chip bags, and loose bills. I watched in disgust as Harvey cooked the leftover heroin on a spoon over a candle, drew it into a needle, and shot it into his vein.

There was nothing genius about Harvey Grand. A man who'd lucked out with an aunt who had married into a wealthy family and was capable of affording lawyers who played the justice system like a child played with a toy.

I lingered for a few more moments, then cautiously edged the closet door open and stepped into the room. Cloaked in a black coverall and booties, I was a ghost, leaving no trace of my presence. My steps, silent and deliberate, carried me past the couch on which the two unconscious prostitutes were sleeping. The scene was a bleak testament to the wickedness I was about to end.

Approaching the grimy lounge chair, I stopped in front of Harvey. His head was tilted back, his wide-open mouth revealing uneven yellow teeth.

Shaking my head slowly, I acknowledged the simplicity of the task at hand. This oceanfront motel was the perfect setting for an "accidental" overdose. Harvey had been partying and sleeping with prostitutes for days, and the motel's ground-floor layout and bathroom window, facing the dark beach beyond, made it easy to enter and leave unnoticed. Nobody would question anything.

Suddenly Agent Richter's voice echoed in my mind: "No Harris crime scene."

I fixed my gaze on Harvey with a mix of disgust and resolution.

"Use drugs," Richter had advised.

A wry smile touched my lips as I delved into my coverall's pocket and withdrew two syringes—one filled with a clear liquid, the other filled with a caramel-hued substance.

I set the caramel syringe on the cluttered coffee table and administered the clear liquid into the median cubital vein in Harvey's arm, precisely where he'd injected his last hit of heroin. Swiftly, I withdrew the needle, securing it safely in my pocket with the cap reattached, ensuring I left no evidence behind.

The moment the Narcan—a medication negating the heroin's effects—coursed through Harvey's system, his eyes snapped open. He gasped for air as though he were rising from the grave.

"What the fuck?" he spluttered as his bloodshot and bewildered gaze locked onto me. The drug had cleared the opiate fog but left the alcohol haze untouched. "Who the fuck are you?" he slurred, confusion written all over his face.

I mustered a seductive smile and picked up the other syringe from the coffee table. "I'm Cindy, remember?" I gestured toward the two unconscious women on the couch. "Jenny called me. Said you were looking for more fun. Twenty for a blow, fifteen for a hit of smack." I waved the needle before him.

He wiped his mouth, which was a mess of saliva, and leaned in sluggishly. "Why you dressed like that?" he mumbled, reaching for the syringe I held just beyond his grasp.

"Got a cleaning gig later at the Sea Lion Motel," I cooed, my voice dipped in fake allure. "Lean back, let me take care of you. That makes fifteen plus twenty for the blow, yeah?"

His response was a grotesque grin. He smelled like semen and whiskey, yet I knelt between his legs, which were spread open in anticipation. "You've gotta try this." I leaned closer, whispering the lie with practiced ease. "Right here, I mean." I pointed at his neck. "In an artery. Hits you ten times harder, sends the gold straight to your head, arms, even your dick."

Harvey's grin widened, lulling in excitement. "Fuck yeah, bitch."

"Good boy," I whispered back, my gaze and steady hands fixed intently on the delicate skin of his neck near his collar bone.

What I didn't share with this sociopathic asshole was that I was aiming for his right common carotid artery, intending for my special mixture to bypass his heart to avoid dilution. Finding arteries was a challenge; unlike veins, they weren't visible, and despite my extensive, costly private education from physicians in the art of anatomy and medicine, my first attempt missed. Harvey flinched as I withdrew the long needle before swiftly repositioning and trying again. This time, I hit my mark. The needle's resistance against the strong flow of blood confirmed it. Bright red blood backfilled into my syringe, mingling with the caramel liquid. I pushed the plunger, injecting the mixture into Harvey's neck. Then I stepped back, watching him closely.

He reacted with a growl of pleasure, his body tensing in anticipation. "Fucking bitch, yeah," he groaned, gripping the armrests of the lounge chair. But his ecstasy quickly shifted to surprise. Then shock. Then horror.

"What the fuck is—" he choked out, his complexion turning a fiery red, his eyes bulging.

"Krokodil," I stated coolly, watching as he collapsed to his knees and clawed at his throat. "A little parting gift from the families of Newcastle. They didn't appreciate the poison you put into their water. And, frankly, neither did I. So the emphasis is on *parting*, I suppose."

Harvey's screams, initially choked, erupted while his red face conveyed pure terror. It was as if flames were engulfing his entire body—which, in a way, they were.

"I modified the recipe, adding more paint thinner and introducing hydrofluoric acid. That explains the platinum needle and special gloves," I said. "This mixture is extremely hazardous and will cause internal corrosion. I also mixed in a blood thinner to ensure my cocktail spreads quickly throughout your body, targeting as many areas as possible until it finally attacks your heart. How do you like it?"

Harvey's screams morphed into a ghastly wail as the drug began corroding his insides at his neck and face. Raw, exposed tissue emerged before my eyes as patches of skin and red flesh seemed to dissolve into the air, transforming him into a figure straight out of a zombie apocalypse.

"Heeeeeelp!" he shrieked, staggering to his feet. In a clumsy motion, he clutched at the nearest prostitute, the one with long blonde hair. She jolted awake to the nightmare of his melting visage and chest—a horrifying blend of red flesh and white bone laid bare.

The woman's frantic scream matched his in intensity as she scrambled away, pulling Harvey with her. He maintained his grasp on her hair as they fled past the large dresser, where I swiftly concealed myself, and out the door. Harvey stumbled along, dragged like a blind man by a service dog. He maintained his grip until he tumbled over the porch steps. The abrupt fall yanked a large strand of hair from the woman's head.

The screams drew a few curious onlookers to the courtyard. Their initial intrigue turned to terror as they witnessed the macabre scene unfolding before them.

Lurking in the shadows of the motel room, I observed as Harvey's last moments unfolded on the grimy concrete of the motel's walkway. A frantic crowd gathered around him. Their desperate cries for help filled the room.

I was about to make my way toward the bathroom window through which I'd slipped inside when I paused beside the prostitute with the gruesomely twisted nose. She had miraculously slept through the entire show. Overdose, or just a deep high?

Gently, with gloved hands, I checked her pulse. It was steady and slow. The situation with her nose wasn't as encouraging; it was jarringly sideways and covered with blood. Even if she made it to a hospital, without top-notch medical care, which I doubted she could afford, it would never look the same. An outstanding plastic surgeon could fix it later, but a woman like her wouldn't be on the client list for something like that.

Her only other option would be for someone knowledgeable to snap it back into place before the swelling began. That would need to happen immediately.

On impulse, I realigned her nose to its natural position.

I didn't stop there. Quickly, I pulled her underwear back up, then put the table's cash into her purse.

As the chaos outside escalated, I slipped through the bathroom window and onto the dark, deserted beach, where the night air—cool and salty—surrounded me. The rhythmic crash of waves and the moon's reflection on the water cast a tranquil spell. Shedding my coverall, I walked up to the edge of the high tide.

Why had I intervened on behalf of the prostitute? Why had her misfortune suddenly become my problem?

The wail of distant sirens intruded upon my thoughts, pulling my mind to Agent Richter. Had that act been for him? A bid to sprinkle a dash of humanity over my actions tonight, knowing this case would inevitably land on his desk?

Harvey's gruesome end replayed in my mind. Richter wouldn't approve, of course, yet part of me reveled in the justice of it all. If I was indeed softening, even if just for Richter's sake, it changed nothing about the aftermath. I wasn't a hero or a knight in shining armor. I was the darkness that hunted monsters, and a single act of kindness to a prostitute wouldn't elevate me from the depths.

That was fine by me.

At the end of the day, my feelings on the matter were ambivalent.

FIVE

Agent Vallery Rose

"Come on!" Agent Vallery Rose huffed loudly, gasping for breath as she landed another blow on the punch bag. This was followed by a forceful side kick. The large red bag, suspended from her basement ceiling, was the final challenge in her rigorous morning routine. For Rose, excellence was the only acceptable outcome in every aspect of her life.

"Come on, I said one more!" she urged herself, sweat flying from her ebony skin as her fists and feet moved with increasing ferocity. "I said," she grunted with each punishing kick as if chastising herself for even considering fatigue as an excuse to stop. "One." Another determined kick. "Mooooooore!" Her final kick sent her to her knees.

Pausing, she leaned forward, trying to catch her breath as she rested her hands on her thighs. A fleeting image of her brother smiling during a sunny day at the zoo crossed her mind before thankfully disappearing.

After a long shower, Rose dressed in her crisp suit pants and white shirt, her gun securely in its holster. Breakfast was the usual affair: organic eggs and gluten-free toast with a cucumber-spinach-apple smoothie, consumed in solitude at the kitchen table of her quaint three-bedroom single-family home in Roxbury. The only sounds were the ticking of the kitchen clock and the clink of dishes being placed in the sink.

As a college graduate with a good job, she could have moved to a suburb with farmers markets and bicycle lanes. But her childhood memories of a loving mother and brother anchored her to every corner here. It wasn't the safest of places, yet she stayed, devoting her free time to community projects and her garden.

After donning her blazer and smoothing down a strand of her bob, she attended to her Glock 19 Gen 5—a top-tier handgun reflecting the FBI's standards for excellence. Every morning and night, she checked the ammunition, locked the slide to the rear for a visual inspection of the chamber (clear), and then cycled the slide to ensure it moved freely. Satisfied with its functionality, she reassembled the gun and holstered it. With a final, contemplative look in the hallway mirror, she reminded herself in a quiet but determined voice, "We get to see what happens only if we don't give up."

With that, she stepped out, ready for the day.

She had barely left the home and made it past her beloved flowerbed with its blooming rose bushes when she saw a parking ticket on the windshield of her black SUV, which was parked in her driveway.

Muttering curses, she pulled it out and waited for—

"Rooooooose!"

The urgent call from an older neighbor across the street amplified her annoyance.

"Rooooooose!" called out the older white man who was limping across the quiet street. Rose tried to ignore him and get into her car. However, he caught up quickly and prevented her door from closing by wedging himself between her and the handle. The smell of cigarettes filled the car.

"You see this, Rose?" With visible frustration, he pointed at the parking ticket in her hand. "Another one, Rose. They gave me another one."

Leaning back in her seat, Rose muttered something inaudible. Then she spoke up. "Billy, please stop putting your parking tickets under my windshield wiper. How many times do I have to tell you this? I'm not a traffic cop. I work for the FBI."

Billy placed his hands on his hips, his demeanor turning defiant. "And that makes you blind to injustice?" he challenged.

Rose exhaled, offering him the ticket. "When it comes to parking violations, yes. Besides"—she raised an eyebrow at him—"I've warned you about parking in front of the hospital when you go to your appointments."

"It's a spot reserved for individuals with disabilities. I'm a disabled vet," Billy retorted.

"And I thank you for your service. But that spot is for ambulances," Rose clarified. "To save people's lives, you know. You're lucky they squeezed by and didn't tow you."

Billy mumbled a disgruntled reply before snatching the ticket with a sharp yank.

Rose shut her door and started the engine, but Billy knocked urgently on her window. She rolled it down, frowning. "Damn it, Billy, I'm going to be late."

"It's Kevin," he said, a hint of defensiveness in his voice as he presented a black backpack to her. "He didn't come home last night. That boy is nothing but trouble."

With another sigh, Rose accepted the backpack, realizing this would make her late for work. But unlike the parking ticket, this problem was of genuine importance. She knew exactly where to find Kevin, who had lately been spending too much time with the B street gang—a choice that had destroyed his good grades.

Rose drove to the local 24/7 corner store, directly in view of a group of young men sprawled on old couches in the adjacent empty lot. As she parked her car, her gaze briefly met that of Hassan, the shop owner, who nodded with concern toward the group. She understood the gesture wasn't out of fear but rather to indicate Kevin's whereabouts.

This part of the neighborhood, one of Boston's last remaining projects, was familiar territory for Rose. She had grown up here, and she was well aware that, despite the hardships, many in this community banded together. They wanted to protect their youth from a nation governed by the wealthy one percent who didn't give a shit about the demise of the other ninety-nine. The community was a mix of young and old from various ethnic backgrounds. However, they had one thing in common: the struggle to survive and pay the bills.

Backpack in hand, Rose got out of the car and made her way toward the group. Almost instantly, the men averted their eyes and mumbled inaudible curses. She knew nearly all of them—men and women from all sorts of backgrounds, but all too deep in the criminal justice system for a simple school diploma to make a difference. In Boston, gangs usually formed based on where they were located, differing even from one street to the next. In Rose's area, a few gangs were racially mixed, mirroring the neighborhood's diversity. This mixing was boosted by the fact that young folks of different backgrounds hung out together in school and local spots.

"Come on, Kevin. Let's go," Rose said firmly to a teen dressed in jeans and a hoodie. "I don't have time for this." She presented the backpack as if it were incriminating evidence in court.

Kevin ignored her, looking at his phone as if she weren't there.

"Dude, it's Nario's little sister," one of the guys muttered to Kevin before shifting his attention back to his phone. The others disengaged, quietly scrolling on their devices.

Rose furrowed her brow at Kevin. "At least have the decency to face me when I'm talking to you, Kevin. Otherwise, I won't let your ass stay with me the next time your grandparents kick you out."

Kevin finally turned, a hint of remorse on his face. "What you doing here, Rose?"

"Getting your ass to school on time."

He shrugged in defiance. "Why bother? My school is a joke. Up in Beacon Hill, their kids get salad bars and MacBooks. My piece of shit school is stuck with metal detectors and PFAS in the water fountains. I don't care about no diploma. There are other ways to make money."

Rose nodded. "Salad bars and PFAS, huh?" The hint of irony in her voice inspired a few grins among the group. "Other ways to make money. I see," Rose mumbled. "Well, if you want to throw your future away over a salad bar and quick cash, then by all means, go ahead. Just do me a favor and don't walk around acting like it's big news that rich people don't give a shit about us small people."

She stepped closer to the group, her presence commanding. "Because, Kevin, we already know that there isn't a salad bar or a MacBook waiting at school for you or anybody else around here. But nobody's going to fight your battles for you. You gotta do that on your own, like all the other kids in your class. Does that suck? Hell yeah, it does. But guess what? That quick cash you make right now won't be worth much when your ass sits in jail, will it? So stop the excuses and get in the car."

Kevin hesitated, scanning the group for support that didn't come.

"Go, man. School is important. We'll catch up later," Vito said.

Rose locked eyes with Vito. A higher-tier gang leader in the neighborhood, he had earned a lot of respect from the younger guys. He was in his late thirties and had outlived more than one gang shooting. The hardship of a life of violence was evident in every inch of him.

Finally, with an eye roll and a series of handshakes, Kevin took the backpack from Rose and headed toward her car. Rose felt a fleeting sense of relief, as she was aware this could have gone differently. She nodded to the boys and returned to her car.

"You know he's right," Vito called out to her as soon as Kevin was inside the car.

"Of course he is," she shouted back, "but we get to see what happens only if we don't give up."

Sliding into the car beside Kevin, Rose sighed. She would be late for work—a fact that unsettled her. That nagging sixth sense in her gut warned her that today wasn't a day to be late. And her intuition was almost never wrong.

SIX

Liam

"And don't you fucking dare talk to the media! None of you. Everything goes through me first," warned McCourt's voice through the phone. I leaned forward, resting my elbows on the desk, which was cluttered with papers. Heather, Cowboy, Martin, and a few other agents were packed into my cramped office. They stood before me, their expressions a mix of anticipation and shock.

"Understood. No one's speaking to the press," I said, giving Cowboy a stern look. "Not a word. I promise," I pressed, my gaze hardening.

Cowboy, trying to play innocent, mouthed a *what* as he raised his hands. Yet this same "innocent" man had blabbed for a low-budget documentary about the College Snatcher, posing in front of a cheesy black cloth backdrop like he was Charles Bronson reborn. McCourt had quietly suspended him for a week, making me play babysitter. Meanwhile, McCourt watched closely through Vallery Rose's scrutinizing eyes.

She entered the room, her forehead creased with concern. "What's going on?" she asked.

Heather put a finger to her lips, signaling for silence.

"Liam, I need that bastard taken care of quietly," McCourt barked, his voice echoing across the room. "No drama. No hiccups. Like a beautiful Sunday stroll with Granny through Boston Common."

"Yes, sir," I responded.

McCourt ended the call without another word.

"Can someone catch me up?" Rose asked as the others began to grumble to one another.

"Harvey Grand. Remember him?" Cowboy asked.

"The well water poisoner?" Rose asked.

Cowboy's grin widened. "He overdosed in Ocean City, partying with drugs and whores."

I watched Rose closely, gauging her reaction.

"Holy shit," she said, hands landing on her hips.

"Nothing 'holy' about it," Heather chimed in. "We've been told his body is in a pretty rough state."

"From the drugs?" Rose asked.

Heather shrugged.

"We're still putting the pieces together," I said, rising. "They confirmed his identity after matching his prints with those we have on file from his time in jail. McCourt wants us to head there immediately on a military plane, retrieve the casket, and deliver it to his aunt somewhere near Boston. The exact location's still undisclosed."

"Why the hell would we do all that with taxpayer money?" Heather asked.

I pinched my lips. I'd wrestled with that exact question the moment McCourt had given me the instructions to retrieve Harvey Grand from Ocean City.

It almost pained me to admit this—almost—but the thought of Harvey being dead gave me an unsettling feeling of peace. He couldn't harm anyone else ever again.

"Harvey Grand was never convicted of any crime," I explained. "His family is fully aware of the accusations against him and expressed concerns about the safety of his remains if they were transported back without protection and under public scrutiny. They've provided evidence of threats to their personal safety."

"So, in short," Cowboy interjected, "the bastard's aunt was a Marilyn Monroe lookalike in her prime and married into one of the wealthiest, most powerful families on the East Coast. Now they're stealing government resources to quietly bring back the body as if nothing ever happened, all because they've lined the pockets of half of DC with campaign donations."

I frowned. Cowboy's crude summary was spot on, but my focus was on minimizing office drama. McCourt was more volatile than ever. His ambitions to become the next FBI director had found new life amid the dissatisfaction in DC with the current director, Helen Finch. Since then, he'd doubled down, staying mostly at the office in DC and weaving a network of informants throughout the FBI to report directly to him. Agent Vallery Rose was his eyes and ears in Boston.

"Thanks, Cowboy," I said, my tone heavy with fatigue. "Why don't you coordinate with Hanscom Air Force Base for our transport? They're briefed and ready to fly us out to Ocean City to collect the body. If everything goes smoothly, we'll be back before our shift ends."

Cowboy snapped a quick military salute and made his exit. I wasn't thrilled about bringing him along, but he wasn't the sharpest tool in the shed, which could be an asset given my arrangement with Leah.

"Heather, Rose, you're coming with me," I continued. "The rest of you, back to work. We've got full support from the military and the local Maryland police, so there's no need to turn this into a spectacle."

"What about the Bay Reaper?" Heather asked. "I was supposed to meet with the Cape Cod police this afternoon to interview a potential suspect."

Damn. I had completely spaced on that. Some lunatic in a skull mask was out there stabbing people along the bay, earning himself the media nickname Bay Reaper. Thankfully, there were no fatalities, but he needed to be stopped. Now.

"Take Martin with you," I directed. "I'll manage with Rose and Cowboy."

Heather and Martin nodded and departed with the rest, leaving me with Rose.

Her gaze lingered on me, probing. "So, we're really doing this? Getting Grand for his rich aunt?" she asked.

"I'm afraid we don't have much of a choice."

"It'll look like we're guarding his remains. The remains of a mass murderer."

"We're safeguarding the public around those remains," I countered. "Harvey Grand made plenty of enemies. If someone attempted to attack his coffin, it could endanger others."

Rose folded her arms, her stance firm. "Everyone here sees this for what it is—a powerful family abusing their influence."

"Maybe," I conceded. "But McCourt's orders were loud and clear, literally, and we'll follow them. This operation stays as quiet as possible. And if, by some chance, someone does target the coffin, we'll be there to handle it. Public safety is our top concern."

Her stance seemed to soften slightly, though I was taken aback by the fact that she'd questioned McCourt's orders, especially given her role as his informant.

As I began tidying the papers on my desk, I noticed Rose hadn't left. Her gaze was fixed on me, expectant. "Is there anything else?" I asked.

Rose pinched her lips. "I . . . overheard an agent coordinating a patrol car for Anna Smith when I walked in."

Shit.

"Yes?" I prodded, feigning ignorance. Until now, nobody had questioned it.

"Well, the Train Track Killer is dead, so . . . why?"

I shuffled the papers into a manila folder, deliberately avoiding eye contact to downplay the situation. "A threat was made to her life. Probably just some teenager messing with us, but better safe than sorry." I looked up just as Rose was about to speak again. "Where were you this morning?" I asked.

Immediately, I regretted it. No one here needed micromanaging except maybe Cowboy. Typically, I didn't question comings and goings; my agents had their reasons. But whatever Agent Rose was chasing with the whole Anna thing needed to stop.

Her expression shifted from inquisitive to embarrassed. "I . . . was dealing with something personal."

"Next time, please call. I need to know where my agents are during duty hours."

"Yes, sir. It won't happen again. I promise."

"Thank you." Rose turned and exited.

As I watched her leave, my thoughts raced. How had Larsen managed this dance with Leah without getting caught? Most of the details of this new collaboration with Leah remained shrouded in mystery.

Harvey Grand's downfall ensured the world was now a safer place, and the fact that Leah had gotten out safely was equally comforting. But the stress of our secret operations weighed heavily. A cunning agent might start connecting dots, and Vallery Rose could very well be that agent.

Cowboy's presence at the door caught my attention. "That's not how you make friends, you know." He jerked his thumb over his shoulder in the direction of Agent Rose.

"This isn't high school. We're not here to make friends. We're here to stop psychopaths and sociopaths."

"Wait, is there a difference between the two?"

I sighed. "Cowboy, whatever you're here for, can it wait? Because today is quite—"

"You need to hear this!" he interrupted, full of joyful energy. The way he stomped in was annoying as hell. I leaned back in my seat and watched as he sat across from me. Silence fell as he grinned, barely able to hold back.

I shrugged. "Soooooooo, you gonna spill the big news or what?"

"You'll never guess."

"You're right about that, so just say it now, and I mean right this second." My patience had run thin.

"Alright, alright," Cowboy said. "I just got a phone call that blew my mind."

I straightened in my seat, as would anyone who was hiding a second identity as a killer of killers. Had Leah gotten caught?

"We all got played," he said, grinning. "Right here in Boston, under our noses, lives one of the worst serial killers of all time."

Every inch of my body tensed. Would Cowboy bring us down?

"The Boston Strangler..." he finally said.

I sank into my chair, relieved. Then his words hit. "The fucking what?" I countered.

"The Boston Strangler," he repeated. "Never heard of him?"

"Do you think I grew up under a rock? I'm from Boston. Of course I've heard of him," I said. "His case involved a series of murders of women in the Boston area between 1962 and 1964. The victims were mostly older women who were raped and strangled. Albert DeSalvo confessed to the murders while in custody for other crimes, but no evidence conclusively linked him to any victims until a DNA test in 2013 connected him to the death of Mary Sullivan. Yet quite a few people believe there might have been a second Strangler because DeSalvo's stories don't add up for all the victims."

Cowboy nodded enthusiastically. "Yup. I'm one of those many believers. And not only did that second Strangler get away, but he actually still lives here in town." He leaned over my desk. "Right under our noses. Like some twisted fairy-tale ending for a sick fuck. Who knows? He might kill again, for all we know."

I sighed. "The Boston Strangler, part two."

"Mm-hmm."

"And somebody called you, huh?" I asked.

He nodded. "A tip."

"A tip," I repeated.

He nodded again, his eyes filled with sparks.

"Cowboy..." I sighed loudly. "Even if there were a second killer, the Boston Strangler killed in the early sixties."

"So?"

"So..." I sighed again. "Let's just say, for the sake of argument, that whoever murdered those women was in their twenties back then. How old do you think that person would be now?"

The wheels turned in his head. I watched his excitement slowly turn to disappointment. "Old?" he asked, like a school kid guessing the answer to a teacher's question.

"Very, very, very old," I said. "Too old to kill anyone. Most likely even dead. Sorry, buddy. Is there anything else I can help you with?"

Cowboy frowned and stood. "Too bad. I grew up watching documentaries about him. The guy is a legend in all the worst ways. I really hoped he'd get caught."

I sympathized with Cowboy. This work could be draining. "We have to focus on those we actually catch," I said, also rising. "And you're doing an amazing job making that happen. I'm glad to have you on the team."

His eyes lit up with pride, and he smiled, about to leave.

"The Strangler..." I tossed out.

"What about him?"

"Just out of curiosity, what did the tip say?"

"Oh, yeah. Some woman called and said her dad talks in his sleep about strangling women. Maybe he's old enough to actually be the guy?"

I shook my head. "He'd most likely be over one hundred years old. Even so, it's a stretch to assume an old man's nightmares make him the Boston Strangler two-point-oh."

Cowboy listened carefully.

"Let's keep this between us," I said. "We have enough to worry about. I don't want any fake news causing panic and distracting us from our current mission. The media would be all over us."

"You can count on me."

"Thanks."

As Cowboy left, I sank back into my chair. Of course, I'd follow up on this lead. It could be nothing, or it could be everything. Most cold cases are solved by tips like this, no matter how many years later it happens.

So, was this how it worked? Leah needed me as much as I needed her. I'd offer most of the leads; she'd take care of them like a dark knight.

If any of this information about the Boston Strangler was even remotely true, the only choice we'd have wouldn't be a warm and fuzzy one. But I could live with that.

SEVEN

I watched closely in Doctor Silver's high-end wound care clinic by the Boston harbor as he amputated a severely infected toe. "It's crucial to remove all the dead tissue to prevent the infection from spreading and compromising the healthy areas," he explained, dropping the severed toe into a metal tray. It landed with a clinical clink.

As he prepared for the next incision, Doctor Silver offered me the scalpel. Calmly, I took it in my gloved hands and followed his instructions precisely to remove the next toe.

"Remarkable work," he said after a moment, admiration evident in his tone. "None of my students have ever demonstrated such precision."

After the procedure was done and the patient gone, I handed him a yellow envelope filled with cash and promised to return the following Monday.

The typical Boston weekend buzz of people danced around me as I walked down the street near the harbor. Then, out of nowhere, the sound of a police patrol cut through the vibrant atmosphere. The officer had pulled over a minivan.

What appeared routine escalated in seconds. From the open window, a shot rang out at the officer before the van accelerated through a red light and plowed into a crowd crossing the street. It mowed them down like a bowling ball sweeping through a set of pins. The van's violent journey ended in a construction zone, where it crashed into a large excavator. The surrounding screams were chilling.

I bolted over to the van and found the driver, who reeked of alcohol, clutching his neck. Blood spurted around a large shard of glass embedded in his flesh. The passenger, an older woman, was dead, her head crushed by an excavator's shovel, which had broken through the windshield. In the back seat, a little girl cried for her parents, oblivious to the real tragedy around her. Her mother was right next to her, unconscious.

"Mimi," the girl whimpered, calling for her grandmother, apparently not knowing the woman was gone. "Daddy and Mommy don't answer!"

My gaze shifted to the man in the front. I briefly swept over the street, taking in the chaos and victims, before returning to him. He was the villain in this tragedy: a man led astray by booze and selfishness, willing to risk everything to avoid the consequences of his actions, even if it meant killing his own child.

"I'm not going back to prison," he gasped, blood bubbling from beneath his hands as they clutched his wound.

I glanced at the unconscious woman in the backseat, wondering why she had stayed with this man despite the threat he posed to her and their child. Had childhood trauma locked her in a cycle of misery, causing her to risk a bleak future for her and her daughter with a man who didn't deserve their love or loyalty?

"I'm not going back to prison," he repeated, gasping through the blood. Even now, he cared only about himself. It was pathetic and disgusting . . . not worth another moment of my time or anyone else's.

"I'm not going back to—"

"You won't," I interrupted, harshly.

"Ma'am, step away from the car! This man is dangerous," a police officer yelled in my direction.

Quickly, I surveyed my surroundings, noting the ring of officers encircling the vehicle, guns aimed at us from a safe distance. Then I redirected my attention to the bleeding man. "Close your eyes," I instructed the little girl.

"I'm scared."

"Don't be," I said. "Darkness is your friend in dark times like these."

Finally, she complied, sobbing softly.

Without a second to waste, I pressed both hands on the glass shard, driving it deeper into the man's neck. He grabbed my wrists the moment he realized I was there not to save him but to ensure his end.

"Don't fight . . ." I whispered into his ear while pressing the glass deeper, cutting myself in the process. "Let them go."

After a few more twitches, he was motionless, his eyes wide with terror, staring right at me.

The police were at my side moments later. "Ma'am, step back!" they shouted.

"He's dead," I told them.

Their attention quickly turned to the surviving mother and daughter.

As I watched the police carry the mother and girl to safety, an overwhelming sense of justice and satisfaction filled me. It was a new yet profound feeling. I had removed a threat, a monster who posed a risk to others and would have continued to do so if not for my actions today.

As the EMTs rushed to aid the mother and daughter, I slipped away quietly, my part played.

The notion of cleansing the world of monsters felt infinitely more fulfilling than any applause I'd received as a pianist. The little girl and her mother might stand a chance in life again. Was that not justice?

Right then, this act of finality, this intervention, felt like the most meaningful accomplishment of my life. Maybe my life had meaning, after all. Maybe the flawed model that left the factory years ago had intentionally been made broken, setting the stage for a dark yet hopeful path ahead.

EIGHT

Leah

My eyes gradually opened, my mind still clouded by remnants of the dream—a vivid memory of my first kill.

I shifted to the edge of the bed, feeling the silk sheets against my bare hips and legs, and gazed out the expansive hotel window of my luxurious penthouse suite in Washington DC. Through the glass, the US Capitol's iconic dome stood as a radiant landmark amid the bustling cityscape. The surrounding gardens appeared tiny from this vantage point, yet they offered a sense of tranquility.

I found myself deep in contemplation. Dreams were foreign to me. I hadn't had them since childhood. But this was the second one I'd had since meeting Agent Richter.

For a moment, my hands almost felt tingly, as if I'd just pushed the glass into that man's neck.

A soft moan broke the silence. The man beside me stretched a muscular arm toward me with a suggestive smile.

I rose and made my way to the large closet before we could make contact. "Thank you. You can leave now," I said, moving to retrieve my clothes from my suitcase.

He sat up, confusion etched across his face. "Now?"

I fetched my purse from the desk and removed an envelope filled with cash. "Yes, now." Handing him the envelope felt as mundane as purchasing a coffee.

He hesitated, his deep brown eyes locking with mine. He was undeniably handsome, embodying the Mediterranean features I favored—a detail well-known to the escort agency. His name eluded me, but at this point, their names were inconsequential. Since Emanuel's death, I never allowed them to linger beyond their purpose: providing me with a brief escape. And this one had overstayed, likely because I'd inadvertently fallen asleep.

"Our transaction is complete," I explained. "Thank you."

"I . . . I wouldn't mind staying a bit longer for you," he offered.

"That won't be necessary. I expect you to be gone after my shower. And I'm quick." I headed toward the bathroom.

The clock on the nightstand read 9:04 a.m. It was highly unusual for me to sleep this late, but then again, dreaming wasn't part of my repertoire either. My appointment with the Smithsonian Secretary, Robert Michaels, loomed at 10:30 a.m., leaving me scant time for breakfast and a shower.

Initially, my interest had led me to the Museum of Fine Arts in Boston to consult with their Egyptologist. However, I shifted my focus when I learned that Emilia Wagner had been appointed as the new Egyptologist at the Smithsonian Museum of Natural History. She was one of the best in the field. Our meeting was scheduled under the pretense of discussing a potential advisory council seat—or, to be more precise, to become a significant donor to the Smithsonian Institution. That would be the most logical explanation for my visit should it ever be questioned. A logical cover was of the utmost importance. Always.

After my shower, I was mildly irritated to find the escort still present. I quickly dressed, donning a bra, a white silk shirt, and a satin cream-colored skirt atop black thigh-high stockings. I'd complete the outfit with black pumps and a luxurious cashmere poncho. Today's makeup would be more natural, complementing my hair, which was neatly tied in a bun.

The escort was still awkwardly standing by the bed, fidgeting like a guilty child. "I'm sorry . . ." he mumbled, our eyes meeting. "But I can't find my phone."

"It was on the couch," I said, watching him rush over and frantically lift the cushions. As he bent over, his sweater rode up, exposing a glimpse of his toned back and the edge of his muscular abdomen.

Instantly, a vibrant heat came to life within me. Psychopaths often sought comfort in lust and sex. It was one of the few things they could truly feel. And I wasn't naive enough to think I was different. But my interests didn't align with those who reveled in violent fantasies. My preference was more run-of-the-mill. I yearned for the intimacy that came with a loving, committed relationship. It was a curiosity that had puzzled me all my life, one that, unlike the logical processes I usually depended on, would likely never be solved.

He retrieved his phone and offered an apologetic smile. "I'm leaving now. Please don't tell the agency I've upset you. They . . . said you're a big deal."

As he walked past, something within me stirred. "Wait!"

He stopped and turned, his eyes meeting mine.

The battle was brief but intense. My craving for another encounter that made me feel alive, the few seconds when I reached that orgasm, clashed with rational thought.

One last time, I thought. *Then he'll leave, and I'll request someone new on my next visit to DC, avoiding any pattern that might attract the Train Track Killer's attention.*

"I'll pay you an additional thousand cash if you fuck me against the glass window."

"What?" He looked surprised, likely more by the abruptness of my request than by its content.

Approaching the window with a view of the Capitol Mall, I outlined my fantasy. "I'll stand here, looking out. You'll embrace me from behind, whisper intimacies into my ear. Act like we're married. Then you'll finger me and tell me how much you want to fuck me. When I'm about to cum, you'll pull my panties down, thrust your cock into me, and tell me that you love me." I turned to face him. "Try to sound convincing. Understood?"

He nodded slowly.

"Good. There's an extra five hundred in it if you get it right."

He pursed his lips. "When . . . do you want to do this?"

"Now, of course," I said, positioning myself at the window, adopting the role of an oblivious bride mesmerized by her new beginning. "I have to leave soon."

My driver was waiting by the dark limousine when I stepped out of the hotel. There was no time for food, but hunger was a sensation I had mastered. I was accustomed to waiting for hours on end, standing perfectly still, just as I had done while waiting for Harvey Grand in his rundown motel closet.

Lost in thought, I gazed out the window as we drove past the majestic buildings of downtown DC. Their imposing neoclassical architecture rivaled the grandeur of Europe.

As if last night's dream weren't strange enough, my mother's words suddenly echoed in my head. They were words she had repeated far too often during my childhood: "Are you stupid? I wish you were never born!"

Reflecting on it now, I strongly disagreed with her assertion that I was lacking in intelligence. In fact, I stood firm in my belief to the contrary. Among the many things I might have been, simple-minded was not one of them.

And yet, I could understand her aversion toward me as an individual and my father's silent complicity. My upbringing occurred long before the concepts of attachment parenting and the mental health movement took root. In the seventies and eighties—particularly in small American towns—a family's reputation, and more so a woman's, adhered to very strict standards. The prevalence of face-to-face interactions meant that social perceptions and gossip played a significant role in determining one's community standing. Against this backdrop, my mother, who placed her social standing in our small town above everything else, saw me as a threat to her reputation and, therefore, a threat to her survival. My father, a modest man who'd managed to marry the prom queen due to his own father's successful gas station business, found himself obliged to support my mother's views. He was always walking on eggshells around a woman he otherwise couldn't have dreamed of marrying.

There was no love between my parents and me. We maintained a relationship that was more transactional than familial. I regularly paid them their share from my wealth as though they had invested in my childhood piano lessons like stocks. A very large dividend, so to speak. They were entitled to it in my mind.

Aside from these financial interactions and the obligatory phone calls from my father on Christmas and my birthday—which I reciprocated on their birthdays until my mother requested I stop—there was no contact.

Though our situation might sound heartbreaking, it was a perfectly acceptable arrangement for us.

And yet, here I was, dreaming about my past and contemplating my unusual childhood for the first time in nearly three decades.

"Ms. Nachtnebel," my driver said, pulling me from my thoughts. "We're here." He sounded curt, like he'd tried to get my attention more than once.

Shaking off my thoughts, I glanced up at the National Museum of Natural History. Its grand neoclassical structure and iconic rotunda were a sight to behold. The sun's bright reflection off its white pillars was dazzling.

"Thank you," I quickly said, slipping out before he could come around to open the door for me. "I'll text you when I'm done. Stay close, please."

As I approached a group waiting at the museum's entrance, I recognized the head of the Smithsonian right away. President Robert Michaels was just as his pictures portrayed: a head of neatly groomed hair with silver highlights and eyes that seemed to sparkle with a genuine love for his work, all complemented by a tweed jacket and dress pants. He approached with a smile that was both warm and eager.

His hand stretched out to shake mine as soon as I reached him. "Ms. Nachtnebel, it's such an honor to have you here," he said. "I mentioned to my wife that you might join our board, and she just laughed. I had to show your assistant's email to her to convince her it was real."

I returned his smile as a woman stepped forward.

"This is Mrs. Emilia Wagner, our renowned Egyptologist," he said.

Mrs. Wagner, who had sun-kissed skin and graying hair, wore a linen blouse and khaki trousers. The ankh necklace around her neck caught my eye immediately. The symbol was the same one the Train Track Killer had left by his victims. My gaze lingered on the necklace as she shook my hand with a vigor that spoke of her passion.

Choosing her felt right. If anyone could help me unravel the mystery of the ankh symbol found with the bodies, it would be Emilia Wagner, a true expert in her field.

"That moment when the whole Colosseum chanted 'La Imperatrice,' I teared up," Mrs. Wagner said, her grip on my hand still firm.

I gently pulled my hand from hers. "Thank you, Mrs. Wagner—"

"Call me Emilia," she interjected. "I've been a fan for ages. I snagged a ticket off a waitlist to your Christmas concert three years ago. It was magical."

Mr. Michaels nodded enthusiastically as if to underline her sentiments. "Your music is right up there with discovering ancient tombs," he joked.

"You're both too kind," I replied with a smile.

"I hope you don't mind that we've invited two other potential donors to join our tour?" Mr. Michaels gestured toward two men engrossed in conversation by the grand museum doors. I was initially reluctant, but the presence of Nabil Adel, the real estate magnate, made their inclusion understandable. His portly figure and thinning hair were overshadowed by a grin that carried the unmistakable hint of power-driven lechery. Adel was as notorious for his tasteless opulence as he was for his tax evasion tactics. Or his affairs with models.

My smile faltered as I observed the person beside him. In his mid-forties, this tall, blond man stood out in an impeccably tailored suit and confident posture, mirroring the appearance of an elegant gentleman from a bygone era. He wasn't overly handsome, but his aura attracted attention, somehow enhancing his presence and rendering him remarkably distinguished. It was a rare gift that undoubtedly served him well in business—and most likely with women.

Mr. Michaels led us toward them. "Let me introduce Nabil Adel," he announced.

After a brief handshake with Adel, I turned to the other man.

"And Mr. Jan Novak."

"It's a pleasure to finally meet you, Ms. Nachtnebel," Mr. Novak said, then gestured toward the museum's entrance. "Shall we begin?" His voice was both commanding and melodious, leaving no room for disagreement.

"Of course," Mr. Roberts said, obediently opening the large doors for Mr. Novak, who, unlike Adel, stepped aside to let the women enter first.

The tour of the museum was captivating. It began in the grand entrance hall, from which we moved through the Hall of Mammals. There, we marveled at the array of life, from diminutive shrews to the colossal African elephant. I paused, looking into the elephant's dark, dead eyes. Such a magnificent creature, wasted on us humans.

"It's known as the Fénykövi elephant," Mr. Novak said, coming to stand beside me. "Named after the Hungarian game hunter who donated the hide. They also affectionately call the elephant Henry, from what I've read."

I continued to gaze at the unfortunate creature's eyes, faux yet sad. They reminded me of the eyes of a serial killer's victim. "Killed solely for someone's amusement," I remarked coldly. "How distasteful and absurd to call it Henry . . . *affectionately*."

For the first time, Mr. Novak smiled. He followed me into the Ocean Hall, where Mr. Michaels was elaborating on the mysteries of the deep sea to Mr. Adel. "You disapprove of violence, then?" Mr. Novak asked.

The irony of his question almost made me laugh. I thought of Harvey Grand and the satisfaction I'd derived from watching another predator dissolve, quite literally. "It's not the violence that disturbs me but the motivation behind it," I replied as I noticed Mr. Adel awkwardly scratching his privates as if no one could see him.

"It disturbs you when it's done for fun?" Mr. Novak asked.

"It's more nuanced than that, but yes, among other reasons," I responded.

Mr. Novak nodded thoughtfully. "Maybe violence is simply in our nature, and we're not so different from animals after all. Many species like cats and dolphins kill for entertainment." He shifted his gaze from the imposing whale skeleton above to a large dolphin model.

"Possibly," I conceded, pausing beside him in front of the dolphin display before moving on to the ancient realm of dinosaurs, where towering skeletons dominated the space. Mr. Novak kept pace with me. "But I would also argue that a species capable of reaching the moon should adhere to higher standards than mere primal instincts," I continued. "Humans have moral reasoning and the capacity for ethical decision-making. This sets us apart from most animals. While certain animals might kill beyond their survival needs, interpreting this as 'fun' could misrepresent their actions. Humans, with our advanced cognitive abilities and societal norms, generally view the killing of others for pleasure as a grave departure from ethical behavior, not as an innate trait."

"Fascinating argument," Mr. Novak admitted. A grin played on his lips as we ventured through the Hall of Human Origins, delving into the intricacies of human evolution.

The group paused before John Gurche's bronze sculpture of a Homo neanderthalensis mother and child. The artwork captured them with profound realism, showcasing distinctive Neanderthal features like their robust build, pronounced brow ridges, and strong facial structures. The mother smiled as she cradled her child.

Mr. Michaels shared a few words about the artist and the sculpture before leading the group toward the skeletons. An eager Mr. Adel trailed behind, inquiring about tax deductions.

I was about to follow when I noticed Mr. Novak lingering by the sculpture. He kept his gaze fixed on it before shifting his icy blue eyes to me. "What do you think we should do with humans who kill for fun? Get rid of them for the good of others?" he asked.

I hesitated, suddenly rooted to the ground. It wasn't easy to catch me off guard; in fact, I could recall only one other person who had managed to do so recently: Agent Richter. The precision of Novak's question struck me, his inquiry as sharp as a scalpel. "Could you clarify your question?" I asked, maintaining his intense gaze, neither of us willing to back down.

Standing a head taller than me, Mr. Novak was an imposing figure. He narrowed his eyes. "Those who kill for pleasure. What do you believe should be done with them? To stop them, I mean."

The gravity of his question remained. It felt as if he could see through the myriad layers of my facade, touching a truth I had kept concealed to most.

I held his stare a moment longer before offering a forced smile. "I think that's a question better suited for Mr. Michaels, not a concert pianist. After all, his halls are the ones filled with death. My own is filled with life and dreams."

A hint of a smile played on Mr. Novak's lips. His intense gaze never wavered from mine.

"Do you have any other questions about the sculpture?" Emilia approached us with hurried steps, her tone that of a worried host. "Did we move too quickly?"

"Not at all," I replied before following Mr. Michaels, bypassing the insect zoo and butterfly pavilion.

"Ah, here we are, the tour's highlight," Mr. Michaels announced, stopping before the grand entrance to the Egyptian exhibit, marked "Eternal Life." The room lay shrouded in darkness, deliberately set to enhance the effect. "It may not be the largest collection in the nation, but we've managed to acquire some of the most prestigious artifacts from Egypt. Loaned to us at a significant cost, so the American public can experience history up close for free, thanks to our generous donors."

Inside the exhibit hall, a dim light shone on the Egyptian treasures, enveloping us in an air of ancient mystery. The darkness highlighted the artifacts on display, their details brought to life under focused beams of illumination. Statues of pharaohs, mummies, and intricate hieroglyphics glowed ethereally, their presence stark against the shadowy ambiance.

"Look at this guy!" Mr. Adel bellowed, his grin wide as if he'd just cracked a fart joke. He was gesturing toward a large mummification display featuring a bull's head and genitals.

I brushed off his childish humor and moved closer to a golden necklace adorned with an ankh symbol made of lapis lazuli gemstones. Its T-shape was crowned with a loop shaped like a teardrop. Inside the glass showcase, it sparkled on a crimson silk pillow like tiny stars twinkling in the night sky.

"Ah." Emilia stepped up beside me, her voice tinged with awe. "The Eternal Kiss. Believed to have belonged to Agathoclea, the favored mistress of the Greco-Egyptian Pharaoh Ptolemy IV Philopator. Stunning, isn't it?"

I nodded. "Is that the ankh symbol?"

Emilia touched the pendant of her own ankh necklace, her fingers tracing its sun-stained contours. "Yes," she responded. "I'm impressed you recognized it."

"What does it symbolize?"

"Most commonly, it's a symbol of eternal life. But its significance can vary with the context. In this instance, we believe it was a gift from Ptolemy to his mistress, Agathoclea. He loved her more than anything else in life. His obsession with her was profound. Legend has it he constructed a magnificent temple for the gods, hoping to persuade them to allow her to join him in the afterlife when he died."

"As in, he planned to kill her upon his own death?"

Emilia nodded. "Such practices weren't rare for the era. Servants were often buried alive with their pharaohs. But Agathoclea and her brother attempted a coup for the throne upon Ptolemy's death. Their plot failed, and she met a grisly end, torn apart limb by limb."

The necklace seemed even more enigmatic as I pondered its history, struggling to connect any threads to the Train Track Killer. "How intriguing. You mentioned it usually represents eternal life. Are there alternative interpretations?"

A wave of pride washed over Emilia's aged face. "Actually, yes."

I leaned in, captivated.

"It's not widely known, even among Egyptologists, but I was fortunate enough to participate in an excavation where we unearthed a rare stone tablet. It depicted a priest's vain daughter, clutching the ankh as though she were gazing directly into it."

While Emelia talked, an unmistakable sense of being watched crept over me. It was just like when I was eight and Larsen had darted between cars, chasing after me. I turned my head slightly and immediately caught his gaze.

Jan Novak.

Shrouded in darkness away from the group, illuminated only by the ambient light reflecting off a nearby mummy, he had fixed his intense blue eyes on me with the precision of a predator stalking its prey. Our eyes locked.

I felt momentarily paralyzed.

"So, although the ankh is most commonly associated with life or eternal life," Emilia pressed on, "in this exceptional case, it signifies a mirror. Its form unmistakably resembles an old-fashioned hand mirror. This interpretation is supported by the sequence of its consonants, ʿ-n-ẖ, appearing in several Egyptian terms, including, as you might guess—"

"Mirror," I said, shifting my attention back to her.

She nodded. "We theorize this interpretation could originate from the notion of the mirror as a reflection of one's true essence or soul."

"To highlight the significance of self-reflection of one's current self and beyond? Like a self-analysis or evaluation?"

Emilia pondered this. Then her eyes lit up with excitement. "Yes. Your interpretation really supports the mirror theory from new angles. Would you mind if I shared your observation with some of my colleagues?"

I glanced back to where Jan Novak had been standing. He was gone.

There was something about that man . . . something deeply unsettling. It wasn't like the darkness I'd come to recognize in the eyes of the monsters I hunted. Still, he had a strange quality that I couldn't quite grasp.

"Well," Mr. Michaels said as we returned to the hall where our tour had commenced, "unfortunately, Mr. Novak had to leave on urgent business. But I hope you align with his belief in the importance of preserving our cultural heritage." Clearing his throat, he added, "As you're aware, access to any Smithsonian Museum is complimentary for everyone. We depend significantly on the generosity of patrons like yourself to fulfill our mission of presenting history to the public."

"Is there anything else we get out of this besides tax deductions?" Mr. Adele asked. His tone was getting on my nerves.

Fed up with his rudeness, I discreetly pulled out my phone to text my driver to be ready outside. "Mr. Adele," I said firmly and impassively, "a donation is essentially a voluntary contribution, given without the expectation of receiving anything in return. What you're inquiring about would constitute a transaction, an exchange where goods or services are traded with the anticipation of something in return. It would have been prudent to acquaint yourself with this distinction prior to attending and enjoying our hosts' precious time."

Mr. Adele looked stunned, then pulled out his checkbook in silence.

Approaching Mr. Michaels and Emilia, I extended my hand. "Thank you for the exquisite tour. My assistant will be in touch with the details of the amount of my regular contribution."

Both Mr. Michaels and Emilia's expressions brightened. "That would mean the world to us," Mr. Michaels responded.

I turned to Emilia. "Should I have further questions regarding the ankh symbol, may I reach out to you?"

She nodded enthusiastically. "Absolutely! Please do."

With a courteous smile, I made my exit.

As I descended the steps, my thoughts drifted back to Mr. Novak. His probing questions about the morality of killing, coupled with his intense scrutiny in the Egyptian exhibit, struck me as profoundly unusual. An enigma surrounded him, one that warranted closer examination.

Then there was Emilia's insight into the ankh symbol.

A mirror.

Why would the Train Track Killer want to reflect on himself and his actions? Was he grappling with his identity, searching for himself, or aspiring to evolve into something more formidable or terrifying?

As I settled into the limousine, my conviction to consult Agent Richter solidified. I knew I had to talk to him. After giving him some time to process the situation with Harvey Grand, of course.

I had no doubt that what he encountered in the autopsy room would disturb him.

NINE

Liam

Cowboy, Rose, and I stood alongside the pathologist in the oppressive silence of the Green Cross Hospital morgue, where a pin drop would have resounded as if it were being played through a megaphone. Harvey Grand's body, or what remained of it, lay splayed on a cold embalming table. The stark metal surface was a sharp contrast to the eerie stillness of the lifeless form it bore. And *form* was indeed the right descriptor for whatever the hell lay before us, as *human being* no longer seemed a fitting term.

What was once Harvey Grand had been grotesquely altered by the acid. The remains were partially dissolved, right down to the bone. Certain areas were more severely eroded than others, revealing exposed tissues and discolored, uneven surfaces where the acid had mercilessly eaten through flesh, muscles, and even bone. The eyeless face, retaining mere remnants of a yellow-toothed mouth torn open in a scream, bore a chilling resemblance to something out of an Evil Dead movie.

The room's dim lighting cast long, somber shadows, lending a macabre emphasis to the gruesome spectacle before us.

"What . . . the . . . fuck?" Agent Rose's voice, muffled yet sharp, cut through the silence like an arrow streaking across the sky. Her hand rose to her neck as if to assure herself that she hadn't ingested poison as well.

The atmosphere was spooky, saturated with the antiseptic scent of a hospital.

Overwhelmed, I tilted my head back to gaze at the water-damaged ceiling, my lips tightly pinched in disbelief.

"Well," Cowboy said, "he did like to party."

Rose and I turned our sharp gazes on him. He responded with a what-did-I-do-now shrug.

"Krokodil," interjected the pathologist, a petite woman named Dr. Giselle Lopez.

"The Russian zombie drug?" I asked.

She nodded. "I've never encountered anything like this." Her voice was tinged with professional intrigue. "We're seeing more cases as Krokodil spreads on the streets across America. Acidic burns down to the bone aren't unheard of with this terrible drug . . . but this?" She shook her head. "This batch is something straight out of hell."

Cowboy stepped closer, snapping on a latex glove that had been in his pocket. "Did they increase the paint thinner or whatever the hell could have caused such a severe reaction?"

As he reached toward the body, Dr. Lopez swiftly intervened. "Don't!" She gestured toward visibly corroded latex gloves on a nearby metal stretcher. "You need butyl gloves, or the acid will burn through."

"Holy shit!" Cowboy hastily retreated from the body.

"What the hell did they spike this batch with?" Rose asked, her voice a mix of horror and curiosity.

I observed silently, a gnawing certainty in my mind that this was not an accidental cocktail. Leah knew exactly what she was doing here.

"Holy shit indeed," Dr. Lopez echoed. "I'm still waiting on the full lab report, but there's only one substance I know of that's potent enough to do something like this. And the fact that it doesn't eat through plastic only confirms my suspicion."

"Hydrofluoric acid," I murmured.

"The stuff that ate through the bath tub in Breaking Bad?" Cowboy asked.

Dr. Lopez nodded solemnly. "Drug dealers throw all sorts of things into Krokodil, including paint thinner, but this is absolute madness. I pray to God this was the only batch of this hellish cocktail."

A heavy silence fell again as we stared at the grotesque remains of Harvey Grand. The yellowish pus, the black holes for eyes.

"Why did it spread so much? Shouldn't it have killed him instantly?" Rose asked.

Dr. Lopez gestured toward an area of the neck, just above the collarbone. "You're right. Usually, we only see burns near the injection site. That's because most of the time, users inject into visible veins. They're easy to find. But this unlucky guy somehow managed to inject into an artery. Unlike veins, they pump blood and drugs away from the heart."

"And that causes . . . *this*?" I asked, gesturing both hands at Harvey.

"Yes," she replied gravely. "As I said, arteries carry blood away from the heart. This means the toxic mix kept circulating through Harvey Grand's body even after he suffered one of the most horrific deaths I've ever encountered."

"So, the heart kept pumping the acid throughout his body even after he died?" Agent Rose interjected, her voice laced with disbelief.

"It looks like it. He was most likely already brain dead, but given the severe damage of the acid, the heart must have kept pumping for quite a bit longer."

"How is that even possible?" I asked.

"Dying isn't like in the movies," Dr. Lopez explained, her tone clinical and somber. "During the dying process, different parts of the body cease functioning at various times, not always in the same order. For instance, the heart might keep beating even after the brain has stopped. Or the liver might still function when the intestines don't. In this case, the heart continued pumping the acid through corroded veins, spreading it everywhere. Once the drug reached the heart, it instantly stopped due to the corrosive effects of the hydrofluoric acid. The acid did its own thing from here on for quite a bit longer."

"Did he . . . suffer much?" Cowboy asked.

"Beyond anything imaginable," Dr. Lopez replied, her face reflecting the gravity of her answer.

Once more, the room sank into a silence punctuated only by the distant beeps of machines and the muffled sounds of hospital staff.

As I stood there, gazing at this shitshow called Harvey Grand, a surge of anger welled up inside me. What the hell was Leah thinking? We'd talked about using drugs.

Whatever happened to a good old-fashioned heroin overdose or even a shot to the head? Both were merciful by comparison. But more importantly, how could I ever trust her with any information again? If that phone tip about the Boston Strangler led us to him, how could I possibly share any of it with Leah? What would she do to him—cut off his head and place it on a spike at the Children's Museum?

This . . . this was unthinkable.

"Jesus Christ." I exhaled loudly, my sigh echoing my internal battle.

My arrangement with Leah was beginning to make me feel like one of those crazy people who kept lions as pets until, one day, Simba got angry.

What had worked for her and Larsen didn't align with my principles. Not in this. Not even close. And there was always the lurking question: Could I end up just like Larsen if I started making waves?

Surprisingly, I felt no remorse over Harvey's death. In fact, when the call came in that a drug overdose victim in Ocean City had been identified as Harvey Grand, an immense sense of relief had washed over me. Leah had a point: An out-of-control sociopath like Harvey was bound to wreak havoc again. Once a monster like him crossed a certain line and was rewarded with a get-out-of-jail-free card and a lucrative book deal on top of that, there was no stopping him, not even with the logic that he wouldn't walk free again. So, Harvey's demise saved innocent lives.

But . . .

I gazed at what was left of his face, where fiery red flesh clashed grotesquely with the yellow-white remnants of wounds.

No, not like this.

Not for Harvey's sake but for my own humanity.

Rose spoke up, shifting the atmosphere entirely. "Eleven," she said abruptly, drawing all eyes to her. "The youngest victim in the Newcastle well case was only eleven months old. His mother, too exhausted to go to the store, made his bottle with boiled tap water instead of bottled water. And now her baby is gone forever."

Shit.

I was a parent myself. My heart shattered.

Cowboy sighed. "Well, she'll be thrilled once she hears that this piece of shit is rotting in hell." A wide grin spread across his face. "Rotting. Literally. You get it? *Rot* in hell."

"That's enough, Agent McCourt," Rose said in a reprimanding tone, beating me to it.

I studied her briefly. The intense look in her amber eyes. The deep frown line between her brows. In moments like these, I found it hard to gauge her stance. Was she relieved at Harvey's demise? Or did she feel deprived of the trial and the justice expected in a storybook-ending court case?

"What happened?" Dr. Lopez asked, her voice tinged with hesitation. "I mean, how did he escape justice?"

Cowboy glanced at me, almost as if expecting me to silence him. However, there was a sense that we owed Dr. Lopez an explanation after sharing this experience with her.

"Some cop screwed us," Cowboy explained. "Before a warrant came in, that idiot searched Grand's home based on some Chuck Norris hunch about the town's nutjob, who happened to be Harvey Grand. He was right about this asshole in the end, but the law doesn't work that way. Not in this country, at least. Right or wrong doesn't matter. The fucked-up wording of the law does."

"Thanks for that . . . colorful explanation, Agent McCourt," I said.

He continued, missing the hint. "His ultra-rich aunt could afford lawyers smart enough to challenge every breath we took. We didn't know about the warrant issue until it all came out. The cops tried to cover it up by forging documents, but the Grand family's million-buck law firm brought all this shit to light. We all agreed to keep this quiet and, of course, to let Harvey walk. That's just how it goes. It's not about the crime you commit but how much lawyer you can afford."

Dr. Lopez looked confused. "How can a single late warrant let a man like him walk?"

"The evidence," Rose clarified, "was inadmissible in court because the search of Harvey's home was illegal. Without it, there was no case against him. There were no witnesses."

"I see." Dr. Lopez paused, lips pursed, then glanced at Harvey's remains with a raised eyebrow. "I guess there might be a God after all."

The loud, insistent ringtone of Cowboy's phone shattered the tense atmosphere in the room. He quickly pulled it from his pocket. As he put the phone to his face, the screen cast a soft glow against his cheek. He listened for a moment, then held the phone slightly away from his ear, cupping the lower half as if it were an old landline. "It's the hospital's reception. Some funeral home, Woods Funerals, is here to collect the body."

I nodded. "Tell them you'll be right out."

"I'll be right up," Cowboy said into the phone and ended the call.

"So, we're not taking the remains back to Boston with us?" Agent Rose asked.

"No, we are," I said. "But the family insisted on having the remains in a coffin instead of some plastic bag."

"A rich-folk-worthy home delivery," Cowboy said. "And we just wag our happy tails."

"All right, can you please bring them down here?" I asked. It wasn't that what Cowboy said was different from what we were all thinking. However, when you wore the badge, there was a big difference between thinking something and voicing it out loud.

Cowboy exited through the double swinging doors, muttering something under his breath—likely, a tasteless joke.

"Did McCourt say what we're supposed to do after we land with the remains?" Rose asked.

"Yes." I looked over at Dr. Lopez, who understood all too well. "Unless you need me, I have a meeting," she said. "Make sure you sign the paperwork on the desk over there before you leave." She nodded curtly at the desk and threw her oversized gloves in a plastic trash can labeled DO NOT TOUCH. HAZARDOUS WASTE.

"Will do. Thank you for your time," I said and watched her leave.

Rose shook her head, her eyes back on the corpse. Then she walked over and picked up the clipboard with the paperwork. She signed it with a pen attached to it by a small chain.

"His family will collect the remains from a small airport near Newcastle where they've got a mansion they use for summer vacation," I said. "We just hand him over at the airport. It's all them from there."

Rose nodded. "Nice."

With a resounding crash, the double doors flew open and slammed against the door stoppers. They rebounded and collided with an ornate wooden casket adorned with golden handles. It was being wheeled in on a stretcher by two older men in sleek black suits.

"What's up," one of them greeted us with a nod.

"Thanks, guys," I responded. My gaze shifted to Cowboy, who lingered in the hallway and looked uneasy as he used a foot to prop open one door.

"Umm . . . guys?" Cowboy said. "You might want to see this."

Rose and I exchanged anxious glances, then stepped into the hallway. There, we were met by a throng of hospital staff, their eyes fixed on us amid a murmur of curiosity. A man in blue scrubs brandished his phone, poised as though he were expecting a celebrity's entrance.

"Shit," I muttered as we retreated back into the morgue.

Rose folded her arms. "Seems our 'covert operation' isn't so covert after all."

"Should we have clued Dr. Lopez in on the whole FBI confidentiality spiel?" Cowboy's sarcasm was only thinly veiled.

"I doubt she's the leak. She's been in the loop longer than we have," I said, frustration threading through my voice as I raked a hand through my hair. "Goddamn it."

Who leaked this?

"Cowboy, call for local PD backup," I continued. "We're going to need a lot more muscle to get us to the airport."

He was on his phone in an instant.

This was a complication we didn't need. The FBI's involvement was supposed to ensure discretion. No public spectacles, no vitriolic protests shadowing the hearse. Definitely no reporters thrusting their microphones at us. McCourt would be livid if this spiraled out of control.

"What's the situation at the front desk?" Rose asked the moment Cowboy ended his call.

He shrugged. "Just a small gathering of patients and staff, snapping photos of the funeral service. No press . . . yet."

"For now," I added, the urgency clear in my tone. "Can we expedite this?" I asked the funeral staff, who had donned protective gloves and were preparing to handle Harvey Grand's body.

"You can't rush the dead," the older one retorted, unfazed and unhurried.

"The dead won't mind if you become the face of the evening news for carrying the coffin of one of the nation's most despised individuals," Rose retorted. "I'd reconsider that so-called wisdom of yours unless you're keen on becoming a public spectacle."

The funeral staff exchanged looks of concern, then hastened their pace considerably.

"Be ready for potential confrontation," I advised, withdrawing my Glock from its chest holster beneath my blazer. I swiftly checked for a smooth slide action and unobstructed barrel, then verified the trigger and firing pin function with a safe dry fire.

Cowboy glanced my way, his expression one of disbelief. Then he turned to Rose, who was completing her weapon's dry fire check. My eyes locked with Rose's, and an unspoken understanding passed between us.

"A team of optimists, I see," Cowboy said.

"Check your weapon, Cowboy," I ordered, holstering my Glock.

He rolled his eyes but followed suit.

"Let's move, now," I urged as the funeral staff secured the coffin with a hefty lock.

Exiting the room, we were met with chaos. The corridor leading to the elevators was crammed with curious hospital staff, their murmurs punctuated by the clicks of their camera phones. This scene extended all the way to the main entrance.

Beyond the hospital's glass façade, a large crowd had gathered, with patients and onlookers blending into a mass of curious faces. It wasn't a riotous assembly yet, but it was too large a group for what was supposed to be a discreet operation.

Outrage erupted from the crowd.

"Fuck Harvey!" a man shouted.

The words sparked a chain reaction, with other voices amplifying the dissent.

"Why are you protecting this asshole?"

"Shame on you!"

Tensions escalated, morphing into a cacophony of indignant murmurs.

We had barely made it out of the hospital when police backup roared in: a fleet of at least ten cars, sirens wailing and lights flashing. Among them was Agent Wilson, the local FBI liaison who had escorted us here. She had waited outside in her SUV.

"Thank God." I breathed a sigh of relief and directed the funeral and our escort vehicles into formation. "Load him up." Then I approached the lead police vehicle. "Appreciate the swift response. Could you have your team form a protective detail around us? We need coverage front and back, all the way to City Municipal Airport."

"Yes, sir," the officer said quickly. "Sirens?"

"All the way. We need to get the hell outta here ASAP."

"Understood."

I navigated to the SUV in which we'd arrived. On the way, I passed Agent Wilson and her partner, who'd been part of our detail. I caught a glimpse of Cowboy attempting to claim the driver's seat, only for Rose to snatch the keys from him and nudge him aside. This elicited a frustrated "Hey" from Cowboy before he climbed into the back seat with a grunt.

"Let's roll!" I announced to our team. Police cars maneuvered past us to form the vanguard of our procession, akin to the tip of an arrow.

Swiftly, I settled into the passenger seat beside Rose. After a quick exchange of determined glances, she ignited the engine, and we joined the escort of police vehicles carving a path for us.

The blare of sirens from the police cars cut through the city noise, clearing intersections as our convoy hastened toward the airport. From the corner of my eye, I noticed a camera crew from a local TV station trying to tail us from an intersection.

"FBI Escorts Notorious Corpse: Public in Uproar," Cowboy quipped, holding an imaginary microphone to his mouth.

I reached for the handheld radio and eyed the conspicuous white van adorned with a satellite dish. "Can someone intercept them and do an ID check to buy us some time?" I asked.

"On it," came the prompt reply from an officer.

I watched as a police vehicle decelerated, strategically positioning itself to obstruct the media van's pursuit.

Our advance continued, with onlookers attempting to capture fleeting images, seemingly enthralled by the spectacle of our mission. But the swift pace of our escort ensured we made it to the airport quickly.

The metal gate to the airfield swung open as our convoy arrived. We sped down the airfield toward the C-17 awaiting us with its cargo door lowered.

A group of airmen in camouflage-patterned utility uniforms hurried down the ramp to meet us. They included Lieutenant Colonel Jason Lewis, whose approach was marked by a cool, deliberate stride. He had personally overseen this mission on the military's end to ensure everything proceeded without a hitch. The balding officer, in his early fifties, made his way over to me as I exited the SUV alongside my team.

"Go get him on board," he commanded his airmen, then paused in front of me to survey the extensive police escort. "Making friends already?"

"I guess so," I replied, maintaining a tone of respect. "How soon can we depart?"

Lieutenant Colonel Lewis glanced back at his men, who were efficiently transferring the coffin to the aircraft. "If you're ready . . . now," he said, his voice imbued with his usual confidence.

"Thank you, sir," I said, then turned to Agent Wilson, the lead of the local agents who had supported our mission. "Thank you."

She nodded, her demeanor professional. "No problem. Good luck," she responded before signaling her team to vacate the runway.

I acknowledged the police officers with a wave before hastening up the ramp to join the others.

"Let's get her off the ground!" Lieutenant Colonel Lewis ordered, standing beside me as the airmen used tie-down straps to secure the coffin to the C-17's expansive metallic floor. The aircraft's cockpit, outfitted with advanced instrumentation, lay at the front. Our passenger seating ran along the windowless sides, underscoring the plane's utilitarian design for military use.

"Got lucky on this one, huh?" Lieutenant Colonel Lewis mused, eyeing the coffin. "Kinda wish our enemies would eliminate themselves. Would save this country lives and money."

"No kidding," I murmured, offering the Lieutenant Colonel a respectful nod before settling down next to Rose and Cowboy. We watched the airmen testing the straps. One of the airmen reached for his phone, aiming for a photo of the coffin, but

Lieutenant Colonel Lewis intervened sharply. "Is that for your one follower on social media, Sergeant Dorfman?"

The other airmen laughed as Sergeant Dorfman stowed his phone back in the side pocket of his camouflage-patterned utility trousers like a beaten dog. Then they quickly took their seats across from us.

I felt the powerful engines roar to life, vibrating through the mighty aircraft's frame. Its acceleration was steady and forceful, pressing me back into my seat. Soon, the plane took off the ground, transitioning from the rumble of the runway to a smooth glide over open air.

The outside noise diminished as we climbed into the sky, embarking on our short journey to the Portsmouth airport near Newcastle to hand Harvey Grand over to his family.

Nobody really talked during the hour-and-a-half flight. While the engines were louder than those on commercial flights, it was more that the cargo had everybody in a quiet mood, exchanging nothing but quick glances and nods.

Everything progressed smoothly until we began our descent into Portsmouth airport. That was when Lieutenant Colonel Lewis pressed the headset connected to the plane's intercom system against his ear. He looked serious. After a brief exchange, he stood and signaled me to join him.

Unfastening my seatbelt, I hurried to the cockpit, where three pilots in military attire operated the controls, surrounded by an array of buttons and displays. "We have a problem, sir," said the senior pilot, nodding out the window.

My gaze followed his and landed on the unexpected sight below. The small airfield had been swallowed by a vast, tumultuous sea of people. A carnival-like assembly of journalists and protesters had besieged the normally tranquil airport. With each foot we descended, the tension in the cockpit thickened.

"Goddamn it," Lieutenant Colonel Lewis cursed before I had the chance.

Goddamn it, indeed. My mind raced. This was what I'd been dreading. The impending media frenzy and the fallout were inevitable, and McCourt's fury would be unmatched.

"Fuck yeah," Cowboy whispered, his excitement barely contained as he and Rose squeezed into the cockpit. His reaction starkly contrasted with that of Rose, whose gaze fell to the metallic floor, her silence heavy with frustration. Unlike Cowboy, she fully grasped the gravity of our predicament.

"Special Agent Richter." Lieutenant Colonel Lewis turned to me. "Awaiting your orders."

I stood frozen, overwhelmed by the sight of the gathering crowd.

"Special Agent," he pressed, urgency lacing his tone as the airfield loomed closer.

The crowd swelled to the point that we could discern the first of many hostile signs: "Rot in hell, Harvey!"

"Would you like us to land or redirect to another airport?" he continued.

I slowly nodded, the weight of the decision heavy on me as I confronted the daunting reality awaiting us. "Let's land," I said.

There was no need to redirect the flight. Regardless of how our operation had come to light, our next airport would most likely look the same. It appeared we had a mole. There was no other explanation for the press's rapid mobilization.

"You heard the Special Agent in Charge," Lieutenant Colonel Lewis instructed his pilots. "Touch down."

"Yes, sir!"

We left the cockpit to take our seats for the last stretch of the landing.

"This is bad," Rose said, shaking her head. Cowboy, on the other hand, cheerfully pulled out a small Ziplock bag from the inside of his fancy jacket. The bag contained makeup, primarily in the form of powders and similar items.

"Hmm?" He offered some to Rose, whose face was a blend of utter annoyance and disbelief.

"You fucking kidding me?" she asked.

"Cameras always make my skin look oily. Gotta look good for the ladies out there," he quipped, then opened the compact's mirror before applying powder to his forehead.

"Unbelievable," I muttered as we touched down, the craft briefly bouncing before coming to a harsh stop.

The airmen instantly sprinted to the coffin.

"Everything from here on needs to be picture-perfect!" Lieutenant Colonel Lewis practically yelled to his men and women. "I don't want to see a single wave or smirk when you carry this coffin to the funeral car. In fact, I don't want to see a single wrinkle in your uniforms or faces!"

"Yes, sir!" they hollered simultaneously.

With heavy steps, Rose, Cowboy, Lieutenant Colonel Lewis, and I lined up at the ramp of the plane that would open any second. A block of anxiety solidified in my chest. This was a nightmare. A disaster.

"Woo-hoo," Cowboy exhaled in excitement, shaking his legs and limbs as if he were ready to step into a WWE fight ring.

"Fuck me," Rose whispered.

"Badges out!" I commanded, affixing my own badge to my belt. "Keep walking. Not one word to anybody! I mean it."

"You can count on me on that one," Rose said.

"Fine," Cowboy agreed hesitantly.

The creak and groan of the heavy metal mechanism reverberated inside the craft as the ramp of the C-17 began to open. Daylight seeped in, slowly flooding the dark interior of the plane with an intense, growing brightness. With each inch the ramp descended, the muffled noises from outside became clearer—the chants of "Rot in hell" growing louder and more aggressive. The camera flashes started as faint flickers but soon turned into a relentless storm of light, each flash stronger and more blinding than the last.

"Still think I'm on a lucky mission?" I asked the Lieutenant Colonel as we stood side by side in silence like allies ready to make it through hell together.

"I'm more wondering whom I have to thank for making my men and women Shakespeare's Othello two-point-oh. The whole nation will hate on these fine airmen." His tone was low, serious.

"I'd say some rich asshole senator in DC," I countered, "but ultimately, the almighty dollar would be more accurate."

"Fucking traitors," he muttered. "All of them."

"Fucking traitors indeed," I mumbled, thinking of the irony here. The monster everyone was clamoring over was dead because of me, yet now everyone saw me as his protector.

The thunder of bright flashes and sound that erupted as the ramp clanged against the concrete was almost otherworldly. A chaotic nightmare awaited us, and there was no other path but straight through the heart of it.

"Let's go," I said, my voice heavy as the coffin settled into position behind us. "Let's bring this piece of shit back to his swamp."

The airmen aligned themselves, three on each side of the casket, preparing to shoulder the burden of carrying one of the country's most hated monsters back to his family as if he were a fallen soldier who had sacrificed himself for a noble cause. Their gazes flicked back and forth between one another. Not a sound was made as Sergeant Dorfman nodded and removed the American flag from the casket. The flag had been mistakenly placed by one of the airmen who'd been unaware of the true nature of the man whose coffin was strapped to the plane's floor.

Having already positioned Harvey Grand's body directly behind their Lieutenant Colonel and the FBI agents, Sergeant Dorfman gave his team one last look, offering them a chance to reconsider their participation. As everyone nodded in agreement, and with the ramp already halfway open, letting in a flood of bright light that seemed to briefly blind him, he reached into his pocket. From it, he pulled out a sticker depicting a human skull with bony hands giving the middle finger above the bold proclamation "Two Wrongs Can Make a Right."

Then he slapped it onto the casket for the whole world to see—a parting gift from his unit, a sinister greeting sent straight to hell.

TEN

Leah

My head gently tilted over the keys as I caressed the final delicate notes of Liszt's "Liebestraum" on a historic Bösendorfer grand piano. This remarkable instrument had withstood the test of time. The illustrious Vanderbilt family had placed it in the very spot where I now had the privilege to perform.

The venue was the Elm Court Estate, near Lenox, just outside of Boston. The Hubble family, current stewards of the former Vanderbilt estate, had invested a fortune into tuning and repairing the piano, ensuring its preservation within the family. Tonight, however, marked a pivotal moment: The piano would become mine. That was the only reason I'd agreed to entertain the whims of the affluent and influential tonight.

The trade-off was worth enduring the indignity of playing their clown for an evening. I had no doubt that Ronald Hubble, the birthday boy turning one hundred today, agreed to let the piano go only because he knew his time on earth was ticking away.

The Bösendorfer was a masterpiece. Not only was it crafted from an exquisite array of woods like cherry and rosewood, handcrafted in Vienna and shipped across the ocean, but it also boasted an original Claude Monet painting on both sides of the lid. A whimsical interpretation of Mozart's "The Magic Flute," it showcased the dreamy, ethereal landscape of an enchanted forest—a tribute to the opera's mystical themes. The soft pastel colors conjured a realm of fantasy, with delicate flowers abloom in the moonlight, akin to the water lilies Monet often painted, all melting into a surreal, magical scene.

My fingers moved softly, gracefully bringing the haunting melody to a close, capturing the piece's dreamlike essence in this final, reflective moment. Its last notes echoed through the grand hall and over the heads of two hundred and fifty elite.

As I rose to my feet and turned to the audience, my gaze effortlessly found Mr. Hubble seated in the front row. His wheelchair did nothing to diminish the presence of the man who had established one of the nation's largest banks and hedge funds. His profound and murky influence was deeply entrenched in the highest political circles. He was the one percent of the one percent, thriving off the labor of the bottom 99.99%. The true American dream.

After exchanging a few pleasantries, I seized the opportunity presented by the cake-cutting and the comedian's performance to discreetly withdraw from the gathering, seeking silence in the vast estate's garden.

Navigating the grand hallway, adorned with a towering ceiling, I felt my phone vibrate in my purse.

Liam.

He had been pressing for a meeting, which I had strategically avoided. He needed more time to process Harvey Grand, and any rushed meeting could only strain the delicate threads of our relationship.

"May I help you?" asked a waitress in a tuxedo with a level of formality that seemed straight from the nineteenth century.

"I'm just looking for some fresh air," I replied, my disdain for these gatherings evident. Despite the lucrative offers, my performances at such events were rare. The aftermath of the Colosseum had prompted me to scale back even more, opting for a period of low visibility. In the US, classical music wasn't as big as it was in Europe and Asia. That allowed me a degree of anonymity among Gen Z as well as freedom from the prying eyes of journalists hungry for tabloid fodder. Maintaining this obscurity was crucial, even if it meant occasionally performing for the insufferable elite who governed this country like farmers watching over a herd of pigs.

The scent of the gardens wafted toward me on a refreshing fall breeze as I approached a set of wide-open double doors. My path took me through a jarring gaming room where classic pinball machines stood alongside modern video game consoles and a bowling alley. For a moment, I forgot the piercing tunes of eight-bit melodies and the assault of flashing lights as I looked up to admire the exquisitely painted ceiling high above.

The illusionistic fresco masterfully deceived the eye, portraying the ceiling as an opening to a clear blue sky. Angels peered down from their celestial perch, lending depth and realism to the scene. Their expressions radiated innocence and joy.

"It's magnificent, isn't it?" Mr. Hubble remarked, his wheelchair quietly brought to my side by his nurse.

I spared a glance at the frail man in his meticulously tailored suit before returning my attention to the ceiling. "It reminds me of the Camera degli Sposi in Mantua, Italy," I said, my eyes momentarily drifting to the gaming room.

"It's a replica of it," Mr. Hubble said. "Aside from its horrendous surroundings," he added, nodding toward the gaming room with a weary smile. He maneuvered his chair to a spot directly beneath the painting, then craned his neck to gaze upward. "This room was once a magnificent library housing a priceless book collection, including a scroll from the Dead Sea Scrolls. But the grandkids wanted to be closer to their bedrooms, so instead of constructing a game room near the pool house, we demolished a piece of history for . . . this."

Silently, I continued to study the painting. The angels' innocent smiles harmonized beautifully with the serene sky and clouds. Then my gaze landed on a darker figure lurking behind one of the angels. It was a boy dressed in rags. He had short brown hair and a face marred by grime. His large brown eyes peered out accusingly from behind his guardian angel. "That figure differs from the original in Italy," I observed, intrigued.

"Impressive, Ms. Nachtnebel," Mr. Hubble said. "Indeed, it does." With a heavy sigh, he fixed a long, meaningful gaze at me. "I assume you're familiar with my story."

I nodded. The tale was well-known. "You began your venture as a teenager, selling mugs outside grocery stores, mugs crafted from clay by a nearby river. After your father's premature death, you persuaded your mother to sell her home, living in a van with your mother and sister so every penny could be invested in a factory. Years later, you became the leading kitchenware producer in the US and the first to import cookware from China. A fairy tale ending for a boy who supposedly began his career by crafting a mug from dirt for his mother's birthday. From dirt to an empire of gold."

Mr. Hubble nodded. "Back then a ceramic mug cost about fifty cents to manufacture in the US and four cents in China. The profits from overseas manufacturing and importing lower-quality items at cheaper rates provided me with the funding I needed to establish Rising Bank and Hedge Funds years later."

"Making you one of the wealthiest individuals on earth," I remarked bluntly.

He offered a brief grin that faded as his gaze shifted back to the impoverished child whose judging eyes stared down at Hubble. "I was eight years old when I made that famous birthday mug for my mother. I understood even then that we couldn't afford a present on my father's salary as a shoe polisher. She wore her worn-out shoes and the same old dress so that the little we had could be spent on us kids. We were so poor, my sister and I would scavenge wood from dog houses and fences in middle-class neighborhoods during winter for heat." A sad smile touched his lips. "The moment my mother unwrapped the old newspaper from around the mug, tears of happiness streamed down her face. I felt an immense sense of accomplishment. All the blisters and burns from shaping the mug and firing it in a fire pit seemed worth it."

"A touching story," I responded, pretending that his narrative had moved me.

His smile vanished. "If that were the end of it, yes. But you see, nobody knows the rest of the story. My mother, she never drank from the mug. I never gave it much thought until one day when I was thirsty and used the mug to scoop water from one of the buckets in our kitchen. The realization struck the moment the mug became wet— the unmistakable stench of feces. I was shocked, and the mug slipped from my grasp, shattering into tiny pieces before me. Somehow, dog feces must have mixed with the mud I collected." Mr. Hubble shifted uncomfortably in his seat. A hint of disappointment flickered across his face. "How could I have not noticed this? Maybe it was the thrill of my mother's happiness over the mug. Or maybe it was because I was so accustomed to stench and filth that I had become desensitized to it." He paused, then shook his head dismissively. "In the end, it doesn't really matter."

He spread his arms wide, his gaze shifting from me to the fresco above.

"What matters is that standing here, in my grandchildren's million-dollar gaming room, so close to the end of my journey, I can't ignore the truth."

"And that is?" I asked.

His eyes met mine with an intensity that felt like a physical force. "That my entire empire was built on shit."

I maintained eye contact out of respect before returning my gaze to the fresco. Silently, I concurred with his assessment.

Mr. Hubble was a pioneer in the movement that had decimated domestic jobs for astronomical profits. Millions of positions vanished, outsourced abroad to child laborers who worked in barbaric conditions. He had played a key role in shifting the political landscape of our nation to favor inexpensive foreign-made goods. This strategy wasn't just about being wealthy; it was about hoarding it all, leaving scraps for the many while a select few basked in opulence. In his wake, Mr. Hubble had left countless boys like the one depicted on his ceiling, silently passing judgment from above.

"Your silence is deafening, Ms. Nachtnebel," he finally said, his voice frail.

"Silence can be complex and multifaceted, Mr. Hubble," I responded, maintaining my composure as I observed the man whose greed knew no limits. His visage caught the lights of the gaming room as if we stood in the pits of a colorful hell. "But in this instance, you're correct in interpreting my silence as agreement."

His expression shifted to one of curiosity.

I gently smoothed a crease from my silk dress. "While I understand the allure of luxury and support it, the very existence of *billionaires* seems absurd in my view. To amass such wealth without genuine concern for those in poverty mirrors a lack of empathy. Billionaires like yourself often support a political system that solidifies your elite status and supports a cycle of hardship for the less fortunate. My stance may not reflect the outlook toward all individuals of vast wealth, but in your case, you're right: Your empire is built on . . . *shit*." My gaze remained fixed on him.

The shock on his face soon gave way to a bizarre admiration, reflected in the grin on his lips. He opened his mouth to say something but was interrupted.

"Leah!" Luca Domizio's voice echoed through the grand hall. He approached me with a smile and gently placed his hand on my back in a gesture of greeting. He was aware of my dislike for cheek kisses and hugs. "I've been looking for you." Luca smiled at Mr. Hubble. "Blink twice if Ronald has kidnapped you to have you all to himself."

Mr. Hubble laughed. "Luca, I'm afraid this time you're off the mark. I believe nobody could kidnap our most beloved wunderkind. She seems quite immune to my charms, if you really need to know."

"I can't believe we've finally encountered a woman who sees right through your crap. Remember Miss Universe?"

Mr. Hubble chuckled. "How could I forget her? If I laugh on my deathbed, only you, my friend, will know why."

Both men laughed.

"Would you mind if I steal Ms. Nachtnebel for a moment?" Luca asked.

"Only if you bring her back to me," Mr. Hubble said with a grin. "Our conversation was very, well, engaging."

"I'll do my best," Luca promised, then walked out with me onto the terrace. He closed the large double doors as I leaned over the white marble patio railing. Its cool touch soothed my warm skin.

"I knew you had friends in high circles," I said. "But I didn't know how high."

"Most of these friendships stem from my darker days. Some of them are sincere. Others are afraid of me. In any case, as a simple government contractor, I can now openly attend their lavish parties. But you already knew you'd find me here, am I correct?"

I remained silent.

"Something tells me that an innocent evening chat isn't why you asked to speak to me after your concert, is it?" He leaned against the railing next to me.

"No."

He nodded. "They're still talking about you as if it were *their* dying wish that you played here tonight, not Ronald's. The Grand family wants to offer you double whatever he paid you to play at their silver anniversary."

The Grands . . .

I couldn't help but grin. How ironic would that be? And yet, no thanks.

He threw a curt nod in the direction of the great hall. "There must be more wealth in this one room than in all of North America combined. I always thought you despised our nation's puppet masters. Lately, you've surprised me, Leah. First, the concert in Italy, and now this."

He was referring to my history of never playing at these parties before, no matter how much I was offered. Even presidents had to come to Boston to see me. But things had changed. There was an enemy out there far greater than any before.

"I'm adapting to new circumstances," I said.

"I can see that. And I'd be lying if I said it doesn't worry me a bit. Are you in trouble?"

I faked a smile. "Always. Do you know a man called Jan Novak?"

"Never heard of him. But I can ask around."

"Please don't."

It was better to lay low right now. I had nothing on Jan Novak other than a strange feeling. Drawing his attention to me by asking around would not be in my best interest one way or the other.

"But that's not why you called me here," Luca concluded.

"No. I need to ask a favor."

"A favor or repayment of my debt?" He smiled.

"Whatever you want to call it."

His smile faded.

"Will you stand by your word?" I asked.

"Of course. I always do."

I nodded. "I don't know when or where, but someday, an FBI agent will approach you and ask for your help. It's important you do as he says."

Luca's eyes narrowed. "Which will be?"

The floral scent of the vast gardens now felt heavy. "Something that might seem horrific at first, but only you can—"

"No, Leah, not that," he said.

He knew. Of course he did. He was one of the smartest people I had ever met.

"Ask me anything else," he said in a harsh tone. "Anything. Money. This house. Any house. The head of anybody in that room." His finger shot toward the great hall I'd played in only moments ago, where the elite were now conversing over $50,000 whiskey about vacation homes in Europe. "But not that," he added, his eyes scowling as he shook his head.

"I'm sorry. This is what I'm asking of you to release you from your debt. Do I have your word or not, Luca?"

He looked at me in defiance.

"Luca," I said, stepping closer, inches away from him. I could smell his cologne. His body tensed at my proximity. For a moment, he seemed distracted, his narrowed eyes widening. "You've never broken your word. Your word is who you are. You've always said so yourself. Do I have it or not?" I asked again, my hand gently grabbing the white jacket of his immaculate hand-tailored tuxedo.

Agony was evident on his face. He resisted a moment longer. Then, after a light squeeze of my hand on his arm, he finally nodded. With force, he turned away as if unable to look at me for one more second.

I knew my request would hit him hard. Perhaps more so than any other request I could have made. And yet, there was no other way.

"I feel played, Leah," he said as he stared at the garden, his back turned to me. "I would never have asked you for the favor in Italy if I'd known the price of it. You know that."

I pinched my lips, looking at the man whom I had indeed played. All I could hope was that the fallout here would make things easier on him once the time came.

But the Train Track Killer would use all his genius against me, pushing me to the very edge of sanity. Checks and balances had to be in place.

My empire, too, was built on shit.

"I'm sorry, Luca."

He remained silent. I lingered for a moment longer, then departed just as my phone buzzed in my purse.

If this were the moment to feel sorrow, guilt, or shame for my actions concerning Luca, I would have embraced those emotions if I could. But, as had been the case so often before, I found myself unable to feel. No matter how much I wished otherwise, I simply couldn't.

For what it was worth, I did feel a sense of deceit. But a war had begun—a conflict against an enemy vast and unseen, a battle that threatened to obscure my distinctions between right and wrong, good and evil, like a blurry watercolor painting in which one color bled into the next. These were the lines that defined morality, the lines that defined me.

In the context of love and war, as the saying went, all was fair—and in this instance, the same principle applied to the pursuit and eradication of monsters.

Including myself.

ELEVEN

Liam

"Two wrongs can make a right?" McCourt yelled at us, spit flying between words like a rabid dog's barks. His piercing blue eyes bore the look of a man accustomed to command, and his perfectly coiffed silver hair complemented his authoritative stance.

The meeting room of the Behavioral Analysis Unit at the FBI Boston headquarters had never felt smaller. The walls seemed to close in on me as the entire floor's unit crammed into the space. A few lucky individuals had snagged makeshift back-row seats by standing just outside the door; they literally couldn't fit inside.

McCourt clutched a copy of the Boston Globe, its front page featuring an enlarged print of the sticker that had been audaciously placed on Harvey Grand's casket. He brandished the newspaper as though it were a wand and he a wizard ready to declare, "You shall not pass."

"This is the last time—I repeat, the last time—I give you jokers a chance to come clean," he bellowed, slamming the newspaper on the table. The motion rattled the coffee mugs on the table's surface. "Because God, Jesus, Jehovah, Allah, Santa, or whoever else you pray to shall have mercy on your pitiful soul if I find out it was one of my own who did this after I leave this room today!"

A heavy silence fell, punctuated by a stifled cough. I avoided eye contact with McCourt. Instead, my gaze briefly met that of Heather, who had spent most of the meeting staring at the table.

"Senator Wheezer is livid," McCourt continued in a weary yet calmer tone as if he were explaining something painfully obvious to children. "And why is Senator Wheezer livid? Because Senator Wheezer just lost five million dollars in campaign funding from the Grand family. And why does that matter to us, you might ask? Well, let me spell it out for you. Because Senator Wheezer personally requested that the Boston FBI ensure the smooth return of Harvey Grand's body. And when a senator, whose political party has recently approved our request for additional funding for staffing, asks us to do something, do we get it done?" He held up the newspaper again. "Or do we take a big juicy shit in his yard in broad daylight?"

He paused to catch his breath.

"The whole fucking nation is now talking about the Grands. They're receiving death threats. Ruth Grand even had to cancel her trip to Paris, and her grandson has been called a 'monster's cunt' at his private school. And why? Because somehow you managed to turn a confidential mission into a national circus. Before you Einsteins took charge, almost no one knew of the Grands' connection to Harvey Grand." McCourt slammed the newspaper on the table once more. "But leave it to us," he yelled. "The nation's brightest and finest. We'll leak confidential information to the press and ridicule one of the most powerful families in the nation with a sticker that sounds like a bad fortune cookie!"

Dead silence reigned as McCourt caught his breath again. He wasn't done. I knew it was just the eye of the hurricane. I used the brief quiet to check my phone quickly. It read 3:29.

Cold chills raced through me.

The hearing for my never-ending custody battle was at 4:30. I had to leave soon. Really, really soon. And to make matters worse, Leah had been ghosting me for a while. At first, she'd simply denied my requests for a meeting, which pissed me off, considering what she'd pulled with Harvey Grand. But then she'd stopped replying to my texts altogether, which drove me mad with anger and a strange sense of worry. Had the Train Track Killer gotten to her? Was he holding her hostage? Would my car blow up soon? Or would I find her head on my pillow like some sick homage to The Godfather?

Relax, I told myself. It's Leah we're talking about here. And that woman was no one's victim. Not even the Train Track Killer's.

"Last chance. Anybody want to come forward?" McCourt said this in a much kinder tone before his eyes settled on his nephew, Cowboy.

Cowboy, who had been doodling on a piece of paper in front of him, took a moment to realize that everyone was staring at him. When he did, he looked up with lost innocence and scanned the room. "Hmm?" he managed, the sound almost stuck in his throat. His eyes, wide with panic like those of a mouse under a cat's paw, found mine. I quickly shook my head at him, signaling discreetly. He understood and shook his head emphatically at his uncle.

"Are you sure, Theo?" McCourt said, his tone still soft.

"Sure . . . about what?" he replied, hastily covering his doodles.

"The sticker, goddamn it!" McCourt snapped.

"No!" Theo recoiled. "It wasn't me. Of course not! I'm an FBI agent. I wouldn't do something like that! If this is about the smiley sticker that was on my desk . . ." He produced a yellow smiley sticker from his jacket. "It ain't on no coffin. Still have it."

The room buzzed with murmurs and sighs. I rubbed my temples.

McCourt stared at Cowboy in disbelief, then pointed toward the open meeting room door. "Everybody, out!"

Agents hesitated, unsure if this was a trap.

"Now, goddamn it!" McCourt barked.

Everyone rushed to get out as quickly as possible. Already on my feet, I caught McCourt's direct gaze.

"Not you. Rose, Richter, Connor, Martin, and Theo, you stay."

"Shit," I mumbled, checking my phone again. It read 3:57. I had to leave immediately to be only five to ten minutes late. "Sir," I said respectfully, "I really need to go. I have my custody hearing at 4:30 and—"

"Then I recommend you stop bickering and sit down again. This will be over quicker if you do as I say."

I caught the empathetic looks from the others. Missing this hearing wasn't an option. These sessions took months to schedule, and Larsen had been killed before he could help get a new judge. I was officially stuck with one of the most inept judges the bench had ever seen. This judge seemed determined to favor Sara, no matter the size of her lies or demands.

So, I remained standing. "Sir, with all due respect, this custody hearing can impact my rights to see my daughter. I would have called in today, but I wanted to respect your urgency."

McCourt looked at me as if he couldn't believe I dared to defy him openly. "It's your choice, Richter, but if you decide to leave now, you might have to explain to the judge how you plan to support your daughter without a job."

I heard Heather's gasp before Martin's.

May all hell freeze over. Had this asshole really just threatened my job? After everything I had done for this unit?

"Sir." Heather tried to stand up for me, but McCourt raised his finger at her.

"Don't you dare!" he said. "All of you. The situation is bad. Really, really bad. If I end up losing my job because of this, I'll make sure to drag down every bad seed along with me. The FBI deserves only the nation's brightest, not its bottom feeders."

Heather was about to say something else, but before she could get herself in real trouble, I sat down and signaled her to do the same. Hesitantly, she did.

I threw McCourt an intense gaze, which he ignored.

Asshole.

"Where are we with the Bay Reaper?" he demanded. "Elections are coming up for Senator Wheezer, and the Reaper needs to be taken off the streets by any means possible."

Heather opened the manila folder she had tucked under her arm. "We interviewed a suspect, Jason Brown. He matches the description in height and weight and has no real alibi except his alcoholic wife's promise that he was at home with her. Both have a record. Misdemeanors. His sister-in-law called the police on him when she found a skull mask identical to the one used by the Bay Reaper in his laundry room during a visit with his wife. Also, one of the victims released from the hospital, Bonnie Marks, identified him in a lineup. After one wrong try."

"Great. So, that's that, then." McCourt's tense body relaxed for the first time since the meeting had started.

"Not really," I dared to disagree, all eyes on me. "We don't have enough to keep him. The witness didn't reliably identify him. No murder weapon was found, and no DNA ties him to any of the victims."

"So?" McCourt countered. "Agent Connor, when you interviewed him, did he say anything damaging?"

Heather straightened in her chair. "Not to me. The police showed me a confession that he apparently signed after seventeen hours of interrogation. When I met with him, he insisted he signed it just so they would stop. He didn't have a lawyer with him either. There's definitely something strange about him and the way he acts, but I can't say for sure if it's the behavior of a murderer."

I nervously checked the time again: 4:10.

Fuck, fuck, fuck.

"Open and shut case, if you ask me," McCourt said.

I locked eyes with Agent Rose. Her calm, almost detached demeanor had gained my admiration earlier when McCourt was yelling at us.

"Sir," I said, trying to sound confident yet respectful. "Can I look into the case a bit more? I haven't had the chance to review the new evidence yet." I couldn't sign my name to anything I wasn't certain about. Especially not if it involved framing an innocent person.

"And you won't need to. Focus on helping the AG nail Brown," McCourt replied, gathering his files from the meeting table.

Yes, God, let me out of here.

"Got it," I said, rising to my feet. There was no point in arguing further. I'd investigate the case regardless of what McCourt said. He might be my boss, and he could make my life hell, but ultimately, we all had to follow FBI rules and a code of ethics. Sending innocent people to prison wasn't part of that. "Is the meeting over?" I asked, my legs almost shaking.

The moment McCourt nodded, I turned and ran.

I knew I wouldn't make it on time, but maybe I'd get lucky. Maybe the judge would be late herself. Or, more unlikely, maybe she'd be empathetic to my situation for a change.

As I raced down the courthouse corridor, my footsteps echoed ahead of me. Faded photos of local monuments under dim lights adorned the seemingly endless hallway. I passed several imposing wooden doors, each leading to a courtroom where people's fates hung in the balance, until I halted before one of them.

My breath caught at the sight of my mom sitting on a bench, her figure small next to the old, grand doors of the courtroom. She was wearing her Sunday best, her usual glittering purse replaced with an elegant black leather one. When she met my gaze, her thin lips curled into a sad smile.

"Oh, Liam," she said, rising from the bench to place a gentle hand on my shoulder.

"Please tell me they didn't start yet."

Her silence was like a stab to my heart with a dull, rusty dagger.

"Well, let's go. I'll explain—"

My hand had already reached the door when my mom pulled me aside.

"You're over an hour late."

"They didn't let me out of work, and then I hit commuter traffic."

"I know," she said, her tone soft and understanding for once. "Dan told Judge Ethel Dunbar as soon as you texted him, but she waited only ten minutes. She said that 'she knows entitled men like you.' Then she issued a default judgment in your absence, favoring..."

Her voice broke off as the doors opened and Sarah and her lawyer walked out. She was arm-in-arm with her TikTok boy toy, looking as if she'd just stepped out of a courtroom TV show. Her hair was in a bun, and she wore glasses—with fake lenses—that matched her suit skirt and pumps. Her brown eyes locked on me as a devilish grin formed on her pink-colored lips.

She slowed her pace, her lawyer already walking ahead, unaware. Then she had the audacity to lean in and whisper to me, "Vanilla, Liam. You'll always be vanilla. You were never more than that. Only now, you'll have to be worthless without your child."

I was practically shaking with anger and frustration. If not for my mom grabbing my arm and the fact that Sarah was already moving again, almost halfway down the hallway, I would have lost my cool and called her out for what she was.

A cunning piece of shit who'd thrown her own child under the bus.

"Where the hell is Dan?" I demanded, a little too loudly, as a passing couple looked at me. I searched the hallway for my lawyer. The man to whom I paid four hundred and twenty-five dollars a fucking hour to prevent this very thing from happening.

"He had to go to another trial," my mom said.

I took it all in. How the hell had this happened? All of this. Sara cheating on me. Taking everything. Me working myself to death for a world that had awarded my case to a sexually frustrated old judge who hated men for the same reasons I now hated my ex: getting played.

"It's just all getting so freaking much," I mumbled as my head fell into my hands. My mom's fragile body pressed against me from the side, her thin arms wrapping tightly around me. I was a grown-ass man, but right now, losing Josie . . . I could feel hot tears in my eyes. I felt nauseated.

"Dan said we'll appeal," my mom said. "He says everyone hates that judge. People have filed complaints against her."

I wanted to play this game more than anything else in the world right now. The "let's talk until there's hope again" game. After all, hope was all we had left when darkness swallowed us whole.

But for some reason, my anger sharpened like a knife, and one name was at the tip.

Leah.

I pulled my flip phone out of my coat pocket and opened it.

Nothing.

No calls, not even a "fuck off" text.

I'd had enough. I was sick of being the kind dumbass. I was sick of playing by the rules of decency and kindness when nobody else gave a fuck.

My arms wrapped around my mom, squeezing her tightly. "Don't worry, Mom," I said, realizing she was shaking. "Dan's right. We'll appeal until we get a real judge with some backbone. I don't care if I have to take this all the way to the Supreme Court. We'll get Josie back."

She nodded, sobbing as if she'd been waiting for me to be strong again before showing her own pain.

"Don't cry, Mom. We can still video-call her whenever we want."

She nodded.

"Actually, why don't you go home and do just that? Josie wanted to talk to you about the essay she wrote in school. It was about you."

"Really?" My mom looked at me with wide eyes. The mascara she'd worn so gracefully moments ago was now smeared all over her cheeks.

I nodded. "She read some to me. It was the best essay I've ever heard. She must've gotten that talent from you. No one else in our family knows how to write like a poet."

"I did win an award for a piece I wrote for our school newspaper." My mom smiled again. Good. "Are you coming as well?" she asked as I pulled away from her.

"Later this evening, I will. I have something important to do for work right now."

She frowned, her mouth opening to snap at me—her old self again—when I quickly added, "It's important to have my work in order and great references from my supervisors for when we appeal and get that new judge."

My mom thought about this, then nodded. "Very true. Things need to be in order and look good."

"Exactly," I said. "Come on, I'll walk you to your car."

She nodded again as she wiped away tears.

As I walked her down the hallway, my hand on her back for emotional support, I promised myself two things.

One, I was done being people's little bitch.

And two, "people" included the genius mastermind who thought she had me wrapped around her finger like a puppet on strings, dancing like an idiot to every pull and tug of her whims.

TWELVE

Leah

The moment I stepped into my townhouse on Beacon Hill, I sensed something was off. The alarm system had remained untriggered, yet the unmistakable presence of someone in the house lingered in the air. Ida was likely already asleep or watching TV in her cottage in the backyard, as she would have greeted me right away if it were her.

I reminded myself to stay calm. My body's first instinct was to release adrenaline, which would have been helpful if I planned to run, but that wasn't my intention.

As though nothing were amiss, I switched on the lights in the hallway and walked upstairs to the master bedroom closet, keeping a vigilant eye on the stairway as I did.

No shadow or movement.

Good.

With a smooth motion, I retrieved the loaded handgun from beneath a pile of folded silk pajamas, then selected one of the garments and put it on.

Maintaining a normal pace and holding the gun behind my back, I descended into the darkness of my study. There, I listened intently for unusual noises, ready to aim and shoot at a moment's notice. I was about to turn on the light when a voice broke the silence.

"It's me, don't shoot," Liam said calmly.

For a moment, I remained motionless at the wide entrance to the study. Then I lowered the gun and turned on the light.

Liam was seated on the Victorian wood bench by the bay window overlooking the back garden. He was dressed in gray jogging pants and a sweat-soaked T-shirt. A hoodie was loosely tied around his hips. A black backpack leaned against the bench on the floor.

"A rather risky move, don't you think?" I asked.

"Maybe. But don't you want to know how I got in?"

I calmly made my way to my desk. "The small cat door in the kitchen, of course. You used a wire to unlock the door from the inside. Then you used the law enforcement code for the alarm system to turn it off. What I'm curious about is, if you knew I was armed, why did you wait until I came back downstairs before you identified yourself? A little idiotic, don't you think?"

Liam's face contorted with anger. "I jogged five fucking miles in the dark, and I'm going to have to jog five fucking miles back to my car. So, don't get smart with me now. I waited here for you because you went straight upstairs to your bedroom, and I didn't want to follow you there like some pervert."

"So, you risked a bullet to the head in the name of decency? Next time, I'd prefer you do something you deem morally wrong over getting yourself killed."

I placed the gun on the wooden desk next to a bottle of wine and a set of glasses, then made my way to the large stone fireplace. Liam watched with curiosity as I built a fire from a small pile of wood beside it before taking a seat behind my desk.

"How can I help you?" I asked, reaching for the bottle of wine and pouring myself a glass. My gaze lingered on the empty second glass, the one I had set out for Emanuel months ago but hadn't removed. It wasn't in anticipation of guests but as a poignant reminder of my failure that had led to his death. A promise to myself to try harder next time, regardless of the cost.

"How can you help me? Let me tell you how." Liam held up the flip phone. "Remember this thing?" His tone was tense and laced with sarcasm. "People use it to communicate, meaning it's a two-way street, Leah. Back and forth."

"So, you thought it was wise to break into my house to confront me?"

"Wise wasn't part of the equation," Liam retorted, stepping closer. "But it was a risk I was willing to take to get a few things straight." His expression softened. "And to make sure you were okay. I was worried."

"Worried?" I raised an eyebrow.

He recoiled slightly. "Yes, worried. I've been texting you for almost two weeks. You rejected every meeting request, then completely ghosted me for days. I was losing my mind, checking your social media and the news for any sign of your death. I even drove past your house a few times. The Train Track Killer is still out there, doing who knows what. So, yeah, I was both pissed and worried, if that's all right."

I leaned back in my chair, watching the flames cast a soft glow on his face. He wasn't particularly handsome, at least not in the way the escorts I paid for were. Still, he had a quality that any discerning woman would be wise to value. That quality was worth more than A-list Hollywood looks.

Loyalty and kindness.

Liam had plenty of it in a world desperately lacking in both.

I grabbed the bottle of wine and poured him a glass before he could decline.

He looked at the glass warily for a moment. Maybe he was concerned about leaving DNA, or maybe he thought I'd poison him. But then he took it and settled into the chair across from mine, on the other side of the desk. He opened his mouth to speak, but I was quicker.

"I thought you needed some time to digest Harvey Grand. That's why I didn't agree to a meeting and stopped replying to your texts. I'm sorry it caused you emotional distress. I'll try to be better about returning your texts."

Liam's mouth closed. He appeared to be satisfied. Then he leaned onto the desk, glass still in hand, his intense look returning. "Thanks. Now, regarding Harvey..." He sighed, shaking his head. "What. The. Actual. Fuck, Leah. Have you seen the man? I mean, have you actually *seen* what he looks like now? Cuz if you haven't, I'm more than happy to show you some pictures. But let me warn you, it ain't pretty. It's bad. Really, really bad."

I let him speak as I sipped my wine.

"Actually, no. Not bad," he continued. "The right words for it would be fucking horrific, Leah. He looks fucking horrific."

"I'm aware. I stuck to drugs, as agreed, but allowed for some artistic freedom."

"Artistic freedom?" he echoed. "Are you kidding me? McCourt was furious. Not only did I get yelled at for this shit, but if the media had found out how bad Harvey really looked, it could have drawn a lot more attention than the shitstorm we're dealing with now. And I have enough on my plate as is!"

There was more than anger here. I wondered what else was at stake for him.

"I apologize," I said.

There was a brief silence as if he hadn't expected my apology and was now searching for plan B.

"Apologize, huh?" he said, much calmer now, like an erupted volcano with no lava left. "That's not enough, Leah. I . . . I can't work like this. I understand Harvey Grand was a monster who had it coming, but what I saw down there in that morgue wasn't a human being anymore."

"He never was."

"Maybe so, but I'm an FBI agent. I can't do it like this, Leah, and nothing you say can change that. If that's something you can't deal with, well, then we've got a problem."

He looked up, his gaze locking onto mine. The flickering firelight cast a warm glow in his brown eyes, intensifying their depth. It was captivating, peering into them. There was an almost childlike innocence in Richter, a belief in a better world, paired with a steadfast determination to defend his ideals. This combination fascinated me. I'd never seen anything like it.

I reached for the wine bottle, inadvertently sweeping over the gun in the process. Out of the corner of my eye, I noticed he didn't flinch. Perhaps, deep down, he knew I'd never harm him.

"All right," I said, my tone devoid of emotion.

"All right?"

"I accept your terms. For now."

He furrowed his brow, then nodded. "Good. Thank you." He downed his glass in one gulp. "Sorry, I was really thirsty. The jog here was brutal." His gaze swept the study as I leaned over the desk to refill his glass, but he placed his hand over it. "No thanks."

"Water?" I offered.

He shook his head. "But it's nice, meeting in an actual home for a change. That whole meeting-on-a-dock-in-the-rain thing isn't as exciting as movies make it out to be. Can't you get the keys to your abandoned factory near the docks so we can meet there? This is the wettest year on record. After our meetings, I have to wear wet clothes all day."

I couldn't help but grin. "I'll look into it."

His lips twisted into a smile. Then an awkward silence fell upon the room, punctuated only by the crackling of the fire.

"Have you discovered anything new about the Train Track Killer?" I asked.

He shook his head, his shoulders drooping. "No, nothing. I've been monitoring the entire train network from New York to Portland for deaths but haven't spotted anything out of the ordinary. What about you? Anything from your meeting with the Egyptologist?"

I shared his feeling of defeat more than I cared to admit. "Nothing substantial. But I did manage to get some additional insights into the symbolism of the ankh. It's commonly associated with eternal life, but the Egyptologist presented a compelling argument that it might also represent a mirror."

"A mirror? Like a reflection of the killer?"

"A reflection of his true self. Maybe as a preparation for the afterlife."

Liam's gaze drifted off, and a thoughtful furrow formed between his brows. "Or he believes these murders will give him powers or immortality."

I leaned back in my chair. "I've been mulling it over, and yes, that's a possibility. But it's only one theory among many. Maybe the Train Track Killer believes that by revealing his true self and making offerings, he'll gain favor with the gods or whichever higher power he believes in."

"Like some twisted version of the Make-A-Wish Foundation?"

"Possibly. If his victims were human sacrifices."

"And the trains? Why the train tracks?"

That question tortured me. I had no definitive answer. "I can't say for certain. There might be a link to his past. Maybe he lived near a train station, or maybe he suffered a traumatic event involving trains. But it's equally plausible that he simply uses them as a means to conceal his crimes. Train police are underfunded and lack a dedicated murder investigation unit. Moreover, they're notoriously inept at seeking assistance from local police. The train tracks could just be a cunning strategy to remain undetected."

"Which he has, for years."

I nodded solemnly. "We must continue to scrutinize old and new files, but I'm afraid he's currently dictating the play, and we're mere pawns."

Liam clenched his fists. I hadn't intended for my words to strike him as harshly as they did, but the truth can have that effect when it isn't in one's favor.

Suddenly, the black and white cat I'd rescued from Emanuel's apartment leaped onto the desk, nearly toppling my wine glass and the bottle. Initially, the arrangement was meant to be temporary, as shelters were full. However, after my assistant failed to secure a home, and the grim alternative was a for-kill shelter, weeks morphed into months. Now, the cat stood as yet another reminder of the failure that had cost Emanuel his life.

"You . . . have a cat?" Liam's face was etched with a surprised curiosity.

"Not really. It just lives here."

"Rrrrrrriiiiiight," he said.

The cat settled on the desk, scattering fur, which I must confess was a significant irritant. Yet, feeling accountable for its situation, I felt obligated toward the animal. Ida and her family loved the cat, but one of her grandchildren was highly allergic, so the cat couldn't live with them permanently.

"I think it wants to be petted," Liam declared as the cat meowed loudly, its large green eyes fixed on me. Ida was overfeeding it, I concluded from its drooping belly.

"I'm aware," I responded, "but it typically seeks Ida's affection over mine."

Liam struggled to suppress a grin, then surrendered to a full-on smirk. "Well, it won't leave until you pet it. Trust me, I had one of those fur-balls before my ex took him along with everything I love."

His demeanor began to darken, the sadness returning to his gaze, so I quickly interjected, "I don't know the proper way to pet it."

The smirk returned to his lips. "La Imperatrice is unfamiliar with the art of petting a cat?"

His mocking tone irked me. "Clearly, I know how to pet an animal. But my concern is that the cat could perceive my actions as insincere and lacking in genuine warmth. That, in essence, would be unkind. No?"

Liam burst into laughter. "For Christ's sake, Leah. Sometimes a damn cat is just a damn cat."

Before I could respond, he stood, leaned over, and softly clasped my hand. I watched in astonishment as he guided my hand in gentle, rhythmic strokes over the cat's soft fur. The contact, his skin against mine, was thrilling. Or perhaps it was the brief drop in his defenses. For a moment, it seemed as if we'd been close for years.

The only sound in the room was the cat's loud purring as Liam continued to guide my hand. Then the cat bounced off the desk and walked into the kitchen, where Ida had arranged a feeding station in an adjacent pantry.

Liam released my arm and resettled in his chair. "See?" he said, still grinning. "It got what it wanted and then dumped you. Totally normal. Cats are fun creatures, aren't they?"

I remained seated, wrestling with how to process what had just happened. Larsen would never have dared to touch me.

But Agent Liam Richter...

Did the presence of this cat in my home make me appear more human to him? The logic was flawed. History had shown that even monsters like Gacy and Hitler could show affection to animals while committing unspeakable acts against humans.

"Can I ask your opinion on something?" Agent Richter inquired as he retrieved his black bag from the floor.

"Certainly, if it's quick," I replied, rubbing the spot where he had touched me.

He produced a laptop from his bag and placed it on the desk between us. "I'm sure you've heard of the Bay Reaper? He's been all over the news."

"I have, but he's not a typical serial killer. His pattern aligns more with a mass shooter."

"A mass shooter?" Liam echoed, concern filling his voice.

I nodded. "Mass shooters often seek notoriety or act from a vendetta against society, as they desire attention for their personal grievances. Their actions are high-profile, aimed at making a statement in public as some form of revenge."

"Some serial killers want that sort of attention too," he pointed out.

"In rare cases, yes. But serial killers typically operate over a longer period, driven by deeper psychological compulsions for power and control, usually away from the public eye."

Liam turned to the laptop. "This is footage of a potential suspect. His sister-in-law found a skull mask identical to the one used in the stabbings in his laundry room. One of the eyewitnesses identified him in a lineup. His only alibi is his wife, who insists he was at home during the attacks."

I watched the video on the laptop. In it, an older man in military pants and boots was led into a cramped police interrogation room. Two overweight detectives flanked him. "Can you fast-forward to the end?" I asked.

"What?"

"The ending, can you skip to it?"

"Um, sure, but the interrogation was quite intense, and we have a confession. Don't you want to see that part?"

"Not really. I have no doubt about the confession, judging by the two GI Joe police officers in the room. Now, would you mind fast-forwarding to the end?"

Liam's gaze lingered on me for a moment. Then he sighed and pressed a few buttons. "Alright, here you go."

I watched as the older man, exhausted and limping, exited the room, handcuffed, the weight of the world crushing his wide shoulders.

"It's not him," I declared, steepling my fingers.

"All right, Columbo, care to elaborate a bit here?"

"Sure. The man in this video limped into the interrogation room. He has a leg injury that I suspect would prevent him from running long distances or even short sprints. Wasn't one of the attacks by the Bay Reaper prevented by a group of young friends, and he fled on foot? You have to be in good shape to outrun younger men."

Liam looked at me, a mix of puzzled admiration and defiance in his eyes. "He could have faked the limp for the interrogation. Many suspects fake injuries to look vulnerable."

"Which is why I asked you to fast-forward. After hours of grueling questioning, he most likely would have dropped the act if it were fake. However, his manner of rising from the chair, shifting weight to his left leg, and using his arms to spare his right leg seemed genuine."

With narrowed eyes, Liam watched the end of the interrogation several times.

"You could always request a warrant for his medical records to confirm or debunk my theory. Hasn't the FBI interrogated him? Typically, your agents don't rush to judgment without solid evidence, unlike smaller police departments."

Liam leaned back in his chair. "We did interrogate him. Not me personally, but a colleague of mine. I usually trust her judgment, and she mentioned having a bad feeling about the guy."

"Understandable given the nature of the crimes, but I would strongly advise basing judgments on facts rather than feelings. Feelings change. Facts don't."

"I actually agree with you. But McCourt is convinced this man is the Bay Reaper. He's, well, not very receptive to other theories, to put it mildly."

"McCourt is an opportunist. The scandal with Larsen and political changes have put FBI Director Helen Finch in hot water. She's on shaky ground. McCourt knows this is the perfect time for him to step up and become the next FBI Director. But to secure his position, he must prove himself to Congress and the president. With elections on the horizon, he sees the Bay Reaper situation as a strategic asset in key battleground states, including those along the Seacoast. Fear has been a potent tool in both classical and modern political climates since ancient Roman times."

"So, who do you think is behind these stabbings?"

"The TV coverage and eyewitness statements describe a muscular male wearing tactical pants and boots, which suggests he might be ex-military. I wouldn't be surprised if the victims' stab wounds matched the size of a KA-BAR USMC Straight Edge."

"A marine knife? You think he could be an ex-marine?"

"Or an Army Ranger. Why would that surprise you? The government dumps active-duty personnel and veterans the moment they exhibit war-induced injuries. Physical or mental. Many veterans struggle to access adequate mental health services. It's led to a silent crisis of untreated trauma and psychological struggles."

He nodded. "Why do you think he isn't killing them?"

"There could be several reasons, but it's possible he's struggling with dehumanizing his victims."

"You mean he's trying to view us Americans as the enemy but is finding it difficult?"

"Possibly. Soldiers often receive training that encourages them to demonize overseas enemies and their cultures. But considering how veterans are treated by our government, it might not be long before he starts seeing fellow citizens as enemies. Once the first body drops, that's when we'll be seen as the enemy too."

There was a brief silence before Liam packed his laptop away. "Thank you for your insights. I should get going. Josie wants to video-call me at eight, and I still have that damn jog back to my car."

As I stood, I tried not to show it, but Agent Richter had managed to surprise me again. The casual way he mentioned his daughter's name, as if I already knew her, made it seem as though he were speaking to an old friend. I harbored no illusions about our working relationship. Agent Liam Richter likely pegged me as a psychopath, as he should. Yet he seemed to have acknowledged that I wasn't an uncontrollable monster like Harris or the Train Track Killer. In his eyes, I was a human being. It shouldn't have felt as good as it did.

Liam slung his backpack over his shoulder and gave me a faint smile. "No more radio silence," he said.

I nodded. "You can get out through the backyard gate. It's dark and leads to a small alley behind my home."

"Thanks, and . . . sorry for the break-in."

I escorted him to the back door in my kitchen. "Do you know a man by the name of Jan Novak?"

Liam paused, scratching his chin, then shook his head. "No, why? Is he a suspect?"

The memory of Jan Novak glaring at me from the shadows of a dark corner in the Egyptian exhibition during my conversation with Emilia surged forward. His eyes had held a glow that, to this day, remained mysterious to me. "He was at the museum tour," I said.

"Did he say anything suspicious to you?"

Reflecting on our conversation, I recalled the peculiar mix of suspicion and innocence in his words, his probing questions about killing killers. "It's difficult to pinpoint. He's highly intelligent, and certain comments sparked my curiosity."

"I could look into him."

"Can you do so discreetly, without anyone knowing?"

"If I handle it personally, yes."

I nodded. "Let me know what you find."

There was an awkward silence. Liam stood in my kitchen, shrouded in darkness, with only the hallway light spilling in. "There... is something else," he finally said.

I waited for him to continue.

"We received a tip about the Boston Strangler."

"The Boston Strangler?" I repeated. "He's dead. Albert DeSalvo has been linked to the most recent victim."

He nodded. "But as you know, evidence suggests there may have been two stranglers, and the second one was never found. An older woman called, saying her father talks about strangling women in his dreams. I traced the call back to Jill Wilson. She's a crime podcast addict and claims to recognize some of the Strangler's victims in her father's mumbling. Her father is Donald Wilson. I looked into his background, and there might be some truth to her wild claim."

"Truth to him being the Boston Strangler?" The information stunned me as much as the fact that Liam had almost withheld it—a sign that trust was now an issue between us. It wasn't surprising, given our work together.

"As crazy as it sounds, yes. Donald Wilson is a retired parking enforcement officer. That son of a gun is old as hell, ninety-three, but besides a recent hip replacement, he seems to be in great health."

I took it all in, every word. Excitement rushed through my veins like lava from a volcano. If this monster were finally brought to justice, it would be a welcome distraction from the Train Track Killer's years of playing me. "Did you look into the parking tickets near the murders to see if his signature is on them?" I asked.

Liam hesitated again, then slowly nodded. "They... match."

My eyes narrowed as a slight grin spread across my lips.

"His tickets can be traced back to several locations of the murders. Even the dates match." Liam studied my face. "He also had a rape charge and a few domestic violence arrests. I could get a DNA test done."

"No. I'll take care of it."

"Leah..."

"I said I'll take care of it. I'll reach out once I have the locations of the missing bodies."

Another moment of silence hung between us. Neither of us spoke.

"Let me know when it's done," he finally said, then departed.

I lingered, watching the door through which he had just exited. I had promised Liam to restrain myself, for now at least. But when faced with a killer, could I truly hold back? I'd never made such a promise before, and the gratification of making monsters endure their own torment was one of the few joys in my life.

So, when I confronted the Train Track Killer or the Boston Strangler, would I honor my promise? If I couldn't, what did that say about me? That I was a monster myself? A threat to Agent Richter and others? Someone he had to eliminate?

The pact I had made with Luca Domizio provided a strange solace. If Liam ever deemed it necessary to act on it, I would trust his judgment completely. It was oddly comforting. There was a certain allure in knowing I would meet my end before becoming a true monster myself.

But for now, I had to plan and execute my next rendezvous with a killer. And, given his age and infamy, there was no time to waste.

When I saw Jill Wilson sitting at her cluttered desk in the living room of her modest three-bedroom in Mattapan, I knew this mission was rushed and riskier than usual. In the old days, I would have taken Donald Wilson away from his house, tortured him slowly until he confessed and revealed the locations of any missing bodies, and then tortured him more to make him pay. But given my promise to Richter and the broken trust between us, such a *modus operandi* wouldn't be wise in this case. I couldn't operate without an ally in law enforcement. The tip from a broken-hearted daughter that led me here tonight was proof of that.

Jill was absorbed in a true crime podcast about John Wayne Gacy on her computer while a dating reality TV show murmured from the television. It was 10:46 p.m. A quick scan of the room revealed an older woman who had devoted every inch of herself to her children and grandchildren. Pictures of smiling faces were everywhere. Yet the absence of any photographs of Donald Wilson—a man with domestic violence and rape charges—suggested he had shattered his family just as such men usually did.

I quietly made my way along the wall until I found a shadowy corner where I could watch undetected. I observed the woman with curly silver hair as she drank coffee. People who consumed coffee at this hour did so to stay awake—either to avoid nightmares or simply to savor the silence of the night. I knew Jill wasn't seeking silence.

We both listened as the podcast recounted John Wayne Gacy's love for his childhood dog, Prince. Growing up in a violent home with an abusive father, Gacy had found solace in his relationship with Prince. This bond was shattered when Gacy's alcoholic father killed the dog. Gacy buried Prince, stealing flowers for the grave, and was said to never be the same.

"It makes you wonder if a monster could be saved after all, or at least be taught right from wrong before their soul is swallowed by pure evil," I said, breaking the silence.

Jill flinched and sprang to her feet, staring straight at me. I wore a face mask and was dressed in a dark coverall.

"You were right about your father," I continued. "He's a monster who killed many women."

"Who are you?" Jill demanded, frozen in place. Panic and fear twisted her face. The podcast continued playing in the background.

"It doesn't matter," I replied calmly, stepping out of the darkness. "I won't hurt you."

Her gaze flicked down the hallway, where her father was sleeping in a room next to the room where one of her granddaughters slept.

"Quite risky to have the girl here with him around, don't you think?"

Jill stared at me for a moment before bolting for her cell phone on the couch.

"No doubt, the police belong here," I said as she fumbled with her screen. "But before you call them, consider what the world will say and do to your family once they discover the monster this house harbors."

Jill froze, her eyes wide in shock. Her gaze locked on mine.

"As I said, I'm not here to hurt you. I'm here to work with you to make things right—things you, your children, and your grandchildren shouldn't suffer for."

A tense moment passed before Jill tossed the phone back onto the couch. "It's true then?" Her voice was low and weak. "He really killed all those women?"

"Not all of them," I said, "but many, yes. Deep down, you know what he's capable of. He did horrible things to you and your mother, and he'd do the same to your kids and grandkids if you let him."

A tear rolled down Jill's red cheek. Another tear followed it. "I don't have to look very deep to know what this man is capable of. He never made a fuss about hiding it."

I nodded. "Yet you care for him in his final years and let him near your kids."

Jill shook her head. "I'd never let him hurt them. He wasn't allowed near us until about a year ago, after his hip surgery went wrong and both legs were amputated due to a bad infection. He ended up in a wheelchair. When the hospital called and told me I was his emergency contact, I wanted to hang up. But when they told me that they'd found him homeless on the street..." Her voice faltered. "I couldn't say no." She shook her head in disbelief, her gaze dropping to the floor. "They said he'd pass soon. But here we are. I don't know how he keeps going. We all thought he was on his way out, so I granted his wish to die in his childhood home. This house belonged to his parents before my mother took it in the divorce. But I guess darkness gives you more strength to live than light does. He'll probably outlive us all."

I stepped closer, slowly, cautiously. "He won't make it till morning."

Jill's head shot up as she met my eyes.

"I'll put an end to this monster. Here. Tonight. The only question is whether you'll look the other way for the sake of your children and grandchildren or fight me for a monster who doesn't deserve another second on this earth."

Jill's tears flowed more freely until she was weeping into her fist. How anyone could still care for a man like this was a mystery to me, but then again, love itself was foreign to me.

"Captain Fuzzy," she said, her voice weak. "That was the name of my father's cat. A stray. He was the only creature my father ever spoke of with warmth in his eyes. My mother told me how my father used to torture and kill other cats in the neighborhood, pierce them with sticks. Then he'd go home and cuddle Captain Fuzzy all night. Captain Fuzzy meant something to him, maybe something some would even call love. How bizarre." She pressed her fist tightly against her lips again. "These poor women, the way he speaks about them in his sleep . . . I don't think a man like my father could ever be saved, not after he crossed that line of evil. Maybe a long time ago, when he was just a boy—before my grandfather beat the last bit of love out of him. If anybody had saved him then, maybe these women would still be alive. Now it's too late."

Slowly, with the walk of a broken woman, she made her way back to her desk, to the podcast that had been running the entire time.

"I'll check on him in the morning like I always do." Tears were still streaming down her face. "What I find, I'll find."

I nodded and made my way past her into the hallway. There, I stopped briefly. "It'll look like an overdose on his pain medication. If he cooperates, you won't find anything but a man who died in his sleep. If he doesn't, you'll need to tell the ambulance in the morning that he had frontotemporal dementia and that he hurt himself before he killed himself."

Her eyes widened.

I quickly added, "Your granddaughter won't hear anything. We'll be quiet in there."

Jill wiped her tears with a heavy sniffle, then nodded. "Nobody will find out who he really was?" she asked.

I shook my head. "It was selfless of you to call the FBI, but this man has terrorized others long enough. I'll find out where the missing bodies of those women are and send an anonymous note to the police with the locations. I'll tell them the killer died a painful death many years ago. Some families might find comfort in that. But there's no need to destroy your children's and grandchildren's lives over this. The world would treat them unfairly. A monster like your father can be a burden for generations to come."

Jill nodded. I was almost down the hallway when her shaking voice reached me one last time. "Thank you," she said.

"Frontotemporal dementia," I repeated. "Tell them he struggled with thoughts of harming himself." Then I listened for any sounds from Donald's room or his great-granddaughter's room next to it. Hearing nothing, I entered his dark room with my backpack of supplies.

I had a feeling this man wouldn't simply talk, so I was prepared: tape to cover his mouth and prevent screams, a local anesthetic to relieve pain when he was willing to cooperate, and ammonia mixed with water to wake him up if he passed out from the pain. I still needed him to write down the locations of the bodies, so killing him right away wasn't my goal. Fortunately, I didn't need any injections to kill him; a little digging into his most recent prescriptions revealed that Donald had enough fentanyl patches to do the job for me. He had ten 50 mcg/h patches—more than enough to kill him several times over.

It wasn't the death I'd wished for him, but with a little luck, this monster would resist and grant me some foreplay before the drugs carried him into hell.

I'd already decided on the method I'd use to make him talk. His legs were gone, but the weapon he'd used against those women was still intact. By that, I meant the weapon between his missing legs.

Cutting it off with scissors would be a hell of a way to persuade him to cooperate.

Agent Richter trusted me not to leave a gruesome scene, but surely he wouldn't mind a small detail like this if it meant we'd be able to recover the missing women for whom many families had been searching their entire lives.

THIRTEEN

Agent Vallery Rose

Rose spotted the black FBI SUV the moment it rounded the corner. She was unloading another pallet of water bottles from the donation van in front of the homeless shelter when Agent Richter pulled up beside her. Setting down the water, she walked over to him.

"I guess now I know two people who might beat the odds and make it into heaven," Richter remarked, his tone a blend of jest and admiration.

"Let me guess. The other person is you?" Rose quipped.

"Me?" Richter chuckled, shaking his head. "No way in hell. I meant my daughter."

"I see. Well, if volunteering a few hours at a shelter were all it took to avoid those flames, we'd have more than four volunteers today," Rose said.

Richter scanned the surroundings—the individuals sitting alone, clutching their belongings, their faces etched with resignation. He nodded toward a woman in a dirt-stained pink ski jacket who was digging a hole by a bush in the front yard. "What's she doing?" he asked.

Rose followed his gaze and sighed when she saw the scene. "Goddammit," she muttered under her breath, then shouted, "Cynthia! Please stop digging holes in the front yard."

Cynthia looked up, then scurried away.

Rose sighed again. "It took me hours to fill those back in last month."

"Why is she doing that?" Richter asked.

"Because our system kicks those with mental health issues to the curb," Rose explained, "and because she believes she's creating tunnels for hobbits. But what can I do for you?"

"Do you have a moment to spare?" Agent Richter asked. "I want to show you something."

Rose checked her phone. "We start handing out meals in two hours."

"You'll be back in one."

"It's my day off."

"I know. That's why I'm offering to trade you an hour today for a whole day off later."

She pondered this for a moment, then nodded and got into the car.

Rose sat in the driver's seat next to Liam, her gaze fixed on the Cape Cod jail. It was a typical East Coast detention center: a discreet brick complex set apart by its small, secured windows and controlled entry points.

Silence had swallowed the car as they sat there observing the entrance.

Among the many thoughts crowding her mind, one stood out: Why on earth had Richter involved her in this side mission? He was well aware of her role within his unit—and the reasons behind it.

Dragging her along felt counterintuitive, and Rose hated unpredictability—in situations and people alike.

"So . . . any family in the area? Agent Richter ventured. "Any hobbies?"

It was another subtle probe, another attempt to connect. "No," she replied, shutting down the conversation. If Agent Richter expected her to open up like a chatty housewife on a daytime talk show, he'd be disappointed. And if he thought she didn't see through his tactics, he'd be even more disappointed. "McCourt will be really pissed about this, but you know that already," Rose said, still focused on the jail entrance.

"I do." Agent Richter sounded unconcerned.

"So . . . why?"

He turned to her as if she had posed the most bizarre question. "Why what?"

"Really?" Rose scoffed, more annoyed than amused, but she added, "Sir."

Agent Richter regarded her with a scrutinizing look.

"I see," she said. "May I speak freely?"

He nodded.

"Since you're so interested in me all of a sudden, out of the many things I could tell you about myself, including the fact that I hate bullies almost as much as I hate cheesecake, there's really only one thing you need to know."

Richter maintained his attentive stare. "Which is?"

"That while people were opening doors for you, those very same people either slammed them in my face or tried to get in my pants. I grew up in an America some people choose to deny exists. A shitshow not in some far-off communist country but right here, in front of our middle-class mortgaged doorsteps."

She had barely spoken the words, and there it was: the haunting memory of gunshots, the vivid image of her brother lying on the ground, his eyes wide with panic, gasping for breath, urging her to run as he choked on his own blood.

She shook it off.

"I need superhero strength in this world to survive"—she steadied herself—"so if you think you can play me, you're wrong."

A heavy silence filled the SUV.

"Now, let me ask you again," Rose said, regaining her composure, her gaze piercing. "Why did you bring me on a mission you knew would piss off McCourt?"

Rose was somewhat surprised when Agent Richter, instead of getting defensive, simply nodded. "Fair enough," he replied, adjusting his position. "Let's get to the point, then."

"I'd appreciate that."

He pursed his lips. "What are you doing at the BAU, Agent Rose? Why has McCourt assigned an organized crime unit agent fresh out of the academy to one of the most demanding units on the force, one that usually requires years of field experience? Even Cowboy has several post-academy years under his belt."

Ah, there it was. Rose knew there was a hidden agenda behind all of this.

"Well, maybe I'm the Michael Jordan of the FBI," Rose quipped. "Maybe McCourt noticed that and decided to put me here straight out of school."

Richter arched an eyebrow.

"Fine," she said, returning to a serious tone. "But here's a question for you first . . . Sir. Does it really matter if the assistant director of the FBI wants to keep a close eye on a unit that's just been rocked by one of the biggest scandals in FBI history? Larsen made the FBI look like shit."

"It matters to me."

"Oh, yeah? I pull my shifts like everybody else and, so far, thought I was doing a pretty decent job at it. Or are there complaints I'm unaware of?"

"No, you've done more than a pretty good job, actually. Quite impressive, given your lack of experience. It's as if you've been doing this work all your life."

For a moment, Rose experienced the unmistakable warmth of pride swelling in her chest. Hearing those words—words McCourt could never bring himself to utter—felt incredibly satisfying.

"Then"—her tone softened—"why does it matter what I may or may not do for McCourt?"

Agent Richter's face turned grave. His gaze locked with hers. "I'll tell you why it matters. Because as long as you roll with my crew, I need to know whether you wear your badge for a man whose ambitions might not always align with what's right."

As if on cue, the front doors of the police station swung open. A stout elderly woman, maneuvering a walker in front of her, emerged. She was followed closely by Jason Brown, who limped. Their dirty, worn clothes hinted at a life of food stamps and struggle. In weary silence, they headed to an aged SUV parked nearby.

"Or," Agent Richter continued, his eyes fixed on the man who had nearly been wrongfully imprisoned for McCourt's ambition, "do you wear the badge for the people you swore to protect?"

Rose watched the Browns struggle to store the walker and climb into the vehicle. For Mrs. Brown, the ordeal seemed to be like climbing a mountain.

"Let's be even more frank, Agent Rose," Richter said.

Their eyes met once more.

"If I were to take a bullet for you—as I would for any BAU agent—will my daughter cry at my funeral over a man who did the right thing, or will her tears be shed for an idiot who died for a power-hungry man's footwoman?"

Rose almost laughed. She had to give it to Richter. Out of all the fake people she had met in her life, he truly radiated that certain glow that all those righteous people with overly high levels of integrity seemed to emit. They were a rare bunch. A needle in a haystack full of bullshitters. And yet. If he thought he could bring her here, spit out a few clever words, and make her betray the man to whom she owed everything, he was mistaken.

"Fair enough." She mirrored his earlier words, signaling the start of an understanding. "But how about this? If I promise you that I wear my badge to protect people at all costs, does the rest matter?"

Agent Richter studied her for a moment, then nodded. "No. For now, that's all I need to know."

"Good," Rose said, igniting the car's engine. "Looks like we're good, then. Or is there another stop for me on this little field trip? Maybe Legoland?"

"Nope. We're good. For now."

Liam

I dropped off Rose at the shelter and drove away. I didn't wait for her to get out of sight before I called Cowboy.

"Sup, man?" His voice bounced through the phone as I pulled around the corner.

I shook my head, annoyed even at the way he answered the phone. "Where are you?"

"At headquarters. Looking for potential suspects for the Bay Reaper. Heather did a deep search and found quite a few veterans in the area who fit the new profile."

"Good. Hey, listen, could you do me a favor?"

"What's in it for me?" he said.

"Are you kidding—"

"Relax, just joking. What do you need?"

I got into my car and closed the door, then turned on the engine. "Agent Rose—"

"Our Vallery Rose?"

"Yes. She was transferred here from Organized Crime. Did you know her before you came here?"

"Nope. Never heard of her, but I can ask my uncle about her."

"I'm afraid that's not what I'm going for here." There was a brief silence. In my rearview mirror, I watched an agent walk to his car.

"I see," Cowboy said. "Well, I still got some friends at Organized Crime. I'll ask around a bit."

"Discreetly."

"Of course."

"Great, thanks a ton—"

"So, what's in it for me?"

"Are you serious?" I snapped. "I'm still not sure if it wasn't you who slapped that damn sticker on Harvey's rotting corpse, and you're trying to play me?"

"Relax, kidding again."

I sighed loud enough for him to hear.

"I got this, boss," he said, taking on the accent of some Italian mafioso. "You can trust me."

I shook my head, sighing again. Why the hell was I recruiting Cowboy for help at all? This would blow up in my face. I knew it.

"Thanks. Keep up the good work with the suspects."

"Yes, siiir," he said.

I hung up and pulled over for a minute. The thought of meeting her again was stirring up some stage fright. These meetings with Leah always felt surreal.

On the other hand, as strange as it was, the prospect of meeting her eased the feeling of being buried alive with work and the ache of losing custody of my daughter. Then there was the Boston Strangler. Did she take care of him? Why didn't she let me know like she said she would?

The surreal world she had created, pulling me along, seemed to soothe my worldly pains, of which I had too many to count.

"All right," I said, heading back to headquarters to leave my phones behind and switch vehicles so I couldn't be traced. "Hope the meeting will be inside this time."

FOURTEEN

Leah

As I stepped into the abandoned rope-making factory, the crunch of broken glass under my feet echoed through the vast, empty space. Gray light streamed in through the shattered windows and reflected off the gloomy brick walls. Above, birds startled by my intrusion launched into flight with a flurry of feathers before leaving behind total silence.

I waited almost thirty minutes, but that was acceptable for these meetings. Or maybe Liam simply didn't annoy me as much as Larsen had.

Finally, he approached me with confident strides. "I'm sorry I'm late, but I had to oversee the release of Jason Brown to ensure the police station followed the judge's orders."

I nodded. "You did the right thing."

"Not according to McCourt."

"Probably not. But you don't work for McCourt. You work for the people under his supervision. Supervisors can be wrong. The well-being of the people is never wrong."

Liam straightened. "Thank you."

I nodded. "Does meeting inside the old factory still appeal to you?"

Liam made his way into the large roping hall. Dust covered the factory machines. Beams of light from broken windows cast eerie shadows over old ropes on the floor. The air held a stale scent of mold and neglect.

"It's dry. And these walls do give me a false sense of security. Although the crumbling roof and the restless souls that are probably haunting this place are a negative."

"I'm afraid I don't believe in ghosts," I said.

"It was a joke," he countered with a smile.

I watched him as he lifted an old metal hook from the debris-littered ground.

"Kinda cool," he said. "What was this place back in the day?"

His childlike curiosity was surprisingly entertaining. "An old rope factory. The proximity to the sea made it a great location. But it filed for bankruptcy in the seventies due to intense global competition from Asian countries and a decline in demand for new ships because of the growing popularity of air travel."

He nodded. "The land must be worth a fortune now."

"I purchased the property in the nineties. Before the real estate development boom outside of Boston. As long as people keep multiplying, real estate will be a good investment."

He picked up a few more objects, including an old typewriter, which seemed to give him the most enjoyment based on the time he spent pressing old keys. I watched him until he looked at me, having put the typewriter back on a rusty desk. "I'm sorry, but I didn't find out much about Jan Novak."

That wasn't surprising. Something told me that Jan Novak was a man of much secrecy. "What were you able to find out about him? I hope you were discreet."

He nodded. "Special Agent in Charge comes with some perks, I guess. Cyber got me into the system without logging in under a name. We do that sometimes when the CIA asks us to access information without leaving a timestamp."

"Good."

"Don't praise me yet. There really isn't much about this guy that would raise any suspicion. No criminal record. No speeding tickets. Two kids. He filed for divorce. She fought, wanting to stay together, but ultimately lost. That's it on the dirty side."

"What about his childhood?"

"He was born in New York to Slovenian immigrants in very poor circumstances. Not much there about his family, but once he started college, there's more. Got a scholarship to Penn's Wharton, which is the most prestigious business school in the world. That's also most likely where he met the contacts to land him his first job as CEO of a small investment hedge fund. From there, over several decades, he did a lot of smart investing that launched him into the top point-zero-one percent. He's filthy rich. Bill Gates level."

I already knew he was extremely wealthy, but the *how* mattered. "Were you able to find out any details about how he accumulated such wealth?"

"Pretty standard billionaire crap. Real estate is a huge part of it. So are the several hedge fund groups he owns. He's one of the elite who get rich by investing in stocks when the economy is good and then get even richer by betting against it when the country is struggling. Most of his money seems to be in technology stocks. I couldn't find specifics. The ultra-rich keep their portfolios very private. He also owns a large water distribution company, Waterfina, which is stocked in pretty much every store in the US."

I processed this information with a grain of salt. Not that I had expected much more, but this really wasn't much. "Was there anything out of the ordinary?"

Liam frowned. "Not really. The only strange thing is that I couldn't find much on him in footage from any government-owned surveillance systems. Usually, you can type a person's name into a face recognition search and find something. An airport, toll cameras, public street, something. Not Jan Novak. There's nothing."

"You won't find me on many of those searches either."

"Exactly. You know the techniques to dodge facial recognition. But does he?"

"Techniques? All it takes is a face mask, and those are common after Covid. These days, it's easy to leave no trace."

Richter frowned. "So, Jan Novak is just a germophobe who wears a mask everywhere he goes?"

"Unlikely. He didn't wear a mask at the museum."

"Then he's dodging them on purpose. And he knows how to. Now, why would Jan Novak do that?"

I thought about it. "I don't think he's dodging anything."

"Why?" Liam asked.

"When you typed in my name, I still showed up on some searches, correct? Most likely in front of the Smithsonian Museum near the mall. That whole area is heavily monitored due to its proximity to the White House."

"What makes you think I—"

Forehead wrinkled, I threw Liam a look.

"All right. I did look you up as well." He smiled faintly. "But Jan Novak didn't show up in any of my searches. Nothing."

"How is that possible?"

"I honestly have no idea. There are only a few very high-profile cover agents and some politicians who don't show up in those searches. Their faces have been blocked in the database for their protection."

"Would a billionaire have access to this special, well, treatment?"

Richter ran a hand through his hair. "Hard to say, but why not? I was assigned to escort a mass murderer as if he were a fallen hero, all because his family is a mega donor. So, I guess, with money, anything is possible. But the better question is, why would Jan Novak feel the need for that? I can promise you something like this would come at a price tag that even the point-zero-one percent would think about twice."

We both looked up as another group of birds flapped their wings high above us before settling on the metal beams of the roof.

"I was hoping Jan Novak would turn out to be nothing more than a man with strange ways," I said.

"Do you really think he could be a serious suspect for the Train Track Killer? I mean, that sounds farfetched. A billionaire going out at night to place innocent people on train tracks."

"Farther fetched than a world-renowned pianist killing serial killers?"

He laughed. The sound echoed in the vast hall. It was good to hear, almost comforting. For some reason, it had been on my mind how much Richter was struggling lately. "Touché," he said. "Do you want me to look into him again?"

I shook my head. "I doubt it would reveal more. If it's really him, we're working with a man of utter genius. An old parking ticket won't lead us to a crime scene in this case."

"So, what do you want me to do?"

"Did you find anything on his personal life? Any memberships, upcoming charitable events?"

"I did. But I don't think it's a good idea for you to meet with him again. He could be extremely dangerous."

"It's admirable that you're worried about my safety, but it's unnecessary. Besides, I wouldn't expose myself to such risk."

He pondered this, then nodded. "All right then. He has a membership to a fancy fitness club in New York. He plays badminton there. It's called The Club."

"Good. I'll take care of it," I said.

Richter furrowed his brow. "You'll . . . take care of it?"

"Yes. There won't be any fatalities, if that's what you're concerned about. But it won't exactly be legal either. Still want details?"

"Yup. Sure do."

"All right. I plan to hire a male escort from the New York area to go to the gym's locker room and look for a gunshot wound on Jan Novak's shoulder."

Liam processed this. "Are you sure you got him in his shoulder that night in the woods?"

"Yes. If Jan Novak has a scar on his shoulder, it's crucial we investigate further."

"Sounds like a low-risk operation."

"You're on board then?" My tone conveyed my surprise.

He exhaled deeply. "No, not exactly. But with all the chaos in my life right now, if I can eliminate the Train Track Killer from my worries by hiring an escort to peep around a gym, then tell me how much. Let's do it."

"It's on me."

Liam chuckled. "Do I look like the kind of guy who takes a woman out and then makes her pay for her own escort spy?"

"Is that a reluctant stance on equality?"

As he stepped closer, his smile broadened. "Damn it, Leah, can't a man just act like a man sometimes?"

I wanted to say something like this had nothing to do with manhood or that I was well aware of his low income and high lawyer fees. However, that would have wiped the smile off his face. I didn't want to do that. But why did I even care?

"I appreciate it," I said. "But it would be better not to leave any money trail that could connect us." I hoped he wouldn't insist on paying me in cash.

"Always one step ahead, huh?" he said. Our eyes met briefly. His smile was warm.

"Anything else?" I asked.

He furrowed his brow. Clearly, he wanted to discuss the Boston Strangler—likely the primary reason he had called this meeting. "He's dead," I announced.

"What?" Richter sounded outraged. "Why didn't you tell me? You said you'd tell me as soon as it was done."

"I said I'd let you know once I had the locations of the missing bodies. That's what I'm doing now."

He opened his mouth to object.

I quickly added, "Donald Wilson gave me the locations of the missing bodies. Next week, I'll mail an anonymous letter to the Boston police, providing those locations and letting them know the killer has been dead for many years. It'll sound like the late confession of an anonymous family member of the Strangler."

Richter took a moment to process all this. Then his anger dissipated. "Doing it this way will protect Jill Wilson's family."

I remained silent.

"How did he die?"

"Peacefully. Fentanyl overdose," I said.

Richter nodded, satisfied.

"With a small hiccup," I confessed.

"What?"

"He might be missing his privates. I had to remove them to make him talk."

"Leah, goddammit!" he exclaimed.

"He was all tough and stubborn at first," I said, defending myself. "It was a clean cut, and nothing else happened to him before he drifted into a deep sleep, crossing into hell. He deserved so much worse."

Richter cursed under his breath, then nodded. "Fair enough. I'll look out for the letter. It'll land on my desk soon after the police receive it. The Strangler was an FBI case." He sighed loudly as if he'd truly made peace with the whole thing. "Keep me updated on the Train Track Killer," he added.

"Of course."

I had already turned and taken a few steps when an impulse made me stop and look back.

"The Bay Reaper," I said. "From what I gathered on the cases, it seems there's a significant chance he might escalate his actions soon."

Liam's eyes narrowed. "Like what? Some kind of mass shooting?"

"Maybe."

The abandoned factory lay silent. Liam ran his hand through his hair again. It was a gesture I'd come to recognize as a sign of stress or uncertainty. "I'll assign every available agent to this case."

I nodded. Then I uttered words I never imagined I'd say to anyone—because I never cared enough to say them, and I always meant what I said. "Be careful."

They were barely a whisper, soft, as if they were breaching a dangerous threshold.

"I will," he said.

I turned and left the factory, then stepped into the somber early autumn day. The gray skies seemed to probe the depths of my soul.

Be careful. Why did I care so much?

The words, which might have seemed trivial to others, held immense weight for me. My usual indifference to others wasn't out of spite or narcissism; I had simply been robbed of most feelings at birth, leaving me emotionally detached. To some, I was a walking tragedy—another label attached to me by the judging eyes of the world.

Yet something about Agent Liam Richter unsettled me, prompted me to think and act beyond my norm. Not from any sentimental, romantic illusion but from a deeper, enigmatic concern. It was almost as if I feared he was the sole person capable of anchoring my humanity, preventing my descent into monstrosity. Who would I be if I were to become the very thing I destroyed?

I had convinced myself that I was incapable of inflicting cruelty on innocents, that I derived no pleasure from the suffering of others unless they were monsters, which I deemed non-human. But I had never harmed an innocent person, so how could I be certain of my emotional response, positive or negative? How could I know the revulsion I'd feel, the shame, if I'd never crossed that line?

You're questioning yourself again, I chastised myself.

And that was his fault. The Train Track Killer.

He was a constant battle, an unseen foe, unraveling me slowly but surely. It terrified me beyond words to realize that the power to stop this downward spiral wasn't within me; rather, it was in someone else. It lay in a man who'd awakened feelings in me that I hadn't experienced since childhood. Or maybe ever.

It defied logic, yet the outcome remained unchanged.

Time and again, I found solace in the fact that I had a contingency plan.

Should I ever lose myself, it would be the person I trusted more than myself who would end my misery, saving not just me but potentially many others.

FIFTEEN

The Club Gym, Manhattan

The upscale male locker room at The Club was a sensory symphony, oozing luxury. Steam hissed gently from the showers, creating a soothing, rhythmic backdrop to the black marble floors and walls. Scents of lavender and eucalyptus drifted from the steam rooms, infusing the air with tranquility.

Around him, a few guys were wrapped up in their post-workout routines, moving with the ease of regulars. The metallic clink of locker doors mingled with the steady hum of activity. Dylan, dressed and sporting damp hair from his shower, leaned casually against his locker. After months of blowing a high-profile member, he had finally secured membership to this prestigious club. The steep thousand-dollar monthly fee seemed a small price, especially because the club had just netted him an easy ten grand. And who knew? It might even lead to snagging a wealthy sugar mama or daddy, which was the real reason he had joined.

He flicked through his phone, looking for a picture of the man he was meant to find here. A smirk crossed his lips as he thought about the simplicity of it all, especially because he could have sworn he'd seen the guy before in this very locker room.

Then the shower door swung open, releasing a cloud of steam. A tall man, lean and muscular, stepped out wearing a white towel around his hips. Another towel hung around his neck, partially covering his chest but leaving his shoulders exposed.

Shit.

It was him.

Dylan reminded himself of the rules. *No pictures. And don't talk to him.*

He quickly glanced at the aged photo again for confirmation. Matching the man here with the picture of a young college student from the nineties wasn't easy. But the tall build, blond hair, and slightly crooked nose left no doubt.

It was him.

What freaking luck! He had come during peak badminton hours, and there he was.

Picking up a shoe, Dylan turned toward the man and slipped it on. He just needed a good look at the man's face and shoulder. Though the man was now standing sideways, several feet away, Dylan was certain it was the same person.

Keeping his composure, Dylan put on his other sneaker. He glanced down and then up again, focusing on his real task: checking if the man had any scars or wounds on either shoulder.

From his position, Dylan could tell the man's left shoulder was unmarked. Feeling like some undercover agent, with adrenaline and excitement coursing through him, he grabbed his gym bag and rose. Then he moved to one of the sinks along the wall, as it offered a perfect angle from which to view the man's right shoulder. The reflection in the mirror confirmed his suspicion.

The right shoulder was just as smooth as the left. No scars, no wounds. Just toned, muscular skin.

That was it. Mission accomplished. Ten grand earned.

But something in Dylan stirred—an adventurous spark ignited by too many action movies or a childhood dream of being a cop. The thrill of the man being oblivious to Dylan's mission added an element of the forbidden, a sensation long forgotten in his career as a seasoned escort. He felt like a predator observing its prey or a villain sizing up a victim.

Walking halfway across the locker room, Dylan found himself right next to the man. He was on his way out when he inexplicably stopped. "Good match?" he heard himself say, as if his voice weren't his own.

The man, slightly hunched, straightened up, revealing his impressive height. Maybe six-two or six-three? Definitely a towering figure of authority and sex appeal. "Excuse me?" the man said, turning around, his hands adjusting the towel around his neck.

Dylan gestured toward the badminton racket leaning against the man's locker. "Good match?"

The man's prolonged stare sparked a flicker of panic in Dylan. Those eyes held the commanding presence of someone who knew he stood apart from the rest. "Yes, thank you," the man finally said, smiling. "How . . . kind of you to ask."

Dylan nodded, a wave of relief washing over him. He returned the smile. "Have a good day," Dylan said, making his exit.

The man didn't respond, but as Dylan opened the door to leave the locker room and glanced back, he saw that the man was still there, still watching him, frozen. Then the door slammed shut behind Dylan.

It was odd but not a concern. His mission was a complete success: no scars, and his cover was intact.

That ten grand was as good as his. Life was looking up. About damn time.

SIXTEEN

Agent Vallery Rose

Assistant Director McCourt's waiting room was the epitome of sleek professionalism, adorned with framed awards and a stylish modern vase. His secretary, a short woman with a timid demeanor and neatly cut hair, was engrossed in her computer at her impeccably organized desk. Rose observed her with a mix of wonder and disbelief. She didn't know how anyone could tolerate daily interactions with McCourt. The few hours Rose spent with him each month were more than enough to test her limits despite what she owed him.

The phone's ring cut through the silence. The secretary answered with a stoic face. "He will see you now, Agent Rose," she said, her eyes fixed on her computer screen.

"Thank you," Rose responded, moving toward the door to preempt the inevitable "Come in" response to her knock.

McCourt's office was spacious and imposing, featuring a large mahogany desk. He sat behind it, radiating authority and experience. The room was lined with bookshelves filled with legal and investigative texts, while the walls boasted framed pictures of McCourt with presidents and other notable figures.

The atmosphere was always the same when Rose was summoned here. A solemn professionalism tinged with McCourt's stamp of authoritarianism. His rolled-up sleeves— pushed to the elbows in a failed attempt to seem approachable—fooled no one, probably not even himself.

Leaning back in his massage chair, McCourt gestured for Rose to sit across from him. "How is the search for the Bay Reaper going?" His icy blue eyes bore into Rose as if he already knew the answers to all the questions he was about to pose.

Her hazel eyes held steady, barely blinking under his intense gaze. "Every available man is on it. Special Agent Richter is giving it all we got," Rose replied.

McCourt nodded dismissively. "He'd better, after the fiasco with our main suspect."

"Sir, I don't think Jason Brown was an open and shut case," Rose ventured, maintaining politeness.

McCourt clasped his hands in silence. She'd struck a nerve. After almost two years of these meetings, Rose could write a novel about his moods and body language.

"Oh, yes, I forgot. You threw that 'release party' for Brown together, like pals who run the show," McCourt said, his tone dripping with sarcasm. "Would you enlighten me again, Agent Rose, about all those years of experience in the field that supposedly made you an expert on suspects and their handling?"

Rose remained silent, knowing this was her best response.

"That's what I thought," McCourt mumbled, now pissed. "The entire Boston headquarters watched Richter defy my orders. With elections looming, I've got senators and the president himself breathing down my neck about this goddamn Bay Reaper."

Rose had stopped wondering why McCourt always omitted FBI Director Helen Finch from these discussions. It was clear he considered himself her successor, so he no longer bothered to acknowledge her.

"Sir, are you suggesting we should've kept Jason Brown in custody while the real Reaper is still out there?"

"Jesus, Rose," McCourt huffed. "Of course not! Do you think I'm an idiot? But with elections just weeks away, holding a suspect a bit longer wouldn't have hurt."

"Yes, sir."

A brief, awkward silence filled the room.

"Richter thinks the Reaper might be planning something big, like a mass shooting?" McCourt asked.

"That's correct, sir."

"Do you agree with him? He seems to have an awful lot to shout about this Bay Reaper."

"I do, sir. Examination of footage of the Bay Reaper from various surveillance cameras has revealed that he's getting in and out of different cars with fake license plates. On a few occasions, he had an AR-15 slung over his shoulder."

McCourt sighed, annoyed.

Rose continued. "We're looking for an ex-military male, aged twenty to sixty, with extensive weapons training and a troubled mental health history. I'm thinking he could have had a medical or dishonorable discharge, which made him hate society. Add in some economic hardships and a lack of access to mental health services, and this could be the disastrous recipe for something big, like a mass shooting."

"Good God," McCourt mumbled. "A major event now would be catastrophic, especially after the Larsen incident. If only Richter, that self-righteous brat, would've listened to me. The whole nation knows Brown is free, and the real killer will now feel pressure to act quickly before we find him."

Rose hadn't considered that.

"What?" he said. "Did you get caught up in Richter's noble heroics? I'm not the old idiot you all think I am. I was playing this game when you two were still in diapers. We needed time, Agent Rose. Time we might not have anymore thanks to Richter's damn hero complex. And where were you in all this? I knew a guy like Richter would stab me in the back the moment I laid eyes on him, but you, Rose, I can't help feeling a bit betrayed by you. Which hurts even more considering everything I've done for you. Everything I've risked for you."

Shit. This was bad.

Rose stiffened in her seat. "Sir, I didn't know Richter's intentions regarding Jason Brown when he asked me to come along on the mission."

McCourt's eyes narrowed. Rose always felt like she was navigating a tightrope in his presence. He had given her this life at the FBI. When fate had pulled the rug out from under her, McCourt had been there to prevent her fall. But that didn't mean he couldn't finish what the person who'd pulled that rug from under her feet had started. The roles were clearly defined here: king and peasant. Cat kills mouse.

"I"—she cleared her dry throat—"I called you right after I dropped Richter at headquarters to tell you what happened. If I'd known his plans in advance, I swear, sir, I would've—"

McCourt stood, signaling the end of the conversation.

Rose sat a moment longer, sweating, then rose too. "Sir, I'll do everything I can to find the Bay Reaper before something bad happens."

"Then do," McCourt said, opening the door for her. "Because if this blows up, I know who I'm gonna land on to soften the fall, Rose."

Rose absorbed his words as she slowly made her way to the door. "I won't let you down, sir, I pr—"

McCourt closed the door behind her before she could finish her sentence.

Rose caught the secretary's glance before the woman returned her gaze to her screen.

This was bad. Really bad.

Rose had known the trip to the jail with Richter would anger McCourt, but she had underestimated how much.

She had to find the Bay Reaper, no matter what. Otherwise, the next time she was called to McCourt's office, it might be to kiss her badge goodbye.

SEVENTEEN

Liam

The relentless clacking of keyboards and murmuring voices formed the new background noise in my life. Urgency filled the air at headquarters, evident even in the hectic way agents sat and rose from their desks. McCourt had okayed pulling agents from the Critical Incident Response Group and the Counterterrorism Division. All were now assigned to catch this guy before he wreaked havoc at some fall festival, of which the Seacoast had no shortage. Not even the news of the death of a suspect in the Boston Strangler case, along with the locations of the missing women, could keep the media or anyone else distracted long enough to shift focus from the Bay Reaper. As sad as it was, the Strangler was a nightmare of the past; the Reaper was the present threat to anyone living on the Seacoast.

I stood by Heather's desk. Cowboy leaned over, listening to her phone call, while Martin ran a search on a potential suspect.

A local resident had handed in her doorbell security footage of the Reaper's attack on a young college student on a Sunday evening in New Bedford, a small port community.

"And you think John Hunt's alibi is solid for Sunday the fifteenth, around 9:31 p.m.?" Heather asked a local detective about the possible suspect.

I watched intently as Heather, phone in hand, nodded and then shook her head at me.

"Damn it," I muttered as she hung up.

"Not him," she confirmed. "Hunt was at an AA meeting. They've even got him on camera entering the church."

"Guess that means we're on to the next suspect on our universe-sized list," Cowboy said. "You know," he continued, furrowing his brow, "it's actually pretty damn sad how many suspects we've got. These brave men and women gave so much for this country, and now they're potential terrorists because no one gave a shit when they came back from war."

We let that sink in, a moment of shared, silent sadness hanging between us.

"Isn't that the goddamn truth," I agreed, reaching for another file from the towering pile. The photo of a middle-aged army vet met my gaze. His dull and weary eyes, along with his three-day beard and unkempt hair, spoke volumes about his battle with life.

"Oh, look who's finally here," Cowboy said as Agent Rose settled into her desk next to his.

"Are you the new punch clock, Cowboy?" Agent Rose shot back.

"Wait, we've got a punch clock at BAU?" Cowboy asked, genuine concern in his voice. "Because if we do, I just want you to know that those afternoons I left early I—"

"Can you be quiet just this once?" Heather interjected. "And go check out that suspect in Roxbury. We don't have time for this."

Cowboy leaned back in his chair in protest. "I already told you, I don't want to go alone. We never go solo. It's one of the most important rules of law enforcement. Never engage alone."

He had a point, but the overwhelming number of suspects made it impossible to send agents in pairs for initial questioning, especially with local police fighting serious staff shortages.

"We're short-staffed like everybody else," I said. "But I respect any agent's request for a partner. Better safe than sorry."

Rose scoffed. "We're dealing with a potential disaster of unknown magnitude, and you need someone to hold your hand? Just avoid entering anyone's house, and call for backup if things get sketchy."

"Amen," Heather said, marking a rare moment of agreement between them. Not that Rose cared, but Heather was quite open about her feelings toward McCourt's mole in our unit.

"There's no shame in playing it safe," I said loud enough for surrounding agents to hear.

As the unit refocused on their work, I felt my flip phone vibrate in my suit pocket. I discreetly checked it. A text from Leah. I hoped it confirmed Jan Novak had the bullet scar on his shoulder, making him a suspect in the Train Track Killer case. The blunt "No" in the text felt like a punch to the gut.

Damn it.

I realized the room had gone quiet. Cowboy was scanning for a volunteer to accompany him. With no takers, I let out a loud sigh, disapproving of such blatant and childish hostilities toward Cowboy. Annoying as he might be, he was now one of us.

I turned to Martin. "Martin, would you do us the honor of accompanying Cowboy?"

"Me?" he asked, looking up from his computer with the innocent expression of a child caught off-guard.

"No, Martin, not you, the other Martin sitting in your chair," I countered. "Now, would his highness please be so kind as to assist us in this matter?"

Martin got up without another word, grabbed his jacket, and followed Cowboy out the door. I could hear Cowboy in the distance, asking Martin if he'd seen the Vice documentary about competitive goldfish racing.

As I made my way to my office, the weight of stress bore down on me. I still had to visit three potential suspects today. It was a burden I had to carry alone, like most agents right now. On top of that, McCourt was so deep up my ass, it was hard to tell where my ass began and his head started. Then there was Leah and me, grappling with the Train Track Killer case, devoid of leads. Worst of all were the godawful phone calls with Josie crying because she wanted to see me while Sarah stood like the Great Wall of China between us.

It was hell. Absolute hell.

With the next family court appointment still three months away, I had to beg Sarah to see Josie face-to-face. At first, Sarah had flat-out refused. When Josie cried non-stop for two days, Sarah had accused me of turning our daughter against her. Ultimately, though, she had given us three hours a month.

I sat at my desk to quickly type the daily report for McCourt. I knew it was simply a way for him to cover his ass if things went south.

Just then, someone knocked at my office door. "Come in," I called.

It was Heather, who walked in with her usual composed demeanor. "A bit edgy today, huh?" She settled into the chair across from my desk.

"What makes you think that?"

Heather raised an eyebrow and nodded at my chest. "You're stashing pens in your chest pocket again."

I looked down, noting six pens there. "Damn it," I mumbled, emptying it.

"And you were a douche to Martin," she added.

"I know. I'll apologize."

I was about to ramble an explanation, but her deep, empathetic sigh stopped me. "I can't even imagine what you're going through right now," she said, her voice soft and comforting. It was the same tone she used with agents on the floor when they needed it.

"We'll catch him before he targets families at some pumpkin patch," I said.

"That's not what I was talking about." Our gazes met. "I have three little monsters myself, remember? Most days, they drive me crazy. Sometimes, I dream about running away to an island all by myself, far from the chaos. But every time I'm actually away, even right now, I miss them. I'd die of a broken heart if I ever lost one of them."

A sad smile crept onto my lips. "I gotta stay positive. I've got another hearing coming up."

Heather nodded and smiled gently. "You'll ace it. And if not, you can always escalate it to the Massachusetts Supreme Court. Get it out of that cunt's hands."

I couldn't help but laugh. "Heather."

She shrugged. "What? I'm a woman. I know a bitch when I see one. That judge needs a boning bad. Let someone mentally stable decide families' futures."

We both chuckled.

A loud knock interrupted us. It was Rose, who stepped right in. The urgency in her face alarmed me.

"What is it?" I asked.

"Another attack. At the Port of New Bedford."

I rose quickly. So did Heather.

"Which hospital is the victim . . ." Heather asked, but her voice trailed off when Rose's face twisted.

There was no hospital this time. He'd finally done it.

His first kill.

"Shit," Heather mumbled.

"Gather every available agent and send them to the Port of New Bedford," I said. "And radio the officers on site not to touch anything."

"Yes, sir," Rose said as she turned away. Heather followed her.

I fetched my rain jacket with the bright yellow FBI lettering on the back. Then I grabbed my flip phone. I clenched it for a moment before stuffing it into my pocket and making my way into the wind and rain. The summer had turned on us Seacoast folks again, leading us into one of the gloomiest falls on record. One full of rain, dark clouds . . . and deaths.

Liam

I led my team of FBI agents down a rain-slicked dock shrouded in dense mist. Fishing vessels, moored on either side, bobbed slightly in the murky gloom. The scene was illuminated by the flashing blue and red lights of numerous police cars, their colors painting vivid reflections on the boats and dock. The intense gazes of the fishermen followed my team all the way to the end of the pier. We stopped in front of the body of a deceased fisherman in his twenties. A soaking-wet cigarette lay not far from his lifeless hand. His yellow rain jacket was stained with blood. His shirt and fishing pants had been cut open, revealing a large, gruesome incision from his lower xiphoid process all the way to his pubic bone. His intestines grotesquely spilled out. They'd likely fallen as he stood during the attack.

Heather, Rose, several police officers, and my agents surrounded the body in solemn silence. In the distance, a boat horn sounded. Meanwhile, seagulls began to peck at the corpse. They were hastily shooed away by anyone nearby.

"Anything new on the Reaper?" I asked, breaking the silence.

A police officer cleared his throat. "A fisherman from one of the lobster vessels reported seeing a man in a skull mask running away just after a loud scream." He pointed toward a rugged-looking boat bobbing in the water. Its crew stared at us.

"I'll gather any possible surveillance footage," Heather said.

"We should interview everyone who was on the dock that night," Rose added.

I nodded. Those were all logical steps, but as I stood there, facing the grim reality of the Bay Reaper's first official kill, I knew it wasn't enough. "Any other ideas? No matter how small or strange they might seem, they could be vital," I said, still staring at the body.

The group fell into a contemplative silence.

"We're running out of time," Agent Rose said.

I looked into the victim's lifeless eyes. Rain drenched his face, and his mouth was agape in a silent scream that mirrored the terror of his final moment before the darkness took him.

"Yes," I murmured under my breath. "We are."

Reluctantly, I reached for the flip phone in my pocket. It was a move I dreaded, asking the unthinkable. However, we needed to stop the Bay Reaper, and for that, I had to turn to her—the smartest person I knew. Our agreement was far from what I was about to make of it.

It was a desperate measure and a lot to ask, but with lives at stake, how could I not?

EIGHTEEN

Leah

My fingers flew over the keys of my prized new Vanderbilt Bösendorfer, adorned with Monet's forest painting on its lid. I was deep in the spiel of Beethoven's "Appassionata," a piece as dramatic and intense as the piano itself. My right hand darted with quick arpeggios, while my left pounded out solid, rhythmic bass notes. Beethoven's genius lay in his ability to culminate these energetic keystrokes into a final, gripping chord—a fury that was now mine to unleash upon the Boston Symphony Hall audience.

This piano, my dramatic companion, would've justified Hieber's push for pricier tickets if I'd agreed to it. The stage glowed warmly, a stark contrast to the shadowed audience.

As always, the audience included Luca, who was seated in his personal first balcony box. Ever the epitome of elegance in his immaculate white suit, he bore a stoic expression.

As applause and my name echoed through the hall, Luca gave nothing away. No claps, no typical red rose. His gaze held mine for a moment in a silent conversation before he vanished from the balcony. In that uproar, our new, unvoiced understanding was clear.

I pitied him and this situation.

Though I didn't agree with or relish his anger, I understood it perfectly.

Turning to the crowd, still basking in the glow of the Vanderbilt, I caught a glimpse of a familiar face.

Jan Novak.

Like a shadow against the bright stage lights, he sat in the far back row, not clapping, just watching me with those intense eyes, like he'd done during our museum encounter.

As I stood, meeting his stare, the curtains closed. I peered through the satin folds, the applause still thunderous. But when I looked again, Novak's seat was empty. I wondered if I had imagined it all.

I leaned over the leather seats of my Maibach and tapped Mark's shoulder, signaling him to pull over. He had steered us down a dead-end road behind the Veteran's Memorial Pool, close to the Charles River. The atmosphere of the park at night was mystical and lonely. Shadows gently danced as moonlight filtered through the trees.

A dark figure hurried over. I rolled up the tinted divider window, cutting off Mark's view, and opened the back door. Agent Richter jumped in, clearly out of breath.

"Sorry, had to jog here," he panted, fanning his sweat-soaked gray T-shirt. Drops of sweat ran down his exposed arms—not the bulging muscles of a weightlifter but the lean, natural strength of a fit man.

I watched closely.

There was something erotic about a fit man covered in sweat, his toned skin glistening.

"How far did you jog?" I asked, texting Mark to take a spin around the city.

"Three miles," Richter huffed.

"Then you're out of shape," I remarked.

He shot me a look. "I bet I'm in much better shape than your old buddy Larsen. Why didn't we meet at the factory?"

"You said it was urgent, and I'm too tired after my concert to drive all the way out there. Besides, there are homeless and drug addicts lurking around the factory at night. I'm not up for dealing with that right now."

Richter glanced at the window where Mark sat on the other side. "Can he hear us?"

The Boston night scene unfolded outside my window as my Maibach pulled onto the city roads. Streetlamps cast a warm glow, mixing with the headlights of the sporadic night traffic.

"He's deaf. Plus, I pay him too well to talk even if he could hear us."

"Right. Well, good," Richter said.

"So, how can I assist you tonight, Agent Richter? I assume this isn't about the Train Track Killer?" I sounded weary. After my concert, I was mentally drained, and Jan Novak was still lingering in my thoughts. What did he want from me?

Richter didn't answer, so I turned to him. He sat up, fixing his gaze on me. "I . . ." His voice trailed off. His lips pinched as he looked away, then back at me. "I need your help."

His raw, vulnerable honesty surprised me. So did his words. Never had I been asked for help like this before. I had no close family relations, social ties, or friendships, and my relationship with Larsen was certainly not one in which he could ask for favors.

Now here I was, sitting across from this sweat-soaked FBI agent with average facial features, highlighted by the dim light of my luxury car.

And he was asking for my help.

In a rare moment, my forehead creased. "What sort of help?" I tried to clear my head. Money?

Political favors?

Or was he asking me to kill someone? That seemed the most logical, given the nature of our relationship. Shockingly, I wasn't necessarily opposed to the idea.

Agent Richter tensed, the gravity of his worries evident in every inch of his body. "The Bay Reaper claimed his first kill. A male fisherman on the New Bedford docks, gutted like a hunting trophy."

I let the information run through my head as I recognized the core of his request for help. He wanted me to help him solve a case unrelated to our agreement of killing serial killers. His notion was understandable, and yet in no shape or form was our relationship that of a detective couple solving crimes together.

"I think there might be a misunderstanding regarding the scope of our arrangement, Agent Richter," I said.

He frowned. "There isn't. I get our arrangement, really. And I promise you, I'm not trying to turn us, whatever *we* are, into some kind of twisted version of Sherlock Holmes and Dr. John Watson, but I need your help, Leah, I really do. This guy . . . he's about to do something big. You said so yourself. And I need to stop him, or else—"

His voice faltered as if he was exhausted.

I observed him closely: the nervous bounce of his leg, his eyes darting out the window and then back at me. His anxiety seemed fitting for an FBI agent on the verge of a mass shooting. One who was also battling an unreasonable ex in court for custody of his daughter. And then there was me, a black mamba promising not to bite.

"You're right to assume that he's planning something on a larger scale soon," I said, maintaining my composure.

Richter looked at me. He nodded. "We've managed to trace him back to his vehicles on several occasions using neighborhood and traffic camera footage." He extracted a rolled-up folder from the side pocket of his jogging pants and offered it to me.

For a moment, I hesitated as if accepting it would cast us into a partnership I neither had time for nor desired.

But then, in silence, I took the folder and pulled out a few crumpled photographs. They showed a man hiding his face under a mask and baseball cap. He was driving various car models, each with a different license plate.

"This is about all the information we have," Liam said. "No one hears or sees much when he strikes. A fit man around six feet tall, dressed in military pants and boots, wearing a skull mask and stabbing people."

I scrutinized the photos: him entering a white SUV, a black truck, a family van— each vehicle brand-new. "The plates are fake?" I asked.

"Yes. It's unclear whether he owns these cars or steals them. The times of the incidents don't match any regional car rental agencies' logs. The makes and models are among the region's most popular ones, but we were able to rule out car rentals. Privately owned vehicles are a different matter. No law enforcement in the world has the resources to consider all these vehicle models as suspect descriptions."

I narrowed my eyes at the photos before returning them. "I have to admit, he's clever. By choosing these particular vehicles, he's exploiting the very dilemma you outlined. It's impossible to narrow down suspects when he's rotating through the country's most popular car models."

Richter's expression clouded with defeat as he took back the photos, his gaze falling heavy.

"But this tactic will hold up only as long as no one uncovers what he's really doing here," I added quickly, unsettled by his defeated demeanor.

"Which is?" He looked at me, a glimmer of hope flickering in his eyes.

"He's exploiting the lemon law," I said.

"The lemon law? You mean the federal legislation that allows consumers to return defective vehicles?"

I nodded toward the pictures he held. "All those vehicles are brand-new, this year's models, except for the van, which is from last year but still considered new if it came directly from a dealer's lot."

"How can you tell just by looking at the pictures?"

"I have a photographic memory. Car advertisements are among the most prevalent on TV and in magazines. An obnoxious yet subconsciously effective marketing strategy."

Liam looked at the pictures in his hands. "Why would he abuse the lemon law to get new vehicles so frequently? Why not steal them? It would be much easier."

"It's easier but riskier too. This man has dedicated considerable time and effort to the logistical aspects of these attacks, hence the fake plates and car switching. Stealing brand-new cars would be too risky for him, given all the work he's invested. New vehicles are traceable if stolen."

Liam nodded. "But if you buy the car, you're the registered owner, and no one would be searching for it. And if you opt out of dealership title handling, you get a grace period to register the vehicle yourself." His tone lightened as if a weight had been lifted. "That's why our searches for stolen vehicles and rental cars turned up nothing. He's been buying them outright."

"Then, after using the car briefly, he tampers with it just enough to suggest a factory defect and returns it under the lemon law," I said.

"Which grants him the right to a full refund or a brand-new car. Just like that, he's set for his next operation. He could be playing every car dealer along the coast," Richter said, a hint of admiration in his tone. "He's driving around in constantly changing, unregistered cars with stolen plates. If he were ever stopped by the cops, he could play ignorant, providing evidence he had just purchased the car. The cops would assume the plate was a dealership error and tell him to register it within thirty days." Richter's eyes widened, a hint of surprise flickering across his face. "What the actual fuck. I've never seen anything like this in all my years."

"He's cunning, which is a disadvantage for you. Especially now that he's made his first kill."

Outside, a raccoon led its offspring into a commercial trash bin in a dim alley.

"Contact all dealerships within a reasonable radius and inquire about recent lemon law claims," I said. "That's how you'll find your suspect. Time is of the essence. He may have already prepared for his large-scale attack."

Richter shifted uneasily. "I need to get back to the office. Is there a darker park closer to the community college? I don't want to make that run again."

I looked at him with slightly narrowed eyes. "The community college? You're parked near Boston Community College?"

He looked caught. Rightfully so. There was only one reason for him to park at the college, which was out of his way.

I nodded. "I see. May I ask how often you're spying on Anna? She's taking classes at the community college, isn't she?"

He sighed. "I'm careful. I promise. The patrol cars protecting her never see me."

"You need to stop this," I said firmly. "Your worry will draw attention."

"Maybe rightfully so," he countered. "I can't just sit back and watch Anna get killed by the Train Track Killer after everything we've done to protect her."

"Hence the police protection, which already seems to draw attention from Agent Rose. Am I not correct to assume that?"

He remained silent.

"You need to stop this. She made her choice, and you're doing all you can to protect her. If others find out the Train Track Killer is still alive and you were trying to hide that fact, it will make things more difficult for us."

"I understand that," he said, "but I can't just do nothing. Can't you try to talk to her again? Tell her to get the hell out of here? She won't talk to me. Last time she saw me, she turned around and left."

I texted Mike to head toward the community college. This was what I got for working with people with actual hearts. "I will if you promise you'll stay away from her college."

Liam nodded.

"Good. Any updates on the Train Track Killer? Or Jan Novak?" I asked as the car executed a U-turn.

"Nothing."

"Are you certain?" I pressed, defeated.

"Sorry. I'm trying, really. But didn't you say that Novak was missing the gunshot scar?"

"That is correct."

Richter's eyes flickered with confusion. "And you're sure it was the Train Track Killer you shot that night? Maybe there was a third person involved, another lowlife like Patel."

I shook my head. "It's difficult to explain, but the man I encountered that night . . . it was the Train Track Killer. I'm certain of it."

Richter frowned. "If you really shot him, and Novak is missing that scar, why is he still a suspect?"

I looked out the window at a homeless man getting into his tent in front of a supermarket. "No monster I've pursued comes close to the Train Track Killer. This man . . . he's one of the most intelligent and cunning people on the planet. He makes no mistakes, never falters. Each action is meticulously calculated, refined. And now we're both trapped in his web. Novak has a certain energy that I can't explain. And I'm *almost* never wrong."

Agent Richter absorbed the information. "Leros," he said, invoking a word Emanuel and I had once cherished privately. "I didn't want to ask back then, given your recent loss, but what does it mean?"

"I've told you, it's old Greek for 'nonsense.'"

"I understand that, but I meant, why that word? What message is the Train Track Killer trying to send by using it?"

The car slowed as we approached a red light.

"It's not about the word's meaning," I explained, "but the fact that the Train Track Killer knows about it. It was an inside joke between Emanuel and me. He sent that message to tell me he's watching." I nearly smiled, remembering the absurd origin of the word, the day Emanuel rescued a kitten and mused about sending messages from the afterlife. "Emanuel said if he died before I did, he'd send a word only the two of us would understand, a sign from beyond. I'm a woman of logical thinking and science. To underline the absurdity of this belief, I chose the word 'leros,' old Greek for nonsense."

"But . . ." Richter struggled, "how could the Train Track Killer possibly know?"

I faced him. "That's the great mystery here. I thought maybe he'd paid someone to follow me that night or listen in on my conversation at the dinner table. But I had the waiters from the night of my dinner with Emanuel interrogated, quite convincingly, and none admitted to being bribed to listen to my conversation with Emanuel."

"But how else could the Train Track Killer know the word?"

A chilling silence enveloped us as we both lost ourselves in thought.

Finally, I spoke. "As I've said, the Train Track Killer is unlike anyone you've encountered or will ever encounter again. That includes myself."

"I was hoping Jan Novak would give us more," Richter said.

"He still might. Maybe he's not the person he portrays himself to be."

"What do you mean?"

"He attended one of my concerts."

"Jan Novak?"

I nodded. "Tonight. And I'm trying to understand why he's suddenly taken an interest in me."

Richter's lips twisted into a knowing smile. "You realize a man might seek a woman's attention for reasons other than murder, especially if the woman is as—" He paused, reconsidering his words. "I mean, is a renowned pianist."

I found it disappointing that Richter had held back his initial thoughts.

"Don't be ridiculous," I countered. "Of course I know that. As a woman, I'm all too familiar with your predatory kind. I understand my value all too well. I represent the perfect trophy for men like Jan Novak. Yet there's something elusive about him, something beyond mere conquest or sexual desire."

Richter's grin broadened. "Do you want me to beat him up?"

I nearly laughed at his absurd humor, but a smile sufficed.

The car slipped into another dense silence as Mark navigated the dimly lit street behind the community college and then came to a stop.

Richter remained seated, thinking. "Leah?" His tone was soft, laden with sincerity. Our eyes locked.

"Would you . . . I mean, the Bay Reaper—"

"No," I replied firmly. "Not as things stand with him as of now."

"But isn't he, I mean, a killer?" he persisted.

I smoothed out a wrinkle on my dress. "I hunt monsters, Agent Richter."

"If he does what we suspect, doesn't that make him one?"

I shook my head. "This is different. The monsters I hunt were born with a darkness so deep there is no hope. Only darkness can welcome them back into the hell they slipped from. Their souls are empty. Their hearts beat for them and them alone. Even what they claim to love is only there to serve them. But this one . . . your Reaper. This one was made by us. He joined the military to make a difference, but he was disillusioned by the very society he aimed to protect. Returning home, he didn't find the embrace of a grateful nation or the helping hand he needed. He found only neglect. The system that was supposed to be his safety net failed him. Your monster wasn't born a monster. He was turned into one by our nation's collective indifference."

Agent Richter's expression was a mixture of sorrow and contemplation. "Then let's hope there's something of him left to save."

"I fear it's too late for redemption. But maybe you can prevent him from truly becoming the sort of monster I would hunt. There would be some mercy in sparing him that."

Richter lingered, then opened the door. He paused to look back at me. "Thank you."

I nodded. As he was about to exit, I leaned forward. "Richter," I said.

"Yes?" He halted, his hand on the door.

"This . . . you and me . . . this won't turn into some twisted version of Sherlock Homes and Dr. John Watson." I cited his earlier words. "That's not the nature of our agreement. I can see why the lines might blur, but my purpose here on this earth is clearly defined. By me. And me alone."

He held my gaze, nodded once, and then gently closed the door.

As we drove away into the night, Richter stood motionless, watching us merge back into the city's illuminated expanse.

NINETEEN

In the crowded command center of our Providence FBI Field Office, I stood with Cowboy, Rose, and Martin. They were at my side like loyal knights at a modern-day round table. The air was heavy, tinged with the scent of sweat, strong coffee, and musky deodorant, laced with the occasional hint of perfume from the female officers. The room buzzed with the presence of every available FBI agent and local law enforcement officer from the Providence area. All of us were armored in bulletproof vests, our faces a mix of focused anxiety and unwavering determination.

Behind me, the whiteboard was dominated by two images of Robert Kirby, a forty-five-year-old ex-Army Ranger who had seen the horrors of Afghanistan, Iraq, and a redacted mission in Yemen. The first photo showed a young, eager soldier, the embodiment of dreams and discipline. Next to it was the current Kirby: a man visibly marked by life's battles, his weary eyes and messy beard telling a story of inner scars and haunted memories.

"Kirby is highly trained in short and long-range combat, skilled in weapons, and a veteran of surviving hostile environments," I began. "The technique he used to gut the fisherman on the docks demonstrates experience in hunting and processing game. He's been through hell, taken several bullets, and even played hero during a suicide bomber attack in Afghanistan, saving two fellow soldiers that day. Medal followed."

There was a short pause. Maybe it was the irony of this hero-turned-villain.

"His family," I continued, "says he sometimes retreats to the woods to cope with mental health issues. It's a pattern they thought explained his disappearance from his construction job six months ago and the spotty contact. Kirby is highly dangerous, so don't let your guard down for a second."

My gaze briefly lingered on the picture of Cindy Boon, Kirby's ex-girlfriend. Her heavy makeup hid her fine facial lines but not the trauma and abuse in her eyes.

I continued, my voice grave. "Last he was seen was by his ex-girlfriend of two years. Put a gun to her head after they'd been drinking all night. Asked her if she wanted to find peace with him or keep walking the flames of hell." Again, my eyes briefly met Cindy's in the photo. Her gaze conveyed the deep sadness of a person too hopeful to quit and too hopeless to believe she deserved love.

"He's extremely cunning and organized. Kirby has been using the lemon law to cycle through unregistered, legally acquired vehicles from dealerships, keeping us off his trail. Until six months ago, he was working construction jobs on and off. He vanished after his mental health and alcoholism took a nosedive post-breakup."

Turning to the Providence police officers, I asked, "Is the perimeter around his home ready to be secured quietly?"

The Providence police chief, a stout man of color in his fifties, gave me an affirmative nod. "We have a team ready. Right before we move in, the team will block off the streets. Wearing the uniforms of the local gas company, they'll advise neighbors to stay inside. Gas leak."

"Amazing work, thank you," I said, nodding appreciatively before addressing the group again. "Kirby lives in an old three-bedroom house on King Henry Lane. He inherited it from his grandmother. We'll approach in unmarked vehicles, keeping it low-key. We have a warrant, so entry will be swift and assertive. One team for each area of the home, surrounding it from all sides first to cut off exit routes."

All eyes shifted to the pictures of the rundown house and yard displayed on the board behind me. My gaze swept over the room and stopped briefly on McCourt, who was quietly leaning against the wall in the corner of the command room. His eyes were on me like those of a spider eyeing a fly in its web.

As if on cue, he pushed off the wall and strode up next to me. "No A-Team bullshit," he announced, his tone authoritative. "If a stray bullet hits old Mrs. Molly pushing her purebred Maltese in one of those ridiculous dog strollers, I will personally make sure the human diaper responsible for this shitshow gets thrown out."

As the tension in the room instantly ramped up, I quietly scratched the side of my head to avoid rolling my eyes at McCourt's 1920s cop drama. But he was the ruler of this land. You either took it his way or got the fuck out.

"This operation goes by the book. Is that understood?" McCourt continued.

"Yes, sir," came the collective response.

"Any questions?" I asked.

A rookie officer raised his hand. "We're supposed to shoot him, right?"

Shit.

I felt for the poor bastard. Cowboy grinned wide in anticipation as McCourt stepped closer, zeroing in on the rookie like a drone locking onto a target.

"I apologize if my A-Team reference was lost on those still being burped when this absurd TV show was captivating America's man-children," McCourt said, stepping closer, now right in the face of the terrified rookie. "So, let me spell it out. With the FBI in charge, this mission won't be a John Wick fantasy. It will be Hermione Granger with a gun and a license to kill. Fucking got it this time, Harry P?"

He took a sudden step back, allowing the young man to catch his breath.

McCourt then addressed the crowd again. "Any real questions?"

The room was dead silent.

"Good." McCourt straightened his necktie. "Then let's go get that son of a bitch before he shoots up a school."

Immediately, the room cleared out.

"The A-Team was a damn good show," Heather said as she passed me on her way out.

"He went too far this time," I agreed. "A-Team is legend."

I was about to head out myself when McCourt shook his head at me and Rose. Soon, only the three of us were left in the room.

"Kill the asshole," McCourt said as soon as the room was clear. "Less paperwork, no sob story in the press about another soldier going to hell. Also, make sure Theo sticks to the back during the raid. If anything happens to that little fucker, my sister will hound me to my grave and continue in the afterlife."

Rose and I exchanged glances as McCourt marched out, not bothering to wait for a response. Her lively eyes brimming with a silent protest against his orders. Then she pulled out her gun and methodically checked it before throwing me a look that screamed, "It is what it is." Finally, she exited the room.

Hot on their heels, I decided that McCourt could go to hell.

I knew what he, and most others, thought of me: Richter . . . the guy from a poor but somewhat decent home, following in cop-dad's footsteps to make him proud. The rule follower.

Mr. Vanilla. Not the hardened cop drowning his old scars in whiskey or seeking hot sex with women whose names he'd forget the next morning.

No.

Richter was a guy who'd go home after work to help with a load of laundry, read to his kids, and then make love to his wife despite the stretch marks and extra pounds lingering after childbirth.

And they were right about that.

But Mr. Vanilla wasn't all of me.

I was also the guy ready to fucking die for a better world and for the people I cared about.

When the loudmouths faltered, I was still standing. In a world gone mad, I was the sanity, the glue holding shit together so everybody else could fuck up and be crazy.

And there was another side to me. New Richter, who worked alongside a genius killer to take down monsters like Harvey Grand. That Richter would do everything in his power to save a guy like Robert Kirby. He'd pay dearly for his crimes, especially the murder of the fisherman, but maybe that could be the end of it—no more bloodshed.

So, yeah. "Fuck McCourt," I said aloud as I caught up with Agent Rose, who threw me a worried look. "If Kirby goes down without a fight, nobody shoots. That's an order," I declared.

TWENTY

Liam

If I had known she was playing "The Swan" from "Carnival of the Animals" at the exact moment we were huddled in the stuffy van en route to Robert Kirby's house, it would have felt like a cosmic connection. A personal soundtrack, as if she knew the path I was on.

I knew nothing of classical music, but my music teacher had played "The Swan" to us back in my school days, and it stuck with me. I found it tragically beautiful. Back then, I asked my teacher if the swan was dying. To me, the melody was serene but filled with profound, unspoken sadness, the end of something once beautiful.

Just like Robert Kirby now.

Or maybe myself.

The van was shrouded in its usual pre-mission silence. Any of us could be the one not coming back.

A young, buff, GI-Joe-looking officer suddenly threw up. We all minded our own business as he apologized into his hand.

I felt my cell vibrating in my pants pocket again. It had been buzzing non-stop since I'd gotten in, so I decided to break my habit of ignoring calls before a mission and pulled it out.

I checked it: five missed calls from my younger sister, Stephanie, and twenty-five texts.

What the fuck.

Panic choked me as I opened the messages. After years in this job, I found that my mind always jumped to the worst. Was it Mom? Josie?

My hands nervously fumbled over the first text, which showed a picture of a woman in her early thirties. Neither pretty nor ugly, she had brown eyes and hair that mirrored her unassuming clothing style.

I read my sister's first text. *We have a fucking sister, Liam!!!*

This made no sense to me, so I continued reading the jumbled texts she had bombarded me with.

Dad cheated on mom, that piece of shit!

This woman found me via some DNA test.

She just showed up at my school, Liam. At my fucking school!

She showed me pictures of dad and her mom. Some childhood pictures. She said we had a brother too, but he died driving drunk or some shit like that.

Liam, call me back damn it! I can't breathe, the panic attacks are back.

I hope dad rots in hell!!! I hate him.

Liam!!!

My head flopped back against the cold metal of the car as my pulse skyrocketed. What the fuck? Was this some kind of joke?

I felt the sweat, the anger, the disappointment, and then the anger again.

"You okay?" Agent Rose's voice snapped me out of it. I looked at her. Her gaze shifted from the phone in my hands then returned to my face. Nobody else seemed to have noticed, as people either prayed or stared at the floor in silence.

"Yes," I lied and tucked the phone back into my vest pocket just as the van slowed down and my walkie-talkie went off.

"One minute to touchdown," crackled a voice.

Inhaling deeply, I unholstered my Glock, feeling its familiar, reassuring weight. Around me, the team prepared their weapons, including shotguns, Rose's favorite. After a tight squeeze in a basement with a shotgun on my first warrant execution, the Glock had become my weapon of choice.

"Thirty seconds!" I announced. The van brimmed with palpable tension. Time seemed to blur. Then, abruptly, the van jerked to a halt, jostling us.

I flung the door open and leaped out into the crisp fall afternoon. The peaceful neighborhood belied the gravity of our task.

A fleet of vans and SUVs converged simultaneously, releasing a swarm of agents and officers. I caught their focused stares and signaled the yard team to surround the house. They moved with military precision, Cowboy among them, as that team was the least likely to see action and could find cover quickly during crossfire.

I led Rose and three other teams. Adrenaline surged through me as we neared the front door. Every sense was heightened; my heart thundered in my chest, my gun aimed, ready for whatever lay ahead.

An officer knelt at the floor, quietly working the lock open with a drill. Within moments, it clicked, barely making a sound.

It was nothing like the dramatic entries you see in movies. We pushed the door open gently, then slipped inside with practiced stealth. The home's hallway was tidy yet dated, with a narrow path flanked by old-fashioned floral wallpaper. I gestured to the upstairs team to move in. We scanned our surroundings, searching for any sign of movement.

Standing guard at the front door, the basement team was set to intercept any escape attempts from the first floor or upper floor. Once those areas were clear, they'd clear the basement.

I led my team into the living room, which had older furniture, all bathed in the soft light from an antique lamp. The upstairs team's footsteps echoed as they cleared each room methodically above us.

The living room was empty, so we swiftly advanced to the kitchen. My heart pounded against my ribcage, and I wondered if it might burst free.

Also clear.

We made our way into what looked like an old dining room. It was also clear but littered with maps and various objects scattered across the aging table. The house felt like a time capsule, as if Robert's grandmother still lived here—outdated, mostly neat except for the clutter of empty liquor bottles, beer cans, and vape pods.

"Upstairs is all clear," came a young officer's voice through my radio just moments before the front door team signaled their intent to enter the basement.

My eyes darted over the chaos: wires, tools, containers of volatile chemicals, and protective gloves and goggles strewn about.

Fuck!

"Don't go downstairs!" I bellowed into the radio, a surge of icy panic gripping me. Without hesitation, I dashed past Rose and the rest, screaming, "Don't go downstairs!"

In seconds, I was in the hallway. For some reason, Cowboy was at the top of the basement stairs. The door was wide open, and other agents were likely descending.

I barreled into Cowboy just as a deafening explosion shook the house. The shockwave catapulted us to the ground. My body slammed against the hard floor. The air turned thick with dust and the stench of smoke and burnt wood. A high-pitched ringing in my ears muffled everything as I rolled onto my stomach, struggling to get on all fours.

The hallway was devastated: walls cracked, a carpet of glass and debris strewn all around.

It was an absolute nightmare.

As my vision cleared, I noticed Cowboy next to me. He was coughing but alive. So were the other agents.

I sat up and looked into space, my gaze finally falling on a family portrait of the Kirbys. It had tumbled from the wall and was now propped against a piece of wood amid the rubble. Sunlight streamed through broken windows, and dust danced in its beams like a flurry of tiny stars over the portrait. The glass was cracked, partially veiling the fading photo of Robert Kirby and his parents at an amusement park. In the photo, young Robert and his parents were joyfully poking their faces through a whimsical face-in-hole board designed to represent a happy dog family. Robert's face appeared in the smallest hole, intended for the baby of the family. His eyes sparkled with the happiness of a child who was going on rides and eating cotton candy with the people he loved. His parents' faces emerged from the two larger holes, portraying the parent dogs.

The words above them, bold and clear, read: "From a happy heart springs a life filled with love and joy."

TWENTY-ONE

Leah

My fingers delicately traced the piano keys, concluding my personal arrangement of "The Swan" by Camille Saint-Saëns. I was on stage, performing a rehearsal run of this weekend's concert. Crystal, the operations manager, and a few stagehands sat in the front row, their eyes fixed on me, awaiting instructions while indulging in the music.

It was strange, but I couldn't shake the feeling that something was amiss. It was as if I'd developed a sixth sense. Suddenly, the jarring siren-like sound of an amber alert cut through the room, emitted from several cell phones simultaneously.

Confused murmurs filled the air as the message was read.

"It's the Bay Reaper," Crystal announced, looking at me through her red-framed glasses. "They've issued an alert for a Robert Kirby and a red pick-up truck, license plate MA3 4BZ."

Marianne, a young stagehand with short hair and a nose piercing, fumbled with her phone. "OMG!" she exclaimed, her face a mix of shock and excitement. "There was an explosion at Kirby's house during an FBI search. Now there's a huge manhunt underway!"

"You're kidding!" Crystal gasped. They all descended into excitement.

I processed this information and then clapped my hands. "Focus, please," I insisted.

Crystal and Marianne looked at me, momentarily confused, as if snapped out of their trance.

"Tell Gregory to retune the piano but this time without the digital tuning device. It makes the notes too perfect. People don't appreciate such sterile precision."

"Yes, Leah," Crystal responded, quickly stowing her phone. "Marianne will go right away."

Marianne shot a "why don't you do it yourself" look at Crystal but then got up and left.

I reached for the cream cashmere jacket beside me on the bench and pulled out my flip phone. Rising gracefully, albeit a bit more quickly than usual, I stepped out of sight behind the stage.

For a moment, I stood there, holding the phone.

A cold tingle ran through my chest. Was Agent Richter injured or, worse, dead? If he was, what a colossal waste that would be. It had taken years to replace Larsen with someone of Richter's caliber. Frankly, I doubted I could find another quite like him.

Richter was a man of integrity, unafraid of facing danger. He was mostly stable and guided by a moral compass intent on improving the world or at least preventing its further descent into chaos. Most importantly, he harbored a naive yet sincere hope in his heart, genuinely believing he could succeed in such a colossal task.

Because of that, he was irreplaceable, especially now with the Train Track Killer still out there.

Was it this realization of Richter's value that sparked something in me?

It was a revelation that not only stunned me but also stirred a flicker of . . . nervousness? Worry?

I picked up the phone and dialed his number. No phone calls ever, we said, and yet here I was.

He picked up.

The unmistakable beeps of hospital machines and background announcements left no doubt as to his location.

"Hello?" His voice was soft, detached from reality.

I stated the obvious. "You're alive."

A pause followed.

"Kinda," he finally responded.

Another brief silence.

"Good," I replied and hung up.

His voice left me with no doubt about his state. The past months would have taken a toll on anyone. Despite his resilience and determination, Richter was human, with his own limits. Something told me that Richter was at risk of rapidly losing steam. With the potential loss of his child, and now, if he'd been injured from the explosion, the combined effect might completely derail him.

The judicial system in this nation was bizarre and deeply flawed. Laws seemed to apply only to the poor, and lady luck was as dependable as a drunk whore.

"Crystal," I called as I returned to the stage.

She instantly stood.

"Please arrange for the attorney general to call me on my cell."

Her eyes sparkled with intrigue. "You mean the United States Attorney General in DC, right?"

I pondered for a moment. "No, the Massachusetts Attorney General."

Low status. He would be more eager to trade favors.

"Sure. I'll call his office right now," she said.

"Thank you," I responded, watching her leave.

TWENTY-TWO

Agent Vallery Rose

"We're working on it tirelessly, sir," McCourt said, his voice dripping with the artificially kind and respectful tone reserved for those above him and the public. He sat behind his large mahogany desk, a barrier between him and agent Vallery Rose.

"I'll do everything in my power to catch Robert Kirby before he hurts anyone else," he said, nodding. "Yes . . . uh-huh. Yes, sir. You can trust me, sir. I understand. Thank you, sir. Thank you."

With that, he hung up, his gaze lingering on the handset he had just set down. Then, with an exaggerated sigh, he said, "What a fucking shitshow."

"I take it that wasn't Director Brooks?" Rose asked.

"Of course not. Helen is finished. She lasted quite a while, given that her nominating party lost the election two years ago. Gotta give the old lady that. But now, the big question is, who'll take her spot once it's official?"

Rose straightened in her seat. "I . . . thought your hard work positioned you well for that role, sir."

"That's what people assumed, yes. But that was before all this shit hit the fan." His tone was surprisingly calm. "Robert Kirby's been on the run for almost a week. A goddamn week. And the whole country's asking one very valid question."

Rose waited for him to continue. When he didn't, she fell into his trap. "What question, sir?"

"Fucking *why*, Agent Rose!" he exploded. "The country wants to know why Kirby's still free, turning the entire Seacoast into a cesspool of fear. What the hell are you guys doing down there? Making TikTok videos? Catching Pokémon around the office? Because it sure as hell doesn't look like you're working on finding Kirby!"

Rose could have argued that every available officer in every law enforcement unit was on this case, pulling night shifts and missing Sunday baseball games. But she knew better than to voice that.

"If Richter had just listened to me." McCourt shook his head. "Or if that person I thought I could trust had reported on him before he fucking freed Jason Brown from jail, we wouldn't be in this mess. At least not at the same time as two swing state elections in my jurisdiction!"

"Jason Brown was innocent, sir," Rose interjected carefully.

"Of course he was, but releasing Brown so quickly forced the real Bay Reaper's hand. The moment that white trash headed home to his bottle and wife-beating, Robert Kirby knew we'd be on his ass in no time. We left him no choice but to act, all while we knew jack shit about him. And the result is one person butchered at the docks and four officers in the hospital from a bomb explosion. One of them missing an arm and a leg!"

While everything McCourt said could be a possibility, it also could be nothing but conjecture. In cases like this, no one could accurately predict what might have happened. Some news stations had actually praised the FBI and argued that finding Kirby so quickly had prevented a larger bomb threat. But those same news stations were now turning on the FBI, blaming it for a missing Kirby with the usual sensationalist headlines that went after clicks and views.

"Sir, is there anything else I can assist you with?" Rose asked.

"Let me think . . . yes. I think there is." McCourt's tone seemed as if he was truly thinking about it, but then he slammed his hand on his desk and leaned forward. "Find! Robert! Fucking! Kirby!"

He sank back into his chair, exhausted.

The room filled with a heavy silence that was oppressive and unbearable. McCourt had a point: The nation was clamoring for them to find Kirby. After a week of fruitless searches, the pressure was mounting, reaching Everest-like heights. It weighed heavily not just on her but on everyone. Yet for Rose, the stakes were personal. Her badge and her position, which hung precariously on the approval of the man before her, now teetered on the edge of his rage.

In a twisted way, she understood McCourt. If his promotion was jeopardized by his agents' actions, it made sense he'd scrutinize his closest ally: her. The logic was obvious, even if ethical matters weren't so clear.

The phone's ring cut through the tension, providing a welcome relief for Rose.

McCourt inhaled deeply, then answered with his forced friendly tone, "Assistant Director Clifford McCourt." His insincere smile disappeared as he rolled his eyes. "Jesus, Bonnie, I've told you not to call me at the office unless it's a real emergency."

A woman's muffled voice barely traveled through the line.

"Theo is an FBI agent, not a member of Congress, Bon. He actually has to work."

The muffled sounds continued, growing in volume.

"No, I can't fetch Jen from kindergarten," McCourt snapped. "I'm the Assistant Director of the FBI, for heaven's sake. Tell Dr. Douchebag to let you off early or I'll have a Medicare audit done on his clinic."

The mumbling on the other end became frantic.

"No, I'm not raising my voice at you, Bon," McCourt said in a tone that mixed frustration with a forced apology. He rubbed his temples as he gestured for Rose to leave.

Rising, she sent a prayer of thanks to McCourt's sister only to feel the weight of responsibility crash back down on her the moment she stepped out.

She knew she had to find Kirby, whatever the cost, or start looking for another job. Which, in her eyes, after everything she had endured to beat the odds and be here, would be the biggest failure of her life—the kind that would haunt her to her last breath.

TWENTY-THREE

Liam

The entire BAU floor at Boston headquarters had transformed into the nerve center for the Kirby case. Following the explosion and discovery of weapons and homemade bombs in the rubble of Kirby's basement, the case's importance was unmistakable. Time was our worst enemy. So were the fucking woods. Kirby's truck had been found abandoned near a boat dock on the Merrimack River north of Nashua. With its door wide open and some weapons left behind, it was clear he'd ditched the vehicle in a hurry, almost as if he'd known that it'd be found, but he couldn't care less.

It seemed likely he'd escaped in a boat. Eyewitnesses had seen a red truck hauling a boat to and from the dock within the past few months.

And that was where we were utterly screwed.

The Merrimack River, with its considerable length and numerous coves, tributaries, and islands, offered a labyrinth of hiding places, complicating our search efforts. The river's open and fluid nature made constant surveillance a nightmare, even for an intense manhunt with our level of resources. The fact that the river led to the bay at Newburyport only magnified our challenges.

Perched on a chair at Heather's desk, I delved into the notes from Kirby's therapist. Cowboy and Martin sat hunched at their desks nearby, piecing together the fragmented notes on Kirby's victims found at his home. The notes had been damaged in the explosion, but it was clear Kirby had targeted his victims deliberately, profiling them like a hitman. Surrounded by a sea of evidence and tips, we focused primarily on Kirby's profiling methods and long, tumultuous battle with mental health. These were our keys to understanding Kirby and, ultimately, finding him.

"This info he's gathered on his victims," Martin said, shaking his head, "I honestly have no idea how he did it. I mean, this is incredible work. The FBI would need a hell of a lot of warrants to gather this much info on people."

"That's the US military for you," Heather said. "We create the best."

"And the most depressed," Cowboy added.

His joke was macabre but true. Kirby's story was a damning indictment of our nation's broken mental health system.

He'd returned home from the Middle East as a shadow of his former self.

Initially, Kirby had fallen into the same trap many veterans did: steering clear of help out of fear of repercussions within the military—a culture where admitting struggle was often seen as a weakness and could cost you everything. But reality hit hard with his first DUI and a series of bar fights. Diagnoses of severe PTSD and a substance-induced psychotic disorder followed. It was then that desperation set in, and Kirby earnestly began seeking help.

What he found was a system in shambles. The laughable wages offered to community mental health counselors had precipitated a crisis. There was a severe shortage of qualified professionals and a revolving door of brave souls willing to tackle the county's darkest problems in return for high student debt and a wage comparable to that of a grocery store clerk—without even the benefit of a store discount.

Self-medicating became Kirby's answer to the haunting nightmares and PTSD: a deadly combination.

"Damn it," I mumbled as I gazed at a photo of a young, hopeful Kirby and then at the broken man our country had abandoned post-war. "These days, a soldier's real enemy isn't in the Middle East. It's right here in his own fucking country." I dropped Kirby's file onto my desk.

Heather, Martin, and Cowboy looked up, their faces a mix of agreement and frustration.

"These bastards in DC send our boys to hellholes to get fucked up for life while their own kids get private schools and vacations in Paris," I spat out. "Why the hell do we still let them do this to us?"

"Bread and circuses," Heather chimed in. "Just like in Roman times when emperors kept the masses calm with free bread and shows. Not much has changed. As long as we have just enough for fast food and cable, we won't grumble."

As we absorbed that, Martin received a call and then hung up with a brief "thank you."

"Local police," he informed us as we all braced to dive back into the case. "A hunter said his cabin was broken into near Concord."

"Is it close to the river?" I asked.

Cowboy rose, phone in hand, and walked out. "I'll be back."

I paid him no attention.

"About two miles," Martin said. "In a pretty secluded area."

I frowned. "Could be something." Though I suspected it was yet another dead end, like the many we'd already chased.

"I'll get a unit out there," Martin said, his voice betraying the strain of stretching our resources even thinner by pulling in another police unit.

The manhunt had been dragging on for days, spanning several states. Support for such a massive operation was dwindling by the minute, from the FBI down to local stations.

"Thanks," I replied, my gaze suddenly catching McCourt approaching us like a hyena scoping out the savanna for injured prey. "I'll be back in a minute," I said as I stood and wove through the maze of desks and chaos, opting for the stairs at the far end to avoid the elevator McCourt was using.

Descending a floor, I headed straight for the Cyber Crime Unit, then made a beeline for a small office at the end of the hall. Griffin had earned his private space through over three decades with the FBI. He barely glanced up from his computer as I entered with a soft knock.

Griffin nodded toward the open window, which was almost as large as a door. A cool breeze flowed through it.

I returned the nod and clambered onto the fire escape balcony through the window, then entered the hidden "break room" that the smokers and vapers used.

Cowboy's eyes met mine. They were filled with a sorry excuse for an apology as he puffed out a cloud of vape. Behind him, agents from Cyber Crime and Organized Crime were chatting, all blowing vape clouds like chimneys.

"How the hell did you get down here so quickly?" I grumbled, pissed that my few quiet minutes were about to be ambushed with bullshit. Still, it beat getting my ass chewed out by McCourt.

"My uncle texted me he was on his way down." Cowboy shrugged.

I shot him a scolding look.

He shifted uneasily, a frown tugging at his lips. "You guys understand that I have to spend time with him outside of work too, right? It's bad right now. Really bad. My little sister's birthday last Sunday was a total shitshow. My uncle pissed off the moms there talking about attachment parenting. Said he's glad he'll be dead when this yoga-app, breastfed-until-college generation is asked to defend our nation. Said they'll all be pointing their guns backward."

"Jesus."

"Yup. Jen told my mom her only wish for Santa this year is to make Uncle Cliffy go away. Jen's five."

Yanking out my crumpled pack of cigarettes, I sparked one up only for Rose to stick her head through the window. "This is the twenty-first century. Who the hell still smokes cigarettes?"

I inhaled deeply. "I'm almost forty. I refuse to leave cotton candy-scented vape clouds behind at serial killer crime scenes. I'm shooting for a Detective Rust vibe here."

Rose emerged onto the balcony, her expression deadpan. "Well, *detective*, McCourt's looking for you."

Fuck.

Cowboy gave her a wry smile. "Ah, Sauron's unleashed his Nazgul, has he?"

Unfazed, Rose marched up to him and snatched his vape pen. "Is this original Cowboy wit, or is ChatGPT scripting for you again?" She inhaled deeply, blowing a cloud of vape in his face, and then coolly returned the pen.

I took another drag of my cig, grimacing at the nasty smell. Fifteen years smoke-free, yet here I was, back at it. The pressure was ripping me apart, and these brief nicotine hits gave me a fleeting illusion of calm and pleasure.

With a frown, I stubbed out the cigarette and then crammed it back into the pack.

"Sir," Agent Rose called out.

I turned.

"We got some calls from residents along the Neponset River. Complaints about a boat and lights in the marshes at night. It's unusual, they say. Never happened before. Thought it might be worth mentioning."

I stroked my chin thoughtfully. "Neponset is right here in Boston. Doesn't fit our search grid. We've been focusing north, Merrimack way, expecting Kirby's holed up in that vast forest."

Rose nodded, but then Cowboy chimed in. "What if the crazy bastard took his boat to the ocean at Newburyport and came back down?"

"On a RIB, in those ocean currents?" I scoffed.

"RIB?" Cowboy looked puzzled.

"Rigid inflatable boat. It would be crazy," Rose explained, rolling her eyes.

Cowboy's face lit up with understanding, then turned to defiance. "So?" he pushed, glancing at the Cyber team like a kid challenging an adult.

The Cyber agents grinned at his antics.

"This son of a bitch is skulking around in a skull mask, stabbing people, luring us with lemon law tricks, and setting up Vietnam-era booby traps. What's wrong with 'crazy' here?"

I locked eyes with Agent Rose, who shrugged in a "sounds far-fetched, but why not" kind of way.

I sighed. Of course, I'd be the one wading through tick-infested marshes to check this out. "I'll go take a look."

Cowboy's grin widened, victory written all over his face.

"I'm coming with you," Rose said.

"Meet me downstairs. If I'm not there in thirty, you might wanna fish my corpse out of McCourt's office."

No one cracked a smile. That joke was a little too close to reality.

"Good luck," Rose replied.

TWENTY-FOUR

Leah

The gloomy sky cast a somber hue, creating a bleak backdrop as I stepped into The Stance, one of the nation's most acclaimed restaurants. It was a typical gray fall day in Boston, with heavy clouds brooding low, diffusing light through the establishment's towering windows.

Inside, it was a world apart. Softly glowing golden light fixtures illuminated the space, while the air was perfumed with the aroma of exquisite French cuisine.

At a prime corner table away from the buzz sat Derek Beckett, the Massachusetts Attorney General. Apart from his pricey suit, there was nothing particularly remarkable about him. His hair, a mix of salt and pepper, was overly styled with gel, which did little to enhance his sharp features or the icy blue of his eyes. He surveyed the room with an unmistakable blend of arrogance and authority. Finally, his gaze settled on me.

His face lit up with an excited smile as he rose to greet me.

I moved toward our table with confident strides. My cream-colored cashmere dress, white coat, and leather gloves mirrored the restaurant's elegance. As I neared, Beckett reached out to help me with my chair and coat—a gesture meant to be chivalrous but one that ended up clumsy as his fingers grazed my skin.

Settling into my seat, I was again struck by how much I loathed lunches like this. I typically avoided these plays of wealth and power. However, today, I was on a mission, and despite the unappealing company, I was determined to leave satisfied.

"I can't tell you how honored I am to receive this rare invitation," Derek said, smiling widely. "The world-famous Leah Nachtnebel."

I mirrored his smile. "A bottle of your Château Lafite Rothschild and your lunch special, please," I said to the waiter after he approached and welcomed us.

Derek's expression betrayed his concern—understandable, given the wine's eighteen-thousand-dollar price tag.

"It's my treat," I declared swiftly, watching his concern morph into delight.

He shifted impatiently in his seat as the waiter uncorked the bottle and poured our glasses. Of course, Derek didn't wait for me, taking a sip and shaking his head in amazement. "Incredible. I've never tasted wine quite like this."

I maintained my smile, though it was becoming more difficult. "I hope you don't mind if I'm direct and address something upfront so we can then fully enjoy our lunch."

"No, not at all," he replied, seemingly astounded at the thought that anything I could say might disturb him.

"Great. Then let me get straight to the point."

He took another sip of wine, more interested in the taste than in whatever I had to say.

"I must confess my invitation to this lunch came with an agenda. I own a property in Hillson County, right in a wetland buffer zone, and I'm planning to build a summer home by the water."

"That sounds delightful," he said. "I've considered something similar near Big Island Pond. I inherited some land from my late aunt up there."

"There's just something about entertaining by the water, isn't there? It appeals particularly to those accustomed to places like the Hamptons."

"Our state will hold its own against such locales," Derek quipped.

"Well." I leaned in to lay on some charm. "I must confess, I've encountered some obstacles with the local judge."

Derek furrowed his brow. "Hillson . . . isn't that Albert's jurisdiction? Albert White?"

"Possibly. But it's also Ethel Dunbar's."

The frown etched deeper into his forehead. "Never heard of her."

"Great. That will simplify matters. The city rejected my conditional-use application, and she's poised to back that decision in court, as she's done repeatedly, favoring an inept village council over the hardworking citizens footing the bill. I don't have the patience for such nonsense."

Derek set his glass down, visibly puzzled. "You want her off your case, or—"

"No, I want her out of the Hillson District Court entirely."

For a moment, Derek's expression was hard to read. "Ousting a judge isn't easy," he said, leaning back just as the waiter served the truffle and wild mushroom consommé. His tone left no room for doubt; he was curious about what I had up my sleeve in exchange.

"I can only imagine. Fortunately, this judge has quite a few complaints lodged against her."

"Maybe so, but complaints are common for judges. Every alcoholic in the state tries to whine over his DUI. Anything of substance?"

"I couldn't say," I replied, poised with my spoon, my gaze fixed on Derek as he indulged in his soup. "But I'm quite sure the vice president would appreciate your commitment to upholding justice, especially in an election year."

The spoon paused in midair as astonishment flooded Derek's face. "The . . . vice president?"

I picked up my wine, twirled the glass, and examined the deep red liquid. "Yes, he'll be attending my concert next month—for the fifth time, I believe. It's a challenge to keep track of all the politicians who attend. But I've reserved two tickets for you and your wife, should you be interested in meeting him."

"The vice president," he said again. It wasn't a question this time as much as a statement of awe.

I gave a nod, gracefully sipping my wine as he burst out with excitement.

"Yes!" His face lit up with anticipation, mirroring the eager excitement of a puppy awaiting the throw of a ball. "That . . . that would be amazing."

I offered another smile; it was almost genuine this time.

"And about your property issue," he said, topping off his glass, "sounds like we've got some digging to do in Hillsboro. We can't let corruption or shady dealings threaten our system. It's supposed to protect everyday folks, not power-hungry judges." After a hearty swig of wine, he added, "Consider it handled."

I'd figured as much, but having him confirm it was part of the game.

Switching gears, I asked, "So, how was Rome? Did you check out the Colosseum?"

As Derek started to babble, I tuned out, my mind wandering to Agent Richter and his Bay Reaper. Was he patrolling the Merrimack River by boat right now? The thought of Robert Kirby stirring up trouble only to vanish into some backwoods seemed off. A mass shooting at a local store? It didn't fit the cunning work he had come up with so far. His actions pointed to something grander.

But piecing that puzzle together was Richter's job. My only hope was that he'd wrap it up fast so we could return to our real work: killing monsters.

TWENTY-FIVE

Liam

"It sounded like the noise came from over there." Mrs. Waver, an elderly resident who had reported loud boat noises to the local police, gestured toward the direction she mentioned. We stood at the edge of the waist-high marsh grasses in Joseph Finnegan Park. This side of the Neponset River was crammed with single-family homes and urban development, all squeezed into thin stretches of parks and walkways along the riverbank. The rain had ceased, but the skies remained a somber gray, continuing the theme of what was shaping up to be one of the gloomiest falls on record.

Mrs. Waver likely noticed my hesitation to venture into the high grasses. So did Rose, who seemed happy to stall alongside me.

"Right out there, near the shore," Mrs. Waver repeated, pointing decisively. The short, stout woman was clad in a wool sweater and a skirt. Her feet were shoved into tiny ballerina flats that looked like they would explode any second. Her voice carried the weight of conviction, as if she'd just unearthed the key piece of evidence in a long-cold case. Her appearance suggested she came from modest means—a local Seacoast family clinging to her parents' home out of pride for her heritage, ignoring the cash its sale would bring in today's market.

She gestured toward the water beyond the endless expanse of marsh grass. Agent Rose gave me a look that silently pleaded for me to challenge the woman, but ultimately, I exhaled deeply and trudged into the grass.

"Damn it," Agent Rose muttered behind me. I turned and watched her pluck a tick from her white business shirt. "I swear, if there's a co-pay for doxycycline . . ." she grumbled.

By the time we reached the edge of the damn marsh grasses, my dress shoes were caked with mud. One sock was now thoroughly soaked.

The river's water was calm and wide. A group of ducks floated under the weight of the sheet metal sky.

"So, what are we expecting to find here besides Lyme disease?" Agent Rose asked.

"You mentioned you saw the boat's lights briefly here at the shore?" I called back to Mrs. Waver. There was nothing. No tracks, no trash—just grass, mud, and ticks.

"Wait a minute," Mrs. Waver said, scratching her curly white hair. "I think it was about a hundred feet to your left."

Agent Rose's glare was lethal. She sighed, hands on her hips. "Mrs. Waver," she called out, her voice strained with forced kindness. "Are you sure it was to our left?"

Mrs. Waver paused, scratching her head again. "No."

"Jesus Christ." Rose extracted her foot from the mud. Her shoes were now soaked and covered in dirt. "We're wasting our time. We should be focusing on the Merrimack River."

My gaze followed the ducks and settled on a larger wooded area in the distance across the river. "Most likely so. And if you think about it, it makes perfect sense to flee up north into one of the least populated parts of the US. But then, why go through all the trouble down here? The stabbings, the dead fisherman, the lemon law. All of that to flee without a big bang? I doubt he's doing all this just to shoot up some tiny gas station near the Canadian border."

Agent Rose paused, her gaze distant as she mulled over the situation.

My phone rang. It was Dan, my lawyer.

"Hello?" I answered.

"Liam," Dan said, sounding almost out of breath. "You're not going to believe this, but Judge Dunbar has been removed from the Hillsboro court."

"What?" I practically yelled.

Agent Rose turned to me. "What happened?"

"They haven't provided any specifics, which is typical when a judge is being investigated for something," Dan explained.

"Holy shit." Despite the cold seeping into my wet feet, the news ignited a fire within me.

"Holy shit, indeed. This is like Christmas, Hanukkah, and Ramadan rolled into one, my friend. Our new judge is Alex White. Tough but fair as hell. Can you come to my office right now? There are documents you need to sign. We have to move fast in case she gets reinstated."

"I'm on my way."

After hanging up, I turned to face Rose. "I need to leave, but let's catch up later at the office. Or you could head home and rest."

"At the office," Rose decided. "But it'll be a few hours."

"Same here," I said, glancing down at my soaked shoes and pants.

"Keep me updated if Mrs. Waver comes up with anything…substantial," I said with a grin. "I'm counting on you to keep scouting the marshes."

Rose flipped me the bird as I took my leave.

Was I joking again? How long had it been since I'd done that?

The excitement coursing through me was unmatched. Dan was spot on—this opportunity was a rare gift. And the thought of having Josie back was indescribable. It had been torture without her. I'd felt like I was running on a beach, kite in hand, trying to make it fly high without the slightest bit of wind.

But the shitshow of a man I had become was dead. I was reborn. Nothing could stand in my way now. Not Sarah, not the Bay Reaper, not the Train Track Killer. Nothing.

TWENTY-SIX

Agent Vallery Rose

Rose was determined to head straight home for a shower. Mrs. Waver had sent her traipsing along the damn river shore for nearly another hour, each time "remembering" where the elusive boat had supposedly anchored at night only to change her mind again and again.

Her legs and feet were a soggy, mud-caked mess, and Rose had already picked off eight ticks from her skin. Another one was audaciously exploring her steering wheel. She itched everywhere, constantly checking another prickling spot for one of those little bloodsuckers. And then there was the stench in her car—the murky, sulfurous scent that evoked wet soil and rampant algae growth. She had to drive all the way back to Roxbury with the windows down despite the rain that now drenched her torso as well. Her hair was a mess too, which irked her since she had just gotten a touch-up relaxer yesterday at Lanette's.

It was dark by the time she made it home. She was turning into her street when she suddenly remembered what Richter had said about the Bay Reaper's strange escape northward—without the "big bang," as he had put it. As much as she loathed to admit it, his words bore some truth.

Why the hell would he go through all the trouble and planning, including an IED booby trap at his home, just to vanish in the woods?

No.

Something was fishy here, beyond her own smelly self and her car.

This truth made her skip her driveway and head all the way up to the old, unrestored historic mansion at the corner of the park.

The paint was peeling from the wooden siding, and dry rot marred its surface, visible even in the dim light cast by the street lantern.

Rose stepped out of her car and navigated the uneven brick walkway up to the sprawling front porch. Inside, music throbbed through the walls as she knocked loudly. She peered through the window, her gaze cutting through the throng of Black, Latino, and White individuals directly to Vito.

He caught her eye and wove through the crowd of gang members to the door.

As he opened it, a blast of loud hip-hop bass surged forth. He gave her a once-over, his eyebrow arching in question.

"Can I come in for a minute?" Rose asked.

Vito gave her another scrutinizing look. The lines on his face deepened. "Nope," he responded, the gold in his necklace glinting under the porch light.

Rose arched an eyebrow. "Afraid I might stumble upon something I shouldn't?" She crossed her arms and craned her neck to glimpse the party through the window.

"No," Vito shot back. "Because you stink, and you'd drag mud all over my new carpet."

"Fair enough," Rose conceded. "Can you step outside for a minute, then? I really need to talk to you."

The unflinching shift in Vito's expression made it clear he was anything but eager for this conversation.

"Please?" Rose added, her tone softening.

Vito paused, considering for a moment, then stepped outside, shutting the door behind him. The clamor from inside was immediately muffled.

He walked over to the porch railing and leaned against it.

"I need some information," Rose said cautiously, leaning beside him against the railing.

"Of course you do, but that doesn't mean I'm gonna give it."

She nodded. "Nothing about you or any other gangs in the neighborhood."

This piqued his curiosity.

"Have you heard about the Bay Reaper?"

A subtle shift in his demeanor betrayed his surprise at her question. "The sick fuck stabbing people while wearing a Halloween mask?"

"Yeah. He blew up his house during a search warrant and is on the run."

Vito smirked. "I guess he don't like you much."

Rose leaned over the railing. "We think he's about to do something big. Really big."

"Like a mass shooting?"

Rose nodded.

"Sounds like typical white people shit. What the hell do you want from me? He ain't gonna find a place to squat in my hood, that's for sure."

"I know. But this one is smart enough to go about it the right way. Tricking people. I was just wondering if you heard anything."

"Such as?"

"Military-grade sales. Stuff to build large bombs or generally just fuck shit up."

Vito fell silent.

"You heard something?" Rose asked, encouraged.

He scowled at the ground.

"Vito," Rose pressed.

"Maybe, but I ain't gonna snitch."

"Well, in that case, maybe I should finally take a closer look at what happens in your shed every other Saturday, which, wait, would be today. You really gonna make me call the cops to search it?"

His anger flared. "You threatening me?"

"Do I have to, Vito? Threaten you to get your help to prevent an attack that could be bigger than the Oklahoma bombing? Do you remember how many people died? One hundred sixty-seven, Vito. One, six, seven. Including kids."

Vito pushed off from the railing. "Damn it, Rose, I knew you were trouble."

"What have you heard?" Rose pressed.

He was still hesitant, the internal struggle etched clearly across his face.

Rose understood his dilemma all too well. In the hood, being labeled a snitch was a fate worse than death. Her own brother had paid dearly for it.

Rose threw her hands up in frustration. "Do I need to remind you—"

"Some white guy was asking about buying Tovex," Vito said.

"The explosive that IEDs are made of? Did you sell it to him?"

"No!" Vito looked offended. "What the fuck, Rose. You hang with the pigs too much if you think your own would sell that kind of shit to psychos!"

Rose took a step forward, her voice softer. "Who would deal with it around here?"

He shrugged nonchalantly, lighting a cigarette. "The Russian cartel, if the price is right. Nobody, if it's obvious the buyer is some FBI-wanted white boy planning to blow shit up."

"Let's say the price was right, that the Russians were willing to sell. Where would they do it?"

Vito met Rose's gaze. "Can't say for sure, but a handoff like that would need time. That stuff isn't easy to get. It's heavily regulated, more dangerous to deal with than drugs. But if your ifs are really happening . . . might wanna start looking south."

"South?" Rose echoed, taken aback. "How far south? As far as the Neponset River?"

Vito remained silent, drawing deeply on his cigarette and exhaling a thick cloud of smoke.

"Fuck," Rose muttered, hurrying down the porch steps, her body radiating with urgency. Nothing was a given, but maybe Mrs. Waver was onto something after all.

She reached for her phone and dialed Richter only to be met with the incessant ring of an unanswered call.

"Rose!"

Rose turned.

"I didn't help you because you played bad cop. I . . ." Vito paused, the emotions evident in his face. "I did it for Nario."

An overwhelming coldness enveloped Rose, that all-too-familiar ache that surfaced whenever someone mentioned her brother's name.

"I still wake up at night when he visits me in my nightmares. But what happened back then . . ." Vito said. "It happened because he was protecting his brothers."

No matter how many years passed, grappling with that truth offered no solace. "Maybe he should have protected his family instead," Rose retorted.

"He did," Vito insisted, his gaze softening. "Just maybe not the right one."

Her expression twisted into a blend of pain and sarcasm. Rose acknowledged his words with a half nod, then walked back to her car to call Cowboy.

"Where the hell are you?" he barked through the phone as she slid into her car.

"Following up on a lead on the Neponset River."

"That old lady seeing a boat at night?"

"Kinda. But there could be more to it. Some guy trying to buy—"

"We have a possible sighting of Kirby near a small town by the Merrimack River," Cowboy interrupted. "I'll text you the location."

"Who's on it?"

"Everybody except Richter. Just called him, and he didn't answer his phone."

"Do you need me? I want to check on this lead."

"All right. You won't make it up in time anyway. Chase your lead. I'll keep you posted."

"Thanks."

The car's engine roared to life as Rose weighed her options: drive north to join Cowboy or follow her gut. Something felt off. She thought about Kirby's madness, his potential route back to Boston via the ocean. Then Mrs. Waver's words echoed in her mind, hinting that the boat might have anchored on the opposite side near a large patch of woods.

She set the car in motion and headed toward the Neponset River.

What if everything hinged on this one tip? She had to pursue it.

Her mood sank as she thought about the daunting marsh grass and the encroaching high tide.

She dialed Richter again. No answer.

Common sense urged her to wait, to let Richter know and join her in pursuing this lead. But deep down, she thought it was likely nothing. And if there was even a hint of suspicion once she reached the river, she could always call Richter or for backup.

TWENTY-SEVEN

Leah

Every seat in the symphony hall was about to be filled. Adjusting the short train of my black evening dress for the night's performance, I entered Luca's box on the first balcony, which boasted some of the best views in the concert hall except for the one opposite us. It was now occupied by the Prince of Qatar and the Vice President of the United States. A nervously rambling Derek Beckett was clearly getting on their nerves.

As always, Luca was the personification of sophistication. His long legs were crossed elegantly. White tux. Hand-tailored.

"What a great honor for you to visit me here, especially with such distinguished company in tow. Aren't you expected over there?" he asked, gazing intently at the box across from his, then at the gradually filling seats below.

"By now, you should know that I am where I desire to be, not where others expect me to be. Usually." I offered a polite smile and nod to the vice president, who reciprocated with a wave.

"To what do I owe this pleasure?" he asked.

"Do I need a reason to enjoy the company of an old friend?"

Luca smiled. "I came to understand that La Imperatrice navigates the intricate games of life at all times."

I settled into one of the gilded chairs beside him. "Who doesn't?"

"That's fair enough," he conceded.

Our eyes locked.

"Are you still angry with me?" I asked.

After a pause, Luca responded, "Disappointed."

"Is that worse than angry?" I didn't know the answer to that. The subtle differences in these emotions were alien to me.

"In my case, no. My anger is far more feared than my disappointment."

I nodded. "Will you join me for dinner? Whenever it's convenient for you."

Luca's gaze shifted forward, deliberately avoiding mine and meeting that of the vice president, who clearly recognized Luca but chose not to publicly acknowledge him.

"Unless you withdraw your last request, I'd prefer not to."

"I'm afraid I can't do that."

Silence.

"Would you still . . ." I asked hesitantly, "look into something for me?"

Luca scoffed. "Ah, there it is. I knew there was a reason for your visit."

Gently, I placed a hand on his forearm. He recoiled slightly from the contact but didn't withdraw. "I did come to invite you to dinner . . . and to ask you about Jan Novak."

Luca still avoided eye contact, but he softened his tone. "What makes you think I've looked into him? You asked me not to."

I withdrew my hand and rose. "For old time's sake. Please let me know what you discover. It's very important to me. Goodbye, old friend."

As I rose and turned to leave, Luca gently caught my arm, his hold as delicate as if he were cradling the neck of a fragile bird. "Stay away from him," he advised, his gaze piercing.

My eyebrows furrowed. "So, you did look into him. What did you find?"

He leaned in. "Absolutely nothing."

I remained silent, prompting him to elaborate as he released my arm. "And that's very unsettling as I always find something, no matter the subject," he continued. "There's been only one other instance where I failed."

"And who was that?" I knew the answer but asked anyway.

His gaze swept over me from head to toe, then returned to the crowd ahead as he turned his back to me.

"You."

TWENTY-EIGHT

Agent Vallery Rose

Rose had been navigating the marshes along the Neponset River for nearly half an hour, her shoes wet and soaked once again. On this side of the river, there was an eerie solitude in the darkness. The sky above was obscured by clouds, eliminating any light from the stars or moon. Her phone was fully charged, yet she was aware that using the flashlight would drain it quickly, so she picked up her pace.

Another mosquito buzzed by her ear. She couldn't stop herself from slapping a palm against the side of her head.

"Damn it."

It was then that she noticed a patch in the marsh grass flattened into a small circle.

As she hurried over, her flashlight revealed patterns of boot prints at the water's edge: a possible sign of someone repeatedly entering or exiting a boat at this spot.

Turning, she aimed her flashlight along a path carved through the grass from the riverbank. It led into a densely wooded area seemingly untouched by human hands. This was likely private property, maybe owned by a business or by wealthy individuals desiring solitude around their mansions—characteristic of the nearby area known for its rich residents and expansive estates.

Instantly, Rose turned off her flashlight and dialed Richter.

Voicemail again. Then the beep.

"SAC," she whispered, "I think I've found something on the Neponset. Kirby might still be here, waiting for a Tovex order from the Russians. I'll call for backup near the—"

Suddenly, a heron burst from the grass in a flurry. One of its massive wings struck Rose in the head. Reflexively, she drew her gun with her right hand while still clutching the phone, which slipped from her grasp. The phone made a sharp *blop* as it hit the water. Then everything was silent again.

"Fuck," she cursed quietly, kneeling at the water's edge to retrieve the device, but her hands found only water. It was deeper than she had anticipated, which aligned with the theory that this could be an ideal location for a small boat like a RIB.

Gradually, Rose's eyes adjusted to the surrounding darkness. It was remarkable how she could be so close to the city and yet so alone.

She considered the distant lights on the opposite side of the river, then the dark woods looming behind her. The sensible decision would be to return and contact Richter and backup using the radio in her car. That was the safer option. But if Kirby was indeed nearby and the transfer of Tovex had already occurred, every minute was vital.

Facing the woods, Rose made her way as quietly as possible down the path left by someone else, leading into the expansive, shadowy forest—a path that could tip the scales of life and death not just for herself but for many others.

TWENTY-NINE

Liam

Dan was an older, short man who resembled a car salesman in an ill-fitting suit. He lacked the aggression of younger attorneys but had a deep understanding of the law, treating it with the familiarity and consideration of a mother caring for her child. He'd worked for my family for decades. Starting as my dad's lawyer, he now represented me.

He organized the papers I'd signed and looked up at me with a smile. "I'll file these first thing in the morning. And call your mom back, will you? She's called me eight times, complaining." He stood up but quickly noticed that I'd remained seated, which prompted him to sit back down.

"Did . . . you know?" I asked, my voice packed with disappointment. "About my half-sister," I pressed, sidestepping any potential evasion.

Dan's expression was a mix of discomfort and regret. "I did."

"Goddamn it, Dan! Did you ever consider telling us?"

"Well, first, there was client-attorney privilege between your dad and me, and I'm bound by that. Your father insisted this remain secret until after his passing. What your mother did with the information afterward isn't my responsibility, Liam."

I straightened in my chair. "Wait. My mom knew about this second family since my dad passed?"

Dan's mouth hung open as if he'd inadvertently revealed the secret ingredient to Betty Crocker's world-famous pumpkin pie. "Your father," he started, his voice softening, "came to me just before he passed, asking that a portion of the inheritance intended for your mom be allocated to his other family. For the children, you understand. Your sister and, I believe, a now-deceased brother."

The revelation was overwhelming. I'd been dodging this reality, burying myself in work, avoiding reflection. But facing Dan, my father's longtime lawyer and friend, brought everything rushing back like acid reflux.

"Your dad was a good man," Dan said.

"That's what I spent my whole life believing, Dan." My voice dripped with malice. "But 'good man' doesn't describe someone who cheats on his wife and creates an entire second family. Actually," I said, rising and pulling out my phone, "'asshole' seems more fitting. Big. Fucking. Asshole. Piece. Of. Shit. To be exact."

Memories of my first conversation with Leah, when she'd probed the clear roles of my parents as if she'd known their secrets, flooded my mind. She'd been right all along.

Dan sighed. "Liam, life isn't always black and white."

"In this instance, it's quite black and white, Dan." I glanced at my phone, noticing the absence of the "5G" signal next to the battery indicator. "I need to go. There's no reception here, and the Kirby case is heating up."

Dan walked me out in silence, not mentioning my father again, which I appreciated. Once the fresh air hit me in the parking lot, my phone lit up with several missed calls, including a voicemail from Rose.

"SAC," her voice played quietly from the voicemail. "I think I found something on the Neponset. Kirby might still be here, waiting for a Tovex order from the Russians. I'll call backup near the—"

Then the voicemail cut off.

A wave of adrenaline rushed through me. I called Rose repeatedly, but the calls went straight to voicemail.

"Shit."

Without a second to waste, I dialed the FBI's internal communication system.

"Special Agent in Charge Liam Richter speaking. I need immediate backup for a potential encounter with Robert Kirby in the Neponset River Reservation Park area. The exact location is unknown. Agent Valerie Rose may be engaging him at this moment and is unresponsive to communication."

"Did you say Neponset River Reservation Park?" came the operator's voice.

"Yes."

"We just received calls from residents about possible gunfire. Local law enforcement was dispatched to the area around five minutes ago, but they're still searching the area. It's quite large."

Fuck. Fuck. Fuck!

"Deploy every available unit and search the park now!" I ordered. "We might have an active shooter."

"Understood, sir!"

I ended the call and leaped into my SUV. The engine roared to life as I sped off with sirens blaring and lights flashing, parting traffic like Moses parting the Red Sea.

I dialed Cowboy. "Cowboy, where are you?"

"Heading back. We followed a false lead on Kirby up north. I tried to call—"

"He's here! In Boston. Near the Neponset River," I said. "Kirby. He never left."

"Fuck," Cowboy blurted. "Rose called earlier about a lead there."

"Where exactly did she say she was going?"

"Just mentioned a potential lead near the river."

"Damn it!" Why didn't she wait for backup?

"We're en route, but it'll be about fifty minutes."

"Coordinate the search location with local law enforcement. I'll meet you there."

I hung up, frustration mounting. This was bad, bad, bad. Kirby, that bastard, had taken his flimsy-ass boat from the Merrimack River down over the dangerous ocean to the Boston area for his final move.

At least I was nearby, as Dan's office was south of Boston. But nearby to where exactly? The Neponset River covered a vast area with miles of nature trails and neighborhoods.

No one but Rose knew exactly where he might be hiding.

Except for Leah.

I told her that I'd never ask her to play Sherlock Homes with me again. But this wasn't only about the life of an agent. It was about countless others as well.

I dialed her.

My dark thoughts filled with hope.

The phone rang a few times, and then she answered.

THIRTY

Leah

My reflection in the mirror appeared unusually fatigued. Seated at the golden makeup table in my personal backstage quarters, I was interrupted by Crystal's knock, which indicated the start of my concert was imminent.

I couldn't get the Train Track Killer out of my mind. The thought of him overshadowed my collaboration with Agent Richter. My focus had been solely on this case. I'd broadened my search from suicides on tracks to all manner of tragedies across the city. Yet the sheer volume of cases was overwhelming. I'd need an entire team just to cover Boston.

Feeling disheartened, I reached for my flip phone, a habit that had become all too common.

No new messages.

Richter hadn't provided any updates on the Train Track Killer.

"Leah?" Crystal's voice echoed in the hallway. It was accompanied by a knock. "Everyone is seated. We're ready."

I stored the phone away and stepped into the corridor.

"A few people didn't show, but we've filled those seats with those waiting for cancellations outside the symphony hall," she said.

I nodded, securing the door behind me. We had taken only a few steps when the distinct ringtone of my flip phone halted me.

I paused, sensing Crystal's concern.

"Is everything all right?" she asked.

I turned, staring at my door. Did he have new information on the Train Track Killer? My gaze jerked down the hallway toward the stage.

I hesitated, torn between my performance and the potential call. Could it wait? But why would he call unless it was urgent?

"Wait here, please," I instructed Crystal as she glanced nervously toward the stage.

Quickly, I returned and shut the door. The ringing continued without pause.

"Hello?" I answered quietly, ensuring my voice wouldn't carry to the hallway.

Richter's voice came through, desperation clear amid the backdrop of sirens. "I need your help."

"Go on," I urged.

"Kirby is here, in Boston. Agent Rose is engaging him in a shootout somewhere along the Neponset River, but her location is unknown."

Using my photographic memory, I visualized the map of Boston, including the Neponset River. My eyes closed momentarily.

"The Neponset River stretches for twenty-nine miles. Provide any details you have."

"Shit . . . um . . . Rose mentioned a potential Tovex deal with the Russians."

"The Russians typically utilize waterways for their illegal transactions. Does Kirby have a boat?"

"We believe so."

I conjured the image of the Neponset River, pinpointing it instantly.

"If the deal occurred along the Neponset, it would likely be near the Baker Dam in Lower Mills. Beyond that point, they'd encounter low water levels."

"Lower Mills area? But where could someone hide out there?"

I concentrated, searching my memory.

"Think, Leah! Please!"

The untouched acres of forest behind the grand mansions near St. Luke Church flashed before me like a vivid photograph.

"There's a large expanse of private woodland behind some mansions right on the river, not far from Baker Dam. Someone could easily navigate through the marshes by boat and remain hidden there."

"St. Luke Church?" Richter echoed, the sound of screeching wheels audible on his end.

"Roger's Lane is a narrow road that leads deep into the woodland at the rear of the villas. From there, it's entirely on foot. You need to wait for backup. Vehicles can't navigate those woods efficiently, and facing Kirby alone on foot is far too dangerous."

"I can't do that, Leah." Richter's voice was urgent.

"Richter, listen to me. On foot, you'll be a needle in a haystack. If you run into Kirby alone, it might take backup too long to find you."

Richter was silent.

"Do not engage alone, Richter," I demanded. "Kirby is likely well-armed."

Another pause, broken only by distant sirens.

"I'm . . . sorry, Leah."

"Liam. Listen to—"

"Kill as many as you can—" he said before hanging up.

I stood there, overwhelmed with shock. But why? Richter's altruistic nature was precisely why I had chosen him. I should have known it might turn against me. I had exchanged a monster for a human, and humans trusted their hearts over logic.

Exiting into the hallway, I found Crystal waiting anxiously. I looked at her, then at the stage. Then I looked the other direction, down the corridor leading to my car, which would transport me to a storage unit in South Boston near the Neponset River. There, I kept a dirt bike, among other escape essentials: cash, a gun, and fake passports.

The mere thought was absurd.

Reckless.

Impulsive.

Unplanned.

Potentially fatal.

If Richter met his end, it would be due to his own heroic foolishness.

And yet . . .

I turned to see Crystal approaching, her face etched with deep concern.

Moments had passed, critical moments that could determine life or death for either me or Richter.

"Cancel the concert," I declared abruptly.

"What?" Crystal's eyes went saucer-wide. "But—"

"I'm not feeling good. Cancel it," I insisted, my tone brooking no argument.

Richter's recklessness astounded me. Agent Rose might already be beyond help. Why would he risk everything without waiting for backup?

Dressed for the evening, I rushed down the hallway and darted through the employees-only passages, then slipped out into the secluded alley where my car was parked.

I ignited my Audi's engine, urgency propelling each movement. Every second was precious. I ignored traffic signals as I sped toward my storage unit on the outskirts of Boston, near the Neponset River.

After bursting through the rundown storage unit's door, I ditched my heels, seized the handgun from the duffel bag, which also contained cash and a passport, and secured the gun inside my pantyhose, ensuring it stayed put below the waistband.

There wasn't time to put on the protective leather suit, so I strapped on the helmet and mounted the dirt bike. Accelerating briskly, I launched out the rear end of the storage facility, which I'd strategically chosen for its protection from surveillance and streetlights. My dress's train billowed behind me like a cape, while the cold wind and light drizzle chilled my bare arms, legs, and feet.

Before long, I encountered a procession of police cars heading for the bridge over the Neponset River, leading toward the wooded areas near the mansions. Despite the imminent arrival of backup, Richter might have already initiated contact with Kirby.

One police car seemed to notice me tailing them and slowed as we crossed the bridge. The rest of the convoy pressed forward. I decelerated and took a side road that led to the eastern edge of the woods.

My bike's light was the sole beacon illuminating the challenging deer paths littered with rocks and fallen branches. Despite the obstacles, I was faster than any on-foot backup approaching from the south. Only a few minutes ahead, but in situations like this, a bullet needed only the blink of an eye to find its target.

THIRTY-ONE

Liam

The muffled sounds of sirens sliced through the darkness of the woods from the south—the direction from which I had entered the densely overgrown area. Gun drawn and pointing ahead, I resisted the urge to call out for Rose, as I feared Kirby might hear me and either shoot or detonate a bomb, endangering us all.

It was almost pitch black as I ventured deeper into the patch of untouched forest on the outskirts of Boston. It felt as if I had stumbled into a hidden, otherworldly realm. The drizzle intensified, with thick clouds obliterating any traces of moonlight.

A branch snapped under my foot, startling birds above and sending shivers down my spine. I quickly refocused on the narrow deer path below—one of countless intertwining trails in this wilderness. Leah was right. With all these paths, there was a real risk that any backup might not arrive in time.

I had hiked the path for a few minutes when I spotted what appeared to be a large rock partially concealed by bushes and nearly crushed by a massive fallen tree.

As I approached cautiously, the silhouette of a black tent began to materialize before me, not far from the rock. It was ingeniously blended with the underbrush as if nature itself had built it.

Holding my breath, I listened intently for any surrounding sounds. With the woods seemingly silent except for my pounding heart, I risked a brief flash of light from my phone.

"Holy fuck," I whispered as the light reflected off the largest IED bomb I had ever seen. It was protruding from a military-grade backpack alongside an M249 Squad Automatic Weapon and a huge pile of ammo. Scattered around were empty food cans, water bottles, ammunition, and IED assembly equipment.

My shock was shattered by a faint, guttural sound—something I might have missed earlier. I swung the flashlight toward the noise and nearly dropped it when the beam highlighted Agent Rose lying on the leaf-strewn ground. Her eyes were wide with terror as she clutched her stomach, her hands trembling over her blood-soaked shirt. She struggled to speak, a gurgling sound mingling with blood.

"Rose!" I exclaimed, rushing to her side and kneeling on the muddy ground.

"Armor . . ." she managed just as the first rounds of gunfire erupted. I launched myself behind the rock as bullets ejected sparks and rock chips under a high-pitched ping.

Then an eerie silence swallowed us.

A whirlwind of sensations overcame me—I was hot, cold, nauseous—as I cautiously peered around the rock. My phone, the flashlight still on, lay on the ground. The dim silver light revealed the figure of a man standing near the tent.

Fucking Kirby.

Without hesitation, I fired.

One, two, three, four, five shots, each striking him squarely in the chest. Picture-perfect, just as I was taught in the academy.

But the anticipated thud of a body never came. Instead, Kirby remained upright, unfazed.

I fired again, three more rounds aimed closer to his upper chest, one possibly near the head. But in the darkness and from this distance, my supposed headshot was ineffective. I was immediately met with a return avalanche from his automatic rifle.

I took cover behind the rock. Rose's word came back to me. "Armor."

The North Hollywood shootout between heavily armored criminals Larry Phillips Jr. and Emil Mătăsăreanu flashed in my mind. I recalled the intense gunfight they unleashed against the LAPD. And now, here we were, in a forest at night. Kirby could shoot us all and then rampage through the nearest neighborhood.

Suddenly, silence again.

Time slowed as I heard the rustle of leaves and snapping branches, the sounds inching closer to my hiding spot. What could I possibly do now? He was armored, armed with an automatic rifle, and likely equipped with night vision. Running for it was a death sentence, as was remaining here.

"Kirby!" I called out, pressed tightly against the cold rock. "The man you stabbed at the docks had a history of rape and domestic violence, so no real loss there. We can get you help. Real help. I promise you, I'll make sure of it."

The snapping of twigs continued.

"Let me get my agent out of here. We can still save her. She's just doing her job like you once did to protect us."

He kept advancing.

A wave of horror washed over me. Would this be it?

"I met your parents," I said. "Your mother . . . she just wants you to know everything will be okay and that she's here for you no matter what."

Silence, then another branch snapped, now alarmingly close to my cover.

"Nothing is okay in this shithole we call America," retorted an empty voice from mere feet away on the other side of the rock.

"Tell me about it," I said quickly. "You're not the only one getting screwed over. My life's pretty shitty as well right now. But we have to keep fighting. If not for ourselves, then for the people who love us."

The sounds halted, presumably from just behind the rock. Had I gotten through to him?

"And you have people who love you, Kirby," I quickly continued.

Silence.

"Your family wants to work with us to get you the help you need. Real help, not just a quick prescription that won't stop the nightmares and pain."

"It's . . . too late," Kirby said, his voice weak and filled with pain. "He's too powerful."

"Who?" I pressed. "Who are you talking about?"

After a brief silence, the dark figure of Robert Kirby emerged from the right side of the rock, maintaining a distance that allowed for effective use of his M249 Squad

Automatic. He was armored from head to toe, his eyes deadly, piercing the night like a nocturnal demon.

"You're just as blind as the rest of them," he concluded firmly. "Someone needs to open your eyes. And that burden falls on me."

He aimed the weapon at me.

Fuck.

My gaze shifted to Rose, whose wide eyes were filled with pain and fear, grasping at the last seconds of life.

I attempted a comforting smile as if to reassure her everything would be all right, either in this life or the next. Then I braced myself for Kirby's final act, wondering if this old dog was worthy of heaven.

THIRTY-TWO

I navigated my dirt bike along narrow deer trails, veering close to the riverbed, the most logical place for a campsite accessible by boat. Branches lashed against my exposed arms as if the trees themselves were trying to thwart my advance, branding me an enemy. My feet were in agony from several barefoot stops on the forest floor as I negotiated sharp rocks and branches—a necessary evil to avoid slipping off the throttle with high heels and losing control.

Soon, a faint light pierced through the trees. I burst into a clearing, instantly assessing the scene: Kirby aiming at Richter, a wounded agent on the ground.

Without hesitation, I emptied my Glock 19's magazine into Kirby. Fifteen rounds fired into his chest with precision and speed.

Yet Kirby remained upright and turned his weapon toward me.

"He's—" Richter attempted to warn, but I was already in motion.

I slammed the bike into first gear, twisted the throttle to its limit, and released the clutch, charging at Kirby with the bike rearing up in full, reckless abandon.

Rat-tat-tat! His shots barely missed me and hit the undercarriage as we collided with brutal force. I was flung from the bike, tumbling over rocks and scraping my skin before coming to a halt. The instant sharp pain in my chest and back left no doubt that I had broken a few ribs.

Kirby was knocked back, his weapon sliding away into the darkness. The bike, now without its rider, skidded to a stop, its engine still rumbling defiantly.

Kirby staggered to his feet and quickly recovered, jumping on top of me to pin me down, his armored weight pressing me into the mud. The silver blade of his knife glinted dangerously close to my neck. It was halted by the edge of my helmet, then cut into my flesh just as Richter slammed into Kirby with the same momentum as the bike, dislodging Kirby's armored helmet.

I staggered to my feet, panting. Kirby, now helmetless and pinned underneath Richter, struck Richter on the head with a rock, momentarily stunning him before pushing him off.

But Richter, who'd found his own rock, rose again.

The two exchanged clumsy swings, dodging blows with difficulty. Kirby, with superior hand-to-hand combat skills, struck Richter across the jaw. He staggered.

As Kirby raised his rock for a decisive blow, I launched in excruciating pain and struck him from behind with my own rock.

My feet felt lacerated, probably embedded with small stones and debris. I was concussed as well, as evidenced by my overwhelming nausea.

Kirby was quick to turn and swing at me, landing a heavy blow on my helmet that sent me tumbling backward. The world spun around me even after I'd landed. But Richter was right behind him, slamming his rock onto the side of Kirby's head. Kirby stumbled but managed to stay upright. With a blank face, he turned to Richter. Clearly, he'd endured pain or been taught to endure it during his time in the military.

It was my turn to dive back in. Richter and I swung at Kirby in a brutal, bloody dance.

Finally, Richter landed the heavy blow that took Kirby down, then leaped on top of him, relentless. Again and again, he unleashed a never-ending avalanche of strikes. Each time, he raised the rock high above his head before bringing it down with savage force.

"Richter," I said, stepping up beside him.

But he persisted, an animalistic scream of raw frustration escaping his lungs.

"Richter, stop!" I demanded, staring into Kirby's face, now awash in a flood of blood. His eyes were wide open, a silent testament to his tragic death.

Richter raised his arm for another blow, so I grabbed his wrist to stop him.

That seemed to snap him out of his frenzied trance. He looked at me in utter shock, then at Kirby's blood-soaked face and gaping head wound.

"Fuck," he muttered, climbing off Kirby, letting the rock slip from his grasp.

He turned away, his face a mask of pain, agony, and disgust, while I stared emotionlessly at Kirby.

"Spare yourself the guilt. This was mercy," I said, words that Richter acknowledged before he rushed over to the critically wounded agent. Her breathing was now shallow and rapid, her vacant eyes staring into oblivion.

She was in shock; her time was running out.

"Rose!" Richter cried out, his eyes scanning her bloodied torso.

I turned to limp toward my bike; I had to escape. The first helicopters hovered anxiously over the woods, their lights scouring the darkness, every visible inch. The barking dogs were closing in. We had a minute, tops, before this place swarmed with them.

"Wait!" Richter called after me.

I knew better than to stop; I had to keep moving.

"Please, help her!" Richter's voice halted me, his desperation anchoring my feet as if they weren't my own.

I turned to face his pain-streaked visage.

"Please save her, please," he pleaded.

I glanced at my bike, then back at him, caught by the raw desperation in his eyes— an emotion that unexpectedly stirred something within me.

"Damn . . ."

With a quick limp, I approached the agent, lifting my visor to see her more clearly. Our eyes locked. Hers were filled with a haunting resignation, as if she saw me as the angel of death come to take her away.

"There's a chance she's still conscious enough to remember all of this," I said, standing motionless as the barking grew closer. "She'll come after me, this one . . . after us. I can see it in her eyes."

Richter focused on Rose, now holding her hand.

"You didn't kill her," I said. "Is this worth losing everything for, including your daughter?"

He stared at her, perhaps envisioning the smiling face of his daughter, a face he would never see again should our secret come to light. But then that moment passed, and he looked back at me. "Save her."

I gazed at Richter, the man I once considered an ally, now potentially the one who could cause my downfall. But then, wasn't this the very reason I had sought him out? To save me from my true self and the dark deeds I might commit in moments like these? If I walked away now, it would be a "real" murder weighing on my conscience, as the monsters never counted.

Quickly, I removed my helmet and kneeled next to her, opposite Richter. "Sit her up," I instructed, pressing my ear against her back to listen to her lungs. "Collapsed lung. Air is trapped in her pleural space, putting pressure on the lung, impairing her breathing."

I held a hand over her shoulders to prevent her from slumping as she desperately attempted to breathe.

"Do you have a pen?" I asked, maintaining my usual calm despite my own pain.

"What?" Richter looked confused, panicked.

"A pen," I repeated firmly.

He frantically searched his jacket pockets, then the front of his suit shirt, and finally pulled out a pen.

I took it and unscrewed it in the middle. Then I tossed aside the upper part, keeping only the chamber of the lower part, which would now function like a short straw.

Rose flinched as I used my fingers to locate the exact spot at the second intercostal space between the second and third ribs along the midclavicular line.

"Go behind her and hold her tight."

Richter positioned himself behind her, stretching his legs out next to hers, with her in the middle.

I used the train of my dress to wipe down and hold the pen, ensuring that I left no prints.

Quickly, I took a rock, placed the empty pen chamber at the precise spot of her upper ribs, and, with one strong swing, drove the pen into her flesh. She mustered a final burst of strength to resist me. If this were a movie, that single blow would have sufficed, allowing the pen to pierce her lungs and miraculously save her life. But reality is no film, and I found myself having to strike the pen multiple times with the rock to embed it fully into her lungs, sunk deep into her flesh like a nail driven into a wall.

Instantly, air and blood escaped through the pen, alleviating the pressure and, more importantly, allowing the lung to partially re-expand.

Rose gasped as the sudden influx of air revived her. She drew long, haggard breaths like she'd just broken the surface after being submerged for too long.

I didn't wait a second longer. I jumped to my feet, rock still in hand, and ran to retrieve my bike. Despite my pain and a broken rib, I lifted it with adrenaline fueled by the barking dogs only moments away.

I mounted the bike and sped into the darkness along the small path I had come from. There was a decent chance that law enforcement hadn't yet encircled the entire woods to focus manpower on the site Richter had sent them to. That would leave my escape route open, especially now that they would find Richter with Kirby dead and wouldn't be looking for another suspect.

Relief greeted me as I emerged onto the bridge where I had entered the woods earlier and found no law enforcement blocking the road. I saw cars with sirens passing, but none seemed to be looking for me.

I drove past them over the bridge, briefly slowing to throw the rock with my prints into the river. Then I increased my speed again.

I was tempted to head straight home on the bike, but this was unadvisable despite the intense pain. I had to return to my own car and then drive home, ensuring my outdoor security camera captured my return in the vehicle I had left in.

I would call Ida to assist me in the basement where I kept all my medical equipment. Then I would heal at home, informing Crystal that personal matters had arisen, and I needed some time to myself.

This wasn't the first time Ida would assist me in the basement. My hobby came with physical dangers, though this was the most severe I'd suffered so far. She never asked for details. I paid her too well, and the money meant a lot to her family. My demise would be hers as well. Her children and grandchildren. Ida would never talk. She was a mother, and silence was a matter of survival for what she loved.

For a brief moment, my mind drifted away from the pain as I contemplated the aftermath of all this.

There was a slight chance that Agent Rose had seen me, maybe even witnessed the entire fight, and would remember it. Of course, there was also the chance that she had been battling for her own life so fiercely that she hadn't focused on the fight with Kirby. Maybe it would all seem like a dream to her.

But there was a real possibility I could soon face legal trouble. Although I could likely navigate any scandal, given that the law often sided with money, predicting the outcome without all the facts was difficult.

No, Agent Rose had now become a liability. A threat to my life and Richter's. One I could have eliminated by simply letting her die.

And yet . . . I felt calm.

The monster deep within me was locked away tonight. Richter had awakened my humanity. He had saved me from myself.

As I huffed my way back to my car at the storage unit, breathing heavily and grunting with immense pain, calmness washed over me.

If I went down because I'd saved a life and not because I'd taken one, I was okay with that.

I was, for once, at peace.

THIRTY-THREE

Liam

The hospital ICU floor was in a frenzy, with journalists, FBI agents, and police officers milling about. The flash of cameras illuminated Agent Rose's room, casting light into the hallway where I was waiting. I didn't need to see it to know the picture being taken: McCourt shaking Rose's hand, handing her an award, his smile fake and slimy.

They made their way out, with Rose being wheeled in a wheelchair by nurses. Machines and a saline drip were attached to her arm. As they emerged into the hallway, loud clapping erupted around her.

Rose was being transferred to a lower-intensity unit. She was still in pretty bad shape but was out of the woods now. Her eyes caught mine as the nurses pushed her down the hallway past me, a small train of doctors and staff following her—all for the cameras, of course.

The story was simple. Rose had saved the day by finding Kirby and helping bring him down, taking a bullet in the process. The buzz was all about her, which she deserved. It was she who had found Kirby before he could take more lives.

"I need to talk to you," I said, trying to stop her briefly as she was pushed past me. However, all she did was throw me a weary look that I couldn't decipher. Of course, she was tired; she'd almost died. But was there something else in that look. Would she talk to McCourt, tell him about the woman who had saved her and helped kill Kirby? Or had she already spoken to him?

Anxious worry formed in my chest as McCourt stepped next to me. We both watched Rose roll past a small group of cops, none of them clapping but smiling dismissively. Typical macho pricks.

"Has she said anything?" I carefully asked McCourt. We watched her all the way to the elevator, waiting for it to open.

"Not much, but I doubt she remembers much anyway. I can't believe you saved her life with a pen. When the hell did you turn into MacGyver?" His gray eyes gave me a cunning, questioning look.

"CPR training. Some guy in the class asked about a trick with a pen he'd seen on TV. The trainer walked us through it, telling us how real it actually was."

McCourt scratched his jaw, shaking his head. To him, this was all wonderful: No bomb went off, nobody was killed but Kirby, and McCourt looked like he knew how to run the show.

"Maybe Jesus is real after all," he said as we continued to look at Rose in the distance.

"Maybe," I countered, discouraged, worried Rose might remember too much, though it didn't seem as if she had snitched on me yet. But why hadn't she? She was McCourt's top dog. This unnerved me almost as much as if she had.

McCourt's eyes fell on the group of male cops and agents. "That's what happens when you let a woman hold a badge," joked one of them, a middle-aged cop. The others laughed right under the nose of a journalist who was walking by them, stopping and noting every word in his notepad.

"Ah, for Christ's sake," McCourt cursed under his breath, "the children are pissing on my moment again." Then he strode over, and I followed. He stopped in front of the cop who had made the misogynistic joke. "What's your name?" he asked with a fake smile that seemed to make the officer think McCourt found his sexist joke funny.

The blond officer smiled wide in response. "I'm Officer—"

"Don't bother, I already know who you are," McCourt said loudly.

Every cop and agent on the floor turned quiet, avoiding eye contact—except for the sexist asshole, who now looked like he was about to piss himself.

"You're the kind of guy who thinks he's a main character," McCourt said loudly. "But the truth is, you're just a child whose Mommy makes you call a fart a 'fluffy,' and now you walk around thinking that being a fluffer is a good thing."

McCourt turned to me as I stood in shock. I was Team McCourt on this one. But damn...

Then McCourt took the badge off the officer's chest. "You can go now. You're suspended without pay." McCourt briefly looked over at the journalist to make sure the man got it all. Then he nodded at me to follow him to the stairs.

When we made it into the quiet of the stairs, McCourt asked, "You think the media overheard me?"

"I'm pretty sure they did."

"Good," he said. "This will go well with the whole 'woke' thing that's going on now. Red hats and tree huggers will love this alike. Gotta be on good terms with both sides of the swamp."

"If you say so, sir," I mumbled.

We walked down the stairs all the way to the first floor.

"Good work," McCourt said. "Killing Kirby saved all of us."

"It was all Agent Rose," I said. "She found him and stopped him. I only helped toward the end, and even that was almost too late."

He faintly smirked. "She's a hell of an agent, that's for sure. I saw that certain something in her the moment I first looked into her eyes. Kids just aren't made like that anymore. It's fucking depressing."

"I think the kids will be alright," I politely disagreed.

"We have a mandatory debrief at four today," McCourt said, changing the topic.

I froze. McCourt turned to look at me. "I have court today. The custody battle," I said.

He stared at me for a moment, then nodded. "I'll see you tomorrow then."

Shit, he was in the best mood I'd ever seen him in.

"Yes, sir. Thank you."

I watched for a moment as he disappeared behind the door into the foyer. There was no way he knew anything. Rose must have stayed quiet, which made my story about killing Kirby by myself when I found Rose the only story there was. Forensics suspected the dirt bike tracks from Leah were Kirby's from when he hauled supplies to the scene. By boat and, occasionally, on a dirt bike.

Nobody questioned anything.

Nobody but, maybe, Rose.

I had no doubt that saving her was the right thing to do, no matter what would happen, but I had a hard time accepting the possible outcome with grace. The mere thought of Rose hunting down Leah and ultimately finding out about us tore me apart. It could ruin my chances of getting Josie back.

If there was one agent in the FBI who could uncover the truth, it was Rose.

THIRTY-FOUR

Liam

It was dead silent in the courtroom. Sarah, her boy toy, and her older lawyer sat at their table next to Dan and me, both of us facing the judge's empty bench. Judge Albert White was in his chambers, talking privately to Josie. My mom and sister sat on the benches behind me, their tension and worry clutching at me like an invisible hand.

Sarah and her lawyer were glancing around the room, their feet tapping in unison. I couldn't blame them. Hell, I was nervous too. The room seemed to be closing in, the walls encircling me. Breathing became a chore. I kept tugging at the tie around my neck, loosening and then tightening it to appear immaculate for the judge.

I checked my phone again.

Still no answer from Leah.

This was a brand-new phone that I'd received via courier at my apartment. As always, it had only one number saved in it—hers. But none of my texts had been answered since the one I'd received over two weeks ago, which only said *Talk soon.*

What the hell did that mean? *Talk soon* as in, *I'm not well, but we'll talk when I'm better?*

Or *Talk soon* as in, *All is great, see you soon?* I had asked this in brief texts, but no response ever came. The fact that her concerts had been canceled until further notice only made things worse. Depending on the moment, I pictured Leah either in her bed in some private hospital setting with a million-dollar concierge doctor team tending to her or in a ditch somewhere, bleeding to death.

Worry and guilt pressed down on me so hard that even the thought of holding Josie again eased it only a little.

"Goddamn it," I mumbled under my breath.

"All rise," the court clerk announced as Judge White stepped back into the courtroom and took his seat. He was an older, bald man dressed in a black judicial robe. Despite his authoritative presence, he seemed approachable and fair.

"Your honor, we would like to petition the court to add additional evidence regarding Liam Richter's deeply disturbing father who—" Sarah's lawyer began, rising quickly to his feet, but Judge White waved him off.

"That's not necessary."

"But your honor—" Sarah's lawyer interjected only to be met with a forceful "I said that's not necessary" from Judge White.

The judge continued. "I have reviewed the entire case and spoken to Josie, who is, quite frankly, one of the most reasonable individuals I've ever encountered in my courtroom. She made it very clear what she wanted, and I can support her wish wholeheartedly as the best for the child."

"Your honor," Sarah tried anxiously, "my daughter is just a child. She doesn't know what's best for her."

Judge White raised an eyebrow at Sarah as if he'd just caught her with her hand in a cookie jar. "Mrs. Richter, considering everything at hand, I would kindly ask you to refrain from speaking. I've heard enough."

"But your honor—"

"I said I've heard enough!" Judge White lashed out at her. "I wanted this to be graceful, for your sake and the child's, but if you want my honest opinion, I find this whole smear campaign you've started against your ex-husband—who has done nothing but try to make this easy for you and your daughter—despicable. First, you cheat on him, then you financially destroy him with your unreasonable demands, which he agreed to—an act of compliance I have never seen in this court before—all for the love of his child. And now, you have the audacity to question your own child's wish to be with her loving father? If I hear one more word from you, I will hold you in contempt of court and sentence you to a fine and a week in jail to think things over."

After staring down a whimpering Sarah for a few moments, the judge turned to me.

"Special Agent in Charge Richter, I hereby grant you joint custody with your ex-wife. I will personally appoint a court social worker as a mediator to ensure the custody schedule is fifty-fifty and without issues. Thank you for the hard work you do to keep us all safe. Your daughter is waiting outside. She wants to spend the weekend with you if your schedule allows—"

I was already on my feet, running out of the courtroom. Thank God, Josie was right there, holding hands with a woman who was most likely a social worker.

"Dad!" Josie yelled, jumping into my arms, tears streaming down her face.

I felt a burning in my eyes. Fuck, was I crying too?

I squeezed her and reassured her that all was good now. Moments later, I felt my mom and sister join our embrace. Both were shedding tears.

"I made chocolate chip cookies," my sister announced, her long, loose hair partially covering Josie's face in our group hug.

"Good God, that vegan horror," my mom remarked dismissively. Josie laughed, and even my sister chuckled.

"Let's go," my sister said, taking Josie by the hand. As the doors swung open again, Sarah, her boy toy, and her lawyer emerged. Josie froze, looking guilty, the weight of her conversation with Judge White apparent in her tear-streaked face.

Sarah's eyes met mine. They were filled with venom. For a moment, I wondered if she'd pull a knife from the fancy designer bag I'd bought her for our fifth anniversary.

"Wait here, sweetie," I told Josie, then approached Sarah. I leaned in, my next words meant only for her. "Do the right thing for once and smile for our daughter, or I'll file for full custody and make you work for your money again."

Sarah's shock was apparent, but then, as if under duress, she smiled widely for Josie.

The relief on my little girl's face, seeing her mother's approving smile, felt like the gates of heaven opening to bless her with peace and happiness.

"Vanilla is the most popular flavor in the world, honey," I said to Sarah. "Don't ever fuck with me again."

I returned to Josie.

What a win.

What a day.

My girl was back.

I was back.

Kirby was taken care of. No more lives were lost this time. And with a bit more luck, Rose might not remember anything at all.

I held one of Josie's hands, and my sister held the other as we made our way to the parking lot. My mother and sister argued about the vegan cookies, which made Josie and me smile. That was when my work phone rang.

"Richter here," I answered.

"Wow. You sound happy. I take it things went well?" Heather asked.

"They did."

"God, I'm so happy for you," she said, her voice trailing off.

"Why?" I asked, slowing my pace.

The silence that followed made me let go of Josie's hand. I gestured to my mom to take her to the car. She nodded, and they walked ahead.

"Heather?" I urged. "What's wrong?"

Heather sighed through the phone. "Fuck. It's . . . it's Anna."

A chill colder than an Arctic storm seized me from within as I braced for her next words.

"She was found dead in the woods."

THIRTY-FIVE

Anna

Ah, so you've come at last. Thank you for caring about me enough to stop by. In a world full of sorrow and horror, your attention to my tragedy means a lot to me. I feel so lonely and scared, it could kill me all over again.

You wouldn't notice me at first, lying where the woods meet the river, at the foot of the cliff. It's cold. Both of my legs are soaked with crystal-clear water that sounds soothing at night but restless during the day. Days have passed, weeks maybe, and the trees have been both a silent witness and an active participant in my slow mission to merge their falling leaves with the dirt beneath me.

Day and night have danced their endless cycle. So have rain and moonshine, washing over me in powerful, cleansing torrents, both leaving their marks on my body, soul, and heart . . . whatever might be left of it.

I've felt the curious nudges of small creatures and a more serious bite by a bear. The cautious steps of rabbits and deer have entertained me. Even the stars have cast their eternal gaze upon me—some of them judging the sins of my past, others sharing my pain, but all of them constant.

Will you shed a tear for me?

You can't say?

Then you have shed too many in this cold world already, and I'll shed one for you.

But if you shed one for me after all, I shall be forever in your debt.

The occasional hikers have wandered close, their voices a distant murmur. They linger for selfies on the cliff, eyes scanning the distant horizon one last time before continuing on their path, oblivious to my tragic story lying mere steps away. They move on, leaving me to the embrace of my utter loneliness.

But today, there's a different sound, a persistent bark breaking the serene quiet. A dog with senses sharper than its human companion has found me. I hear the owner's approach, a mix of anger and urgency in their footsteps.

Ah, there you are, I think the moment he stops and his wide eyes stare at me in horror. I don't know you, but I'm sorry it was you who found me. I'm sorry your day filled with nature's calming peace has turned to darkness.

Forgive me that a sense of relief is washing over me as your shaking hands dial 911. Forgive me that I might visit you in your dreams. But maybe now, thanks to your discovery, I can finally find peace.

Suddenly, the scene around me shifts. Do you see it? The police crew invades, blue and red lights slicing through the calm I've found here. You see, the EMTs don't even pretend to save me. I'm already long dead. My body left to rot in this world, my soul in another, watching.

The officers stand around, their eyes reflecting the weight of a world where darkness like this happens. "Look harder, he left a mark," I wish I could tell them as one silently prays for me, for the soul speaking to you right now.

See how the investigators swarm, collecting evidence, cameras flashing, intruding on the peace of this lonely spot I'd come to accept. But they're missing it, aren't they?

The ankh symbol.

His signature, hidden under a rock.

Suddenly, an officer stumbles across it by accident, his foot slipping on the rock where the mark was left. However, there's no shock, no realization. Just a quick photo of the symbol, and then they move on, stepping all over the very clue they need.

They leave, making all this noise, blind to what they should be seeing. They take what's left of me, but here I am, still with you, still by this creek.

Days pass.

Then I sense her before I can hear her steps.

My angel of darkness.

Have you come to save my immortal soul? Will you get the revenge I crave and deserve?

I see *he* has brought you here.

The two of you like predator and prey, trapped in a violent storm.

So, he joined us after all? But does he truly accept his part in this heartless world?

As my spirit is pulled away, I'm filled with an aching need. I haven't seen how it all ends. Will you watch for me to see what happens?

Please tell me in a prayer once it's done so I can rest for all eternity.

THIRTY-SIX

Leah

Wet twigs snapped under my feet as I followed the hiking trail in Bigelow Hollow State Park toward the creek where Anna's body had been discovered about a week prior. It was yet another gloomy day; the wet canopy teemed with ravens and their ominous caws—a fitting soundtrack for the grim scene that awaited me. The familiar yellow "do not cross" crime scene tape still sectioned off the last part of the trail to the creek and the small rocky cliff from whose base her body had been recovered after several weeks.

This would be the first time I'd seen Richter since the Kirby incident. He had been hounding me over the phone, requesting meetings. However, as I was still recovering from two broken ribs, stitches on my cut feet, and two on my neck—the spot where Kirby had pressed his knife—I wasn't up for it.

When I emerged into the clearing, he was standing by the edge of the creek, lost in thought. I had no doubt he would blame himself for Anna's death, though he had done everything within his power to prevent it. That was just the kind of man he was.

He turned the moment I stepped closer, his intense gaze meeting mine.

"I see you're well," he said, sizing me up, his eyes briefly lingering on the small, visible wound on my neck.

"Well enough," I replied.

He nodded. "I'd be mad about you forbidding me to check in on you, but I'm just too freaking grateful to you."

I tilted my head.

"Josie . . . that was you, wasn't it? The miracle of having Judge White take over my case."

"No gratitude necessary. It was in my own best interest to alleviate some of your stressors."

He smiled, but the smile vanished as he walked over to where Anna's body had been discovered. "Forensics found no sign of struggle," Liam said, his voice laced with guilt and sadness. "They detected benzos in a hair sample that corresponded with the time of death. No weapons, no witnesses. Anna was ruled a tragic accident."

Of course, she was.

"It seems he has moved his operations from the tracks to the rivers, which gives him a hell of a lot larger canvas than before," I concluded. "We're talking thousands of miles of rivers and creeks on the East Coast." It was a hard truth to digest. "If the body wasn't Anna's, who knows if we would have realized it was him behind this."

Richter shook his head, unable to fathom the enormity of the enemy we faced.

But something seemed different about Anna's murder. It was as if the shift in scenery from rail to river made it less significant for him. Less personal.

"I went over the college security cam. We can see Anna leave the campus by herself in the opposite direction of where the patrol officer watching her was parked. As if she knew the risk and didn't care."

I was about to speak when a branch snapped behind us. Agent Vallery Rose stepped into the clearing. The moment she saw me, her hand moved to the gun in her chest holster. In reflex, Richter threw himself into harm's way, drawing his own weapon.

Rose paused, looking at him and his hand on his gun. Then her gaze snapped back to me. "You . . ." she said. "You're the woman who helped kill Kirby that night!" Her grip on her gun tightened. Confusion and fear flared in her eyes as if she were a cornered deer.

"Rose!" Richter said firmly. "Remove your hand from the gun."

"What?" she asked, betrayal washing over her. "What's going on here?" Her hand was still lingering on her gun. Richter's hand remained on his own.

Slowly, I stepped closer to her, relieved that she still hadn't drawn her gun as the distance between us closed.

"Rose," Richter said, his voice cautious. "Let's talk, but lower—"

"If I wanted you dead, I wouldn't have risked getting caught to save you," I said, stepping in front of her. "Now let go of the gun. You already know that you don't have the upper hand here." I pointed to the yellow pus mark on her white shirt. "They put you on the wrong antibiotics. May I?"

Her head twitched back as I reached for her collar, pausing for her nod of consent. Gently pulling it down, I exposed the bandaged bullet wound on her upper chest and lifted the dressing. The wound was stitched but swollen and oozing with pus.

"Did they give you Azithromycin?"

She looked at me as if all of this were a dream, then nodded.

"Call your doctor and ask for Cephalexin. Otherwise, you'll need to start wound care treatment soon." I let go of her shirt and moved to stand beside Richter near where Anna was found.

Rose slowly removed her hand from her gun and straightened her shirt before joining us at the crime scene, maintaining a healthy distance. "Who the hell are you?" she demanded. "And why did you ask me to come here?"

Richter, too, removed his hand from his gun, slightly easing the tension. "That's a question I'd also like answered," he said, his tone marked by frustration.

I circled the scene under their vigilant watch, then halted where the small ankh sign was etched into the rock near the river. One had to consider it carefully to associate it with the ancient symbol, as its carving had a certain natural rawness. However, upon direct inspection, there was no doubt.

"Do you recognize this?" I asked Rose, gesturing toward the symbol on the ground. She approached slowly, then shook her head.

"It's the Train Track Killer's signature, the Egyptian ankh symbol," I clarified. "He leaves it at all his crime scenes."

Rose recoiled slightly, her eyes examining the ground. "But that's impossible. Patel is dead."

Richter cursed under his breath as he threw me a "what the fuck are you doing?" look as sharp as an arrow. He took a step closer. "Patel wasn't the Train Track Killer," he said. "He was just some guy who we suspect worked with him. Or, more likely, was used by the Train Track Killer as some sort of footman."

Rose scoffed. "That's ridiculous. Are you guys smoking peyote or something? The Train Track Killer is dead. And the only real question here is, who is this woman and why the hell did she kill Kirby?" She turned to me. "You CIA or something?"

An intense silence settled over us. Once again, Liam used that moment to throw me another gaze, this one even more threatening than the last. "Leah, no," he said.

"I'm . . . not part of the Central Intelligence Agency," I said.

Richter stepped closer. "Leah." His tone was low and filled with warning.

"Nor am I part of any other law enforcement or government agency."

"Leah, don't!" His voice grew even louder.

I briefly looked at him, then faced Agent Rose. "I kill people, if you want me to be honest and precise."

"Leah, goddamn it!" Richter cursed. "Stop!"

"I kill serial killers," I clarified, ignoring Richter. "Harvey Grant was one of my more recent works."

Rose laughed, but the moment she looked at Richter, the way he ran his hand through his hair, every muscle tense and anxious, the laugh was smacked right off her face.

"Leah, what the fuck!" he cursed at me. "Have you lost your mind?"

I took a step closer to Rose, who was now backing up slowly. "I'm quite busy and not good with emotional encounters. So, let's skip straight to the point. The man who killed Anna and countless other people is still out there. He's a genius mastermind who not only has played law enforcement for years but won't stop killing until he's taken out. I take you for a woman of facts and logic, so instead of going back and forth trying to convince you of something so outrageous it would top the JFK assassination theories, I propose you go back to the office and do your own research."

Rose, who looked as if she was ready to call in for support any moment, now seemed curious.

Slowly, I pulled a paper out of the pocket of my cashmere coat and held it up to her. "You'll find the ankh symbol I showed you here today at every single one of these murder scenes. Carved into the tracks close to where the bodies were found. He stages his murders to look like suicides. Just like Anna." I nodded toward where her body was found. "He won't stop killing until someone makes him. An arrest is out of the question. He's too genius to get convicted in our useless courts. Especially since I believe he might have extreme wealth and power."

Rose stood still for a moment before her amber eyes shot to the paper in my hand. She suddenly grabbed it from me and looked at the names and locations of deaths written on it. "You're the pianist, aren't you? I saw you on TV," she said.

This threw me off. The question seemed out of place, given everything I'd just said. I nodded as I held her gaze.

She responded with a sarcastic smile, then peeked at Richter, who stood frozen in shock. "Is it true?" Rose asked him. "What she says?"

His gaze dropped to the ground before returning to hers. For a moment, they stared at one another. Then he nodded, brief and quick.

"Mm-hmm. So, let's say all of this crazy shit is true," she said. "Why are you telling me?"

"I thought that was evident," I countered.

She thought about this for a moment, then frowned. "You're worried I saw you at the Kirby crime scene and will tell McCourt about it." She sounded disappointed, as if she'd hoped to have been called here today for a different reason. Which there was.

"There are other benefits for you to know," I said. "The Train Track Killer is one of the most genius humans who has ever walked this earth. An extra pair of hands and eyes could be beneficial in the task of killing—"

"Stop!" Rose cut me off. "This is insane! Even if all of this is true, what makes you think I won't arrest you? If you really kill people, bad or not, you belong behind bars just like them!"

Richter ran a hand through his hair, his complexion pale.

"You can certainly try to bring me to justice," I offered. "But what evidence do you have? I'm the world's most famous virtuoso. Besides resources for a legal team that will greatly surpass the skillset of the government's lawyers, I have friends in powerful positions. You, on the other hand, have nothing. The scandal could destroy my career and cause enormous problems within the FBI and its reputation. The situation with Larsen would be nothing compared to this. But you strike me as a woman of logic. Would that be an outcome you deem worth the short-term gratification of arresting me? The FBI in shambles. The Train Track Killer still out there, killing and killing until the day he dies."

Rose's gaze fell onto the paper in her hands again, the names.

"Rose, listen to me," Richter said, throwing me an angry look. "Leah is the only chance we have to get rid of this monster. I know how you feel. I was where you are right now. Torn between black and white, right and wrong. Good and evil."

"So, what happened?" she asked, her tone accusing. "I mean, to the man I thought you were. The one fighting for the people of this country against the bad guys."

For a moment, I thought Richter would cave at that—he'd probably asked himself the same question. But, instead, he looked her in the eyes and said, "He's standing right here doing just that."

This threw Rose off. Her eyes blinked rapidly, but then she shook her head. "This is crazy, Richter. If this woman is telling the truth, what makes her so different from the Train Track Killer? She's just like them. A crazy killer. And killers can't be trusted!"

It was a good point. So, instead of arguing her logic, I decided to give her the one thing she needed to even consider the offer I was about to give her.

"I don't need your trust, nor do you need mine," I said. "I have arranged a safety net for Agent Richter in case he ever needs to end our partnership."

Richter's eyebrows rose. "What are you talking about?"

I glanced at Rose, then back at Richter. "There's an associate of mine, Luca Domizio, a former mob boss. He's agreed to kill me if the FBI approaches him for that purpose. Nobody knows about this. Nobody but you two."

"What!" Richter's disbelief was palpable. "Luca Domizio? Kill you?"

Ignoring his astonishment, I moved past them, positioning myself at the edge of the creek. "Time is running out," I said. "I suggest you take action, Agent Rose. But consider the innocent victims before you do. You might regret the bed you've made for yourself when you have to keep adding names to the list. I assume you're the type of person who might go mad over the fact that you missed the chance to stop one monster by leveraging another. It will eat you up from the inside. Just like your brother's death did."

Rose remained silent, grappling with the line I had crossed, before throwing her hands up in frustration. "Fuck this, I'm going to McCourt," she announced and stormed off.

"Rose!" Richter's voice was full of desperation. "Rose, wait!" he continued as she disappeared, leaving the tranquil silence of the woods behind.

But that tranquility was short-lived.

"What the fuck, Leah!" Richter exploded. "You're jeopardizing everything. Destroying us both!"

"Quite the opposite," I countered calmly. "The risk of her spotting me at the Kirby scene was too significant. She's persistent and cunning enough to eventually connect the dots. We needed to act before she convinced herself that pursuing me was the right thing to do."

Liam gazed into the distance, his head shaking in disbelief. "This is bad, Leah. A complete disaster. I just got Josie back. Now this. Rose is going to tell McCourt."

"Not if we can demonstrate the immense necessity of eliminating the Train Track Killer. A woman of her integrity will logically examine the facts I've provided. If she reaches the conclusion that everything I've said is true—"

"She might come around?"

"Or at least remain silent until the Train Track Killer is dealt with."

"And then what?" Richter pressed.

"We'll see. You've put us in this position by saving her life."

The words caused Richter to recoil.

"Maybe she'll come to appreciate that before she goes to McCourt," I said. "After all, I've never harmed a real human being."

"Is it true?" Richter said, his tone calmer, almost tender. His eyes locked with mine. "The thing with Luca?"

I remained silent.

"Goddamn it, Leah," he swore, his hands balling into fists. "Don't you think we need to discuss any assassination plans you're making?"

"No. Not if it's aimed at me. Or you," I replied, logical and detached.

I noticed a mix of emotions in his gaze—pity, sadness?

He dismissed it, looking in the direction Rose had vanished. "I don't like any of this."

"I know, but it's our only option. We must stop him, regardless of the cost. And we can't afford her flanking us when we're at full-blown war with him."

I took Liam's silence as a sign of agreement.

"She's not like me," he finally said. "Rose. She might betray us. Destroy us. Something's going on with her and McCourt."

"I know. But unless he has something that could threaten her life, there's a chance she might come to terms with the fact that our goals aren't so different. He's going to kill again soon. Every moment he's free, the threat of death lingers. She understands that. More so than any promotion McCourt might give her."

"How can you be so sure?" Richter asked.

"I can't. But in the woods, she chose to risk her life by chasing down Kirby before backup arrived. And just like you, she thought it was the right thing to do to save the lives of others." I smiled faintly. "Where is your trust, Agent Richter? She can't trust me. I agree with her. But you . . . you can. For now, at least."

He pinched his lips as we both looked toward the spot where Anna's body had been found. Unlike Liam, whose face was marred by sorrow and guilt, I had accepted her fate the moment Anna refused my offer to escape. Her death was sealed then and there. Also unlike Liam, I was able to interpret her end as a sacrifice for the greater good. We had another victim, another clue. He was now active along the rivers, and if Agent Rose was anything like Richter, Anna's death might have enlisted another ally for our cause. Sure, this new ally was more unpredictable than Liam and could turn on me at any moment, but as long as I maintained my strategy, she posed no threat to us.

With this new lead, I could practically taste the trail of blood in the air. Now all I had to do was follow it. No matter the cost.

THIRTY-SEVEN

Rose

On her drive to headquarters, Rose was more certain than ever that she would walk straight into McCourt's office and tell him everything. As crazy as it all sounded, she couldn't let this slide. With Ms. Nachtnebel's identity now known to her, she could establish some sort of connection to Kirby's crime scene. Or Harvey Grand. Maybe a lie detector test, maybe some blood at the Kirby scene that would reveal her DNA. Rose could turn over every rock that could have possibly touched that woman during the fight with Kirby.

She was a hell of a woman, this Nachtnebel. Rose had to give her that.

But the audacity to bring up her dead brother as a psychological tactic . . . like a looming threat of failure on her end.

It wasn't until Rose was already in the elevator that she felt the paper in her coat pocket—the paper that Leah had handed her.

Might be a good idea to check on those names. Better to have something concrete for McCourt when she talked to him about this.

So, she went straight to her desk instead of McCourt's office. What followed was absolute madness.

At first, there was nothing. No ankh sign was visible in the crime scene pictures, which were horrendous. Rose was pissed off that she had to look at them. However, once she examined a picture of Emma Mauser's body a second time, she found it.

The damn ankh symbol was right there, carved into the tracks! It was tiny, but once she knew what to look for, she had no doubt about it.

After that, she discovered the symbol at another crime scene. That meant Rose now had to drive to the other crime scenes to make sure this symbol was really there as well.

And it freaking was! At every single location on the list. It took a lot of her sick days, but she found each one.

Rose wasn't sure how long she sat in the woods on the tracks of the last crime scene. But she just sat there, in disbelief.

The Train Track Killer was real. And worst of all, not only was he still out there, but he was one of the most cunning and monstrous killers she had ever heard of. As much as Rose hated it, Leah Nachtnebel was right. Should Rose do something that would contribute in any shape or form to the killer's success in murdering more people, she would never forgive herself.

She had to stop this sick fuck, no matter the cost.

But how could she know what the right thing to do was? The FBI was a powerful force, surely more powerful than a pianist and Richter, no matter how genius the pianist might be. But then, why didn't the FBI know about the Train Track Killer in the first place? After all these murders?

Rose spent the rest of her day at the office looking into Leah Nachtnebel, the world-renowned pianist. She was rich, pretty, and—from every article Rose could find—a genius.

People compared her to Einstein and Tesla, to Mozart and Beethoven. Rose wasn't into classical music, so she'd never heard much about her, but now she had no doubt that what Leah had told her was the truth—including the fact that she would be a very hard person to bust.

So, just let her do her thing, then? Keep killing and hope she'd get rid of the Train Track Killer?

It was early evening. Rose was still hovering over her desk at the FBI headquarters when she noticed something strange in the file of Emma Mauser, a young woman killed after disappearing from a college party in Philly. As with all the other murders, the train track police had initially deemed the murder a suicide. However, closer inspection of the file's police report revealed that the word "homicide" was crossed out and "suicide" written above it, signed and dated by Officer Wagner from a station outside Philly where the body was found.

She pulled up the file on the computer. The forensic report clearly stated "suicide." Something was off here.

Quickly, she picked up the phone and called the Philly police station. "Agent Vallery Rose from the Boston FBI headquarters," she said to the secretary on the other end. "Is Officer Wagner on duty?"

"Hold on a minute," the secretary replied, putting Rose on hold. "He is," she said again after a minute. "Would you like me to connect you?"

"Yes, please."

After a brief wait, a low male voice answered. "Officer Wagner speaking."

"Yes, hi, this is Agent Rose from Boston FBI headquarters. I'm calling regarding the death of Emma Mauser. Does that ring a bell?"

"Phew," Wagner sighed. "That's one of those cases I'll carry with me until my last breath. Don't look at the crime scene pictures unless you have to. What trains can do to the human body . . . horrible. Truly horrible."

"Too late, I'm afraid," Rose said as she glanced over the picture of the dead woman's body on her desk. "But I was wondering if you could answer a question."

"I'll try my best."

"In your report, you initially wrote homicide as the cause of death but then crossed that out and marked it as a suicide. Could you tell me why?"

"Yes. When I wrote the report, I swore the coroner at Jenkins Hospital told me he suspected foul play. But then my chief called me in and told me it was a mistake on my end. He showed me the coroner's report on the computer, which clearly stated suicide. So, I corrected the original document. I had no clue you had a copy of that."

Rose pondered this for a moment. "I see. Well, we pulled the copies of the original files for a different investigation," she lied, assuming it was Richter who had pulled the original files' copies while hunting his killer in secret.

"Oh, okay. Not sure why you're looking into this case, but I usually don't make mistakes like that. I could have sworn the coroner told me he suspected foul play. I think he mentioned rope marks on her wrists or something. I'm not in some sort of trouble here, am I? Please tell me Netflix isn't making a documentary out of this, and I'm going to look like an idiot in front of the whole country."

"Nah, nothing like that. Just finishing up some paperwork on an old case and wasn't sure about the correction."

"I see."

"Why did you never double-check with the coroner?"

"Honestly, between us, we're understaffed and pulling double shifts all the time, so mistakes are very possible on our end."

"I hear you. Same here. Same, but different. Well, thanks, Officer. Stay safe out there."

"Thanks, you too."

Rose stared at the file on her desk, then at her computer. In no time, she was looking up the coroner's report, which clearly stated suicide. Then she dialed the number of his hospital.

Shit, she was already more invested in this case than she had wanted to be.

After a few back-and-forths, she was transferred to Dr. Clark Post.

"Dr. Post," he answered.

"Yes, um, hi, this is Agent Rose from the Boston FBI headquarters. I'm combing through some suicide cases in your area in search of a missing person."

Why the hell was she lying to him? Was she already working on the case with the "killer" squad?

"Do you remember the Emma Mauser case?" Rose asked.

"I do," Dr. Post confirmed. "Terrible tragedy. The body was horrific to work on. Very messy case. The family personally contacted me on that one."

"Really? Why is that?"

"Well, for some reason, they thought I had deemed the case a suicide—"

Rose straightened in her chair.

"But I told them that I didn't."

"You didn't?"

"No. I clearly stated in the paperwork that homicide was possible due to rope marks on her wrists. Also, the motive for the suicide didn't add up to me. She'd never used drugs before, but her system was full of opiates."

Drugs in the system of a non-user. Just like Anna.

Shit.

"Why? Is there still a problem with my report? I thought it was fixed."

Shit. He didn't know the death was still described as suicide? What was going on here?

"No, no," she lied. "I was just curious about the officer's original report and why corrections were made."

"Good luck," he laughed. "You can find discrepancies and corrections in every case out there."

"Very true."

Suddenly, horrific guilt overcame Rose. Did the family think their daughter did this to herself when it was actually murder? How could Rose keep such a painful secret to herself? It felt like deception.

"You said the family knows about this mistake?"

"Absolutely. They made quite a fuss about this. But as sad as it is, it doesn't really change much. No other evidence points to homicide. I'm afraid my findings were not enough to keep the case going one way or the other."

"Well, thank you. Hope you get to go home soon."

"Me too. Have a good evening."

"Thanks, you too."

Rose hung up, deep in thought. Why the hell did the computer files still deem the incident a suicide, contradicting Dr. Post's real opinion? The files were also missing the rope marks on the wrists that he mentioned.

He was right that discrepancies in files were common, but this was not a minor mistake. How had this been handled so poorly?

A quick search revealed why: because the file of Emma Mauser was labeled *Active investigation, not to be released.*

"God, please, fucking no," Rose cursed under her breath as she stared at the computer. Did Richter have a hand in this? This kind of shit was usually reserved for a handful of files of great political importance or of three-letter agency involvement to protect national interests. Not some murder on small-town train tracks.

Something was off here. Really, really off.

Rose had picked up the phone again to request the original copy of Dr. Post's report when her heart nearly stopped.

Straight ahead, by the elevator, was McCourt. He wasn't the problem, but who he was with certainly was.

Fucking Special Agent Jack Rice, that piece of shit.

The shock caused the handset to slip from her grip. It landed on her desk with a loud bang.

Jack Rice. Head instructor of interrogation tactics at the FBI academy.

The man who had nearly destroyed her life. And he was here, with McCourt.

It was a nightmare.

She was already on her feet, watching as if this were an out-of-body experience. Rice left using the stairs but not before turning and throwing her a hateful glare.

Then he was gone.

McCourt, on the other hand, stood by the elevator, staring straight at her. His face was like the calm before the storm.

Rose was by his side in moments, the air in her lungs deflating quickly. "S-sir," she stuttered, looking at the door Rice had just disappeared through. "May I ask—"

"Come with me," was all he said.

He led her back to his office. Rose stumbled after him like an idiot. She knew why he had paraded Rice in front of her like this. It was all part of his psychological warfare.

Something bad had happened on McCourt's end. It might be the end of her FBI career. Maybe even jail time.

McCourt took a seat in the wide massage chair behind his mahogany desk. The Arab princes and presidents shaking his hand in photos behind McCourt stared at Rose as if they were his army.

"Sir, may I ask—" Her voice broke off. God, it was so freaking hot in here. She was sweating. "May I ask what's wrong?"

McCourt frowned. "Wrong? Why would anything be wrong? You risked your life to save this pathetic unit, which unfortunately includes me at its helm, so I wanted to do something for you in return."

Desperate, Rose tried to analyze what he'd just said. Was he being sarcastic? Sincere?

He pushed a manila folder toward her, then leaned back in his chair. "For you," he said.

Carefully, Rose pulled it closer, opening it as if a bomb might detonate inside. A sigh of shock escaped her lips when she saw the contents.

It was her lie detector exam from her application to the FBI. The one she'd spent weeks training for so she could successfully lie about her past—and pass.

"Sir?" Rose asked, confused.

"This is what Rice used to report you to me, wasn't it?"

Rose nodded.

"The one where you lied about that incident in your childhood. To be precise, the question of if you've ever killed before."

The horrific scene of the worst moment in Rose's life washed over her like a tsunami. She couldn't stop it from replaying in her mind. The shots came in through the downstairs window while she played in her room upstairs. The blood. The tears. The screams. Her dead mother and wounded brother in the living room. Nausea overcame her at the memory of the little girl—her—looking into the eyes of her dead mother. Bullets had riddled her mother's body and the wall behind her, causing the glass of the window to shatter into a million pieces.

"Run." Her brother coughed up blood, too badly shot to speak a full sentence. His eyes stared past Rose, knowing his fate. "Run, Boo-girl," he coughed over and over, using the nickname he'd given her. Her first word had been "boo" on Halloween.

But Rose did not run.

Instead, she grabbed the gun in his twitching hand. And when the man in the black ski mask entered the home, machine gun in hand, his eyes landing on her, she didn't run. She wanted to, having never been more scared in her life, but when the man ignored her, stepped over her dead mother, and pointed his machine gun at her brother's head, Rose did the only thing she could think of.

She emptied the gun into the man until there were no bullets left to shoot.

Now, many years later, she was sitting in front of the lie detector test she'd lied on. The one she'd passed to be chosen to attend the academy: one of the few chosen out of tens of thousands of applicants.

She had worked so hard for this. The terrible foster homes, high school, and college.

But the dream hadn't lasted long. Karma had pulled off the unthinkable: The same police officer who had processed Rose's statement after the shooting was the one leading the procedures training course at the academy.

He instantly recognized Rose and spoke about her to Rice, saying how happy he was to see her come so far after such tragedy in her childhood. It didn't take long before Rice uncovered Rose's lies in her application. As a seasoned son of a bitch, he interrogated her and found out the truth—every dirty little detail that the police never found. When the cops arrived that day, they concluded her brother had killed the intruder before he died. They asked Rose if she had taken the gun out of his hand when everybody was dead—hence the fingerprints. She wrongfully confirmed this with a simple nod.

Scared to death, and a child, she worried she might be sent to prison.

"It's the only copy of it," McCourt said, tearing her out of her thoughts. He was analyzing her every breath. "The one on the computer is already erased."

Rose stared at the file. The file that should have gotten her kicked out of the academy and charged with a felony for lying to a federal agency.

"I never understood men like Rice. Insecure little cunts," McCourt continued, steepling his fingers. "The day he approached me with your case, I could tell he was a slimeball. He left a trail like a poisonous snail. Any good mentor who scouts a flaw in one of the best trainees we've had in years would have looked the other way.

"I mean, look at the applicants we had in recent years. Gen Z. An overly sensitive and entitled bunch who are more interested in TikTok likes than real life." He scoffed. "When Rice stomped into my office thinking he was about to unveil another Watergate, it actually pissed me off. It's not like you did anything I wouldn't have done myself. Quite the opposite, in fact. You were cut out to be an agent from the old days when the badge meant more than hashtags. I mean, how many little girls do you know who would have had the courage to do what you did? Picking up that gun and shooting the man who killed your family." He leaned forward, elbows on the desk. "The balls to do that, Rose. Not many people I know would have done the same. Especially not a worm like Rice."

Rose glanced at him, then nervously looked at the file again.

"And yet," McCourt added, "the one thing I never understood in this whole thing: Why did you lie about it in the first place? It was self-defense, was it not?"

"If I were born on Beacon Hill, it would be," Rose mumbled, a comment McCourt fortunately didn't catch.

"What was that?" he asked.

Of course, she wouldn't repeat those words. Nor would she launch into a rant about how Rice had it out for her the moment she won against him in a target shooting event during training. The contempt she saw in his eyes from that day forward. The eyes of a misogynistic prick who probably went home and took out his frustrations on his abused wife. McCourt wasn't blind to social and economic injustices, but he showed little concern for them.

"I . . . was scared," she finally answered truthfully, without elaborating.

McCourt frowned, then nodded. "Did they ever find out who was behind the hit?"

He hadn't bothered to spend even a few minutes on the case files of the incident. Classic McCourt.

"They did. It was a rival gang hit. The Critters on fourth."

"Mm-hm." McCourt nodded. "Animals."

At least on that, she could partially agree. It wasn't that simple, but what the Critters had done that day went against even the hood's code. They didn't shoot her family as a revenge attack but simply because her brother wouldn't snitch about the location of a warehouse full of "goods." The real fucked-up tragedy about all this was that the Critters later joined forces with her brother's gang, the past deaths "forgiven." Her brother became a famous tale of loyalty to death.

A tale Rose refused to tell that way, ever.

Her brother's death was murder, nothing else. It was the reason she'd worked so hard to become more than just another statistic. She wanted to change the country, make it a better place for others, and she wouldn't settle for less than the best in the field—the FBI.

Rose's eyes narrowed at the file in front of her. How could such a small thing hold the power to destroy her?

"We get to see what happens only if we don't give up," her brother had always told her.

Would she let a man like Rice ruin her future and everything she had worked so hard for?

With newfound confidence, Rose grabbed the file, then looked straight at McCourt. "Am I to assume this is mine now?" she asked.

"It is. Rice won't ever be a problem again. Nor will anybody else. Sometimes, files just get lost. It happens more than you'd think at three-letter agencies."

Rose nodded, her grip tightening on the papers that held the keys to her destruction and, now, her freedom. "Why are you doing this for me?" she asked.

McCourt shrugged. "Why wouldn't I? You just saved the day, and the agency needs great agents like you. *I* need great agents like you. Trustworthy agents willing to do the job, whatever that might be. To protect the agency's best interests."

Or, more likely, *his*.

But for now, Rose was okay with this deal; asshole or not, nothing he'd asked of her so far was truly a sacrifice.

"Thank you, sir," she said, and she meant it.

McCourt acknowledged her with a slow, meaningful nod. "Well, why don't you go home and get some rest? We need you to look your best for the award ceremony."

Slowly, she rose, file in hand. With a faint smile, she turned and was about to leave when McCourt leaned forward in his seat.

"Oh, one more thing, Rose."

She turned to face him expectantly.

"That night, with Kirby," he began, his eyes piercing her like bullets, "was anybody else at the scene with you and Richter?"

The smile vanished from Rose's face. "Sir?" she said.

"Careful, Rose. Richter might think I'm an idiot, but unless he can show me his medical degree, I can't shake the feeling that something is amiss here. That procedure that saved your life—I was told that most of the doctors at the hospital wouldn't have been able to perform it. They were in awe of how a simple FBI agent without medical training was able to execute a procedure only one of their best surgeons could do, without killing the patient. Of course, I shrugged it off, supported his lies. It's the best story for them and the public. But *best* doesn't do it for me."

Rose's heart hammered against her chest. Of course, he wanted something in return from her. This wasn't just a meeting to reward the agent who'd prevented one of the potentially biggest mass murders in recent history.

This was a test.

The possibility of another copy of the file in her hand crossed her mind. Now she felt stupid. How had she ever trusted or believed in this man? She would have to be his footwoman for all eternity.

"There were also those dirt bike tire marks, which it's argued Kirby must have left while gathering his ingredients for his bomb recipe, but I find that rather . . . well, a bunch of horse shit."

Rose stared at him, her hands shaking. Would she be the downfall of the woman who'd saved her life and helped kill Kirby?

"You see, Agent Rose, trust is a two-way street." McCourt nodded at the file in Rose's hand.

Her mind raced with questions and answers, lies, worries, and regrets.

"I need to know I can trust you," McCourt added, his voice hypnotizing like that of a snake charmer. "Because if I can't . . ."

The walls of the room seemed to close in. What about the Train Track Killer? Would she become the sad prophecy Leah Nachtnebel had predicted so bluntly at Anna's crime scene? The snitch who helped the Train Track Killer by taking out his enemies?

Snitch. Her brother and mother had paid a heavy price for his silence. If silence was golden, maybe talking was diamonds?

"Because if I can't trust you, I don't need you, and if I don't need you, the FBI doesn't either," McCourt continued.

The file crinkled beneath Rose's grip. She could barely breathe, bile rising in her throat. Why did life always play her dirty? Why couldn't she just catch a break for once?

McCourt locked eyes with her, his gaze now threatening.

"So, let me ask you one more time, Agent Rose. What the hell really went down that night?"

THIRTY-EIGHT

Leah

I was practicing tomorrow's program on my Vanderbilt Bösendorfer on stage at the Boston Symphony Hall. My concerts had been canceled for weeks until I healed enough to sit for an hour with only moderate pain. When I finally did, I arranged a string of fall concerts to accommodate those who had refused a refund and opted for a replacement ticket—which was practically everyone.

A moderate wave of pain struck my ribcage, enough to make me flinch but not enough to stop my play.

I pushed through Chopin's "Revolutionary Étude," which demanded fierce left-hand dexterity for its relentless, stormy arpeggios, symbolizing turmoil.

Not until I finished the entire piece did I allow myself to take a deep breath. I tried to ease the pain with another Tylenol.

Crystal and Mr. Hieber were watching from the first row of seats. They were both worried that I'd cancel this weekend's concert, that I'd come back too soon.

They were right, of course, but the fuss my absence created was not in my best interest. People had laid flowers in front of my home and the symphony hall. There were so many flowers that the news stations started to pick up on the story. I needed to put an end to the drama.

I hit the last notes of the piece, sweat dripping onto the keys. Shortly after, Hieber and Crystal rose to their feet, applauding.

"Wonderful, Leah," Hieber said, his tone dripping with insincere friendliness. "We are all so relieved to see you healthy and well."

I adjusted my choker necklace, which hid the scar from Kirby's knife until a plastic surgeon could see to it.

"I'm certain you are, Hieber," I replied coldly as I rose to my feet. I planned to practice at home for the rest of the day. The only reason I had come here was to approve the tuning of the piano, as tomorrow included several important guests from the music world.

I was about to leave when Hieber rushed onto the stage. "Leah," he panted, "I wanted to ask if we might place a special guest in your personal box next to Luca Domizio's."

I raised an eyebrow at him. That was quite an audacious request considering nobody but myself had a say over this box. "And who would that be?" I asked.

"The Assistant Director of the FBI, Charles—"

"McCourt," I finished, my eyes narrowing.

This could mean trouble.

Had Rose talked to him after all?

A coincidence?

Or . . . had Liam tried to find a way out of the current situation? Was his worry about losing his daughter greater than his hatred for the Train Track Killer? How could I blame him for that?

"You know him?" Hieber asked.

"No."

Hieber rearranged his scarf. "Well . . . would it be okay if we assign him your box? Unless you have someone else in mind you wanted to invite, then—"

"You can give him the box."

Hieber smiled, likely having secured some favors in return for clearing the box for such a high government figure.

"Anything else?" I asked.

"No, no, thank you. Go get some rest. Tomorrow will be epic."

Epic.

I didn't agree with that choice of word, but I understood what he was referring to: the large live screen outside the symphony hall. To honor my recovery, the mayor himself had arranged to have the street blocked during my concert to allow a crowd to follow along on a large live screen.

My gaze moved up to the box McCourt would be placed in, right next to Luca.

The fact that I had not been arrested or questioned yet indicated he could seek a private conversation with me. But why?

"I'll see you tomorrow," I said as I made my way back to my car. The soft drizzle of another fall rain embraced me like a cool greeting. It was refreshing and grounding.

Whatever McCourt wanted, I would deal with him. I had never really met the man, yet I knew everything about him.

Selfish.

Narcissistic.

Arrogant.

While many despised those traits, I had no personal feelings toward them one way or the other. On the contrary, those traits would make handling him all the easier, as men like him could bend a thousand ways.

None of them were noble, which was fine as long as they did the trick.

THIRTY-NINE

Liam

Cowboy and I were south of Boston, watching the entrance of the Green Hill funeral home. Its ridiculously large and bright neon cross was nearly blinding. We were leaning against the car, the rain having just stopped. It was a bit cold, but the inside of the SUV felt claustrophobic, as if it were cutting off my air supply.

This whole thing with Anna weighed heavily on my soul. Another young girl gone. Her death made me feel like my work was pointless.

"They say stress kills people," Cowboy remarked, blowing out a stream of vape from the pen he was sucking on.

"Yup. Working with serial killers can do that. But I'm an FBI agent, not some B-list model who can quit his job and start dancing on social media."

"FBI or not, you're too old anyway," Cowboy said.

I frowned at him.

"Although the ladies might dig the whole broke-ass-down-on-his-luck agent vibe. If you get some Botox on that forehead and your eyebrows microbladed, you might be able to shave off a few years."

"What?"

I watched as Cowboy admired his reflection in the mirror of our SUV. "I just got my own brows done, and the ladies are in love with them."

"Fucking Christ," I mumbled. "You said you'd be quiet if I let you tag along."

"If you believed me, that's on you."

I ignored him. A strange silence fell between us.

"I'm really sorry about Anna," he finally said, his tone serious. "You know, you're not the only one who feels like we failed her. Like it was all for fucking nothing. I mean, why the hell did she do it? Why kill herself?"

Initially, I expected Cowboy to start laughing and say something stupid. However, when he remained silent, staring at the ground with sadness in his eyes, I placed my hand on his shoulder in a fatherly gesture.

"None of this is on you," I said as his eyes met mine. "It pains me to admit it, but you're doing an incredible job at the BAU. We're lucky to have you here in Boston."

His eyes lit up as if this acknowledgment was all he ever wanted. Then, suddenly, his gaze drifted off into the distance. "What the fuck is this shit?" he asked.

I followed his gaze to find Anna's uncle and aunt stepping out of the funeral home. They appeared worn and disheveled, with baggy clothes and faces that bore signs of hardship. At first glance, compassion stirred within me, leading to thoughts of how I could help. However, my second thought was less kind when I noticed the urn they were carrying.

Or the lack of it.

Instead of holding a beautiful urn, the older man, dressed in sweats and a bomber jacket, held a plastic bag wrapped around his wrist. Undoubtedly, the bag carried Anna's remains. He leaned over and opened the bag only to close it again with a coughing sound.

Cowboy tucked his vape away and was about to storm over, but I held him back. "It's not our place."

"They have her in a freaking plastic bag!" he protested.

"I know." The words felt like acid in my throat. "But it's not our place to tell them how to deal with a loved one."

My intentions of walking over and expressing my condolences were completely dashed when Anna's uncle tossed the remains in the plastic bag into the back of a black pickup truck.

"What the fuck," I cursed, barely able to hold myself back now. This man deserved a good beating.

"People are animals," Cowboy spat.

We watched in disgust as they drove off. My heart raced with rage. For a brief moment, I saw Anna in front of me, vibrant and alive, laughing like she did with her friends on campus when I watched her a few times in the distance from my car.

"This is fucking terrible," Cowboy mumbled. "Just fucking terrible."

Without another word, he got into the passenger's side of the SUV, where he sat like a pouting child.

I took a deep breath, trying to process all of this. Deep down, I had hoped this would give me a bit of closure—shaking hands with her family, apologizing that I wasn't able to do more for her. It would have helped with the anxiety caused by Rose's absence from work and her silence in response to my texts.

But now, life had revealed itself as another bad rollercoaster ride: too many downs, none of them fun.

As I got into the car, my phone rang.

McCourt.

"Shit," I muttered, staring at the screen.

"My uncle?"

I nodded, then accepted the call.

"Can't be good this late on a Friday," Cowboy said too loudly.

"Tell Theo to keep his whining to his therapy sessions, not my phone calls," McCourt said, loud enough for him to hear. Cowboy rolled his eyes.

"Sir?"

"Where are you?"

"We were attending Anna's funeral."

"The suicide case? Why?"

"Thought it might reflect well on the FBI considering she was a survivor of the Train Track Killer."

"Good move. Will make us look sensible and caring."

Prick.

"Well, I need you to join me at the Boston Symphony Hall tonight."

The phone nearly slipped from my grip as my mouth fell open. My stomach turned a thousand times over. "S-sir?" I stuttered.

"The Boston Symphony Hall. I got tickets for tonight's performance. Rose will be there as well. It's a work thing. I'll meet you at headquarters around eight. We'll ride together. Don't be late."

And just like that, he hung up.

I sat there, staring into nothingness out the window, paralyzed. Did he know? Had Rose talked?

This was bad.

"Did he say I can come too?" Cowboy asked.

Cowboy must have overheard everything. I ignored him.

"I mean, the pianist is really hot."

My mind was a whirlwind of panic. Sweat beaded on my forehead. I envisioned it all. The worst-case scenario: Josie visiting me in prison. The best-case scenario: all of us simply enjoying the concert, nothing more than a treat for his Kirby stars.

"Hello?" Cowboy persisted.

"I don't know, Cowboy, call him," I said as I started the car.

"He didn't say anything about me coming too?"

"I said I don't know!" I snapped. "Fucking call him, all right!"

Cowboy looked at me, shocked.

"I'm sorry," I apologized.

He just gave me a curt nod. "No worries. Tonight really fucked with me too. On second thought, can you just drop me off at home? I don't feel like being anywhere near my uncle right now."

"That makes two of us," I mumbled.

FORTY

Leah

I was wearing a new dress gifted to me by Rilloni, one of the most renowned designers in the world. Its sleek, figure-hugging black Japanese silk cascaded down to mid-thigh. I usually preferred dresses with plunging necklines and low, open backs, but this one perfectly hid the bruises on my back and chest while adding a touch of class and seduction with a hemline that boasted a flirtatious slit. Completing the ensemble was a delicate golden belt cinching the waist. It enhanced my curves and sculpted a striking silhouette, perfect for tonight's special performance.

The cool breeze of a Boston fall evening greeted me as I stepped outside to meet Mark, who had already opened the door for me. That was when I saw Luca's black limousine parked in front of my front yard's metal gate. His driver got out and opened the door to the back of the car, signaling me to get in.

I smiled at Mark, who nodded and closed my door. Then I walked over to Luca's limousine and got in.

He was in his usual immaculate tuxedo, holding a small pink flower that differed from my usual gift—a red rose.

"How kind of you to pick me up," I said with a smile. "Our quarrel pains me."

Luca looked at me, his expression hard to read. "I wouldn't have missed tonight's performance for anything in the world. Every moment with you is worth a thousand lifetimes, La Imperatrice." He stretched his hand to offer me the flower. I accepted it, inspecting it curiously.

Its bloom was exquisite. Vibrant pink petals, soft and velvety to the touch, contrasting strikingly against the lush green of its stem and leaves.

"This can't be . . . a Middlemist Red," I murmured, genuinely surprised by the treasure in my hand.

"I wouldn't dare bring you anything less tonight."

"But there are only two left in the world. Billionaires and presidents have failed to secure a clipping from it."

Luca observed me silently as I marveled at the beautiful flower. "They call it Middlemist Red despite it actually being pink," he said. "But the more fascinating mystery is its extinction from its native country as well as anywhere else in the world. Only two plants have survived in botanical gardens, and nobody knows why."

"What an intriguing secret it holds about its own demise," I commented, sniffing its fresh floral scent.

"Indeed," Luca said, his eyes fixed on me. "A priceless mystery right in front of all of us, yet nobody dares to push too hard in a search for answers, fearing it might be unforgiving and decide to take away even the little we are blessed to have."

I met his gaze.

"A riddle that might never be solved," I remarked with a smile. Then I grew serious. "I always enjoyed our time together, Luca. As much as I am capable of enjoying anything this world has to offer me. My ability to do so is, well, hindered."

"I know." Luca smiled, offering comfort. "I have enjoyed our time together too, La Imperatrice. My trade comes at a heavy price. Your music is the one thing still able to stir emotions in me, the one thing that keeps me from questioning if I'm already dead. I wanted to thank you for this precious gift."

I met his intense gaze with a respectful nod.

He smiled. "But now, let's shift to lighter topics. I've formed an opinion on Cziffra's obsession with Liszt, and I'm eager to hear your thoughts on it."

FORTY-ONE

Liam

The car ride to the symphony hall was unbearably awkward. Rose was driving the SUV, I was in the passenger seat, and McCourt was in the back. I tried hard not to stare at either one of them, attempting to act normal, but in the rare moments when neither was looking, I discreetly wiped my forehead.

Had Rose talked?

Or was this a coincidence, and McCourt genuinely wanted to reward his two "best agents" with a rare treat, just as he had explained when I met up with them at headquarters?

Neither of us was dressed in concert clothes, but our formal work suits would blend in enough to ensure we didn't stick out.

We parked the car. I was about to get out when McCourt pulled his gun from his holster. I froze. His eyes locked on me as he lifted the gun and handed it over. "Put that in the glove compartment for me, will you?"

I nodded and complied.

"Put yours in as well. We don't need them here tonight."

Rose threw me a glance before handing her gun to me.

When I hesitated, McCourt narrowed his eyes at me. "Or do we, Agent Richter? Need guns tonight?"

"Of course not," I said, placing my gun in the glove compartment. What else would I be doing with it anyway? If they planned to arrest me tonight, I wouldn't engage in some crazy shootout. I would quietly let them cuff me and take me in. No innocent guests would be endangered by me.

On our way to the balcony, McCourt trailed me and Rose as if watching our every move. This made it impossible for me to pull her aside to talk privately.

We entered the balcony where I'd sat when I'd first seen Leah play. My heart took a dramatic leap when I noticed Luca Domizio taking his seat in his balcony right next to ours. He didn't glance over. It was as if none of us were worthy of his attention.

"I heard she's quite something," McCourt said as we took our seats. He grabbed the program and skimmed it. I finally managed to catch a longer gaze from Rose, whose amber eyes looked troubled.

"Leah Nachtnebel. I've never heard her play. Up until recently, I didn't pay her much attention," McCourt continued. "I didn't really give a fuck, to be honest. I heard even the president holds her in high regard, along with pretty much every major player in DC. It takes a certain person to not only do well in this world but actually contribute to its script. That's quite something. You've got to give her that. Right?"

"Sir?" I asked, perplexed.

McCourt grinned at me. "We all have a role in this world's play, Richter. Some of us are main characters, like Leah Nachtnebel. Others are merely extras. Most don't even get to be part of the play at all. They watch from their seats and clap along like idiots. Their existence is unnoticed. Their sparks too weak to ever start a fire."

He glanced at Rose, who kept her gaze fixed on the red curtain of the stage. Then he turned and looked straight at me.

Right then, the lights went out. There was a bizarre moment of utter silence in the room, like the calm before a major storm or the eye of a deadly tornado, all while McCourt still stared at me.

The large red curtains opened to reveal the Monet grand piano. Leah walked onto the stage, looking stunning. The hall rose to its feet as thunderous applause washed over us like the apocalypse. It felt like the Olympics of the classical music world, even more intense than when I had first witnessed it. Every breath I took felt heavy and dangerous.

I broke free from McCourt's gaze and watched Leah bow. Her eyes briefly found mine as if she were telling me it would all be alright.

McCourt leaned over and said to me, "What is your role in this world, Richter? Main character, extra, or not even worth giving a fuck about?"

FORTY-TWO

Leah

My fingers moved on autopilot, playing Maurice Ravel's "Gaspard de la Nuit," then Bach's "Goldberg Variations BWV 988," followed by Claude Debussy's "Clair de Lune."

My thoughts had completely drifted off. The look Richter gave me was unsettling. He attempted to hide it, but the stress etched on his face was as clear as permanent ink. I had considered why McCourt was in my concert hall—everything from a post-concert interrogation to merely an admirer's attendance, which I doubted. The reality was, all possibilities were still in play, with none yet realized. There was no point in worrying. Things would unfold as they did, and I would respond as necessary, as circumstances required. It was as simple as that.

Halfway through the concert, just after I finished Chopin, Richter's intense gaze bore into me like a fresh cattle brand. Resisting the urge to meet his eyes, I focused back on the piano to begin the next piece.

Suddenly, the hall's silence broke into murmurs. They were sparse at first, but they quickly grew. I peeked out to find a man storming through the seated guests. He wore a tuxedo, yet his rugged features stood in sharp contrast to the formal attire.

Suddenly, somebody screamed right before a growing chorus shouted, "Gun!"

I leaped to my feet as chaos erupted. People rushed toward exits, and some even clambered over the stage. In an instant, the gunman leaped onto the stage, gun poised and aimed directly at me. He advanced steadily.

It was strange, but I was oddly calm. I looked for Richter. His box was now empty except for McCourt, who was still seated. His calmness left no doubt about his involvement in this. He knew everything. And now, he was asking for my head.

My gaze shifted to Luca, who stood there motionless. My days were numbered, as were my minutes, but not my seconds. So, in the final moments before I went to hell, I scanned the crowd for Richter. Why did I want him to be the last thing I saw? When I spotted him hanging off the first balcony toward the end of the concert hall, where the distance to the floor was shortest, a wave of emotions washed over me. Excitement? Joy? I wasn't sure.

Had I grown soft? Had I inconveniently and illogically attached myself to a dying breed of man? Whatever the case, I was grateful to be able to leave the world like this.

Feeling something.

Anything.

As he fought his way through the crowd of guests rushing for the exit—people falling, tumbling, screaming—our eyes finally met. I couldn't help but smile.

It didn't even matter if he'd been the one who told McCourt everything and had asked Luca to follow through on his promise to kill me. I understood why he would have done it—to protect his own well-being and, more importantly, his daughter's. Given Rose's awareness of the entire situation, I had become a liability in his eyes.

And although I wished he would have allowed me to at least kill the Train Track Killer first, I not only forgave him but was grateful he'd been a part of my life. Before him, I was truly dead inside. Now, I was fortunate enough to die with feeling, almost as if I had a heart like a normal human being. Nothing special, nothing broken. Just a normal model exiting the factory of life.

"Thank you, Richter," I mumbled with a smile on my lips. He was only feet away from the stage, where the gunman was now ready to fire. "Thank you."

FORTY-THREE

Liam

I pushed, shoved, and even elbowed, fighting my way against the tide of people desperately trying to escape.

I felt like a salmon swimming against a current of sharks; every second was a lifetime. From the corner of my eye, I caught a glimpse of McCourt calmly standing on the balcony, a smile on his face. Not far from him, Luca Domizio was sitting in his seat, his face grave and serious.

Then her green eyes locked on mine, her figure illuminated on stage against a backdrop of darkness.

The emotion in her eyes, coupled with her faint smile, shattered me. Forgiveness.

She was forgiving me. She thought I was the one who had arranged this, likely to save myself.

"Leah!" I screamed as I finally broke free from the crowd and reached the stage. "No!"

Desperation surged through me as I leaped onto the stage. The gunman to my right, Leah to my left, I did what instinct dictated.

As the gun fired, I threw myself between them, pulling her to the floor, trying to cover as much of her body with mine as I could.

The collision was harsh, and the impact on the floor stole my breath. I wrapped my arms around her, clinging tightly, attempting to shield her from further harm. A second gunshot tore through the silence of the hall.

Was I hit?

I wasn't!

Fuck . . . was she?

Silence stretched on for heart-stopping seconds before I loosened my grip around her chest and waist and raised my head. My eyes darted around only to spot Rose near the stage, looking like she was ready to take on the gunman bare-handed. Just a few feet away, the gunman lay lifeless on the stage, blood pooling around him. He had shot himself. But twice?

I looked back down at Leah as her green eyes met mine.

"Are you shot?" I needed to know.

"No," she answered, her tone shockingly calm and steady. "You?"

I shook my head. "Are you hurt?" I yelled over to Rose as I quickly got to my feet. She shook her head, her sweat glistening in the stark stage lights.

Then the gurgling sounds reached us from the damn first-floor balcony.

"McCourt!" Rose shouted as she pulled her phone from her jacket. "Agent down. We need an ambulance and immediate backup at the Boston Symphony Hall," she barked into the phone.

I gave Leah a puzzled look, then raced after Rose out of the hall to ascend the stairs to McCourt. When we reached the balcony, he was slumped off his chair, gasping for air, each breath heavy and strained with evident pain.

"Shit," I muttered as I stretched his legs out on the carpeted floor. He had taken a clean shot in the middle of the chest. His chances were slim.

I ripped off my jacket and pressed it firmly against the wound.

"Police!" came shouts from officers below.

"Up here!" I yelled back. "Rose, get them up here."

In all the chaos, my gaze dropped to the stage, where Leah stood tall, fearless, proud, and strong as always. She stood beside the dead man, her expression devoid of emotion as she looked down at him. Then her gaze lifted, not to me but to the man in the box next to us.

Luca Domizio.

He stood there, eerily still, returning her stare. Then, just as the first officers arrived at the balcony, he turned and cast a brief, dismissive glance at me and McCourt before disappearing as if all this were nothing more than a dream.

Or, in this case, a nightmare.

FORTY-FOUR

Leah

I was sitting on the couch in my private quarters at the symphony hall, surrounded by Liam and police officers pressing for a statement.

"Can we please give Ms. Nachtnebel some space?" Liam asked. "We can go over her statement again tomorrow."

The officers left the room, though the EMTs lingered a bit longer. "Are you sure you don't want to go to the hospital for a thorough check-up?" asked one of the EMTs, a young woman with a caring aura.

"Quite certain, thank you," I replied.

She nodded, then packed up her equipment and exited with the other EMTs.

The room was now empty except for the two of us.

"You okay?" Liam asked.

"Yes."

He nodded and looked down at his hand, which was shaking. He stuffed it into his pants pocket. "You know it wasn't me who did this, right?" he whispered loudly, stepping closer.

I hesitated, then offered a faint smile. "Your actions on the stage spoke for your innocence."

"It was fucking McCourt or Rose," he muttered, his words punctuated by inaudible curses. "I saw McCourt on the balcony when all hell broke loose. He was sitting there calmly, grinning like a villain from a bad sci-fi movie. He must have asked Luca Domizio to make good on his promise to you. But why didn't he? Why did Luca turn on McCourt instead?"

"I'm not certain," I replied, "but I'll find out."

A knock sounded, then Rose entered the room.

Liam confronted her. "You have some fucking nerve to show up here."

"Richter," I interjected, but he didn't back down. Instead, he closed the door behind Rose, standing in front of it as if to block her exit.

"Did you do this?" he demanded, his tone menacing. "Was it you who asked Luca Domizio to kill her?"

Rose, normally confident and bold, appeared diminished, shaking her head meekly.

"Liar!" Liam hissed.

"I swear I didn't do this," Rose said.

"So, you didn't run to McCourt like the loyal pet you are?" Liam shot back.

"Fuck you," Rose said. "I don't owe you anything." She took a step toward him. "Last time I checked, I'm not the one killing folks in secret. I'm on the right side of the law here."

"Did you tell McCourt or not, you fucking snitch? I swear, if you're lying to me—"

"I had no choice," she interrupted, her gaze falling to the floor. "I didn't want to, I swear. And I never thought that crazy bastard would try to have her killed. Honestly, I didn't even believe this whole business with Luca Domizio was real. But McCourt blackmailed me. He . . ." Her voice faltered, but one look at Richter's judgmental eyes spurred her to continue. "He has dirt on me."

"And what could that possibly be?" Richter pressed.

It took her a few deep breaths to muster her strength. "I . . . lied on my application. An instructor at the academy found out and reported it to McCourt."

"So, to save yourself a job, you almost ruined my life and had Leah killed?"

"This job is all I have."

"My daughter is all I have, and I got close to never seeing her again tonight. Might still turn out that way if McCourt survives."

Richter's shoulders relaxed as the room grew silent.

"What does he have on you?" I asked.

Rose bit her lip.

"Mind sharing that parking ticket or AI-generated college paper crime with us?" Richter asked.

"I shot the man who killed my family," she spat at him. "McCourt helped me cover it up back when my instructor approached him about it. I thought it was to help me, that he saw something special in me." Rose slumped in disappointment. "But instead, he turned me into his puppet."

"So, you told him everything," Liam said.

She nodded, her eyes shadowed with shame. "I really didn't want to. I've felt like shit ever since."

"Must have been really hard on you," Richter remarked.

"Yeah, Richter, it actually was. Especially after I'd already investigated the train track suicides. For days, I drove around, frantic. To find out that everything she said was true." Rose nodded toward me. "They all bear the ankh symbol, just like Anna's crime scene."

The air suddenly felt cold.

"It's the craziest thing I've ever seen, but you're right," Rose continued. "The Train Track Killer is still out there, playing his twisted games, and it might be a lot worse than you realize."

I rose to my feet. "What do you mean?" I asked.

"The computer files don't match the paper files," Rose said.

Richter stepped away from the door, moving closer. "That's not true. I've seen the files. They match."

Rose nodded. "The paper files printed from the computer and the computer files match, of course. But they don't match the original file of Emma Mauser by Officer Wagner."

I exchanged a bewildered look with Liam, seeking clarification.

"What original file?" he asked.

"One of the officers at the train station police noticed a discrepancy in his report," Rose said. "He was convinced the coroner had mentioned to him that he, the coroner, suspected homicide after finding rope marks on Emma's wrists."

"Rope marks? That's not in the file I read," I said.

"That's because Officer Wagner corrected his report by hand in the original file to match the computer file. We somehow ended up with his original file at headquarters."

"Larsen must have requested it and failed to notice the discrepancy," Richter concluded.

"Larsen?" Rose asked, raising an eyebrow.

"So, how can you be sure the computer file is incorrect?" I asked, sidestepping the Larsen issue.

"I called Dr. Post, the coroner. He was unaware that his report states suicide on the computer. He believes it indicates homicide."

"That makes no sense," Liam said. "Why would his file be altered on the computer?"

Rose shrugged. "I was hoping you might have an answer. You guys have been at this much longer than I have."

Liam's gaze lowered, his forehead wrinkling. "Only top-secret classified files are manipulated like that. We're instructed to ignore discrepancies when a three-letter agency is involved, for national security reasons."

"But wouldn't more families notice the discrepancies in the cause of death and raise an issue?" Rose asked.

"Some did," I said. "That's how my previous partner in the FBI first became aware of the Train Track Killer. A complaint from a very persistent family reached higher levels within the FBI. Nothing concrete has resulted from it yet, but it put the murders on my radar."

"And not much is likely to come of it ever," Rose interjected.

Both Liam and I turned our attention to her. "What do you mean?" Liam pressed.

"I mean that most of the files are marked as active investigations with instructions to block their release to the public. Nobody outside of us even knows what's really in those files. Somebody has altered them and blocked them without anybody really knowing."

"But," Liam said, "why would non-political death cases be altered by us or any other three-letter agency? They hold no information that threatens national security."

My thoughts raced. "The more interesting question isn't why they're blocked, but who's behind the blocking."

Liam's face contorted as if a sudden, distressing thought had struck him. "Kirby! He had extensive files on all his victims, information you'd normally need a warrant to obtain. It was as if they were handed to him by a government agency. And right before he died, Kirby told me that *he* was too powerful. I thought he was talking about a voice in his head, but now . . ."

Rose's eyes widened. "You're suggesting someone fed Kirby those files to manipulate him? Play him like a puppet? Maybe even tipped him off when we were closing in on him?"

The pieces of the puzzle were aligning slowly but unmistakably.

"Patel," I declared with newfound clarity. "He was a pawn that the Train Track Killer used against us. It's possible the same person manipulated Kirby too."

Rose's voice trembled with disbelief. "But how could anybody possibly orchestrate all of this? Are you saying that the Train Track Killer might be an FBI or CIA agent?"

I had considered this, but it didn't align with what we knew. "No, I don't think so. The killer's behavior is too unpredictable for a federal agency employee, who would need to maintain regular work hours and can be tracked. But it does make me wonder, who or what outside of the government could have the ability to manipulate official documents? Be everywhere at once—constantly listening and watching."

Rose and Liam stared at me, their expressions a mix of anticipation and confusion.

"Think about it," I pressed. "Leros. Emanuel and my code word. We wondered how the Train Track Killer had accessed that personal information without someone feeding it to him."

Liam mulled over my words. "What if Emanuel provided that information himself?"

I shook my head. "I'm certain that's not the case. He had no reason to do that. I paid too well, and he enjoyed his work with me."

"Then how else could he have known?" Liam asked.

Pondering this, I posed a question, "How can anybody see and hear everything without being physically present?"

"Wiretaps?" Rose suggested.

"But you need someone to actually wear them," Liam said.

"Maybe he pays for access to security footage," Rose proposed.

"Or the Train Track Killer owns a security company," Liam said. "Many security firms now incorporate indoor cameras with sound."

I tilted my head. "Jan Novak holds a significant fortune in the tech sector. But owning a security firm wouldn't grant him or anybody else the ability to alter or block FBI or other law enforcement files."

As I mulled this over, the fragments began connecting in a rapid, chaotic dance in my mind.

Then it struck me.

"The tech sector," I murmured. "Which branch in the tech industry, privately owned, remains shrouded in secrecy and is almost never discussed in the media?"

There was only one answer.

"It infiltrates every aspect of our lives," I continued, "managing the content of every moment we're captured on camera or speaking on the phone."

Liam's eyes widened. "My God. The cloud!"

"The cloud?" Rose asked, puzzled.

"It's the biggest cash cow in the tech industry," I explained. "Amazon's entire worth hinges on its cloud services. So does Microsoft's. And neither are the biggest players in the field. They hold only a tiny margin in the industry."

Richter scratched his head. "A few weeks ago, I read about a major new contract between the NSA and the largest cloud storage provider in the world."

"Which is?" Rose asked, her curiosity piqued.

Silence hung in the air.

"I see," she said, pulling out her phone to do a quick search. She read for a moment, then recoiled slightly. "Og . . . Ogledalo?"

"Ogledalo Corporation?" I repeated, feeling a chill spread through my veins.

"Ogledalo," she repeated, confused. "Does that mean anything?"

"It means 'mirror' in Slovenian," I said. "Or, metaphorically, 'ankh,' in this context."

"What?" Liam and Rose said at once.

"Ogledalo Corporation," I mumbled as if summoning a demon. "It's named after the symbol that the Train Track Killer leaves at crime scenes. The largest cloud computing storage company in the world. It's storing information from phone companies to banks all the way to the National Security Agency's darkest secrets."

"Jesus," Rose whispered. "That's a hell of a lot of power. Who in the name of God would be granted such ridiculous leverage?"

Richter did a quick online search on his phone, then shrugged. "The owner or board members aren't named publicly."

We still needed more evidence, but that strong feeling in my gut was undeniable.

The concert visits. The meeting at the Smithsonian Museum. The ability to block facial recognition. The missing files on him... and the large wealth in tech.

I walked past them and flung the door open. The hallway had already cleared of officers.

"Where are you going?" I heard Liam call after me.

Both Rose and Liam were on my heels as we moved through the hallways and into the busy foyer. Scattered around were officers, EMTs, and a few concert-goers who were being questioned. Some of them cast relieved glances my way when they saw I was unharmed.

Liam and Rose appeared hesitant about being associated with me out here, as was evident from their quick scans of the surroundings. However, they were two federal agents in a crowd of law enforcement following a shooting, so their presence wasn't out of the ordinary.

I stopped to graciously accept the well-wishes of some guests. Then I walked a few more steps, right into the middle of the entrance hall. Rose and Liam stopped next to me, bewildered, scanning the area as if I'd lost my mind. Other people were beginning to notice, sneaking sidelong glances at me.

"What the hell are you doing?" Rose asked, her gaze not meeting mine.

I tilted my head upward, directing my gaze toward the security camera of the Boston Symphony entrance hall. I looked straight into it, then smiled.

Triumphant.

Fearless.

Provocative.

"I'm just saying hello," I explained to Liam and Rose.

"Saying hello? To whom?" Rose asked. Both she and Liam were now also staring straight into the camera.

All three of us stood there, side by side, like the Three Musketeers taking on an invisible enemy from above.

"Saying hello to whom?" Rose pressed again.

"To Jan fucking Novak," Liam said on my behalf, his face shifting into that of a Viking ready to take on hordes of Roman legions.

As we all stared into the camera, it dawned on me. The real fight had finally begun. The ultimate battle that would determine my and Liam's fate and now Rose's as well. It was going to be a fight of life and death.

There was nothing I wouldn't do to win the overall war against one of the mightiest monsters alive. But if we were to stand a chance, I needed the same commitment from Liam and Rose.

It would take everything we had to bring him down.

And that was perfectly fine by me.

Let him come.

After all, we kill killers.

FORTY-FIVE

Jan Novak

Deep in the underground cloud computing storage center of a large compound belonging to Ogledalo Corporation in New York state, Jan Novak, the embodiment of power and wealth, sat in his windowless office. All crucial storage was underground, with the buildings above used primarily for storing parts and housing the offices of low-security-level employees. And, of course, the enormous team tasked with securing the most valuable information-gathering system on earth. One that was more valuable than gold mines. Or Area 51.

With strategic planning, Ogledalo Corporation had decimated most other cloud services by aggressively slashing its storage fees and outbidding competitors until it controlled over ninety percent of all US cloud storage. It was a mistake that its clients were too late to rectify. These clients included the CIA, the NSA, the IRS, ICE, banks, telecommunication firms, internet providers, security companies—the list was endless. Ogledalo Corporation knew what you "sexted" to your ex just as it knew who shot JFK.

Jan Novak leaned forward in his chair, examining his reflection in the mirrored walls of his office, every move captured like a window to his soul. Like a modern form of the ankh.

The wall opposite him was lined with screens as thin as glass, showcasing cutting-edge technology not yet on the market. These screens presented information from the cloud, pulling whatever he needed at the moment. The setup made his office feel like a futuristic space station.

His company employed only the brightest and most genius computer scientists in the world, often provided by the NSA itself.

Deep in thought, he swiped his finger over the touchscreen desk in front of him, all while petting his one-eyed rescue dog with his other hand.

It was early morning, but the first item on his agenda was reviewing last night's footage of the shooting at the Boston Symphony Hall.

He watched as a gunman shot Assistant FBI Director McCourt and then himself on stage during a concert by Leah Nachtnebel. Agent Liam Richter had tried to protect her, but that had turned out to be unnecessary.

But what fascinated Novak the most was the moment Ms. Nachtnebel stepped into the entrance hall and came back into view of the security camera. Looking straight up, she smiled into the lens as if she knew Novak was watching. The directness of her gaze, the knowing smile—it felt as if she was peering right at him.

He paused the footage, sitting there in awe.

There was no doubt. Her green eyes were seeking him out. This was for him. A message.

But why reveal that she'd finally found him?

"Mr. Novak," his suit-clad young secretary called out as she stepped inside. "The CIA director is waiting for you to sign the papers for the updated storage agreement."

He didn't even look at her, just waved her off. "Tell him to wait. I'm busy."

"Yes sir," she said without the slightest hesitation, then left.

Jan Novak leaned over his desk, narrowing his eyes at Leah Nachtnebel and the two FBI agents she was dragging along.

Those green eyes were staring through all the walls between them. She was smiling even though somebody had almost shot her.

He couldn't help but grin back at her. He had always feared this day would come—the day he would become the target of someone as brilliant and determined as he was. The fact that she had actually uncovered his identity was nothing short of marvelous. Especially considering the extreme measures he had taken to erase the scar on his shoulder. The skin graft surgery had cost a fortune and been performed by a team of the world's top plastic surgeons, all paid in cash to keep his identity hidden.

And yet, she had found him.

This woman.

A dark angel.

A genius.

A monster that was now coming for him. And, in her mind, there would be only one ending for a killer more powerful than the president.

That would be death.

But he wouldn't go down without a fight. His work was too important. Not the company. His other work.

"Brilliant, Ms. Nachtnebel," he murmured in admiration. "Let the games begin."

EPILOGUE

New York, 1981

Mojca and Anton spent hours on the train, endlessly looping the city, re-tracing the same route through New York. They sat silently, watching the sun's last rays glimmer off the high-rises surrounding them.

The joyful sound of a giggling girl nearby captured their attention. Mojca watched with a mix of jealousy and sadness as the girl's father playfully tickled her side while her mother watched with a fond smile.

As the train slowed into the station, Anton grasped Mojca's hand. "Let's get off here and head back home. One of them must be in jail by now."

Mojca nodded as his gaze lingered on the happy family across from them.

Anton tightened his grip around Mojca's hand as they got off the train and crossed the station's platform to catch the train for home.

"I think we should pick up some chocolate and chips and watch Wonder Woman tonight," Anton suggested.

Mojca's mood brightened. "Can I have some cola too?"

"Only if you promise not to stay up all night again, bombarding me with questions about Ancient Egypt and why cats lick their butts."

A genuine chuckle escaped Mojca—a stark contrast to the forced ones on the train when Anton tried his jokes too hard too soon.

As they watched the train approaching in the distance, Mojca felt a tremor in his hand. He instantly knew his own hand wasn't trembling. In sheer panic, he looked at Anton. His brother's eyes had rolled back as if a demon were possessing him

"Help, he's having a seizure!" Mojca shouted as Anton's violently shaking body fell forward onto the train tracks, almost pulling Mojca along with him. "Help!" he screamed, looking left and right at the crowd that had gathered and was now staring at the horrific scene. "Please help my brother!"

Mojca's voice shattered the silence, but no one moved.

His eyes darted to the train thundering toward them as his unconscious brother violently seized on the tracks.

"Why is nobody helping?" he cried out. Hot tears streamed down his face as a sharp pain choked his breath, leaving him gasping for air. But the large crowd merely gawked, unwilling to help, captivated by the unbelievable scene unfolding before them.

Thoughts of terror and blame raced through Mojca's mind. This was all his fault. If it weren't for him, his brother wouldn't have forgotten his coat with his medication at home.

Without a second to waste, Mojca leaped onto the tracks. The train's loud horn blared a stark warning that it couldn't stop in time. As things stood, it was set to claim not only Anton's life but Mojca's as well.

Desperately, with only seconds left, Mojca pulled at his brother's heavy body. "Help! Please help!" he screamed over and over again.

But the train drew nearer, and the onlookers did nothing but stare.

Mojca pulled relentlessly, bargaining with God and the mighty pharaohs to never lie or do anything bad again if only they would help save the one person who loved him— the one person who had always been there for him, the one reason he still wanted to wake up each morning.

The train was moments away from striking them with the force of a bomb. An odd sense of relief suddenly mixed with Mojca's horror. At least, the train would kill him too. Because without his brother, no other soul on earth could possibly feel the profound and hollow emptiness as Mojca would.

FINAL KILL

PROLOGUE

"Momma?" The man's low voice churned like gravel into his cell phone. His gold front tooth flashed as he spoke. "I'm ... I'm watching her again."

An exasperated sigh resonated from the other end, followed by a pause.

"Pookie," an elderly woman finally responded with authority. "No, no, no, Pookie. No, I says."

The man's brown eyes narrowed at the prostitute at the far end of the dimly lit alley. Her ample breasts nearly spilled out of her skimpy dress as she leaned into the rolled-down window of a newly arrived car. The dress barely covered her curves, leaving little to the imagination about what was underneath.

A surge of desire thundered through the man's cock, a wave of lust threatening his control. The urge was so intense he nearly stepped out from the shadows to claim her in full view of anyone who might see, including the driver of that car. But a deep, shuddering breath steadied him.

"Momma..." A growl rumbled from his throat as he watched the prostitute climb into the car and bend over the driver's lap. Her head began to bob up and down in quick succession. "The devil is back. I can't tame the devil inside me anymore, Momma."

"Yes, you can, Pookie," the woman's voice came through clenched teeth like a desperate prayer. "Listen to the voice of our Lord Jesus, Pookie. The devil is a filthy liar. He plants those sinister thoughts in your mind. You must—"

Pookie hung up and turned off his cell.

The prostitute climbed on the man's lap, riding him energetically, her long blonde hair bouncing in rhythm with her movements under the faint glow of a nearby streetlamp.

This thirst. It was overwhelming. Consuming.

For weeks, he'd watched her. The way she fucked and fucked and then drove back to her trailer, where her mother cared for her children while she indulged in her sins. There was something addicting about this one.

He needed her. The devil wouldn't stop tormenting him until he did as he was commanded. The fight was over. Pookie knew he'd lost.

Immersed in the shadows, he observed the woman step out and snatch the cash from the man. With practiced ease, she wiped the semen off her thighs with a tissue as the car drove off.

The urge intensified, making him tremble like a puppy in the bitter cold. Oh, all the things he'd do to her. And how it would make him feel.

The thrill of her screams. Power. Control.

His lips twisted into a smile.

But a sudden feeling of being watched made Pookie whip around. Was that a shifting shadow? Was it her?

That strange letter flashed vividly in his mind. Mailed to him from an unknown sender. Whoever had sent it knew who he was and what he did ... yet he was still free. No arrests. Not even a call from the cops.

After praying to the devil about it, Pookie had concluded that his dark lord himself had sent the warning. To protect their work, of course.

"One of your kind has broken the pact of evil and turned on her own," the letter read.

The message included a photo of a renowned pianist—not his type. But he'd manage. Women were weak and useless unless they brought him pleasure.

He glanced back down the alley where the prostitute was counting her earnings. Tonight belonged to her. But after that ... the pianist would get what she deserved.

ONE

Leah

This wasn't a piano recital. It was a battle.

I pounded Beethoven's Appassionata into the keys in front of me like it was a duel to the death. Jan Novak consumed my thoughts day and night. Sleep eluded me, and though I forced myself to eat, I continued to lose weight. No matter how I approached the situation, I had nothing to take on a man with such power.

I knew it was him.

He was the Train Track Killer.

My gut told me so, and the evidence we'd gathered was persuasive enough for me. But Richter and Rose had doubts. They were hesitant because of the missing gunshot wound on Novak's shoulder. I understood their concerns. Their thought process and happiness—unlike mine—were heavily based on emotions. Inadvertently killing someone who wasn't the Train Track Killer would devastate them.

And it was risky for me as well. Killing an innocent person could turn me into the monster I hunted. Yet that fear was fading.

But why? Had the Train Track Killer pushed me to the edge after all these years?

The confrontation with Jan Novak in the forest replayed in my mind. He'd placed Anna on the tracks. I'd fired, striking him in the shoulder. He'd clutched his shoulder, crumbled to one knee, and then escaped with Patel's help.

And heaven only knew how many other demons Jan Novak had recruited for his sick games. All-seeing. All-hearing. Almost godlike, Novak knew everyone's moves—who did what, where, and when. He had the power to manipulate people like chess pieces. The sky was the limit.

My fingers slammed onto the keys as the finale began. I played it at almost twice the speed, seeking exhaustion as much as releasing frustration.

When the last note echoed through the mighty Boston Symphony Hall, I sat in silence, surrounded by thousands of empty seats.

My eyes fell to the spot on the stage where my attacker had taken his own life shortly after shooting McCourt. I'd canceled my concerts until further notice. People had come to lay a sea of flowers at the symphony hall and my home. Much to my annoyance, they held hands, singing "Kumbaya." What nonsense.

But my days on the stage were far from over.

The attack had skyrocketed the demand for my concert tickets. And although the news coverage seemed to be waning, the attention was still overwhelming. It would fade quickly—the world had too many tragedies to dwell on mine for too long—but for now, it was exhausting.

"Leah."

Crystal's soft voice pulled me from my thoughts. She had endured what could only be described as a hellish few weeks—managing my PR and dealing with Hieber. I'd tripled her salary. It was perhaps the only reason she'd stayed.

I lifted my head to look at her. With her bright red glasses and hair, Crystal was the only splash of life in the vast, silent concert hall.

"I've managed to get rid of the journalists in front of your home and the symphony hall. I've also asked your driver to wait for you at the back exit. Do you need anything else from me? Otherwise, I'll go home."

"No. Thank you. Please go home and rest."

She nodded.

"And take the next week off. I'll make Hieber work for a change."

She grinned. "Thank you."

Then she lingered awkwardly, like a child hoping for a second scoop of ice cream.

"What is it?"

Crystal bit her lip.

I sighed. "No, Crystal. Please, not again."

"But, Leah, you need protection. All Hollywood stars have bodyguards."

"I'm not a Hollywood star."

"You're a star in the world of classical music. And somebody just tried to shoot you."

"My answer remains the same. I can take care of myself."

Crystal bit her lip again. It was a habit she fell back on when she was afraid to speak up.

"Talking about security," I said as I rose. "The symphony hall ... did we switch security companies yet?"

She nodded, clearly puzzled as to why I'd instructed her to change our security service provider for a smaller, pricier company. Crystal didn't know that the new firm was one of the only companies in the entire U.S. that didn't use Jan Novak's cloud storage. And I was tired of him watching me. Tired of his very existence.

"That'll be all, then." My tone left no room for argument. "Take two weeks off," I added, grabbing my cashmere coat from the piano bench.

I checked the time. Nine thirty-one.

The cold night air brushed against my face as I stepped out the back door and headed toward my car. Immediately, I sensed a presence in the dark alley behind me. I slowed my pace and reached for the gun in my purse.

For the past week or so, I'd felt like I was being followed. A strange shadow behind a tree at night outside my home on Monday. Evil eyes staring at me from under a hood on a crowded Boston street on Thursday.

Calmly, I turned, gun drawn. But no one was there. At least, not anymore.

"You okay?" Richter's voice came suddenly from behind me.

I kept my gaze on the dark alley a moment longer, then tucked the gun back into my purse. "A bit risky approaching me in public like this, don't you think?" I asked. I looked into his tired brown eyes. Behind them was a man I knew I could trust to always do the right thing.

"Nah," he said playfully, flashing his FBI badge. "Just checking in on a victim and a main witness to McCourt's attack. And to be honest, it's kinda nice to meet in the open like this. Makes it all feel—"

"Less wrong?" I interrupted.

He frowned. "Easier. That old rope factory is far out, and I almost got jumped by a homeless guy last time we met there. Tried to bite me but ran off when I tackled him."

I strode toward my limousine, where Mark was holding the door open. As I climbed in, Richter remained motionless outside. I raised an eyebrow at him just as Agent Rose approached, balancing two coffees in her hands.

"We've been here for a while," she said, handing a coffee to Richter as they got in.

"Thanks, Mark," Richter said as if they were old friends.

I told Mark to drive around Boston. He nodded, closed the door, and slipped behind the wheel. With a soft click, he shut the privacy divider before the car smoothly pulled into motion.

"Why did you wait outside?" I asked. "You could have just texted me to meet up."

"I did," Richter said. "You didn't reply."

"The piano is loud," I said quickly.

That was true. But lately, I'd also been lost in thoughts of Jan Novak.

"Did you do a deep dive into Novak?" I asked. Meetings like this were reserved for sharing crucial information. And meetings with Rose specifically targeted the Train Track Killer. She wasn't involved in our other endeavors: hunting serial killers. For now, everyone seemed content with that arrangement.

"He's tougher to get information on than the President," Rose said, adjusting her suit jacket with one hand while holding her coffee in the other.

"We're trying to keep a low profile," Richter added, "so I'm calling in favors from cyber and even a friend at the NSA."

"On paper, his life reads like a fairy tale," Rose continued. "Some poor kid who worked hard and made billions."

"But?" I prompted.

"But his Oscar-worthy story starts from college," Richter said. "Before that, there's nothing. The only thing we know about his childhood comes from a college entrance essay. In it, he mentions arriving in New York as a kid with his Slovak immigrant parents. And that's pretty much all we have."

"What about his birth certificate?" I asked. "School diplomas? Hospital records?"

Richter shook his head. "Nothing. His past is pretty much a mystery."

"There are no mysteries," I said. "Everything has an explanation."

"And some people go the extra mile to find that explanation." Rose handed me a document. "This is a list of Jan Novak's shareholders. Apparently, the U.S. government forced him to split up his cloud storage company before practically handing him control over every aspect of our American lives, making him the closest thing to God since Jesus."

"How tactful of them," I said.

"Don't give them too much credit," Richter countered. "Every single person on this list is a mega-donor to the dirtiest in Congress."

I scanned the names and pictures of ten men. All old. All filthy rich.

"Surprise, surprise," I muttered.

"Do you recognize anyone?" Rose asked.

My gaze narrowed on Ronald Hubble. "I do."

Rose and Richter exchanged hopeful glances.

Richter leaned forward. "Do you think you can get some information? Discreetly?"

"Me? No," I said. "But I might know someone who can."

"Good. We need more proof that Jan Novak is the Train Track Killer." Richter ran his hand through his hair. "Or any proof at this point, actually. A disgruntled high-class prostitute. A pissed-off shareholder. Even the smallest lead would help."

"I assume Jan Novak canceled his gym membership?" I asked. "If he's had skin grafts to remove the bullet scar, there'd be a scar on his chest somewhere. He could have been hiding it under a towel when we first had him followed in the locker room. We focused only on his shoulder."

Rose shook her head. "Too late for a second try. He canceled his membership, and there's no legal way to make him strip down. As powerful as he is, he could be caught red-handed with a bloody knife over a dead body and still have the connections to avoid a court order for a physical like that. Even inviting him for a chit-chat at the office is impossible based on what we have. Trying anything like that would be textbook career suicide for both of us."

Richter opened his mouth as if to speak, but then his phone rang.

"Agent Richter." He listened intently, tilted his head, and stared upward. "Good God. Can you ask her to come back tomorrow?" After another pause, he sighed. "No, no police. I'm on my way."

"Please don't tell me the Night Stalker raped another woman," Rose said.

Richter shook his head as he pocketed his phone. "Thank God, no. Some mother of a missing prostitute is causing a scene in front of our headquarters. Security called me before the cops arrested her."

I listened closely, curious about the Night Stalker.

"Good," Rose said. "We really don't need bad publicity right now. The bureau is having a good streak. Do you want me to take care of this?"

Richter shook his head. "No, you've got a big day tomorrow. Go home and rest. I'll handle this."

Rose nodded, then furrowed her brow. "So, what happens now? How does this work? Do we just talk things over, and then you drop us off at home like an Uber until we have more information on Novak and regroup?"

I texted Mark, who instantly pulled over.

"Not quite. You can get out here," I said.

Richter smiled. "Feels like a one-star ride-share. Still, beats a rainy dock any day."

"Mm-hmm." Rose placed her hand on the door handle.

"Wait," I interjected.

Both turned to me.

"I think ... I'm being followed."

"By Novak?" Richter asked, his voice concerned.

"I don't know."

"Why would he follow only you?" Rose asked. "Why not go after all of us? Kill us or at least get us fired—whatever it takes. He knows we're on his trail."

"I wish he'd come after me," Richter said. "If I see him outside my house at night, that's all the reason I need to put a bullet in his head." Suddenly, he tensed. "He wouldn't go after my daughter, would he?"

"No. He won't hurt her," I assured him. "Children are sacred to him. The Train Track Killer isn't an out-of-control sociopath like Grand or the College Snatcher. He's calculated. Everything he does has a purpose, a reflection of what he aspires to be. He has never hurt a child. It would go against who he is. Everything he built."

Richter ran a palm across his cheek in thought. "People can act out of character when they're cornered."

"I doubt he feels cornered by us," I said. Silence followed the heavy truth of that statement.

"I wonder if we should have stayed under the radar," Rose said. "Used secrecy and the element of surprise as our weapons."

I leaned back, gazing out the window as a drunk couple stumbled past on the deserted streets of downtown Boston. "There's no secrecy with a man who sees and hears everything and has the government in his pocket. If he knows we're on to him, it might force him to make a mistake to protect himself. I recommend you get the FBI's cloud storage contract with Novak's firm terminated as soon as possible, or he'll know every breath you take."

"That will be ... quite a mountain to climb," Rose said, opening the car door. After a brief silence, she stepped out.

Richter scooted over but then paused, fixing a deep, searching look on me. "Why do I get the feeling you're up to something?"

"I can't say. I'm hardly the right person to ask about interpreting your feelings."

He studied me. "I'm serious, Leah. Is Novak getting to you?"

I met his gaze. "He doesn't have that power over me. No one does. Except myself."

"Do you want me to watch your house for a while, see if someone's following you?"

I managed a faint smile. "Cute," I said. "But that won't be necessary."

Richter nodded, then got out and closed the door.

As Mark drove off, I mulled over Richter's question. Not his offer to camp outside my house like a scene from an undercover cop movie. Rather, his suspicion. Richter seemed to have acquired the ability to see right through me. It was something nobody had ever managed to do.

And that was a problem—because he was right. I did have plans for tonight.

TWO

Liam

I was sitting next to Mrs. Moore on the cold stone steps in front of FBI headquarters. I'd invited her inside, but she'd declined, saying her grandkids were asleep in the car parked in front of us. It was a chilly fall night, and the air felt crisp. She wore a sweater with an image of a dog drinking wine. Her white hair looked unkempt and neglected, and she had dark rings under her swollen eyes.

"I'm sorry I called your security 'assholes,'" Mrs. Moore said, wiping away tears. "It's just … I don't know what to do anymore. The police don't care. Nobody seems to care that my daughter is missing." More tears began streaming down her face. "I thought Nathalie worked night shifts at the corner store. That's what she always told me. Then the police said all these things about her. Called her a cheap prostitute."

I stayed silent.

"But in the end, what does it even matter how she earned money for those kids' clothes and food? She was an amazing mom. She had so much love in her heart. No matter what she did, she is still my child. Or was…"

I gently placed my hand on Mrs. Moore's shoulder. "We don't know for sure that she's gone."

"But I can feel it. The darkness that swallowed her. Took her out of the light. It's like a piece of my heart has been ripped out. And the kids." She nodded toward the car, where I could see a glimpse of a blonde scalp in the car seat. "They can feel it too."

Of all the burdens that came with being an FBI agent, dealing with families was the most heart-wrenching.

"I'm a parent too," I told her. "And I can't begin to imagine what you're going through right now." Mrs. Moore's crying intensified, and I strengthened my grip on her shoulder. I glanced at the rundown car with the kids inside. "But the kids need their beds. As much of their normal life as they can get."

Mrs. Moore used her sleeve to wipe away her tears.

"How about I get on this right now, and you all go get some rest? I'll give it my all, I promise."

Mrs. Moore's swollen, red eyes lifted to mine. She stared at me as if trying to figure out if I was all talk or really meant it. Finally, she nodded and rose to her feet. So did I. But instead of walking to her car, she tilted her head back and looked up at the night sky.

"We're not supposed to outlive our children," she said softly.

"No, we're not. But until we find a body, there's still a chance she's out there. Alive."

Mrs. Moore kept staring upward.

"I hope so. Because God be my witness, I won't be some forgiving, sweet old lady if we find my little girl dead in some ditch." Her voice quivered. Her eyes met mine again as tears streamed down her face. "I'll carry hatred and rage in my heart until the very last breath I take. And I'll pray to God, Satan, or anybody else who'll listen to bring nothing but pain and misery to whoever did this to my daughter."

I nodded.

Many people judged a parent's abilities by their financial success or educational background. But from what I'd seen on the job, real love wasn't reserved for parents with material wealth or a polished resume. It was also in the mom who played Uno with one hand while holding a cigarette in the other, or the mom who lost her temper during her kid's tantrum in the parking lot but covered them with kisses and hugs before bed.

"Thank you," Mrs. Moore finally said, her voice hoarse.

"Of course. I'm sorry you're going through this. Let me know if you need anything. Just call my cell."

As I watched her drive off, a dark feeling settled in my stomach.

Mrs. Moore could be right. A missing prostitute, ten days gone. All signs pointed toward the worst. I'd still give it my all, hoping for the best. But if all was lost and we found a body, at least Mrs. Moore and the kids would have a grave to lay their flowers on. To some, this meant something. And I'd do all I could to give the Moores at least that.

And maybe more.

If her daughter had really been murdered and I found out who did it, her killer might get the brutal end he deserved.

I happened to know someone good at that sort of thing. And I had a feeling Mrs. Moore would be okay with it.

THREE

Disturbingly, I found myself enjoying the thrill of lurking in the shadows. I stood in a narrow alley between two imposing townhomes on Beacon Hill, just across from Leah's mansion. Was this the same thrill that drove serial killers when they stalked their prey?

I'd been here for over three hours, and the deserted streets felt apocalyptic.

A twinge of guilt washed over me for not telling Leah or Liam about my decision to tail her. But when she'd said she was being followed, I knew doing nothing wasn't an option. My secrecy wasn't meant to deceive or betray her—it was to ensure the mission's success. Real-world surveillance was nothing like its fictional portrayal. Parking a car in front of a house for days was a surefire way to attract attention. And tracking someone else's stalker posed an even greater challenge; stalkers were already on high alert.

So, the first rule of my mission to find out who was following Leah was secrecy.

I was mentally prepared for a long night of nothingness when Leah's Audi emerged from her driveway. It was after midnight. Where the hell was she going?

I sprinted to my car, which I'd parked behind a store at the first intersection out of Beacon Hill. Sure enough, Leah's car paused at the intersection's red light. I slid into my seat and waited for the light to turn green. Pulling out of the parking lot, I began following her.

She drove west through the city, heading toward the Children's Hospital. Then she pulled over and parked on a dark residential street.

I watched in shock as Leah Nachtnebel, the world-renowned pianist, emerged from her car, utterly transformed. She now sported short blonde hair, a skimpy mini-dress, and a leather jacket. Heavy makeup concealed any trace of the elegant artist I knew. Even her nose and eyes looked different.

She walked about a mile before arriving at The Thirsty Monkey, a dive bar on a dimly lit corner. Its neon "OPEN" sign flickered wildly. The bar's broken windows told of better days gone by.

Without hesitation, she pushed through the bar's door.

I pulled over and turned off my lights and engine. The area was relatively quiet, but I still blended in perfectly with the occasional car and late-night pedestrian.

As I watched people come out of The Thirsty Monkey for a cigarette, a feeling of worry overcame me. I had no idea what the hell Leah was doing here, but something deep down told me it wasn't a night of karaoke.

388 | S. T. ASHMAN

Pushing open the door to the bar, I was hit by a blast of loud music and the stench of cigarette smoke mixed with the greasy aroma of chicken wings. Slurred voices and clumsy laughter echoed from the crowd of drunks scattered around the dimly lit room. Its walls were plastered with broken neon beer signs and sun-bleached band posters. The tables were scuffed, bearing the scars of endless rough nights. In the corner, an old jukebox gathered dust.

I hadn't even reached the bar before the first drunk man leaned into my path and asked if I wanted a drink. I ignored him and ordered a whiskey from the overworked bartender, who acknowledged me with a nod while continuing to fill another order.

"Hey there, pretty," a man in his forties reeking of booze said as he leaned against the bar next to me. "Can I buy you a drink?"

"No." I grabbed the glass of whiskey from the bartender and was about to turn when the man blocked my path.

"Why not?"

I glanced at the barbecue sauce stains on his white shirt. His half-shut eyes indicated he was one step away from being blackout drunk.

"I'd rather not say," I replied, trying to walk around him.

He blocked my way again. "You think you're too good for me?" he slurred.

I drank about half of my whiskey in a smooth swig, then sighed. "Of course I do. It's not even the fact that your fingers are yellow from cigarettes, or that your breath stinks, and you don't know how to eat chicken wings, which literally don't require utensils."

The man's eyes widened as disbelief washed over his flushed face.

"Quite frankly, what disgusts me the most is the wedding band mark on your finger. Your hand is tanned except for the white where you usually wear the ring. You took it off when you came here. So if you want to sleep with anyone tonight, it should be your wife, who I personally don't think deserves the horror of having someone like you in her bed."

His brows furrowed. "You arrogant cunt."

I smiled as I finally managed to pass him. "Thank you."

It took another rejection before I finally got a seat at a high table in the middle of the bar. Every now and then, another hopeful adventurer tried their luck. I turned them all down, though I'd craved good sex ever since Emanuel died. Not that I'd find it in this bar anyway. And I wasn't here for fun.

I was here to be seen.

I was here as bait.

It took less than an hour for Leah to stagger back out of The Thirsty Monkey.

"What the hell is going on?" I mumbled, straightening from my slumped position behind the wheel of my parked car.

For a moment, I was concerned she might attempt to drive in that state, but then she stumbled away from the direction of her car.

Once she'd turned the corner, I followed her on foot, leaving plenty of space between us.

A few streets later, Leah made her way into Ramler Park, a small public area known for its tranquility and flowers. Its secluded walls of bushes swallowed her instantly. When the street was clear, I walked around the park, then climbed the black metal fence to enter through the bushes. Not far from me, Leah sat in the darkness on a bench near a fountain, smoking a cigarette and looking at her phone. The screen lit up her unfamiliar face, adding an eerie layer to an already strange night.

I was about to reveal myself and ask what the hell was going on when a dark figure darted past me to my left, hiding behind a nearby tree. A rush of adrenaline surged through me, and I quickly took cover behind a bush to stay out of sight.

Fuck.

Was that Jan Novak? It was too dark to tell.

I drew my gun and peeked at Leah again. She continued scrolling on her phone, seemingly oblivious. What the fuck? Was she trying to get raped or killed?

Then it dawned on me. She wasn't drunk or clueless or suicidal.

She was on the hunt. But who was she after?

My grip tightened around my gun as my heart quickened. I readied myself to bolt toward the tree to my left and confront whoever was hiding there. But then, out of nowhere, another shadow emerged from the dimly lit street, moving with a confident stride.

A man, perhaps in his late thirties, swiftly walked down the path toward the fountain where Leah was sitting. There was something creepy about him. Maybe it was the way he didn't slow down. Leah was still engrossed in her phone. Didn't she see the man approaching?

The creepy guy adjusted his pace, striding even faster toward Leah. Before she could look up, he grabbed her and wrestled her to the ground, pinning her beneath him.

I glanced to my left to ensure the man attacking Leah and the figure hiding behind the tree weren't one and the same. The dark figure was still there, watching everything unfold. Was that a golden shimmer I just saw from the shadow? It was tiny, almost as if it had come from his mouth. A gold tooth?

If I burst into the open now, the man hiding would see me and escape. But I couldn't just stand by and let Leah get hurt.

Damn the stalker. I had to act.

I was about to jump into action when, suddenly, the man on top of Leah let out a scream. In seconds, the scene on the ground had completely changed. The man had rolled off, screaming in pain. Leah jumped on top of him as the glint of a knife flashed. She drove the blade down quickly and with force.

I watched, frozen, as the knife struck him two more times.

What the fuck was wrong with me?

I had to get out there and stop her.

Now, goddammit!

I was an FBI agent. And the man on the ground with her most likely wasn't even a serial killer. Everything here pointed toward an attempted rape, which was now turning into a murder by the supposed victim.

My gaze shot to the man behind the tree. He was still there, watching, the golden shimmer from what I thought looked like his teeth now constant.

Then, all of a sudden, he rushed off.

"Shit!"

What now? Stop Leah? Run after this man?

My phone vibrated. The flip phone.

It was her number.

A text.

FOLLOW HIM!

Leah

From the corner of my eye, I saw two shadows darting through the park—one after the other. One of them was probably Rose. Good. She'd gotten my text and followed my instructions.

I snapped my attention back to the Night Stalker. In the brief moment I'd been distracted by my phone, he'd managed to slip out from under me and roll me onto the gravel. My eyes locked onto the whimpering man. Should I just end him now? A few more quick stabs or slit his throat?

This was uncharted territory, dangerously exhilarating. A rapist. No murders—yet.

I got to my feet and drove my knee into his back, pinning him to the ground as he squirmed and tried desperately to crawl away. His pleas for mercy pierced the night, but I was unyielding. I'd already sunk the blade into him five, maybe six times. Still, he'd survive if I walked away now.

"Not so much fun when you're the one pinned down, is it?" I asked. "I heard the youngest of your rape victims was only fourteen, right?"

My gloved left hand clutched his thick hair and yanked his head back to expose his throat. Thanks to a hacker I'd paid on the dark web, I'd tracked down the famous Night Stalker in less than two weeks. The idiot had boasted about his rapes in an exclusive forum, a sanctuary for perverts like him, hiding behind anonymous usernames. These depraved scumbags chatted about rapes like nerds talked about video games. During one of their twisted chats, they'd pushed the Night Stalker into planning his next rape at this park—famous for the migratory birds that paused here to drink. "Rapes n' chirps," they'd called it, laughingly. They told him to follow a drunk woman from the Thirsty Monkey. So, I'd decided the last laugh would be mine.

Night after night, I'd waited here. And now, here he was, just as he'd promised. Rapes n' chirps. No mystery on his end—just a sick fuck living out his twisted fantasies.

But the real question was, what the hell was I doing here?

This man wasn't a killer. He'd shattered women's lives in other ways, stealing their confidence, their self-worth, their peace of mind, and, for some, their will to live. Wasn't that a form of murder too? Maybe. But he wasn't my usual prey.

Without realizing it, I'd placed my knife against his throat. The blade pierced his skin slightly.

He begged and whimpered like a coward, which only fueled my desire to kill him. But if I did, what then? The monster lurking within me—would Richter finally see it and sever ties?

I sighed, then rolled the Night Stalker over. Annoyed, I yanked down his pants and, in a few swift cuts, severed his penis.

A screech of agony tore from his throat before he slumped into a half-conscious state, mumbling incoherently.

"Quite small for a man acting so big," I said calmly as I tossed the severed penis into the fountain. Then I walked away through the bushes, avoiding the main paths.

I ducked into a dark alley to wipe the blood from my neck and arms. My mind spun with questions. I knew Rose had been following me ever since I'd left my house. But why hadn't she intervened tonight? Would she report this to Richter? It didn't matter; he'd probably figure out it was me anyway.

I took off my wig, letting my real hair fall loosely over my shoulders. Then I pulled a pair of leggings from my purse and slipped them on, tucking the dress in like a shirt. I looked like a completely different person—enough to make it back to my car, which I'd parked in a blind spot away from security cameras.

As I walked, my mind wrestled with the night's events. Something inside me was shifting, and I wasn't sure if it was for better or worse. Tonight felt different—off. The target, the method—everything was out of place. Sparing the Night Stalker's life felt like a shallow gesture of justice. For the first time, I found myself wondering whether I was truly driven by a sense of justice when I hunted monsters. Or was it the thrill that kept me going?

Rose

I followed the man down the street. He was clad in a dark sweater and a baseball cap, and he walked calmly to fit in with the occasional dog walker. Unaware of my pursuit, he likely believed he had successfully stalked Leah and was now nonchalantly continuing on his way. He acted as if he were on a Sunday stroll, not a man who'd just witnessed a murder.

Crossing to the other side of the street, I tailed him for another block, then watched as he climbed into a red pickup truck. I paused to memorize his license plate. A chilling thought struck me: Whoever he was, he was good at what he did. The plate was probably fake. Panicking, I scanned my surroundings.

Just then, a police car drove past, heading away from us. I turned and sprinted after it. Before long, the officer noticed me. He stopped the car and rolled down the window, his expression a mix of confusion and irritation.

"Why are you chasing me?"

"FBI," I panted, flashing my badge. "That red truck at the end of the street—follow it, pull him over. Record his face and license with your body cam. Make up some excuse for why you pulled him over, then let him go."

"What?"

"Now, goddammit!" I snapped.

The officer flicked on his lights and took off.

From a safe distance, I watched the officer do as I'd instructed. Good. Even if this wouldn't directly point to Jan Novak, we were one step closer to catching someone. And maybe Leah would be able to get this man to talk.

But what about the rapist in the park? He was probably dead by now. Strangely, I didn't feel a thing for him. I didn't take any joy in his death, but I also couldn't muster any pity. Maybe that's why I hadn't stopped Leah.

I wasn't sure who that guy was or exactly what Leah was doing, but there was a real chance she'd picked up a new hobby—one that wasn't just about killing serial killers. One that involved taking out any kind of bad guy.

I shook my head. None of this was good. As much as I wanted to stay out of it, I had to talk to Richter—ASAP.

FOUR

Liam

Cowboy and Rose stood next to me. We were staring through the window of a private patient room on the Intensive Care Unit floor of Mass General Hospital. The strong smell of disinfectant mixed with the rhythmic beeps of hospital machines.

On the other side was a man in his late thirties. His face looked tired but was in pretty good shape otherwise—something one couldn't say about the other half of him.

"Well, who gets a gold star for this masterpiece?" Cowboy asked. "Chopped his dick right off. The doctors couldn't reattach it. Apparently, there were fish in the fountain that nibbled on it for too long."

"Jesus," I grumbled. "How sure are we he's the Night Stalker?"

"Very sure," Rose said. "A DNA sample connected him to eight of the Night Stalker rape victims. His name is Terry Patterson. Thirty-four years old, works as a mechanic for a local garage. Loner. Coworkers described him as strange. Pedophile kinda type, one of them said."

"He said that, literally?" Cowboy asked, grinning.

"Yup. Literally," Rose confirmed.

"If it looks and talks like a duck, eh?" Cowboy's grin widened.

Rose threw him a scolding look, then continued. "Patterson woke up for a few hours yesterday and denies any wrongdoing. Told the cops that he was hooking up at the park with some woman from a bar called Thirsty Monkey. Then, out of nowhere, she stabbed him and chopped his dick off."

"Well, ain't that a plot twist," I said, narrowing my eyes at Patterson.

Cowboy grinned. "More like a happy ending. Grand. Patterson. That guy strapped to the tree in the woods a few months back. It's almost like some higher power is finally doing some spring cleaning on Earth."

Not some higher power.

Leah.

Staring at Patterson, I couldn't help but wonder if this was her work. It had her signature all over it, except for the fact that Patterson was still alive. But Cowboy didn't need to start connecting the dots here.

"Grand killed himself with drugs. Woods guy was a cartel crime," I said.

"This one, though, has an artist behind it," Cowboy joked, nodding at Patterson. "There won't be a single sane person on this planet who'll feel sorry for this guy. Especially not the fourteen women the Night Stalker beat and raped. The youngest was only fourteen."

We continued watching Patterson for a moment.

"So, what do you want us to do about all this?" Rose asked.

"What do you mean?" Cowboy interrupted before I could respond. "Don't tell me we're going after the woman who did this to him?" His eyes were wide with disbelief.

I sighed. "We have to conduct a fair and legal investigation, Cowboy. So please go and talk to the police about their reports and possible witness statements they recorded."

Cowboy lingered, defiant.

"But if nothing comes of it, don't waste any other resources or time on this. We'll just wait for the woman to step forward herself. Ok?"

He grinned. "Yes, sirrr!" Then he walked off.

Rose and I lingered as I shifted my gaze from Patterson to her. Did she know anything about this? She seemed a bit on edge. Conflicted. Still, it seemed unlikely that Rose and Leah had teamed up behind my back to hunt down rapists and pedophiles.

"What's wrong?" I asked.

She looked at me for a moment as if she wanted to say something, then shrugged. "Nothing. Well, the meeting later, it's going to be a bit ... fucked up."

I nodded. "Are you sure you want to do this? I can always step in for you."

Rose shook her head. "No. I'm gonna be fine."

"Just let me know if you change your mind. I gotta get Josie now, but I can drop her off at my mom's if you have a change of heart."

"Thanks, but as I said, I'll be fine. I'll call you after the meeting."

I nodded and Rose left.

I watched as she made her way down the Intensive Care Unit hallway, dodging doctors and nurses who were moving around like busy ants.

Something was off about all this. Why hadn't Rose asked if I thought Leah was behind this? My gaze wandered over to Terry Patterson—or what was left of him. I wasn't disturbed by any of it. Like Cowboy, I agreed that he deserved this. Living the rest of his life without the weapon he used against those poor women was only fair. Still, a heavy clump of worry was forming in my stomach. Was Leah prowling outside her usual hunting grounds? Serial killers required months to years of digging to find and dispose of. But rapists and other lowlife criminals were so plentiful in this country, the corpses would pile up sky-high. And so would the trail of evidence. Cowboy was already beginning to form the idea that someone was out there taking care of monsters. If Leah was picking up a side hobby, I had to talk to her. Now. Before our cover got blown and I was sent to jail before the Train Track Killer was caught.

I checked my phone. It was one in the afternoon. I had to pick up Josie, but this ... this couldn't wait.

FIVE

Leah

I made my way through the lush garden of the mansion situated on a private pond just outside Boston. It was a warm and sunny fall day, and the air smelled of grass and roses.

Luca was sitting on a bench overlooking the pond, where a group of ducks swam peacefully.

"I didn't think I'd ever see you again," he said without turning.

I slowed as I made my way around the bench. "How did you know it was me?"

He lifted his eyes from the pond and fixed them on me. "You're the only person who my men would allow to walk around freely on my property. They'd never dare to deny you any wish."

"Unlike you?" I said as I sat next to him. Dressed in a white suit, he appeared immaculate as always, but his face looked tired and deprived of life.

For a moment, we fell silent, listening to the quacks of the ducks and the warm breeze rustling the leaves of the trees.

Luca shook his head. "I know I've failed you. I broke my word when McCourt approached me, asking for the impossible. The impossible promise I made to you. To kill you if anyone ever came to ask for it. But for what it's worth, this is the first time I've broken my word in over sixty years. The first time since I broke it all those years ago and cost my older brother his life in a run-down Italian neighborhood in Boston."

"Sixty years. Unfortunate to break such a streak," I said.

"It is indeed. But at least this time, it saved a life I care about."

I remained silent, giving him space to continue.

He drew a long breath, as if reliving a painful memory. "Times were hard back then," he said, his voice weighted with something dark. "We all did what we had to do to survive. I was just a kid when my brother crossed the Moretti family and made me swear to keep his meeting with the Pallini boys a secret. But when the Morettis showed up at my father's shoe polish shop, pressing me for answers, I told them for a dime." He looked away, regret casting shadows over his face. "I took that dime and ran off to buy ice cream. They shot my brother for his betrayal. I didn't know they'd kill him. But that day, I learned what it means to keep your word."

"You never told me this story," I said.

"That's because I later killed every single one of the Morettis. Except for the women and children, of course."

I nodded. "I'm sorry for your loss."

"It was a long time ago. Yet it'll haunt me until the day I die. Even more since I broke my word to you." He turned to look at me. "But I'd break it a thousand times again to save one of the greatest pianists who ever walked this earth."

We fell silent again. I inched closer to him on the bench.

"I need your help."

He leaned forward, a spark of the man I'd once known returning to his eyes. "Anything," he said, his voice firm.

"Your friend, Ronald Hubble. He has something of great value that I need."

Luca looked surprised. "Ronald?"

I nodded.

"Name it. I'll get it for you."

"It might not be that easy. I'm not talking about a piano or painting. I'm talking about the entire share of a company he's invested in. I need his seat at the shareholders' table. It's of great importance to me."

Luca took a moment to process my words before a slight smile crossed his lips. "Let me guess. That company would be owned by Jan Novak?"

I couldn't help but smile back. "I did miss our conversations. Your sharp mind."

"No friendship in the world could make Ronald Hubble give up such a powerful investment. Even if he's dying, his legacy means more to him than heaven and earth."

"Then make him," I said, my voice flat. "You can keep the shares. I only need a power of attorney to attend the meetings. Acquiring those shares would be a financially significant move on your part. You know they hold more than just monetary value—they hold a seat at the table with the most powerful men in the world. And those shares also come with the most powerful weapon in the world."

"Knowledge?" Luca asked.

"Knowledge," I repeated.

Yet he hesitated. I leaned back on the bench.

"Why did you ask me to play for the mafia in Italy?" I pressed. "You knew the risks. If the media found out, my career could have ended overnight. You have everything you could want here in America. Riches, power. So why? What could the Italian mafia possibly offer you that made risking my career worth it?"

Luca paused, lost in thought, his gaze drifting away. "I'm sorry I asked that of you. Truly, I am. But it was of great sentimental value to me."

"Sentimental? In what way?"

He sighed, a shadow of old memories crossing his face. "After I killed the Moretti family all those years ago, I found myself at odds with the Italian mafia. I broke our code of honor, but by then, I was too powerful for them to touch me here in the U.S. So they banned me from ever returning to Italy. If I did, they'd kill me on sight."

"Even now?" I asked, intrigued.

"Italians don't forget. We are of Roman blood," he replied with a hint of pride.

"I see," I murmured.

"Arranging a private concert by 'the Empress'—someone who has turned down kings, queens, and presidents—was a gesture of such immense respect to the current Don that I hoped it would erase my past sins. I wanted to return home, to smell the olive trees, to visit the family I still have there before I die."

"Well, you're welcome for the favor," I said bluntly.

After a brief silence, Luca narrowed his eyes at me. "If I was to get these shares ... will this ... make us even?"

I nodded.

"Consider it done then," he said, his intense gaze locking onto mine.

I stood to leave, but he gently caught my wrist. "Will you stay a bit longer?" he asked, his voice hopeful as he released his grip. "I've missed you so."

"I'm afraid I have another engagement today," I replied. "But let's do dinner soon?"

His face brightened. "How about Luigi's? He keeps tuning that old piano for you. Swears his grandma's soul is in that thing."

I smiled. "People are peculiar." I turned to leave but then stopped and glanced back at him. "McCourt."

"What about him?" Luca asked.

"Please, leave him alive. For now, he might be useful to me."

Luca hesitated, conflict flickering in his eyes, then nodded reluctantly. "If that's what you want. But he'd better stay out of my sight."

"He will," I assured him. Then I made my way through the lush garden and back to my car.

SIX

Liam

I was sitting in my car in front of the metal-gated driveway of Leah's townhouse mansion. My mind raced as I gripped the steering wheel with both hands. The street was covered in flowers and candles that Leah's fans had left as a show of support. So far, the story was that a criminal had planned an attack on McCourt from the start. Luca had been clever enough to hire a man with a criminal record and schizophrenia to carry out the assault. No one questioned the scenario of a mentally ill attacker targeting a high-profile FBI agent at a concert. And now the world mourned Leah—the tragic genius who'd endured so much trauma.

"Dad," Josie called from the passenger seat, her voice tinged with annoyance.

"Hmm?"

"I thought you said you had to talk to the woman in this house."

We'd been sitting here for a few minutes as I went back and forth about bringing Josie anywhere near Leah. But my visit to the Night Stalker this morning had left me seriously worried about Leah picking up a side gig that could endanger us all. And she wasn't answering her phone—again. That worried me too. Something had been off with her ever since Jan Novak had entered our lives.

"I do need to talk to her," I finally said.

I spent another moment just sitting there.

Josie cocked an eyebrow. "Well, usually people move their legs when they want to get somewhere. If you need to talk to her, you'll have to start by opening the car door. Then, you use your legs to walk to the house."

A proud grin spread across my face. "Sarcasm, first class. Just like me. Love it."

"All jokes aside, the movie starts in thirty minutes, and I don't want to get stuck in the huge candy line again."

I sighed, gave it one last thought, then opened the car door.

"Don't open the car for anybody. I'll lock it and take the keys with me. If some weirdo knocks at the window, you call me. Where's your phone?"

Josie pulled it out of her backpack and held it up for me to see.

"Good. It'll only be a minute."

I quickly walked through the entrance next to the metal gate and knocked on the door. To my surprise, Leah herself answered. A flicker of astonishment crossed her face.

"Another risky check-in on the shooting victim?" she asked, stepping aside to let me in.

"Something like that," I said, leaving the door wide open so I could keep an eye on Josie. Leah followed my gaze to the car, where Josie was watching us.

"Hmm," was all she said before stepping into the office off the hallway. "So how can the poor victim help you today, Agent Richter?"

"Well, first off, by guaranteeing me that you aren't the artist behind the Night Stalker's attack by the fountain."

Leah leaned against her desk. She wore a cream-colored pantsuit, and her long, dark hair was pulled up in a lazy bun. She looked stunning, as always.

Her green eyes found mine. "I'm afraid ... I can't do that."

"Leah, what the fuck?" I sighed in disbelief and stepped in front of her, keeping my voice low. "Do you have any idea how dangerous this is? For you? For me and Rose? What's going on with you?"

Much to my surprise, she had no snappy reply. She just looked at me as if she, too, was searching for an answer to my question.

"People are starting to notice that bad guys are having a rough streak," I said. "Not enough for anyone to connect the dots yet, but if this becomes your new side gig—with all the fucked-up people out there—we'll have enough dead bodies to wrap around the earth twice."

"That doesn't sound like a bad thing," she said.

"Leah, I'm serious. I didn't sign up to be Robin to your serial killer Batman."

"Good. Because I'm not planning to involve you in any of this."

"I'm already involved," I countered. "Not only is this dangerous, but the margin for error is too close for my comfort."

Her eyes narrowed at me as she studied my face.

I exhaled heavily. "This is also taking energy away from Jan Novak. We need to focus on him. It'll take all we have, and even that might not be enough. Do you really want to risk the chance of bringing him to justice for the sake of your new hobby, or whatever the hell this is?"

There was a brief, intense silence.

"Rose found out who's following me," she finally said.

My head jerked back in surprise. "Rose? What? When?"

"She texted me shortly before you came here. I was about to set up a meeting for tonight."

"How did she get that info?"

"She followed me after our meeting."

This was outrageous. "After our meeting? You mean before you chopped off the Night Stalker's dick? Did you know about this?"

Leah shook her head. "Not until I noticed her following me to the park."

"This is dangerous. Why the hell is everybody starting to do side missions?"

"Because it needs to be done."

I threw her an angry look. "At least people could tell me about these things."

"I'm telling you now. It made sense to follow me. We needed to know who my stalker is."

I thought about it, then nodded. "Fine. Then tell me. Who is it?"

"I haven't gotten much information on him yet, but he seems to be a turkey farmer west of Boston. Carl Carr. He drives a red truck with the license plate MA 3333. The plate is fake, but we have his address from his driver's license."

"Carl Carr?" I repeated. The morning was full of surprises. Then it hit me. "A red pickup truck?"

Leah nodded.

I drew my phone from my suit jacket and called Cowboy. "It's me," I said. "Remember Mrs. Moore and her missing daughter? Can you check surveillance cameras near Fifth and Riley? Where Nathalie Moore disappeared on the twentieth? We're looking for a red pickup, MA 3333."

"Sure thing," Cowboy said.

I hung up.

Leah watched me curiously.

"Just a hunch ... but not a good one," I said.

She had opened her mouth to say something when the sound of piano keys echoed into the office from the library across from us.

Both of us hurried over. My hand was on my gun when we found Josie sitting on the grand piano's bench, looking over her shoulder at us with the stare of a kid who knew she was in trouble.

"Josie!" I yelled.

Her eyes widened. "I ... I'm sorry. I just—"

"I told you to stay in the car!" I shouted again, my voice louder and harsher than I intended.

Josie froze, fear washing over her.

"Richter..." Leah reprimanded me as Josie's eyes welled up with tears.

"I was looking for you," she mumbled. "The movie, it was getting late. Then I saw the cat by the open door—I'm sorry."

"Fuck," I muttered as I walked up to her and placed a hand on her shoulders. "I'm sorry, Muffin, Daddy is just..."

What could I say? *Daddy is just worried about you meeting a serial killer who kills serial killers?*

"How about we get going, and you can get whatever candy you want? No limits."

But the crying didn't let up as Josie buried her face into my stomach.

"I'm sorry," she kept saying. "I followed the cat and saw the piano. I started playing at school, and I'd never seen a piano like this."

I rubbed her back, feeling like the biggest jackass. "I know, Muffin. Daddy is so sorry."

"You must be Josie," Leah said, her eyes still giving me a scolding look as she spoke. "My name is Leah."

Josie immediately stopped crying. She turned her head to Leah. "You're that pianist, aren't you? The one my dad watches on TV all the time," Josie said.

Leah smiled gently. "I'm afraid the cat has left, as you can see," she said, glancing around her elegant piano room. "But I heard you're learning to play the piano?"

Josie nodded, wiping her tears with her sleeve. "For my dad. He watches you all the time."

Jesus. How could I have been such a jerk?

"I see. Would you like me to play something for you?" Leah asked, catching me off guard.

"Really? For me?" Josie asked in disbelief, wiping her eyes one last time.

"Of course. It would be my pleasure."

"You don't have to," I interjected. "We're actually late for the mov—"

"Please, Dad!" Josie cut me off. "Please!"

Leah and I locked eyes. She gave me a look—the one all women have when a man is being a complete idiot.

"All right," I agreed.

Josie jumped up from the bench and grabbed my hand, her face lighting up. We watched as Leah took her seat behind the grand piano.

"I'm afraid I don't know any children's songs," Leah said quietly. "But I did hear a lullaby on the radio once that stuck with me. It's rather sad, though."

"That's okay," Josie replied. "I'm sad a lot when my mom and dad fight, and I was sad when I couldn't see my dad anymore."

Her words pierced me like a knife straight to the heart.

"I can understand how the thought of losing your dad could feel overwhelmingly sad," Leah said softly. "There's a song called 'You Will Be Okay' by Sam Haft. I think you'd appreciate the piano version by Annapantsu."

She settled at the piano and began to play, her fingers gliding over the keys. Then she sang, her voice rich and haunting. It was the most amazing voice I'd ever heard.

The melody filled the room, wrapping us in a tapestry of sorrow and solace. The song was about facing darkness and the inevitability of endings. It spoke of the fading of life and the stark weight of silence. Yet, amid all the despair, it offered a promise—that even when everything went to hell, when she was gone and the world seemed to collapse, those left behind would find a way to be okay.

As she reached the final, heartfelt notes, Leah lifted her gaze from the piano. Her piercing green eyes met mine, leaving me breathless.

Josie and I stood there, frozen after the last echo faded into silence. I was an utter mess inside. Emotions swirled through me: guilt for Josie and all she'd been through. Sadness for Leah and her tragic life, as well as for myself—for the man I'd become or, more likely, the man I'd always been without knowing it.

A murderer.

Even if it was bad people. I was still a killer.

But I felt something else—something I couldn't put a finger on. Or something I was too scared to think about.

Suddenly Josie started clapping. "That was amazing!"

Leah smiled. "I usually don't sing, so I hope you both still enjoyed the piece. It's a simple song to play, so if you keep practicing, you'll be able to play it soon."

"Can I hear another one?" Josie begged.

"Oh no, Muffin, we really need to go," I said. "And Leah is busy."

"Your dad's right. Maybe next time," Leah said.

"Okay," Josie said, disappointed.

On the way out, I stopped and looked back at Leah. "Thank you," I said.

"It was my pleasure. I'll talk to you soon, Agent Richter."

I nodded. Our issues weren't resolved, but now wasn't the time.

As Leah closed the door behind us, Josie and I walked to the car. I was deep in thought about both the song and our conversation before it.

"Dad?" Josie asked as we passed through the gate. Her voice was soft and curious.

"Yeah?"

"I think ... she played that song for you," she said, her brow furrowed in thought.

"What makes you think that?" I asked.

"The way she looked at you," she replied, her eyes searching mine.

I smiled softly and shook my head. "Nah. That song was for you, Muffin. It was all for you."

SEVEN

Luca

Luca opened his arms wide for an embrace as he made his way through Ronald Hubble's grand bedroom. His smile was sincere, creating a bizarre contrast to his mission.

Ronald had been bedridden for a few weeks. Doctors and nurses buzzed around him as he vegetated on death's doorstep, too afraid to let go of the spectacular life he'd been granted.

"I was hoping you'd show up with a bottle of Pappy Van," Ronald huffed, using the electric controls on his bed to adjust his position until he was sitting upright. He looked like a ghost, pale with dark rings around his eyes. Yet his mind still seemed sharp.

"I did." Luca smiled. "But one of the pretty nurses took it from me before I entered."

Ronald's blue lips split into a cheeky grin. "I should have picked them by their brains, not their looks."

Luca watched as one of the pretty young nurses came to check his vitals and then left.

"No, you did well," he joked, sending Ronald into a coughing laugh.

Ronald's eyes flicked to the chair beside the bed, then shifted to Luca, who remained standing.

"Why do I have the feeling you aren't here to visit an old friend?" Ronald asked in his weak voice.

"Because you and I know each other too well."

"What is it then? How can I help you in my last days before I go to hell?"

"Ah, there's no such thing, my friend. But if there is, I'll be joining you soon enough." Luca's expression turned serious. "But you're right. I'm here for more than a visit. I've never asked you for anything, my old friend. Not even when I took care of that whistleblower who would've ruined your family and brought your empire crashing down."

Ronald's eyes narrowed. "But you're asking for something now, aren't you?"

Luca stayed silent.

"I see. Well, it's not a big surprise. I always knew you'd come calling for a favor someday. I just didn't think it'd take this long."

"It took this long because you never had anything I wanted," Luca shot back.

"But now I do," Ronald said.

"Now you do."

"So what is it? What does the mighty Luca Domizio want from his old friend on his deathbed to repay an old favor?"

"All of your shares in Obligato Corporation," Luca said, adjusting his white suit jacket. "I'll pay you for them. Market value."

Ronald lay there for a moment, silent, before ripping off his oxygen mask. "Let's skip the whole you-must-be-joking shit. I know you're dead serious. What I don't get is how you can seriously ask me for this. You know I can't do that, Luca. This company ... it's not like the others. And the fact that you're asking for it only proves you know that. This investment isn't just about money—and, by the way, my shares are worth over a billion. It's about the seat at Novak's table, a stronghold of power only a few in this country will ever hold. My son will take my place there and continue our legacy."

Luca let out a sharp, sarcastic breath. "Ben is an idiot. The only tables he'll ever sit at are the poker table and the judge's bench—to settle all the lawsuits against him."

Ronald didn't argue. "Ask for something else," he said, his voice firm.

"I'm afraid, my old friend, I'm asking for this. I'll have to ... insist. And you know what that means."

Ronald started coughing violently, then took a deep breath from his oxygen mask to calm himself.

"So after all these years," he huffed under the mask, "you now threaten me. Our lifelong friendship gone. For power. Greed. My legacy destroyed."

"Those shares will hardly destroy your legacy. If you upset me, on the other hand, that will. Everything you see with your tired old eyes will be gone. Hubble will be a name of tragedy and ruin. I'll pay you a decent sum for the shares. And you'll still be filthy rich after that. Now, do I leave here with those shares? Or do I leave with your family's ruin?"

"Higgins," Ronald wheezed, coughing violently as if this might be his final breath. "Higgins will arrange the paperwork and have it to you by this evening."

"Thank you," Luca replied.

"Get the fuck out," Ronald growled. "I never want to see you again."

Luca let out a short, disbelieving laugh, his brows furrowing. "You really believe that out of the two criminals in this room, I'm the evil one, don't you? Meanwhile, you robbed hardworking families of the roofs over their heads for your own gain. You took the little they had to feed their children because towers of gold weren't enough for you. I stayed in the shadows where I belong. But you, my friend—you feasted on women and children and honest men."

Turning his face away, Ronald pouted like a stubborn kid.

Luca nodded. "Farewell, old friend."

"I'll see you in hell!" Ronald shouted after him as Luca made his way toward the door.

"You can count on that," Luca muttered, flashing a flirtatious smile at the nurse as he left.

EIGHT

Rose

McCourt's office seemed bigger. It was as if the walls had stopped trying to close in on me.

McCourt was sitting across from me, popping pain pills in silence. I had to give the old bastard that. He was resilient. The gunshot wound was a clear shot through his chest. No arteries, no internal damage. Lady luck was on his side once more. Kind of ironic, considering how many good people she passed every day without making a stop. After the incident, which had been deemed an attack by a mentally ill drug addict, McCourt was hailed as a hero by both the reds and blues in Congress. No FBI director had ever been elected so fast. He'd run the bureau from Boston while the new assistant director represented him in DC for a few months until he was fully healed. Then McCourt would pack up and ship to DC to be right in that swamp.

"Congratulations on making FBI director," I said. "Sorry I missed the ceremony in the hospital. Looked really good on TV, though. Like that of the surviving hero who'll lead us to great victories."

With a swig from a water bottle, he swallowed the pills. "Cut the bullshit, Rose. What do you want?"

I smiled. It felt incredible to be out from under his thumb. The constant pressure. The feeling of being controlled. Gone.

"I think the bigger question is what you want. I assume staying alive and holding onto your position as FBI director are at the top of that list."

McCourt narrowed his eyes. "So you're part of all this now? Them?"

"It's complicated," I said.

"There's nothing complicated about how you betrayed me. The bureau. The badge."

"You must know," I countered calmly.

A heavy silence settled over the room as I stood.

"No need to drag this out," I said. "Operations continue as usual. We catch bad guys. The only difference is, there'll be no sniffing around in the BAU or the Boston Concert Hall. That's it."

"Oh, that's it, huh?" he shot back.

"Pretty much. You can still play the big boss. But if I were you, I'd tread carefully. Your little arrangement with Luca Domizio didn't exactly go as planned. You'd better steer clear of pissing him off for a while."

His eyes flared with a mix of disbelief and fury.

"And maybe check under your car for a bit," I added. "You know, for bombs. I think Luca Domizio agreed to leave you alone, but with the mob, you never really know. From what I've gathered, he seems quite fond of the pianist you tried to have killed." I turned toward the door.

"Fucking bitch," I heard McCourt mutter as I left his office. But to me, it wasn't an insult. Not the way he said it, laced with defeat and rage. He was like a child throwing a tantrum, with no other way to vent. In this context, it was almost a compliment. Maybe the only time in my life when being called a bitch felt like one.

With a grin, I walked past the secretary. "Have a good day," I said, "and make sure he remembers to take his pills. The FBI needs him in top shape."

My smile faded as I took the stairs down to the BAU. I had texted Carl Carr's info to Leah before I'd even talked to Richter about it. And then there was the hospital, where I'd had the chance but hadn't told him about Leah and the Night Stalker. What really troubled me, though, wasn't Richter. It was why I hadn't said anything. Did I feel like I owed Leah for the McCourt incident? Or for saving my life? Or, maybe worse. Did I, deep down, support her missions, no matter what?

I was dancing with the devil now, fully caught in the tango. And the thing about dancing with the devil was that once you started, you didn't get to decide when the music stopped.

NINE

Leah

Carl Carr.

I'd been waiting in those woods for hours, watching the sun slip away behind Carl Carr's turkey farm. I was wearing a black coverall, and I'd brought my bag of goodies in case my hunch about my stalker turned out to be true. Richter was still waiting for the results of hundreds of hours of surveillance footage. But I had all I needed to visit Carl Carr and scout out the farm under the cover of night. This man had stalked me for weeks. It was time to return the favor.

As twilight faded, I followed a narrow deer path through the woods. It led straight to a field of turkey barns surrounding a small, old farmhouse.

Emerging from the woods, I was enveloped by the night sounds and smells of the farm. Soft gobbles and clucks of turkeys mixed with the faint hum of distant machinery. The air smelled like grain and turkey manure. Large holding houses loomed in the dark, their structures casting long shadows across the open fields. In the back, a meat processing facility stood out with a single bright light outside, creating a stark contrast against the darkness.

I made my way to the small, rundown farmhouse not far from the holding houses. Its white paint was peeling, and weeds grew tall around it.

I approached it, stepping carefully to avoid making any noise. Dim light from inside flickered through the gaps of a flowery curtain. I peered through the window. An old woman sat in a worn armchair and smoked a cigarette. Her face was deeply sun-tanned and lined—a testament to a life spent farming. She wore a faded pink nightgown that looked like it was from the sixties. Her eyes were fixed on the television, some old movie in black and white.

Next to her was a man in his thirties, lounging on a battered sofa. He looked unkempt, with a scruffy beard and long, oily hair. His overalls and denim shirt needed a wash. He stared at the screen, occasionally glancing at the old woman as if seeking some form of approval.

Leaving the farmhouse behind, I made my way toward the large processing facility and stepped inside. The metallic stench of meat—thick and repulsive—hit me. Despite the overhead lights buzzing faintly, the place was deserted. No workers. No cameras. Curious. Very curious.

I kept close to the wall, moving carefully, until I spotted a red door at the far end of the machinery room, where turkeys were being ground into meat. The door was reinforced, solid steel, and locked tight. Far too secure for a place like this.

Quickly, I used my tools to unlock it. Then I slipped inside. The small room was dusty and filled with cleaning supplies. To most, it would look like a janitor's closet. But that heavy steel door had me on edge. Why go to such lengths to guard a few rags and buckets?

I swept the room with my flashlight, its beam cutting through the dust. That's when I found them—faint but distinct footprints, leading to a rug in the center of the room. The prints looked like they belonged to a man about the size of the one I'd glimpsed at the farmhouse. And they stopped right at the rug.

I shut the door behind me and lifted the rug. Beneath it, I found a wooden hatch—the kind used to access hidden basements. It took some effort, but I managed to pry it open, revealing a set of wooden stairs leading down into darkness. A chill ran through me as the stench of feces and death hit, along with the cold certainty that something dark was waiting below.

I'd been right to come tonight.

And I'd be right to end whatever this was.

My flashlight illuminated the wooden stairs as I descended. Noise dampers lined the reinforced walls. When I reached the dark room at the bottom of the stairs, the reek of rotten meat hit me, forcing me to gag. But what I saw next in my flashlight's beam hit me even harder than the stench.

Fresh blood mingled with dried stains, splattered across the walls and floor in a gruesome tapestry. Metal hooks dangled from the ceiling. One of them pierced a decomposing human leg, crawling with maggots that wiggled and squirmed. I swept my flashlight to the left, revealing a long wooden table covered in tools—a blood-soaked chainsaw, a rusted axe, and a set of butcher knives, their blades stained and dulled from repeated use.

A metallic clinking of chains echoed to my right, and I spun my flashlight in that direction. The beam landed on a chained, naked woman huddled in the corner of the room, her body trembling. She blinked rapidly against the sudden brightness. Filled with fear and desperation, she murmured pitifully beneath the duct tape covering her mouth. Next to her was a large shelf containing several jars, each with a preserved human head inside it. All women, swollen and soaked from having sat in the solution for a long time. Their eyes, opened wide in horror, matched those of the woman chained to the wall. The agony of sitting here in this hell, all alone, in the dark, was unthinkable. She was still alive, but her blonde hair was sticky with blood, and it looked like someone had cut chunks of flesh from her arms and legs. The exposed areas were swollen and oozed pus.

I was about to rush over to the woman and remove the tape from her mouth when a groaning sound from the red door at the top of the stairs echoed down into the room.

Quickly, I turned my flashlight off and squeezed between old boxes under the stairs.

The light snapped on, casting a harsh glare down the staircase. A tense silence followed, as if the person above was straining to hear any sound. The wooden stairs creaked ominously above me as someone descended slowly, step by step. Each heavy footstep thudded, echoing through the quiet.

I grabbed the gun from my bag, ready to shoot. Carl Carr had probably noticed the door was unlocked. His slow, cautious steps confirmed my worries.

He was looking for me. And if he looked long enough, he'd find me.

I had only one option.

When he was right above me, I aimed the gun upward and unloaded the entire magazine through the wooden steps. He screamed as his body tumbled down the stairs. With practiced ease, I reloaded my gun and carefully emerged from my hiding spot.

I found Carl at the bottom of the stairs. He was clutching his chest and grunting in pain. But he wasn't entirely out, maybe still able to fight. I changed plans and ran over to the table with the tools. There, I grabbed the axe.

"You cunt," Carl Carr spat, his moment of brave defiance fueled by the flicker of evil in his dark eyes. "I'm not afra—"

Before he could finish, I swung the axe high above my head and brought it down on his right ankle, severing his foot. Blood sprayed across my face as his scream ripped through the air.

"I don't need you to be afraid," I said coldly, wiping the blood from my forehead. "I just need you to be in pain."

His screams filled the room, unrelenting.

"In just one strike. Would you look at that," I mumbled to myself. He was immobile but not dead. Just what I wanted.

Calmly, I checked the door at the top of the stairs. He'd locked it behind himself.

Perfect. Nobody would hear his screams.

"Please stop!" he cried.

"Shut up. We're just getting started," I said, scanning the table of tools. I spotted a roll of tape and grabbed it to cover his mouth. He was too busy sobbing over his severed foot to put up much of a fight. When he started crawling toward the stairs, I took advantage of his desperation and taped his legs together just above the stump.

He managed to worm his way to the base of the stairs, so I decided to take his arm too. My first swing missed, and it took a few chops to sever his arm at the elbow. His screams turned into desperate sobs. Then he went still.

"I hope the bastard didn't die on us," I said to the woman in the corner. Her eyes were wide with a mix of horror and satisfaction.

I checked his neck for a pulse.

"No, just passed out," I said, grabbing a rope from the table. I tied it around the stumps as a tourniquet to slow the bleeding. He'd been shot a couple of times, but from what I could see, there were only two bullet wounds—one in the shoulder and one in the leg. Neither was bleeding too badly. Technically, he could survive all this.

"Where does he keep the keys to your chains?" I asked.

The woman nodded toward the table.

It didn't take long to find them nestled between a bloody knife and a rotting finger.

For a moment, I stood there, staring at her. This was a problem. A witness. But it was too late to worry about that now. This was the first time I'd ever saved a life before taking one, and I found a strange satisfaction in it. So much so that a warmth spread through my chest—a warmth that might have been happiness. Or maybe joy?

"I'm going to remove the tape from your mouth, okay?"

She nodded, her blue eyes wide, a mix of fear and hope.

"Thank you," she choked out, sobbing the moment the tape was gone. "Thank you, my guardian angel. Thank you."

Guardian angel...

The irony hit me, considering I'd just hacked off a man's arm and foot. Then I noticed the small silver cross around her neck. She must be religious.

"I'm going to unchain you now, but you need to promise me you won't run. He can't hurt you anymore, understand?"

"Yes, I promise," she wept, her tears flowing freely.

I used the keys to release the chains from her wrists and ankles. The moment she was free, she sprang up—not to run, as I'd expected, but to throw her arms around me in a desperate embrace. The foul odor of urine and feces filled my nostrils as she clung to me, squeezing so tightly that she forced the air from my lungs. Yet that strange, warm glow inside me remained.

I stood there, my arms dangling motionless by my hips, frozen, as the naked woman sobbed into my neck, thanking me over and over again. Nobody had ever hugged me like this before.

Finally, I gently pushed her off and grabbed her by the shoulders. "I need you to focus now. We don't have much time, you understand?"

The woman nodded.

"I have two options for you," I said calmly. "We can call the police, and this monster might survive and will be arrested. The horror of all of this will publicly haunt you and your family for the rest of your life. You'll never be able to leave the house without people taking pictures of you. And the police might come looking for me."

The woman's blue eyes stared straight into mine.

"Or?" she said, her tears dying down.

"Or I'll take care of this monster. Nobody will ever find him. As of now, the police don't know who he is or what he's doing. It'll look like he just left his old life behind. People disappear all the time. And you ... you run back home and tell your family whatever lie suits you best. To explain your temporary disappearance."

Surprisingly, she didn't need time to think about it. "Kill him," she spat as her gaze wandered to Carl on the floor. "Make it painful."

I nodded. "Go now. Use the woods to get to the road. Make sure nobody sees you."

But instead of fleeing, the woman slipped her silver cross necklace over her head and placed it into my bloody, gloved hand.

"I have no use for—"

"Thank you from the bottom of my heart," she said, closing my hand around the cross. "I have two kids, and thanks to you, they still have a mom. Even if she's now a broken one, they still have her."

Then she turned and bolted toward the stairs. I watched as she snatched a dirty dress from the floor and pulled it over her head. In a flash, she was up the stairs and gone.

I stood there, clutching the silver cross necklace in my bloody fist. She'd called me an angel and hugged me. And, for a moment, it had felt ... good. But as my gaze shifted back to Carl Carr, I remembered what I truly was.

A monster.

If I had more time, I'd make Carl Carr feel every ounce of my rotten core. But time was a luxury when one was committing murder.

I walked over to my bag by the stairs, deliberately stepping on Carl Carr as if he were nothing more than a rug. He let out a pained groan and twitched slightly. In a rare moment of sentiment, I slipped the silver necklace into my bag. Not that it would suddenly make me religious or give me a warm feeling every time I saw it, but leaving it here didn't feel right.

Frowning, I pulled out my phone and dialed Richter.

He answered immediately. "Are you alright?"

"I found a woman with long blonde hair and blue eyes in Carl Carr's hidden basement. She might be your missing prostitute. She'll be home soon."

"You what?" his voice echoed back.

"I still have to deal with Carl Carr. No help needed. Resume business as usual."

"Resume business as usual? Leah, this—"

"Oh, one more thing. I got the shares to Jan Novak's company. Tomorrow, they hold a shareholders meeting, which I'll attend. I'll meet with you after that."

"Are you kidding? What the hell—"

"I don't mean to be rude, but I have to go."

"Leah, wait!"

"Don't eat turkey for a while."

"What? Goddamn—"

I hung up and turned off my phone.

Richter was upset. Of course he was. But lately, I'd found myself caring less about consequences. It was as if Jan Novak was taking hold of my mind, clouding it.

Carl Carr groaned, tearing me away from my thoughts.

I walked over to him and pulled the tape off his mouth.

"Mama ... help me," he huffed weakly.

"Stop that, you piece of shit. Your mama won't help you. But I'll make it quick if you tell me why you were following me."

After a moment of defiant silence, Carl Carr coughed up blood. He looked like he was about to pass out again, so I stepped on the stump of his arm.

"Aaaaaa—!"

"You know I can keep you alive for weeks down here. Stop by every night, just to torture you and take a piece off you inch by inch, starting with your dick."

Carl Carr whimpered like a child.

"We could even bring your mama down here. Show her your work. Make her watch. I mean, she kinda already knows what you were doing down here, doesn't she?"

He kept whimpering, so I grabbed the axe and dragged it over to him.

"Fine, let's just get to work."

"W-w-wait!" he stuttered hysterically. "The devil. The devil told me a-about you."

I sighed. "What utter nonsense." I lifted the axe high above his leg.

"Wait! No! It's true!" he screamed, finding a new will to live.

I paused.

"He sent me a letter and picture of you and warned me about you. I know it was the devil. He watches over me. Warned me. Said you turned on your own. That you're a traitor." He spat the last two words in disgust.

I almost laughed as I lowered the axe. "Turned on my own? Ridiculous. You're not my kind. You're a monster from pure darkness. I'm a monster walking in the light."

"I ... I need help." Carl started crying. "My arm. I'm bleeding. Please call an ambulance. I'm really hurt."

I lifted the axe again. "Well, aren't you slow, Carly boy. That's the whole point of it."

"Wait!" he begged beneath his tears. "I told you about the letter. What are you doing?"

"Chopping you up, of course, so I can carry you over to the meat grinder. You're too big for me to carry you. I'm petite."

"You're crazy! Somebody, help! Heeeeeeeeeeelp!"

I dropped the axe with speed onto his upper thigh. After a few strikes, I'd chopped it off.

It would take a few trips, but I ignored him as I taped his mouth shut again and began hauling his severed leg up the stairs to the meat grinder. Disposing of Carl Carr in a meat factory seemed like the most fitting end. Sure, I could leave him down here, but I didn't want the heads of the women in those jars to spend another minute in this bastard's presence.

Grinding him up would be quick and clean. No trace of him left behind. And in a sick, twisted irony, Carl Carr would finally serve life rather than take it.

Tonight, there wasn't enough time, but in a few weeks, once the dust settled, I'd try to return and bury those poor women's heads somewhere peaceful in the woods, far from this hellhole. It wouldn't be a happy ending, but in a fucked-up world like this, it would have to be enough. For now.

TEN

Liam

Rose and I were waiting in an SUV not far from the Moores' trailer. It was already three a.m., but after Leah's call, I had to see for myself if Nathalie was safe. And Rose had insisted on tagging along the moment I'd texted her.

"So, what else did she say?" Rose asked, her eyes locked on mine, concern creasing her brow.

"That's all she said. Carl Carr was taken care of. And if the woman in the basement was Nathalie, she'd be home safe soon."

Rose sighed. "So how does this work, exactly? I mean, this whole taking-out-serial-killers thing. This isn't exactly covered in the FBI training manual. So far, it seems a bit ... well, risky."

I ran my hand through my hair. It had been months since this business with Leah had started, and I still had no idea how it was supposed to work. How the hell did Larsen operate like this? Or had Leah changed? Had she gotten more out of control? Leah should have run this mission by me first. There was no pattern, no order to anything anymore, and I had a feeling Jan Novak was the reason why Leah was becoming more aggressive. But Rose didn't need to know any of that. We needed her on board without doubts—or at least with more commitment to us than against us.

"There isn't really much to it," I said. "We find bad guys. She disposes of them."

"Mm-hmm. Disposes of them," Rose said. "Just curious. What evidence do we have that Carl Carr was really a serial killer? Did she say anything about that? Because the guy in the park—"

"Yeah, let's talk about the guy in the park," I cut her off, facing her.

Rose's gaze dropped to her hands.

"Because I'm still a bit confused about all of that, to be honest. How exactly did you come by the information about Carl Carr again?"

"I ... I followed Leah after our meeting. So I could catch her stalker and get his ID. Worked out quite well, if you ask—" Her voice broke off the moment she saw the look on my face.

"Yeah. Worked out great, didn't it? Especially the part where you knew Leah stabbed the Night Stalker and decided not to mention it. I assume that was to protect her?"

Rose's lips moved as if to respond, but no words came out. Finally, she spoke. "It wasn't like that. And it's not like she needs protection. I followed her to catch her stalker. Everything else that happened ... it just happened. And I knew you two would sort it out eventually. Aren't you supposed to be a team or something? You're acting like I should know exactly how to handle situations like these. But guess what, Richter?

There's no manual on how to operate in an office with serial killer coworkers, okay? But I'm still here, no?"

I nodded. "Yes. You are."

"Then please tell me Carl Carr was the bad guy we were after because if I'm responsible for the brutal murder of some random—"

Rose stopped mid-sentence when a shadow emerged from the dark road.

Nathalie!

She was hurrying along the narrow flower path to her trailer's porch. There were only a few streetlights, which made it hard to see her face, but the limp and the way she clutched herself told a story of horror. She stopped under the porchlight, which illuminated her blood-soaked blonde hair. She was wearing a large jacket, probably given to her by someone on her way here, but her legs, exposed beneath the blood-stained mini-dress, bore what looked like deep, ragged wounds as if something had gnawed at her.

"Fucking Christ," Rose muttered, gripping the car door handle, ready to leap out.

I grabbed her arm. "Wait!"

We watched as the door opened. Mrs. Moore and Nathalie fell into each other in a tearful embrace.

"It's her!" Rose said. "I can't believe it. It's really Nathalie! Fucking Carl Carr. We gotta talk to her."

"No." I shook my head. "Nathalie didn't call the cops. It would be suspicious for us to be out here in front of her home at this time. We have to wait and see what the Moores tell us about what happened. Nathalie might never mention Carl Carr to protect Leah and her family from the media."

Rose leaned back in her seat as a loud breath escaped her lips. "This ... is nuts, Richter."

We watched as Nathalie and Mrs. Moore closed the door to the trailer.

"Pretty much," I agreed. "But it also feels pretty damn good, doesn't it? Seeing Nathalie back home. Carl Carr gone. I know it's wrong. And yet..."

Rose's gaze met mine. "It does feel pretty damn good."

For a moment, we just sat there and let the beautiful feeling of Nathalie returning home alive sink in. She had been through hell and would carry scars for the rest of her life, but she was alive. If she was half the fighter I made her out to be, they'd be alright someday.

"So what exactly happened to Carl Carr?" Rose asked. "It would be nice to retrieve the missing bodies of the other women from his farm. I have a feeling this was a thing for that sick fuck."

"I've thought about that," I said. "But we need to give this some time, let things cool down. I'll pull Cowboy off the search for the truck. In a few months, we'll come up with a plan. Maybe something like a hiker's dog finding evidence on Carr's property."

Rose nodded. "You said Leah got the shares to Jan Novak's cloud firm?"

"Yes. She'll meet us after she attends that shareholders meeting with Jan Novak."

Rose crossed her arms. "I don't want to jinx it, but things might be looking up for us."

"Amen to that," I said.

"Might even get some sleep tonight," she added, smiling faintly.

"Wouldn't that be a plot twist for these two burnt-out, emotionally drained, walking-on-the-sword's-edge FBI agents?"

She smiled. "It would, indeed."

The car engine kicked on with a roar as I turned the key. "Just don't eat any turkey meat for a while," I said.

Rose's smile vanished. "Jesus fucking Christ, you serious?"

"'You don't look a gift horse in the mouth,' my German grandmother always used to say," I said.

"I guess not," Rose responded as I pulled the car onto the road.

ELEVEN

Leah

Dressed in a hand-tailored white pantsuit and carrying a Hermès Birkin, I walked into the heavily guarded underground hallway of Obledalo Corporation. The setting felt more like a secret military base than a corporate office. My hair was styled in a sleek chignon, adding a sharpness to my look. Walking beside me was Ronald Hubble's lawyer, Jeff Higgins. He was a short, elderly man well past his prime and seemed almost out of place. We approached a massive metal door guarded by two men in black suits standing sternly in front. To the side, a young woman sat behind a desk, typing on a computer.

As soon as she spotted us, the woman jumped to her feet. "You can't be here!" she exclaimed, her voice laced with shock as the men beside her tensed, hands hovering near their weapons.

Higgins, cool and composed, retrieved a document from his suitcase and handed it to her. "This is Ms. Nachtnebel," he stated firmly, "the representative for the new owner of the Hubble family's shares in Obligato Corporation. Mr. Hubble sold them very recently. Now, tell those men to open the door or risk a lawsuit for denying a shareholder the ability to attend a corporate meeting."

The woman's eyes widened as she scanned the document. Then her gaze lifted to meet mine. "Ms. Nachtnebel, I apologize for this incident. We take security very seriously around here. I hope you understand."

"Of course," I replied smoothly.

She nodded to the guards, who reluctantly stepped aside and opened the wide metal doors.

Higgins stood still until I glanced at him. He shook his head in response.

"Only you can enter, Ms. Nachtnebel," the woman said in an apologetic tone.

When I stepped through the doors and into the grand meeting room, its sheer scale instantly struck me. Warm light from crystal chandeliers bathed the space in a soft glow, reflecting off polished mahogany walls adorned with intricate carvings. Illuminated cases lined the walls, showcasing ancient Egyptian artifacts. To the side, a sophisticated bar, stocked with top-shelf spirits, stood next to a cluster of plush leather armchairs and a velvet sofa. This cozy lounge area sharply contrasted with the imposing dark wood table gleaming under the lights in the center of the room. High-backed chairs with rich red upholstery flanked the table on either side, giving it a regal feel. To the left, four elderly men sat in impeccably tailored suits, exuding an air of arrogant authority. I recognized them immediately—America's wealthiest and most influential figures, mega-donors to politics, representing both old and new money.

On the right side of the table, three men sat beside an empty chair, presumably reserved for Hubble. At one end of the table, a larger chair was occupied by a man whose back was to me. On the opposite end sat Jan Novak. Dressed in an elegant suit, he radiated power and confidence. His sharp blue eyes surveyed the men around the table. Clearly, he was the one in charge.

As I stepped inside, the room buzzed with a heated discussion. None of them noticed my entrance.

"China slashing its cloud storage prices in half is a direct attack on Obligato," said Edward Wallace, whose tall frame and silver hair boosted his commanding presence. He owned one of the largest airplane companies in the world. His voice brimmed with urgency as he continued: "They're aiming to secure contracts with our allies. Sensitive information in China's hands would be catastrophic!"

"Absolutely," agreed Thomas Whitmore, his gruff voice matching his stout frame. He came from old money, as his family had made their fortune in the late 1800s through oil and railroads. His eyes flashed with anger behind gold-rimmed glasses. "But some of our allies are willing to risk it for a cheap price. Just like when Europe ran to Putin for his cheap oil, not even realizing the power he'd gain over them. Truly idiotic."

"We all know what happened next," said Harold Lytton, his voice low. He was a thin man, always calm, with a neatly trimmed beard. He ran a massive beef business, feeding half the world. "Putin invaded the Ukraine, and Europe had to beg the Saudis for oil while we drained America's emergency reserves to stabilize global markets and help them get through the winter. We can't let them make the same mistake again."

"Fucking idiots," snapped Richard Caldwell, whose booming voice cut through the room. His white hair and dominant presence made him hard to ignore. As heir to the world's largest pharmaceutical empire, he had the confidence of someone used to getting his way. "This isn't just about national security. It's about global security," he added, taking a sip of whiskey.

The argument intensified as I approached. It wasn't until Jan Novak rose from his chair that the room fell silent. His piercing eyes locked onto mine, betraying a mix of shock and cold calculation. All eyes turned to me.

"Well, if it isn't the world-famous Ms. Nachtnebel," Jan Novak announced, his voice slicing through the stillness with surgical precision. "I must admit, I'm quite surprised to see you ... *here.*"

"I'm here to attend the shareholders' meeting," I replied calmly.

"Ms. Nachtnebel," Thomas Whitmore said, rising to greet me with genuine warmth. He shook my hand as three other men followed suit. "That attack was awful. My wife and I were so relieved to hear you came out unharmed. She thinks you're the closest thing to Jesus. We were at Mr. Hubble's birthday concert, and being so close to the piano was an experience like—"

"I'm afraid this is a closed meeting," Richard Caldwell cut in, his tone sharp as he stood to face me. "For shareholders only. There must be a mistake. Please excuse us."

The men who had greeted me quickly returned to their seats, visibly uneasy after Caldwell's authoritative interruption.

"There is no mistake, Mr. Caldwell," I replied. "I'm here on behalf of Domizio Investment Corp, which now holds Mr. Hubble's entire share of Obligato Corporation. And with that, the empty seat at this table."

"Luca Domizio bought Ronald's shares?" muttered Thomas Whitmore, disbelief clear in his voice. "How is that possible?"

"It's quite simple," I said. "Luca Domizio wanted the shares. Now he has them."

I walked to the vacant seat amid the murmurs of the group. Jan Novak's gaze followed my movements. A smile played on his lips the entire time.

I pulled back the empty chair and was about to sit when Novak nodded subtly at Caldwell. "Why don't we welcome our new member to the table by offering your seat at the head, Caldwell?" Novak suggested. "Right across from me."

The room fell silent. Richard Caldwell, likely the wealthiest in this room after Jan Novak, was a man who had influenced and sponsored the last few presidents. He wasn't accustomed to this sort of treatment.

"My seat?" Caldwell echoed, his voice laced with confusion and disbelief. "But I own the most shares after you—nearly double what Ronald Hubble had."

"You do indeed," Jan Novak replied smoothly. "But ... I'm afraid I have to insist. As the only woman at this table, Ms. Nachtnebel should be made to feel welcome, sitting right across from me."

Caldwell scanned the room, searching for support, but found none. With a slow, reluctant motion, he began gathering his papers.

"That won't be necessary," I said, sliding into Hubble's old chair. "It's just a chair. You can sit back down, Caldwell. Let's get back to discussing China's advancement in the cloud storage industry."

Jan's grin widened as he leaned back in his seat, his attention fixed on me.

Caldwell cleared his throat, clearly irritated. "Ms. Nachtnebel, now that you're here ... maybe you'd like to enlighten us on how to solve this problem?" His voice oozed with condescension. He was trying to catch me off guard. To him, I was just a woman, out of my depth.

All eyes turned to me, brows furrowed and curious.

"Well, I might not represent enough shares to decide the matter alone," I began, "but I'd suggest raising our cloud storage prices domestically while lowering them internationally for our allies who are seriously considering China's offer."

Caldwell laughed. "We can't raise domestic prices high enough to offset the discount needed to stay competitive internationally. And cutting prices without making up for it would hurt shareholder profits unless we cut workers' benefits or salaries—something Mr. Novak strongly opposes. Any seasoned businessman knows you have to balance what you take with what you give to maintain profit margins. It's basic math. Unlike music, which is more like child's play with sounds—no real structure, no logic, just whatever feels good at the time."

A few men chuckled. I waited for them to finish.

"Quite simple math indeed, Mr. Caldwell," I replied smoothly. "Which is why we could offset the international price cuts further with a targeted tax break for the tech industry, specifically cloud storage. I estimate a point-five percent tax decrease should cover it, though it could be closer to point-forty-four percent if I'm not mistaken?"

Caldwell hesitated as the room's curiosity shifted toward him. "Are you a comedian too now, Ms. Nachtnebel? Who's supposed to fund this tax break?"

"I'm not naive enough to think it would come out of your pocket," I said. "Otherwise, you'd just accept a lower profit margin after reducing prices for our allies internationally without raising them domestically. From what I've gathered, those margins are still more than substantial. But given your company's history—such as those recent government contracts that inflated medication prices to boost profits after two record-breaking years—I'd bet you'll find a way to pull funds from a social security program to cover the proposed tax break. Food stamps. School lunches. Medicaid. Your choice. Make the poor poorer but safer, right? That's what you'll tell yourself while you sail the world on your nine-hundred-million-dollar yacht. By the way, I completely agree with the public—the large ivory dolphin sculptures placed along the railings on the first deck are a tasteless monstrosity."

The room fell into dead silence. Caldwell's face was as red as a lobster. Not that I took any pleasure in any of this. The idea that another social program would be cut just to make the rich even richer was repulsive. But this wasn't my company, and someone else would have made the same suggestion anyway. The world worked that way, and my battle was with a different kind of monsters. For now.

Caldwell opened his mouth to speak, but Jan Novak cut him off. "I see now why Luca Domizio trusted you with his seat," Jan said, a faint smile playing on his lips. "Shall we vote on Ms. Nachtnebel's proposal? All in favor, raise your hand."

Everyone in the room, except Caldwell, raised their hands.

"It's decided then," Jan said, rising from his chair. "Well done, Ms. Nachtnebel. Be sure to send Luca Domizio my regards and congratulate him on his wise choice of representation. We'll meet again next quarter."

The men stood and chatted among themselves as they scattered. I was heading toward the door when Jan Novak stopped me.

"Quite impressive, Ms. Nachtnebel."

"There's nothing impressive about greed," I replied.

"Yet here you are."

Standing close, he towered over me by nearly a head. He was slim but muscular. Not classically handsome, but his power, influence, and confidence radiated off him in waves. Even I could feel the pull. Had I not known the monster he truly was, I might have found myself drawn to him.

"I'm here for many reasons," I said. "Some of them you might not like."

"Try me. I might surprise you."

"Not many things surprise me anymore, Mr. Novak."

"Challenge accepted. Will you join us for a drink?"

"Another time," I said. "I have another engagement today. I'll see you at the next meeting."

I turned and walked away, but his footsteps followed close behind. He wasn't the type of man used to hearing the word "no."

"Let me walk you out," he said, holding the heavy metal door open for me. "It was good to see you again. It's been a while since our very interesting conversation at the Smithsonian Museum."

"It has indeed," I said. "Yet I have a feeling you saw me more often than I saw you." I locked eyes with him. He held my gaze without flinching. Unfazed and playful. Nobody ever did that except for Richter.

"May I invite you to dinner at my house this Friday then?"

I could almost hear Richter screaming *no*. That it was too dangerous. That he would come along. But I was who I was.

"I would be delighted," I said as I looked into his icy blue eyes.

Strange.

I'd thought seeing him again would spark a fire of hatred within me. He'd killed Emanuel. Shouldn't I slit his throat right now, right here, no matter the consequence? Yet as we stood there, just as we'd done back at the museum, I failed to see the monster in his eyes.

Jan Novak was truly one of a kind. A master. Of everything.

"It's settled then," he said.

"Jan!" Caldwell shouted from the metal doors. "Could we have a word, please?"

"Of course," Jan responded.

"Why do I have the feeling that I'm the root of this 'word,'" I said.

Jan chuckled. "Because you are. Ruffled quite some feathers. But you're a shareholder's representative and free to speak your genius mind. I'll handle the children. Don't worry."

I nodded.

"Friday then," he said. "I'll have my driver pick you up at your house."

"I assume you know where I live."

"Of course I do," he said, his grin vanishing.

Then he turned and disappeared through the metal doors.

For a moment, I looked down the hallway of the most modern tech facility I'd ever seen.

This dinner with Jan Novak could be the step forward we needed to gather the proof to catch him. Or it could be my end. He could kill me, and nobody would be able to prove anything.

I wondered if I should mention the dinner to Richter. I already knew he'd be against it. Yet open disagreement with him wouldn't break trust. Hiding things from him would. Especially after the Night Stalker incident. And Carl Carr.

I didn't have my phone, which I'd been forced to leave at the entrance of the building—no electronics were allowed. But as soon as I had access to it, I'd text Richter for a meeting tonight. I had a feeling it would be among our most tense ones yet.

TWELVE

Liam

"No. Absolutely not, no way," I said in a tone that should have left no room for debate. However, I was talking to Leah. "You can't meet him for a private dinner at his house. It's out of the question."

We were in her study. It was late afternoon, and Rose was late.

Leah sat behind her desk, leaning back in her chair, her eyes drilling into me with a cold, merciless stare. For a long moment, she said nothing, just watched me in silence.

"It's too dangerous," I continued when she didn't respond. "What would stop him from killing you and dropping you in some river like he did with Anna? I wouldn't know for weeks what happened to you. Maybe months. There has to be another way."

Another moment of silence stretched between us. It was broken only by the crackling of the fire in the fireplace.

"Are you done?" she finally said.

"No." And I wasn't. "After everything we've been through together. Everything we survived together. You think I'll just let you get killed over caviar and a bottle of fancy whiskey? Just keep attending those meetings. Something might come up."

Leah rose. "Something did come up, and I intend to take the chance."

I stood from my seat across from her desk. "Leah. Be honest with yourself. Don't you see how dangerous this is? This is madness."

"Of course I do. But we need to know if Jan Novak is the Train Track Killer. You said you want real evidence. I plan on delivering it to you."

"But not like this. No," I countered. I could barely control myself. How could she do this to our mission? To us as a team? Without her, our work to rid the streets of monsters was over.

"Larsen and I hunted the Train Track Killer for years before you came on board," she said. "With no leads. Nothing. He's not like you or me. Don't you understand what we're dealing with here? Do you want him to continue murdering innocent people? Like Anna. Hundreds and hundreds more of them. Gone."

This stuck me. Of course I didn't. Of course I wanted him dead as much as Leah did. But not like this.

"Besides," she continued. "If Jan Novak wanted us dead, we'd all be dead. Or at least fired. Have you ever asked yourself why he doesn't just call in a favor and have both you and Rose removed from the FBI altogether? Publish some scandal about me in every news outlet owned by his rich friends?"

"Of course I have," I shot back. "Many times. And none of it adds up."

"Then you know we're running out of time. This might be our only chance to get the evidence we need to prove he's the Train Track Killer—before he decides we're no longer fun and wipes us out. We need to move now. If I can confirm he's the killer, I can finally rid this world of one of the worst monsters ever to walk it."

The room fell into silence once more. She was right, as always. And I hated that I'd known it all along. But why was it so damn hard to let her go, knowing she might be sacrificing herself?

"Besides, if he kills me, you'll be able to connect him to the murder. I know you will. You know where I am. If I disappear, you'll go after him publicly. I'm not Anna. The world will care if I disappear. Jan Novak is powerful, but not even he can make a world-famous pianist disappear without a trace if a hungry FBI agent is on his heels. You'll get him. If anybody can, it's you, Richter. I have faith in you."

A wave of ice-cold dread washed over me, settling deep in my gut. Was this her strategy? Getting herself killed for the greater good of taking down Jan Novak? Sure. In this fucked-up world, it would be an honorable sacrifice. A killer for a killer. One life for saving hundreds. But something deep inside me couldn't accept this.

"No," I said, shaking my head. "No, Leah, please don't do this."

Her forehead furrowed as she slowly circled the desk, finally stopping in front of me. "Why defy logic, Richter? Is there another angle I fail to see that prevents you from accepting this mission?"

She stared into my eyes. Inches away from me. I could smell her perfume. I wanted to say something but just stood there like an idiot. Lost. The way she laid it out made sense. So why fight it? Had I grown attached to a killer? Was I creating some fucked-up version of Starsky and Hutch after all? But after all we'd been through together, could anyone blame me?

"No, Leah … I can't sanction this suicide mission."

Her green eyes narrowed as the air between us became suffocating. For a split second, her hand lifted, reaching for my arm. Instinctively, I stepped back as if her touch might turn me into something else—something from which I could never return. She noticed, of course. Which only made it worse.

A sudden knock on the door shattered the tension, startling us both.

Without a word, Leah crossed the room and opened the door for Rose.

"Sorry I'm late, but I had to write a shit ton of fake interview reports about the shooting at your concert to explain why Richter and I have these meetings at your house." As they walked into the study, Rose handed a few papers to Leah. "Here are the copies for you to read so our stories about the interviews match."

Leah accepted the papers and placed them on her desk. The room fell into an awkward silence.

Rose looked between Leah and me, her brows raised. "Did the old married couple fight again?" she joked, though the heavy air quickly smothered her words.

"I'll drive you so Novak knows I'm not far," I announced as I walked toward the door. "And that's what I'll do no matter what you say."

"Drive her where?" Rose asked as I walked past her.

"Leah will bring you up to speed. I'm late to pick up Josie for bowling."

Without glancing back, I left, pulling the heavy door of Leah's Beacon Hill mansion shut behind me. I made my way to my SUV, which was parked just beyond the gate. The air was still heavy with everything unspoken.

I hated how much this mission messed with me—how it angered me, worried me, made me sick to my stomach. Thoughts of Leah being raped, or drowned in some river, spun through my head. And then there was her stare. Those intense green eyes, just inches from my face.

If he laid even a finger on her—if he so much as pulled a single strand of her hair—I'd shoot him. Literally, I would.

I couldn't let my mind wander down the path of how she'd get the evidence we needed. It wouldn't come from small talk. There was only one way to confirm that he had a skin graft, and it involved him taking off his shirt. Which probably meant she'd have to take hers off too. For a monster. Forced to sell herself out like an enslaved prostitute.

My fist pounded against the steering wheel. Once. Twice. Again and again.

"Fuck," I muttered, tipping my head back against the seat and staring at the roof of my car as helplessness coiled tightly in my chest. I felt sick.

I had to do more. No, I had to do everything. This would be the first and last time Leah would risk her life for this murdering psychopath.

I had to be ready to act the moment she walked out of there alive.

Doubt weighed on me like an anvil. I was nobody compared to Jan Novak. What was I even trying to pull off? Arrest the most powerful man in the nation? It would cost me my job. But if Leah was willing to risk her life to stop this killer, to save more victims like Anna, what kind of coward was I to worry about my career?

No, the moment she had the evidence to tie him to the Train Track Killer, I'd act. No matter the cost.

And there was only one way.

With an army of loyal people. People who weren't slaves to money like Congress was. People who still gave a damn about the world. Convincing them wouldn't be easy. It would take a hell of a lot of effort. But if Jan Novak was taken down in broad daylight, that alone would send a message to his allies: cut him loose, make him too dangerous to be associated with.

It was a crazy mission, no doubt. But inside that house was a woman ready to sacrifice her life and her body to make the world a better place.

And I'd do the goddamn same.

First, I needed an ally. Someone who'd proven his loyalty to Leah more than anyone else.

Luckily, the answer was simple.

Luca Domizio.

THIRTEEN

Leah quietly took a seat behind her desk and started reading the papers I'd handed her. I studied her fancy study for a moment. The large fireplace. The antique books on the mahogany bookshelves along the walls. I walked over to one that caught my attention.

The Bible.

I pulled the large book off the shelf and opened it. It was heavy as hell. A handwritten manuscript with ornate illustrations, bound in leather with metal clasps, showcasing exquisite calligraphy and craftsmanship.

"You don't strike me as religious," I said, wondering why I was even still here. I should have left with Richter. Instead, I was wandering around as if I were more loyal to her than to him. Which concerned me to the core.

"I'm not religious," she said. "In fact, I don't put my faith in anything beyond the immense strength we all possess—the strength to achieve extraordinary things. But as you know all too well, some of those things can descend into pitch-black darkness. That's the nature of human potential. It's capable of both brilliance and horror."

I absorbed the weight of her words, my brow furrowing slightly. "Why have a copy, then?"

"This is a rare version of the Bible that includes the Lost Gospel—possibly one of the oldest fully transcribed copies in existence. There are only two like it. It reads like the most brilliant fiction novel—if you can read Aramaic."

"What's the Lost Gospel?" I asked.

"The Lost Gospel is a 1,500-year-old manuscript that was excluded from the conventional Bible. Some interpretations suggest it contains hidden references to Jesus and Mary Magdalene having a child. However, mainstream scholars and the Catholic Church largely regard it as a fictional narrative involving biblical figures rather than a historical account of Jesus's life."

"Hmm. Interesting. Well, it would make sense for Jesus to have a child..." I mumbled.

Leah looked up from the papers. "Why is that?" she asked.

"I mean ... who'd be a better dad than Jesus?"

To my surprise, Leah smiled. "I never thought about it that way."

I quietly set the book back in its place and nodded toward the door through which Richter had just walked. "So ... what was that all about?"

"I'm going to meet with Jan Novak for dinner this weekend. Richter objects, of course, but at this point, it's the only way. We might be running out of time. I don't know how much longer Jan Novak will let us interfere with his life. To be honest, it's a mystery to me why he's put up with us for so long."

I nodded.

Leah lifted an eyebrow. "No objections?"

I shrugged. "It's the most logical strategy on our end. You can always kill him if he tries anything stupid."

"Interesting," Leah said, leaning back in her chair, her eyes still on me.

I was ready for her to ask why I hadn't told Richter about her and the Night Stalker, but instead, Leah pointed at an empty glass of wine.

"Would you like some?"

I shook my head. "No, thank you. I only drink on Thanksgiving and Christmas."

"I see."

Warm memories of better times washed over me. "My mom used to drink wine only on Thanksgiving and Christmas. Every year. It drove my dad crazy when she went to the store and bought the really expensive wine. She told me that alcohol killed more good people than bullets and that this was her rare treat."

Leah filled herself a glass. "If alcohol kills good people, I have nothing to worry about," she joked.

I couldn't help but smile.

"Sounds like your mother was a wise woman, though," she added.

"She was. She was the kindest and strongest person I knew."

Had I just opened up to Leah Nachtnebel? The woman who brutally murdered bad guys? I never opened up to anybody. My memories were mine.

"Sorry. I didn't mean to sob on you," I said.

"Not at all," she responded. "I personally don't attach myself to memories, those of others or my own, but I enjoy good stories about good people."

I held her gaze for a moment before looking away. I was beginning to understand why Richter was so drawn to her. There was something about her—something that made you realize, almost instinctively, that she was different. Special.

"So you're meeting Jan Novak for dinner. Did you consider that men act irrationally when they feel cornered?"

"Yes. But I don't think Jan Novak feels corn—"

"I wasn't talking about Jan Novak," I said. "I was talking about Richter. I think he's starting to take this whole thing with you personally. Richter's the kind of man who gets attached—to memories, to people. He'd do anything for those he cares about."

She fell silent, taking a long sip from her glass. "I doubt Richter would be foolish enough to get attached to me. He doesn't see me as anything more than what I am."

I wasn't so sure about that.

"Why did you choose him in the first place, if I may ask? From what I've gathered, Larsen seemed to get the job done," I said.

She hesitated. "Larsen ... yes, his performance was satisfactory. But there were other issues with him."

"What kind of issues?"

"He was a killer. Like the ones we hunt. I gave him a chance to prove he'd truly changed, just as he'd tried to convince me. But he failed that test. Miserably. Richter, on the other hand, has qualities that Larsen lacked. Qualities..." She exhaled slowly.

"Qualities I lack. And there's no better judge than someone who truly believes in a better world. Even if that sounds like something from the back of a cereal box."

I nodded. "Fair enough. Just make sure you take into account that Richter's judgment might be clouded with sentiment." I turned toward the door. "Thank you for the drink offer."

She remained silent as I made my way out.

And with that, our plan to take down the Train Track Killer was set in motion.

A genius mind would meet another. A killer would meet another killer.

As I walked back to my car, the sun faded into strong orange hues across the sky. I had no idea how any of this would end. But I'd ride it out. As my brother always said, we only get to see what happens if we don't quit.

FOURTEEN

Liam

I pushed open the heavy wooden door of the Italian restaurant. The warm scent of garlic and herbs welcomed me as I stepped inside. Dim lighting gave the bustling dining area a cozy atmosphere.

The carpet muffled my footsteps as I made my way to the back room.

Looking sharp in a tailored suit, Luca Domizio sat at a round table covered with a white tablecloth. He was eating pasta and sipping red wine across from an older man who was enjoying the same meal.

As I approached, Luca looked up and dabbed at the corner of his mouth with a white napkin.

"The FBI seems to be rekindling its old flame for me," Luca said, his voice smooth but cold. "I didn't like it then, and I don't like it now. I suggest you leave before I call my lawyer and have you fired."

"Don't flatter yourself. It's hardly a spark," I said. "But you might want to hear what I have to say."

He looked me over, unimpressed. "I doubt it."

"We have a mutual acquaintance ... who needs help."

Luca leaned back in his chair, studying me for a moment. "Antonio, give us a minute," he finally said.

"Of course. I'll get more wine from Luigi." Antonio stood and cast an arrogant glance my way as he walked past, then closed the door behind him.

"If you think your relationship with our mutual friend will impress me or make us allies, you're wrong," Luca said. "I'm aware of her odd fondness for you, but frankly, I neither understand nor share it."

I sat down across from him. "Good. Because, frankly, I don't understand or share her fondness for you. But I'm not here for myself. I'm here for her. She's in serious danger, and the fact that you took out McCourt and secured the shares for her tells me you might be willing to help. So can we cut the bullshit? I don't have much time."

Luca sipped his wine. "I deny everything you just said. I had nothing to do with McCourt's shooting."

I sighed, fearing this trip would be for nothing.

"But," he added, "I'll admit, we do share a very special friend. She asks for favors when it suits her. I don't worry too much about it. Her judgment has always been exceptional. A true genius. I prefer to stay out of things unless she asks me directly. And when she does, I'll do whatever is needed."

"Fair enough. But things have changed a lot in the past few months. A threat has emerged—someone with both the power and the will to harm her. And, as crazy as it sounds, this person might be her equal in every way."

"You're speaking of Jan Novak, aren't you?" Luca said, his voice serious.

"Jan fucking Novak," I confirmed.

He pressed his lips together, then sighed. "A very powerful and dangerous man indeed. People look at me and think I'm the bad guy. The truth is, there are plenty of men like me out there. But Novak ... men like him are rare, maybe one in a generation. It would be wise to stay far away from him. Even people like you and me."

"Well, as you know by now, she didn't."

A flicker of despair flashed in his eyes. "No, she didn't. And if that woman ever made a mistake, this might very well be it. But as I said, Leah writes the rules for her life. Unless she asks me, there's nothing I can do about that, or I would have already."

"Fine," I said, standing. "Just remember that I tried. When we find her face down in a river a few months from now, stiff, cold, and blue. Remember that I was here, trying to save one of the greatest musical virtuosos of our time, taken from this world—and from you—by a man who could have been stopped. Because whatever you think you know about Novak doesn't even scratch the surface of what he's truly capable of."

Luca's eyes sparkled dangerously at me.

"Funny," I continued, my voice dripping with sarcasm as a chuckle escaped. "Here I was, thinking Leah Nachtnebel's music might be the last thing that gets you excited when you open your tired old eyes in the morning, still searching for reasons to drag yourself out of bed. Years of murder can dull the senses, make you feel dead inside. So I figured you'd go to great lengths to protect that last real spark in your lonely life. Your kids have cut you off, haven't they? No wife stuck around. But what do I know? Maybe there's still enough in your fancy, empty life to keep you jolly. Plenty of pumpkin patches in full swing, eh? Hardly a match for the melodies of a prodigy like Leah. But then again, what would a peasant like me know about the finer points of life?" I turned, ready to leave.

"Wait," Luca called after me.

I paused, then slowly sat back down, a smirk of victory tugging at my lips.

"What do you want?" he demanded.

"Thought you'd never ask." I took a deep breath. "I'm ... planning to arrest him."

A sudden, deep laugh erupted from Luca. "Jan Novak? Absurd. You might as well try to arrest the president."

"If the president turns out to be a serial killer as well, I just might do that," I said.

Luca's laughter faded. His eyes narrowed as he studied me with newfound curiosity. "If you think Novak is the first sick fuck among them, you're too naive for that badge you flash around," he said. "Most powerful and rich men have some sort of disgusting hobby, and most of them never pay the price for their actions." He shrugged. "The law doesn't apply to the ultra-rich, just like in the days of kings and their subjects."

"Maybe so, but you see, in this case, Novak is messing with the wrong peasant. With enough public involvement, even a commoner like me can make quite a fuss. And as fate would have it, something more powerful than kings and queens has formed in this world. Social media. A direct voice to the people. If you gather enough of us, even kings have to care about the laws again."

Luca frowned. "You want to start a public war with Novak?"

I grinned. "Picture a huge crowd of cell phones pointing straight at him. An army of police officers and FBI agents at my back. Not even Jan Novak or the president could keep that spectacle secret."

"You're really serious about this," Luca concluded, almost in admiration.

"I am."

He shook his head. "Seems like a huge fucking headache if you ask me. Why not just get rid of Novak in, well, simpler ways?"

"That would be the easier method, yes. But it could also complicate things. Nothing is as it seems with Jan Novak. So far, he has held all the cards in his hands. I need to talk to him, force him to make a mistake. I'm an FBI agent, not Al Capone. I can't just start shooting suspects without proof—proof that I need now. All of our lives could be in great danger—hers, other agents', mine, and ... my daughter's. There's no time left for games."

Our eyes met.

"A public arrest of Jan Novak," Luca said. "A spectacle like that would raise a lot of questions and draw attention. Surely, it would also be a quick way to make a lot of enemies for very little return. All this might go nowhere."

"The media brought Epstein down. And he had some powerful sickos on his little island too."

"Indeed he did. And I wish you luck with your plans. But I don't see how a simple construction company owner like myself could be of help in any of this."

"Simple construction company owner, huh? Didn't we say no more games?"

Luca grinned. "We did."

"Good. Then let me tell you how you can help. I need you to have a large group of people ready at the scene of the arrest. Filming every second of it. Saving it online to any data storage company that doesn't use Obligato. As a weapon for the media and social media apps."

"You could pay any homeless fifty bucks to record the arrest. You don't need me for that."

"I need people who are willing to treat the arrest and evidence with the utmost ... well, respect. People who can be trusted to post the evidence on every social platform in this world or delete it. People who do what they're told no matter what."

Luca pondered this for a moment, then narrowed his eyes as he fixed his gaze on me. "But that's not all you need, is it? You need something else from me." He took a sip of his wine. "No more games, remember?" he added.

"You're right." I took a shallow breath, my words catching in my throat. "I ... I also need to know how far your arms reach into the Secret Service."

"The Secret Service?" Luca raised an eyebrow. "Are you planning your crazy mission at the White House or something?"

"No, of course not," I replied.

"Then why mention the Secret Service?"

"The location of the arrest might be tricky. We'll need to strike during a private fundraiser. Jan Novak keeps a low profile, mingling only with the ultra-rich and influential. The next fundraiser that could draw him in might have some very big names on the guest list—potentially as big as the vice president."

Luca shook his head. "Well, in that case, I don't think I can help you. It's only logical that some of my acquaintances will be there. Bullets could fly, and I'm not eager to turn allies into enemies. Dead business partners aren't exactly profitable."

"Nobody will get hurt. That's why I'm here. In case the vice president will be there, I need the CIA to stand down. Focus on getting him out of there. Prevent him from helping Novak so the arrest can take place."

"This is madness. Even if the CIA stands down, what about the police and your own men? Won't they listen to the vice president if he tells them to stop this nonsense?"

"I'll handle the police and the FBI."

Luca sighed. "Let's say, against all odds, you manage to pull this off. David hits Goliath one more time with his little slingshot. Have you thought about the consequences for yourself? A mission this reckless would be career suicide. You'd kiss your badge goodbye. You might end up in prison. Or worse, dead. And if by some miracle you survive, I couldn't risk having you around talking. Do you understand what I'm saying?"

I met his gaze. "I do. But Novak ... if he is who I think he is, someone has to stop him. Not just for Leah but for many others. Including my daughter. Nobody touches my daughter. Nobody. Do you understand?"

Luca folded his hands in his lap as he studied me.

"Nobody will ever know you were involved if that's what you're worried about," I said.

"Don't be ridiculous," he scoffed. "Very few things worry me, and upsetting a bunch of rich old men isn't one of them."

"Then help me save her."

Silence fell between us.

"Leah..." he finally said. "She knows nothing about this, does she? You see how this could feel like a betrayal. That's a risk I can't take. Not again." He looked away. The weight of past mistakes hung between us.

"I'll tell her everything before the mission. I promise."

He nodded slowly. "Still, for now, I won't be part of your Rambo fantasy."

I frowned.

"But," he added, "if you somehow manage the impossible and rally enough fools at the FBI and police to turn fiction into reality, come see me again. I've been known to change my mind about things that interest me. And I have to admit, your crazy mission is ... very interesting."

I grinned. He was right. This was crazy. I knew it. He knew it. But crazy might be the only weapon I had against Jan Novak, and Luca was sharp enough to see that my plan might be the only option.

I was by the door when I turned one last time. "Thank you."

"Don't thank me yet," Luca replied. "But do grab some pasta on the way out. It's the best in town."

FIFTEEN

I wore a red cocktail dress that hugged every curve, with matching heels and a daring slit up my leg. My hair was pulled into an elegant bun. My makeup was flawless, and diamond jewelry caught the light as I moved.

The crisp autumn breeze brushed against my skin as I pulled my cashmere coat tighter around me. As I stepped out of my townhome, the limousine that Jan Novak had sent pulled up to the curb. Before I could reach it, I spotted Agent Richter leaning against the hood of his black SUV, parked just behind the limo. He was in his usual FBI suit, his badge on full display.

The limo driver got out and glanced between me and Richter, looking confused.

"Thank you, but I already have a ride. We'll follow you," I said.

The driver nodded and got back into the car.

Richter's eyes moved over me, concern flickering across his face. Without a word, he opened the passenger side door for me, then got behind the wheel. I slid into the passenger seat, and we followed the limousine.

The tension in the SUV was thick, and the silence between us stretched on.

"You got a gun in there, right?" Richter finally said, nodding toward my red purse.

"That and a few more things," I replied.

He nodded. Silence fell again.

"Are you upset with me?" I asked, glancing at him as he focused on the road.

"I'm not upset, Leah. I'm worried. What if he hurts you? Kills you? You said it yourself. Jan Novak is unlike anyone else. Nobody knows what's going on in the head of a psychopath like him."

"I might have some insight into that," I replied.

"So enlighten me. What exactly are you after tonight?"

The scar from a skin graft, I almost said but stopped before I had to explain how I planned to get that information from him.

"I'm ... not sure yet. But I have a feeling he invited me for a reason. Novak doesn't strike me as a man who wastes time. This might be our only chance, Richter. We've gotten almost nowhere. The shareholders meeting was supposed to get us a lead. Here it is."

He exhaled, the sound long and frustrated. "I was hoping for something ... different."

"Me too."

"Just promise me you'll kill him the moment things feel off."

"That's a promise I can easily make," I said, smiling faintly.

The tension lifted slightly as he smiled back. "Good. I won't be far. If Jan Novak tries anything stupid, it'll be the easiest shot I've ever taken."

"I'll keep that in mind," I said.

We followed the limousine out of Boston, then turned onto a narrow, private road lined with dark trees. After a few more minutes of driving, we'd passed all the other houses in the area.

"Looks like private property. God, this is huge. Right out of Boston, it must be millions," Richter said as we pulled up in front of a large brick mansion that looked straight out of Downton Abbey.

"My estimate would be around a hundred million dollars."

Richter shook his head as we stopped in front of large marble stairs leading to wide-open double doors. Burning torches lined the pathway as if this were an episode of The Bachelor. At the top of the stairs stood Jan Novak, dressed in an elegant tuxedo. I noticed Richter's hand clutch the steering wheel tightly.

"Richter ... don't. It'll be for nothing, and he'll get away."

Richter exhaled, nodded, and got out of the car. He opened the door for me before Jan Novak, who was already descending the stairs, had the chance. I stepped out, watching as their eyes met.

"Agent Richter," Novak said with a smile. "I didn't realize you'd be joining us tonight. I'll have another plate set at the table."

"That won't be necessary," Richter said before I could respond. "I'm just the driver." He turned to me, his tone shifting. "I'll be close by. Call if you need anything." Without warning, he pulled out his phone and snapped a photo of us. The flash momentarily blinded Novak. "For the album," Richter added with a smirk. "Uh-oh. Caught you mid-blink."

Novak smiled faintly, then extended his arm toward me. "Shall we?"

I threw Richter a glance before I locked arms with Novak, who led me up the stairs.

Inside, the grand entrance hall was even more imposing than I'd imagined it would be. Vaulted ceilings soared overhead, and frescoes of mythic scenes stretched across the walls. The polished marble floors reflected the flickering light from candles mounted along the walls. Instead of the knight's armor that one would expect in such a grand space, ancient Egyptian artifacts dominated the room. Their golden hues cast a warm glow over everything.

Novak noticed my curious gaze as I took in the unusual decor. "You know how fond I am of Egyptian history," he explained, his voice echoing slightly in the expansive hall. "My collection is the biggest in the world."

I stopped in front of a large golden mirror shaped like an ankh. It had a smooth oval top and cross-like arms. Its gold frame gave off an ancient feel. "You seem to be especially taken with the ankh symbol," I said. "It represents a mirror, doesn't it?"

"It does indeed," Jan Novak replied. "A window to our souls, exposing who we truly are behind all the smiles and frowns, the shouting and laughing, the words spoken in truth and the ones in lies."

I nodded slightly. "What do you see, Mr. Novak, when you look in the mirror?"

"A man who's getting older," he joked. "But please, call me Jan."

He led me farther into the mansion. Eventually, we stopped at a large dining hall set for an intimate dinner: candles flickering, silver cutlery shining, and wine glasses catching the light.

"And beyond that?" I pressed. "What does it show about your soul?"

Jan pulled out a chair for me and leaned in close to my ear. "That's a secret for another time. We don't want to cut dinner short before it's even begun, do we?"

I watched as he walked to a smaller side table where various dishes were laid out—an assortment of simple yet elegant foods. He picked up two plates, already prepared, and set one in front of me before taking his seat. Then he poured red wine into our glasses.

"Everything here is grown in my own gardens," he explained. "I prefer simple, well-prepared food over the fancy trash they serve at a Michelin star restaurant."

I was surprised to find the starter was a basic garden salad.

"I sent the staff away so we could talk freely," he continued. "But that also means I'm your waiter tonight. I hope you'll enjoy the vegetarian menu. I know you like mushrooms and watermelon, so the chef prepared a cold watermelon soup and mushroom risotto for the main course."

A chill ran down my spine. Mushroom risotto was the first meal I'd ever shared with Emanuel. Was this just a coincidence?

"Thank you. I do like mushrooms. It's almost as if you know me so well," I said.

He gave me a small nod and sat across from me. "So how did the famous Ms. Leah Nachtnebel end up on the board of a tech company?" He sipped his wine before starting on the salad.

I took a bite myself. It was easily the freshest, most flavorful salad I'd ever had. The herbs were likely picked only hours ago, and even the lavender vinaigrette tasted homemade.

"My interest is more in the company's owner," I said, wiping my mouth with a napkin before taking a sip of wine. I placed the glass back on the table. "Eagle Cabernet Sauvignon 1992," I noted. "You shouldn't have."

Jan raised his glass. "Only the best for my daring pianist, who's going to such great lengths to uncover mysteries no one else would dare to dream about."

Our eyes met. "And what secrets would that be ... Jan?"

Jan rose to his feet and cleared the starter to place the mushroom risotto in front of me. For a moment, I stared at it, memories of Emanuel flooding me. Where was the rage? The hatred I'd felt every second before I looked into Jan's eyes for the first time at that museum? In some ways, it felt like a betrayal.

"Agent Richter," he said, taking his seat across from me again. "That's quite interesting company to keep. Is it business-related? Personal?"

My eyes met his. "It's nothing of the romantic sort. But my relationship with him is a secret I'll keep tonight, as you seem to guard so many."

"Touché," he said with a charming smile.

We started the course. It was outstanding—the food, at least. Not so much my attempts at getting anything useful out of him.

"Carl Carr," I said, deciding to go straight at it. "Does that name ring a bell?"

Jan briefly furrowed his brows, then continued eating. He held his fork elegantly as if he were some sort of duke. "Why do you ask?"

"I was wondering if we have some acquaintances in common."

Jan's gaze flickered. He appeared to be considering whether to cut through the bullshit. Then he leaned back in his chair and took a slow sip of wine. "I know many people. I'm certain you do as well. Carl Carr ... hmmm. It's almost like it rings a bell, but then it slips me."

This was going nowhere. I placed my napkin onto my plate to signal that I was done with dinner. His eyes followed the gesture, and he quickly rose.

"Do you know how to dance?" he asked.

"I don't dance."

"I'll teach you." He walked over and offered me his arm. I accepted and followed him into a gigantic library where a fire crackled in a large stone fireplace. Slow jazz music played from speakers in the walls.

Jan guided me to the center of the room, then placed one hand gently on my bare back. The other one wrapped around me. Pulling me close, he began swaying us side to side, leading me into a slow, careful dance. I caught the scent of his expensive aftershave—rich with notes of cedar and leather.

"I hope you don't mind the music choice, but I'm personally not a big fan of classical music."

"Not at all," I said, resting my hand on his chest. I could feel the lean muscle even through his tuxedo. This—between the fireplace and the dancing—was headed in only one direction, and I wasn't going to stop it. Talking had gotten us nowhere.

"I apologize if I'm a bit rusty," he said, his hand gently moving up and down my back. "I haven't danced since my divorce."

"You're quite good at it," I replied. "Just another hidden talent of yours."

"I'm trying very hard to impress you. Something extraordinary brought you back into my life, and I'm not going to sit by like I did after we met at the museum." He pulled me closer, his chest pressing against mine. "I know you won't believe me, and I almost can't believe it myself, but our meeting back then—it really was by chance on my end."

I tilted my head back, searching his eyes. I couldn't tell if he was lying.

"Do you believe in fate?" he asked, leaning in, his lips almost brushing mine.

"I don't," I replied just before he kissed me. His kiss was full of desire: confident and sure.

I should have felt repulsed. Angry. Or at the very least guilty. Something uncomfortable. But all I felt was the usual emptiness.

And lust.

That unmistakable heat rising between my legs. It had been too long since I'd allowed myself to feel anything close to pleasure. Months, to be exact. And for someone like me, a psychopath, repressing primal urges for too long could be dangerous.

I caught sight of the couch near the fireplace.

Without a word, I pushed him backward onto it. He landed in a sitting position as I climbed on top of him, spreading my legs over his hard cock.

He grabbed my hips eagerly, guiding me as I started moving against his erection. Quickly, I began unbuttoning his shirt, my breath shallow with anticipation.

The scar ... the reason I was here.

Unbuttoning Jan's shirt was taking too long, so I tore it open, sending buttons flying. As he sat beneath me, bare-chested, everything stopped. My eyes searched his chest, where I expected to see the bullet wound.

No scar.

I checked higher, near his upper chest. Still nothing.

I searched his skin again and again, but all I found were faint patches of discoloration, barely noticeable, stretching across his chest, over his shoulder, and up toward his neck. It could have been anything—a healing sunburn or natural discoloration from birth.

If this was a skin graft, it was a true masterpiece.

"Impossible," I muttered. I knew I'd shot him in the shoulder. I was sure of it. There was no doubt in my mind, not even now.

My gaze dropped to a small scar on his lower abdomen, no more than four inches long. But that couldn't be it.

"Did you find what you were looking for?" Jan asked, confidence dripping from every word. He didn't move an inch.

In silence, I stared at the small scar, frozen. Defeated.

"A parting gift from my father," he continued calmly. "When I tried to stop him from stabbing my mother. One of many times, unfortunately."

I looked into his eyes. For the first time, I saw something. There were feelings there, flickering in the depths. Jan wasn't dead inside like I was. He was a monster but one who could still feel.

"Maybe ... I'm not the man you think I am," he said, his voice softer now.

I should've left. Right then. Instead, I stayed, my thoughts drifting to the hardness pressing between my legs. For a shameful moment, the urge to fuck him crept in. The need for release, for something, anything, was almost unbearable. I craved the sensation, the quick thrill of getting off. It had been too damn long since I'd let myself feel pleasure.

Jan groaned, gripping my hips and pulling me closer. I was about to give in, ready to let it happen, when thoughts of Richter flashed through my mind. Guilt hit me like a truck, mixing with the shame that finally, finally washed over me.

I felt something.

At least for Richter, if not for myself or Emanuel.

Jan's hand moved to his zipper.

I rose abruptly, stepping away from him. Emotionless, I adjusted my dress, making myself presentable again. "You might fool the world, but I know who you really are," I said, grabbing my purse from beside him.

He calmly zipped up his pants. With a faint grin, he sat there, watching me with those same eyes—like I was exactly where he wanted me.

For a moment, I considered grabbing the gun from my purse and putting a bullet in his head. It wouldn't mean a damn thing to me. But with the little I had on Novak, that might end my relationship with Richter—and with it, our partnership, which I wasn't ready to lose.

"Thank you. That was quite an interesting evening," I said, turning to make my way to the double doors.

Of course, he didn't chase me. "Oh, we've only just begun," he called out as I strode through the grand entrance hall and out the door.

As I descended the wide steps, I was surprised to find Richter leaning against the SUV, waiting. He looked at me with a frown.

"Let's go," I said, climbing into the car with him.

We drove in silence for a few minutes until we hit the main road. Finally, Richter cleared his throat, careful, hesitant. "Please tell me it's him so this wasn't all for nothing."

"It is," I replied, not a single doubt in my mind.

"Did he admit it? Or did you ... see the scar?"

I shook my head.

"Fuck," Richter muttered, gripping the steering wheel tighter. "Fuck!" He said it louder this time, his hand raking through his hair—something I'd seen him do a hundred times by now.

"It gets worse," I said, my voice steady. "The way he spoke to me. He knows who we are. He knows everything. I'm sure of it."

"Then it's time for us to act," Richter said, urgency creeping into his voice.

I turned to him. "What do you mean?"

"I mean the time for games is over. I mean it's time to make things uncomfortable for him. Create a rift in his perfect world. A rift so big it'll hit his closest allies. Distance them from him. Push him to make a mistake."

"And how are you planning to do that?" I asked.

He was hesitant, then nodded. "An open arrest. In front of the whole world."

I stated the obvious. "That's impossible. We don't hold that power over Jan Novak. Not even the FBI holds that power over him. At this point, nobody does."

"You're right. The FBI doesn't hold that power. At least not by itself. But with allies, it can be done. It will be done. The whole country will watch as Jan Novak is dragged away in handcuffs. We'll put it all over the news and social media. If we shout loud enough, people will notice."

"You'd lose your job overnight."

"I'm not worried about my damn career. I'm worried about my daughter. And ... other people I care about."

This was madness.

Our eyes met. "Richter, please listen to me. Arresting him in broad daylight—"

"We did it your way, Leah. Now we do it mine."

This plan was impulsive. Almost impossible to pull off. I opened my mouth, but Richter was faster.

"How much longer do you think we have before we start finding more corpses in the river? A nice little ankh carved next to them."

I stayed quiet, letting his words sink in.

"Exactly. After tonight, can you really say he won't hurt us? That it won't be Josie we find floating facedown in a river next? He's playing us, Leah. He probably even knew you'd be looking for that scar. Hell, I wouldn't be surprised if he sent Carl Carr to kill you."

He wasn't wrong. Novak was in control of this game—setting the rules, toying with us for as long as it amused him. I'd thought coming here would get me answers. Instead I'd left with more questions than I could count. Questions like why I still couldn't see the monster in him. Why his touch hadn't repulsed me. Though it hadn't made me feel warm and safe, either. But I'd almost fucked him like some wild animal.

"Do you trust me?" Richter's voice broke through my thoughts, his tone serious.

Our eyes locked.

"Do you?" he asked.

Trust? I'd never trusted anyone. Not even myself. But Richter...

"I do," I said, realizing in that moment that it was true. "But if we go through with this arrest, he'll come after all of us. And he won't hold back."

Richter nodded, his grip on the wheel tightening again. "Let him come. I'd rather face him head-on in a fist fight, knowing he's coming, than be caught guessing. I'll have a bullet with his name carved into it, ready for him. Hell, I'll carve an ankh right next to where this asshole drops dead." He exhaled sharply, shaking his head. "Let's take him the fuck down. All we need is one slip-up when we question him. Turn him into the Epstein of murder in the public's eyes. Make him nervous. Corner him for once." He glanced over at me, his eyes hard. "Because you were right about one thing. We're not the predators in this hunt. And if you're not the predator on a killer's playground, there's only one outcome."

"Death," I said, my voice flat.

"Death," he echoed before silence swallowed the car once again.

SIXTEEN

Liam

The dimly lit meeting room buzzed with tension. Chief Murray, stocky and weathered, sat at the long table, his eyes sharp with the same no-nonsense attitude I'd seen during the College Snatcher case. Beside him, Lieutenant Colonel Jason Lewis sat rigid, military discipline carved into his posture. He'd been the one to recover Harvey Grand's charred remains from Ocean City. McCourt, sitting farther down, was silent, his simmering frustration clear in every glance.

Agent Rose sat alongside them. All eyes were locked on me.

As I stood at the head of the table, their stares felt as heavy as lead. Behind me, the evidence board displayed Jan Novak—elegant, composed—as well as the gruesome photos of the train track murders, each marked by his twisted ankh symbol.

The air felt stifling, and the untouched water bottles on the table only heightened the tension.

Murray's voice cut through the room. "So you're telling me this Great Gatsby wannabe is a serial killer dumping people on train tracks? Why the hell haven't I heard about this?"

I kept my voice steady. "The investigation's been kept quiet because Novak is extremely well connected. He's as powerful as the president. His company manages data from Granny's doorbell camera all the way to secret military bases."

"And he has access to all this information?" Chief Murray asked.

I nodded. "He does."

"Is it safe to talk here then?" Lieutenant Colonel Lewis asked, concern lining his features.

Rose shot a glance at McCourt. "The FBI recently ended its contract with Obligato and switched cloud storage providers," she informed us. "It was quite a fight with some members in Congress, but we managed to pull it off."

"And your evidence links him to the crimes?" Murray leaned back in his chair. "In over fifty years on the job, I've never seen anything this insane."

"It does," I replied. "Unfortunately, we live in a world that's produced monsters like Hitler and Dahmer. As crazy as it sounds, it's real."

Lieutenant Colonel Lewis frowned, disbelief etched across his face. "I've been to war more times than I can count. To think a monster like this could hide behind greedy U.S. government officials ... what the fuck was it all for?"

"For the people," Rose cut in. "The same people we're trying to protect by taking down Jan Novak."

"That's all well and good," Chief Murray said, his voice heavy with skepticism. "But if what you're saying is true, how the hell are we supposed to stop him? Any arrest would be blocked by his powerful friends. The evidence we've got might be enough to haul Bobby from down the street in for questioning, but not a man like Novak."

"We're not entirely powerless," I said, locking eyes with McCourt as he pressed his lips together in frustration. "We're part of the system that protects him, and right now, Novak's not getting any sanctuary from the FBI. With this meeting, I'm hoping he won't find refuge with the Massachusetts police or at Hanscom Air Force Base either. It's the closest base to Boston, and it would be responsible for any airborne aid requested during an arrest."

The room fell silent again.

"This mission is a death sentence for my career," McCourt spat, anger flashing in his eyes.

"And 'no mission' is a death sentence to our integrity," I snapped back.

Our brief clash caught discreet glances from Lewis and Murray.

"Look at this man," I said, pointing at Novak's picture. "He's likely one of the deadliest serial killers in history. He's killed indiscriminately—men, women, the young, the old. Who knows when he'll start targeting children? We all have families. Imagine someone you love being laid out on train tracks, knowing the killer walks free. Have you seen what a train does to a body? I spared you those pictures today, but one family found parts of their son's body a mile down the tracks from where the crime happened."

I took a breath, steadying myself, then continued. "I called this meeting because the FBI won't sit back while this monster kills like it's a stroll through Boston Common. We swore to protect the people of this country from enemies, foreign and domestic. Jan Novak is one of the worst domestic threats we've ever seen."

I gestured to the door. "If you want to walk out and save your career, I won't hold it against you. Do it now before we get into the details. I get it. I have a kid who needs a roof over her head too. But remember, I called you because you can make a difference and more so because I trust you. And I trust that when Novak's pile of bodies keeps growing, you'll regret not doing everything you could to stop him. Right now, to achieve that, we need to arrest him for questioning."

The silence in the room felt weighty. For a moment, I thought Murray would get up and leave, but he just leaned back, deep in thought.

Rightfully so.

Here I was, asking these men to risk their careers. Their public images. Their legacies. But stopping Jan Novak was more than just a mission or duty. It was the only way.

"So what do you propose?" Lieutenant Colonel Lewis asked.

Rose got up and handed a printout to the three men. "Our greatest weapon in this arrest will be the public eye. Jan Novak is attending a private fundraiser near Provincetown. Senator Wheezer will be there, along with the … vice president."

"The vice president?" Chief Murray repeated, his wrinkled forehead creased with shock.

"Yes," I said. "But that'll work to our advantage. We need to let Jan Novak's allies know that associating with him can cost them their elections. We need to make him nervous. Corner him. And to do that, we need to get as high up in the swamp as we can. A few senators won't send a very strong message."

"How do we make sure this won't end up in a shootout between us and the Secret Service?" Murray asked. "Because I'm not willing to stop a murderer by becoming one."

For a second, I let his words sink in. My eyes briefly met Rose's.

"We have a source in the Secret Service," Rose said, "who will make sure the agents on the ground pull the vice president out the moment we arrive. He won't be around to possibly interfere with Novak's arrest."

Chief Murray nodded slowly. "Senators depend on police protection. And since Provincetown's in Massachusetts, that protection falls to me."

I met his gaze in agreement.

"We're hoping Hanscom Air Force Base will stay unresponsive to any requests from Novak's allies," Rose said. "No troop movements, no air support. You're the closest base, and it would buy us some time."

"We'd also need a police helicopter to retrieve the target and drop us off at a location that we'll communicate to the pilot on the scene," I said. "The police use helicopters daily. If we were to request one through the FBI, it could raise some eyebrows."

"What about witnesses?" Lieutenant Colonel Lewis asked. "If your goal is to make this a talked-about arrest, it won't work. Staff at these high-level events sign non-disclosure agreements, and no phones are allowed."

"Our mentioned ally will arrange for a catering service we can ... well ... trust," Rose said. "The source will take over the contract from the current catering service with an offer they can't refuse."

I almost laughed at the irony of Rose using those words on a mission involving a mob boss.

"We have only one shot at this," I said. "If we don't get anything from Novak out of the interrogation or the media doesn't pick up on this, then he walks." I put my hands on my hips, a silent gesture of frustration. "And we'll all be fired. Ruined. Our careers destroyed beyond redemption."

McCourt sighed loudly and shook his head, but he held strong. His eyes met those of Chief Murray and Colonel Lewis, who leaned forward on the table, deep in thought.

"So..." McCourt drawled, his voice dripping with doubt, "how sure are you, really, that Jan Novak is the Train Track Killer?"

I thought about the murky waters of the gunshot wound, the ankh symbol and Novak's strong connection to it, the name of his company. But above all, I thought about Leah, the smartest person I knew. I'd asked if she trusted me, and she'd said yes. And this street went both ways. I trusted not only her judgment but my own gut feeling. I'd seen something in his eyes the night I'd dropped off Leah at his fancy mansion. Something that told me, as clear as the blue sky, that Jan Novak was the Train Track Killer.

"I..." I paused. "I'd stake my career on it. If he's the killer—and I know he is—I'll get the truth out of him during that interrogation, and we'll save countless lives."

"And if you're wrong?" McCourt shot back.

"If he's not the Train Track Killer, he can cry about his arrest to his thousand-dollar-an-hour therapist and sail off on his billion-dollar yacht to find closure. No real harm done. At least my career would have been gambled on something worth losing it over. Simple as that. *Que sera, sera.* But I'll sleep at night knowing I did the right thing."

Lieutenant Colonel Lewis started nodding as if he'd just come to a conclusion. "I can only speak for myself," he said, "but when I joined the Air Force, I did it to serve the people of this country. Not to protect a bunch of rich sick fucks hurting the people I swore to protect." Something shifted behind his eyes, a darkness settling there. "When they made my airmen carry that bastard Harvey Grand's remains like he was some kind of fallen hero, they took something from us. Our honor. Our pride. At least in the public's eyes. My men and their families received hate messages—hell, even death threats. All because of some dirty politicians. So if I go down for taking out another sick fuck that these dirtbags are trying to protect, at least I'll go out with a big fucking smile on my face."

I gave him a firm nod.

Chief Murray let out a heavy sigh and shook his head. "Fuck it. As crazy as this is ... I'm in."

Relief washed over me. Rose and I exchanged a glance. For the first time, I noticed the beads of sweat glistening on her forehead.

"Under one condition," Murray added. "I'm coming along on the mission, so the blame falls on me, not my men."

"Of course," I said. "The same goes for our agents. They'll simply follow my orders with no more details other than the target. No shot will be fired, no matter what."

Chief Murray and Lieutenant Colonel Lewis exchanged a look, then turned toward McCourt. He rose slowly, leaving the papers untouched on the table. "It's settled, then," he said. "Gentlemen, good luck. We're gonna fucking need it." He didn't wait for a response before striding out of the room.

Lewis and Murray shifted their gaze to me.

"He was just named FBI director. This hit him hard," I explained. "But we're moving forward as planned. Rose will fill you in on the mission details. Will you excuse me?" I hurried out after McCourt, catching up to him just as he stepped into the elevator. I slipped in beside him before the doors could close.

"You're fucking crazy," McCourt barked, jabbing the button for his floor.

"Keep your voice down," I snapped.

"This is career suicide, and you know it," he growled. "I'd rather have Luca Domizio shoot me than get dragged through the media as a lunatic. If this blows up, Congress will make us look like idiots too stupid to hold their own dicks when they piss."

I slammed the emergency stop button, halting the elevator, and stepped in front of him. "Cut the shit. We all know you're just like those scumbags in DC who jerk off people like Jan Novak to keep their power."

McCourt pressed himself against the elevator wall, his eyes widening.

I leaned in closer. "But here's the deal. You're going to stay quiet and play along like a good boy. And if this mission goes south, you're taking the fall right beside me. Got it?"

Shock flickered across his face, his sass crumbling.

"Because if you don't," I continued, "I'll make it look like you were the grandmaster behind everything with Leah. Hell, I'll make you the mastermind behind all the shit that went down with Larsen too. I'll testify that I was just following your orders. I'll have Rose testify about you blackmailing her."

"But ... but none of that's true," he mumbled, panic creeping into his voice.

"You trying to kill Leah is true. You blackmailing Rose? Also true. But above all, the fact that you'd let a murderer like Jan Novak walk to save your own ass? That's why I'll destroy you. And if you think quietly losing your job and rotting in your fancy Nantucket beach house is bad, let me remind you that your other option is prison—where you'll be taking it up the ass from the guys you put there until the day they finally kill you."

I stepped back and hit the emergency button to get the elevator moving again.

"If I were you, I'd shut the fuck up and, for once, do something selfless," I added.

Moments later, the doors opened to reveal two agents, who stepped inside.

"Thank you, Director McCourt," I said, all smiles and respect as I stepped out. "Hey, guys. Hope to see you for drinks later tonight." I flashed a smile at the agents, who nodded and promised to be there.

And just like that, Mission Career Wreckage was officially in motion.

SEVENTEEN

Liam

I stood in front of the men's bathroom mirror at the FBI office, staring at my reflection. My hands were clenched tightly around the edges of the sink, my knuckles white from the grip.

Dressed in a suit and bulletproof FBI vest, I looked every bit the agent ready to take down Jan Novak. Yet doubts crept in. Was this crazy? A mistake?

My gun was secure in its holster on my hip. If all went well, it'd remain there all day— unless Jan Novak tried to hurt anybody.

The bathroom door swung open, and Cowboy stepped in. "It's time," he said.

I took a deep breath as a mix of adrenaline and anxiety coursed through my chest.

"Can't you give me more details than the target's name and picture?" Cowboy begged again like a child. "I thought we're a team."

"We are. But it's for your own good. You're just following my orders. Got it?"

Cowboy muttered something under his breath as I stepped out to meet Rose by the elevator. She looked as anxious as I felt. We exchanged a glance, with no words needed, then stepped into the elevator.

It carried us down to the garage, where a line of ten FBI SUVs sat idling, their engines rumbling. Inside each, agents were prepped and ready to roll.

"Let's fucking do this," I said as I slid into the passenger seat of the lead SUV. Rose was behind the wheel. Cowboy took his usual spot in the back.

Tension hung in the air as our convoy cut through Boston's streets. Every turn and acceleration was charged with purpose. The hum of powerful engines echoed through the city, creating a relentless symphony of urgency.

Pedestrians turned their heads, their eyes widening as we sped past. Some reached for their phones and snapped photos of the black line of SUVs blowing through red lights and weaving through traffic like an unstoppable force. Cars parted for us, their drivers staring as we surged ahead.

When we hit Route 1, the scene shifted. About fifteen police vehicles were lined up along the roadside, forming a wall of authority just outside Nahant. The peninsula was known for its sprawling mansions and old money.

As we neared the line, Rose maneuvered the SUV to the front of the convoy. Chief Murray rolled down his window when we pulled up beside him.

"You're not messing around," I said, glancing at the row of cop cars.

"Figured we'd skip the formalities," he replied, a grin tugging at his lips. He was suited up in a bulletproof vest, just like I was.

I adjusted mine, feeling the weight pressing against my chest. "Might as well make 'em sweat for a change."

"Let's do this. Let's take this bastard down," Murray said, his voice low and full of grit. He turned to his radio and barked orders with sharp authority. On his command, the line of police cruisers surged to life, sirens blaring, red and blue lights slicing through the morning fog.

Our SUVs joined his fleet like a black wave crashing forward.

Together, we tore down the road toward Nahant, ready for whatever awaited us.

As our fleet drove through the outskirts of the city, Senator Wheezer's waterfront mansion loomed ahead on its cliffside perch. When we had neared the massive iron gate, a line of Secret Service agents in sleek black suits stepped forward and halted our advance—just like Luca had warned they would.

I swung the car door open and stepped out, authority in every movement. "FBI! Open the fucking gate!" I barked, leaving no room for hesitation.

The agents exchanged confused glances but quickly obeyed, swinging the gates wide open.

We rolled up the long white gravel driveway and pulled to a stop in the middle of a lavish garden party. The rich mingled over champagne and caviar while the delicate notes of violins serenaded them. That serene bubble shattered the second our caravan arrived. Panic rippled through the crowd as shocked murmurs rose. The partygoers' faces twisted in fear and confusion.

I jumped out. Rose and Cowboy were close behind, with Chief Murray at my side, leading a small army of police and FBI agents. We marched through the stunned elites, who parted like a sea of diamonds and silk until we reached him.

Jan fucking Novak. Flesh and blood.

He stood there, cool as ice, sipping champagne as chaos swirled around him. Beside him, the vice president looked stricken, his thin, wrinkled face tight with alarm. Senator Wheezer, red-faced and trembling, looked ready to explode.

"Get the vice president out of here!" Chief Murray shouted.

Secret Service agents rushed to surround the vice president and quickly guided him toward the black limousine.

"What the hell is this? How dare you!" he yelled, but his protests faded as the car sped off.

"What is going on here?" Senator Wheezer demanded, charging toward me, his face flushed.

I shoved him aside and faced Jan Novak. "Jan Novak, you're under arrest for suspicion of murder."

"Are you insane? Stop this madness!" Wheezer yelled at me, his voice desperate. "Jan, I'm so, so sorry. Don't worry, I'll fix this!"

Chief Murray grabbed the senator before he could interfere more. "Get out of the way, or I'll arrest you for obstruction," Murray snapped.

My hands shook as I pulled out the handcuffs. Novak's eyes met mine. The arrogant grin was still plastered on his face. "You have the right to remain silent," I said, locking his wrists behind his back. "Anything you say can and will be used against you in a court of law. You have the right to an attorney. If you cannot afford an attorney, which I fucking doubt, one will be appointed to you."

He didn't resist, that fucker, just stayed as calm as ever.

Out of the corner of my eye, I spotted the catering staff recording everything—just like Luca Domizio had promised. The vice president's limo was long gone. God bless that old son of a bitch. Domizio had kept his word.

"Let's go, you piece of shit," I muttered, dragging Jan Novak by the arm toward the open field where our helicopter was supposed to land any second. But just as I moved, Murray's phone rang.

He answered, and his face tightened with dread. "Fucking shit!" Murray cursed, slamming his phone shut. "The police helicopters are all tied up, responding to a shooting at a gas station."

"We're not going to make it to the factory by car," Rose said. "The vice president has probably already called for reinforcements from the nearest military bases. Colonel Lewis might hold off on his orders and buy us some time, but the others will respond. We'll never get out by land."

Fuck. Fuck. Fuck.

I scanned Murray's face for a plan, but he had nothing.

"Lady luck turning on you already?" Novak sneered, enjoying every second of the chaos.

"Shut up!" I snapped, feeling the crowd of guests press in tighter around us. Mumbling, demanding that we let Jan Novak go.

Sweat dripped down my face, and my pulse hammered in my ears. We wouldn't make it far without air support. If we didn't get Novak out now, the whole mission would collapse—our asses hauled off in cuffs while Novak waved goodbye with that disgusting grin on his face.

"Let him go right now!" Wheezer demanded, yanking free from Chief Murray's grip. His face was twisted with rage. "Your careers are over! Don't you idiots know who I am?"

I barely heard him. Everything blurred.

My career? Over. Rose, Chief Murray, Lieutenant Colonel Lewis? Done. And Leah? Probably dead—killed by Novak in some twisted act of revenge.

I'd never imagined my downfall would come on a manicured lawn at some pretentious garden party.

My grip on Novak's arm started to slip as defeat settled in. Rose hissed a string of curses under her breath. We were so damn close. So fucking close. Life had screwed me over before, but this—this was the worst. Everything I'd fought for, everything I'd sacrificed, would be erased. All for nothing. And this bastard would walk free. Exhaustion hit me like a freight train. How easy it would be to just let go. To stop fighting. Let fate have its way.

But just as my fingers began to slip from Novak's arm, a deafening roar shattered the chaos—the unmistakable thunder of helicopters.

Rose, Murray, and I shot each other shocked looks. My head snapped up as five Air Force helicopters ripped across the sky, their blades slicing the air. Party guests screamed and ducked for cover as tables flipped, champagne flutes shattered, and chaos exploded around us. The helicopters hovered low, whipping up a storm of debris, and then descended onto the open lawn, kicking the panic into overdrive.

"Is that the fucking U.S. military?" Wheezer shouted, his voice cracking with disbelief. "Our military?"

I couldn't help but grin as I caught Chief Murray's eye. Satisfaction lit up his wrinkled face.

"For the record, I know exactly who you are," I yelled over to Senator Wheezer, who was now crouched like a scared child, hands over his head. "But you forgot who we are. We're the people who put you in power to serve us—not the other way around. So don't ever insult the U.S. military again, you greedy piece of shit."

I shot him a wicked grin as I stared at his wide, shocked eyes. If I was going down, I might as well go out with a bang.

I yanked Novak toward one of the helicopters, then spotted Colonel Lewis in the front seat next to the pilot. I shoved Novak inside as Rose followed. Cowboy was about to hop in, but Rose pushed him back as the helicopter lifted off.

"Figured I'd make sure my last mission counts," Lieutenant Colonel Lewis yelled over the deafening roar of the blades. "Let these bastards know where the U.S. military stands when this shit hits the fan."

"Oh, they'll know," I shouted back, handing him a piece of paper with coordinates. "Please drop us off at the first location, then send the other choppers to the second. That'll buy us more time."

He nodded sharply.

With that, we lifted off, the chaos below swept into the whipping winds of the helicopter's blades. This was probably my last day as an FBI agent. Especially given that Rose, Leah, and I had agreed to interrogate Novak at Leah's factory—far from government eyes. That decision alone would bury my career. Taking a suspect to private property instead of a federal facility or FBI headquarters? There was no coming back from that. My career was over.

But the chances of Novak talking? Slim to none. The smug grin on his face told me that he was thinking the same thing. What that arrogant bastard didn't know was that it wasn't me he'd be up against.

It would be someone far more persuasive.

The only person on this planet who could break him.

So I grinned right back.

EIGHTEEN

Leah

I stood in the shadow of the dark hallway of the old rope factory that I owned outside of town. The stench of urine lingered—a testament to the homeless who sought refuge here. Their makeshift mattresses and trash bags were scattered beneath graffiti-covered walls.

When I heard the distant thud of helicopter blades, I was impressed. Richter had actually pulled it off. He'd managed to bring Jan Novak here on a mission that was close to suicide.

My grip on the gun tightened as I watched Richter and Rose drag a handcuffed Jan Novak into the expansive factory hall. Richter believed I could make Novak talk, but I saw only one inevitable outcome.

One of us had to die, and it wasn't going to be me.

My time as a famous pianist would surely end, likely in a high-profile prison. But I held no attachment to the life I'd led—not the crowds chanting my name, not the luxurious life that came with it, and especially not my personal life. I'd never been foolish enough to hold myself in high regard. Even if I told myself that I was different from Carl Carr or Jan Novak, I was still a killer. And today, I realized just how tired I was—tired of the hunt, tired of the games. Tired of waking up each morning fighting the same fight.

The only regret I harbored was for Richter, the trouble this brought him, and the possibility that he might not see his daughter for a long time.

Glass crunched under my shoes as I strode down the corridor and headed into the hall of abandoned machinery where Richter, Rose, and Novak were waiting.

Richter was the first to notice me. His eyes darted to the gun I now aimed directly at Novak.

"Leah!" he yelled, pushing Novak toward Rose. "No! Don't!"

Jan Novak's eyes—an icy blue—met mine. His demeanor was calm and composed. "I have to say, this is quite impress—"

I squeezed the trigger.

The gunshot rang out. The bullet bounced off the factory walls before the sound faded into silence. Richter spun around, expecting Novak to drop—but he was still standing. Rose, panic written all over her face, glanced at Richter, then turned to me, her eyes wide with shock.

I kept my gun steady, smoke curling from the barrel. "The next bullet goes right between your eyes unless you answer me—truthfully," I said, my gaze fixed on Novak.

He frowned briefly, then found his cool, old self. "Is this the moment in movies when they make deals? Well, I guess here's mine. Uncuff me, and I'll answer your questions. Otherwise, do as you wish."

Rose and Richter exchanged glances.

"Uncuff him," I said.

"I don't think that's a good idea," Rose muttered, looking at Richter. But after a tense moment, he nodded. With a sigh of protest, Rose uncuffed Novak. He rubbed his wrists, then straightened his tuxedo jacket like he wasn't standing in the middle of his doom.

"Your turn," I said, my gun still pointing at Novak. "Why did you send Carl Carr after me?" I bypassed the question of whether he was the Train Track Killer. That would be confirmed by his answer to this one.

"I didn't send him after you," he said.

My finger tightened slightly on the trigger as I stepped closer, now only a few feet away. I'd shoot him—no doubt about that.

"Wait!" Jan said quickly, his eyes watching my every movement. "Let me finish, please."

I narrowed my eyes but eased up on the trigger slightly.

"Here's the problem with your perception about all this," Novak said, his tone calm, almost patronizing, like we were students who'd fumbled an easy equation. "Carl Carr—I didn't send him after you. I sent him *to* you."

Richter and I exchanged confused glances. "We don't have time for this bullshit," Richter snapped. "You're the sick fuck putting people on train tracks, aren't you?"

Novak didn't flinch. "My dear Agent Richter, life *is* a game. And today, you've played yours in ways I couldn't have imagined. Quite frankly, I'm impressed. Utterly stunned." He began clapping slowly, the sound echoing through the hall. "Bravo. Really. You've made today quite the headache for me. A career suicide mission for you, of course, but your passion, Agent Richter—it's remarkable. I'm starting to see what *she* sees in you."

"Answer the fucking question!" Rose barked, her voice cutting through the tension.

"But I just did," he countered. "Carl Carr—I didn't send him after you but *to* you."

Richter's hands trembled as he drew his gun, the weight of the moment etched in his face, tension tightening every muscle. "This is all the proof I need," he muttered, aiming at Novak. "If you don't do it, Leah, I will. I can't let him hire some top-notch lawyer and walk. Not after what he did to Anna and all the countless other lives he's ripped apart. He won't stop. He's sick. He'll do it again and again. We all know that."

"Richter, wait!" I snapped. Something wasn't adding up.

He shot me a troubled look. His gun was still trained on Novak, but he lowered it slightly.

"What do you mean you sent Carl Carr to me?" I asked, turning toward Novak. "You knew what I'd do to him, didn't you?"

"Of course I did," Novak said like it was the most obvious thing in the world.

That lingering question, the one that had gnawed at me from the start—why I'd never seen the monster in Novak's eyes—fought its way to the surface. And when a possible answer formed, a sickening knot of horror twisted in my gut.

"Let's move this along, shall we?" Novak said, his hand sliding toward his pocket. Instantly, three guns were on him.

"Oh, please. You really think I'm stupid enough to pull a gun like this is some Patterson novel?" His hand moved slowly and pulled out a phone. "Like I told you, I'm not who you think I am. And here's the proof."

He walked over to a rusty metal table, set the phone down, and propped it up against an old typewriter.

"You might want to come closer," Novak said, his voice smooth and unsettling. "It's about Anna—sweet Anna. A little memoir about her life."

"You sick fuck!" Richter shouted, his voice trembling with rage.

I moved toward the metal table, my gun hanging loosely by my side. Deep down, something told me the real enemy in this room wasn't Jan Novak—it was whatever waited for me on that phone.

"Access personal storage file labeled 'Complete.' Play video one hundred fifty-three," Novak instructed calmly.

"Password?" the phone's robotic female voice responded.

"Mojca," Novak answered.

The phone turned on and played a video of what looked like a college party. At first, it showed the floor and the feet of people dancing to rap music. Then the camera shifted up to show a teenage girl held down on a couch by several young men and ... a younger version of Anna.

"Fuck the slut!" Anna shouted with an excited grin as a young man walked up and tore down the girl's panties. He rammed himself inside, moving his hips wildly to the girl's screams.

Richter and Rose approached the table, watching in horror as one man after another raped the poor girl, all while Anna laughed and helped hold the girl down.

"Fuck that slut, she likes it!" Anna shouted.

"No..." Richter whispered, stumbling backward, his face as white as snow. "No!" His voice rose into a desperate shout as he spun away, hands gripping his head, trying to block out the horror. "This can't be real! NO!"

Rose's hand flew to her mouth, stifling a gasp as her wide eyes filled with shock and disbelief.

I stood frozen, my mind struggling to process what I was seeing. The world I thought I knew was ending right in front of me, crumbling into chaos I couldn't escape.

"Stop!" the girl kept screaming as man after man raped her.

"That girl's name is Sunny Loyd," Novak declared. "A high-school student who snuck out at night with her friend Anna to attend a college party. She later committed suicide. It broke her family. Parents divorced. Father is now an alcoholic and lost his job. Mother is in and out of mental institutions."

"You're a fucking liar!" Richter roared, grabbing Novak by the suit, his fists clenched tightly. "This video is fake!"

Novak didn't even blink. "Play video two hundred and two," he said calmly.

Another video started, this time showing Mr. Mauser, one of the first train track victims. The image flickered on the screen, horrifyingly real.

Video 202 looked like store security camera footage. Mauser was in a parking lot, pulling a little girl into his car.

Richter's grip slackened. He let go of Novak and stepped toward the table, his eyes fixed on the phone as if he was seeing the truth for the first time.

Then another video played, showing Mauser in a different parking lot, guiding a different girl into his car.

"He liked them young," Novak remarked coldly as another video of Mauser played. This scene was similar. Mauser and a little girl disappeared into his car, though this time Mauser was carrying a princess balloon.

"Turn it off," Rose demanded, her voice trembling with barely contained rage.

Novak, unfazed, adjusted his jacket with an eerie calm. "Already had enough? I've got plenty more. Considering the work you three do, I thought you'd appreciate my collection a little more. Personally, I admire what you bring to this world."

"I said *turn it off!*" Rose screamed, lunging forward. She snatched the phone and hurled it to the ground. The screen shattered with a sharp crack, but the videos kept playing, their flickering glow casting eerie shadows over the room as Rose collapsed to her knees.

I stood frozen, my gaze locked on the broken phone, unable to look away.

Then Richter snapped. His fury boiled over as he grabbed the edge of the table and flipped it with a thunderous crash.

"Fuuuuuuuuuuuuuck!" he bellowed, his voice echoing through the hollow factory.

I wanted to move, to place a hand on his shoulder, but something held me back. Instead, I turned my attention to Novak, locking eyes with him. His stare was steady, unshaken. "As I said, I'm not who you think I am."

And he wasn't.

That was why I'd never seen the monster in his eyes. That was why the rage I should've felt toward him had always been absent.

Jan Novak wasn't a monster.

He wasn't the Train Track Killer—despite placing those bodies on the tracks.

He was ... *a version of me.*

A dark justice dealt to those who did wrong. Maybe not serial killers but clearly people who deserved justice in one way or another.

And Jan Novak administered this dark form of justice. As dark as mine, just less selective in his targets.

For all those years, I'd hunted myself.

The distant drone of helicopters resonated through the hall as the lines between good and evil blurred into a morally indistinct haze.

They were here.

Novak's allies. They'd found us.

But none of it mattered anymore. We'd sacrificed it all.

And all for nothing.

"Well, this was fun," Novak said, his tone as steady as ever. "But I think my ride's here." He walked past me, then paused. "I really enjoyed our dinner the other night. Let's meet again. Maybe we can have, well, a bit more fun next time." Novak strode confidently toward the door. He was almost there when Richter sprang to his feet, his gun aimed at Novak's back. Richter's hands shook. His face was a twisted mix of rage and despair.

Novak stopped but didn't turn around.

"There were other ways to handle Anna," Richter shouted, his voice cracking. "She didn't have to die. And her grandmother ... you had Patel kill her grandmother!"

Novak slowly turned, just enough to glance over his shoulder. "If it had been the first time Anna had drugged a girl at a party, maybe. And if it were the first time her grandmother had lied to protect her, maybe. But you see, Agent Richter, the world isn't as black and white as your simple law enforcement perspective might suggest. There are layers to this, complexities you can't begin to grasp. Most people can't even be honest with themselves." Novak shrugged, his voice smooth. "They hide behind lies and convenient stories, burying the truth so deep they forget it's even there. You think you're getting to the bottom of this? You're barely scratching the surface. It's best to leave those matters to people who understand them. People who know everything about them."

Richter's aim stayed locked, the barrel trembling ever so slightly.

"Liam," I said softly, stepping closer. I placed my hand on his outstretched arm, slowly guiding it down. "Liam," I repeated, my voice gentle and steady.

He resisted at first, but then, like a man crushed by the weight of the world, he gave in, his arm lowering as if in defeat.

I squeezed his arm in silent support, then turned to Novak. "What about Emanuel?" My voice was level, controlled. "Why did you kill him? What could he possibly have done to deserve that death on the tracks?"

Novak's eyes locked onto mine. "That," he said, "is a question you'll need to ask someone else."

His words hit me like a gut punch. Novak hadn't killed Emanuel? But if he hadn't, who had?

Without another word, Novak walked out, disappearing through the door.

The three of us stood there, staring after him, the weight of the revelations pressing down like a suffocating fog.

We waited for the storm to crash down on us. Gunmen, army, helicopters, something. Any second now, I expected armed men to burst in, arrest us, or worse, open fire. It made sense to get rid of us. It was what I would have done.

"Are they gonna kill us?" Rose asked. Her voice was calm, almost eerily so, as if she'd already accepted that this was how it would all end.

"Probably," I said, glancing over at Richter. I wanted to say something to him, something meaningful. Maybe that in all this darkness, meeting him somehow made it worthwhile. But the words never made it past my lips.

Seconds ticked by. Then a minute. Maybe two, maybe three.

No gunmen came. The thudding of boots and the hum of helicopters faded into the distance until there was nothing but an empty, unnerving silence.

We stood there, frozen in place, as if time had stopped. Trapped in this crazy limbo, unable to move or speak.

Finally, Rose pushed herself to her feet. "I guess we're gonna see tomorrow after all. What ... now? What the hell are we supposed to do?"

Richter's eyes locked onto mine, searching for answers I didn't have.

At that moment, all I had were questions.

Who was I, really?

I'd already diverged from hunting serial killers when I'd attacked the Night Stalker. Was I really so different from Jan Novak? Did my two wrongs actually make a right, especially now that the man I'd hunted and wanted to kill had turned out to be another version of myself?

It had all seemed so clear when I'd thought Novak preyed on the innocent and I hunted the guilty. But who decided what made someone a monster? Me?

And then there was Emanuel. Who killed him? Why?

"What now?" Richter asked. "What do we do now, Leah?"

"I..." My voice faltered, the words dissolving into the space around us, echoing off the factory's cold, lifeless walls. "I don't know."

NINETEEN

Liam

Rain pounded against my SUV, which was parked in the empty lot of a hiking trail. Lieutenant Colonel Lewis and Chief Murray yanked open the doors and climbed into the back seat. The storm outside matched my dark, brooding mood. It had been a few weeks since Jan Novak's arrest, and after weeks of tense texts, this meeting had finally been called.

Chief Murray slammed the door shut. "What the hell is going on?" he barked. "I'm tired of sitting around like a goddamn caged animal. Are they coming after us, or are we going after Novak again? I'm sick of doing nothing. Something has to happen soon, or I'll lose my damn mind."

Murray had risked everything to arrest Novak. But that was before we'd known what Novak really was—a monster similar to us.

Killing men like Harvey Grand and Carl Carr had been simple. Black and white. But this? Novak was a puzzle with no clear answer, and that moral gray area gnawed at me. It made everything murky, filled with questions none of us could answer.

"They found him before we could extract anything useful," I lied, keeping my eyes on the rain streaking down the windows. "Nobody's come for us so far, and we all still have our jobs. My gut says there's a silent deal in place. Pretend it never happened. Stay quiet, act normal, don't release any footage of the arrest, and in return, we keep our freedom and jobs."

Murray snorted. "Sounds like a lot of guessing to me. There's been nothing on the news about the arrest. But that makes him even more guilty, if you ask me. If he were innocent, they'd have formal investigations so far up our asses, you'd see it in our eyes."

Guilty. Murray was right. Novak *was* guilty. But of what, exactly? Killing a child molester like Mauser? Or a rapist like Anna? How could I justify protecting Leah after she'd taken down the Night Stalker but condemn Novak for doing something eerily similar?

Since that day in the factory, my mind had been spiraling with questions as dark as the night. I didn't have the courage to dig into the details of Novak's other victims— what they'd done to deserve their fate on the tracks. After Mauser and Anna, I just wasn't ready. Or maybe I was simply scared. Scared I'd stop judging Novak for the monster he was. Scared I'd stop judging him at all.

"I still have the footage from the arrest," I said. Luca had secured the phones from his people who'd recorded the event. "As long as we hold onto that, we're safe."

"I don't give a damn about my safety," Chief Murray growled, his eyes blazing with fierce determination. "I'm not a coward. I want Jan Novak gone. Arrested. Dead. Whatever it takes. He's a killer hiding behind powerful friends and a mountain of cash.

He's my enemy now. Enemy number one. And I'm not the type to let scum like him shit all over justice. I'll keep pushing until things are set *fucking* straight. I'm the Massachusetts State police chief, for Christ's sake. Novak doesn't walk!"

Lewis nodded. "I'm with Chief Murray. We can't let Novak live like a king while he's out there playing Jack the Ripper."

Innocent people.

I sighed. For a moment, I thought about telling them everything. About Leah, me, Novak. But then what? It was a lot to assume they'd be willing to follow me down that path. Leah's pursuit of dark justice was one thing. But Novak? His story was murkier, much harder to justify. And as of now, I wasn't even sure I was on board with the things he did.

Outside, the rain pounded against the roof, its rhythm relentless.

"For now, we keep our heads down," I said, staring at the drops streaking down the SUV windows. "They haven't come after us, and jumping into another mission would be reckless. Novak didn't give us anything during the arrest. But I promise, I'll find something—something significant. If we rush this, we'll all get locked up. And if that happens, Novak will shit on justice ... and on us."

Chief Murray's eyes narrowed at me. I recognized that look. He could see right through me. He'd spotted my stalling tactic like a gambler spying a neon Vegas sign. Lewis was likely aware as well, but unlike Murray, he was the patient type, accustomed to military strategies that simmered over years.

"You'd better," Chief Murray said, reaching for the door handle. "Because if you don't, I will. And this time, Novak will be taken care of. Maybe even get hit by a stray bullet during an arrest. Wouldn't be the first time it happened. Wouldn't be the last."

He left.

Lewis lingered a moment longer. "You'd better come up with something fast. When you asked Murray for help, you dangled a blood-soaked cloth in front of a bloodhound. Can't call him off the hunt now." He hurried out of the car, disappearing into the rain as he dashed to his SUV. I watched as both vehicles pulled away, leaving me alone with my thoughts.

I pulled out my flip phone.

After the silence that we both needed, Leah had texted me a few days ago. She wanted to meet. I told her soon. And soon was now.

I stared at the screen, my fingers hovering over the keys. I started to type, asking when she wanted to meet. Then, second-guessing myself, I deleted the message and snapped the phone shut with a frustrated click.

I leaned back, my mind drifting.

Jan Novak had changed everything.

He'd made me question my partnership with Leah. Question myself. And that scared the hell out of me.

Rose had pretty much taken time off, said she'd let things play out for now and thrown herself into other cases. I wanted to do the same, but the memory of Anna's cold, blue body clashed violently with the video of Sunny Loyd's rape.

What Anna had done was unforgivable. Inexcusable. But had Novak truly delivered justice by killing her? Deep down, I wasn't sure.

Leah didn't seem to be wrestling with the same doubts, and that worried me as well. She'd already crossed the line when she'd gone after the Night Stalker. Now, with Novak in the picture, this could spiral into something far worse.

I had to talk to her. Now.

I grabbed the flip phone again, ready to text her. Before I could, my work phone rang. Cowboy was calling.

"Special Agent in Charge," he said cheerfully. "You won't believe this. But the red truck you made me look into?"

I'd completely forgotten about that. Carl Carr was already dead, but Cowboy didn't know that. He must have continued going through thousands of hours of surveillance footage from the area where Nathalie had disappeared.

"About that—" I began.

Cowboy cut me off. "I found his truck on footage. On the fucking night Nathalie disappeared."

I rubbed my temple with my free hand. "Cowboy, Nathalie is back home. She said she ran off with a man who promised to marry her, but he dumped her. Surprise, surprise. Now she's back home."

"I know that. But leave it to Cowboy. Bang-bang!"

"Cowboy, not now, I—"

"Thanks to Nathalie's disappearance for whatever reasons, I was able to connect his truck to three other sites where prostitutes disappeared. And those women are still missing."

I straightened in my seat.

"You know how you always tell me to be more independent and think outside of the box?" Cowboy continued. "Well, I did. And hit the jackpot. That guy Carl Carr ... I think it's time to pay him a visit."

Shit. Shit. Shit.

"Richter?"

"Yes, yes, of course. Good work."

"Bang-bang. Leave it to Cowboy."

"Um, hey, listen. Let's not jump the gun quite yet. He might just be some pervert. We don't have anything that makes him a real suspect or anything. Not in the eyes of the court, and we're too busy right now to bust consensual sex. Prostitution or not. That's a cop problem."

"I think there's more to it. I think we really need to pay this guy a visit. I already called him, but his mom said he's not home right now."

I ran my hand through my hair. "You ... spoke to his mom?"

"She answered the phone. A strange woman, if you ask me. Talked a bit with her. Gives me 'College Snatcher mom' vibes. Remember? The crazy one with the dead stuffed cats all over her place?"

"Taxidermized, not stuffed."

"Yeah, whatever. Creepy as fuck."

Shit. This was bad. I couldn't let Cowboy get any closer. "All right. Keep trying to get a hold of Carl Carr to get him in for an interview. But that's it. We can't waste time on this right now, you hear me? Your uncle is breathing down my neck." I knew that would go nowhere. Carl Carr was gone. For now, this was good enough.

"Got it. You can count on me."

"Good."

"One last thing," he said just as I was about to hang up.

"Yes?"

"The Night Stalker."

"What about him?"

"He got out on bail. His mom sold her condo and paid the $200,000."

"Are you fucking kidding me?" I said. "I told the state's attorney that $200,000 was a joke for what that piece of shit did."

"You and every woman in this country."

Could the day get any worse? Fuck! If Leah found out, she'd make sure the Night Stalker was dealt with. It would be ugly. It would be messy. And the fact that Cowboy was sniffing around might complicate things.

"I need you to go over his bail conditions and meet with the state attorney first thing tomorrow," I said, my frustration roaming free. "Until he's found guilty and locked up, I want everything: ankle bracelet, daily check-ins with the police, passport surrender, drug testing, no-contact orders. Throw the damn book at him. And make it hurt. You hear me?"

"Loud and clear. I'll give him hell."

"Good."

He hung up, and I slipped the flip phone back into my coat pocket. I'd text Leah later. Right now, I needed to devise a plan—a plan for Novak. Cowboy. Murray. And now the fucking Night Stalker.

I had to figure out where I stood before I talked to Leah, especially on the matter of killing. After all, she was at the root of all this. At least on my end. But she was likely my only solution too.

TWENTY

Liam

As I pulled into my reserved spot in the condo's underground garage, my headlights swept over a figure standing just outside the parking space. The brief flash of light revealed a woman. Instantly, I recognized her from the picture my sister had sent months ago.

It was my half-sister—the child my father had conceived behind our backs with another woman.

I cursed under my breath. Of all the days for her to show up, it had to be this one. The last thing I needed was to deal with family drama after the kind of day I'd had.

With unsure movements, she stepped aside to let me park. I killed the engine, sat there for a moment, and then opened the door and stepped out.

"Liam?" Her voice was small, trembling with insecurity. Instinct from the bureau kicked in, and I found myself scanning her from head to toe.

There was no mistaking the fact that she was my half-sister, but the woman standing in front of me wasn't the same as the one in the photo. The picture showed a fresh-faced, hopeful girl. But now? Red, swollen hands from years of drug use and a missing tooth told a story of a hard life. Her makeup was caked on as if in an attempt to hide the damage, but it only amplified the contrast between her appearance and the church-like outfit she wore. It seemed that she was desperately trying to make a good impression.

It hurt to see her like this. To see her trying so hard. For me, of all people.

"Hey," I said, locking my car. The beep echoed through the garage, hanging in the awkward silence between us.

"I..." she started, her voice faltering, "I'm Lucy, your half-sister. I'm so sorry for showing up at your place like this. I know our sister said you both didn't want any contact right now. But..."

I pinched my lips. This was true. I had enough on my plate without family drama, especially with Josie's court case having just wrapped up. I couldn't—didn't want to—get involved in this. Not now. Maybe not ever.

"How did you find me?" I asked.

"A coworker at your office gave me your address when I mentioned I'm your sister."

"Cowboy," I mumbled in annoyance. How could he just hand out my address like that?

Frustration must have been written all over my face, as Lucy took a step back, her gaze dropping to the floor. "If now isn't a good time, I could come back another day," she offered.

I sighed. "Yeah. I'm really sorry, but now is actually not a good time." I tried to keep my voice kind, hide the exhaustion of the chaos in my life.

She nodded. "I'll come back—"

"It might be better if I reach out when I have more time," I interrupted.

Disappointment washed over her face, visible even beneath the heavy makeup. It hurt me to see her hurt, but this was exactly the drama I couldn't handle on top of everything else right now. Goddamn Cowboy. Goddamn my cheating asshole father.

"It's not you. Really," I said. "I'm busy at work right now. Please don't take this personally. Karma treats me like shit sometimes. I'm not one of her favorites. Never was, never will be."

She smiled faintly. "I know all about that. Karma don't like me too. She's a sneaky bitch, that one."

I nodded. "Well, I'll catch you later, if that's alright?" My tone was sweet, honest.

"Yes, yes, of course," she said, brightening slightly. She handed me a paper with her contact information. "I work nights at the nursing home, but I'm free during the day. Call me anytime."

"Thanks," I said, pocketing the paper. Then I watched as she left through the garage entrance and disappeared around a corner.

I didn't have much time to dwell on the encounter. My eyes locked on a black BMW in an employee parking spot.

My heart started racing as I headed over, each step faster than the last.

No need to text Leah.

The dark angel of justice was already here.

TWENTY-ONE

Leah

Richter climbed into the driver's seat and shut the door with a heavy thud. Dark circles hung under his eyes, and his hair was a mess. He looked like a man who hadn't slept in days.

"I didn't mean to intrude on something personal," I said, nodding toward the spot where he and his half-sister had been talking.

He rested his head against the seat. "Leah, you and I have faced things darker than my half-sister showing up out of the blue. You didn't intrude."

I nodded. "I'm not an expert on family matters. I don't really have a family. But a lost sibling trying to reconnect ... isn't that a good thing?"

"I don't know." His gaze shifted to the window. "At first, I thought she'd just add more chaos to my life. Add fuel to the fire. But now that I think about it..."

"About what?"

His eyes turned back to me. "Now I think I might be the mess. I'm the fire. And anyone who gets too close is going to get burned."

I let his words settle for a moment. "We have that in common," I admitted. "Now more than ever."

Our unspoken fears filled the silence between us.

"What are we supposed to do now, Leah?" Richter finally asked, his voice low. "Keep going like nothing's changed? Take him out? Or worse ... join him?"

I'd been dreading that question. The truth was, I didn't have an answer. Not one that would satisfy him, anyway.

"I mean," Richter continued, "our mission. Are we really so different from Novak? Or have we become monsters too, playing judge and jury, blind to the fact that we're only human?"

I shook my head firmly. "No. We're not like Novak. The people we've taken down were serial killers—pure evil." My voice faltered as the memory of the Night Stalker crossed my mind. Quickly, I pushed it aside. "If you're questioning what we did, try to remember Harris and those college girls. The frozen head at the crime scene. Or Harvey Grand. The bastard poisoned a baby. An innocent baby."

"I do remember them," Richter shot back.

"Good. Make sure those memories stay with you for the times when you doubt yourself." I sighed. "I never told you what I found in Carl Carr's basement, but trust me, it was pure evil. The kind of evil you can feel in your bones. And Nathalie? She's alive because we stopped him. Does that mean nothing?"

"It means everything," he said, his gaze locking with mine. "It's the one thing that keeps me going through all this. And I don't regret Carr, Harris, or Grand one bit. I sleep just fine knowing we got rid of them."

"But?" I asked.

Richter exhaled slowly, running a hand through his hair in frustration. "But what Novak did ... if I'm honest, Leah, how is it any different from what you did to the Night Stalker?"

That question hit harder than I'd expected. It was the one I'd been dreading, worried that Jan Novak would wedge himself between us like this.

"I didn't kill the Night Stalker. That's the difference," I said firmly.

Richter seemed somewhat satisfied with that answer, though doubt lingered in his eyes.

"No, you didn't. And thank God for that. Because as much as I wish I could stop thinking about it, there's something about Anna's death that doesn't sit right with me. She deserved to rot in a cell, but killing her?"

I nodded, knowing exactly what he meant. Not because I felt the same way about it but because I'd chosen Richter for this very reason—for his empathy. His unwavering moral compass.

In moments like this, I needed him. To justify why I was alive, doing what I did. To keep me on the right path. But though I trusted his judgment, I was incapable of feeling the way he did. Of feeling much of anything.

"Anna was underage at the time of the rapes. She most likely wouldn't have gone to jail," I said. "Not even received a fine."

"So are you saying her death was justice?" Disbelief filled his voice. "Like Grand and Carr? Are we really comparing serial killers to a girl who did something terrible but never killed anyone?"

"I'm not saying that. But Sunny Loyd is dead because of what Anna did. Isn't that a form of murder too?"

Richter's eyes shot to mine. Something sparked in them—agreement? Or was it disbelief?

"Don't you feel the slightest bit of sadness over the whole thing with Anna?" he asked. "Nothing at all?"

I looked away, unable to meet his intense gaze. If I answered him, I'd be honest, and I knew he wouldn't like it.

"Richter, what's done is done. Why do the details matter?"

"They matter to me, Leah. Novak is out there playing God, handing down Old Testament judgments, and that should scare you as much as it scares me. So I'll ask again: Is there anything you can muster for Anna? Sadness? A sense of injustice? Goddamn pity for the pathetic girl she was? Anything?"

I stayed silent.

"Leah!" His voice rose, frustration boiling over.

"No," I said firmly. "No, Liam, I don't. I don't feel anything for her. Anna didn't just watch the horrors that happened to Sunny Loyd that night. She held her down while man after man violently raped that poor girl. Now Sunny's dead. Suicide. And her parents will probably join her soon. So no, Liam, when I think about Anna lying at the foot of that river, blue and stiff, I don't feel sadness. I feel justice. And a bit of relief that it wasn't me who got to her first. And you'd do Sunny Loyd's family—and yourself—a favor if you saved your tears for the victim."

The silence in the car was suffocating. We stared straight ahead.

"I'm not saying you're wrong," he finally said. "But I don't know if I can continue like this. Something about this feels different, no matter how hard I try to convince myself that it isn't. Novak ... I don't know if he's right or wrong, but I do know I can't keep going like this if we end up following his path."

A wave of panic shot through me. Was he considering quitting?

Suddenly, I realized I'd called him Liam again, just like I had in the factory when he'd almost shot Novak. Sitting here now, I wished he'd pulled the trigger. Or that I had.

As if my body weren't my own, my hand moved, resting on top of his. The warmth of his skin sent a toxic rush of excitement through me.

The realization struck me like a live wire: I cared for Agent Liam Richter.

He didn't pull away. His eyes softened, calming as they finally lifted to meet mine.

"What does it matter if Novak's right or wrong?" I asked. "We don't have to be him. We can keep doing what we've always done. Let him go his way. Maybe Anna's death weighs on your conscience, but what about people like Mauser? After you watched him drag little girls into his car. Do you feel bad about his death too?"

Liam didn't hesitate. "Fuck no. I'm a dad, for Christ's sake. If one of those little girls had been Josie..." His voice cracked.

I nodded.

"The Night Stalker..." he said. "You never told me why you did it."

The memories flooded back. That night, alone with my thoughts and slightly intoxicated.

"I was up late again, going over the train track murders. It's all I did most nights back then. The news was playing in the background, and they aired an interview with one of the Night Stalker's victims. The terror in her eyes, the tears ... I felt so powerless against Novak. That feeling turned into rage. And then ... it became a voice. For her and for all the others he hurt."

Liam placed his hand over mine. There was nothing romantic or sexual about it—at least not on his end. It was a gesture of understanding, sympathy, friendship, and support. It meant a great deal to me when almost nothing else in my life mattered.

I wondered if that was all he needed from me—to see the human side of me every once in a while.

"I'm not mad about what you did to The Night Stalker," he said. "But I'm relieved you didn't kill him. Our work with serial killers is so black and white. But Novak ... I'm not convinced, Leah. And I need you to promise me that what happened with the Night Stalker, that attack—it won't..."

"It won't happen again," I interrupted, knowing what he needed to hear. To keep our work going. And to keep him in my life. "After that day in the factory," I continued, "I wasn't sure who I was anymore. Am I just another monster like him? Or am I the monster, and he's the justice the world needs? But now, sitting here, I realize it doesn't matter. I need to continue my work. If you're with me on this, I'll take that as a sign that I'm still on the right path."

He looked at me, his eyes searching for something in mine. Then the tension in his face eased as he sighed. "As much as I hate it, I think we need to talk to him."

"Novak?" I asked.

"Yeah. We need to find out what the other victims did to end up on those tracks. I might not agree that Anna deserved to die, but people like Mauser ... that's a different story. Novak's methods are brutal, but if we want to figure out what to do with him, understanding his reasoning could help. Don't you think?"

"You want to find out if we should go after him or not," I concluded. I honestly had no feelings toward killing Novak if that was what Richter really wanted. "Has it ever crossed your mind..." I trailed off.

"What? To ask Novak if he knows of any other serial killers still out there? His company possesses almost god-like powers."

I nodded.

"Sure did. But I'm worried that would force us into making him an ally," Richter said.

"Not a bad trade-off if we catch them faster."

"Not bad at all. Until he kills someone innocent. For now, I have to treat Novak like any other psycho time bomb. Maybe some guy cuts him off in traffic. Dead in a river. Then what? Are we responsible for that? For not stopping Novak when we had the chance?"

Liam pulled his hand away from mine. The shift in conversation was clearly unsettling him. I regretted steering it in that direction.

"Well, for now, let's stay away from him as much as possible," I said. "Until we find out more about the other victims from the train tracks. I'll talk to him at the next shareholders' meeting."

Richter nodded slowly. "Yeah. That would help a lot. Thanks." He reached for the door handle.

"Wait," I said.

He paused, turning back to me.

"I actually came here to invite you to my Christmas concert. You and Rose. I've got a ticket for McCourt too, just to keep things from looking suspicious."

His eyebrows lifted in surprise. "I heard it was sold out. Tickets are going for record prices after all the cancellations."

I smiled. "It's my concert. I think I can financially weather the loss of three ticket sales."

A small grin tugged at his lips. It was a glimpse of the Richter I used to know—before Novak, before everything changed on the day of the arrest.

"It would defiantly make the FBI look good. And we need that right now," he said softly. "Might bring some normalcy back. Maybe even help with Rose. Help her move on ... or smooth things over."

"We could also go over some new items on the agenda," I said casually.

He cocked a brow. "New items on the agenda?"

My attention drifted to a couple stumbling into the garage, drunk, kissing wildly, unable to keep their hands off each other. "I've been paying hackers to surf the dark web for me. It's tedious and time-consuming work because these perverts are extremely cautious, and websites pop up and disappear daily. But it's showing promise."

Liam tilted his head. "Dang. Is that how you found the Night Stalker?"

I nodded.

"And you think we could use that to find other serial killers?"

"At the very least, it could help us follow up on leads faster. We could access sensitive information like Jan Novak does. It's illegal without a warrant, obviously, but building our own network could be useful, especially if we decide Novak is an enemy, not an ally."

Richter smirked. "Hackers. That actually could be a game-changer. Like having our own FBI cyber unit, but without all the red tape—no warrants, no rules."

"It would definitely trample on privacy rights," I said.

"Well," he shrugged, "those perverts lose those rights the moment they surf the dark web for murder porn. Not exactly 'green flag' guys, don't you think?"

I couldn't help but smile at that.

Our eyes shifted back to the drunk couple, now practically having sex against the side of their car. Richter shook his head, amused.

"What?" I asked, teasing. "Not proper?"

He laughed. "Nah. It's not that. Just thinking back to when I was still that carefree and fun."

"You're still fun," I said with a faint smile.

"Oh yeah? You mean between the murders, shootouts, and mental breakdowns? When I don't look like a walking piece of burnt charcoal?"

I laughed. "Some women find men who carry the world attractive. I think they call them 'well-seasoned.'"

He threw me a sarcastic smirk.

The drunk couple clumsily climbed into their car, and the engine roared to life.

"Oh, hell no," Liam said, tearing open his door. "I'd better stop them before they kill somebody."

"You do that," I said, watching as he rushed over and pressed his badge against the driver's side window.

I watched their exchange from a distance—the man stumbling out of the car, apologizing, practically begging. The woman, trying to prove she was sober, attempted to jump on one leg only to lose her balance and fall to the ground.

Then it hit me again.

The strange feeling I'd had earlier when Richter's hand had rested on mine.

It was comforting, soothing, like a wave of warmth and relief washing over me.

Maybe I was a monster, like Novak. Maybe I had been all along. But standing there, watching Richter, I realized something. As long as he kept me walking that fine line in the twilight, just one step from falling into complete darkness, it didn't matter anymore.

Novak.

Good.

Evil.

Me.

None of it mattered. Not as long as Richter was guiding me through the shadows like the first light at dawn.

TWENTY-TWO

Liam

The rapid-fire clicks of camera shutters echoed around the cramped, run-down bedroom. Cowboy stood beside me, chewing gum obnoxiously loud. The two-bedroom apartment in Dorchester looked like a bomb had gone off inside it. Clothes and dirty laundry were strewn across the floor like discarded memories.

In the center of the room, a large mahogany-framed bed dominated the space. On it, a woman lay motionless, her faded T-shirt and sweatpants soaked in blood. Her eyes, wide open, stared into nothing.

Next to her, slumped against the bed frame, was a man. A bullet hole gaped in his skull, a gun still loosely hanging from his limp hand. His head drooped forward like that of a rag doll, his chin resting on his chest.

I knelt beside the woman, my gloved fingers just inches from her vacant blue eyes. The sour stench of blood and sweat clung to the air, thick and oppressive. I leaned closer, meeting her empty gaze. "You get a shot of her face yet?" I asked.

A forensic tech, wrapped in a white coverall and booties, snapped his camera once more and nodded. "Got it."

With a slow, deliberate movement, I closed her eyes. The finality of it settled in the room like a weight. For a moment, she almost looked peaceful—if one ignored the exit wound on the side of her head, where the bullet had torn through her skull.

I stood, my gaze shifting to the man on the floor. He wore boxers and a wife-beater. The blood-soaked fabric clung to his skin.

Taking a deep breath, I glanced at Cowboy. His jaw worked the gum as if he were a cow chewing cud. Rose was tied up in a meeting. That left the two of us to represent the FBI here.

"Lie to me," I muttered, already knowing this wasn't going to be clean.

Cowboy cracked his neck, gum still popping between his teeth.

"Just tell me it's not the Night Stalker," I clarified.

Cowboy shrugged. "All right, it's not the Night Stalker."

I sighed, my frustration mounting. If Leah found out about this...

"Fuck," I muttered, placing my hands on my hips.

"Thirty-six-year-old Caucasian female," Cowboy read from his notepad. "Regina King. Worked the register at a local grocery store. Around one a.m., an unidentified white male in his thirties—"

"Cowboy, I know damn well it's the fucking Night Stalker."

"Oh. Right. Okay. So around one a.m., a not unidentified white male called Terry Patterson, AKA the Night Stalker, entered with a key and argued with the victim.

Neighbors didn't call it in 'cause apparently arguing wasn't out of the ordinary for those two."

"Did anyone hear the gunshots?"

"Nope. Probably 'cause he didn't shoot her until morning. Jackhammers and trucks from the construction site outside drowned out any noise."

I'd noticed that on the way in. It was loud as hell.

"Still waiting on some tests," Cowboy continued, "but looks like he shot her around ten a.m., then turned the gun on himself."

Suddenly, Rose burst into the room, her strides quick, her gaze sharp as it landed on the Night Stalker's body. She caught her breath.

"Shit," was all she said.

Cowboy shot her a frown. "What're you doin' here? Thought you were filling in for Miller over at Violent Gang?"

"I am. But McCourt wants another pair of eyes on this."

"Why?" Cowboy's brow furrowed.

"Because this shitshow happened a week after he got out on a two-hundred-thousand-dollar bail," Rose said, her tone clipped. "For violent rapes."

"Yeah." Cowboy nodded, lips tight. "That."

I shook my head, disbelief churning in my gut. "Fuckin' hell. A violent rapist. Two-hundred-thousand-dollar bail. Did we make sure our recommendation to deny bail got to the judge on time?"

Cowboy nodded. "Yep. All on file. We even objected after the bail was set."

Rose clenched her jaw. "I hate to stab the DA in the back, but we'll need to leak our objections to the press."

Both Cowboy and I turned to Rose, eyebrows raised.

"Let me guess," Cowboy muttered. "My uncle's idea?"

Rose nodded. "Yup. He tried to get a hold of you," she said, looking at me. "Wants to see you, now."

I nodded, understanding perfectly. This was bad. Every drug addict in the streets got held longer than this guy, and now an innocent woman was dead because the system screwed up.

My gaze drifted to the bedroom across the hall. It was lined with movie posters and skateboards. Cowboy followed my stare.

"The kid. Where is he?" I asked.

"He's with his biological dad. Shared custody with the victim," Cowboy said.

"Thank fuckin' God he wasn't here when it happened," I muttered.

Cowboy's expression darkened. "Don't thank the Lord yet. The kid is the one who found her. With his dad. When he dropped the kid off."

A heavy weight pressed on my chest, and my lungs struggled to fill. As I stared at the woman's pale face, a knot tightened in my gut. "Jesus. What a shitshow."

Cowboy's face twisted into a frown. "Feels like we failed her, doesn't it? This didn't need to happen."

"No, it didn't. But it's not on us," I said firmly. "We didn't pull the trigger. We tried to stop him. Told the court to hold him. We did what we could."

"Not everything," Cowboy muttered, locking eyes with me. I knew what he meant. "If that woman in the park had just kill—"

"Stop it," Rose snapped.

Silence fell between us. It was broken only by the click of cameras and the voices of officers securing evidence.

"If you keep going down the 'what-if' road, Theo, it'll eat you alive," I said, my voice soft.

He nodded slowly, letting it sink in. "I'll talk to the neighbors, make sure the witness statements are solid. The family's gonna sue, no doubt, and when shit hits the fan, the FBI better be squeaky clean on this."

"Good," I said, feeling a sense of pride in how far he'd come. "Smart thinking."

Cowboy smirked. "Don't tell me you're starting to like me, boss."

"Let's not get ahead of ourselves," I joked, but everyone at headquarters, including Cowboy, knew how fond I'd become of the little prick.

He chuckled but lingered.

"Is there something else?" I asked.

"Remember the guy with the red truck you asked me to look into? Carl Carr?"

"Not that again," I said.

"Wait. Hear me out," Cowboy said. "I talked to a prostitute who swears she saw him the night Nathalie disappeared. She said—"

"Jesus." I sighed loudly enough for him to get the message.

"All right, maybe not now," Cowboy said. "We'll talk later."

"Thanks," I muttered.

Cowboy nodded and left.

Rose stepped closer. "Can I talk to you outside for a minute?" she asked.

We moved down the hallway, where it was quiet. Both of us glanced around a few times, making sure the coast was clear.

"What are we gonna do now?" Rose asked, hands on her hips, worry written all over her face.

"What do you mean?"

She stepped closer, right in front of me. "Don't do this, Richter."

I exhaled sharply. "What do you want me to say?" My voice was a harsh whisper, my eyes flicking around to ensure no one overheard. "That I feel like we failed this poor woman? That she'd still be alive if Leah had just killed that piece of shit? Like Novak does?"

Rose took a deep breath, her gaze dropping to the floor. "I ... feel lost, Richter."

I blinked, caught off guard by how quickly she'd surrendered. Deep down, I wanted her to fight me on this, tell me it was good that Leah hadn't killed the Night Stalker. Give me some reason to believe in the system again—a reason that I currently couldn't see.

But she hadn't. Maybe she couldn't. Just like me.

Yet, it was my job to lead, not to crumble into doubt. I had to stay strong—or risk breaking beyond repair.

"Listen." I placed a hand on her shoulder. Her eyes snapped up to meet mine. "We saved Nathalie, didn't we?"

She nodded, though the weight on her face remained.

"And God knows how many more are alive because Grand and Harris are dead. We need to focus on those victories, not the losses."

The tension in her shoulders eased just a little.

"We saved a lot of people, Rose. Mothers like Nathalie, families who deserve to survive a glass of water from their taps because assholes like Grand are dead." I paused, my eyes locked on hers. "Can I count on you?"

Her expression tightened. I had to offer her a way out too. Forced loyalty was a ticking time bomb.

"If you're not up for this, it's okay," I continued, my tone gentle. "Go back to being a regular agent. Let me and Leah handle the ugly side of things. No shame in that. Honestly, part of me wants you to walk away, Rose. Save yourself. One more life saved."

"No." The answer came sharp, with no hesitation. "You can count on me."

I searched her eyes. Then I nodded and pulled my hand away.

Rose turned, checking the hallway again, making sure no one was close. "What about Leah and Novak?" Her voice was low, but it carried the weight of the million-dollar question.

I exhaled through my nose. "I'll handle Leah. I'll talk to her. She won't do anything reckless. She's the smartest person I know. The Night Stalker won't change that."

"And Novak?"

"Well," I exhaled. "We'll dig into his victims. Find out who they really were. Until then, we lay low."

Rose nodded firmly.

Suddenly, Cowboy stumbled around the corner. "You're still here?" He blinked at us.

Rose and I exchanged glances. **Fuck.** Had he heard anything? The construction noise outside was loud, but still...

"Did you talk to the neighbors?" I asked.

"Yeah. Mrs. Jones, down the hall, didn't hear anything. But I'll keep working my way through the damn building. Make sure nothing ugly shows up later."

"Good. Agent Rose, I'll see you at the concert tomorrow?" I asked, loud enough for Cowboy to catch.

"Yes, I'll be there."

Cowboy frowned. "Wait. What concert?"

"Leah Nachtnebel," I said.

"The ... pianist?" He raised a brow.

"Yup," I confirmed. "McCourt thought it'd be smart for us to show up. Strength in numbers after what went down."

Cowboy's frown deepened. "And nobody invited me? That woman's a ten!"

Rose rolled her eyes. "Maybe that's exactly why nobody asked you. After what happened, we have to look professional, Cowboy, not collect a harassment complaint from Leah Nachtnebel. I'll see you guys at the office."

She turned and strode down the hallway.

"What the hell!" Cowboy called after her. "You think I'm some out-of-control dog? I know how to make a smooth move on a woman! I'm a green flag guy, Rose! *Green!*"

I shook my head. "I'll see you at the office."

As I walked past the victim's apartment, I stopped and stared into its short hallway. Another motherless child. Another innocent woman, gone. Her life snuffed out because of the Night Stalker—a violent rapist whom the courts had let walk free.

Leah was still on my mind, too.

I had to tell her about this. Sooner or later, she'd find out, but the real question was, what were the consequences of all this? We'd agreed to stick with serial killers and let the courts handle the other scum. But where had that gotten us?

The world wasn't just upside down anymore. It was twisted beyond repair. Chaos had become the new baseline, and insanity was its weapon of choice.

And then there was Novak. If he'd been handling the Night Stalker, Terry Patterson would be dead, either strapped to the train tracks or floating face-down in a river. An ankh symbol—Novak's signature—carved neatly beside him.

But was a lunatic killing people on train tracks really a better choice, let alone justifiable?

As I made my way down the hallway, the voice in my head was loud and clear. No matter how hard I tried to drown it out, it kept repeating the same damn thing.

If Leah had killed him, Regina King would still be alive.

TWENTY-THREE

Rose

I tugged at the collar of my suit, trying to get some air. This whole situation felt off. McCourt and I sat in the VIP box next to Luca Domizio. Both of us were here for Leah's Christmas concert. It was the spectacle of the year. Across from us, the biggest names in politics and commerce filled the seats—people like the newly reelected Senator Wheezer, who shot us a hateful glance.

We looked ridiculous, sitting in suits with our badges hanging from chains around our necks. Then there were Luca and McCourt, who exchanged glares like two kids about to fight on the playground.

"Can we at least pocket these damn badges?" I muttered. "Feels stupid wearing them like we're at a crime scene."

McCourt shifted in his seat. "You think I enjoy this? I'd rather be dealing with an active shooter. But orders are orders." He popped a pain pill just as another reporter called his name. We both forced a smile as the camera flash went off, temporarily blinding us.

I glanced at the empty seat beside me—the seat where Richter should've been.

"He'd better get his ass here soon," McCourt grumbled.

"He said he's finishing something at the office. He'll be here," I assured him.

McCourt let out a sharp laugh. "Yeah, he'd better. This? All of this? It's his mess. And they damn well know it."

I leaned forward, intrigued. "You hear anything about the arrest?"

McCourt rolled his eyes. "Kid, I've been doing this for over thirty years."

"So? Spill it."

Silence had hung over the Novak situation ever since the arrest. No firings, no inquiries—nothing.

McCourt leaned back, a smug look crossing his face. "Doesn't matter. If you think we're not gonna pay for this down the line, you're too stupid to wear that badge."

His ability to piss people off was impressive.

"Can you skip the drama and fucking talk?" I asked, my patience thinning.

McCourt's eyes flicked toward a reporter approaching us.

"Or else I'll make a scene," I threatened, nodding toward the journalist. "Let's see how your masters like that after all the effort to make the FBI look good tonight."

We both flashed fake smiles for another picture. Once the reporter left, McCourt muttered curses under his breath. "Novak," he finally said.

"What about him?"

"I heard he's the one who saved our asses."

I blinked. "Novak? Why the hell would he do that?" My thoughts started racing. I'd assumed the silence was due to the video evidence we had of the arrest. I thought people were avoiding a scandal. "Is he scared we'll leak the arrest to the press?" I asked.

McCourt snorted. "Scared? Novak? Of what? We don't have shit on him. His lawyers and allies would chew us up and shit us out like a laxative. You ever hear of the Billmart heiress? Killed people driving drunk—fucking twice, that alcoholic cunt. Didn't face a single charge. You think anyone cares about some trailer trash dead girl in a river when the killer's a billionaire funding half the politicians in DC?" He chuckled again, this time with a provocative edge.

I brushed off his insult. "So why did Novak stop us from getting fired?"

McCourt shrugged and popped another pill. "How the hell should I know? Word is, he stopped the formal hearings—or, more likely, a bullet in our heads."

Shit.

I had to talk to Richter and Leah. Novak had something cooking. No way was he protecting us out of kindness. He had a plan, and whatever it was, I wasn't going to like it.

My gaze drifted back to Richter's empty seat. The concert hall was filling up. People were taking their time, chatting.

My eyes wandered over to Luca Domizio. Dressed sharp, champagne in hand, he oozed arrogance. He wasn't watching the crowd. His focus was locked on the stage. I followed his gaze.

And then I saw her.

Leah.

Just a shadow, blending into the backstage darkness near the velvet curtain, but I knew it was her. No doubt about it.

Fuck.

Was she looking up here? At the empty seat where Richter should've been?

I yanked out my phone and dialed Richter's work number. Straight to voicemail. I tried his personal number. Same.

"Where the hell are you?" I muttered, my eyes flicking back to the stage just as Leah's shadow disappeared.

This concert was her olive branch, the chance to get things back on track. If Richter didn't show up, who knows what would happen? The man she'd spared had just gotten out on bail and shot his fiancée.

When I grabbed my burner phone, McCourt sneered at it with obvious disapproval. It rang a few times before I got a generic text: *Can't talk right now. Call you right back.*

"Trouble in paradise?" McCourt smirked.

"Just pop another pill and shut the hell up," I snapped, forcing a grin for the latest journalist to take a picture.

That smile was harder to fake. Something felt off.

But as long as Richter showed up before the curtain dropped and Leah spotted him here, we'd be fine.

No need to panic.

Not yet.

TWENTY-FOUR

Liam

I was wrapping things up at the office while constantly checking my phone, making sure I left on time. The whole floor was dark except for the light spilling from my office. I was the last one left.

But it was the weekend, and Regina King's ex-husband and parents had already hired a lawyer. While I wanted justice for them as much as they did, the focus now was ensuring that everyone understood the FBI had fought tooth and nail against releasing the Night Stalker on bail.

I shut down my computer, grabbed my jacket, and was ready to head out when my personal phone buzzed.

I expected it to be my mom or Josie. But no—Lucy's name flashed on the screen.

"Shit," I muttered, pocketing the phone. I'd told her I'd call when things settled down.

I turned off the light, stepped into the hallway, and started for the stairs. It buzzed again. Lucy.

Pushing the call aside again, I started wondering if it was important. When I'd met her, she hadn't seemed like the pushy type.

The phone rang for a third time as I reached the stairwell.

Lucy.

"Damn it," I grumbled. I hesitated, then answered. "Hello?"

"Liam?" Her voice was so soft, I barely heard her.

"Yeah, hey. Everything okay?"

There was a short pause. "Yeah ... sorry for calling you like this, but I just wanted to say, well, thank you for the other day."

My alarm bells went off. I'd been on this job long enough to hear the weight behind those words. I could feel the crisis hiding in her tone.

I leaned against the wall, feeling the tension building. "Thank me? For what? What's going on?"

She sniffled.

"I'm so sorry to call. I just didn't have anyone else." She paused. "No. This is unfair to you, I'm sorry I ca—"

"It's fine, Lucy. Really," I said quickly before she hung up. "What's going on?"

A long silence hung between us before she spoke, her voice cracking. "My mom ... she passed. The funeral was today. She was the only person left in my life."

"I'm ... so sorry."

"No, don't be. I know what she did to your family. The woman who had an affair with a married man. She knew all about you and your mom. She kept trying to get your dad to leave. Maybe that's why I was the only person at her funeral today. But it still hurts, you know?"

"Of course it does." I swallowed hard. "I mean, I didn't know her, but my dad ... he must have seen something special in her to have an—"

My voice trailed off. For some reason, I couldn't finish. A heavy silence followed.

"Where are you?" I finally asked.

"It doesn't matter. I just wanted to say thank you for being kind to me."

"Lucy, whatever you're feeling now, it can get better."

Another heavy pause.

"Did you know you have a niece?" I said out of the blue. "Her name is Josie. She's amazing. You two would get along."

Lucy's laugh was bitter. "Funny, isn't it? You think the world's this messed-up place, and then you look in a new direction and see true kindness. That direction was you, Liam. I'm sorry for everything my mom did to your family. God. My brother. My mom. Me. Maybe it's fair that a family that wasn't ever supposed to exist doesn't anymore. Thank you, Liam. I hope life will treat you kinder soon. You really deserve it."

"Lucy, wait—"

The line clicked dead.

My heart pounded as cold sweat slicked my forehead. I tried calling her back, but it went straight to voicemail.

"Fuck!"

I sprinted back to my office and flicked the computer on. Each second it took to load felt like a lifetime. Finally, I was able to do a quick search on her. As soon as her address popped up, I called 911.

"There's a possible suicide attempt at twenty-three Gulp Street," I said into the phone as I left my office. "Lucy Folbs. Send an ambulance now."

I hung up and leaped to the stairs, hitting the garage in record time.

"Please, God, please."

I jumped into my car just as my phone buzzed. It was Rose. Shit. The concert. But this was more important.

I ignored the call, turned on the siren, and sped out of the garage. Another call from Rose. I quickly shot back a standard text: "Can't talk right now. Call you right back." Then I dialed Lucy again.

Nothing.

"Goddamn it, Lucy!" I shouted to no one as I floored it, racing against time.

I slammed my hand against the steering wheel, frustration boiling over. This was exactly the kind of drama I didn't need. And yet, maybe it wouldn't have happened if I'd let Lucy into my life when she'd asked.

I grabbed my phone and called the police again to make sure they were on it. Relief hit when the dispatcher confirmed a unit was on the way.

Each turn felt like slow motion. My mind spun, and questions pounded in my brain. Was any of this real? Leah, Lucy, Carl Carr?

By the time I pulled up to the scene, there was just one cop car. The officer inside was likely finishing up paperwork. I screeched to a halt in front of him, then practically jumped out of the car before it had fully stopped.

"Where's the ambulance?" I yelled, rushing toward his open window.

The officer glanced at my car, its flashing lights still on, then back at me. "Already on the way to the hospital," he said calmly.

"Was she alive?"

"Yes."

I froze. My head tilted back, and I stared up at the cloudy night sky. The weight lifted off my chest.

Thank God.

I could breathe again. The tightness in my lungs was finally releasing.

"Which hospital?"

"I think they said Hyde Park General," the officer said.

"Thanks."

I didn't waste another second, just dove back into my car and punched the hospital into the GPS. The concert had probably already started, so there was no point in calling to interrupt it.

I'd wait until it was over and apologize to Leah. She'd understand. She had to.

This was more important right now.

TWENTY-FIVE

Leah

The final notes of my improvisation on *O Come All Ye Faithful* echoed through the sold-out concert hall. I'd chosen a few classic Christmas pieces for tonight's crowd, adding my own signature touch, and the crowd's reaction didn't disappoint. The applause thundered. Chants and whistles filled the room. People wiped tears from their eyes, and the ovation lasted longer than any I could remember. Tonight wasn't just a performance—it was my return after the shooting.

As I stood under the spotlight, bowing to the crowd, my eyes drifted to the seats reserved for Rose, McCourt, and Richter. Rose and McCourt were there, but Richter's seat remained empty.

A pang of disappointment hit me. Why wasn't he here? I caught myself overthinking it, telling myself it didn't matter. But it did. It was ridiculous how much it bothered me.

After forcing a few more bows and smiles, I left the stage and walked quickly toward my artist's suite.

After everything that had happened, tonight was supposed to be a symbol for the three of us—a reaffirmation of our work and how we had to adapt to keep going. The plan was to talk in my dressing room right after the concert.

"Leah, Senator Wheezer and the mayor want to congratulate you in person," Crystal said, hurrying after me as I strode down the hallway.

Of course Wheezer did. He had no idea about my connection to the arrest. Novak had kept quiet—for reasons I still didn't understand.

"I'm tired. Tell them another time," I said, my tone final.

Crystal knew better than to argue. She nodded, slipping away.

I entered my dressing room and closed the door behind me. My eyes went to the flip phone on my golden vanity. Any messages from Richter? I grabbed it and checked.

Nothing.

Then a soft knock came at the door.

"Crystal, I said I'm tired," I repeated.

"I ... I know," she stammered through the door. "But there's a man. He insists that you want to see him."

Richter?

I rose quickly and made my way to the door. When I opened it, I found a confused Crystal—and a face I recognized: Jan Novak's driver. He wore a crisp, dark suit with a neatly pressed white shirt. His face was lined, with thinning gray hair combed back, and a quiet, stoic expression.

My eyes narrowed. "Where is he?"

"Waiting for you outside," the driver answered.

I glanced at the flip phone on my makeup table, then back at the driver. Novak had been silent for weeks. In fact, he'd never made direct contact before. But considering he held more cards than we did, hearing him out seemed wise.

I grabbed my coat from the hanger by the door and slipped into it. "Let's go," I said, brushing past Crystal, who stood frozen in confusion.

The driver, dressed in a crisp suit and cap, led me out the back door of the concert hall and into a quiet alley. Parked there was a sleek Maybach, its polished surface gleaming under the streetlights.

The driver opened the back door, and there he was: Jan Novak, dressed casually in jeans and a wool sweater. Beside him lay a neatly folded pile of women's clothes: jeans, a sweater, and boots, all looking eerily similar to his outfit.

I hesitated, surprised by his appearance, but then regained my composure. "I take it you didn't attend the concert," I said as I stepped closer to the car.

"No," Novak replied smoothly. "When I told you I don't care for classical music, I meant it."

"Fine by me," I muttered.

But something made me pause.

I turned once more, looking back at the concert hall's door. I was half-hoping, half-expecting to see Richter burst through, to come and stop this. Stop me from walking into something dark, something inevitable.

But the door stayed shut.

I nodded and stepped into the Maybach. The door closed behind me with a weighty thud as if sealing a new chapter in my life.

"So," I asked, meeting Novak's gaze, "where to?"

A confident smile played on his lips. "I've got a surprise for you."

"I don't care for surprises."

"Oh, you'll care for this one. Believe me."

TWENTY-SIX

Liam

I rushed up the concert hall's stairs, dodging the few remaining elegantly dressed attendees. Almost everyone had left.

When I reached the balcony, I found Rose. McCourt was gone.

My eyes scanned the empty hall, then flicked back to Rose.

She gave me an accusatory look. "Where the hell were you?" she demanded as she followed me into the hallway and down the stairs toward the backstage area.

"Busy," I said, my voice heavy with exhaustion as I tried to shake off the lingering memory of the night's events.

I tugged at the backstage door. Locked. But then a violinist stepped out, and I quickly flashed my badge, slipping through without a word.

"Richter!" Rose called after me, struggling to keep pace as I charged ahead.

When I noticed she had stopped, I turned.

She approached slowly, arms crossed. "Where were you? McCourt was unbearable, and Leah wasn't happy you didn't show."

"I know," I muttered, taking a deep breath. My eyes met hers briefly before they dropped to the floor. "It was my sister."

"The one in college?" Rose asked, her face softening.

I shook my head. "It's complicated. But anyway. My sister. She ... she tried to kill herself."

Shock spread across Rose's face. "What? When?"

"Right before the concert. She called me to say goodbye."

She blinked slowly, the weight of the words sinking in. "Jesus."

"Yeah."

"Is she okay?" she asked quietly.

"She's alive," I replied. "I went to the hospital. But she said she didn't want to see me. I'll try again tomorrow with Josie."

Rose remained silent.

"Come on," I said, motioning toward Leah's room. "Let's talk to her so I can go home. I'm really fucking tired."

"Of course," Rose said just as Crystal appeared. I would have recognized her red hair and glasses from a mile away.

"Agent Richter!" Crystal greeted me with a huge smile, a light blush coloring her cheeks.

Rose rolled her eyes.

"Good to see you, Crystal," I said, forcing a polite smile.

"What are you doing here?" she asked.

"The FBI director wanted us to personally thank Ms. Nachtnebel for hosting us tonight," I explained.

"That's sweet of you," Crystal said, "but she's already left."

"Left? Already?" I asked. Rose and I exchanged glances. Leah usually remained after concerts, making sure no fans lingered for autographs or photos. "Where did she go?"

Crystal shrugged. "Some limo driver picked her up right after the concert. She seemed to know him. They left together."

My stomach twisted. I exchanged another glance with Rose.

"Thank you," I said, forcing a smile at Crystal before turning to walk with Rose toward the entrance hall.

Once Crystal was out of sight, Rose stepped in closer. She kept her voice low. "Please tell me it's not who I think it is."

I cursed under my breath and pulled out my phone. It rang, but Leah didn't pick up. "Nothing," I muttered, hanging up.

Rose let out a sharp breath. "We could head back to the office, track the limo with traffic cameras."

I shook my head. "Won't get us far. He's probably taken her out of Boston by now."

Her forehead creased with worry. "He won't hurt her, right?"

I hesitated. "I don't think so."

Murder didn't seem like Novak's move when it came to Leah, at least not tonight. Picking her up with his driver in front of witnesses felt too bold, too sloppy. He could've tried to kill her quietly a dozen times already. She was safe—for now.

Rose nodded slowly, absorbing my logic. "So what now?"

"As much as I hate it, all we can do is wait."

She exhaled through her nose, then tried a smile. "Get some rest. You need it. I'll let you know if I hear anything."

"I'll do the same."

She leaned in, smirking. "Who knows? Maybe we'll find Novak face down in a river tomorrow. If anyone can pull it off, it's her."

I let out a dark chuckle. As messed up as it sounded, it would make things easier. "Don't give her ideas," I muttered.

Rose threw me an innocent look, her grin not fading. She placed a hand on my shoulder. "Let me know if you need anything."

I nodded and watched her walk away.

Today had been a shitshow, like most days since Harris had been killed in those woods over a year ago. But if this was my life now, the only thing I could do was keep moving forward—*falling* forward was more like it—until things got better. Or until my head was next on the railroad tracks.

TWENTY-SEVEN

Leah

We hit Route 1 North and left Boston behind. The car had been mostly quiet. I had questions, of course, but Novak answered only when he wanted, so I remained quiet.

"You're not scared?" he asked as I stared out the window, watching the closed businesses blur by.

"No."

He grinned. "I expected a million questions by now."

"Why bother? You seem to talk when it suits you."

Silence fell over the dark limo until he shifted in his seat. "Fair enough. I feel chatty now. Ask away."

I turned to face him, doubt creeping into my expression.

"I mean it," he said, catching the look. "Ask whatever you want. I'll answer truthfully now that the secret's out."

"Anything?"

He nodded. "Except one question."

"What's that?" My brow furrowed.

His hand tightened briefly around an object in his hand. It was the first crack I'd seen in his confident facade since I'd known him. He shoved the object into his jeans pocket. "I won't talk about the meaning of the tracks or the ankh. They're connected."

Just like that, he'd admitted he was the Train Track Killer. I already knew that, of course, but it was strange to hear the confirmation this way.

"All right," I said, straightening up. "How long have you been entertaining your ... hobby?"

He frowned, thinking. "About fifteen years now."

Longer than I expected.

"How did it start? Your first murder?"

"I don't call it murder, but fine. Let's not argue over labels." He took a deep breath. "Back then, I'd just secured a big contract with the largest home security company in the world. It was the investment I needed to make my company the largest cloud storage firm in the nation. But soon after that, people at Obligato started reporting crimes caught on the security camera footage we stored on our cloud. The company that rented the storage didn't want to report them after we reported the incidents. They were afraid it'd hurt business. Lead to the loss of customers. People wanted protection from other people's crimes but not their own. So they stayed quiet."

"Of course they did. The almighty dollar is hardly a secret."

He nodded. "See no evil, hear no evil. As long as the cash comes in."

"But not you."

He shook his head. "No. Not me. At first, I played along. Couldn't afford to lose the contract. Money talks, not ethics and fuzzy feelings. But then we contracted the biggest online storage provider in the nation. They became a subcontractor under us to cut costs. The cloud is expensive. Soon after that, one of my IT techs flagged a violent rape at a man's home. The man had recorded it and stored it on his computer, which synced its data with online storage on our cloud. We'd seen bad things before, but this one..." Novak's face darkened, disgust and anger mixing in his expression. "This man raped a woman he'd paid for from a sex trafficking ring. And he did it ... with a knife. Somehow, the poor thing lived for over an hour, enduring this horror over and over again. Then she finally died. I was never so relieved to see somebody die."

I narrowed my eyes at Jan, watching him relive the memory. He looked distant, disgusted, but mostly angry.

"I paid the guy a visit at night. Shot him straight in the head while he slept. It was so easy. I knew everything about him—his routine, where he ate, even the church he went to, singing songs to Jesus before he went home to rape and kill women." Jan shrugged. "I felt nothing but justice as he lay there, motionless in a pool of blood. My only regret was that he left this world too quickly. Without pain."

Was that why he'd chosen the train tracks? To squeeze out every ounce of fear? To inflict upon them the horror of being tied down and staring at an oncoming train? But something told me there was more to the tracks than that.

"I've always had this feeling of disgust," he continued, "this rage toward people who do wrong." He balled a fist. "Something in my childhood burned it into me, like branding cattle. You must feel it too, right? This thirst for justice. Your work's close to mine."

I thought back to my first kill: a man who'd plowed his car through a crowd to avoid jail, taking innocent lives with him. The satisfaction I'd felt driving that shard of glass into his neck was undeniable. The peace his family would feel once the tears dried and they realized they were finally free.

We left the highway, and the road darkened as we turned onto a more rural stretch. We had to be about an hour north of Boston. Houses became sparse, blending with farmland.

"I understand why you use men like Patel to do the dirty work," I said. "If they get shot, no loss. Genius move. But what about Kirby? He wasn't a monster. He was the sad result of a corrupt and failing system. Why groom him for something so dangerous? That bomb could've killed innocent people."

"Kirby was a troubled soul. When I first noticed him, he was already planning a mass shooting."

"Before you met him?" I raised an eyebrow.

Jan nodded. "My software flagged his texts to a friend about shooting up a mall. Anything suspicious—whether it's a message, phone call, or video—gets flagged and sent directly to me."

"You go through all that? For the entire nation? That's impossible."

"I work day and night, but even then, I barely make a dent. The darkness in this world is beyond imagination."

I couldn't help but feel a strange sense of admiration. The cold-blooded monster I'd always thought Jan Novak to be didn't exist. The more I saw of him, the more the puzzle pieces fell into place. They revealed an operation far beyond anything I could've imagined.

"So you redirected Kirby's anger into a bomb attack?"

Jan's jaw clenched. "Not at first. When I found Kirby, he was ready to leave this world in all the wrong ways. But I gave him purpose. Showed him glimpses of what the world could be."

"You fed him targets from your system?" I asked.

"I did. Every one of those targets deserved it in one way or another. And the more people Kirby stabbed, the more he believed in the mission. Like he forgave himself for the terrible things he'd done in the name of our government. He started using his skills to cleanse the world, like something out of an action movie."

"And the bomb attack?"

"It was planned for a meeting of high-profile pedophiles on a private yacht docked near Boston. All of them are tied to human trafficking. Names you'd never hear in that context but faces you'd recognize from TV and government. Kirby was willing to sacrifice himself for something that meaningful."

For a moment, it felt like Richter and I were the villains, stopping Kirby from wiping out those predators. But then...

"Nice story," I said, locking eyes with Jan. "But Kirby was a ticking time bomb himself. He didn't need a mission. He needed therapy. A chance to rebuild his life. You could've stopped the shooting and gotten him committed to a psychiatric hospital. Instead, you sent him on a suicide mission. Trapped him in the hell he was trying to escape."

"He volunteered. It was his idea," Jan shot back.

"And yet, he shot Agent Rose when she confronted him. Almost killed Richter and me too. You can justify my death, sure, but Rose and Richter? They're not like Anna, Carr, or Mauser. They're nothing like you and me."

Jan's eyes narrowed, and a flicker of betrayal crossed his face. Of course he wouldn't agree. A few moral arguments meant nothing when his methods were so efficient, so effective.

"Fighting fire with fire only makes the flames bigger," I said. "What other outcome is there?"

"Then how do you exist?" he asked as the car pulled into a dark, empty parking lot. He turned away, looking out the window. "Don't you fight fire with fire, Leah? You don't seem to mind the scorched earth you've left behind so far. Why question mine?"

I reached for the pile of clothes next to him. "I assume these are for me?"

He stayed silent as, unfazed, I slipped out of my concert dress and into the jeans and sweater. Then I stepped out of the car and into the cold night air. Whatever he wanted to show me, I knew it was waiting somewhere in those dark woods.

"The difference between my scorched path and yours," I said, turning to face him, "is that what I burn to ash never deserved to exist in this world. You, on the other hand, are a wildfire—swallowing everything in your path without mercy."

I caught myself speaking like Richter. Did Jan notice? I never felt remorse for people like Anna or Kirby. But I understood the logic behind Richter's doubts, and I defended them like they were my own.

"What if Kirby's bomb had killed the innocent waitress on that yacht, just trying to make a paycheck while serving rich pedophiles? How do you justify that?" I asked.

Jan Novak got out of the car. His flashlight cut through the dark as we stepped onto a narrow, overgrown trail. The path was rough. Tangled roots and damp leaves made it barely visible under the beam's flicker as we moved deeper into the woods.

"Some things can't be justified," he said, "but they're sacrifices for the greater war. Like friendly fire between allies. Shooting down a helicopter because you thought it was the enemy. A mistake, sure. But do you stop the war on terror over one misstep? Or is the greater good too important to count every single life?"

"I'm familiar with the Doctrine of Double Effect," I said. "Allowing harm as long as it's an unintended consequence of achieving a good outcome, as long as the harm isn't the goal and the good outweighs the bad."

"I live by it. So do you, even if Agent Richter tries to pull you away from this destiny."

The trees and brush closed in around us. The night was dense and silent. Not a single house was in sight. Rocks and branches crunched under our boots as we passed several "Private Property" signs.

"You're wrong about Richter," I said firmly. "And the doctrine is flawed because it lets people justify morally questionable actions just because they claim good intentions. The harm is the same, whether it's deliberate or not. Richter and I live by a much simpler doctrine: the one where monsters are taken out, no innocents harmed. Smaller-scale justice. But even a bathtub fills if the drops keep coming."

Jan stopped and looked at me. His flashlight pointed at the leaf-covered ground. "And who's going to tell that to Regina King?"

My eyes widened. "Regina King?"

"Yes. Or her son," Jan continued, "who'll never see his mother again, except for the image of when he found her? Brains splattered across the bed every time he closes his eyes."

I fell silent, feeling the icy sting of betrayal creep into my chest.

"What?" Jan asked, feigning surprise. "Richter didn't tell you that the Night Stalker shot his fiancée yesterday? He got out on bail, courtesy of the justice system we're all supposed to trust. Then he shot her hours later."

My fists clenched, nails digging into my palms. Was this true? Why hadn't Richter told me right away? Was he afraid of the rage he knew I'd feel, the justice I craved? Was that why he hadn't shown up to my concert?

Was I shaking? Surely, it was just the cold.

"How much longer will you lie to yourself?" Jan pressed. "This hope that you and Richter are meant to be? I get it—creatures of the dark crave the light. But night is night, and day is day. You can't change that."

I started walking again, ignoring him. If Jan thought he could bring me out here and manipulate me like he'd done with Kirby, Patel, and Carr, he was dead wrong. I lived by my own choices. My thoughts, my reasoning—they were mine, not shaped by anyone's mind games, not even someone as cunning as Jan Novak.

We walked in silence for another twenty minutes or so until we reached a small, decaying wooden hut in a clearing. Moonlight bathed the rotting boards, highlighting the two broken steps leading to the porch.

"What's this?" I asked.

"My surprise, of course," Jan replied with a smile. "Come on, you'll like it."

I followed as he stepped over the crumbling stairs and onto the porch. Without hesitation, he moved straight to the door, which was locked with heavy chains. One by one, he unlocked them with a set of keys. The chains clattered to the floor.

He pushed the door open and disappeared inside.

I froze.

That hut.

Something told me that whatever was inside could change my life forever.

Instinctively, I glanced back at the trail, half hoping—no, almost expecting—that Richter would appear, grab my arm, and pull me back to his world.

But why was I putting so much hope in him?

I'd always been alone. From my first breath to this one, standing on this rotting porch. No one was forcing me to stay. I could turn around, walk away, and return to my own mission, my own sense of justice.

And yet, as if something beyond my control was pushing me, I stepped inside.

The stench of feces and mold closed in around me.

Jan's flashlight swept across the room. It revealed a row of people tied to chairs, their mouths taped shut. Six men and one woman. Their clothes were dirty, some torn, and the stench of sweat and piss hung heavy in the air. The horror in their wide, pleading eyes was unmistakable. Their bodies trembled as they struggled against the ropes. They moaned and shifted in their chairs. But I didn't flinch as I met their gazes. Their fear sank into the darkness that already lived within me.

I felt nothing for them. Nothing.

"Remember that chat on the dark web? The one the Night Stalker held so dear?" Jan asked, approaching an older, bald man who was bleeding from the forehead. He wore cargo pants and work boots. A badge identified him as a school janitor. "This is the one who liked to brag about the baby porn."

Jan's eyes gleamed as he pointed to the next man. "And him? He's the one who said he had a little girl at home whom he did things to at night, things his wife doesn't know about."

The skinny man was in his thirties and had a long, scraggly beard. He blinked rapidly and shook his head, denying everything with an almost believable enthusiasm.

"They're all here, the men from the chat. Coordinating everything was a bit interesting, as we had to retrieve these people from all across the US, but as always, where there's a wallet, there's a way. Do you want me to introduce them all to you?"

I shook my head. My eyes landed on the woman all the way to the left.

"And her?" I asked. "What about her?"

Jan nodded. "Ah, yes. Carole Traylor. She helped the cartel set up fake photo shoots for kids. She pretended to be a photographer and told the parents to leave so the kids could act 'more natural.' When the parents came back, they'd find an empty room. Kids gone, sold into human trafficking."

I narrowed my eyes at the woman. Her bleached-blonde hair was greasy and unkempt. She rocked back and forth as she watched us, tears streaming down her face, smearing her mascara into dark streaks like shadows of guilt. She was begging for her life, trying to scream through the tape. For a moment, I saw Nathalie again—when I'd found her in Carl Carr's basement. But then I remembered the innocent horror in Nathalie's eyes—that of a victim. Carole's eyes lacked the same innocence.

Jan swung the flashlight to the corner of the room, where red canisters of gasoline glistened in the beam.

I didn't need to ask questions. It was obvious.

Novak grabbed the first canister and began pouring gas over the woman. Then he moved to the old man beside her.

I just stood there. Silent. Watching.

The man's T-shirt read "Spread the Love."

"Him, I actually know," Jan said, grabbing another canister and dousing a man in silk pajamas. "From a fundraiser. He works in Senator Wheezer's office. Small world, huh?"

The man thrashed in his chair, desperate, but the ropes held him tight.

The room reeked of gasoline as Jan emptied several canisters over the group, soaking them. Then he grabbed one more and walked over to me. "You ready?" he asked. Unfazed. Cool. Almost jolly.

I stood there a moment longer, then nodded and stepped outside.

Jan followed, trailing gasoline out of the hut, down the steps, and toward me.

I stopped about thirty feet from the hut.

We stood together in silence, listening to the branches swaying in the wind, an owl hooting somewhere in the distance—and, of course, the muffled screams coming from the hut.

I should've run. Maybe even killed Jan with the gun I'd slipped from my coat and into my back jeans hip trim. But aside from knowing I wouldn't stand a chance in a physical fight if he grabbed my wrist in time, I realized I didn't want to run.

I didn't want to stop this.

The rage over Regina King's death at the hands of the Night Stalker was still too raw. I felt responsible. In some way, I even blamed Richter. It was his voice in my head that had stopped me from killing the Night Stalker when I'd had the chance.

My leg twitched as if some part of me was still telling me to run. To return to the moral compass I used to follow. The one that Richter carried for me like a torch in the dark. To kill monsters. Serial killers. Not just people who did horrific things.

There was a difference, wasn't there?

At least, according to Richter.

And yet...

My eyes locked on the silver lighter that Jan had pulled from his pocket and was holding in front of me. His hand was steady, waiting. For a moment, I stared at the lighter. Then I grabbed it and flicked it open. The small flame danced in the wind. Without another second of hesitation, I dropped it onto the gasoline trail.

In seconds, the flames ignited and raced toward the hut. They crept inside and onto their targets. The muffled screams grew louder as fire burst through the windows, then up through the roof. Raging flames swallowed the house in a violent blaze that ascended to the sky.

It was almost incredible how long it took for the screams to die down.

And still, we waited. Watching. Until Jan pulled out a pocketknife and started carving the ankh symbol into a nearby tree.

I watched, fear lingering in the back of my mind.

Richter.

His name tore through my mind, and a sharp sting of loss stabbed deep into my chest. I hurt. Real pain. Shocked by the intensity of the emotion, I almost checked for a blade.

But then that familiar feeling washed over me—the same twisted satisfaction I felt when I killed killers. And in that moment, I realized my dark prophecy had at last come true.

To be fair, it had probably been a hopeless task from the start. And I'd just been too sentimental to see it. Like the little girl in the library all those years back, hoping she'd feel something one day.

In the end, Richter had failed to save me.

I'd become the monster I'd always been.

TWENTY-EIGHT

Liam

I sat in my office, empty eyes fixed on the flip phone in my hand. It had been a week since the concert, and after four messages and several calls, Leah still hadn't gotten back to me.

When I heard a knock at the open door, I shoved the phone into my pocket.

"Got a minute?" Rose asked, stepping through the door. The way she quietly shut it behind her told me nothing good was coming.

She sat across from me and dropped several manila folders on the desk.

"Violent Crimes Unit got a call a few days ago about those bodies in the woods. Remember?"

"Yeah. A hiker and his dog got lost in Bear Brooke State Park and found an old hut that had burned to the ground. Six men, one woman inside. Our Violent Gang force supervisor thinks it was arson." We were the largest FBI office around, so my desk was littered with crimes from all over New Hampshire, Maine, and Massachusetts.

"Yes. Ellis also thinks the La Mano Roja cartel is behind it," Rose said, flipping open a folder.

"Burning snitches and people in debt is their calling card," I said. "Last year, we found five burnt immigrants in that factory in Boston."

Rose nodded. "Well, I was just wrapping up a meeting about the incident at Bear Brooke State Park with Ellis down at Violent Crimes when the DNA results of the victims came in."

I leaned back in my chair, my eyes narrowing at the folders. My gut tightened. I hoped her next words wouldn't confirm what I was now thinking.

"The problem is..." she continued, flipping open one of the folders. A mugshot of a bleached-blonde woman in her twenties stared back at me next to a charred pile of what might've been a living body at some point. "This one. Carole Traylor. She has a history of human trafficking."

I tensed. It was cartel-related, so there was still a chance it wasn't what I feared.

"Cartel crime," I said, almost convincing myself.

Rose opened another folder, revealing a bearded man in his thirties. "Then there's this guy, Roger Miller. Registered sex offender from Nebraska."

I stared at the images, feeling the hope drain out of me. My tie suddenly felt tighter. "What about the others?" I asked.

She opened another folder. "Three are still unidentified, but this one? Daniel Justling. He's got several violent rape charges. All of the victims were minors." Rose looked at me, her eyes sharp. "Three victims with criminal records. Burned alive in the middle of the largest state park in New Hampshire, in a hut nobody even knew existed.

What I need to hear from you now is"—her voice dropped—that you've heard from Leah. That everything between you two is fine, and this is just a cartel hit. That these victims having a record is just a coincidence."

Silence hung between us. I leaned back, staring at the folders. "I can't," I muttered, the words slipping out before I could stop them.

"Yeah," Rose said. "That's what I thought."

I leaned over the table and flipped open the other three folders. Charred bodies labeled "John Doe #1," "#2," and "#3" stared back at me.

"We don't know who they are yet?" I asked.

Rose shook her head. "Our forensic odontologist and anthropologist are on it."

I kept my eyes on the photos. The images almost carried the stench of burnt flesh.

"We should have their names soon," she added. "The new databases should help speed that up, thanks to the cloud."

I shot her a look, my brow furrowing.

"So let me just state the obvious," Rose said, her voice lower. "I'm guessing these other three bodies have a record too or some sick hobby nobody knows about yet. Child porn, murders, rapes, who the fuck knows? But you know where I'm going with this, right?"

Of course I did. This had emerged shortly after Jan Novak had picked up Leah from a concert.

Rose pointed at the folders. "I think they did this. Together."

I leaned back, my gaze still fixed on the pictures. "Anyone at Violent Gang suspect anything out of the ordinary?"

"No. Everyone's convinced it's La Mano Roja. Even if all the victims have skeletons in their closets, it still fits the cartel's signature. Human trafficking and burning people alive are classic La Mano Roja. Like they did in Boston last year. And with the buses of immigrants arriving in the city from the south…"

I nodded slowly.

"So?" Rose raised an eyebrow. "Do you want me to do anything about all of this?"

I thought about it for a moment. "Like what?"

Rose threw her hands up and leaned in closer. "I don't know, Richter! Why are you asking me?" She dropped her voice even further. "This isn't what I signed up for."

"So what do you suggest?" I asked. "Opening an investigation on Novak and Leah?"

"On what grounds? We've got no evidence whatsoever. We'd go down. You and me. People would think we're crazy. Taking Novak down without Leah would be harder than taking down the president. And Domizio might kill us the moment he saw us turn on her." She took a deep breath as if bracing herself for what she was about to say. "So why even bother? I mean, do you even think what they're doing is that bad?"

I opened my mouth, then shut it again. I didn't know what to say. I wasn't even sure where I stood anymore. Should I care that they'd burned some perverts who'd molested kids? Did anyone?

"If I'm honest," Rose whispered, her eyes dropping to the folder. "I don't feel bad for any of them. Not even the woman. Her record … she got only four years for helping traffic kids because there were only witness statements and no hard evidence. When she was arrested, no kids were found at her residence. She probably went right back to it after she got out. Just look at her assets. The Porsche. The house. All cash-bought. So if you ask me"—Rose looked up at me, her eyes glinting—"let Leah and Novak do their thing. Like some twisted couple from hell. And you and I ... we go back to being agents, ignoring the occasional weird cases with their signatures all over them. Nobody will question a thing. They don't know what we know."

I just listened, her words pulling me in like a cobra swaying to the movements of a flute.

"We're in pretty deep, Richter. But if there was ever a time for us to stop this, it's now. I'm ready to be a real FBI agent again. Get the bad guys. With what we've got here at the bureau." She leaned back in her chair, her gaze still locked on mine. "Let's be the good guys again."

Maybe Rose was right.

And maybe Leah was right too.

Maybe we could exist with similar missions but in different ways.

Maybe I'd been riding that high horse for too long, looking down with my morals like some wannabe saint. Regina King had changed everything for me. We'd left it to the system, and now she was dead. I had no doubt that she'd still be alive if Leah had killed the Night Stalker when she'd had the chance. And God knows how many kids had been spared now that these sick bastards were reduced to ashes.

But I couldn't just move on, pretending nothing had happened. Who knew what Novak had told Leah, what methods he'd used to pull her into this mess? She'd trusted me, and I wasn't the kind of man to let her down. Especially not after she'd saved my life. I'd stop by her house as many times as it took until I got the chance to talk to her.

Slowly, I nodded, then closed the manila folders like they weighed a ton. The moment they snapped shut, the temperature in the room seemed to drop back to normal.

"You're the Special Agent in Charge of the Boston FBI," Rose said.

She wasn't wrong. I spent most of my time with the BAU and trusted my unit supervisors to run things their way without my assistance. But I was in charge, after all.

"You could keep me in Violent Gang a little longer, just to make sure everything stays quiet around this case," she added. "They could use the help."

"We could too, with Heather on maternity leave." God bless her. She was having another baby, and she was greatly missed.

"Violent has Higgins and Moore out on long-term disability. Higgins got shot on the last mission, and Moore had a stroke at a barbecue."

I knew all that. We were short on agents everywhere right now, but Violent Gang was definitely feeling the blow harder.

"Yeah," I said. "You might be right. Stay there for a bit."

She nodded, then stood, leaving the folders on my desk. As she reached the door, she paused. "One more thing," she said before turning back. "Cowboy met with Carl Carr's mother."

I stiffened. "He fucking what?"

"I heard him talking to Martin about it. He's got this whole theory about Carl Carr being a serial killer."

I let out a loud, annoyed breath. "For Christ's sake."

"Martin didn't bite. Told him to drop the crap and focus on the job. But you remember what happened the last time an FBI agent went rogue chasing a serial killer nobody else believed in."

Of course I did. Back then, I was Cowboy, and Larsen … he was sitting right where I was now. The sense of déjà vu was eerie. "Shit," I said. "I'll think of something. In the meantime, can you babysit him for a bit?"

Rose rolled her eyes.

"Take him to Violent Crimes. Partner up with him on BAU cases," I said.

"Oh, come on. Like cop partners?" Rose protested.

"Yep, like cop—"

The door flew open without a knock, and Cowboy stuck his head in.

"…partners," I finished.

"Did I hear 'partners'?" Cowboy asked.

"Jesus Christ, ever hear of knocking?" I asked.

Cowboy grinned and knocked on the wide-open door.

I sighed. "What do you need, Cowboy?"

"Oh, yeah." He shuffled some papers in his hands. "Remember Carl Carr?"

Rose and I exchanged glances.

"Good God, Cowboy, no, no, no," I said. "I don't have time for this. From what I heard, Carr's gone. Ran off or something."

"Yeah, that's what his mother told me, but something doesn't add up. Ever since you told me to check the traffic cameras on his red truck, I've had a weird feeling about him."

"Cowboy…" I started.

"And now look at this." He fumbled with the papers. "His truck was parked near the pianist's concert hall, and then near her house, multiple times over two weeks, right after Nathalie disappeared."

"Cowboy," I said again, firmer this time, more aggravated.

"We've got it all on camera. A guy like him? Into classical music? Nah. I think he did something to Nathalie that she won't admit. Too scared to tell us. And now he might be planning to kidnap—"

"McCourt!" I snapped, my voice echoing around the room.

Rose shot me a sharp, scolding look. Cowboy froze, his eyes wide.

But this had to stop. Now.

"I just heard you went to Carl Carr's mother despite me telling you to stay away. Is that true?" Anger edged my voice.

Cowboy nodded.

"And now you're here, showing me days of research on something I told you to drop. Is there really no work to be done in the BAU besides chasing a guy who pays for *consensual* sex? No killers? No rapists? Did the world suddenly turn into all love and gummy bears while I wasn't paying attention?"

The silence was heavy, dead serious. Cowboy cleared his throat. "No, sir. It didn't."

"So there *is* actual work to be done at the BAU, then? Work that your coworkers have been doing for you while you're off on a side quest like this is fucking FBI Zelda Two Point Oh? Regina's family is suing the state, the DA is trying to blame our reports for their failure to keep him in, we've got a guy out there who might be imitating the Night Stalker, Martin just told me about two women found dead in a month, both in doll wigs, and you haven't lifted a finger for any of it?"

I glared. I wanted him to feel my anger.

"Because you want to track down a man who hasn't been charged with a single crime, for the disappearance of a woman we *found*? A woman who told us she ran off with a guy?"

Cowboy's face fell. His eyes were wide, embarrassed, full of doubt. And the worst part? Deep down, I knew he was right. He just wasn't allowed to be.

"I'm ... I'm sorry, sir."

I took a deep breath, trying to steady myself. I saw flashes of Larsen yelling at me for prying into Leah Nachtnebel. Right here, in this same damn chair. Only back then, she was the bad guy, and I was the good guy. Right?

"Good," I said, keeping my voice calm. "You'll work on cases with Rose for a bit."

"You mean supervised like some kid?" Cowboy protested. However, when he saw the shock on my face, he backed down. His gaze dropped and shifted to Rose as if he were a scolded kid ready to leave the principal's office.

"Anything else, sir?" Rose asked.

"No." I felt like a piece of shit, but I needed him to stop. If anything, chasing Leah now was dangerous, especially with Novak involved.

Rose nodded. "All right. We'll talk to the police about the two dead women with the wigs, then see if Violent Crimes needs help with anything."

"No," I said, stopping them. It was better to keep Cowboy away from that crime scene for a while. I had no idea how active he'd been behind the scenes. "Focus on the victims with the wigs. Martin's handling the new serial rapist. We need all hands at the BAU."

If Leah and Novak were working together, we'd have to switch back to our old investigation tactics. Hopefully, they were smart enough to avoid active FBI cases. God knows there were enough other bad people out there for them to hunt—people whom no one would miss.

"Yes, sir," Rose said.

Cowboy nodded, and they both left.

I watched them go, shaking my head. How the hell had Larsen managed this for so many years without anyone finding out?

I grabbed the folder on the burnt woman and opened it. Her mugshot was rough. She looked wrecked.

With a forceful snap, I shut it again.

Maybe it was time to go back to normal, to let Leah and Novak do their thing. But first, I had to talk to her. The decision to break things off wasn't mine—it was hers.

And I wasn't ready to let her go. The nagging emptiness in my chest made that painfully clear.

TWENTY-NINE

Rose

It had been almost two weeks since Cowboy and I had started working together—or, more like, since I'd started babysitting him. Things almost felt normal again. The world was still fucked up, and I was still part of the FBI, trying to patch up whatever cracks I could.

We'd just wrapped up interviews with the families of the two dead women. The family of Claudia Wayne, the young nurse found dead while wearing a wig, lived outside Boston. We were driving back to the office when I noticed Cowboy wasn't taking the turn back into town.

I raised an eyebrow. "We heading to a petting farm or something?" I glanced at the rearview mirror as the highway faded behind us. The barren trees looked like skeletons against the gray sky.

Cowboy smirked, but then his expression darkened. "Claudia's family lives close to something I want to show you." He shook his head as if trying to clear the thought. "Weird. Feels like a sign."

I shot him a look. "A sign? What the hell are you talking about?"

Cowboy's grip tightened on the steering wheel as he exhaled. "I ... need to tell you something. But you can't tell Richter."

I leaned forward, the seat creaking. "Cowboy, no. Absolutely not. No. No. No. I don't want to hear—"

"I talked to Nathalie yesterday," he blurted out.

I jerked in my seat and turned to him sharply. "You fucking what?"

He raised a hand as if that would douse the fire rising in me. "I had to. Something's wrong. I feel it in my gut. Richter's always said to trust your instincts, right? That your gut is half the investigation. Well, I did, and I'm on to something big." Cowboy's jaw tightened with frustration. "So I don't get why he won't back me up! He treats me like a child, Rose. That high-profile arrest at the mansion? The one where you guys flew off in a helicopter like James fucking Bond? 'Just forget about it, Cowboy. Top secret—nothing for the kids,' right? 'Fuck Cowboy. He's just here for everyone's amusement.'"

A curse slipped through my teeth as I fought against the pity creeping in. "Don't say that. You're a hell of an agent, and Richter believes in you, Cowboy. He does. He's just under a shit-ton of pressure. This isn't the Wild West, no matter how much we joke about it. Mistakes cost lives."

Cowboy's eyes stayed locked on the road ahead and the landscape stretching out in front of us—bleak fields, dry and empty.

"You trust Richter, don't you?" I pressed, hoping to break through his stubbornness.

"Of course I do."

"Then you know Richter would take a bullet for you. For all of us."

He glanced at me, and our eyes met.

"He's not perfect, but if there's one thing I know about him, it's that he's not in this for himself," I said. "He does what's right for others, always. He's working himself into an early grave to make a tiny difference. That's a unicorn right there."

Cowboy's gaze drifted back to the road. His lip twitched as he bit down. Then he let out a long breath. "Shit. Maybe you're right. Maybe this is all bullshit."

I reached over and squeezed his shoulder. "Doesn't change the fact that you did good work, though. Really."

He nodded slowly, his eyes distant. "Well, we're here anyway. Might as well do this last thing—"

"Here?" I cut him off, my body tensing as we turned a corner on the country road. The land stretched out ahead of us, revealing a large, desolate turkey farm. The grass was withered, the fences sagging and broken. "Theo, no!" My voice was sharp. "Turn around."

"One quick stop, Rose. After this, I swear, I'll stop." He pulled up the road, past outdoor pens crowded with sickly-looking birds, their feathers ragged and barely clinging to their bony frames—products of mass production.

"This is a waste of time, Cowboy. Richter's gonna lose his shit."

He parked in front of the meat processing facility, killed the engine, and looked at me.

My gaze shifted from the rundown white farmhouse with its cracked windows and back to Cowboy.

"That's why you're not telling him," Cowboy said, getting out of the car.

Sweat beaded on my forehead. It dripped down as I rushed after Cowboy into the meat processing facility. The cold, sterile air hit me like a wall. It was filled with the sharp scent of raw meat and disinfectant. Stainless steel tables lined the room. The place buzzed with activity, but the workers—most of whom looked like they were from overseas—kept their heads down, focusing on their tasks, barely noticing us.

"Cowboy!" I snapped, grabbing his arm. "What the hell are you doing? We don't have a search warrant!"

"We don't need one. Mrs. Carr gave us permission, remember?"

"No, I don't remember that. I've never even met her."

"She takes a nap in her house around this time."

"What? How often have you been here?"

"Two, maybe three times. Mrs. Carr always invites me in. Last time, she showed me around until we got to that red door at the end of the facility. She refused to let me see inside. She walked me back to the house with some bullshit excuses."

"What about cameras?" I shot back, hoping to stop him.

Cowboy shook his head. "No cameras. She told me that too. Don't you think that's strange? A large turkey processing plant with no surveillance? What's Carl Carr hiding?"

We stopped in front of a red metal door.

"Looks locked," I said, hoping to end this insanity.

"That's why I had a key made from a picture I took of the lock." Cowboy smirked as he pulled out the key.

I stood there in disbelief as he slid it in. The lock clicked open.

If I'd ever thought Cowboy was all bark and no bite, that was now a thing of the past.

"Oh look," he said, pushing the door open. "It's unlocked. Just like Mrs. Carr told us." He shot me a sly, knowing look.

"Cowboy, they'll take our badges for this."

"Nope." He stepped into the room. "Not if I'm right about what's in here. Old, sweet Mrs. Carr will pretend she had no idea about the red door's secrets. She'll go along with our lie that she gave us permission to look around freely. As a testament to her innocence."

The small storage room looked ordinary—shelves lined with dusty cleaning supplies, and a worn rug spread across the floor. But I couldn't shake the feeling that something was off. That red door—it didn't belong.

"Nothing here," I said, sweeping my arm around the room. "See?"

Cowboy wiped a finger across a dusty bottle of detergent. "Maybe."

"Maybe? What the hell do you mean *maybe*? There's nothing! Let's go before she wakes up." I threw my hands in the air, frustration boiling over.

Cowboy stood still, his hands on his hips, looking defeated. But then his eyes narrowed and locked onto something on the floor. "Wait."

Without another word, he yanked the rug aside, revealing a hatch in the floor. My pulse quickened as he pulled it open and shined a light into the abyss. Instinct kicked in. I drew my gun, following his lead, the tension building in my chest.

I silently cursed everyone: Carr, Richter, Cowboy, Leah. All of them.

It was too late now. Carl Carr's secret was about to hit every news channel in the country.

As we descended the dark, narrow stairs, the smell of feces and rotting meat slapped me in the face, making me gag. Blood stained the walls and steps. At the bottom, Cowboy's flashlight flickered, nearly slipping from his hand.

"Fucking shit," he choked. I followed the beam of his flashlight, and my breath caught—a shelf lined with human heads, floating in jars.

"Shit," I whispered, horror clawing at my throat.

Cowboy snapped out of his trance, swinging the flashlight wildly, as if expecting Carl Carr to lunge from the shadows at any second.

"All clear," he gagged, the flashlight revealing nothing but us and the remains of the women.

I pulled out my phone, already dialing. "Jesus Christ. I can't believe this."

Cowboy lowered his gun and swallowed hard, likely bile.

"Carl Carr," I said, keeping my voice steady. "He's not starting over. He's on the run."

Cowboy nodded slowly. "That piece of shit."

I called in for a search warrant and the arrest of Carl Carr. And for backup.

At least if people thought Carr was on the run, no one would suspect he was dead— by Leah's hands. No body, no evidence. Carl Carr was just ... gone.

"Mrs. Carr must've lied to you the first time you contacted her. Bet he was still here, and she warned him we were onto him. So he fled."

"That makes the most sense. That old, evil hag. Who the hell protects a monster like this?"

"A mother," I said, my voice flat, emotionless.

I stood next to Cowboy, my gaze locking onto the grotesque sight. The heads, with their swollen eyes and lips, suspended in fluid, looked like zombies. It was horrific.

And yet, I couldn't help feeling a sense of dark satisfaction. Carl Carr had left this world in great pain. "Let's call Richter from upstairs," I said, my eyes still on the jars.

Cowboy clenched his jaw and gave a small, resigned nod. "I trusted my gut, just like Richter told me to," he mumbled, repeating the words as we made our way back up the stairs.

"You did," I said, trying to make my voice comforting. "You did."

As fucked up as this whole situation was, and would be, Cowboy had been right. If Carl Carr were still alive, Cowboy would've been the one to have stopped him and saved lives. And at least now, the body parts of those poor women could leave this house of horrors. Just like Nathalie.

It would be a nightmare to clean up, and the real consequences were yet unknown. But Richter would find some comfort in this too.

At least those women could finally rest in peace. Now they were free.

THIRTY

Liam

It was an overcast day, and the Boston Zoo was nearly deserted. Lucy, Josie, and I stood by the wombat enclosure, watching as the fluffy animal climbed a branch.

"Oh. My. God!" Josie gasped. "This is the cutest thing I have ever seeeeeeeen!"

"It's cute as buttons," agreed Lucy. They both broke into high-pitched murmurs as they tried to contain themselves over the furry, walking teddy bear.

"Dad!" Josie called, spinning toward me. "You don't think this is cute? Are you made of ice or something?"

I couldn't stop thinking about Leah. It was constant. I didn't eat. Sleep. I'd stopped by her house and even the concert hall a few times, and each time, her maid or Crystal had turned me away without a word from her. My texts, my calls—ignored. Every damn one.

"Daaaaad!" Josie insisted.

I cracked a smile. "It's pretty damn cute."

"I heard wombat poop is cube-shaped," Lucy said, her tone casual.

"No way." Josie laughed, her eyes wide.

"Seriously." Lucy nodded. "So the poop doesn't roll away. It helps mark their territory."

Josie almost doubled over laughing, then caught the look on my face as I watched the wombat in its enclosure.

"I'm sorry," Lucy said, looking unsure. "Was that inappropriate?"

Josie rolled her eyes. "It's not you, Aunt Lucy. Dad hates zoos. We don't usually come here. He feels sorry for the animals, you know, being stuck in cages."

Lucy nodded. "Looking at it like that, it is kind of sad, especially for the big cats and elephants."

"Yeah," Josie agreed, her voice quieter now.

"Oh no," Lucy said, glancing between us in horror. "Did we come here because I suggested it, and you didn't want to say no? I'm so sorry. I—"

"It's a zoo, not a cigar lounge," I cut in, trying to ease her nerves. "Don't worry about it. We got to see cube-shaped poop."

Josie and Lucy grinned. It had been a week since Lucy had been allowed to leave the residential mental health facility during the day. This was good for her.

"Dad, can I get a pretzel?" Josie asked, eyeing the food truck down the path.

"Of course," I said, handing her a ten. "You want anything?" I asked Lucy.

She shook her head. We both watched as Josie sprinted off.

"How are you holding up?" I asked, turning back to Lucy.

"Pretty good," she said, glancing down. "I feel awful that I did this, to be honest. It's so embarrassing."

"Don't say that. There's nothing to be embarrassed about."

She nodded, though her gaze stayed distant. "They drill it into your head that suicide is a permanent solution to—"

"Temporary problems," we both finished. We shared a knowing smile, both of us amused at how overused the phrase had become.

"Thank you, Liam," Lucy said, her voice soft. "For being here for me. For letting Josie into my life."

"Nah, nothing to thank me for. You belong with your family, even if it's a bit of a fucked-up one."

Lucy laughed, but it faded quickly. "I didn't always deserve to be here with you and Josie." Her face tightened as if old demons were clawing their way out of the past. "I did some pretty bad things when I was using. It was hard growing up with a mom who resented us. She blamed us for our dad never being around, like his screw-ups had taken the shape of two kids. We were constant reminders of his mistakes. It was too much for David—our brother. He died of an overdose right before I went to rehab and quit. I've been sober over ten years now, but the past"—she let out a sharp breath—"it still haunts me."

"We've all done things we're not proud of," I said, a wave of guilt washing over me. If she only knew what I was wrapped up in with Leah.

"Not like me," she muttered. "You've probably pulled my record? It's fine if you did, I just—"

"I didn't," I interrupted. "I thought we'd start fresh. If there's anything you want to tell me, that's your call."

"Do you believe people can really change?" Her eyes found mine. They were glassy with unshed tears, filled with doubt, shame, and sorrow.

For a moment, I wasn't sure. But standing there, looking at my sister—someone who'd been the tragic product of our asshole dad, the pain and regret so clear in her eyes, yet fighting to be better—I knew the answer.

"I do," I said quietly.

She held my gaze for a beat longer, then wiped her eyes. "You're a good man, Liam. If the world had more of you, it wouldn't be so fucked up."

I was about to make a joke when Josie stomped back, her face red with frustration. "Fifteen bucks!" she fumed. "He wants fifteen bucks for a pretzel." The ten I'd given her trembled in her hand. "Fifteen, Dad!"

"Jesus," I muttered, reaching for my wallet to hand her another five.

She pushed the ten back at me. "No way. I'm not buying into that rip-off. Told him I wanted a pretzel, not a share in the pretzel company."

Lucy and I exchanged amused glances as Josie crossed her arms.

"Let's go to the goats," Josie announced.

"She's so much like you," Lucy said, a grin tugging at the corner of her mouth.

"Yeah." I shook my head with a smile. "That train's left the station. Sarcasm's in her DNA now." Just then, my phone rang. I answered. "Richter."

Rose didn't waste time with pleasantries. Cowboy. Carl Carr. It was bad, and I had to leave—*now*.

I hung up, rubbing my temples. My life was a circus, and every day was a new act.

"Everything okay?" Lucy asked, concern crossing her face.

My mind raced. How the hell was I going to handle this? If Nathalie didn't talk, we could frame it as Carr on the run. Rose probably already had. The way she'd mentioned Carr's arrest warrant suggested that she was around others and was giving me our way out.

"Is everything okay?" Lucy repeated, snapping me out of it.

"That was work," Josie said, stepping in. "Happens when your dad's in the FBI, saving the world." Pride filled her voice. She had so much understanding for a kid her age. I couldn't help but grin at her. "He's about to tell us that he has to leave," she continued, grabbing my hand. "And that's okay." She looked up at me, her eyes shining. "He's tired all the time. But he still does so much with me. When I'm an adult, I wanna be just like him."

I squeezed her hand back, the lump in my throat rising.

But if she knew where I was headed—off to a crime scene to cover up the brutal murder of a serial killer by Leah Nachtnebel—would she look at me the same way?

"I'll drop you both off," I said, clearing my throat. "Sorry about that."

"All good." Lucy smiled. "This has been one of the best days of my life."

THIRTY-ONE

Leah

I walked out of the concert hall through the back door. Once I was outside, my breath hung in the winter night air. Novak's Maybach sat idling by the curb. It was parked in front of my own limousine, where Mark waited behind the wheel. My steps slowed, then picked up again. Piles of dirty snow, left by last night's storm and the snowplows, lined the sidewalk like forgotten barricades.

Novak's driver, dressed in a sharp wool coat and suit, opened the door. I climbed in, pulling my cashmere coat tighter around my waist as I settled into the seat. It was our first meeting since the hut incident in the woods. I'd known he'd reach out again, but I hadn't expected it to happen like this—just as before. I sent a quick text to Mark, telling him to follow us.

Exhaustion weighed on me. I hadn't slept in days, my mind tangled with thoughts of Richter. I'd watched from the window as Aida had turned him away. I'd hoped— *wished*—he'd ignore her, storm the house, and find me. But then what? It would probably be our last conversation, filled with accusations and disappointment. He'd finally see me for what I really was.

And that look would haunt me forever.

"Can I ask you something?" I said.

"Of course," Jan replied smoothly.

"Do you know who killed Emanuel Marin?" I asked. Maybe, at least, that haunting mystery could be solved.

"No," he answered, a little too quickly.

I narrowed my eyes, unconvinced. He had eyes and ears everywhere—including on me. Was this just another one of his games?

"If you're planning another mission like last time, I'll have to cancel," I said, my voice icier than the night outside. "This way of communication doesn't work for me. Neither does our collaboration if this is how you picture it."

Novak nodded. "Fair enough. But there's no mission today. I want to show you something else."

I raised a brow.

"Nothing like last time," he added. "I promise."

I smoothed a wrinkle in my black evening dress. "I'm too tired for this, Jan."

In those dark woods, Jan Novak had handed me an opportunity, a way to truly make a difference in this twisted world. But it had also taken something from me, something I hadn't realized I held more dear than my thirst for justice.

Richter.

"It won't take long," he assured me.

I thought about it, then nodded.

"Has Richter contacted you yet?" he asked, his gaze locking onto mine.

I held his stare. It was none of his business, and my silence made that clear. "What is it you want to show me?" I finally asked.

The car cut through Boston's narrow streets before heading into the quieter outskirts. Trees thickened on either side as we left the city behind. The sound of commercial freight trains rumbled somewhere in the distance. After a brief drive, we arrived at a secluded stretch of commercial train tracks cutting through the forest on Pine Street near Wilkers Manufacturing.

We both stepped out, and Novak, ever the gentleman, offered his arm. I reluctantly took it as we made our way toward the tracks. My heels sank slightly into the soft earth, and the crunch of fallen leaves underfoot echoed in the stillness. The faint smell of damp moss and pine lingered in the air. We walked along the tracks, passing a few weathered wooden benches that seemed out of place in the wilderness. Ahead, a rundown station waiting house loomed in the darkness, its roof collapsed—a relic of an old commuter station long forgotten.

Jan came to a stop near one of the wooden benches, positioned by a small clearing along the tracks.

"Remember when I told you not to ask about the train tracks and the ankh symbol?"

I nodded.

"Well, tonight, I want to tell you a story about a poor immigrant family from Slovenia," Jan said, gesturing toward the benches. It felt like an invitation to his own home.

I sat down. Through my cashmere coat, the cold wood pressed against my legs.

"They had two boys," he continued, his eyes fixed on the darkened tracks ahead. "Mojca and Anton. Both often wished they'd never been born, at least not to those parents. The drinking, the beatings, the screaming ... endless fights." He paused, the memories darkening his expression. "Anton, the older one, he could've escaped. He was smart and kind. Had that rare something about him that drew people in. He could've run off and started a better life. But he stayed. For Mojca. He took care of his little brother. Made sure he had shoes, a coat for the cold weather, and food. When things got bad at home, Anton took Mojca to playgrounds in the summer and museums in the winter. He loved his little brother with all his heart."

I watched as a faint, bitter smile tugged at the corner of Jan's lips. It was like he could see the boys playing in front of him.

"Their favorite place in the world was the Egyptian exhibit in town. At night, before the nightmares came, they'd talk about the stars and the old gods, just like in ancient Egypt." He still didn't look at me, his gaze now locked on the tracks. "One day, after another bad fight between their parents—knives were involved, which wasn't unusual—Anton found Mojca outside in the bitter cold. Barefoot. Anton rushed inside and grabbed his brother's shoes and coat. They spent the day wandering, waiting until it was safe to go home."

His voice cracked. He walked toward the edge of the tracks, his hand slipping into his coat pocket, clenching into a fist as if he were holding onto something.

"They were on tracks just like these," Jan said quietly, "when Anton had a seizure. He had them occasionally. Their mother smoked and drank through both pregnancies. But Anton, selfless as always, had grabbed Mojca's shoes and coat that day instead of his own jacket, where he kept his medicine."

His voice grew tighter, strained.

"During his seizure, he collapsed onto the rails at the station. Mojca screamed for help as he leaped onto the tracks, desperately trying to pull his brother off, but Anton was too heavy. He tugged and strained, tried and tried. The train wasn't even in sight yet. There was enough time to help. But people ... they just stood there. Staring. Watching. Like heartless statues."

He pulled out a silver ankh necklace. The pendant dangled in the dim moonlight. His eyes—filled with sadness and hate—stayed on it.

"When the train hit, only one boy survived. The boy and his brother's favorite possession." Jan slipped the necklace back into his pocket, then turned to meet my gaze.

I sat there, feeling the weight of his story sink in. Anton and Mojca. The accident on the tracks. The meaning behind the ankh. "You ... are Mojca," I said quietly.

Jan didn't answer right away. His expression was cold. "It's horrific what a train does to the human body. Especially one so small," he finally said. The sadness in his eyes faded, replaced by flickers of pure hatred. "People ... most of them are rotten inside. No soul. No heart. They need to face that truth. Confront their demons and leave this world knowing that they've been seen for who they truly are."

I held his stare, the tension between us almost tangible. "The Ankh. It's a mirror," I murmured. "But instead of reflecting what people want to be seen, it reveals their true selves. Their darkest sins."

Jan's hand slipped from his coat pocket. The movement was slow and deliberate. "I told you I wasn't who you thought I was. But now that you know the real meaning of the ankh, maybe I can be."

I stood and took a step toward him, but my phone buzzed in my pocket, pulling me back to reality.

Richter.

I should have ignored it, but my hand had already moved to retrieve the phone. Under Jan's watchful gaze, I opened it and read the message. *Can we talk now?* A picture of Nathalie sitting alone in an interrogation room was attached.

Jan's voice cut through the silence. "Why does he hold such power over you? I see it every time I look into your eyes. Him. I see him in them."

I slipped the phone back into my pocket. "I apologize, but I have to go. I'll call my driver. No need to drop me off."

Jan stayed motionless, his eyes fixed on me as I turned to walk away. I didn't need to look back to feel his gaze; it was heavy, lingering. He must have thought I was cruel for leaving so abruptly, especially after he'd opened his heart to me. Should I have said something, pretended to feel something for him? But how could death itself ever become anything more than a messenger of misery?

I was who I was.

And yet, the timing of the text couldn't have been worse. Jan would surely take this personally—maybe even as a rejection.

But I had to meet Richter.

It was time.

Time to face him.

Time to make him see or lose him forever.

THIRTY-TWO

Liam

As I slipped the flip phone back into my pocket, my eyes shifted to the screen. Nathalie was there, sitting in the FBI interrogation room, waiting under the harsh lights. Leah wouldn't talk to me about the hut in the woods, so maybe this would add some pressure.

It was after 10 p.m., but Cowboy had arranged this meeting with Nathalie, marking it as *urgent*. To him—and everyone else—Carl Carr, suspected serial killer, was still on the run.

To Cowboy, Nathalie was a key witness, just too scared to talk while Carr was "out there." Sometimes, a lie made as much sense as the truth. The heads in Carr's basement, linked to missing prostitutes, were enough to fuel that narrative. One surveillance clip from a liquor store camera even showed him with a woman from his basement—proof that Cowboy had latched onto. I couldn't block this interview, especially not when Nathalie had agreed to talk again.

I leaned back in my chair, my gaze on Nathalie through the screen. She looked so different now. Short hair. Clean. Wearing a decent coat. Her file said she was working at a local grocery store, and she had enrolled in online classes to become a teacher.

It almost made me grin. A former prostitute and serial killer survivor teaching kids? Finally, someone with something useful to teach about this world: how to spot the real monsters. How to survive.

My eyes drifted to the manila folder on my desk. I opened it for what felt like the thousandth fucking time.

Carole Traylor.

Her bleached-blonde hair. Blue eyes that had gone from haunted to accusing in the past few days—and I couldn't explain why.

No.

That wasn't true.

I knew exactly why.

My sister.

Her suicide attempt. The zoo.

After we'd talked at the zoo, I'd decided to look her up in the system. I had to make sure she hadn't been involved in anything that could hurt Josie. And she hadn't lied about her dark past. She'd been the getaway driver in an armed robbery. An elderly woman was stabbed and later died in the hospital from a heart attack. The DA cut her a deal. Rehab instead of jail if she identified the others. She took it.

And here I was.

Staring at the burnt remains of a woman with a past. Just like my sister, whom I'd somehow found it in my heart to forgive. She'd turned her life around—sober for ten years, working at a nursing home where she was known for her kindness and loving treatment of the residents. Many of them would be all alone without her. Now guilt ate her alive. There was a genuine desire for redemption.

If I'd found it in my heart to forgive her, how could I condemn Carole Traylor?

Some digging had revealed that Carole Traylor had been a victim of human trafficking too. How much of a choice had she really had when the cartel had told her to get those kids? Who was I to decide her crimes were worth a death sentence while I granted a second chance to someone I cared for?

I tilted my head back and stared at a dried leak in the ceiling.

"SAC?" Cowboy's voice broke the silence as he knocked on the open door. "Nathalie's waiting in the interrogation room."

"I'm coming," I said, standing.

If Nathalie talked, this would go from fire to a full-blown inferno. She'd never seen Leah's face, but she'd heard her voice. And we already had footage linking Carl Carr to Leah—him stalking her. If Nathalie mentioned a mysterious woman killing Carl, it wouldn't be long before Cowboy's gut would lead him on another trail. The same one I was on. The one that had led me to Leah. And now right back to me.

"I'm coming," I repeated, hiding the dread that threatened to creep into my voice. Part of me almost wanted it all to come out. To end this mess. At least then, I'd know who I was again. Know right from wrong. The burden of judging over life and death lifted off my shoulders.

It was heavy.

Maybe too heavy for any human to carry so easily.

THIRTY-THREE

Nathalie

Once the agents entered, the FBI interrogation room felt small, as if the walls were creeping in. The flickering overhead light didn't help. It cast an uneasy glow that I'd seen too many times before.

I'd been in rooms like this plenty of times. But this time was different. This time, they were after *her*. The woman who'd pulled me from the pits of hell. The one who'd killed that monster.

I had to stay strong. For that angel God had sent me.

I'd never been arrested, but I'd been questioned, and I'd lied to cops more times than I could count, always covering for the other girls. I could do it again. I had to.

I took a sip of the coffee I'd brought with me. Street smart. Never take a drink from cops.

We all knew that trick. They'd swipe my DNA and tie it to something from Carr's basement.

Across from me sat two agents. One was in his late thirties. He had brown hair and even darker eyes. Agent Liam Richter. His presence was odd—calm and comforting.

Next to him was Agent Theo McCourt, the one I already knew. Blond. Younger. Restless energy radiating from him. Ready to make things happen right now.

"You're not hot?" McCourt asked, nodding at my gloves.

I shook my head.

"You want another drink?" He glanced at my coffee.

Another head shake as I put the empty cup into my coat pocket. "I recycle," I lied. "Global warming."

His sigh gave away his frustration. "So..." McCourt started. "You know why we called you in?"

Richter glanced at him before turning back to me, his voice warmer. "Thanks for coming in so late, Nathalie. I know you have little ones at home. And just for the record, this isn't an arrest. You're not in any trouble. We just want to chat. See if you can help us save lives."

I shifted in my chair. "I guess it's about that serial killer again? The one Agent McCourt said is on the run?"

Richter nodded. "Carl Carr."

Agent McCourt slid a picture across the table—the monster who'd kept me locked in his basement for weeks. The man who'd done things to me even the devil would flinch at.

My chest tightened, and my heart pounded as I stared at him. The bastard who'd carved out chunks of my flesh while I was still alive. To eat them.

My gloved hands clenched in my lap. The taste of bile crept up my throat. Was I about to throw up?

"I know you're scared, Nathalie," McCourt said, watching me closely. "But there are other women out there who could be next. We need your help to stop him. Now. Before he can hurt anyone else."

If Carr were still alive, I'd have sung like a bird. But I knew he wasn't. Thanks to her. The woman who'd done what no one else could: saved me. I owed her everything. There was no way I'd betray her.

I leaned back, keeping my voice steady. "I really hope you find him," I said almost casually. "But I don't know how I can help."

McCourt's eyes narrowed, and he slid another picture onto the table. A red truck parked in a dark alley.

"Know this place?" he asked.

Like the back of my hand. Fergy Avenue. The alley where clients parked to find us.

"No," I lied. "I don't think so."

His lips pressed tight. "Let me help you out. This is Carl Carr's truck. Parked right around the corner from where you were working that night. The night you disappeared."

"Ran off with a man," I corrected. "Another loser, promising the world, delivering nothing but a pile of shit."

"Mm-hmm," Agent McCourt mumbled sarcastically. He added another picture— me at a convenience store, buying coffee and a chocolate muffin, right before it all went down. "That you?"

I shrugged. "I don't remember." Pulling my hair aside, I revealed the scab where Carl Carr had slammed me with an iron bar. "I tripped that night. Freak accident. Hit my head. Things were blurry for a while after."

The room was charged, filling the space like an invisible weight.

"Did he do that, Nathalie?" Agent McCourt asked.

I shook my head.

"I know you're scared, but lying to a federal officer is a crime, right, Nathalie?" Agent McCourt said, turning "bad cop."

"Agent McCourt..." Richter's tone was a quiet warning.

"And lying to me means Carl Carr keeps doing what he's doing, Nathalie. To others."

"McCourt." Richter's voice was firmer now.

McCourt took a deep breath, barely holding it together. "So let me ask you again." He tapped the photo of Carr. "Have you ever met this man?"

I refused to look at the monster's picture again. Instead, I stared straight at McCourt.

"Why protect him?" he continued. "If you're scared, we can help. Help you get that college degree. Help you provide for your kids. Help you keep them all safe."

My heart pounded, and my gaze dropped to the table. For a moment, I thought about telling them. What if they found out, and I got a record for lying? I'd stayed off the system for years, working the streets, and now things were finally falling into place. Could I risk it all?

"Nathalie," McCourt said, softer now. "I'm here to fight for you. Let me help you and your family." His finger hovered over Carr's picture. "Please. Have you ever met this man?"

Silence hung in the room. Maybe I wasn't as strong as I thought. Maybe it was okay to let someone else fight this battle. Carry the weight of this dark secret.

My mouth opened before I could stop myself.

"No," I said, my voice steady. Its strength surprised me.

McCourt's hand slammed down on the metal table, rattling it. "You're lying!" he snapped. "I can see it in your eyes."

Richter's voice cut through the tension. "Theo! A word." He nodded toward the door as he stood and opened it wide.

"I'm really sorry, Nathalie," Agent Richter said, his voice softening. "It's been a rough few days. We just need to find this man before he hurts anyone else."

I forced myself to meet his eyes. "I understand. Don't worry."

His lips pressed together in a brief acknowledgment as he stepped aside. "It's late. I'm sure you're tired."

Without hesitation, I hurried out into a dimly lit hallway. My mother stood there, her face etched with worry, arms open and waiting. Her coat hung loosely around her as she pulled me into a warm hug. Tears burned behind my eyes. I tried to hold them back, but the horror of seeing Carl Carr again was too much.

"Let's go, my little Peanut." Her words were soft and comforting as she led me toward the elevator.

We stepped inside. As the doors began to close, I glanced up for the first time since leaving the room.

Standing at the end of the hallway was Agent Theo McCourt, watching me like a hawk, his eyes narrowed. He didn't even look at Richter, who was still lecturing him.

The doors shut, and a chill ran through me.

He knew.

He fucking knew.

And he wasn't going to give up easily.

THIRTY-FOUR

Leah

When I opened the front door and saw him standing in the pitch-black night, I turned and walked into my study. I didn't know what to say.

Liam quietly shut the door behind him and followed me.

The fireplace was burning, its flames casting orange shadows across the walls. I switched on the desk lamp so I could see him better—his face, his eyes.

He made his way to the fire and stared into it.

"Nathalie's sticking to her story," he said, his voice low.

I moved around the desk and sat down. For a while, we remained silent. I watched him stand by the fireplace, his gaze lost in the flames. The quiet between us felt like a wall. It was as if we were both afraid of what would happen once the words were spoken.

"They say," he began, his voice low, "when your body's on fire, you might pass out in a minute or two from inhaling hot air or toxic gases like carbon monoxide. Your lungs get scorched, or the smoke suffocates you. But before that happens, your skin starts to melt—every nerve ending screaming as the flames eat you alive. And death? If you're really fucked, that can drag out for five to ten agonizing minutes." He turned to look at me, his eyes dark. "Five to ten minutes. That's a hell of a long time to burn alive, don't you think?"

"Definitely one of the more painful ways to die," I agreed. "If those rapists didn't want to burn, they shouldn't have worn flammable clothes."

"Nice one," he said, his tone dripping with sarcasm.

He pressed his lips together, then pulled a thin, rolled-up manila folder from his coat pocket and dropped it onto the desk in front of me. I glanced down and opened it to reveal the mugshot of the woman from the hut.

Caroline Traylor.

I braced myself for one of our usual arguments. For his anger. But instead, he just stood there, his eyes locked on the picture of the woman.

"I ... don't know what's right or wrong anymore," he said, his voice steady but quiet. "However, I do know I can't keep going on like this. Won't keep going on like this."

The room felt heavier with the silence that followed.

"You're not like them, Leah," he finally said, shaking his head. His gaze found mine. For a split second, I thought I'd see disappointment, maybe even disgust. But instead, there was only sorrow. And as twisted as it was, hope. Was that for me?

"You're not a monster like Grant, Harris, Carr, or ... Jan Novak." His hand reached across the table, landing gently on mine. The warmth of his touch burned deeper than the flames in the fireplace ever could. With his eyes on me, his gaze pierced into shadows that I didn't want anyone to see.

"We don't hurt good people, Leah. You and I, we save them."

His hand lingered, heavy with meaning. Then he hesitantly pulled it away and stepped back.

A soft meow broke the tension. Liam looked at the cat that was rubbing against his leg. A faint smile curved his lips as he crouched to pet it. "Does the cat have a name yet?" he asked, his tone lighter.

I shook my head. "No."

He straightened up. "Josie thinks Hope would be a good name."

I almost laughed. "Hope? In this house? Living with me?"

He shrugged. "She's a kid. Whatever hell they go through, they usually hold onto the good in the world ... until they grow up."

I frowned. "A remarkable strength," I said.

His brown eyes glanced at the folder, then caught my gaze again. "I'll ... talk to you soon," he said.

I knew what he was really saying. He was giving me time to think.

I stood as he left. His figure disappeared down the hallway before the front door clicked shut.

For a moment, I stared at the picture of the woman in front of me. What was it that Richter saw in her that I didn't?

Pushing the photos aside, I sat and started reading through her file. Her story was anything but ordinary: a teenage girl running away from an abusive home only to fall into the clutches of sex traffickers. By the time I'd finished the first few pages, I could sense the darkness in every chapter of her life.

Sure, I understood her life hadn't been easy. She'd been a victim once. But did that excuse her choices? What did her past matter when she'd gone on to harm others? Kids had gone missing because of her, and they would've continued to disappear if she were still alive. She had a choice: her life or theirs. What kind of argument was Richter trying to make? I knew he'd rather die than harm an innocent child.

"Of course I would," I could almost hear him say. "But that choice isn't so easy for people who've been trapped in hell their whole lives."

And he had a point, logically. I didn't feel anything for Caroline Traylor, but it made sense that people who hadn't experienced her kind of suffering couldn't easily judge her actions by their own standards.

I shut the folder with a snap and leaned back in my chair.

The way he'd talked to me. Even the way he'd tried to appeal to my humanity with ... this. He hadn't given up on me, not even after the hut incident. He might never work with me again, but he still believed I was something more than a psychopathic killer.

Though he'd shown me this courtesy, I wasn't sure I could extend the same grace to myself. That night in the woods—it had changed me. My work with Jan meant something. With his power, we could make this world better. Save thousands of innocent lives.

I could set boundaries with Jan. For Richter. Focus on serial killers and psychopaths, just on a larger scale. Would Richter really oppose that? Was I missing something? Was my inability to feel and think like a normal person clouding my judgment again?

I felt like that little girl in the psych ward all over again.

I'd learned to feel a few things, thanks to Richter, but I still didn't understand them. Like rain trying to explain to fire how it nurtured life while drowning out the flames at the same time.

Maybe rain and fire both had a place in the world—just not together.

I grabbed the folder on Carole Traylor and walked over to the fireplace. Without a second thought, I tossed it into the flames. The paper curled and darkened as the fire devoured it.

I felt nothing when I looked at that woman's picture. Her file was also full of missing girls she'd lured in. Witnesses had seen her with the kids, but there hadn't been enough evidence to send her away for life. Four years. That was all she'd gotten. Four. Years.

And then she'd gone right back to it.

Richter's point about her tragic past left a bitter taste in my mouth. Sure, she might've been a victim once, but when she burned, she was the predator.

When I'd burned her in that hut, all I'd felt was justice.

Nothing else.

If Novak came back to me after how I'd left him at the station, I'd have killed for him again. Over and over.

This was who I was.

This was Leah Nachtnebel.

THIRTY-FIVE

Liam

Three months later

I stood in my office as agents milled around. Dead silence filled the air. I was on hold with the Trace Evidence Unit within our Laboratory Division. A witness had come forward on the tip line, reporting a man who'd backed into her car in the parking lot where Claudia Wayne had gone missing. The witness said she'd seen a woman matching Claudia's description in the man's car. The woman's head had been resting against the window, and her eyes had been closed. She'd been either sleeping or passed out.

We'd tested paint scrapings from the witness's car against those of a van that a neighbor had called in after we'd released a picture of the offending vehicle—and the offer of a reward—to the media. The van belonged to Gerald Smith, a middle-aged landscaper from Roxbury.

My gut told me we were close—so damn close—to catching the sick bastard who'd raped and killed two women and put doll wigs on them.

"Lab just confirmed it," the voice on the other end crackled. "The paint. It's a definitive match."

A surge of adrenaline shot through me, and my heart pounded against my ribs. "Good work," I said.

"Go get him."

I slammed the phone down a bit harder than necessary. The agents nearby turned to look at me, anticipation on their faces.

"Gerald Smith. It's him!" I announced. "The lab confirmed the paint match. We've got our guy!"

A ripple of excitement swept through the room. In an instant, the team sprang into action.

"Everybody to the equipment room to gear up," I commanded. "Matin, get me a warrant. We move in ten!"

As everyone hurried to prepare, I grabbed my FBI jacket. Despite the electric energy rushing through me, my hands were steady. This was it: the moment we'd been pushing toward for weeks.

We pulled up to Smith's house just as the midday sky cast a gray, dark winter hue over the dilapidated neighborhood. The house stood out even among the other worn-down homes. It was a sagging two-story structure with chipped paint that might have once been green. The lawn was overgrown, weeds choking what remained of a cracked walkway leading to the front door. A battered van—the one that had hit the witness's car—was parked in the driveway next to an old pickup loaded with rusted landscaping tools.

We moved in silence, fully geared with FBI vests and identification jackets. Firearms drawn, we advanced toward the house, each step deliberate. An FBI agent trained as a locksmith crouched by the front door. His tools glinted faintly in the dim light.

As I waited for the door to be unlocked, I scanned the surroundings. The neighborhood was eerily quiet. My eyes drifted to the side yard. Something caught my attention: a rusty swing set behind a leaning fence.

A knot formed in my stomach. I prayed the kids weren't here. They were supposed to be with their grandmother this weekend, but she hadn't picked up when we'd called on our way here.

I glanced at Rose, who caught my eye and faintly shook her head. She was thinking the same thing.

A soft click signaled that the door was unlocked. Rose turned the knob slowly and pushed the door open inch by inch. We slipped inside, where the worn carpet muffled our footsteps.

The stench of stale cigarettes clung to the room, with something even fouler lingering beneath it. Discarded pizza boxes and empty beer cans littered the floor, mingling with dirty clothes and broken toys. The dim lighting cast long shadows, and every corner was a potential hiding spot. I swallowed hard, fingers flexing nervously around the gun's handle.

I signaled to the team to spread out. Rose and Cowboy took a left toward what looked like the kitchen while I moved straight ahead down a narrow hallway.

Suddenly there was gunfire.

Wood splintered near my head as bullets tore through the wall. I dove behind a large closet in the hallway.

"FBI! Hold your fire!" I shouted.

More shots answered.

I pressed myself tighter against the wall behind the closet, my mind racing.

During a moment when the gunfire had paused, I heard the sound of crying from a room farther up the hallway to my left. It was most likely the living room. The kids—they were here!

"Your kids are in the house!" I yelled. "Gerald, stop shooting!"

A brief pause, then another round of bullets. He wasn't listening.

I locked eyes with Cowboy, who was waiting down the hallway near the front door, close to Rose. She peeked out from behind a doorway, her expression grim. We were pinned down, and any aggressive move could put the children at risk.

Taking a deep breath, I steadied myself. "I'm going for the kids," I said to Rose. "Hold your fire."

She nodded slightly, her eyes conveying both trust and concern. "Hold your fire!" she shouted to the other agents.

I launched myself from the cover and sprinted up the hallway to the living room. Bullets whizzed past. One slammed into my vest with a force that knocked the wind out of me. Pain exploded across my ribcage, but I pushed through, adrenaline fueling me like a jet.

I burst into the cluttered living room and spotted two small children huddled together on a stained couch. The boy, around three years old with tousled brown hair, clung tightly to a slightly older girl. They held each other close as the flickering glow of the television cast an eerie light over their tightly shut eyes.

"Sh-sh-sh. It's okay," I whispered, forcing calm into my voice. "I won't hurt you."

Their eyes met mine. A flicker of hope pierced the fear as I scooped them into my arms.

"Close your eyes again and hold on tight," I instructed.

Without wasting a second, I moved toward the nearest exit: a large window next to the TV. Hugging the kids close, I turned my back to the glass and kicked it out with my heel. The window shattered outward. Shards rained down as I shielded the kids with my body.

Behind me, gunfire erupted anew. Splinters flew as bullets tore into the wall against which we'd just stood. I leaped through the opening and landed hard on the unkempt lawn.

"Agent down!" voices shouted nearby.

"Get the kids!" I yelled back.

Hands reached out, and I quickly transferred the children to waiting arms. They were rushed away to a spot behind a vehicle.

I pressed myself against the exterior wall, breathing heavily. The pain from the bullet impact throbbed dully. Blood trickled from minor cuts, but nothing felt serious.

Inside, the chaos continued. Sharp cracks of gunfire echoed through the house, then abruptly fell silent.

"Suspect down!" Rose called out.

"House clear!" Cowboy added moments later.

Relief washed over me. I closed my eyes, giving myself a second to regroup.

"Call for an ambulance for the kids!" I shouted as I pushed off from the wall.

Rose and Cowboy emerged from the front door. Their faces glistened with sweat. Rose's usually neat ponytail was disheveled, with strands of hair sticking to her forehead. Cowboy's eyes were bright, and his cheeks were flushed.

"You okay?" he asked, eyeing the torn fabric of my vest.

"Another day, another dime," I replied with a wry smile. "I'll live."

Rose glanced at the cluster of vehicles where the kids were being tended to. "The children?"

"Scared but okay," I assured her. "Just some scratches."

She nodded. "I'll arrange for social services and a trauma counselor."

"Good."

Cowboy stretched out his twitching hand. "Adrenaline's wearing off," he said with a shaky laugh. "I'm getting soft. Too much desk work lately."

I held up my own hand, a faint tremble visible. "Keeps us on our toes."

He checked his phone and grimaced. "Ah, man. I gotta bail."

I raised an eyebrow. "What the hell? Seriously? Forensics will get here soon."

"Got a ... thing," he said, a mischievous glint in his eye. "Didn't expect to be playing hero this morning."

I smirked. "Date?"

He shrugged.

"Go on, get out of here before I change my mind," I said, waving him off.

"You're the best, boss." He grinned and clapped me on the shoulder. "Except for that time you—"

"Already changing my mind," I said.

He laughed. "Don't let him die before he approves my PTO," he said to a group of agents coming out of the house as he headed off.

"He has to approve mine first!" one of the agents hollered after him.

As I watched Cowboy jog toward his car, a small smile tugged at my lips. Then, turning back, I surveyed the scene. The forensic team was already arriving as the police put up tape to section off the home from nosy neighbors.

My gaze drifted to the kids. They were sitting in the back of an SUV, wrapped in blankets. Rose was speaking to them softly. Their faces were pale and their eyes wide, but they were alive. And safe.

A heaviness settled in my chest. Their mother had passed away from cancer not long ago. Now, their father was gone too. They had a grandmother who cared, who'd been fighting for custody, claiming that Gerald was abusive to her daughter and the kids. Maybe now they'd get a chance at a better life.

But the road ahead would be hard. Trauma like this didn't fade quickly.

I sighed and removed the vest. A sharp pain flared where the bullet had hit. I'd have a hell of a bruise tomorrow.

Then suddenly, in all of this, Leah's face flashed in my mind.

It had been two months since we'd last spoken. Two months of silence, yet not a day had gone by that I hadn't thought of her. The unresolved tension between us followed me like my shadow. So far, there had been no bad surprises. No burnt bodies in the woods or floating in the river. Not that this couldn't happen again soon, but today, for a brief moment, the world felt a little safer. Today we'd made a difference. The FBI had saved lives. And maybe, just maybe, there was hope for finding a way forward. Both with Leah and within myself. One without Novak. Something more sustainable. More bearable.

I took a deep breath. The cool winter air filled my lungs.

"Agent Richter," a voice called out.

I turned to see one of the medics approaching.

"Let's get you checked out," he said.

I nodded and followed him toward the ambulance. As I walked, I cast one last glance at the kids.

This was why I did what I did.

For moments like this.

Despite the chaos, despite the pain, today was a win. And that was enough for now.

THIRTY-SIX

Leah

I stood in the dark alley, the winter air biting at my bare legs and arms. My wig felt tight, hiding the real me beneath shoulder-length brown hair. Blue contacts masked my green eyes.

The muffled thump of club music pounded through the walls, but out here, in the cold night, the world felt as lifeless as a graveyard.

Marcus, my escort, pressed me against the brick wall. His hands slid around my waist. "You're so beautiful," he whispered, his breath warm against my neck.

But all I could think about was Richter: his brown eyes, the way he'd watched me as the flames from my study's fireplace had flickered across his face, his gaze heavy with something I couldn't name. It haunted me. Every second.

I shoved Marcus off. His confusion was immediate. "What's wrong?"

I reached into my purse and pulled out an envelope stuffed with cash. Two thousand dollars. High-class escorts didn't come cheap, but they were clean and well-educated. The agency was picky for its wealthy clientele. "Here," I said, my voice cold. "You can go now."

"What? But—"

"I said you can go." The finality in my voice left no room for discussion.

His eyes darted from my face to the money. After a brief pause, he snatched the envelope and disappeared into the night.

I turned and walked back into the club.

The noise hit me like a wave. The bass pounded in my chest, and the strobe lights flickered, casting quick shadows over the sea of bodies moving to the beat. I slipped through the crowd, blending into the chaos, and headed straight for the bar.

A man in his mid-twenties, with messy brown hair, sidled up next to me. "Can I buy you a drink?" he asked, barely audible over the music.

I shook my head and signaled the bartender for a drink.

The brown-haired man didn't waste time, just moved on to the next woman—stumbling, drunk, barely able to stand. I narrowed my eyes. I'd seen him before. No. I *knew* him.

His name was Rhodes Walker. I'd read about him in police reports, deep dives into the dark web. He was the reason I was here tonight. Women had accused him of drugging their drinks, but the police had dismissed it. Not enough evidence. Just a bunch of "claims," they said. Case closed.

But I wasn't the police.

Watching him, I felt a familiar spark of anger. At one time I'd hunted real monsters. Now I played with scum. It wasn't the same, but it made a difference. And after the meeting with Richter, no matter how certain I'd felt when I'd burned Caroline Traylor's file and body, I was here. Lost. Confused.

Both Jan and Richter had made their cases. Now what?

Both had tried to reach out. One with roses, daily. The other with silence, then a single text.

I saw Rhodes slide a drink under the bar just long enough to spike it before handing it to the stumbling woman. His movements were casual, practiced.

Before she could take a sip, I was there. I shoved her aside, ignoring her annoyed protest, and stepped up to Rhodes. "I changed my mind," I said, stepping in close with a slow, deliberate smile. "I'd love a drink."

I took the glass from his hand and pretended to take a long, slow sip. My eyes were locked on his.

He grinned. The predator, oblivious to his own trap.

We spent the next hour together, blending into the crowd, talking about nothing, just like people in clubs do. His conversation was insufferable: sex, women's bodies, endless crude remarks.

Each time he handed me a drink, I excused myself to the bathroom and dumped it down the sink. He kept watching me, waiting for his drug to take effect.

Eventually, he leaned in, his voice low and sleazy. "You wanna fuck? In my car?"

Of course, the pig didn't even bother to offer a real bed.

I swayed a little, pretending to be tipsy and out of it. "No," I slurred. "I wanna go home."

"Alright, let's go," he said.

We slipped out of the back entrance. Our breath hung in the cold night air, visible in misty clouds.

I staggered a few steps ahead, feigning a stumble, when Rhodes grabbed me roughly and slammed me against the same wall where Marcus had pinned me earlier. His hand shot to his zipper, and he yanked it down. In seconds, his hard cock was pressing against my stomach.

"Bitch, suck it!"

He grabbed me by the head and pushed me onto my knees. I scanned the dark alley to confirm we were alone, then quickly reached into my purse and pulled out plastic gloves.

Along with a plastic tube of hydrofluoric acid.

Rhodes glanced down as I slipped on the gloves and twisted off the cap.

"What the fuck is this?" he asked.

"Well, Rhodes..." His eyes widened when I called him by his real name. Sober. "Let's not drag this out, you disgusting prick."

He froze, realization dawning in his eyes. "What the hell are you talking about?" He tried to zip his pants back up, but I grabbed his limp cock tightly.

"All those drugged women. I have the drugs in the drink. Your prints. Enough to send you to a prison where they kill rapists like you."

His face paled, and his cocky grin faltered as panic took hold.

"Now listen carefully. You'll tell the police that a crazy homeless attacked you and did this to you," I hissed.

"Did ... what?" he whimpered, paralyzed by fear like a frightened child. A coward, through and through.

"Trade your weapon for your life," I said coldly, dumping the acid on his exposed cock. I quickly took a large step back and closed the plastic container before any acid could hit me by accident.

Rhodes's hysterical screams came almost instantly as the acid began eating away at the flesh of his dick. His hands shot to his crotch, only spreading the burning to his fingers, making it even worse.

I watched as Rhodes collapsed to his knees, screeching for help.

It felt good. Not as satisfying as killing would feel but sufficient for now.

I slipped away into the night, his desperate cries echoing behind me. A cold wind hit my face as I rounded the corner.

Richter crept into my thoughts again.

Would he approve of this? Was this what he wanted from me—a tame version of the monster?

Jan would accept me for who I was. We could thrive together, fueled by rage.

But out here, in the biting cold, with the distant echoes of panicked shouts, I realized justice wasn't what I craved anymore.

The feelings I'd been searching for since I was a little girl weren't about justice at all. It dawned on me that killing killers—this relentless pursuit—had just been a distraction from my own lonely, pathetic life. A desperate way to make myself feel *something*. Anything. In helping people, even through dark means, I'd found just enough to force myself out of bed each day.

But now it all seemed almost foolish compared to what Richter had stirred in me. Rage and murder couldn't hold a candle to the depth he'd unearthed.

Liam Richter could make me feel sadness—real sadness—and that strange warmth that might even be joy.

And now I'd lost it all.

Sacrificed it to the fire of rage that had fueled me for so long.

Was it too late?

Had I already pushed Richter beyond the point of forgiveness? I knew his moral compass, how high his standards were. He'd warned me after the Night Stalker incident, but I'd kept pushing, letting Novak pull the strings to manipulate me like a puppet master.

Like Kirby. Like Patel. Even Carl Carr.

By the time I reached my townhome, looking like I'd just come back from a Symphony Hall rehearsal, I'd decided to contact Richter.

But I didn't make it past the kitchen.

My eyes landed on a small tablet that Ida had left on the counter with a note.

This was left for you. Thank you, it read.

A cold weight settled in my chest.

Jan Novak had taken my silence for refusal.

He'd reignited the games.

And this time, I didn't have a choice about joining his deadly dance.

THIRTY-SEVEN

Liam

I lay in bed, wide awake at 2:30 a.m., staring at the ceiling. It was completely silent. Josie was with her mom this week, and sleep wasn't an option. My mind was a mess of racing thoughts.

It had been a few days since Gerald Smith's arrest—or, rather, his shooting. Things were running smoothly, and the FBI was getting praise nationwide for wrapping up the case so quickly. *Well, who gets a gold star for this masterpiece?* I thought wryly.

The kids were with their grandmother now. Maybe, with enough love, time, and therapy, they'd be okay.

But Leah was a different story.

I'd reached out to her on the day of the incident at Smith's place, but she'd never responded.

Suddenly, my flip phone buzzed on the nightstand. I shot up and grabbed it.

It was Leah. As if she knew she'd been on my mind again.

We need to talk. Now. Bring Rose. Don't meet me at the house. Meet me at Gerald Smith's place. Avoid main roads with traffic cameras.

I stared at the message. This wasn't good. Something was off.

I jumped out of bed, threw on sweatpants and a sweater, and slipped into my shoes before racing out. I dialed Rose as I went.

As much as I hated to admit it, a surge of excitement rushed through me at the thought of seeing Leah again. Maybe we could finally sort out some of our issues. Maybe she was ready to work with me. Ditch Novak. Dial things back.

Or maybe she wasn't. But I couldn't let my mind go there yet.

THIRTY-EIGHT

Leah

I waited inside Gerald Smith's residence, dressed in boots and a coverall to avoid leaving any trace of DNA. The kitchen was a mess. Old takeout boxes and empty beer cans littered the countertops and floor. Light from the street poured through the window, casting long shadows across the room.

At around 3:30 a.m., I heard a car pull up and park outside. Moments later, Richter and Rose entered the house, flashlights in hand.

"Leah," Richter called in a sharp whisper.

"I'm here," I answered from the kitchen.

They walked in, their faces tight with worry and anticipation.

"What's going on?" Rose asked. "Why are we meeting here?"

"It won't raise his suspicion if you're seen visiting a recent crime scene," I explained.

"Whose?" Richter pressed. "Novak's?"

I nodded. "We can't be seen together right now."

"What happened?" Liam asked.

"Hard to say. The last time I spoke to him was the day we met in my study," I said. "He told me about his past—his childhood and how his brother died on the train tracks while everyone just watched."

Rose sighed, her shoulders slumping. "So the ankh is some kind of twisted punishment symbol? To make people pay?"

"There's more to it, but we don't have much time." I set the tablet on the counter. Its glass screen reflected the dim light from the street outside. A green indicator flashed, signaling that it was charged. Ready for games, videos, news—or, in our case, something far more sinister.

"What's this?" Liam asked as they moved closer.

"Ida found this tablet on my doorstep today," I said, tapping the screen. The display lit up with a serene mountain background. I quickly navigated to the video gallery and hit play. "I texted you right after I watched what's on it."

Security footage from a coffee shop began to flicker on the screen. Its light reflected off Liam's and Rose's tense faces.

We watched as Agent Theo McCourt stepped into a farmhouse-style coffee shop. He ordered a coffee, then sat and scanned the room with caution. About a minute later, the door swung open, and a blonde woman walked in.

"Shit," Liam muttered, his eyes widening.

"Please tell me that isn't Nathalie," Rose said, her hands planted on her hips.

The video cut out and transitioned to another: McCourt and Nathalie at a Chinese restaurant—chatting, laughing.

A third video loaded, stitched together like a cheap, hastily made trailer. This time, we watched Theo McCourt and Nathalie strolling through a park. McCourt was giving it everything he had—smiling, flirting, throwing out jokes, showing empathy in every glance and gesture.

The video skipped ahead to show McCourt buying Nathalie a drink and fries from a food truck. Then the tone shifted. Their conversation grew tense. Nathalie stood there, her arms crossed, her face uncertain. She wasn't being defensive—just on the verge of revealing something, clinging to a thread, barely holding back a dark secret that was ready to spill.

Then she said something. There was no audio, but it didn't matter. Cowboy planted his hands on his hips, his face tilted upward, and paced in front of her. We all knew what Nathalie had confessed.

The fucking truth.

"Goddamn it!" Richter snapped.

The weight of everything—her confession, the videos, and what it all meant—crashed down around us.

"Why the hell did Novak send you this?" Rose demanded in a tight, tense tone.

I chose my next words carefully. "I think you need to get a hold of Agent Theo McCourt and Nathalie as soon as possible. Right now, in fact."

"Goddamn it," Liam said again, pulling his phone from his coat pocket. "I'll call Nathalie. You contact Theo."

Rose pulled out her phone. Her fingers moved swiftly as she dialed.

"Hello?" came a woman's voice through Liam's phone.

"Mrs. Moore, I'm so sorry to call you this late, but is Nathalie at home?" Liam asked.

"Yes, why?" Mrs. Moore's voice had a worried edge to it.

Liam let out a long breath, gathering himself. His tense shoulders eased a little as his eyes met mine, then flicked to Rose. "We might have had a sighting of Carr," he lied smoothly. "I'm going to arrange for a local patrol car to be stationed outside your house. Don't be alarmed if you see them there for the next few days. Just make sure all the windows and doors are locked at night."

"Okay," Mrs. Moore responded calmly. It was clear she wasn't worried about Carr. She likely knew he was dead. Yet she played along, just as her daughter had. Only she didn't know how deep this all went. That her daughter might have placed herself on the hit list of other psychopaths.

"I'll keep you updated," Liam assured her.

"Thank you."

Liam ended the call, then dialed his contact at the local police department. His voice shifted into formal business. "This is Special Agent in Charge Liam Richter. I need a patrol car stationed at fifty-five Exeter Street tonight to cover the Moore residence. Please coordinate with me on this."

He paused as the officer on the other end responded.

"Yes, thank you," Liam said. "I'll send my contact information for follow-up." Liam hung up and turned to us. "It's set. They'll have eyes on the house tonight. Anything on your end?" he asked Rose.

She shook her head, her expression tightening with worry. "No answer. He's not picking up."

"Fuck," Liam muttered, his frustration simmering.

"Why the hell is Novak doing this?" Rose snapped, dialing McCourt's number again.

"There could be many reasons, but the most obvious would be to protect the work," I said.

"Just like Larsen did," Liam muttered, his jaw tightening as if he could barely stomach the words.

"The work?" Rose asked. "I thought Novak was killing only bad people. Theo isn't a monster. He's one of the good guys."

"We don't have time to make sense of a psycho's twisted mind," Liam said, his voice taut with urgency. "We have to find Theo. I'll check his house."

Rose didn't hesitate. "I'll check the office. He's been working nights lately."

They darted toward the hallway, their footsteps quick and urgent.

"Wait," I said.

Both of them froze mid-step, then turned to face me.

"I'm afraid you won't find him at home," I said. "Or the office."

The weight of my words settled in the room. Liam strode toward me, eyes wide, searching for answers.

"You should check the hospitals," I said. "Or the morgues." I added the last part quietly.

"What?" Rose's brow furrowed.

"Theo McCourt's death wouldn't carry symbolic value for Jan Novak," I explained. "It would ... look like an accident. To Jan, it would be more of a necessary casualty. Quick. Humane. Something that wouldn't raise questions."

They both stared, but it was Liam's gaze—cold and full of blame—that pierced through me. His hand hovered over his phone while his brown eyes bore into me. They flickered with panic tangled with sadness and something heavier: regret.

Regret directed at me.

I hadn't pulled the trigger on Agent Tony Russo or Theo McCourt, but pulling Liam into my dark world had demanded more of him than he could bear.

Or maybe it was more than I could bear to watch him endure.

Jan Novak had stripped away the one thing I held dear, and I'd realized it too late. It was Liam Richter.

A cold knot tightened in my stomach as this truth hit me like a wrecking ball.

There was no turning back. No salvation for me.

Maybe two wrongs could make a right. But who decided what that right was?

My mother's face flashed in my mind as Liam spoke frantically into the phone, instructing someone to search for Theo McCourt in every hospital across Boston—no, all of Massachusetts.

A childhood memory flashed in my mind. My mother's long, sharp nails dug into my small shoulders. I was just a kid, soaked to the bone, and I had accidentally tracked mud onto the rug.

"When you play in shit, you get dirty, you stupid girl," my mother yelled before slapping me across the face. Back then, I'd thought she'd meant the mud. But now, as crude and simple as those words had seemed, I finally understood.

How could I have ever denied such a simple truth?

No matter how hard you tried, when you played in shit, you got dirty.

Rose had already left, her focus entirely on dialing hospitals. She didn't waste a second on me.

Liam lingered, phone in hand, as if he wanted to say something but couldn't. We stood there, trapped in a silence that felt like an eternity.

I took a tentative step toward him. "Liam—"

"Don't!" His hand slammed against the counter. The sound cut through the tension like a whip.

The silence returned, heavier this time. It felt like torment.

That little girl from the psych ward had finally found what she'd been searching for her whole life—only to destroy it.

To destroy him.

"I swear," Liam's voice trembled, "if Novak hurt—" He broke off, his anger barely contained. After a steadying breath, he tried again. "Killing someone innocent like Theo goes against everything we've fought for, Leah. Don't you see that?"

"I do," I replied quickly.

His gaze darkened. "I hope so, because I swear on everything I hold dear, I won't stand by and let Novak slaughter innocent people for his twisted vision of a better world. If Theo gets hurt, I will kill Jan Novak. And when I look into his dead eyes, it won't feel any different than with any other serial killer we've taken down. Because at the end of the day, Leah, that's what he is—a ruthless killer who hides his twisted mind beneath a polished exterior, like poison wrapped in silk.

The pain in his eyes left no doubt—this wasn't just a warning. It was a promise.

I couldn't hold his gaze any longer. My eyes dropped to the floor. The weight of his disappointment was too much to carry.

"Next time you see him, tell him I'm coming for him," Liam growled.

Without another word, he spun around and rushed out the door.

I stood there, rooted to the spot, my chest tight with a pain so sharp it nearly stole my breath.

I'd done all this. Played God and paid the price as a human. And now there was only one solution. Two wrongs had to make a right one more time. Just one more time.

It would take some planning. It would take everything I had. But the puppet had to become the master.

I owed it to Richter.

I owed it to the world.

And I owed it to myself.

THIRTY-NINE

Liam

I floored the gas of the FBI SUV, its siren screaming as I tore through city streets. Leah had probably been right, but I had to see it for myself. A flicker of hope kept me pushing. Maybe Theo was just asleep, his phone off.

The GPS guided me through the winding roads of Newton. Each turn cranked up the tension. My chest tightened as I pulled up to a modest condo complex. The SUV screeched to a stop.

I stormed up the walkway and pounded the front door so hard, the small frame rattled. "Theo!"

Nothing. No sound, no movement.

Without thinking, I rammed my shoulder into the door, then followed up with a barrage of kicks. Adrenaline overrode all reason. "Theo!" I shouted, my voice bouncing off the quiet street as lights flicked on in neighboring homes.

I didn't give a fuck.

"Theo!" I yelled again. Each kick sent splinters flying as the door frame started giving way. With one final hit, the door cracked open and slammed against the wall. Wood chips scattered across the floor.

I charged inside, where a suffocating silence hit me. Dark, quiet, spotless. It was too perfect, too homey. Typical Theo—everything was always over the top. An FBI agent through and through.

"It's me!" I called, pushing into the living room. "It's Liam!"

I swept through the kitchen, then the hallway, scanning the two small bedrooms. Empty.

He wasn't there.

The frustration drained out of me, replaced by an overpowering dread. I staggered back, my body hitting the hallway wall, my legs buckling as I slid to the floor. Hands pressed against my head, I fought for breath.

"Goddamn it, Theo," I muttered, my voice cracking.

This was on me.

What the hell had I thought would happen? Playing God, deciding who lived and who died, challenging the most powerful man in the nation.

Self-loathing crashed over me like a king tide. And yet, even now, I couldn't bring myself to hate Leah.

Despite everything, I found a way to hope she wasn't the monster that even she thought she was.

Was this insanity? Had I finally crossed the line into madness?

The scream of sirens yanked me out of my head. Lights flashed through the cracks in the door. My heart sped up as an officer shouted, "Police! Hands where I can see them!"

A flashlight blinded me, and I squinted as the beam stabbed through the hallway.

"FBI!" I said, forcing calm into my voice. "Agent Liam Richter. This is Agent Theo McCourt's residence. I'm reaching for my badge, alright?"

"Richter, is that you?" A familiar voice echoed down the hall. Another flashlight found my face.

"Thompson?" I called back, trying to place it.

"Yeah," Officer Thompson replied. He switched on the light to reveal his stocky frame and thinning hairline. Three other officers stood next to him, guns lowered. "It's alright, boys. He's FBI."

I stood up, shaking off the adrenaline. "Good to see you, man." We exchanged a quick handshake. Thompson and I had a history from a murder case years back. "We're looking for Agent Theo McCourt," I explained, urgency creeping into my voice. "Carl Carr's still out there. Someone called in, said they saw him around Boston tonight."

Thompson's face darkened. "I'll make sure everyone's on alert for that bastard."

I nodded and was about to ask if there had been any accidents involving an agent when my phone buzzed.

Rose's voice came through, panicked.

"We found him! Mass General Hospital!"

"I'm on my way!" I snapped, cutting her off before she could tell me if Theo was dead or alive. I didn't want to hear it. Not yet.

I bolted out the door and jumped into the SUV.

Sirens blared as I floored the gas and sped toward the hospital.

There was still hope. And, by God, I held on to it.

I found Rose waiting in the large entrance hall. Silence pressed in from every corner.

"What happened?" I demanded, nearly colliding with her in my rush.

"Car accident. It happened around nine p.m."

"At fucking nine? Why didn't anyone call us? He had his badge on him."

Rose's face tightened. "He just came out of surgery," she said, her voice strained. "They think his brakes failed—while going seventy-five on the highway. The trauma team fought for hours. His heart stopped twice, but they shocked him back both times."

I stood there, words choking in my throat. The frustration, the guilt, it all crushed me. I fought against the tears burning in my eyes. My chest tightened with every breath.

"So he's alive?" I said.

Rose's eyes flickered with hope for a second, though her expression remained tense. "Yes. But he's in a coma. They said it's serious. Really serious."

The brief relief that had sparked inside me died out, replaced by a sinking weight in my stomach.

"Come," Rose said softly, "I'll take you to the doctor. He'll explain everything."

I followed her, barely aware of the people and nurses we passed, their faces a blur. The sterile scent of antiseptic hung in the air, making everything feel colder.

"We have to call his mother," I said.

"I already did." Rose's voice was quiet but firm. "Before I called you. I thought his mom should know as soon as possible. In case..." She didn't finish the sentence. She didn't need to. "She's on her way. So is McCourt."

"Good. Well done," I said.

Rose dipped her head in acknowledgment, though her eyes stayed ahead.

We met up with Dr. Goldman on the ICU floor. He looked fresh out of his residency—mid-thirties, still wearing blue scrubs and a surgical cap. Fatigue lingered in his expression.

The hallway was quiet except for the steady beeping of machines from nearby rooms. The smell of disinfectant was stronger here, almost suffocating.

"Liam!" A woman's voice echoed down the hallway. I turned just as Bonnie, Theo's mom, rushed toward us. Tears streaked down her pale cheeks, and her short, tousled hair looked like she hadn't slept. Dressed in a loose sweater and jeans, she crashed into me, her sobs muffled against my chest.

"He's still alive. There's hope," I said, though the words felt hollow in my mouth. It was as if I was saying them more for myself than for her.

She nodded, trembling in my arms.

"You'll be able to see him soon," Dr. Goldman said, his voice calm—almost too calm for the gravity of the situation. "He took a significant hit to the head. It's honestly a miracle he survived the impact. We managed to stop the bleeding, but there's one artery we're monitoring closely. Once we're sure it's stabilized, you can go in."

Rose's head dropped into her hands. For a moment, she stayed like that, her shoulders shaking slightly. Then she straightened up, forcing herself to hold it together, to stay strong. "Will he wake up?" she asked, her voice tight, barely above a whisper.

Everyone turned to Dr. Goldman.

"We'll have to wait a few days and see," he said. "Right now, it's too soon to say. But he's a fighter, that much I can promise you. Don't lose hope."

I swallowed hard. My hands were shaking. I realized I hadn't stopped trembling since I'd gotten the call.

Dr. Goldman glanced down at my leg, his brow furrowing. "Come with me for a minute," he said. "Let's get that stitched up before it gets worse."

I glanced down, only now realizing that my pants were torn. A large, dark bloodstain had spread across my shin. I must have cut myself kicking the door in.

"I'm fine," I muttered, but Dr. Goldman's raised brow made it clear he wasn't buying it.

"Go with him, Liam," Bonnie insisted, her voice strained. "Rose and I will grab some coffee and call my brother."

I nodded and watched them walk away.

"Just follow me," Dr. Goldman said, gesturing ahead. "This won't take long."

"Thanks," I said, trailing behind him.

My head throbbed, and nausea churned in my stomach. What the hell would I do if Theo didn't make it? The thought pressed down on me, but I shoved it aside. I couldn't afford to go there—not yet.

As long as he was breathing, there was hope.

But hope in itself wasn't enough. Not without fuel. It had to be fed and sustained, like everything else in life.

And this hope would last only if Jan Novak was taken care of.

In any way possible.

FORTY

Leah

I was parked near Josie's school. The rain fell steadily against the windshield. It was the day of her school play—some adaptation of *The Three Little Piglets*.

The bare trees lining the street stood like eerie shadows against the gray sky. Their twisted branches waved like skeletal arms in the wind.

I sat in the driver's seat of the Beamer—Emanuel's Beamer, the one I'd bought him. The leather was cold under my skin, and the dashboard cast a soft glow in the dark. I'd never gotten rid of the car. It was as if I'd known it would serve a purpose again someday.

And that day was today.

I glanced at myself in the rearview mirror. I was dressed to be seen: an evening dress, black and sleek, clinging to my body. The fabric shimmered subtly with each shift, and the deep neckline revealed just enough to be both sexy and classy. My lips were a defiant shade of crimson, vivid against the paleness of my skin. My hair fell loose over my shoulders. I never wore it like this, but today was different. Today I chose to be free.

The rain stopped, and I kept my eyes on the entrance to the school. It had been two weeks since Theo McCourt's crash. Two weeks since the investigation had claimed that there was no foul play, that the brakes on his car had failed.

But I knew the truth.

So did Liam and Rose.

We hadn't spoken since. Theo was still in a coma, fighting for his life. But I knew that Richter was devastated about it. I saw it in his face every time I closed my eyes, and I promised him that I would make things right. That Jan Novak would be taught a lesson—in a language he understood.

Then I saw them—Liam and Josie—walking out of the school, hand in hand. They looked happy. Josie, in her little piglet costume, beamed up at him, her cheeks flushed from the excitement of her performance.

For a fleeting moment, I wondered what it would have been like to have watched the show with them.

Would I have sat next to Richter in the school auditorium, the warmth of his presence grounding me? Would I have smiled as Josie performed, my chest filling with that quiet, aching joy? I could almost hear Richter making a joke about the school orchestra's awful music, and I'd whisper back that it was indeed an assault on the senses. We'd laugh quietly only to be shushed by some annoyed parent sitting nearby.

For a moment, I let myself feel it: the life I could've had, the one I'd always craved. But then the familiar, hollow emptiness returned, sharp and cold.

Gray nothingness.

I was never meant to walk that path.

No.

That wasn't true.

People could choose to change, to do the work needed, and then walk any path they wanted. But I'd chosen something else. There was only one road left for people like me. Monsters.

And tonight, Jan Novak would learn that too.

I watched as Richter and Josie got into their car, still talking, still laughing. I sat there even after they'd driven off, long after the last parents and children had left. The school was empty now, the brick walls darkened by the clouds.

I wanted to stay in that moment for as long as I could.

But I had to acknowledge that it was gone.

That it was time.

Time to face Jan Novak.

FORTY-ONE

Leah

I sat across from Jan Novak in his grand dining room. The long mahogany table gleamed under the soft glow of crystal chandeliers hanging high above. Egyptian artifacts adorned the walls alongside priceless paintings, one of which looked like an original Monet. The air was filled with the scent of polished wood and subtle traces of exotic spices from the kitchen.

Jan's mansion, nestled on the outskirts of Boston, overlooked manicured gardens that faded into the dense forest beyond. The sky had cleared, and a silver moon shone through the tall, castle-like windows. It cast a cold, ethereal light across the room. In the enormous stone fireplace, a fire crackled softly, sending warmth through the air.

Unlike our last encounter, we weren't alone. A server dressed in a tailored vest moved with quiet efficiency, setting plates down with care. Everything about tonight screamed luxury ... and control.

Jan, of course, looked impeccable. His black suit—sharp and flawless—fit like it had been stitched to his skin. His crisp white shirt stood in stark contrast, and not a hair on his head was out of place. His calm demeanor bordered on icy, though I could sense the subtle tension in his posture. Beneath the polished surface, he was wondering if I'd truly chosen him after what he'd done to Richter.

"You can go now," Jan instructed the waiter as the man poured wine into our glasses. The waiter nodded, then left.

The salad in front of me was artfully arranged: thin slices of heirloom tomatoes, vibrant reds and yellows, topped with microgreens and delicate edible flowers. It looked perfect, like everything else in the house.

"I'm glad you decided to join me tonight," Jan said, picking up his fork and taking a bite.

I picked up my wine glass but didn't drink. Jan's eyes flicked up, and a faint crease formed between his brows.

"So you're upset with me after all," he mused, dabbing his lips with the white napkin that had been resting on his lap.

I set down my wine glass deliberately and met his gaze. "I am." My voice was cool but firm. "Very much so."

He leaned back, studying me. "You disapprove of the handling of Theo McCourt, then? Sacrificing one life to save hundreds?"

I shrugged. "Not really. I see the logic. McCourt's accident itself doesn't bother me much."

He nodded, his eyes darkening. "But..."

Silence settled between us. My gaze held his.

Tonight wasn't about emotions. I felt no rage toward him. No hate. I'd meant every word when I'd said that McCourt's death was a logical solution to the problem. And that McCourt himself meant nothing to me.

But McCourt meant everything to the one person I cared about—and protecting that person from the reckless spiral that would follow Jan's attack was what tonight was really about. That recklessness could get him killed, and I couldn't allow that.

"Ah," Jan finally said, the corners of his mouth lifting in a cold smile. "My bad. How dare I upset Agent Liam Richter."

I kept my voice level. "It's more than upsetting. What you did to him—"

"Yes, to *him*, indeed." His expression turned grim. "And I hated it. Every moment of it. McCourt didn't deserve that. He was on our side. But you understand that my hands were tied, don't you? If anything, I did it for you. McCourt would have hunted you relentlessly." He shook his head. "You and I, we don't live by Richter's naive code of morals. We can't afford to. No. Not people like us. You and I, we're soldiers in a war."

I nodded slightly and picked up my fork. I couldn't disagree with him—not now. Not when he had to believe I was on his side.

Luckily, I agreed with the things he said. Most of them.

"Promise me you won't hurt Richter," I said, keeping my tone measured. "And I promise you, I'll never see him again. End whatever childish hope there had ever been between us." I took a bite of the salad, though my attention never left him.

Jan paused, watching me closely, searching my face for any hint of a lie. After a tense moment, he picked up his fork again. "I promise as long as he leaves me alone."

"He will," I replied quietly.

Jan's eyes lit up, and a wave of excitement washed over him. "Now that we've resolved that ... unpleasant matter, I have something for you."

I glanced down at the plate, surprised by the abrupt change in tone.

"We'll finish dinner in a moment," he said, his voice light. "Come, don't make me wait. I'm quite excited to show you."

He reached out, gently took my hand, and guided me through a door that led from the dining hall to the library. The room was like something out of a historical movie—bookshelves stretched to the ceiling, filled with antique volumes that had probably never been touched. Egyptian artifacts filled this room as well—golden figurines, a scarab amulet, and several busts of pharaohs. A fire crackled in the large stone fireplace, casting flickering shadows across the luxurious space.

The life of a billionaire. As beautiful as it was absurd.

Jan stopped in front of an exhibit case, his grin almost boyish in its energy.

My eyes widened when I saw the necklace—the same ankh necklace I'd admired at the Smithsonian Museum during our first meeting. It was golden, inlaid with lapis lazuli gemstones, and shaped like a T crowned with a loop. On its crimson silk pillow, it glittered like stars against the night sky.

"The Eternal Kiss," I whispered, awe creeping into my voice.

Jan moved behind me, his breath warm against my ear. "It belonged to Agathoclea, the favored mistress of the Greco-Egyptian Pharaoh Ptolemy IV Philopator," he murmured. "His obsession with her was legendary. He built temples for the gods, hoping they'd allow her to join him in the afterlife. Stunning, isn't it?"

"Agathoclea..." I echoed, watching as Jan lifted the necklace. "She tried to take the throne with her brother after Ptolemy's death. They failed, and she was torn apart limb by limb."

"Most great men's downfall is a woman," Jan joked softly.

"Most great men's downfall is the man himself," I countered.

His grin widened as he placed the necklace around my neck. It felt heavy and cold. Just as he reached to clasp it, I stepped away, slipping out from under his arms.

His eyes flashed with surprise.

"I ... I can't accept it," I said.

The enchantment from moments ago dissolved. Jan's face hardened.

"Not yet," I added quickly.

His expression shifted. Curiosity replaced the coldness. He placed the necklace back on the silk pillow, then turned to face me. "Why is that?"

"Because now you'll need to come with me," I said, my tone steady. "Just like you asked me to go with you to the tracks, to show me who you really were. Now it's my turn to show you who I really am."

Jan studied me. Finally, he nodded slowly. "Very well," he said. "Lead the way."

FORTY-TWO

Liam

I stood on my small balcony, staring up at the moon and stars shimmering in the clear night sky. It was almost nine. An icy breeze brushed against my skin. It carried the faint scent of the city below.

I should've been dead tired, considering that I'd been up every night since Theo's accident. But sleep wouldn't come. Not tonight. My mind was too restless, my thoughts racing like a freight train that couldn't be stopped.

Guilt weighed heavy on my chest. Anger too. Yet something else lingered beneath it all.

Worry.

For Leah.

It was strange how things had shifted once the first wave of anger subsided. At first, I couldn't even look at her without feeling regret. After those videos had played in the kitchen, I'd stared at her with pure frustration, wishing I'd never met her. In my mind, she was the reason for all this chaos. I'd blamed her for everything. Larsen shooting Toni. Theo's accident. The bodies that piled up as our lives spiraled further into darkness.

But if I was honest with myself, none of that was her fault.

She hadn't pulled the trigger on Toni, nor had she tampered with Theo's brakes. Leah was just another pawn in the same deadly game I found myself trapped in. The difference was, she'd been playing it much longer. When I'd joined, it wasn't because she'd dragged me in. I'd chosen this path. And time and time again, she'd risked her life for me.

I gripped the cold railing, my knuckles turning white. She'd saved me from Patel, risked everything when I'd begged her to save Rose in the woods with Kirby. She'd never asked for anything in return except for my help in hunting down monsters.

Sure, we didn't always agree on the methods. I could never bring myself to kill someone like Carole Traylor. And especially not Cowboy.

Maybe people saw it as weakness, maybe as self-righteousness, but I refused to accept a world where we sacrificed innocent lives for the so-called greater good. Who the hell got to decide who'd be sacrificed? What if it was someone we loved? Would we still feel the same about making that choice if it were their life on the line?

I couldn't sanction that.

But Leah. Leah had a different moral code. She saw the world in black and white: monsters and victims. And though I'd questioned her judgment more times than I could count, part of me understood her.

A sharp jolt twisted in my chest, cutting deeper with every breath.

I had to see her.

Talk to her.

To make sense of it all.

She was the only one who could understand my pain. After all, she carried the same burdens, wore the same scars. And if, in the end, we couldn't see eye to eye on the mission or the lives we took, if our paths had truly split, at least we wouldn't part as enemies. Not like this.

I tilted my head back, letting my gaze linger on the moon a moment longer. Its mystic silver light bathed the world in a strange, ethereal glow as if offering me some kind of strength.

I took a deep breath, letting the cool night air fill my lungs before I exhaled slowly. Then I reached for the flip phone in my pocket. I was ready to call her, ready to bridge the silence that had grown between us.

But before I could type a single word, my phone buzzed in my hand.

A text.

My pulse quickened. Adrenaline surged through my veins as I stared at the screen. It wasn't from Leah. It wasn't from Rose. It was from an unknown number.

I opened the text, my heart pounding, a sense of unease settling deep in my gut. When my eyes scanned the message, a chill crept up my spine.

Fucking hell.

The game wasn't over.

It was only just beginning.

FORTY-THREE

Leah

I drove my car down the lonely country roads, the dense forest lining either side like looming shadows. The rhythmic hum of the tires on the uneven asphalt was the only sound that broke the silence of the night. Jan hadn't been suspicious at first, but when I took a sharp turn leading away from Boston, I saw him glance out the window.

His expression tightened. "This isn't the way to your home," he said, pulling out his phone. His fingers flew over the screen as he typed something quickly, then slid the phone back into his pocket.

"No," I replied, my eyes fixed on the dark road ahead.

"Then where are we going?" His tone was calm, but I could feel the unease creeping in, like a chill in the air.

"You'll know soon," I said, my voice cold and detached, as if the decision had been made long ago.

We drove in silence for a few minutes. The forest seemed to close in on us, the trees taller and darker, their branches curling overhead, grasping for the car.

Almost casually, Novak nodded to himself as if he was finally piecing it together. "The tracks," he said softly. "You're taking me to the tracks."

"Yes," I confirmed, keeping my eyes forward.

He nodded again, a faint shadow of a smile pulling at the corner of his mouth. "What for?"

"To show you who I really am."

The unease thickened between us like a fog, but I kept driving until the road narrowed. We turned onto Pine Street, the winding forest path that led to the tracks. The same tracks where Jan had once told me everything about his past.

I slowed the car as we neared the crossing. The pale moonlight cast an eerie glow on the silver rails ahead as if the ground itself were pulling us toward some final, inevitable destination. With a sharp turn, I steered the car directly onto the tracks, then positioned it to face the direction from which the train would come. I turned off the engine.

The sudden silence hit like a blow, deafening in its finality. The trees loomed on either side. The moon hung above us, cold and indifferent.

I reached under the steering wheel and flipped the switch. A loud click echoed through the car as the doors locked, sealing us inside.

This car was built to trap people. The locks, the bulletproof windows, the reinforced frame—I'd had it all installed to make sure no one would get out. Not even Novak. There was nothing he could do to get out of here. Nothing.

We sat in the dark, listening to the soft rustling of leaves in the wind, the calm before the storm.

Jan glanced at me, his brow furrowing slightly. "Not what I expected," he murmured, reaching for the door handle. He pulled, but the door didn't budge. His hand slipped from the handle, and he leaned back into his seat, his face calm, though his eyes were calculating. "The door won't open," he said after a moment. "Even if I were to take the keys from you by force? Or flip that switch again?"

I shook my head. "No."

"And the windows ... if I rammed my elbow into them, the glass wouldn't break, would it?"

"Bulletproof."

He gave a curt nod toward the tracks. "How much did you pay the train driver to hit us at full speed instead of braking?" A hint of admiration crept into his tone.

"He asked for one hundred thousand. I gave him five. I figured the guilt of killing someone might weigh heavy on him later."

A strange calm settled between us—the kind of stillness that comes before a storm.

We sat there, motionless, as the first faint horn of the approaching train echoed through the night. It was distant but growing louder each second. The ground trembled slightly—a reminder of the raw power rushing toward us.

"You said you wanted to show me your true self," Novak said, his gaze meeting mine, cold and unwavering. "Is this it? Your true self?"

His icy blue eyes betrayed disappointment but also a strange sense of relief. Maybe it was the same relief I felt—knowing it was all about to end. Knowing there was no need for pretense anymore.

"Yes," I replied, my voice just as cold as the night around us. "This is me. The real me. You can kill me now if you want. I won't resist. The train will do the same in," I checked my watch, "about a minute. It doesn't matter to me how I die, one way or another."

He studied me for a long moment, his face unreadable. "So this is how it ends?" he asked.

I nodded, feeling the weight of my decision settle heavily on my chest.

He let out a low, humorless laugh. "This ... all of this. It's for him, isn't it? You figured he'd come for me, so you're killing me first. To save him from himself. And from me."

I shook my head, my eyes fixed on the silver rails ahead, gleaming in the moonlight like a path to nowhere. There was something almost beautiful about it—the clarity, the inevitability. And the silence that would follow. The peace of never having to wake up again, never having to force myself to face another day of a hollow, lonely life.

"It's more than just for him," I said quietly. "Don't you see? You and me ... we can tell ourselves whatever we want, but at the end of the day, we're just like them. Like Carl Carr. Patel. Harris. Grand. When you tried to kill Agent Theo McCourt, you revealed a dark part of yourself. Something all monsters carry: the ability to kill innocent people without remorse. You and I are monsters that don't belong in this world. And the only way to stop a monster is to kill it. I know you understand that."

He remained silent, so I pointed at the tracks ahead. "I carved an ankh on the tracks right over there for you. The mirror. It wasn't just to reveal people's true nature, was it? It was also for your older brother, Anton. To guide you to him when it's time. Like a path to the afterlife. Am I right?"

Novak's lips curled into a faint smile, one of admiration, even respect.

"I wish you would've let me put that necklace on you," he said softly. "It had found a worthy owner again after thousands of years of waiting."

I drew in a deep breath as the train's headlights appeared in the distance. Its beams sliced through the darkness like two enormous stars, growing closer with every heartbeat. The low rumble of the train's engine grew louder, the air vibrating with its approach.

"Just so you know, I'm not angry about any of this," Novak said, placing his hand on mine. "It makes sense, considering who you've always been. To me. To this world. To yourself … and even to him." His eyes locked onto mine. They were steady and sure. He leaned forward slightly, his voice almost tender. "Do you want to come with me?" he asked as if he already knew the answer. "To meet my brother?"

I shook my head, my gaze never leaving the blinding headlights of the train thundering toward us. The sound of the horn was now deafening in the night.

"No," I said. "I don't want to go anywhere. I hope there's nothing after this. No smiles. No tears. No love. No hate. No afterlife. No rebirth. Just … nothingness." I felt a sharp ache in my chest as the weight of my lifelong loneliness pressed in from all sides. "I'm not sure I could bear to live another life as lonely as this one."

The train was almost upon us, its light blinding, the sound of metal on metal screeching louder than anything I'd ever heard. My heart raced, but my mind was calm. The ache in my chest sharpened, but I welcomed it—his final gift.

The gift of feeling.

"I guess I'll find out soon enough if peace is finally possible," I said with a bittersweet smile.

Not much longer. Just a few more moments, and it would finally be over. My dark flame extinguished. Black nothingness swallowing my rotten heart and soul.

The end.

Finally.

"Peace," I mumbled, the word barely escaping my lips.

"I'm afraid not quite," Jan suddenly said, his voice cutting through the roar of the train. "I hope, with time, you'll forgive me."

"What?" I asked, confused, my eyes snapping to his as the train loomed just seconds away.

"Sixty." He smiled warmly, squeezing my hand one last time. "I told him if he hit the passenger side of the car at sixty miles per hour, he could get you off the tracks."

I stared at him in shock. The train's blinding lights and ear-splitting horn filled the car, drowning out everything else.

Jan spoke his last words. "I'm not Mojca, by the way—I'm Anton. My little brother somehow managed to push me off just before the train scattered him along the tracks. Never forget what we're capable of when we truly want something, whether out of love or hate. Nothing compares to the sheer will we carry inside us. The ankh... you'll understand it in time."

Then, in the blink of an eye, he shot back in his seat.

Before I could react, headlights from an SUV appeared out of nowhere, speeding toward us on the passenger side.

"No!" I screamed, my voice tearing from my throat as the SUV slammed into the car just as the train collided with the front. The impact ripped the world apart.

The car spun violently, tumbling over and over. The airbag exploded in my face. My head slammed into the side window before whipping back with merciless force. Everything was a blur: metal, glass, darkness. Flashes of images burned into my mind. Novak's side of the car ripped away, the train tearing through metal like paper. Another spin. Another impact. I was certain that I'd die, certain the end had come, until the car finally came to a tumbling stop and slid a few more feet on its side.

I lay there, barely conscious, barely alive.

"Liam," I whispered, the name slipping from my lips before I realized that I'd spoken. My voice was weak, barely audible, each breath a struggle. "No," I begged with the little strength I had left.

I wasn't afraid to die. I wasn't even afraid of living another life of utter loneliness again. But right now, the only thing I feared was that the train might have killed Liam.

And I'd die never knowing.

The one thing I'd tried to protect might be gone.

What a tragic and pathetic ending.

Even for a monster like me.

Then the world began to spin, and everything faded to black in the blink of an eye.

FORTY-FOUR

Liam

The pain was unbearable. I hung with full force against the seatbelt, my car flipped upside down, the world a twisted mess of smoke, fire, and darkness. Blood dripped steadily from my forehead, smearing against the airbag as I struggled to focus. My breathing was labored. Each shallow inhale sent a stab of agony through my ribs. The coppery taste of blood filled my mouth.

I coughed, wincing as I fumbled for the seatbelt buckle. My hands were trembling, clumsy, and the world spun as I hung upside down. The buckle seemed to weigh a thousand pounds. No matter how hard I pressed, the damn thing wouldn't budge. It was jammed—or maybe I was just too weak to force it open.

Every movement sent fresh waves of pain through my battered body. My vision blurred as I turned my head, and the muscles in my shoulders screamed in protest. Through the haze, I saw that the train had traveled a good distance before stopping. It was now a monstrous silhouette in the far distance.

Then I saw Leah's car—or what was left of it.

Flames engulfed the vehicle, creeping toward her like a predator closing in on its prey. The fire hissed and crackled, flapping from the wreckage like a large tongue. Thick, dark smoke swirled into the cold night air.

"No," I mumbled through the pain, panic settling in my chest.

I pushed against the seatbelt buckle again, this time gritting my teeth in frustration. My hand slipped. I tried once more, pressing down with all the strength I had left. Finally, with a loud click, the buckle released.

I slumped down onto the airbag, collapsing in a heap. My entire body felt like it had been beaten with a sledgehammer. Broken ribs? Probably. My legs wobbled as I rolled out of the car and hit the cold ground. Every breath burned, but I forced myself to stand. My vision swam as I stumbled toward Leah's car.

The impact with the train had sheared off the passenger side where Novak had been sitting. The flames were spreading fast, hungrily crawling from the undercarriage toward the hood.

Without hesitation, I reached for the door handle, only to yank my hand back as the heat from the metal burned my skin. I hissed in pain and shook my hand, the skin already blistering. But I couldn't stop.

"Leah!" I shouted hoarsely. My chest felt like it was collapsing, but I didn't care. I had to get to her.

Ignoring the pain, I grabbed the door handle with both hands and pulled with everything I had. The heat was unbearable, the fire growing, turning the car into a furnace. My hands were shaking, the skin peeling as I yanked at the door again and again. Then it hit me—the entire passenger side of her car was gone. Dazed and barely thinking, I stumbled around the hood, slipping past the crumpled wreckage. The fire roared hotter on this side, but there it was—an opening. A way in.

Smoke filled the air, burning my lungs. The fire was everywhere, but I covered my face and leaned into the wreckage. The flames licked at my clothes and skin.

The heat was overwhelming, suffocating, but I pushed forward.

Finally, I saw her.

It was hot as hell, the inferno creeping dangerously close, but it hadn't reached her yet. At least, not entirely. The car's interior was like a gas stove, the fire boiling from below, reaching higher. Leah was slumped in the driver's seat, motionless. Blood stained her face, and her body was limp against the seatbelt.

My stomach twisted in fear. Was she dead?

I pulled at her seatbelt, but it wouldn't budge. My fingers were numb, and my body was shaking as I fought against the buckle. That goddamn seatbelt again. "Leah!" I coughed, choking on the smoke.

Then, through the chaos, I heard Rose's voice cutting through the roar of the flames. "Richter!"

She appeared beside me, her face set with grim determination. Without hesitating, she pulled out a pocketknife. The fire burned her hands as she sliced through the seatbelt in seconds.

"Pull!" she screamed, her voice raw.

Together, we hauled Leah from the wreckage, my muscles burning with every pull. We dragged her across the ground, away from the inferno, collapsing onto a patch of grass by the tracks.

"Are you okay?" the train conductor shouted from a distance, running toward us.

I ignored him and kneeled beside Leah. My burnt hands trembled as I pressed my fingers against her neck, desperate for a pulse.

If she was dead...

The seconds stretched out painfully as I waited for a sign—any sign. My breath caught in my throat. Then I felt the faintest thump beneath my fingertips. A pulse. Weak but there.

Relief washed over me like a flood. I gasped, pulling her limp body into my arms.

Rose knelt beside me, her eyes wide with panic.

"Is she alive?" she asked.

I nodded, my throat tight with emotion.

Rose nodded and pulled out her phone. "We need an ambulance at the train crossing on Pine Street, near Wilkers Manufacturing. A train has collided with a vehicle." She hung up and turned to the conductor. "Are you hurt?"

"No," the man replied, his voice trembling.

"Good. Step back and wait by your train," Rose ordered, her tone sharp as she knelt beside me again.

We sat there in silence, staring at the wreckage. The flames danced in the distance, casting eerie shadows over the twisted metal that was now Novak's final resting place.

"In some fucked-up way, this might be the ending we all needed," Rose murmured, her eyes fixed on the burning wreckage.

I wanted to agree. I wanted to say yes, as if we were in a movie where a neat, happy ending resolved everything. Novak dead. Leah alive. We could twist the narrative—two lovers stranded on train tracks, their car giving out at the worst possible time.

But deep down, I knew it wasn't that simple.

Novak had texted me the location where Leah planned to kill him. He'd even told me how to save her. It left an unsettling taste in my mouth. Even in death, Novak was pulling the strings, the puppet master playing his final game from beyond the grave.

Had he planned all this?

But why?

"I hope this really is the end," I muttered, my eyes narrowing as I stared at Novak's crumpled, burning wreckage. "Jesus, Allah, Buddha, or even the goddamn devil ... I'll offer my soul in exchange for this being the fucking end of it all. The end and nothing else."

FORTY-FIVE

I was sitting in the sleek, modern meeting room of Obligato's underground compound. Polished black marble floors reflected the soft overhead lighting. Egyptian art lined the walls. It was the kind of place that felt cold, impersonal—designed to impress but reveal nothing. Novak's touch was everywhere, a strong reminder of him at every turn.

On either side of me sat cunning lawyers, their expressions unreadable as they reviewed the contract I was about to sign. They were the best money could buy—the kind who could get OJ off.

Across the table, FBI Director McCourt and Senator Wheezer sat with an older, tired-looking federal attorney. The lawyer looked every bit the government official: cheap suit, worn demeanor. Bottles of water were neatly placed in front of each chair, the labels perfectly aligned.

McCourt was arrogant and unreadable as always, while Wheezer grinned with that familiar mix of slime and forced charm.

Wheezer's eyes darted to the pen in my scarred hands—a lifelong reminder of the night I'd pulled Leah from the burning car.

My lawyers nodded, signaling that everything was in order.

I signed several copies of the contract, the one that would officially reinstate Obligato as the FBI's cloud storage provider.

As the lawyers handed over the signed copy, Wheezer beamed. His voice was irritatingly cheerful. "It feels like coming home," he said, his eyes gleaming. "Especially after Obligato's generous donation to our superfund for the next race." He leaned forward, lowering his voice as if to share a secret. "If I can ever help you with anything—"

"That will be all," I said, standing.

A glance passed between McCourt and Wheezer. For a moment, Wheezer's smile faltered, but he quickly recovered.

"Yes, yes, of course. I'm sure you're busy here. Thank you," he muttered, clearing his throat. He flicked his eyes toward McCourt, waiting for him to echo the sentiment.

With a forced smile, McCourt added, "Thank you."

Wheezer clumsily handed the signed contract to the federal lawyer, who shoved the papers into his briefcase. Making one last attempt at a dazzling grin, Wheezer stumbled out of the meeting room like a fool, his lawyer trailing behind him.

McCourt stayed behind.

I didn't move as I watched the others leave.

"You can go now," I said to my lawyers.

Almost in unison, they rose like robots and left.

McCourt scanned the room one more time before looking back at me. "I bet they pay a hell of a lot more here than at the FBI, don't they?" he said, not even pretending to make it a joke.

I didn't respond. I didn't need to. "When I said 'you can go,' I meant you too," I said, cold and detached as I gathered a copy of the contract for my records.

When he didn't move right away, I shot him a hard look. He held my stare, almost daring me to show who was in charge.

"I meant now," I repeated firmly.

A few more seconds passed, but then he rose, knowing full well I could ruin him with one phone call.

He walked toward the door but stopped when I spoke again. "One more thing," I said.

He turned around.

"If I need anything, I'll let you know."

His face tightened with anger—he couldn't hide it—but he forced a smile before leaving.

I stood and straightened my suit. A soft grin tugged at my lips.

McCourt was right. As much as I sometimes missed the badge, this job paid a hell of a lot more than the FBI ever had.

FORTY-SIX

Liam

I sat beside Theo in what used to be his childhood bedroom. Bonnie had turned it into a space full of medical equipment, sterile surfaces, and the constant hum of life-support machines. The walls still held memories of his younger years—a few posters from Led Zeppelin and Playboy. But now the room felt like a cold, clinical space. The air smelled faintly of antiseptic mixed with the aroma of scented candles—something his mother had insisted on. She'd read somewhere that smell was important for people in a coma. Bonnie was always searching for the next hidden miracle that could help bring Theo back to her.

None of this would have been possible without Leah's generosity. For months, I'd lied to Bonnie, asking for bills and telling her that the FBI was covering the cost of Theo's care. In reality, it was Leah who'd hired the team of private nurses and the world's top brain surgeons. She was determined to do whatever it took to keep Theo alive for as long as his mother believed in his recovery. Every day, physical therapists came by to work on his muscles, moving his limbs so they wouldn't atrophy.

And every day, Theo lay lifeless on the bed, his body thin and motionless except for the rhythmic rise and fall of his chest as the ventilator pumped air into his lungs. The breathing tube in his mouth moved with each inhale—a constant reminder of the fight we were still in. His face was pale, his features drawn in, and though he was technically alive, it felt like I was talking to a ghost.

"It's crazy, really," I said, continuing my story about the documentary I'd watched the previous night. "I mean, who the hell keeps chimps as pets? At first, it's all fun and games. They dress them up like kids, teach them tricks. But it always ends the same way." I shook my head, recalling the vivid 911 call from the documentary. "One day, the chimp snaps, and out of nowhere, it tears them apart. Sometimes they even eat parts of their owners—usually the face and genitals."

I paused, looking over at Theo, hoping for some flicker of response—anything. But his chest kept rising and falling, the machines continuing their steady rhythm.

"People never learn. They think they can control nature, but they forget that animals like that ... they're wild. No matter how much you think you know them, they can tear you to shreds." I laughed bitterly. "Almost sounds like me and—"

Marcia, the young physical therapist, entered quietly. She'd been working with Theo for weeks, moving his limbs and keeping his muscles from wasting away.

She gave me a small, understanding smile as she approached the bed. "It's time for his muscle strengthening," she said, her voice soft but professional. Marcia began moving his leg gently, speaking to him as if he could hear her. "I'm going to pull the blanket down now, Theo," she said, her hands moving with care. She went through her routine, working each muscle, flexing and stretching his limbs as though willing life back into him.

I watched her, feeling the familiar ache in my chest. "Thanks, Marcia," I muttered, barely above a whisper. Turning to Theo, I added softly, "You behave."

It was always the same—a routine that gave me the illusion of control in a situation in which I had none. The guilt sat heavily on me, a constant presence I couldn't shake.

Theo had been too good at his job. And now, here he was, reduced to a shadow of the man he'd been, all because he'd tried to do the right thing.

I couldn't stay any longer. If I did, the guilt would paralyze me like it always did.

Rising to my feet, I glanced one last time at Theo. Then, without a word, I left the room, carefully closing the door behind me. The house was silent. Bonnie was still at work, and Theo's little sister was at school. It felt so empty. Too empty.

I made my way outside and stepped onto the porch. For a moment, I stood there, letting the silence of the street wash over me.

Then I turned to look at the doorbell camera. The small black lens was mounted next to the door. I stared straight into it, locking eyes with the unseen watcher on the other side. I held my gaze for a long, quiet moment as if I was trying to send a message—something unspoken.

Without a word, I turned and left.

FORTY-SEVEN

Leah

The sterile, glass-walled room felt cold, almost clinical, as I sat at the sleek desk of Obligato's underground compound. The faint scent of disinfectant clung to the air, barely masking the metallic smell that lingered on my burned skin. The glossy surfaces revealed my reflection: partly burned face, bandages peeking out from under my shirt sleeves where my arms and hands still bore the marks of that night. The light overhead was harsh, bouncing off the touchscreen desk in front of me.

I stared at the monitor on the wall. Liam's face filled the screen. He stared back at me through the camera with unwavering intensity. Even at a distance, there was something about him—steady, unflinching.

Before I could get lost in the image, the sound of confident footsteps echoed through the quiet room. Rose strode in, her presence commanding. Quickly, I tapped the touchpad to make the video of Liam disappear.

"Here's a copy of the FBI contract," Rose said, placing the file on the glass desk, whose surface glowed faintly from the technology embedded beneath. The entire tabletop was a touchscreen, modern and futuristic, like everything else here. "Strange that we have to work with this man now," she added, her tone tight.

"McCourt or Wheezer?" I asked, picking up the contract.

"Both," Rose said, her lips pulling into a grim line.

"McCourt is a good puppet, and Wheezer won't last. He'll be replaced in the next election," I said, gazing at the contract. "The donation wasn't for him. It was for his younger assistant. He'll make a push next year. The old fool just doesn't know it yet."

Rose nodded knowingly. Her sharp eyes assessed the room, the situation—everything, as usual.

"Have you made any progress on the system yet?" I asked, setting the contract down. Jan had named the AI system Seshat, after the goddess of writing, knowledge, and wisdom.

"Not much," she admitted, her fingers gliding across the touchscreen. With a few swift movements, a large folder system materialized on the glass wall across from us. Its digital contents were reflected in a cascade of blue light. Jan Novak seemed to have coded her himself. The code is genius—really. None of our staff knows much about her. Jan was the only one who truly knew how to operate her."

I frowned as the weight of this revelation settled in my chest. It would take months just to understand the basics of this massive AI system—a program designed to operate Obligato's vast cloud storage. It was enormous. Navigating it felt like David fighting Goliath—only this time, without the slingshot.

Another one of the secrets Jan had taken to the grave.

He hadn't survived the crash, but what baffled me was how he'd known about it beforehand. He'd sent a text to Liam, warning him, giving him the precise location where it would happen. I remembered the moment when Jan had typed something into his phone just before we'd reached the tracks. That must have been the message.

But something else haunted me: the fact that Jan had left me everything. As if he'd always known that I'd take his place. As if grooming me for this role had been part of his plan all along. His words echoed in my mind: *I hope you'll forgive me.* He'd told me this when he'd confessed that death wasn't in the cards for me yet. Peace wasn't in the cards yet.

It almost felt as though he'd saved himself by turning me into him.

Under my leadership, the company had done well—profits steady, the public façade intact. And with Rose's help, I was slowly learning how to navigate the company's vast cloud.

But the real question wasn't if we could use Seshat, but how we controlled her and what we'd do with the information she provided.

That question burned inside me as much as the thought of Liam Richter did.

I'd stopped my concerts after the "accident" on the tracks. The burns on my hands weren't severe enough to end my career or affect my ability to play at my usual level, but Obligato consumed all my time, and stepping away from concerts gave me space to let things settle. It kept me out of the public eye for a while. Naturally, the world was heartbroken, but after the train track tragedy, no one dared to push me back to the piano.

The official story was that I'd been Jan Novak's girlfriend, and we were headed to a vacation home when the car stalled on the tracks. The FBI had been following us, acting on a tip that Carl Carr was planning to make an attempt on my life. Theo McCourt had previously identified Carr on footage near my residence, raising concerns about him stalking me. It all made enough sense to avoid further questions. Nobody had ever heard of Jan Novak or his powerful company to begin with.

To the public, it was just a tragic accident. I was just another virtuoso who was living a life touched by misery.

In his will, Jan had left both the company and his estates to me. Another sick twist.

Luckily, Rose had accepted my offer to help run Jan's company. I trusted her completely, and after everything that had happened, going back to the badge wasn't an option for her. But she wasn't ready to give up the work either. So here she was.

For Liam, things were more straightforward. He'd stayed with the FBI. The badge was his way of fighting for justice in this world, and it always would be.

Rose interrupted my thoughts, her voice sharp and controlled. "As crazy as it sounds, Seshat helped me with something for once—the missing girls from the border. She wasn't even playing games like last time. She led me straight to them. Navigated the cloud with me."

This made me uneasy.

Not the fact that we might have found the missing girls from the truck full of illegal immigrants. A man had taken the underaged girls from the truck for sex trafficking after they'd crossed into the US.

What shocked me was hearing Rose talk about Seshat as if she were sentient.

And to be honest, maybe she was. When ask a question, Seshat responded like a top-notch lawyer, always careful to avoid leaving a trail of evidence. Her answers were never straightforward. They always led to more questions, and you sometimes spent hours getting the information you sought only to discover new questions in the process. If you asked her to open a file on Liam Richter's camera footage, she'd first remind you that this wasn't ethical or legal without a warrant. That was when the chase began—a conversation through the keyboard or voice command, back and forth, until you either outsmarted her or presented your request in a way she deemed acceptable. Legal or not.

Rose handed me a manila folder. For a moment, my eyes lingered on the burn scars on her hands—remnants from the fire that had nearly taken both our lives. My brow furrowed as I looked down at the folder. I wondered why she hadn't just pulled it up digitally on the screen.

Rose caught my look and shrugged. "Old habit," she said.

I grabbed the folder and opened it, then flipped through the papers inside. For a long moment, I sat there, frozen. It wasn't the content that shocked me—it was the decision I wasn't ready to make.

Rose watched me, her eyes piercing. "What are you going to do?"

I lifted my gaze slowly to meet hers.

"Are you going to give this to Richter or take care of it yourself?"

"I ... honestly don't know yet."

FORTY-EIGHT

Leah

A warm spring breeze from the ocean carried the scent of salt and seaweed. Seagulls circled high above me, their cries sharp as they scanned the endless blue for fish.

I sat on the weathered bench by the old rope factory, a place where Liam and I had met many times before.

My stomach twisted with a strange mix of anticipation and anxiety.

I heard his footsteps before I saw him. His shoes scuffed softly against the wooden dock, his shadow stretching out beside mine, long and thin in the sunlight.

As Liam sat beside me on the bench, a faint smile played on his lips. His brown eyes sparkled in the sun, and he wore his usual suit—minus the jacket and with his sleeves rolled up.

He looked more relaxed than I'd seen him in a while, though a shadow lingered behind his gaze. Theo's ghost still haunted him.

"Sorry I'm late," he said softly. "Josie had a parent-teacher conference."

I mirrored his smile. "How's her piano practice going?"

"She's obsessed. Plays every day. And I think you're to blame. She watches your performances on YouTube. I had to buy a real piano last month because she said her keyboard wasn't helping her develop finger strength. The damn thing was over $6,000."

"Sorry," I said, my grin widening. "But she's actually right about that."

He shook his head, a playful gleam in his eyes. "Why do I get the feeling you're not sorry at all?"

We laughed, the sound light but tinged with tension—something unspoken between us.

"She's begging me to ask if you'd listen to her play," he said hesitantly, as if he already regretted the words.

"It would be my pleasure."

Liam smiled faintly.

"When you're less busy, of course," I added, offering him an easy way out.

"Yes," he said. "When I'm less busy." Then he tilted his head. "Actually... she has her first concert next month. At my place. Nobody will be there but my half-sister and me. Josie invited the whole family, but my ex said hell no, and my mom and other sister don't go near my half-sister." He sighed. "Just a normal, fucked-up family."

"I see."

"Well, anyway, if you'd like to join us, feel free. It won't be anything fancy, and you're probably busy—"

"I'll be there," I cut him off.

The sound of waves crashing against the rocks below filled the silence that followed. For a moment, everything felt peaceful, as if the world had stopped turning and it was just us.

I savored that feeling.

Every second of it.

But the peace was fleeting.

My hand rested on the manila folder beside me.

There was work to do.

Liam's way, this time.

I'd learned my lesson the hard way. I couldn't let the monster inside me take control again—not after everything we'd been through. Not after the crash. Not after whatever Jan Novak had possibly set in motion from beyond the grave.

I handed him the folder. My heartbeat quickened, and I almost regretted it, but I knew it was the right choice.

Let him handle it his way. Make him feel like a good guy again.

Liam took the folder and flipped it open, furrowing his brow as he scanned the content. "If this is accurate, we might be able to intercept a truck transporting human trafficking victims from Texas to New York tomorrow," he muttered.

I nodded, my voice quiet but firm. "It could even lead to the missing girls. The ones taken from the border. Same cartel."

His eyes stayed glued to the pages. He was deep in thought, planning every move in his head.

Then he rose abruptly, the folder clutched tightly in his hands. "I need to get on this immediately."

I stood up and nodded.

Liam paused, pulling a folded piece of paper from his pocket. As he handed it to me, our fingers brushed, and a strange energy passed between us.

I unfolded it and frowned. "What's this?" I asked, staring at the name written across the page.

Liam's expression darkened. "What do you mean? It's Massimo Chandler. The inmate at South Bay House of Correction you texted me about. You asked me to look into him."

A chill ran down my spine. "I didn't send you that text."

He stared at me, his face a mixture of disbelief and alarm. "What do you mean? It was texted to my flip phone. Only you and Rose have that number."

"I didn't send you anything," I repeated, my voice steady though my mind raced.

Who had sent him that name? And why?

Liam shook his head, snapping himself out of the confusion.

"We'll deal with this later," he said, raising the folder slightly. "I need to move on this now."

I expected him to leave, to rush off and handle the case, but he didn't. Instead, he lingered, his gaze shifting as if debating something.

Without warning, his hand reached for mine—a slow, deliberate motion. His touch was warm, seeping through my skin like fire. An electric surge shot through me, tingling all the way to my fingertips.

My eyes dropped to his hand, noticing the burn scars etched into his flesh—the same as mine, the same as Rose's. A permanent reminder of that night—the night I killed Jan Novak to save Liam Richter. The night he almost died saving me.

"Thank you," he said quietly, his voice soft. Our eyes met, and in his gaze, there was no anger left, no hatred, not even doubt—only warmth.

"For... what?" I asked softly.

His lips curved into a smile, not the sharp one I'd grown used to, but something softer, almost tender. His fingers squeezed my hand gently, and in that moment, I knew something had shifted. Liam was finally accepting me for who I truly was. Maybe, just maybe, we could be a team again. Not like before, but something better, more uncertain—a place where justice, morality, and loyalty blurred together.

"I'll call you as soon as I can," he said, his voice taking on urgency. "Wait for me before you talk to Massimo Chandler."

I nodded and watched as his hand slipped away, leaving a strange emptiness where his touch had been.

He turned and walked briskly down the weathered dock. His silhouette shrank as he neared his car, which was parked by the old factory.

I stared after him, my mind a whirlwind of confusion, worry, and something else—something darker.

Who texted Liam this name? Was this another one of Jan Novak's twisted games? Had they already begun?

My eyes drifted to the name scrawled on the paper in my hand.

Massimo Chandler. South Bay House of Correction.

Liam had told me to wait, but my instincts told me otherwise. As I made my way down the pier, I was already dialing Rose's number.

"Hello?" she answered.

"It's me," I said, my voice sharp. "I need you to call in a favor with the district attorney."

"What do you need?"

"An informal visit at South Bay House of Correction. Off the record. No cameras. Have Wheezer arrange it with the DA, and remind both of them of our donations."

"Okay," Rose said slowly, intrigue coloring her tone. "Who do you want to talk to there?"

I glanced once more at the name on the paper. My fingers tightened around it.

"Massimo Chandler. And I need more than just a room to chat."

FORTY-NINE

Leah

South Bay House of Correction looked like any other institution—a concrete fortress, cold and unfeeling, bathed in harsh, sterile lights. The building loomed like a monument to hopelessness. Its narrow, barred windows seemed determined to block even the faintest sliver of light.

I sat in my limousine, the engine humming quietly beneath me. Through my tinted windows, I watched the prison's back door swing open. A tall man in an orange jumpsuit shuffled out, heavy chains shackling his wrists and ankles. He was flanked by several armed guards, each keeping a close eye on him as they approached my car. The man's gait was sluggish, and his massive frame moved like that of a bear. Even from here, I could see the crude sneer plastered on his face.

Mark, my driver, opened the door to the back seat, allowing the prisoner to clamber in. The man's grin widened as he lowered himself onto the leather. Immediately, the stench of sweat and unwashed skin filled the confined space.

"You can leave us," I said, my tone cold as ice.

The guards exchanged uncertain glances. One of them opened his mouth to object, but I cut him off with a sharp look.

"Now."

With a reluctant nod, they backed away from the limousine, closing the door behind them.

The man's grin spread even wider. He reeked of filth, his sour breath polluting the air. "You wanna fu—"

"If you insult me with your primitive vulgarities," I interrupted, my voice as sharp as a blade, "I'll tell the guards to shoot you the moment you step back into that prison. They'll say you attacked them. Trust me, the fact that I have the power to sit here with you should make it clear, even to your small brain, that I'm telling the truth. So, are you getting shot today, or are you making some cash?"

The grin vanished. Massimo's eyes widened, and his macho walls crumbled in an instant. He muttered something, his voice barely a whisper.

"I can't hear you when you swallow your words like a child," I said, my patience wearing thin. "Speak up."

His breath was rancid, his body a walking reminder of decay. Every inch of him made my skin crawl.

"Cash," he grunted, louder this time. "I choose the cash."

"Good." I nodded. "Now tell me everything you know about the man who was pushed in front of the train on the Green Line last year."

A knowing smirk tugged at the corners of his cracked lips.

"Don't know his name, but I can tell you it wasn't no crazy homeless guy that did it."

Sarcasm dripped from my voice as I leaned back in my seat. "And how did you come to this brilliant conclusion?"

Massimo chuckled, shaking his chains as he wagged his filthy finger in the air. "First, the money."

I rolled my eyes and tapped sharply on the window.

The guards, who'd been waiting nearby, were at the door in seconds, ready to haul his ass back to his cold cell.

"Get him out of my car," I demanded.

"Wait!" Massimo barked, panic lacing his voice. "I'll talk!"

The guards looked to me for confirmation.

I nodded, and they stepped back, closing the door once again.

"Jesus fucking Christ," Massimo muttered, shifting uncomfortably in his seat.

"I'm not your Jesus," I said coldly. "Talk or get the hell out."

Massimo rubbed his hands together, the chains rattling softly. "I know it because I'm the one who pushed him onto the tracks."

For a second, time froze. Rage seared through me like a wildfire, burning every inch of my restraint. My fingers itched toward the gun in my coat pocket. I should just spray Massimo's filthy brains across the leather seats, the warmth of justice splattering my face.

But not like this. Not yet.

I took a deep breath, forcing the fire back down.

He could die later. Slowly. Painfully. An inmate could do it for almost nothing—just a favor, a whispered promise. But for now, I needed this piece of filth alive.

"Why?" I asked, my voice cold and detached.

Massimo shrugged like he was talking about the weather. "Nothing personal. My boss paid me to do it, so I did it. At first, he just told me to keep an eye on him. But when that fuck boy started talking to the FBI—"

"Shut up." I cut him off, his voice grating on my nerves like broken glass. "Get out."

He opened his mouth again, but I slammed my hand against the door. The guards didn't hesitate this time. They ripped the door open and grabbed Massimo, pulling him out of the car.

"Wait! You lying bitch! You promised me money! I need the money!"

The guards twisted Massimo's arms behind his back, forcing him to the ground as he kicked and cussed. A few punches from the guards, and his resistance crumbled, but his voice didn't.

"I need the money!" he screamed, blood dripping from his nose, his eyes wild with desperation. "It's for my daughter! She's sick! She has cancer!"

The words hit me, slowing the world around me. My gaze narrowed as I looked down at him. His face was bloodied and bruised, barely recognizable.

"You need the money for your daughter?" I repeated, my voice soft but laced with venom.

Massimo nodded weakly, his body trembling from the pain. "Please. I'll never get out of here. I just want her to have the money. She needs treatment. She's sick."

I stared at him for a long, quiet moment, watching as his body sagged, beaten and vulnerable. The desperation in his eyes reminded me of all the killers I'd faced before—pathetic and broken in the end. I should have felt something, maybe pity, but I didn't.

"You're going to die in here, Massimo," I said, my words slow and deliberate. "Painfully and slowly. And I'll make sure your daughter never sees a cent. So she can meet you in hell soon."

His eyes widened in horror. "You lying cunt! I'll kill you! I swear I'll kill you!" Quickly, the guards yanked him to his feet and dragged him away. His screams echoed until he was gone. Tonight, I'd arrange for another inmate to shank him. Let him bleed out. All for pennies.

As the limousine pulled away, I exhaled, calming the fury that had bubbled beneath the surface. I would send the money for his daughter's treatment. Of course, I would. She didn't deserve to suffer because of him.

But he didn't deserve to know that.

As I stared out the window at the fading prison, I gathered myself. Massimo had been the one to push Emanuel, but he hadn't ordered it.

Someone else had.

And I'd pay that someone a visit.

Tonight.

FIFTY

Leah

It was a warm spring night, and the air was thick with the scent of blooming flowers and leaves. The sky above was clear, the stars scattered like diamonds against a black velvet canvas. The moon hung low, casting a silver glow over the mansion's expansive garden porch. I approached, my steps silent on the grass. The wind rustled the nearby trees, causing their leaves to whisper secrets in the dark.

Luca sat alone on the porch, where the flicker of candlelight danced across his sharp features. He was listening to one of my recordings: *Beethoven, Quasi una fantasia, like a fantasy*. The melancholy strains of the piano floated through the night air. A half-empty glass of wine rested in his hand, and he slumped in his chair, staring off into the distance. No one else was around, and I'd approached unseen. Seshut had pulled the footage from the cloud, so I knew every blind spot in his security system.

When my shadow fell across the porch, Luca didn't flinch.

"Do you think Beethoven would have cared?" he said. "That people renamed one of his greatest works *Moonlight Sonata* after his death?" Luca's voice was low, contemplative. "I've thought about it a lot since you brought it up." He swirled the wine in his glass, staring at it as if it held the answer. "Do you think it would have mattered to him, knowing his music is pulling these beautiful emotions from people in ways he never intended? Under a name he didn't choose?"

He shook his head, but the motion was uncertain, as if even he didn't believe his own question.

"Maybe Beethoven would be delighted," he continued. "Or maybe ... indifferent."

He didn't turn. He didn't need to. He knew it was me.

I stood there, looking at the man I'd once called a friend. Someone who had, in his twisted way, almost cared about me more than anyone else in this ruthless world.

Almost.

But that loyalty had come at a cost.

"Beethoven was known for his mood swings and rage," I said, my voice ice-cold. "If he knew that people who'd never played a single key of music had the audacity to rename his masterpiece after he was gone—if you really need to know—he'd be *really* fucking pissed."

"Yes," Luca mumbled. "Yes, I think you're right."

"Why?" I pressed. "Why did you have Emanuel killed?"

Luca finally turned to face me, his dark eyes heavy with exhaustion. He looked more human than usual. His suit was as immaculate as always, but his expression betrayed a weariness I'd never seen before.

"It wasn't personal, Leah. It had nothing to do with you." He set his wine glass on the table. "I placed Emanuel with that escort agency knowing they'd send him to you. He had everything you liked in a man. My only intention was to keep an eye on you."

"You mean to have him report back to you," I corrected coldly. "About my affairs."

"To protect you," he insisted, his voice soft but steady. "My intentions were good."

"Then why did you kill him?"

Luca sighed deeply and leaned back in his chair. "You already know the answer, but you want to hear it from my lips, don't you?"

I said nothing, waiting.

"He was talking to the FBI."

"He never told them anything," I shot back.

"No, he didn't," Luca agreed. "But he didn't tell me about his meeting with the FBI. Others did. And that, I can't tolerate. Not in my line of work."

I clenched my fists, my thoughts racing. Emanuel hadn't betrayed me. He'd kept secrets, yes, but they were out of loyalty to me. He'd abandoned Luca for me.

Luca and I locked eyes again in a long, tense gaze. His voice softened as he spoke. "It wasn't personal, Leah. I hope you can forgive me."

I tipped my head back, looking up at the stars, trying to find some meaning in their cold, distant glow. I thought of Jan and Emanuel. But as always, it was Liam's face that haunted me the most. What would he think if he found Luca dead? Would this be the end of everything I'd fought for?

And yet … what if Liam never found out it was me? Luca had plenty of enemies. Any one of them could be blamed for this.

Then the text came to mind. The one sent to Richter by someone else, connecting Massimo and now Luca to Emanuel's death. Another mystery left unsolved—one of many since Jan Novak had entered my life.

Was Jan still pulling the strings? Was every move, every breath, part of a larger game he'd set in motion? Was he testing me, even now, from beyond the grave?

I turned abruptly, ready to walk away.

But Luca's voice stopped me cold. "I'm the only person who will ever accept you for who you truly are, Leah. Do you really want to be alone for the rest of your life? I did all this for you."

His words hit hard.

That last part.

That he did it all for me.

It was exactly what Jan had said about killing Theo McCourt. But was it really true? Was any of this really for me? If that were true, why had Richter never made such choices for me, always leaving my fate in my own hands, even when it could cost him?

As if pulled by invisible strings, my body moved on its own. My hand slipped into my pocket and wrapped around the cold metal of my gun. In one swift motion, I pulled it out, turned, and pressed the barrel against Luca's forehead.

"You didn't do it for me," I said, my voice steady. "You did it for yourself. If it were for me, you would've fucking asked."

Without another word, I pulled the trigger.

The shot echoed through the night, startling a flock of birds from a nearby tree. Luca's body slumped forward and slid lifelessly from the chair to the ground. His wine spilled onto the porch.

I stood there for a moment, feeling nothing. No relief. No satisfaction. Just the cold, empty silence that followed death.

Then I disappeared into the quiet of the night, my mind racing. Liam burned in my thoughts.

What if he found out I killed Luca? Would he turn against me?

No.

He wouldn't.

For the first time, a strange confidence settled in. I felt it deep inside.

Our relationship didn't form through rainbows and pony rides, but through beasts and ghouls. We had been to hell and back, yet here we stood—cracked but unbroken.

Liam finally understood who I really was. He knew I'd never harm an innocent person. Not someone like him, or Josie. Or Rose and Nathalie. Not even Theo McCourt, despite the threat he posed to me. I'd always protected those who needed it and saved the ones who couldn't save themselves.

Granted, I did it, well, my way. But Liam didn't see me as a monster anymore. He saw me as the villain who killed them.

He finally understood the difference between the two. Monsters and villains.

One you had to kill. The other... was a bit more complicated.

Rose had started accepting me, too. God knew why, but she did. As long as I kept killing the ones who deserved it—violent criminals—maybe Liam would not only accept me but stand by me. Maybe the broken girl who grew up in psych wards could have it both ways.

Deliver justice.

And have him.

I reached my dirt bike and flipped on the headlights. As I kicked down the lever to start the engine, a huge buck appeared in the beam. It stood just a few feet away. Its massive antlers glistened. Something about them caught my breath.

The tip of the antlers.

The tip of the left side curved into the shape of an ankh—a symbol I knew too well. It wasn't a perfect resemblance, but if one looked closely enough, it was there.

The buck stared at me with deep, black eyes before turning and disappearing into the forest.

I smiled at the beauty of it, then cranked the throttle.

If Jan was still playing his game, then let him come.

I knew who I was.

I was a killer of killers.

And on a killer's playground, there was only one rule.

Win and live, or lose and die.

THANK YOU!

My Beloved Readers,

Thank you for being part of the *I Kill Killers* family. The journey of this series hasn't been an easy one, but with your support and encouragement, I kept going. I want to thank you from the bottom of my heart for that. I wouldn't have completed the series without you, nor would I continue to write without you.

I hope you'll join me on my other adventures. We will always be rebels in the literature world, and our books will always be wild.

That's an Ashman promise.

I am so grateful to you.

Thank you. ☺

Make sure to follow me on Instagram, TikTok, Facebook, or join my Facebook Group: *Ashman's Dark Thriller Facebook Group.*

Contact: hello@ashmanbooks.com

Thank you for your support.

ABOUT THE AUTHOR

S. T. Ashman is a writer who once delved into the criminal justice system as a psychotherapist. This role gifted her with a unique insight into the human psyche—both the beautiful and the deeply shadowed. She considers herself a crime-solving enthusiast, often daydreaming about being the female version of Columbo, solving mysteries while rocking a trench coat. Her writing audaciously defies norms and promises to keep readers engrossed in a nail-biting adventure.

When she's not busy crafting suspenseful tales, she's chasing after her nap-resistant kids, binge-watching TV with her husband, or ... actually, that pretty much covers it.

She aims to bend your brain, tickle your intrigue, and leave you pondering long after the last page. Come join her on her journeys.

Printed in Great Britain
by Amazon

54563955R00324